Recounting

Luis Goytisolo

RECOUNTING
ANTAGONY: BOOK I

Translated from the Spanish by Brendan Riley

DALKEY ARCHIVE PRESS

Originally published in Spanish by
Alianza Editorial as *Recuento* in 1973.

Copyright © 1973 by Luis Goytisolo
Translation copyright © 2017 by Brendan Riley
First Dalkey Archive edition, 2017.

Library of Congress Cataloging-in-Publication Data
Identifiers: ISBN 9781628971729
LC record available at https://catalog.loc.gov/

ILLINOIS
ARTS
COUNCIL
AGENCY

Partially funded by a grant by the Illinois Arts Council, a state agency.

www.dalkeyarchive.com
Victoria, TX / McLean, IL / Dublin

Dalkey Archive Press publications are, in part, made possible through
the support of the University of Houston-Victoria and its programs in
creative writing, publishing, and translation.

Printed on permanent/durable acid-free paper.

RECOUNTING

For María Antonia

I

THE ROLLING THUNDER OF the detonations came booming back down the valley, and above the hills, amid the smoke that seemed to be rising from the woods, you could just glimpse the flash of cannon blasts. Two motorcycles and several dun-colored trucks came advancing slowly along the highway, and at the crossroads, a group of soldiers was maneuvering an artillery piece. There was also an officer mounted on a white horse, prancing, galloping back and forth with his saber unsheathed; an officer mounted on a white horse.

Ramona wound up the gramophone and put on a record, but Aunt Paquita immediately removed it, making the needle screech. Once set in motion, the gramophone couldn't be stopped and the turntable kept on spinning until the spring wound down. They were all there in the front part of the house, in the drawing room, with the shutters half-closed. Whispering. *Kyrie eleison. Christe eleison.* The dining room, by contrast, gave onto the back porch, where there was plenty of light. La Quilda was with her family, downstairs on the first floor, and Felipe said that they had used their mattresses to cover the windows.

The rumor is the Committee members have left town, they said.

When they went outside they could still hear some cannons firing in the distance, some random shots. They'd opened the windows wide, laughing and crying, embracing one another, and out in the street they shouted and sang and everybody raised their arms, ran, pushing and shoving, running after the soldiers toward the plaza. The soldiers were tall and they walked very quickly, with blanket rolls, soft rope-soled shoes, and cooking gear hanging from straps, a flood of rifles, and the slow, measured rocking of their elbows. La Quilda caught Ramona in her arms

3

and Ramona began to cry, too, but no one paid her any mind. There were tons of things scattered everywhere, old clothes, books, crockery shards, and the school building was deserted with straw strewn about the floor. Nor was there anyone to be found in the militia headquarters, where Felipe and Padritus scrounged up some tins of sardines and condensed milk, and in an abandoned car in the yard they found a pair of binoculars. At the fork in the road, a column of brown trucks followed the highway, leaving the town behind. *Mira los moritos*, they said. There go the Moros.

Felipe was also marching. And Padritus. Really quite well, said Papa. They were drilling on the soccer field, with wooden rifles, and at last they all marched in red berets and blue shirts. Behind the soccer field was a line of bare gray poplars without leaves. Really quite well. The chubby sergeant was barking orders at them, and Papa went to see him in the mornings and they chatted sitting out in the sun, in the yard outside the militia headquarters. The garden was spacious and damp, labyrinthine, and the branches of the shrubbery formed a sort of shady cote over the dark smooth ground.

This hand grenade is a bomb.

Pere Pecats was killed by a bomb. There had been many deaths. There were stories, a little boy twisting up a fuse or playing with some ammunition or pointing a pistol at another one or fiddling with a grenade, etcetera. The hiding place was underneath the steps in the orchard where there were two bayonets, a rifle without a bolt, a Russian cap, a helmet with a bullet hole, a gas mask, gleaming artillery shells, and especially, bullets, bullets for pistols, for rifles, for machine guns. The town children also had their own and they'd had to dig trenches. People said they went hunting toads, they'd fill them with gunpowder and blow them up. Felipe had learned to remove the powder from the rifle shells. Blowing up fuses in the Valley of the Riders of the Purple Sage was more fun than picking cabbages and beets for Pere Pecats.

A lot more fun. But raw beets tasted very good, eaten in bites, a little prickly, very juicy. They pulled them up from alongside the road at the edge of the field, fat and pale like bacon, and waving them over their heads, Felipe calling: Pere Pecats! Pere Pecats! Or he ran ahead through the winding rows of cabbages, mature and densely whorled, all of them calling for Pere Pecats. And Pere Pecats came out shouting and swearing, but he was twisted and hunched over and couldn't run. In other gardens you had to post a lookout; Padritus and Felipe climbed the trees, and Ramona gathered pears and apples in her skirt. Chestnuts could be carried in hand baskets, but you had to hide them underneath mushrooms picked in the woods. La Pilate and Nieves would thread the strawberries on really fine blades of grass so that when they ate a whole string of them together they tasted more delicious. The water at the falls shone in the sun and Pilate took off her shoes and waded along the bank. Felipe fished for crabs with a butterfly net. Nieves wasn't there. The stones were slippery, and in the quiet pool the water floated still over a bottom carpeted thick with brownish leaves. At dusk those still pools were frightening, the water opaque. Pilate was going to the militia dance.

Pilate whistled furtively to Padritus, and to Nieves and Felipe and Lalo. At night.

The lightbulb glowed dimly, reflected in the window glass, isolated and radiant beneath its opalescent platter. El Mon had brought two squirrels and a skinned rabbit; he was a large, red-haired man, with a goiter. La Quilda bent over the hearth, black and big-nosed as a witch. Papa said that was no rabbit. It's a fox, he said. He traded some soap for a hen from a woman who came with La Quilda. The woman haggled, saying the soap was not very foamy. She pulled the hen out of a basket, by its feet, but it had a fine-looking head; she laid it on her forearm caressing it, all puffed up like a feather duster, furled crest, the eye furious. The kitchen gave onto the porch and the fields were covered in snow. La Quilda sank her shears into the hen's body, she singed the feathers, laughing; she felt around in the entrails until pulling out a yellow, nubbly, clustered, botryoidal lump of flesh. There was also the decapitated duck staggering round the kitchen, silhouetted against the reddish black of the hearth.

La Quilda came upstairs to help Nieves when she had to

butcher some animal. She lived downstairs, on the ground floor. She came heavily dressed, and when a package of food arrived she ate the thickest slab of ham. El Mon was her sweetheart, el Mon-Jamón; he had a rifle and a balaclava.

Snow. They walked obstinately, small and red, with chilblains, their necks retracted, shoulders stiffly squeezed together, hands in pockets, scarves hanging down their backs, socks slipping loose down their calves. The schoolhouse was alongside the road, and Felipe had to pass by the house of Señor Daunis. Señor Daunis was really skinny and he wore a long overcoat, cinched tight, with the lapels turned up. He was tubercular and you had to keep away from him. From Pere Pecats, too; Padritus said that Pere Pecats threw a stone at him, in the plaza. He often went to the bar. He cursed at the children and threatened them with his fist. He talked to himself and limped, and everybody teased him.

Señor Daunis stayed hidden and he managed to avoid being seen by the Committee members. Like the priest who lived above the tobacco shop and the two nuns from Can Vidal. Papa said that in Barcelona they wanted to shoot him because he attended Mass and he owned a factory. He had many kids of his own that nobody wanted to play with, because they had tuberculosis, and they were often very hungry. He was a widower. They said that the river had frozen over.

The divine Mozart, said Aunt Paquita.

And Ramona put on a record. She was seated on the wicker sofa, next to the gramophone, swaying her legs. Aunt Paquita wondered what that pain could be. She came over at night, to listen to the radio, sometimes accompanied by Miss Lourdes, blonde and thin, with plucked, painted-on eyebrows. They were studying a Michelin roadmap, tracing along with their finger, taking off their eyeglasses, hunched over the map. They were chatting: the Reds, checkpoints, avenues, the jail, in disguise, devoutly Catholic, words spoken in undertones. A table lamp topped by a shade with amber flecks. Let your cousin sit in the rocking chair, she said.

Grandfather wasn't listening to the radio. He was still at the table eating, methodically, indifferent as a cactus, as a lichen-furred stone. Grandmother, on the other hand, was moving about, helping; she was wearing a flowered dress, black and white. They got off the bus, in the plaza, and they walked together slowly, arm in arm: Grandfather came out of his room in his pajamas, his face creased by the pillow, his eyes squinting, his hair white and tousled, clearing his throat. For dessert there was watermelon, enormous slices of red watermelon, and grandfather spat the black seeds out onto his plate, one by one. The dining room was fresh, luxuriant with plants, the shadows of the leaves quivering on the ceiling. Ramona danced in the parlor and everyone applauded. She wound up the gramophone, put on a record and danced. Dance with Ramona, they said.

My lovely darling, said Papa.

The parlor window opened onto the street; the sunlight came in only during the morning. The furniture was dark, wicker, and the records had to be stacked atop the console, neatly ordered. There were many: Ramona, Matonkiki, the *Jupiter Symphony*, etcetera. The record sleeves were mostly alike; gray paper, with a dark blue drawing of a Negro band playing for several couples.

Does Ramona belong to Ramona?

The Valley of the Riders of the Purple Sage was very green, with rows of poplar trees running down the hillside. Beyond, the gully was choked with brambles and bushes. You crossed over the creek on a footbridge of logs thick with dark moss. Padritus was unbuttoning his fly; he had to drop his pants. Ramona took off her underpants, she lay down in the grass. Look how it gets big and hard, she said. They examined Ramona's little hole, compared themselves and all that. They took turns masturbating. Lalo, going last.

Following the creek led to the river. There the meadows widened out, smoothly extended, and there were piles of wet logs stripped of their bark. Downstream the river flowed swollen and foamy, and you had to shout over the sound. Pilate was there; she hiked up her skirts and stepped in to wet her feet in the shallows. Cold, cascading waters, of melted snow. The slow quiet stretches lay further down. The water sounded throughout the valley and the sun shone resplendently on the dew, oh my dew. The slopes were covered with beech trees, and higher up, above the shadowy fern-covered slopes, on the talus scree slopes, the mountain peaks stood out, sharp, naked. Crabs eat the dead.

Pilate was ironing on an ironing board set up in the kitchen, in Aunt Paquita's house. She was singing absentmindedly to herself, sometimes answering, wondering aloud. *Soñar dientes, muerte de parientes*, she said. *Soñar muelas, muerte de abuela.* Teeth gnashing, cousins passing. Molars grinding, grandma dying. She brushed on rouge, singing softly to herself, she curled her hair, daubed on eye shadow, lipstick, the butterfly blossomed from the chrysalis. She danced in the militia men's house. Nieves had a sweetheart and didn't go. The music could be heard from out in the street, but to see them you had to go into the dark garden, lie in wait in the hedges, crawl through; the iron gate was open. They were dancing in a brightly lit room, with crystal chandeliers, and some couples were leaning over the railing, shouting and laughing, jostling one another. Thinking about your desires I'm going to lose my mind; it takes my breath away. Ramona stumbled, dazzled by the windows.

Felipe spoke with one of them. The day was cold with a white sky. The militia men had kindled a small fire in front of the fence and they were eating sitting on the ground, around a blackened pot.

Are you hungry? he said.

And also: these are lentils; take them if you want them, if not, leave them.

He was unshaved, with his cap tilted to one side and his cape over his shoulders. Another was scratching inside his boot with a bayonet.

More arrived. They camped next to the road, among the chestnut trees, and the smoke from their fires drifted about like a fog, level with the bare branches. There were also refugees, dark and bundled up. And a file of prisoners. As they passed by they looked toward the parlor window, they gestured to show they were hungry. One of them got jabbed with the butt of a rifle. Downstairs, in Quilda's house, they were lodging a woman and a little boy who had one eye bigger than the other. She said they were from Málaga.

And make sure you don't wander off, said Papa.

They said that the Reds had shot down a plane, a fighter, that it had been going to crash right on the railway line, shot down in flames. And the kids in town found a dead soldier, floating in a quiet bend of the river, all tangled up in the brambles under the water; he was half-rotted away and there was no way of telling if he was a Red or a Nationalist, an infiltrator. Or a deserter. Or a Russian. Barely sunk in the quiet shallows, the water like a clearer air upon the bottom like marmalade; the crabs. Padritus said that he had seen him and Aunt Paquita slapped his face for telling lies. They were whispering, their ears glued to the radio, and in the parlor Ramona was dancing about aimlessly. Felipe was not going to school; he came in chewing on a beet, excited. Yes, the bunch of them from the Valley of the Riders of the Purple Sage. And there were others, from the *colonia*, the summer houses, from the town.

The boys from Puig Sec caught Padritus and said that if they caught him again they were going to hang him from a tree, over a bonfire. Besides, it was a question of spying on Señor Daunis. The garden was fenced in and from there, at nightfall, it was easy to make it to the verandah; then you had to spy through the window standing up, everyone silent, waiting in vain for it to happen again. The one time that, peeking through the window, they saw Señor Daunis crouching on the bed, naked, shaking his left hand very fast, between his thighs, his right hand behind, the crooked fingers twisting back and forth, his thumb sunk into his ass. They could hear a muted boom and people said that was the sound of cannon blasts.

A completely clear day, with the sun softening the brown fields, the sharp snowy mountain peaks. In the dining room the windowpanes were shaking and through the trees' naked branches you could clearly make out the cannon flashes, smoke rising from the hills. And the motorcycles, the brown trucks, the cannons; they were motorcycles with sidecars. And the officer on the white horse galloping with his saber unsheathed. They found Pere Pecats under some thickets, blown apart by a hand grenade. They said it was an accident, that he'd been drinking and it went off on him, or that the Moros had done it, that the Moros hadn't understood what he was shouting.

He slept in the room next to the parlor: he was in his uniform, with glasses and red beret. I'm the chaplain, he said. *El páter.* Nieves drew a bath for him. He spoke with a hand on Felipe's shoulder, and the others laughed, seated around the table. He brought out a glass jar with little white pears in syrup. There was everything, bananas, preserves, and at the town hall they were handing out small loaves of bread.

A Mass was celebrated in the plaza, facing the sun, the rose of epiphany. Many people wore red berets and blue shirts; chatting in groups, intoning couplets, serenades, and *el Carrasclás*, the Nationalists' favorite song. They sang, faces to the sun, forming little choirs, celebrating. *La victoria fue tuya porque así lo esperaba cuando muerta de pena, a la virgen rezaba tu novia morena. ¡Tu novia morena! ¡Tu novia morena!* The victory was yours because, dead from sorrow, you longed for it so, your brown-haired girl prayed to the Virgin, your brown-haired girl! Your brown-haired girl!

Señor Daunis hugged Papa, and Miss Lourdes told again the story of her father, who died in Africa when he was about to be promoted to commander. Father Pascual's soutane stood out on the steps of the church. Swordsmen presenting arms, shining bayonets, golden braids, glory, incense and victory.

Uncle Pedro arrived with gifts. They're some views of Genova. And I've got some records with all the hymns. He also had a uniform, a green beret and a kind of cape. They were gathered talking in the garden of a villa, out on the sunny lawn. There were wicker chairs and a gramophone playing. There was a woman who was smoking.

Is Barcelona the biggest city in Spain?

Does it have a harbor and a park and trolley cars and subway trains and buses and cinemas?

Are the Reds still in Vallfosca?

Are there animals in Vallfosca?

Miss Lourdes gave classes in embroidery and German, and Aunt Paquita offered to teach singing to the summer girls from the colonia. They came back from their hike, feeling somewhat hot, sweaters knotted around their waists, and they passed by under the window singing, young and healthy, walking slowly hand in hand, the song about the five roses. It was a splendid day, springtime. Rosebuds and blossoms, flowers and fruits like fresh hot coals.

The troops passed by, tight columns of trucks bristling with rifles, armored cars, artillery pieces, and only the chubby little sergeant remained. Pilate had already gone and Aunt Paquita was searching for another girl. They cut Pilate's hair very short, a crewcut, because she was a Red. Aunt Paquita managed to get them to let her go, on the condition that she leave town. They said that when she got on the bus she was crying, her head covered with a scarf. Nieves told us.

There was a picnic. Grandma was there, and Uncle Pedro brought lambs. Grandma got busy preparing things, hunched over, the white bun in her hair coming undone. Don't vex me, she said. Nieves and Quilda were helping her, and Aunt Paquita was coming and going and telling her not to worry, that it was more than all right, Doña Gloria. There were many guests. And Ramona was dancing in the front room and everyone was applauding, etcetera.

II

THEY PRAYED THE ROSARY in the chapel throughout the whole month. The rosary, and then came the *Memorare* and the theme for reflection. The prayers, mortifications, offerings, and sacrifices carried out in the course of the day were recorded in the columns of a small folder, everyone kneeling down, leaning on the back of the pew ahead; there was always someone who'd forgotten their pencil. For each good work you put in a grain of wheat and they said that with the flour ground from those they'd make wheaten hosts. The little children were the last ones to enter, but they sat in the first pews of the left nave, dedicated to the Virgin. They processed forward along the center aisle, genuflected before the altar and turned toward the left, slowly, with a flower in their hands, *rosas d'abril*. They sang, encouraged by a priest. *Venid y vamos todos con flores a porfía, con flores a María, que madre nuestra es.* Come forth and we will all go together with flowers in abundance, with flowers for Mary, she who is our mother. The organ played up in the loft and the setting sun filtered through the narrow windows, mysteriously coloring the gloom. They also filed out two by two, blessing themselves with the holy water in an endless succession. Father Palazón was praying, motionless between the two extended lines, impassive as a Roman before the wild wind that fluttered his soutane. Nevertheless, when their gazes met, it made him glance away.

The altar of the Virgin was adorned with wreathes of white flowers. The following month they decorated the altar of the Sacred Heart with red flowers, in the right nave, but exams were upon them and—it was said—one individual visit sufficed during recess, a simple Credo and some short prayers in the secluded light of the shrine.

I'm very devoted to the Virgin of Montserrat, said Gomis. Well, I'm for Saint George.

A priest had been listening to them, and smiled. They hung up their classroom smocks, put on their jackets, picked up their pencil cases, books and notebooks, satchels. Gomis was a day pupil and in the afternoon he went home with the boys who took the bus. He wasn't leaving, he was going to wait for his grandmother. They got off in silence, in orderly fashion, and did not break ranks until reaching the caretaker's lodge in the park. Felipe was finishing later on.

He explained it all to her, occasionally asking her opinion, assuring himself that she was listening to him. They bought comic books at the kiosk, in front of the trolley stop, and they started reading them on the street, absorbed, sucking on mint popsicles, not stopping sucking on them except to exchange some comments. They didn't have much time at midday but in the afternoon they had a soda at La Granja, sipping it directly from the bottle with a straw. One day, Felipe and his friends spotted them and invited themselves, pulling up a chair. They stopped going to La Granja; they were going to a bar, although the bar stools didn't spin round. He carried her satchel and she carried the bag with the snack in it.

Nieves prepared them breakfast and grandma stood in line to buy bread. She also took charge of the rationing and kept the ration books in the upper drawer of her dresser inside of a brick-colored folder. She counted the coupons, naming off items: sugar, oil, meat… *No me amoines,* she said. Don't bother me. Nieves bought the rest in the market except when the delivery boy came from Vallfosca. The basket! The basket! he shouted from the gate, and everyone crowded out into the garden. They pulled out the sack tied with a cord to the mouth of the basket. Look, Raúl, look at this chard! Look at this escarole!

He ate breakfast in the dining room, with Felipe, and then they went out together. For morning recess he took half a baguette with olive oil and sugar, and for afternoon recess, the other half and a tablet of household chocolate. Gomis brought a green thermos with hot chocolate and a cold veal sandwich; the bread, white, from the black market. He began to eat during class; he raised the lid of his desk as if he was looking for something and snuck a bite. Do you know what "fetus" means? he said.

On Thursdays, by contrast, there was communion and Nieves prepared him an omelet sandwich and a hydrogen peroxide bottle refilled with milk with coffee syrup and a lot of saccharine. The bottle had a rubber washer fitted snugly round the porcelain top and it sealed tightly thanks to a wire clamp. He didn't eat breakfast until after Mass, during a brief recess, and amid everything an hour sped by like no time at all. With the prayer book open between his hands he contemplated those lines of imitation stone, the arches and columns painted as if they were cut marble, the stucco capitals, the golden reliefs. He always tried to be able to sit next to the middle aisle and did what he could to be one of the first ones to receive communion. There were two priests distributing the hosts, moving back and forth, now converging, now moving apart along the length of the communion rail. His priest was moving faster, barely leaning forward between the altar boys, the Ciborium against his chest, his glasses refulgent with light. All for nothing: he rubbed his upper lip with his fingers wet with saliva. He returned to his place and knelt down, palms against his face, his fingers slightly parted to see. They were still filing up along the central aisle, two by two, toward the chancel, the congregants with their sky-blue sashes, crowding round the steps, making way for those who were standing up from the communion rail, taking their places, getting back up in their turn, and returning along the side aisles with their hands joined and their eyes lowered, their knees dusty. He squinted his eyes and the rays of light from the candles intensified and grew until blocking out everything else; he could see nothing else. *Ser após- tol o mártir, acaso, mis banderas me enseñan a ser*, they sang. To be an apostle or martyr, perhaps, my flags show me what to be.

For confession on Wednesdays he went to a different priest each time and confessed the same thing. Then, kneeling in his place, he dragged it out as long as possible, as if the penance given was very heavy, and before returning to class he took a long turn round the deserted park, at most a visit, someone's relatives wandering along beneath the plane trees on the avenue. He strolled the quiet paths, a careful open labyrinth between close-growing plants, and as he walked along the blackbirds fluttered around with their flutelike trills, then flew away. In front of the building was a great rectangular esplanade, bare. The sound of singing, voices in chorus, and from the kitchens floated gusts of a pleasant aroma of roasted coffee beans.

Others did the same, a lively, swarthy boy with vaguely Asiatic features. But he stayed in the church with his group, whispering, laughing quietly in undertones, and on their way back they ran pushing and shoving and chasing one another. His last name was also suggestive: Vélez de Guillén. He looked at him furtively and during games he liked to be on the same team with him. One morning they happened to reach the front door of the school, on the way to the patio, at the same time. He was able to catch up with him, and matched his stride, commenting as naturally as possible on some fact which concerned them both, some common problem, most likely some type of ironic observation about their classes or teachers, something that would establish between them both a certain climate of solidarity. It was getting late and they were huffing. Vélez de Guillén glanced quickly at him, he considered his jacket too long, his golfing trousers too long and too wide. So young and already wearing hand-me-downs? he said to him.

Felipe was on the roller hockey team and he went to practice on Sundays; he kept his gear and uniform in his closet, locked away, and his whole bedroom smelled like a locker room. On the walls he had stuck up pictures cut out from magazines, photos of cars, movie actresses. In the afternoons, coming out of school he played ping-pong in the back room of a bar. Sometimes he brought his friends; their voices could be heard joking and talking, shut up in his room. They horsed around in the garden without listening to his grandmother, paying her no mind, trampling the lilies. Then they waited until grandma went into the little WC underneath the archway of the stairs, and at a signal from Felipe, they pulled the chain from upstairs, by opening the little hatch that gave directly onto the water tank. They also set out bait for her, some hard crust of bread on the little vestibule underneath the wall lamp. Grandma walked by shaking her head, and when her eyes fell on the bread crust, she would pick it up. What does "bait" mean? On Thursdays, between Mass and manners class, after recess, the morning passed by quickly. In the Assembly Room, Father Palazón spoke to them about how they must behave themselves in each circumstance in life, at the table, when visiting, and how and when they must practice their personal hygiene and change clothes, how to go to bed and to get up in the morning, for example, how to get undressed, and in what order, so as not to be, in any single moment, completely naked. First the shirt and the undershirt, so as to immediately put on the pajama jacket and, only then, to begin to undress from your waist downward, shoes, socks, pants, underpants; and so, the same for getting dressed, but in reverse order.

They had the afternoon off. And he went out with his grandmother; they didn't say anything in the house, but they were going to the cinema. Like on Sundays, when they said that they were going to the movie at the school, but they went instead to the one in Sarriá, the one that the week before had advertised a better selection of movies. Grandma forgot the money and they had to go back to look for it and they missed the beginning. Don't grumble anymore, please, she said. I just forgot. And after supper, when he was already in bed, he started to cry. What do you want? That I kneel down and beg your forgiveness? Well look, there it is. And she knelt down by the side of the bed with her arms outstretched and he pulled on one of her hands so she would stand up. Papa came in. Come on, enough games, he shouted. Go to sleep.

When they had guests the kids ate by themselves, in the small living room; almost always macaroni and roast beef. There they could re-read comics and talk about them. It seems almost impossible that they managed to escape from the steel men, she said.

The most exciting thing is when they almost discover them. Thanks to Zarkov.

I know I wouldn't have been able to stand it, not likely. I get nervous just looking at them.

She talked to him about when she was a little girl, about the games she played, her baby brother, the other little brother who died, about the vacation house in San Gervasio that they had torn down to make way for an apartment building, about a dog she rode like a horse, about a swing; she explained how they went riding in a phaeton, that her Aunt Marta published poems under a pseudonym, that her father, for Lent, bought them cream puffs. She stored the bread crusts in her dresser, a black piece of furniture, overstuffed, with brass handles and fastenings that smelled slightly of bread. The drawers were deep, difficult to open and close, and they were full of bundles of letters and postcards, folders, little boxes, holy cards and scapulars, lockets, medicines, a sewing kit, her missal and mantilla, some purple garters, keys for who knows where. On the marble top stood family portraits in oval frames, two slender vases, and a candelabra, and above, hanging from the wall, an engraving of Moses and the burning bush.

She was searching for the ration booklets, pulling out ribbons and funeral cards, papers, expired ration vouchers. One afternoon she forgot the money and they couldn't buy popsicles; she emptied out her worn-out coin purse. Forgive me, child, she said. I must have left it at home. On the way back he made her carry his schoolbag and he rang several bells in a row. She caught up with him when she rounded the corner, without daring to turn her head, hunching over, more than ever, in order to go faster, quite worried. They'll yell at us, they'll be furious. She was searching through the drawers, muttering, unable to find her pills. After eating she used her napkin to cover a piece of bread, a fruit peel, and while they were getting up from the table, she hid it in the cuff of her sleeve. Felipe arched his eyebrows, smiled. Then she went out into the garden to shake out the tablecloth, whistling; the sparrows knew her whistle and flew down to peck at the crumbs. Felipe elbowed him. Come on, let's go trap her, he said. They barged into her room.

Here's some food, he said.

Food? asked grandma.

Yes, we brought you a little bread.

Ah, thanks.

They spied her half undressed, flaccid and shapeless, with her petticoats raised, adjusting a garter, and she covered her breasts. There were little bouquets of acacia blossoms in the vases on her dresser, the four candles in the candelabra burning, lighting up the engraving, the burning bush. Felipe was hiding in the hallway; a voice was heard.

Gloria! Gloria!

Grandmother opened the door, squinting. Francesc? she said. Francesc? Who's asking? She moved as far as the vestibule, hiding the banana peel.

Nieves took charge of picking up the food rations and kept the ration booklets in the kitchen table drawer. But sometimes later on she still went, without ration vouchers, to pick up what had already been picked up, standing in the bread line. One day they telephoned, with a warning. Papa shouted. As if we didn't have enough headaches already! he said. She didn't come to pick him up at the school door either and he came running home, ringing doorbells. Now he didn't cry like the first time, when she mistook the hour and he found himself alone when the lines of children all dispersed at the school gate. They had given him a smock with a number embroidered in red above the pocket—1017—and they lined up on the patio, in front of the building; a large smock, somewhat stiff, not like the one Vélez de Guillén had, that fit him like it was tailor-made. Many of them already knew each other and they chatted until the priest made them be quiet; it was a gray day and the ceiling globes were illuminated. They sat him near the back and then they passed out the school supplies. His desk partner put his books in order, and his folders; he had a leather case with colored pencils. My brother knows how to light up his farts, he said after a little while. And also: the Americans shoot bales of cotton over here in shells, like that, *pzzztt*, right over the ocean. My father buys whole batches of it.

Gomis was a tiresome boy, with a thick nose and sleepy eyelids, who sort of smelled like butter. They also got together at recess, and during lineups. They talked about all the movies;

Gomis had seen almost all of them. Another thing was that the caretaker's boy from their building had a lot of comic books and they traded with each other. He was a boy who was a little older, but not any bigger, brown-haired and angular, with a wolfish air about him. He made deliveries for a pharmacy and used his tip money to buy second-hand comics that he later resold or traded, two for one. The pharmacy was next to the school gate, and Manolo, in a moment, took out his comics, and spread them out on the sidewalk. Grandma poked around in her coin purse, then paid. And on Thursday afternoons she accompanied him to the cinema. They came back hand in hand, reciting the list of his classmates in alphabetical order.

Farré
Farré
Fernández
Fernández
Ferrer Gaminde
Ferrer Gaminde
Fisas
Fisas
Folch
Folch
Fuster
Fuster

Not anymore now. She disappeared, and Papa called on the phone. Let's go, we've got to track her down, said Felipe. They found her—they said—standing in line in front of the back door of a convent, with all the beggars waiting for the free soup. She was shuffling along singing, how happy we are the two of us living in our little paper house. She was with several people, with her heavy stockings half-fallen, drooping pleats above her gray felt slippers.

Papa and Uncle Raimón were closed in the study talking and Papa raised his voice. Uncle Raimón quieted down and, when he came out, patted them very quickly on the back, kissed grandma on both cheeks, all in a hurry; straightened his overcoat, with a tic in his chin, put on a hat with the brim turned down and hiding his flexible hands in his pockets, left through the garden sort of swaying back and forth, with a long adhesive stride, as if he feared to fall down or make too much noise. Papa was shouting. Is it my fault that when he was young he spent all his inheritance? Is it my fault he decided to follow music? I would've liked to have been a bohemian, too! Aunt Dolores was a horror, and our cousins a bunch of kids with black circles under their eyes who stank like piss. There were secret family meetings and grandma said: I'm half-crazy, Raul. You're all very attentive to me, but you're making me crazy with so many questions. The notary came by today.

They accompanied her to the taxi, a taxi with a gasifier; they loaded her suitcase and a bundle of clothes tied with several straps. She wore an overcoat and a black hat festooned with artificial flowers, and she limped a little, surely owing to the fact that she had bunions and her shoes pinched her feet; Papa also got in the taxi. Don't cry, they said. She'll come back soon. They cleaned out her chest of drawers and put everything in order. They pulled out the moldy crusts of bread, the scraps of rotten fruit, and some macaroni wrapped in newspaper.

The fact is, he's a blood relative, said Papa. And I'm nothing more than collateral.

Felipe was parting his hair in front of the mirror, tilting his head; he daubed it with green gel. Aunt Dolores has had another boy, he said. You know what she called him? El Pitoletas. He seemed very relaxed. He bought cigarettes and on the way out from the school he was going to wait for the girls from Sacred Heart. Do you say *jodear* or *joder*? Fucker or fuck?

They were also going to a Catholic school. They went in through the back part of the garden, which gave on to a stream, and you had to slip through a spiny hedge and past a dry palm branch. That was as thick as a real forest, and then there were paths bordered by toadstools and ponds and a hanging bridge and an enormous grotto with stalactites. Hidden among the laurels and the cedars and the pittosporums they spied on the little girls who were playing in a small plaza, around a small tiled pond with a spraying fountain, its sliding shadows rippling in the sun, now low, which was filtering through the hedges, yellow beams among the leaves and a large butterfly fluttering above. They watched them running and shrieking and chasing each other and hiding behind the columns of the huge porticoed hypogeum which led into the grotto with the stalactites, under the domes where everything echoed like in an empty room. And then, when the nun's handclaps signaled the end of recess, they saw them pass over their heads across the hanging bridge which swayed and oscillated mischievously, flooded with that parade of pink legs that disappeared up into the depths of their skirts.

Look, look, said Manolo.

But you can't see anything.

Damn. Even their panties.

So what? Panties cover everything.

More exciting, much more, was to arrive at the orchard, at the far end of the garden, and steal something, even if it were a persimmon, without the gardener seeing them. They said that he had a shotgun that fired rock salt. He also had a German shepherd, which he kept in a chicken coop, and he only let it out at night.

It was the Month of Mary and the chapel was hung with white garlands. They prayed, some of them a complete mystery with their arms outstretched, the rosary hanging between their fingers. Then they informed him that Father Palazón wanted to see him and he stepped out of the line. Father Palazón was waiting for him in his office with many windows, standing next to the table. He stared at him for intolerable long seconds before speaking, serene, peaceful, his clear features, his short smooth hair combed forward. Are you sure that you're making honest confessions? Are you sure that you're not holding something back, that you're not hiding something you're ashamed of? Why, Raúl, why are you so stubborn, if God also knows it? He continued smiling, barely, static, he seemed like Julius Caesar, and he avoided his gaze in fear, as if blinded. How, how was it possible. And the priest was saying to him that there was still time, and that besides he also now had a great responsibility, that his father needed him, that the most important thing was to conserve his purity, his modesty. Your brother isn't bad, but he gets caught up in bad company. You're wiser and you shouldn't imitate him because he can't give you anything more than a bad example. The corridor was long and it was empty, with after-dinner odors. The side passages led off to the classrooms, voices, the reflections in the glass, the Latin declensions.

On the patios were burly plane trees, like stone, forming ample naves, domes of boughs. It was forbidden not to play, to just stand around, so that if you wanted to chat you had to take advantage of coincidences, like getting a drink of water or stopping in front of the lavatories at the same time. The priests walked back and forth on the terraces, along the balustrades, and there was always someone accompanying them. The walls were high and they scaled them by following the slope, crowned by a small roof of glazed tiles, but in spite of everything the ball got away and then they opened the side gate, made of black iron, and they went out, looking at the steep street, the few passersby. When recess was over they lined up in a hurry and after the second bell everything went silent. The gym teacher appeared at the balustrade flanked by priests. *¡Por el Imperio hacia Dios!* he shouted. For the Empire toward God! And over the tightly formed lines, all of them with their arms uplifted, was raised an immense cry of *¡Arriba España!*

When they all stood in line, he didn't like to have Gomis behind him, who would put his hand on his shoulder when they told them to salute; he didn't like it and he shook him off since when, on one occasion, as he was raising the top on his desk, Gomis wiped a fat sticky booger on the edge on his side. Gomis was always touching himself, and then he would sniff his fingers. He got poor grades and didn't even know how to copy by hand. Everybody shunned him, quarreled with him. He's a girl, they said. The priests punished him and when they meted out punishments with the ruler he was always one of those who got smacked. They ended up moving him to a separate desk, where he kept a cardboard box with caterpillars, silkworms. He spent classes with his head resting on his crossed arms, indifferent and listless. He didn't have anything to do with Manolo either, he said that his father had forbidden him to. And Manolo said: wait till I get my hands on him.

They went out together every Sunday. Manolo knew the cinemas where they showed the best movies, some of them all the way across town, buildings more like garages, the facades covered with gaudy posters resembled some shattered decoration. The atmosphere was murky, almost fermented, and the crowd shouted at the hazy screen and shook the rows of seats. Guys who looked like soldiers who'd just crawled out of the trenches. After the show, back out in the street, they discussed the convenience of learning Morse code. And they never missed a single neighborhood festival, the stalls and booths for the fair set up, according to the season, in various streets and plazas. Manolo led the way and he tried to not let him out of his sight when they all poured onto the streetcar together, separated by jackets and overcoats, with some woman's purse crushed into his face. And a tit that she tried in vain to protect with the lappet of her overcoat; underneath she wore a red sweater and a fine necklace, a very tight sweater, pleasantly perfumed. The light was ashen and the street was wide and monotonous, the neighborhood with its dirty houses, interminable walls, sharp corrugated uralite roofs, telephone poles and wires.

They also went to the cinemas in Sarriá. And when they came out they pretended to shadow someone suspiciously, each one on either side of the street, and at a distance as if they didn't know each other. Above all, when they followed the newspaper deliveryman, named Papitu, who they said touched little boys. And then, at home, during dinner, he acted reserved, as if embittered, and he swilled down his milk, as if he were getting drunk. And the next day, during recess, at the school that they called the cage, he talked about the teachers in a low voice, as if they were the warders in a prison and they were planning to start a riot. He carried a pistol tucked into his waistband, and when they were trading picture cards, he handed them over like a spy. And Vallfosca was India or the Wild West, and he was preparing his traveling gear.

Manolo didn't like reading novels. Not even the ones about the Coyote. He said there were too many words. And they could never agree about comic books. He preferred *The Phantom* over *Flash Gordon*, and *Juan Centella* over *Jorge y Fernando*. And just like Felipe, he liked *Tarzan* better than *Merlin the Magician*. And they traded punches. In Sarriá. While they were buying comic books and anise cigarettes at the newsstand, watched over by the old woman across the counter, they leaned forward far enough that, when they chose to, they could cram something into their waistband, under their sweater.

For Holy Thursday they visited several churches in Sarriá and Bonanova, they compared monuments, the altars framed by cascades of flowers, with tall, slender palm fronds, upright, lightly tousled. No cars on the streets and the families strolled along leisurely, enjoying themselves, united and at rest; greeting one another, smiling. Many uniforms in sight and women all dolled up with their black mantillas and ornamental shell-shaped combs, loose folds of lace. They shunned acquaintances, Father Palazón, who was coming out of a convent accompanied by another priest. The church smelled strongly of incense, of wax, and the people knelt before the purple banners, listening to the prayers of the nuns that floated in from the cloistered choir. But Gomis saw them in the atrium, they saw each other; he was with his family and his eyes shone and he, suddenly, malign and satisfied. Manolo didn't say a word either; they continued thus a while more, as if without the desire to talk, and they said goodbye right away, the two of them very pissed off and dejected.

In order to see the procession, the slow pass of the hooded figures and penitents, they went to Las Ramblas. Manolo said that in his house there had been a big blowup with his older sister. She goes out with a lot of guys and my mother finally ended up just having a look at her and discovered that she already had it open. What open? Her pussy, stupid! Sometimes you really seem totally stupid.

He also spent Easter in Vallfosca, with Papa and his aunt and uncle, and then they visited the churches in two or three different towns, in a horse-drawn trap. They heard the *De Profundis*, they attended the Tenebrae. El Polit and La Merè came out to greet them, and their dogs recognized him right away. But the field was cold and naked, silent, and even the smoke from the farmhouses seemed lifeless. It wasn't like in summertime, and walking on the mountain with shoes and socks, with his city clothes, made him feel uncomfortable, out of place in those woods, pallidly sunny, without birds. The farmers went about heavily dressed, with sheepskin coats and hunting jackets, and the women covered with scarves, their faces red with cold. Also, El Mallolet served as an altar boy, dressed in red and white, and he went around with the *caramellers* in their processions, in such a way that they hardly had a chance to see each other. He went with them from house to house, and when they finished singing, it was he who passed the hat and collected the money people threw to them. He asked him if Rosalía was still his girlfriend, Rosalía, slender and silent, all eyes, always following him around. Rosalía? said Mallolet. I couldn't care less about her! He didn't know what to say, what to do; the days were short, the time flew by. The same as when, at Christmas time, El Polit showed up in Barcelona with two chickens and sat down in the little sitting room, corpulent and ruddy-cheeked, stiffly formal, with his black beret tightly on his head, with his overcoat open, unbuttoned, owing perhaps to it being too tight for him. He clapped his gnarled hands, big-knuckled, with scratches. Well, Raúl, he said. *¿Qué fotem?* How the hell are we doing?

On Easter Sunday *la mona* that Gregorius had ordered for Felipe arrived. A little house of almond croccante with chocolate eggs around it and candied egg yolk spun on top. Or a fruit basket made of almond croccante with chocolate eggs and candied fruit. Or a chocolate hen inside an almond croccante basket. Raul didn't get a *mona*; his godfather was Uncle Raimón. On the other hand, for Palm Sunday, Aunt Paquita gave him a decorative palm frond, *un palmón*, with a big silk bow and hanging decorations, little sugar figurines. They went to the parish church, and along the way, each one was looking at what the others were carrying and, once in the church, they had to compare heights, to see who had the tallest one, and at a specific moment, always unannounced, to strike the floor with the stem until it splayed, to see who made a better broom. Then they hung it with taut wires from the balcony railings, light, ivory-colored, ruffled dismay.

Manolo whistled from the street and he came out; they went to the nuns' garden, to the cinema, to kick the ball and mess around. Every time he talked to him about Vallfosca, Manolo fell into a bad mood. He said that his grandfather also had a country house, in Aragón, a big stone house, with a patio and a coat of arms above the door. It seemed like it bothered him that Raúl had gone away. When they went on a spiritual retreat in Manresa, he had gone with him to buy adventure novels and real cigarettes and a bottle of moscatel wine, some things that would help to offset, in the solitude of the cell, the effect of the sermons, death, condemnation, hell, a botched confession, and a sacrilegious communion. But going to Manresa meant an excursion and a few days less of class. But that's pretty wild, man, I'm not sure that's such a good idea, said Manolo. I'd be really careful. Some of those priests are real vampires. When they opened the tombs in the convents, they found a lot of children's skeletons.

Sometimes he got mad for no particular reason. Manolo raised his voice, almost shouting, as if he wanted people to hear him, and he said things that made no sense. Goddamn it! Well if you don't like it, that's too bad, you idiot. So there. They went their separate ways. It was All Saints' Day and they went through a cemetery as if being carried along with the flood of all the other visitors. They followed the dusty paths, between white blocks of burial niches, with crowns, with flower vases, with portraits and burning candles, with marble plaques, with iron rings; they read the inscriptions. There were loudspeakers broadcasting Gregorian chants and the cypresses stood out black and dry against the whitewashed walls, against the chaotically confused pantheons, cupolas and crosses, iron railings, stone statues. They stumbled upon a funeral and, lost in the respectful crowd, they could see a little, startled, the lid being raised for the last time, a black coffin, with sparkling incrustations. The harsh sunlight made the mourning clothes seem more intense, and the hot wilted flowers, stems drooping, smashed chrysanthemums, gave off a poisonous smell. And the next day—or the day after—Gomis said to him: Manolo's gone. They arrested them for being thieves. They were

in the middle of a lesson and he didn't finish telling him until
later on. Each night Manolo's father went into the pharmacy
and stole a few pesetas from the register; the pharmacist wound
up discovering him, he spoke with the owner of the building
and they forced him to move out before midday. My father says
that they've even been too good to them, he said. He explained
himself in an affected manner, his eyelids heavy with delectation.

Alright, so what do you have to tell me?

He went back there, and on one of his meandering walks he
was able to see the new caretaker carrying out the trash cans.
He also wore a striped shirt but he was younger and didn't have
a sickly face. He observed him for a while from the corner pretending that he was waiting, bored, just as if he had agreed to
meet someone.

He went alone into the nuns' garden. He crept along, pushing
his way through the foliage, spying, fighting and conquering,
destroying the plants with blows from his fists, rushing forward
in sudden charges or strides, branches, enemy weapons. And he
explored the grotto: it was the Cave of Sesame from the story
of Ali Baba and the Forty Thieves.

Coming out from school he bought packets of picture trading
cards at the kiosk, movie trading cards, from *The Thousand and
One Nights*. They all had their own collection, and he bought
them not so much to fill up an album as for having a chance to
trade his doubles with the others. It was forbidden and you had
to do it underhandedly, in the schoolyard. The one he especially
liked was that card showing María Montes dancing, arching
backwards, showing her tits. Gomis said that Virginia Mayo was
better built, that he'd seen a naked photo of her. Liar, they told
him. Vélez de Guillén preferred Ivón de Carlo.

Vélez de Guillén shared a desk with him and they helped
each other. His mother was young and elegant, and his father
walked with him on his arm, like a friend. He saw the three of
them strolling by with the rector, during recess. Afterward the
boys in the gang gathered round to slap him on the back, to tell
him that he was sure well-protected, and he pushed them away,
with a smile. They got together at every recess and when school

got out for the day they took the same streetcar. They had their own private jokes, allusions that only they understood. But one day he also invited him over, he invited him to his saint's day party that they were going to celebrate on Sunday afternoon. He answered that he couldn't make it, that he already had a date, something to do with his cousins.

Before dinner, chores finished, he followed Eloísa around the kitchen, peevish, excited. And the Carthaginians came and wiped out the Greeks and the Romans wiped out the Carthaginians and the Visigoths wiped out the Romans and then the Moors came along and wiped out the Visigoths. Beat it, go on, get out of here, said Eloísa.

It was raining and it was still too early to go to the cinema. From the study he stared out into the dark rainfall, a May thunderstorm that came sparkling down wildly over the garden, over the lilies thrashing about. Windows fogged up from his breath, a pale gray vanishing in which it was so much fun to draw something. He searched around curiously a while in the wardrobe, checking the jackets to see if he could find some forgotten coin in the pockets. Then he went back into the study. He took down a large edition of the Bible and, seated on the floor, below the window, he looked through the engraved illustrations, Joseph and his brothers, Moses and the Pharaoh's daughter, the Parting of the Red Sea, the Death of Moses on the peak of Mount Nebo, and especially, the chaste Susana. He sang to himself softly and with the nail on his index finger he enlarged an already open hole in the plaster of the baseboard.

The house had two stories and a terraced roof, and balconies whose iron railings interlaced in the form of tiny bouquets, like along the gate, with a gray dried palm frond like the one in his room. The rust had run down and stained the house's yellow facade, the flowered friezes, the festoons. The staircase was short and two large ceramic planters, with gray cacti, stood guard at the pilasters at the gate. There were two planted rows of three acacia trees; the tree grating was made of four quarter-sections, half raised, and weeds sprouted up through the sparse gravel. Besides lilies there were old woody lilacs, some volunteer

pittosporum, and in the backyard, a plum tree. The greater part
of the neighboring houses—Villa Gloria, Villa Hortensia, Villa
Josefa—also had their own small gardens, their hedgerows overgrown with wisteria or honeysuckle, a neighborhood of quiet
streets, badly paved. Nearby there were enormous tracts of open,
fallow land, gullies, clearings scarred by paths, barren fields, trodden down with footprints, which, in good weather, resounded
with the shouts of small children.

III

UNCLE GREGORIO HAD GOTTEN to the house before them. El Polit told him that at the station, when they got into the trap, and of course, like any other afternoon of any other summer, they found Gregorio in the garden, seated next to the table, with his coffee already cold, his newspapers, and his pouch of shag tobacco. He never gave any warning, just made up his mind abruptly, and sometimes that's what happened, they would find him waiting there for them; everything depended on what the weather was like in Barcelona, on the withering heat, and, in this latest instance, for example, on a simple desire to enjoy the long beautiful evenings. Usually, however, they were the first ones to arrive. Later Aunt Paquita came up, and the cousins, around the beginning of July, and Aunt Paquita stayed there until September, although Ramona and Pedro stayed at the beach all through August, just like when Uncle Pedro was still alive. Uncle Gregorio would also be leaving early and not returning until early September, when the grapes started coming in; he always went to the same place, a spa where the weather was cool. By contrast, Montserrat and Juanito came up in August, and on the fifteenth Montserrat threw a party. There were many guests, and around tea time more people began to arrive, groups of summer vacationers, some of them practically strangers. Montserrat brought her little girl, but she almost always left her in the care of Aunt Paquita, who was family. Both Ramona and Pedro, along with Felipe, all went out with the boys and girls from the summer colony.

In the trap, as they drove alongside the creek, Polit brought them up to date. He talked about the drought, explained that Jaumet was no longer working at the house, that Chispa had died of distemper, and that Estrella had thrown a litter of fourteen puppies. They asked him for news, and he summarized the

31

year's most important events. He gave them the gossip from the neighboring houses, from the town, and he complained about the crops. He caught up the reins softly and, now and again, shooed away the horseflies with his switch. He answered reticently, smiling, squinting his scanty blond eyelashes while Raúl, seated alongside him, watched the softly variegated hills, the vineyards, the cherry trees loaded with red fruit, bent over, near bursting. So many cherries! said Eloísa. Behind, coming more slowly, progressively falling behind, the trap with the luggage was following them with a boy riding atop—Ramón or Jaumet or Mario—a horse-drawn cart loaded with trunks and suitcases, everything necessary for spending the summer there. Soon the reeds would be so high, bending close over the road, they would brush the cart's canopy. Then the road turned up and away from the creek, and right there, for a moment, you could see just a flashing glimpse of the house's rooftop, just before heading into the woods. There the branches were all a tangle and the roof didn't appear again until just at the end, right before they reached the garden. Uncle Gregorio stood up and, a few yards away, two showy hoopoes took flight, fluttering their wings like fans. His shirt was stained with coffee and he was wearing some slightly baggy, blue-and-white striped pants, his belt loose, his fly buttoned halfway. He swatted him with his folded newspaper, then took him by the shoulder, explaining to him, for example, that that morning he'd witnessed an amazing fight between a lizard and a snake. They entered the house together, chatting. Soon it was time to go exploring, to inspect his dominions, the very quiet bedroom which smelled uninhabited, the warm porch, the attic, the dark corners of the garden.

He would meet with Mallolet in the evening, when he came back from the field. They generally met up at Polit's house, and sat together in the driveway, among the farmhands awaiting their dinner. Polit busied himself taking care of the animals and he didn't return until just before dinner was ready; he appeared in the doorway, barefoot and bare-chested, his belly sticking out, moving slowly. If he was in a good mood he started picking on someone, whomever was talking at that moment. Sometimes he kept quiet; he drank a long thin stream of wine from the *porrón*, and then rolled a cigarette. The mosquitoes were out, and they only turned on the outside light to push together several mismatched tables, set out the plates, the bread, the wine, and the bowls of salad. They sat down at the table and then Mallolet left, but Raúl stayed chatting until they called him home for supper. Can Mallol was further up the road, on a steep slope above the valley. They also met there when it was cool, on the threshing ground, but the older brothers were there, too, and they never left them in peace. They gave Mallolet a hard time, but made fun of Raúl, too. Wait till the Russians come, you'll see how they make you snap to, you lazy ass, that's the only thing you do well, lazing around. The crickets chirping sounded like a faint bell ringing and, as the day cooled into evening, the tawny owl would begin hooting, a sign, they said, of the coming autumn. La Mallola repeated that they were waiting for Emilio. She said it in a letter, oh, yes, he was arriving the day after tomorrow. She was sorry for not being a very good cook, worried that his parents might think she didn't take good care of him. At mid-morning he ate a thick slice of bread smeared with tomato, and a plain omelet, and she scolded him because he was reading a novel at the same time. He swallowed, hardly chewing, his arms resting on the table, encircling his plate, his gaze descending the page fixedly, from line to line. At these hours the women were alone in the house, Mallolet's mother and sister-in-law, and Raúl listened to them waiting for Emilio, assuring them each day that he'd already had breakfast. So much studying, they complained, so many books. Emilio stood up suddenly. Dammit, he said, my revolver jammed. And Mallola, possibly half asleep as she knitted, started, told him he was a little bit kooky. Emilio left his novel on the sideboard, the pages dog-eared, and got his shotgun. He was taller and skinnier than Raúl and never really got tan; he wore a dress shirt with the sleeves cut off for the summer, and for a belt he wore a dark, thick enviable leather cord. They went hunting all morning, through the woods, along the creeks, shooting at blackbirds, crows, magpies, the way they had once gone out with their air rifles. There was a game warden with a gun and they didn't dare to go hunting in the fields and vineyards, the lower mountain, the field with hot stones and brambles, aromatic, where they could always end up flushing out some bunch of partridges. Mallolet went with them on Sundays; Raúl lent him a shotgun on the sly and the three of them went out together. Mallolet shot randomly, seemingly not aiming, and then went searching uselessly among the bases of the trees, among the shrubs. Emilio, however, shot at least as well as Raúl. They went into the woods separately, without making noise, listening, watching the branches for a sudden flutter or whirl among the leaves. They would definitely shoot something.

They said that Uncle Pedro's shotgun was the best one. An old Holland, with double triggers, but better than the newer ones. Uncle Pedro hunted by stalking his prey, along the creek, around midday when the pigeons went to water at the millpond. Aunt Paquita insisted on accompanying him and she returned delighted, explaining how she'd managed to frighten them all. Uncle Pedro feigned that he was only pretending to scold her, as if in protest, but he was a poor actor, and you could see that he really was irritated after all. He made some sweet, funny face and then started using the ramrod, squinting and frowning down the gun barrel. Aunt Paquita sighed, reclining on a bench in the gazebo, fanning herself. So what I don't understand, then, Uncle Gregorio told her, is why you spend the whole day spraying that Flit up and down, everywhere. Why spare pigeons but not mosquitoes if they're God's creatures too? He laughed with his belly, his eyes malicious, squinting through the glasses he wore for his myopia, his hair gray and uncombed, like a pelt. And he explained how he'd pissed straight into the mouth of an anthill until the damned ants abandoned it completely, in a mad rush. Aunt Paquita ended up getting mad. For the love of God, Gregorio, don't be such an ass, she said. She stood up and left and when she came back out it was to dust off and clean the glass on an oval picture frame, medium sized, a tacky, garish picture of the Assumption. Uncle Gregorio had found it: Mercè prayed before a reproduction of *La Gioconda*, the Mona Lisa—some calendar page, surely—that she had framed in the dining room. It was a

Sunday, after coming back from Mass. There was no room in the trap and Raúl came back walking, with Uncle Gregorio, and they sat in the shade of the plane trees, in front of Polit's house. Mercè also came back walking, with Eloísa, but they stayed behind chatting on the porch of the church and arrived later. By the shortcut you could go quicker and they were already there when the cart passed by in the distance at a good trot and slipped into the lush overgrowth of the garden. They waved. Polit was coming back from the field, his feet covered with mud, his pants rolled up, his faded t-shirt some uncertain color; some boy was with him. Mercè showed them the picture, the heavenly Virgin in celestial blue, the choir of angels, and she stroked the smooth frame; she said that it was beautiful, better than the other. They appeared circumspect. *Prou*, said Polit, enough. They chatted under the plane trees while the dogs went sniffing around and licking themselves, playful, sleepy, in a state of semi-erection.

A luminous morning, with a clean, dry wind. Mercè gathered in the clothes from the line, the white crackling of the dry bedsheets, the wide pants stretched out even wider, full of patches, stiff like pasteboard, just like the shirts.

Mallolet and Emilio appeared with their air rifles and also sat down on the stone bench, against the wall, looking listless. The house—*la masía*—was built of stone, and it seemed—with its doors and windows framed in brick—more like an industrial building or a small train station from the turn of the century than the large old farmhouse it was. The outbuildings were built perpendicular to the sides of the main house: the cowshed, a long aisle with seven or eight cows all lined up along one side; the pigsties, a succession of low enclosures, the majority unoccupied, empty and airy, gray with dust; the horse stalls with soft floors, warm and dark; the grape presses and wine cellars, the roofs made of corrugated asbestos panels, the excessively large storerooms containing old, outdated incubators, complicated artifacts, of some uncertain use, all in a jumble alongside the grain hoppers and the sacks of nitrate. As a whole, the buildings bordered a rectangular patio enclosed on three sides from which, there below the plane trees, the visibility was poor. You could barely make out the wide fields at the end of the valley, the stubble, and beyond, the hills and woods, the vineyards, the dark dusty green of August.

They followed the creek bed a while and then they went up into the woods, fanning out in silent advances, from thicket to thicket, creeping along until reaching that rock, sometimes signaling with the rifle barrel to stay alert, a gesture of intelligence, the same as when the hero moves and a German soldier sneaks up on him, or a Japanese sniper pops up from his hiding place, and in the moment when they draw a bead on him a shot is heard, and the hero turns just in time to see the Japanese soldier keel over and, from behind another rock, a companion waves at him silently, smiling, raising his rifle. Some Sunday, on the way back, they swam in a pool, first making good and sure that there was no snake on the bottom. They smoked a cigarette lying out in the sun and they whiled away the time naming the colors they could see with their eyes closed, as they squeezed their eyelids shut. Red, yellow, purple, black.

They soon grew tired of the creeks. Above their heads, the foliage was still, slack in the sun, the birds seemed to have disappeared. They climbed up a slope, through the thickets, and came out into a vineyard with young, well-pruned vines. They ate warm, sour grapes, still a bit green; they parted the leaves, picking the fattest grapes from each bunch, from each vine. Then they set their air rifles to one side and rambled about for a while. Emilio had made some bolas and they argued about the best way to throw them for greatest accuracy, and they tried unsuccessfully to get them to wrap around the trunk of a tree. It got late. Dammit, man, said Emilio. His parents had come to spend the weekend and they were waiting for him to have lunch, and he had to be with them. In the late afternoon, nevertheless, they let him go with Mallolet to the dance in the town. But then the one who couldn't go was Raúl. They had guests, people from the summer colony, and he had to stay home. Or he had to return a visit or accompany Felipe and his cousins to a children's tea party, by bicycle. Emilio and Mallolet came back after it was already dark, when it was time for supper, the two of them acting very rowdy and, as it were, in cahoots. They said that Rosalia had let all the boys feel her up.

Summer people. They were joking, wandering about the garden, through the house, leaning on their elbows on the porch railing. In the gazebo there were trays of canapés, pan con tomate y jamón, pitchers of lemonade and horchata and, for the adults, sangría. The adults gathered there mostly, and on the croquet pitch, from which they could hear dry thock of the mallets. They also strolled out as far as the reservoir, to the most hidden spot, a small stream which flowed across the transparent water, grown thick with shadowy algae. The paths crossed at irregular intervals, with the odd stepping stone here or there, and in the little clearings there were concrete benches, hefty, made to look like split trunks. The ivy covered the flower beds, spread out like a lawn; it climbed up the tree trunks, hanging from the boughs. The wooded area was thick and dark, lime trees, cedars, yews, cypresses, dwarf palms, pines, the boughs grown close together, pressing tight against the barely visible house, enveloping it like some tangled nest. It was a three-story house, imposing, salmon-hued, and the roof, very steeply pitched, was of glossy blue ceramic tiles. The chapel lay to one side of the house, with its own entrance, although there was also an interior passage which communicated with the vestibule. Now it was no longer used, but when his aunts and uncles were little they had a priest-in-residence all summer long, and there was Mass every day. The last time it had been used was for Papa's wedding.

Beyond the vestibule, the staircase rose in a tight turn, naked, with gray balusters, illuminated by a skylight. Upstairs there were opalescent glass windows and the shadowy rooms were still dormant, darkened by the thin blinds rolled down, sliced by thin strips of light. The floor was paved with small tiles bearing a concentric geometric pattern in muted tonalities. The walls and ceilings were whitewashed, and the lime masked the moulding, the stucco edgings, making the highlights that had once been a different color nearly imperceptible. In the sitting room, symmetrically arranged around a small table of pink marble, there was a sofa and two ample armchairs with cretonne slipcovers.

There were also small, triangular corner tables, Isabelline chairs, wicker armchairs, a piano, a rocking chair, and, on the console table, in front of the mirror, a crystal bell with a bouquet of dried thistle, pieces of nacre and everlastings. Two deformed silhouettes stood out behind the frosted glass, their laughter audible. Raúl continued examining the house, going upstairs, up to the dormer windows in the attic. The interior rooms were dark, with built-in shelves and wardrobes, and the water trickled in the uralite tanks. Below the inclined plane of the roof, a narrow passageway, with tiny floor-level windows, ran along the outer walls, opening right onto the canopy of the trees. The western side was warm, the dusty floor littered with dead, dried-out flies and butterflies. There were a few odds and ends, some furniture, trunks, and, forgotten in the corner, Uncle Raúl's terrifying wheelchair, a reclining chair with bicycle-type wheels, all covered in cobwebs. By means of a very steep, narrow wooden staircase you could climb up as high as the lookout, a small tower with four windows through which it was possible to go out onto the roof and, clutching the guy wires for the lightning rod, reach the slippery, translucent skylights. Below, you could glimpse the hidden corners of the garden, and beyond, ensconced among the plane trees, Polit's house; then, the folded slopes behind the stubble field, the compact pine groves, the cork oaks. On the croquet pitch an argument was unfolding, with the players all gathered around a wicket, leaning on their mallets.

The most important party happened on Montserrat's birthday, on August fifteenth. That's also when we celebrate the Ascension of Montserrat, she said. It was Montserrat who had the chairs in the garden painted white, as well as the iron parts on the pedestal tables, and bought lawn chairs with striped canvas and cushions in bright colors. They chatted in the gazebo, and Juanito talked about a friend that had even seen a party of Maquis just a hundred meters from the spa, strolling about quite casually with their machine guns. He complained about the government's ineptitude, about everything. He used to dress for the city, a linen suit, perfectly ironed, generally navy blue or white, and his shoes were white and black, with a basket weave pattern. He sat with his knees very close together and the tips of his feet touching one another; occasionally he threw one leg over the other and then took the opportunity to pull up his sock, to smooth out the ankles. With Uncle Gregorio, when the time for coffee came, the conversation came alive and he talked about lots of different things in a very general way. It usually lasted until around mid-afternoon, when Uncle Gregorio stirred them up once more before leaving to take a stroll. Raúl called the dogs and accompanied him. They left the others all in a heated wrangle, Juanito very insistent, attacking the Regime, explaining the rude remark by Duchess Somebody to Franco's wife, highlighting the betrayed ideals of the Renovación Española, agreeing with Uncle Pedro, both of them monarchists first and foremost. But what the fuck are you all complaining about? they heard Montserrat shouting. If you'd spent the war like I did, in hospital after hospital, then you might have something to say. But the only ones who really have the right to complain are those who gave their life for the cause, like our brother. She spoke in a lofty voice, pushing back her chestnut-colored hair, brusquely, her face contorted by bellowing, and surely Uncle Pedro had to reemphasize the vitally important idea that someone remain in the rear guard for the purpose of organizing. My darling niece, please, let's not be so simplistic. People took sides, established alliances; if they'd let the Russians and Japan, if the Americans weren't so stupid, if instead of obliterating Germany, Germany, Germany. Uncle Pedro's words filled his mouth, and he savored them like a spoonful of honey or jam. Juanito was an Anglophile and he disagreed. He turned back to Raúl.

Alright, kid. So how are those studies coming? he said. Are you already learning Greek?

He didn't listen to Raúl's answer. Pensive, looking away, he hummed a few bars, shook his right foot resting on his left leg. When he smiled he showed very clean teeth. He arose late and spent half the morning in the bathroom; Uncle Gregorio was sure he dyed his hair. He went about impeccably shaven, but the oddest thing was his being so tanned without ever sunbathing. His only breakfast was a cup of coffee under the lime trees. Good morning everyone, he said, waving his hand slightly. He always pronounced his words with a certain difficulty, concentrating to avoid making mistakes. Papa and Uncle Gregorio were discussing the possibilities of trying out some reasonable way of making money by selling off the property.

Look, Jorge, said Uncle Gregorio. It's one thing to do the math for the milkmaid and it's something else to start a dairy, a model farm or whatever you like. If you're not planning on living here all year round to manage the business directly, then you'd better stop dreaming.

Dreaming? said Papa. Do you think Papa was dreaming when he built all this? You know as well as I do that he did it, precisely, with a view to creating a model community farm. And now it turns out that was just a fantasy?

Juanito cleared his throat, said that the important thing was to keep in mind the profitability of the investment; he fidgeted with the corner of the handkerchief poking up from his blazer's breast pocket. By the way, he added, where do the farmers sell their products?

After eating dinner, if the night was nice, he went out to the garden with Uncle Gregorio, far from the bright lights of the house, and they lay down in some small clearing, free of trees, to gaze at the sky. They watched the stars, the constellations, and how they turned and shifted as the summer passed. Sometimes Montserrat also came out and sang very softly, to herself, her arms crossed behind her neck making a pillow. Papa would come out but then quickly go back inside again, saying it was cold. And Raúl positioned himself to stare straight up at the zenith, without any nearby reference, and ended up getting vertigo from the sky. The earth was fresh and from the deep hollows came the sound of water running between the trees, and the hooting of the owls, the song of the nightingales, and the chirping of the crickets, which sounded like falling stars.

Later, after Montserrat and Juanito had left, they criticized them. Papa more critical of Juanito, and Aunt Paquita more critical of Montserrat, or Monsina, as she called her: her habits, that she went out around there with soldiers and big shots. Besides, she's got quite a vocabulary. She uses some words and expressions totally inappropriate for a woman. The fact that her marriage failed justifies nothing. How can she raise her daughter with the way she's acting lately? What's she going to learn, the poor little thing, besides barracks talk? Apart from her fling with the German, which has been a disaster, you could see that coming a mile away. He was just an adventurer, a player, a Don Nobody. It was obvious he was going to disappear all of a sudden the same way he showed up, just as easy as you please. They were in the dining room, seated around the table, and Uncle Gregorio was serving himself some salad.

Montserrat's like me in that way, he said, concentrating carefully on choosing the best leaves of lettuce. She likes what's fresh, green, and tasty.

Well, all I can tell you is that, if the little girl turns out to be a woman like God commands, it won't be for the example and the late nights of her mother.

What about him? Papa said. How's he going to have authority over his sister with the gluttonous life he leads, every night at the cabaret and all that, chasing floozies? Excessive behavior only leads to moral, financial, and even physical ruin. Sexual abuse ruins a man more than anything else; some men go crazy from doing it so much.

I don't think that in Juanito's case these effects are appreciable, said Uncle Gregorio, cheerful as a mischievous gargoyle. In the end, it's only natural for a man. It would be worse if he went the other way.

Papa smiled, incredulous.

The other way? I saw one of those years ago, on a streetcar. He spoke, and even moved, just like a woman.

He said that instead of expending energy, what one had to do was accumulate it, that that was why Juanito was so lazy, a person without willpower. Grooming himself, having fun, and not working a lick the whole damn day ... the best way to live. Sure.

If that's supposed to be some passing reference to me, Jorge, you're wasting your time, said Uncle Gregorio. Your opinions roll right off me. When you talk about doing things the way I have, what you really mean is that I've not accomplished a thing; by my age you'd be much richer.

Inevitably, someone dredged up the theme of the old mansion on Calle Mallorca. The millions it would be worth now if it hadn't been sold and knocked down to build an apartment house. Aunt Paquita still lived in one of the flats. The millions the land would now be worth. The responsibility carried by Raúl, Uncle Raúl, the father of Monsina and Juanito, as the oldest brother. His crazy blunder.

They went out for a walk, with the dogs, and Uncle Gregorio gave him some background information. Doc, Chisa, Estrella, c'mon, c'mon, shouted Raúl. Even the annoying Balet came along, who was always following at his heels, a yellow dog, an Irish setter mix, with a regal profile, a rosy snout, and a faggot's yellow eyes. The other two trotted along on their own, sniffing around. And he told him the secret, the story of when Juanito almost lost his inheritance, about how one day some kind of chorus girl just showed up at Uncle Raúl's house saying she was pregnant, and how Juanito, although he swore he had nothing to do with it, ended up having to pay. By then Uncle Raúl was already a paralytic, but he was wise to everything going on; he said that Juanito would never receive any inheritance from him as long as he was in a state of mortal sin, and he sent him packing off to Montserrat, for spiritual exercises. Uncle Gregorio had some binoculars slung across his chest bandolier-style and a staff of peeled acacia wood for a walking stick. Generally they went along the creek and then they followed a fern-shaded path to reach some freshwater spring. The pipe was iron and the water poured out onto a circular font, sunk down to the level of the earth, partially covered over by the thick fallen leaves. There were rough stone benches, curving round following the sinuous slope, and they sat down at the foot of the tall plane trees, contemplating the trembling boughs. The trunks were covered with hikers' carvings, and there were remains of bonfires, ashes, blackened stones, a crumpled rusty can. Uncle Gregorio brought out some bread and chocolate, the tablets a little bit softened inside the silver paper.

America, he said.

He encouraged him to leave, to emigrate like his grandfather, but not to Cuba, not even to Argentina, where everything had already been done and practically no opportunities remained, but to Venezuela or Brazil, a country with a real future. In the interior the climate is good, and you can raise cattle. What are you going to do in Spain? If I were young again … They talked about Mato Grosso or Los Llanos like a shared memory, a landscape familiar to them both. None of that, by contrast, seemed to interest either Emilio or Mallolet; they barely glanced at the maps, and the idea of the three of them emigrating together attracted them no more than any other theme of conversation. And Raúl buried himself in his atlas, with its tracts on cattle farming. When they finished their snack of bread and chocolate, Uncle Gregorio drank a little fresh water from the spring and then he rolled two cigarettes.

What about Africa? asked Raúl.

The mill was a bit further down, in a hollow. He went there alone, following a little-used cart track, with the wheel tracks nearly hidden in the grass. The mill was in ruins, roofless, mostly a collapsed mess of fallen stones, and through the wall grew a tangled copse of holm oak. Nevertheless, a section of it had been rebuilt, and you simply had to untie a slender cord to open the heavy wooden door. Inside, the floor was covered with a thick bed of dry, fragrant grass, a bare room, with iron rings set into the walls. The window looked out onto the creek, to a spongy mass of ferns over which butterflies flew and the light poured through green, filtered; an ideal spot. He shut the door.

Once he brought Mallolet and Emilio along and, hiding his excitement, he proposed that they make the place their general headquarters. It's also the perfect place for casting out bad spirits, said Emilio. Mallolet was the least interested; any place is good enough for me, man. Raúl immediately regretted bringing them there but, fortunately, they seemed to have forgotten it and he stopped insisting. Emilio paid them no mind; he talked to himself, shouting, as if he were performing some comedy, rattling off classifications from botany class. Mallolet finally told him to shut the hell up. Sometimes you act crazy, he told him. And

Emilio let out a wild cackle. His mother had come to visit for
a few days and every afternoon she made him study. She sewed
on a sewing machine in the living room, with Mallola, and they
talked nonstop for hours. Mallola watered the floor in a zigzag,
emptying the water jar, and then sat down to thread a needle,
the clothes on her knees. They sewed sitting very close together,
with their glasses pushed on tightly, taking long pauses to laugh
heartily, while the daughter-in-law, sitting apart from them, simply smiled. Then the sewing machine whirred again. The shutters
were closed tight against the sun and the flies.

The boy's going through a growth spurt, said Emilio's mother.
And he'll be just as hairy as my husband. If you saw him…

She spoke slowly, concentrating on her work. Mallola spoke
about her daughter, who would now be the same age as Emilio.
Lately, they were just saying, there was a cure for tuberculosis.
Quiet, woman, hush up, said Emilio's mother. They'd known
each other since they were young, since Mallola was in Barcelona,
working as a maid. They were reminiscing, and when at last the
two of them toppled over, struggling friskily, as if they were tickling each other, the others just stared at them. Mallolet and his
brothers worked for Polit on the thresher and they all went out
together, with the dogs. They were winnowing on the threshing
ground, enveloped in a whirl of rough sunny bright chaff, and
a hand from Valencia who kept the horses walking round on
the hay spread out on the ground was singing jotas. Raúl and
Emilio accompanied the ones who were going out to the field,
to bring in the sheaves. Someone stupidly tried to frighten them
with stories of scorpions hidden among the haystacks. At mid-
afternoon they rested a little and the porrón of wine made the
rounds from hand to hand. The roof of the house stood out in
the distance, above the green mass of the garden, shining in the
sun. And while Mallolet amused himself by masturbating his
dog, Raúl questioned Polit. Polit contracted the fissure of his
lips. A sad affair, he said. The Mallols, he said, have suffered a
lot. During the war, when the oldest son departed, Polit promised to celebrate his return with a dinner, a really fine dinner. It
took him a few years to return, to return from the concentration

camps, pale as a ghost, and he was only back a short time before
he died, and he pulled his sister right along behind him because
she contracted tuberculosis from him; and they didn't celebrate
anything. They'd been harassed a lot and, even now, none of the
family had a license for guns. They've suffered a whole lot, he
repeated. Mallolet wasn't really named Mallolet, nor his father
Mallol. But because they lived at Can Mallol, they also called
the old man like that, and the old lady was la Mallola, and the
youngest one, Mallolet, even though his name was Quim.

They continued bringing in the hay, and it was almost night
now when Polit stood up straight and, with his arms akimbo,
said it was time to pack it in. Let's go, boys, he said. They drove
back in the cart along the shadowy roads, leaning against the
sheaves, contemplating the sky turning every moment more
colorless. Later, seated on the stone bench, against the wall,
the stories and ramblings continued. That very night, probably,
Polit recounted the circumstances of his imprisonment, after the
Nationalists arrived, the diverse anecdotes about his being held
in the town school until he was paroled, thanks as much to the
deliberate intervention of Aunt Paquita and the sergeant as his
own ability to mount his own defense, having argued that even
if he could be held partly responsible for the fact that the church
had been turned into a warehouse, it was certainly the lesser of
two evils, in fact because if nothing else, the structure itself had
been spared from almost surely being burned to the ground.
They called Montserrat the sergeant, a nickname that dated,
said Polit, from the time she went about wearing the Red Cross
chief's uniform. Even now she always came over to talk a little
while, to hash things out with Polit face to face, and Polit followed her lead, they knew how to understand one another. Now
and then she got the urge for making jam and then they saw her
arrive out of breath, loaded down with fruit. She dropped the
basket and sat down with her legs extended, her hair loose, her
face dripping with sweat.

You, you don't say a word, you're too restrained, said Polit.

Shit, what about you? said Montserrat. If you had a little
more self-restraint you wouldn't have such a gut on you.

Raúl stayed with them while they ate dinner, until they shouted for him from his house. On the other hand, Juanito, like Ramona and Pedro and even like Felipe, sometimes left without even having come over to say hello. Besides, more and more they all came less frequently to Vallfosca, and for less time; Juanito, at the most, came for a few days around the Feast of the Assumption. Ramona and Pedro preferred the beach, and Aunt Paquita lamented her loneliness, but she continued to allow them to spend long stretches in Palamós, with Uncle Pedro's family. Felipe did the same, barely staying at all; he went to Puigcerdà, to a friend's house, and Papa said that he had a semi-serious girlfriend there.

A girl from the Roura family, wealthy, well-connected people. He started following her and, from the looks of it, she hasn't discouraged him.

What do you expect, said Aunt Paquita. They're spring chickens now. It's natural at their age they get interested in each other.

Spring chickens? said Uncle Gregorio.

I'm not saying this because he's my son, but Felipe really is a very good boy. Well, and Raúl, too, of course. Just you wait, wait and you'll see how he also starts to step out. Isn't that right, Raúl?

Felipe refused to give explanations. He shut his bedroom door and wrote letters. He transformed his room, he traded the bed for a cot, the nightstand for a three-legged stool, he removed the mirror and left the walls blank without any photos or clippings. When he was at home he hardly left his room; and if he did it was just to take a stroll in the garden. One afternoon he came into Raúl's room. Go on, go on, he told him, and Raúl tried to resume his reading—a study about the adaptation of diverse European beef cattle breeds to tropical climates—under Felipe's watchful gaze. Felipe had stretched himself on the bed and was smoking a cigarette. After a bit, nonetheless, he asked him if he wouldn't like to play tennis. At your age you'd learn right away. I've got extra rackets and we could go together. It feels really good, y'know? And, look, you also get to talk with people besides, and all that. He also asked him what he was planning on studying when he finished high school.

I don't know, Raúl said, shutting his book. Maybe Law.

Of course, man. Law is really good, said Felipe. It's a career with a lot of options.

Then he proposed to go to town by bicycle, to take a look around. He helped him straighten the part in his hair, made him put on a clean shirt. But, man, take off that fishing hat, it's ugly as hell.

It took them a while to find the other kids, gathered under the pine trees at an apartment house, on the outskirts of town. They were planning a nighttime exploration of the cemetery and the girls were shrieking. What we've got to do is plan another day at the beach, said one of the girls. They talked about their last outing; the sea wasn't far, you could glimpse it once you crested the hill, but it was very steep and you had to pedal really hard. Someone recalled when Celia fell.

And they all got a prizewinning view.

You're all so fresh, you've really got a lot of nerve.

The same thing happened every September. They were all a little fed up with outings, with hiking to picnic at one spring or another, always the same ones, lately, and having to pedal more than two hours to get to the beach, and the parties, and afternoon teas which every family gave, occasions on which Javi Solans would inevitably end up singing those green eyes, most beautiful poppy, it's impossible, my life, to live so far apart. Looking at Celia as he spread his arms wide, at the most meaningful moments. They grew tired of the mid-afternoon walks, of the jokes and even of the grudges and gossip that had been growing throughout the summer, and the conversations grew ever more boring and rambling. And then September arrived and although they still had a whole month ahead of them, it was as if the summer had already come to an end. The ones who'd flunked some class had to cram and, in some cases, leave early for Barcelona, to take private classes. The thing is I'm flunking math, I'm sinking, said an older boy, almost as old as Javi Solans. And they talked about movies that had just opened or the ones advertised in the papers, yet to premiere. And in spite of the fact that everything pointed to the start of a new school year, the urge to depart, to be already in Barcelona, to see other friends, classmates, to go to the cinema or shopping, to get outfitted for the autumn, was practically contagious. The same process as in June, when everybody was arriving, but in reverse.

Only Raúl seemed to like September, now that he need not accompany Felipe to a town that was emptying of summer vacationers, now that Emilio had left and Mallolet was busy helping with the grape harvest. Going out walking alone he discovered that the spots which years earlier had seemed mythically distant, which when he went with his cousins required a whole day for the outing, with backpacks, picnic baskets, bakelite dishes, folding cutlery, and thermoses, he could now reach them with an autonomy and speed that not even Mercè herself could believe when she saw him return before lunch, back already.

Faker, you're just a faker.

They served more drinks, horchata, beer. In the background, Raúl listened without loosening his grip on his glass. Suddenly he crossed eyes with Felipe and guessed that he was going to be mentioned. This guy is a real Don Juan, he heard him say. He's got a whole girls' school in love with him. Everyone looked at him. He tried to meet their expectant gazes, smiles of sympathy and encouragement; he drank quickly. None of it was true. Perhaps, if he ran into a group of schoolgirls, they laughed and made a fuss, or rather, if he ran into one alone, he saw her walk by very stiff, tense in her uniform, upright, head held high, staring straight ahead; but nothing more. And he didn't even really like them, nothing in them attracted his attention, their too-chubby legs, flat chests, and big bottoms, but not tight and pretty, only large and, in any case, shapeless, their faces undefined, looking self-conscious, with some irritating little pimple, the result of the very changes of the age, as well as an unrestrained passion for eating pastries. No, they were unconvincing despite their attempts to approach him and walk on by, hieratic in appearance, but uptight, ears eagerly wide open: useless, completely useless. The one he really did like was Celia, nicely tanned by the sun, with her hair mussed up and her mouth thickly painted with lipstick. She wore a long yellow bodice with

Japanese sleeves and when she raised her arm it revealed the soft hair in her armpit, the gentle swelling of her tit. She, evidently, had noticed it herself, and frequently repeated the gesture: she leaned back, hooked her hands behind her neck and laughed.

He also observed her during Mass, on Sundays. Celia always sat in the last pews, among her friends, wearing her cardigan and mantilla. Sometimes she picked up her missal and pretended to read, but the most attractive thing was the expression on her face when she returned from taking communion, her full lower lip slightly moist, her eyelids half closed. Raúl stayed with the other boys, standing against the back wall. Papa and Aunt Paquita, however, invariably occupied the front pew on the left. They drove in the trap, arriving early so that, as Aunt Paquita desired, there would be no need to whip the horse. Raúl preferred to walk, taking the shortcut. He left later but arrived first, in time to witness—one of so many among the onlookers—the sudden arrival of the cart in the church plaza, Aunt Paquita seated up front, black and erect, covered in veils like a saint, facing the driver. The boy jumped to the ground and helped them get down, while some acquaintance, some older lady, approached and greeted them cordially. The horse stamped, agitated by the crowd surrounding them, by the cars that kept appearing, and the boy had to dash forward and grab its bridle. The summer people huddled together in groups, exchanging greetings, and the townspeople, standing slightly apart, commented on them, observing their clothes. Then they heard the bells ring again and they began to enter the church. Raúl stayed behind in the background, remaining at the entrance to the atrium, and as soon as some straggler came in, he took advantage of how slowly the door closed to slip out. He lit a cigarette and, dazzled by the sun, went into a bar, on the other side of the main street. He took a seat next to a large window from where he could watch the whole plaza. The main room was long and deep—with echoes and fluid transparencies, like an aquarium. Beyond the back of the room a small door opened onto the patio, onto a violent cascade of blue bellflowers. There were rows of small tables and, facing the marble counter, two men were talking, their voices intermingling.

Closer, with a vermouth on the table, Uncle Gregorio was staring at him silently, from above his open newspaper. *Caramba*, Raúl, he said. He invited him to join him, to order a vermouth for himself; Raúl felt uneasy and couldn't quite relax.

Really hot, isn't it?

Yes, said Raúl. But it's nice here.

They smiled after a while and Uncle Gregorio patted him on the back, delighted.

Look, the truth is I haven't moved from this spot. What color harnesses were the priests wearing today?

Green, I think.

They watched the sparrows in masterful possession of the whole deserted street, in broad shadow, and their conversation developed pleasantly until people began to filter out of the church. Then Uncle Gregorio paid and they let themselves be seen in the plaza. The people emerged slowly, looking for one another, planning for later, the ladies from the summer colony closing their purses and folding their mantillas, gathering under the shade of the plane trees, florid and ostentatious, while some began to wander off, reanimating the side streets of the old town through which, on other Sundays, Raúl went walking before Mass was quite finished. He wandered through the quiet town, among deep doorways and tiny windows, lichen-colored walls, corner patches with sunflowers, hanging geraniums, radiant climbing plants. All that warm quietude was like a siesta that would inevitably be destroyed when the soft trilling and cooing from the chicken coops and dovecotes was drowned out by the sudden hubbub rising from the plaza, and Raúl had to go back and rejoin the crowd.

In Barcelona there was no problem, and when he sometimes accompanied Mireya to eleven o'clock Mass, at the Pedralbes monastery, he joked implacably in a muted voice, making scathing observations for her benefit. She said that, more than anything, she went there for the marvelous beauty of the place, for the organ music, and then, as they strolled around the outskirts she let him grope her. In the afternoons he would take her to a bar with reserved tables and dim lighting and background music. He bought himself a lighter and sunglasses and helped himself to a gold-plated cigarette case which Felipe never used. He usually smoked black tobacco, but when he went out with Mireya he bought loose blonde cigarettes and refilled the case. Now in the bar, he opened the case to offer her a cigarette and, as he'd seen in a film, lit his at the same time as she lit hers, from the same flame. He blew out a slow and penetrating mouthful of smoke, and then put his arm around her shoulders.

During the week they could hardly see each other; Mireya had classical dance classes in the late afternoon and her father had forbidden her from dallying afterward or to arrive home any later than nine o'clock sharp. She was really fine and wore her hair in a long, thick braid, and she seemed older than her years. She talked about the box seats at the Liceo, about other boys, about an old engineer. I really like you because you look so young, she said. And one afternoon, upon leaving school, Raúl took a chance, slipped into Madame Rita's, where—people said—no one asked your age. He hung around outside until some man went in and then, slipping into the salon, sat down by his side to make it look as if they were together. He sat there a while, sunk down in the worn velvet sofa with mushy springs, examining the whores one by one. Especially attentive to the right way to disappear with them, how you had to act, in the manners and customs of the place, in the words and gestures. The whores chatted and laughed, they caressed each other, they fanned the sweaty naked parts that showed through beneath their nylon folds, approaching him now and then, repeating snatches of some song. Too late. It was the time for exams, he was finishing the year, and Mireya was holding out, resisting his advances, proving to be obstinate and distant; she said she was fed up with dark bars, mezzanine tables, and private rooms, of always hearing the same records, all that business of let's go for a stroll and maybe we'll see each other later. He saw her riding on the back of a moped, softly clutching the guy driving, and he managed to not let her see him when they came to a stop a few meters ahead, waiting for the light to change. The afternoon was waning and Raúl kept walking round the streets submerged in Sunday quiet, sticking his head into the bars with

the most activity, stopping in front of the entrances to the caba-
rets and the whorehouses, trying to get a look inside. He made
up his mind sitting in his threadbare velvet corner: a very dark
woman, with thick eyebrows and puffy eyelids, her lips almost
blue with the shadow of a mustache at the corner of her mouth.
They went upstairs to the next floor; the hallways, very old and
silent, slightly illuminated by gray globes, smelled like warm
laundry. Raúl struck up the conversation with some random
phrase, doubtless premeditatedly cynical, meant to facilitate
the preliminaries, the problem of whether he should undress or
undress her or both things at the same time and in which order
and starting where, thus advancing all questions about how to
proceed, as if this wasn't his first time at all. But she didn't ask
anything. She climbed on top of him, on all fours, offering him
her ass, wrapping her arms around his thighs, warm, slippery,
sticky, wet, her hanging breasts tinted by the dim red gloom.

I'll do something that you'll like, she said.

He told Mallolet about it the first chance he got, and Mallolet,
with sly eyebrows, said he'd done the same. He explained what
the brothels were like in the country towns and they got into the
details, of how often, how many times, and for how long. I do
it my way, quick, said Mallolet. He called his brothers and they
kept talking with total freedom, as if among friends. They were
on the wall around the threshing ground and the brothers related
their experiences. Anecdotes of when they were in the military
service, principally, until Mallola called them in for supper. And
when Emilio arrived a few days later they received him with great
excitement, tossing him allusions, discriminating hints, holding
back as long as possible from telling him exactly what they were
getting at. Emilio protested, he assured them that he'd done it,
too, yes, already, and that everything went smoothly, all right,
although, just afterward, he'd felt some pain. But his story wasn't
quite coherent, and they all ganged up on him. The quarrel
left them tired and conciliatory, and they changed the subject.
There was only one more year to finish high school and it was
pleasant to make plans, to map out the future, in which everything was reduced to knowing how to endure nine more months.

Nine months and there would be no more lining up or Mass or smocks or sneaking cigarettes sitting on the toilet or Sundays spent doing equations, and—the most important, including outside of school—nothing that smacked of still being a schoolboy. For Emilio, however, those considerations seemed to matter very little; what worried him was his college career, his studies, his future, and they talked seriously. He'd arrived for the summer very changed, taller, and of course now he shaved every day. People said his father was earning a lot of money, that he'd been lucky, that being an electrician included the possibility of turning his work into a full-fledged business installing electrical systems. But Emilio insisted that his real ambition was to study medicine. Yeah, yeah, bullshit, said Mallolet. He was leafing through comic books without paying much attention to what they said, getting impatient. And they went for walks, the same as other summers. There were still some cherries hanging on the picked-over branches and from the fig tree in the vineyard hung large young unripe figs—pale, insipid fruit, not like the figs in September, sweet and oozing, with soft skin white as curds, bursting at the touch, with red fissures, among the dark, rough leaves. They argued about the annual town fiestas; the feast of San Ireneo fell on Friday, but Mallolet was sure that the best time was always Saturday night. They agreed to meet for a walk, to check out the dance.

In the gazebo, Uncle Gregorio was balancing in his chair, leaning back with his feet resting on another chair, pensive, the thick gray hair tufting out of his half-open shirt. Was he, perhaps, watching the clouds, distant as he seemed from the conversation? Upon the table, his eyeglasses folded, the newspaper, his pouch of shag tobacco, an empty cup, with golden-yellow coffee stains.

He eschewed the noise of the evening street parties. Or fled the humid heat of Barcelona. Or from Leonor, scolding, bossy, and grouchy, always upbraiding him for being absent-minded, for not washing or changing his clothes enough, for his love of making a mess in the kitchen, for his bad habits. She's always got to be complaining about something, he said. Such a good woman that she's unbearable. It was better in Vallfosca.

Fiestas? he said. That's for people who work.

He complained about the heat in Barcelona, the nighttime
fiestas, the bright glow from the bonfires and the fireworks, the
music and the explosions that didn't let him sleep a wink all
night. I've come running back here. What I wasn't counting on
is the mosquitoes being so bad up here this year. Aunt Paquita
was also there, tired from the trip, increasingly strict, fulfilling
her devotions, a practice—the precise one—for every occasion:
the Holy Hour, the five Saturdays of the Immaculate Virgin,
the five Sundays in honor of the five wounds of Saint Francis,
the six Sundays of Saint Luis Gonzaga, the seven Sundays of
Saint Joseph, the nine first Fridays of the months, the fifteen
Tuesdays of Saint Anthony... Fulfilling, accumulating indulgences, speaking of the particular protection enjoyed by those
who wear the scapular as well as those who carry a simple rosary
in their pocket, always ready, discretely put away, recounting still
the horrific death of Voltaire or the irremissible condemnation
of Isabella of England. Her rosary beads were olive pits from
an olive tree in Gethsemane, and she slipped them between her
fingers. Then she would play the piano, a tall black piano with
sconces for candles, more out of tune every year, the keys worn
and broken from being hammered on one summer after another.
Her waxen fingers, like slender bamboo shoots, would play Liszt,
Chopin, and Beethoven, and Papa would inevitably say that
Paquita played with great feeling.

On the feast of Saint Irenaeus it was the first Friday of the
month. Aunt Paquita and Papa drove the trap into town to
take communion. It was probably then, when the Mass was
concluded, when the rumor began to spread that Rosalía had
aborted her baby. Emilio told Raúl, very excited. Later, at night,
at Polit's house, they learned more details; that she'd been three
months pregnant, that the hemorrhage had been stopped, that
the hemorrhage had continued, that she had done it with a
knitting needle, that she'd done it with a stem of rue, with an
ivy leaf, that the doctor made his diagnosis by slicing open a frog
and examining its entrails, that just like in the case of Toni, and
unlike the case of Mariona, etcetera.

Well, of course, said the Aragonese. Who in the hell could you hold responsible if the girl, starting with her brother on down, has whored it out more than a mother hen?

Yes, playing, always playing, and now look, said Mercè.

She was carrying in the plates, the silverware. They had switched the lights on, and Polit, sitting on the stone bench, yawned hollowly, with his arms tensed. Raúl listened to the frogs, the croaking like a broken gurgle that reached them from the pond. And I was counting on her for the dance tomorrow, said Mallolet. He was touching it through his pocket.

They had a good time at the town's annual festival, *la fiesta mayor*. They saw Polit with his daughter and his son-in-law, who lived on the coast; he was wearing a new beret and a white shirt, his belt cinched low beneath his paunch. He called them over, invited them to have a cognac; the outside tables were packed and they had to drink it standing at the bar. There were people from all over the region, summer vacationers, groups arrived from other towns who filed along in tight lines past the fair's booths and stands. By contrast, the area under the awning was still fairly lifeless: rows and rows of empty seats and the orchestra playing for a few couples. Two or three little girls from the summer colony drew near and waved to Raúl, mischievous and shy at the same time, while Emilio and Mallolet watched and waited to see. They adopted a casual air, apparently impertinent, but it showed that they were bored, that they wanted to invite themselves over. Then they kept on bumping into them, too many times to be accidental, and Raúl finally pretended not to see them. They returned to the shooting gallery and won more cigarettes and a little bottle of some horrible alcoholic concoction. They drank beer and ate clams, and in another bar they invited them to have some wine; Mallolet said that he liked the clam best of all. It was hot, they were sweating. Now at night, under the dazzling bright awning, Mallolet danced with a girl from the town dressed in pink, but it didn't take long before they saw him coming back, pushing through the crowd, laughing like crazy, infecting them with his laughter. They laughed and pushed each other, and Raúl felt invincible. On the way back they ran into Polit driving the wagon—the land yacht, they called it—and he let them load their bicycles in the back and climb in. Dammit will you listen to me! shouted Emilio from the back, turning his back on them, with his legs hanging outside bumping along. Polit knew some *habaneras* and they ended up singing, all four of them, saluting in chorus the passing cars that lit up the shadowy turns of the highway. It was like the summer before, when the mountainsides caught fire and everybody worked together to put out the fire; Polit had a small barrel of wine with a bamboo reed spigot and they drank and came back singing, too, and Raúl didn't notice how much fun they'd had until it was all over.

On Sunday it was even hotter, a hazy, muggy morning, clouded over, with a quiet dry glare, like ashes. Raúl lent them the shotguns and they went out, he was carrying Uncle Pedro's gun. They talked about the night before, about Rosalía. And they managed to shoot something: Raúl got an old rook that he ended up shooting to pieces among the cork trees with their gray branches. They met up at the edge of the woods. Just ahead, in some spot among the dark, undulating vineyard, the partridges were singing. It was a few feet away, hardly past where the hill began to slope down, when they heard a voice cry Halt, immediately followed by a shot, brief and cutting. The game warden was coming after them, also coming down the hill, trampling the vine shoots, the barrel of his rifle smoking lightly.

Halt! he repeated.

They looked at each other. The game warden, said Emilio. He saw him running off, to the side, dodging the grape vines, escaping. Another shot sounded and Raúl looked back, jumping sideways, plunging between the twisted vine stumps. Mallolet hadn't moved, he stayed frozen in the same spot, in front of the warden, with his arms raised. He heard the ground crunch and a rustling of leaves, and he saw Emilio crawling toward him from a little ways further down. He caught him, he heard him say. They heard a third shot and the guard's voice shouting at them to put down their guns and stand up. C'mon, up! Raúl noted the taste of dry earth between his teeth. They stood up, maybe with their hands raised. The other two approached, slowly, Mallolet in front, pale, his mouth hanging half-open, his face slack, as if he didn't see them. The game warden, a short ways behind, came toward them with his rifle level, aiming from the waist. He was breathing heavily, hunched and sweating beneath his discolored flat cap. From Vallfosca, eh? he said. He picked up the shotguns and they set out marching, the three of them ahead of him, silent.

They found Papa in the garden, under the shade of the lime trees. Uncle Gregorio came out immediately, putting on his glasses, and also Aunt Paquita, still wearing her mantilla. Papa began to apologize, to say that he'd already warned Raúl. He promised that they would not do it again. He talked with the game warden about the town mayor, about the parish priest, about a prefect who was a friend of his, he offered him a drink, some refreshment. The warden shook his head no; he said that, apart from the fact that none of the three boys had a hunting license, hunting at that time of year was a crime, in the middle of the closed season, when the animals were still with their babies. Eloísa, her eyes wide, frightened, followed the scene from a respectful distance in the background. Then Uncle Gregorio intervened, he took the fellow aside. C'mon, fella, let's talk, that's how people understand one another, he said. They talked a while. Then they saw Uncle Gregorio reach for his wallet.

They went toward Polit's house.

Idiot, said Raúl. He wouldn't have dared to shoot us.

Chicken, said Emilio. Faggot.

They all met up later. What happened? asked Mercè. The hands, just in from the fields, resting, a few shaving by the water tank. And Polit, sweaty and potbellied, barefoot, his pants rolled up, in a t-shirt.

This guy sure is a sissy.

Suddenly Mallolet pulled away, ran to hide in some empty stall in the barn. They chased after him, and in the sudden gloom they could barely see him against the back wall, kneeling in the bed of straw, crying. Polit appeared behind them, on the threshold, surrounded by yellow light, arms akimbo and a straw between his teeth.

Let's go, he said. You two, scram.

IV

COMING DOWN TO Las Ramblas meant not only a change of streets but also, and above all, a state of mind. You noticed it the moment you left Plaza Catalunya, for example, starting to take those first steps under the fluid river of plane trees, strolling, falling into step with the crowd, slow and tight, in full play of searching gazes, advances, grazing you, brushing up against you. A leisurely atmosphere of gentle warmth that only thickened when, further on down, the street narrowed between the flower stalls and the calm air of the long afternoon smelled faintly like lilies. The people emerged from their places of business and there was something like drunkenness or fever in all that coming and going, light clothing, perspiring skin, in that ebb and flow without any fixed direction which could just as well sweep them along to the porticoes of the Plaza Real as to the taverns along Escudillers, on the right-hand side, map-wise, north of Las Ramblas, while, imperceptibly, the first street lamps and the first flashing signs flickered to life. Or else toward the left, southward, taking Conde del Asalto or Arco del Teatro, toward Calle San Ramón, San Rafael, San Olegario, Tapias, Robadors, confusing alleys and side streets with their little dives which stank of hashish, alleys where, as it grew dark, the shining lights isolated the ground floor businesses, the red doorways, the worn, narrow pavement, the filthy paving stones, high-heeled shoes, bulging hips, necklines, long manes of hair, painted eyes, a succession of bars, of turf marked off and intensified by cigarette smoke. From Calle Tapias you could emerge onto the Paralelo Boulevard, wide and luminous, plastered with handbills, dreary, but the boulevard didn't get lively until later, when the shows started, and they decided to head back through El Raval, still barhopping, drinking cold wine, slightly sour. Now fewer people were on the street; they began to hear songs sung in chorus and there were characters hanging around on the corners, waiting for something. Only Las Ramblas was still as lively as before, as at any hour of any day. A salty breeze, smelling like the port, wafted among the plane trees, phantasmal in the neon light, thick with birds perched quietly among the leaves. And there, on the patio outside some bar, closing time caught them as if by surprise. They were cleaning up, and the roaring of the cars cranking up their motors right along the sidewalk, and the rolling metal shutters clattering down, was deafening. The side streets had gone dark and unidentifiable groups invaded the sidewalk mixing with the dense trickle of cars and motorbikes and their fitful procession heading up Las Ramblas.

They were tireless. Later, walking along the bland, quiet streets of the Ensanche, they kept on talking and arguing. Sometimes Leo got a kick out of adopting suspicious attitudes to startle the sleepy night watchmen. They laughed. They talked and expounded. First they all walked Federico home, and then Leo accompanied Raúl or Raúl accompanied Leo, and they ended up taking a streetcar, clear and empty. As Raúl entered the house, the light in Papa's room switched on, and when he passed by the door, slightly ajar, he heard a cough, the agitated stirring of a spoon against a glass. But not until he returned from the bathroom did he hear him call : Raúl, he said. Yes, said Raúl. It's very late, son. Where have you been? He looked at him sitting up in bed, wearing a faded shirt with unbuttoned cuffs, clutching a glass of milk. At Federico's house, Papa, said Raúl. And Papa would say : the Quintana boy? He would say that he'd met old man Quintana, a true personage, that the Quintana family were people of great wealth and social standing.

Federico preferred gin and then it didn't take long for his tongue to loosen up, for him to get involved in conversations. He insisted on stopping by Los Maños or the blind men's bar, la Gran Bodega, where small-time pickpockets, thieves, thugs, and con men gathered around the ash-gray wine barrels fashionably turned into tall tables and porróns of *vino verde*. ¡ *Viva la policía*!

he shouted. And the gray-haired man, who was explaining that he came from Melilla, turned around with a bitter look on his face. What d'ya mean, you? The ones nearest them stopped talking and there was a sudden tension of bodies, of pale hands, of heads close together, of shabby berets, of skulls with dark spots showing through scanty hair. Leo intervened. He said, *Viva la policía.* Why? asked the gray head. Because they keep order, said Leo. Fine, said the gray head. But let's hear it in a different tone of voice. I didn't like how that sounded. We understand each other, right? He turned back to his friends. Don't let those little pipsqueaks fool you. Out in the street Federico started singing and Leo said again that the truth is always subversive. He was the one who guided them through the night, who knew all the obscure joints to visit, who decided what they were going to do; Federico didn't know how to find his way anywhere. Let them put me in chains, he said. I want them to arrest me and clap me in irons. Los Maños was a vast smoky space, with a flimsy door and a counter with burners and stews in casseroles. A worker from the slaughterhouse came in and sold the owner a heavy package of cow entrails, which he brought wrapped in pink, dripping newspapers. Afterward they ran into an old man who was gathering up papers and stashing them in a sack; he stood bolt upright on a corner and, as if bursting out of his wide winter jacket, stared at them sweetly, with large, crazed eyes.

A direct experience of reality, immediate, tangible, epidermic, life on the jagged edge, raw naked life inside a whorehouse, a brawl on Saturday night, a roundup of whores, two or three night watchmen or *guardia civil* clubbing some drunkard, an argument between a whore and her pimp, sordid bars, each one with its regular customers, a pack of blind men selling lottery tickets, for example, or pickpockets and petty thieves, or dope dealers, or whores, or just simple jerk-offs, or queens, more whores, more drunks, the foggy assurances of some man who fought along the Ebro, or so he said, the eyes of a whore kissing a marine while she counted the money right behind his blond neck, things you could never learn in a family setting, nor in residential neighborhoods, nor at university, unique experiences, in the face of which all the habits and principles of their own class were just a charade.

The twenty-first of June, Leo had not accompanied them, perhaps still studying for some exam. In the upper part of the city they heard isolated explosions and, occasionally, the trail of a rocket sparkled across the golden afternoon. A neighborhood procession wound through the streets around Los Maños, people playing music and various characters dressed up in peasant clothing, with oversized wooden spoons and suckling pigs and lambs carried over their shoulders. From each bar people came out to present them with bottles, and two or three boys passed around the traditional red Catalan cap—*la barretina*. After another band—now one in uniform—following the chairman, following the large candles and banners, with the priest, came a double file of young boys, and then, preceding the dress uniforms which closed the parade, isolated, haughty, enveloped in veils and redolent of crushed broom, displaying the emblems of virginity and martyrdom, the Saint—an adolescent girl, her chewing gum the only flaw in her performance. They were enraptured by the sylvan scent of those yellow handfuls of broom that people threw before her, as if they were pieces of gold; several whores fell to their knees. What this saint is doing is called unfair competition, said Federico. They followed along the streets draped from side to side with undulating streamers, and now near Las Ramblas, in a quiet and sophisticated bar, with soft music, dimly illuminated by colored lightbulbs, they met up with Adolfo Cuadras. He was with a friend and he made room for them at the bar. Alright boys, he said, have something to drink. To his right there was a swirl of loose straight hair and a pair of eyes gazed at him from over a shoulder, above a shoulder strap.

I already met this guy. Don't you remember?

No, said Raúl.

At Adolfo's house, silly. This last winter.

This autumn, said Adolfo Cuadras. This is Nuria Rivas. Then she had only just started at university, she'd had her hair in braids and didn't say a word.

He introduced them to at least a few other fellows and to a girl whose name was Luisa or María Luisa and who said that she was celebrating her saint's day. She's the saint, said Federico, but the others didn't understand his jest, and he blushed. They were joking, and Nuria, with her back to the bar, sitting astride the stool, closed and parted her knees beneath her mini-skirt. She nodded to Federico. And this one? she said. Is he one of those quiet types? She talked freely, dropping the occasional swear word, loose tongue and casual manners. It was fun; they were in another bar, surely somewhere around Calle Escudillers, and everyone insisted that they not leave. It's Luisa's turn to pay tonight, they shouted. And Luisa laughed and repeated: look you're all going to end up drunk. Nuria was hanging on Adolfo Cuadras's arm.

What I don't understand is why you all have to drink so much, she said. One drink does it for me.

Well, each to his own, said Adolfo Cuadras.

They ate something in some kind of grocery with mountains of sandwiches displayed on the counter and legs of ham hanging from the beams, lean, dark, like mahogany. Federico had ordered another gin, and Raúl noticed that Nuria's shoulders were lightly freckled.

I can't forgive you for not even remembering me, she said. You look like you're wondering, did I go to bed with her?

Well, really, that's the first thing to get straight, said Raúl.

And Federico said: so you were a virgin then? They ended up at Nuria's house, in the living room with the doors closed and the windows open. They talked about families, parents. She sat facing him, perched on the arm of a chair, with one thigh resting on the other and her elbow against the backrest, next to Adolfo Cuadras's head. She stretched a strand of hair toward her mouth, without even looking once at Raúl, then suddenly she stood up to change the record. Adolfo Cuadras barely joined in the conversation; he was smoking a pipe, listening, his neck against the headrest. On the sofa, Federico was explaining that it was a solemn moment, because it would take another three hundred and sixty-five days before the sun would once more precisely intersect the Tropic of Cancer. He tried to play the piano and dance with Luisa, but in the end he started wandering around. The apartment seemed spacious; there was a predominance of wood and, in the corner with the fireplace, there were bookshelves and copper knickknacks. Come back again whenever you feel like it, said Nuria. Just pick up the phone.

For the evening festivities the three of them went out. On the eve of the feast of San Juan the city was lit up by the splendid glow of bonfires, by the volleys of fireworks, disintegrating in partial and discontinuous images, fleeting, chaotic, angular, beneath the explosion of the rockets and the rain of sparks and the fizzling star castles and the brilliant flaring sparklers and the zipping eruption of a brick of firecrackers, a chain of explosions, zigzagging through those compact blocks deafeningly loud, shooting through like intermittent hot coals in the blackness. Breathing in the clouds of gunpowder, little by little, the low sky going quiet in a soft smoky cardinal red blur. It was muggy and the streets shone brightly, thronged with boisterous turbulent revelers, tangled up in the shredded streamers and splashed confetti. Along the sidewalks, the bars were illumined by the deep hues of Chinese lanterns, vibrant fringed streamers, and little paper flags. They found a spot in the corner of the bar, next to the fan. The owner was wearing a red cardboard fez and his wife a cap of pink silk paper that went very well with her whorish face, whose reflection in the metal butane canisters looked far more beautiful than the real thing. The music played louder than usual.

What are we doing here? said Francisco. We'll just run into boring old Count Adolfo. This place is his personal fiefdom.

Adolfo Cuadras? said Leo. What've you got against him?

He's a spoiled little prick, said Federico.

Well, he doesn't seem like a bad guy to me, said Leo. All things considered, he's one of the best guys at the university.

No way, said Federico. He's an asshole. Besides, he smokes a pipe.

In the Plaza del Teatro someone gave them a more-or-less-phallic-shaped mauve balloon. There were booths selling flat

cakes—*cocas*—brightly lit by candle lanterns, stands selling hats,
cane flutes, scarecrows, party hooters called *espantasuegras*—
designed, as the name implied, to frighten anyone's mother-
in-law—fake mustaches, and shrill toy trumpets. Revelers con-
verged on the spot from every direction. It felt like there might
be a big brawl, and then some drunken guy tried to get everybody together, to make them listen. Well, here we are, in the
navel of the world, said Leo. And he proposed that at dawn they
go to the open-air cafés in Barceloneta, then watch the sunrise on
the beach, among families and couples and sticky used rubbers
tossed onto the sand.

They asked about Teresa. Federico said she was clever and
very good-looking. Why don't you go out with her?

What about you? said Leo. Why don't you take her out,
instead of sitting there all quiet in the corner?

She's only got eyes for you, said Federico. And she'll end up
chasing you. One of these days she'll jump you in the fitting
room, and then you'll have to marry her.

Raúl had run into her that evening when, in the fading
afternoon, he went to pick up Leo. Entering the building's
vestibule he heard her calling him and turned to see her running
across the street, a hanger in her hand. She was wearing a light-
colored housecoat, sleeveless, buttoned in the back, and some
light sandals loose at the heel. Hey you, she said, let's see if
you tell Leo to let me come out with you guys. She preceded
him through the damp shadows, up the steep stairs, and on
each landing the gray clarity of a small open arch at floor level
highlighted her too-chunk calves. They were all in the loft; their
father was cutting, piecing sections together in shirtsleeves, with
his glasses on, and her sister was at the sewing machine. The
canary was twittering in its cage to one side of the window, and
Raúl could glimpse a still sunlit terrace roof where poor boys and
girls were hanging small Chinese lanterns and paper streamers,
and testing their record player. Federico arrived and, with shy,
elusive eyes, sat down next to Leo and lit a cigarette. The brother-
in-law also showed up, smelling of lotion, his bluish cheeks
freshly shaven, his already gray-streaked hair perfectly wavy; he

listened in silence. Then he reappeared in shirtsleeves, hairy and
taciturn, and the first explosions could be heard outside in the
streets. Teresa and her sister sat apart whispering together, Teresa
leaning her elbow on the machine, sewing the seat of a pair of
pants. Her father paused and, looking over the top of his glasses,
suggested something cold to drink. Are you hot? he said. And
then they said yes, and started to laugh. We're very hot, said
Teresa. She touched her forehead, and the other pretended to
cover her sister's mouth.

Alright, alright, said their father. Instead of talking, go get a
few beers. What are you doing with your arms crossed?

They drank beer, the sister drank soda pop, and they
explained to them that they were planning to go and eat *cocas*
on Montjuich, all of them, including the children. Teresa said:
maybe it'll bring me good luck and I'll get a boyfriend and, then,
we'll get engaged. They laughed again. C'mon, you, that's enough
already, said her sister. Watch out or you'll turn into an animal.
The worktable was a dining room table and there were disordered
patterns lying underneath heavy pairs of scissors. The radio was
in the corner by the sofa bed, between worn-out chairs, atop a
small table covered with a runner that hung over the sides like
a shawl, slack and faded, with a fringe of yellow beads. And the
father was saying:

Listen, Ferrer, I want you to understand me: first and foremost, I'm a humanist. And what that means is that I'm for the
human being. I believe in progress, and that the world, sooner
or later, will take a leap forward, the same way that water, when
it reaches the boiling point, turns into steam. And after this leap
forward—call it revolution or whatever—a new era will begin,
a society without classes will be born where each person will be
provided for according to their needs. That's where the world
is going, toward socialism, and you people, the educated ones,
the technicians, the scientists, are the men of tomorrow. Not us,
we already tried once and we failed, precisely because we weren't
prepared. You see, I'm the first to say it, and I've fought, and I've
done time in jail. And my son-in-law, he was very young then,
but he had an ideal and he was always on the front lines, he'll tell

you the same thing. We didn't serve for nothing, and we can only show you, with what we did, the things you shouldn't repeat.

Don't worry, what's got to be done the next time is perfectly clear, said the brother-in-law. And that'll sure be a good fiesta. A really big one, I mean.

He spoke brusquely, contentious, and if they asked him some question he looked at them with suspicion. The father waited, letting him finish, and afterward, as if closing a parenthesis, moved to conclude the sentence where he'd been interrupted. Their memories contrasted, and the conversation concluded by drifting toward anecdotes about the Civil War: the assault on the Atarazanas barracks, the disorder in the Republican camp, Teruel, the fall of Alicante, the retreat, the jails, the firing squads. And at last when Leo stood up, the father stood up, too, his voice uncertain, his eyes feverish, searching. Excuse me, he said. Forgive me if I waste your time with my stories. I'm not someone who's had a lot of schooling. I can't measure up to you either in studies or in culture, but all these things I'm talking to you about are things that I can pass on because I've lived them. And I believe that you, who are the men of tomorrow, need to know them.

It was a season of fires. Not a day went by without hearing, at some moment, the fire engines' sirens fading into the distance. The newspaper covered the string of fires, reporting how in such and such a warehouse, or industrial plant, at such and such a number on this or that street, in spite of or thanks to the opportune and effective intervention by the firemen, etcetera. Raúl read in the shade of the plum tree, in the back part of the garden. He arose late and, while he ate breakfast, Eloísa gathered up the fallen plums. She said that they were the best and she complained about the birds that, even before dawn, flew down to eat them. When she felt like chatting she sat on the steps, with the plums hammocked in her apron, and after some innocuous question she made him put aside his reading and they talked a while. She told him that when she went to the market no one could believe that her hair was natural, that thick braid rolled up like a crown with which now she fiddled around tenderly, chubby and satisfied. Raúl made her some joke about men and she assured him that however much they flirted and teased her she didn't even bother to look at them. Men! she said. They were questions and responses already well-known, commentaries already commented, a chat that always observed the proper tone. How old must she have been? Fifty-something, beneath that appearance at once both infantile and coquettish? Thursday and Sunday afternoons she went out, mysteriously. To see some relatives, she said.

Once in a while a new plum fell and if Raúl was alone it didn't take long for him to hear the stirring of the birds among the leaves. Then he took a stroll, going up through the neighborhood to where the streets ended, cut short by the slopes of dry grass; then he climbed the sinuous paths and from some steep slope along the barren hills he contemplated the immense city, sunken in its lowering haze, shot through with sun, with the moraceous bulk of Montjuich rising up in the distance.

Around mid-afternoon he usually met with Federico. Leo was out of town since the feast of San Pedro, even since before, spending some days in the village. And one night Federico invited him to his house; he asked him over the phone, sounding quite casual. They put on records, lazily slumped in padded leather armchairs, and a maid served them whiskey on the rocks. It was a quiet, impeccable room, and the adjoining dining room, just a step or two slightly higher, also gave the sensation of hardly ever being used. They dined facing each other in the middle of a long oval table, and the chandelier above their heads seemed to be a cascading spider of shimmering tears. Federico explained to him that his family had left for summer vacation; he spoke little and smiled as if concealing some joke, as if mulling over some hidden complicity. Afterward they went out, but without Leo the usual bars didn't feel the same; they didn't know how to get involved in conversations, how to provoke the most unthinkable situation with a single phrase. They felt flat, extinguished, out of place, and now returning home, sleepy, they agreed that they had to discover some new place to go.

And it ended up happening on its own. A woman with a very affected voice answered the phone, and Nuria took awhile to pick up. Oh, yes, come over right away, she said. I've been having the worst afternoon; I read the same paragraph three times and I still don't even get what it says. They'd had quite a lot to drink and Federico got carried away. Nuria greeted them at the door in blue jeans and a black shirt, her eyes bright, like a sprite; the vestibule smelled of blonde tobacco and, further inside, they heard the sound of heels, on the parquet floor, walking away. They went up to the attic on the top floor by an interior staircase. Nuria running, her light, straight hair sweeping her shoulders. Here, we'll be by ourselves, she said. It was a large, comfortable room, with the bed set into a set of shelves, with oaken doors and, facing the terrace window, a spacious desk covered with books and papers. Outside on the terrace there were two or three canvas chairs and a portable record player, and the view from the edge, at the railing, was dominated by a compact panorama of rooftops and terraces. They drank gin, and Nuria pulled out a lighter that felt heavy in her shirt pocket and spoiled the line of her bosom.

I like your shirt, said Raúl.

It's my brother's, said Nuria. Since he's getting taller, his things fit me really well now, so I wear them.

They smoked sitting on the floor, hugging their knees. Federico looked through the records by himself, as if to kill the time. Leo Ferrer, he murmured. You like Leo Ferrer. And suddenly he asked: if you smoke why don't you drink? And she said: are you stupid or do you just say stupid things? Federico started laughing. Look how mean she treats me, he said, and pouring himself some more gin he listened to them talk, his face flushed, with smiling heavy eyelids. What did they talk about? Nuria was cracking jokes, abruptly, aggressive, and Raúl followed the game. As it grew dark they turned on the light, under the awning of brown heather, and Nuria stroked her Siamese cat, a keen, inscrutable cat. Someone mentioned Adolfo Cuadras. I love him very much, said Nuria. I've known him since I was a little girl, from the summertime, and he seemed so much older to me. She said it now in the doorway, when they were leaving. And then Señor Rivas arrived, cordial and expansive, from playing tennis a while or, at least, with the look of having done so; he held open the elevator door meanwhile he stretched out his hand to them like a friend. A youthful man, his hair beautifully white in contrast with his tanned skin, his eyes the same as Nuria's, and from the threshold he still smiled at them, with one hand resting on the nape of her neck.

Immediately, Federico said:

You liked her, tell the truth.

What about you?

Nope, you first: tell the truth, admit it.

Well the thing is she's not bad at all. She's got something that makes me pretty horny.

Well I prefer Santa Luisa, she gets me much hornier. This one is a cautious, sober girl: a little bourgeois Catalana, modern, with her cats, her record albums, and her little intellectual dabbling. No doubt she's a disciple of Count Adolfo. Santa Luisa is a lot more funny, she's more real, more feminine. Why don't we go out with her?

The next time he went back to her house alone, also around mid-afternoon, and he suggested that they take a walk. They went to the Plaza Real and had something to drink under the arches, contemplating the short wheeling flight of the pigeons whose shadows flowed across the yellow facades in the setting sun, as if tossed up suddenly into the air. They generally met there to talk, seated on any terrace under the arches, and afterward they strolled Calle Escudillers for a while, stopping here and there for tapas. They also walked around the south side of Las Ramblas, toward Calle Robadors, past whores who gazed after them and characters who stopped to look at her, make comments, softly sing suggestive snatches of song as they walked by. They stepped into a bar, and in the reddish glare, the people opened a small space to let them in. Raúl smoked a bit mechanically, barely hearing the observations she was sharing with him, covering her from behind with his arm reaching to the bar. Hey kid, he heard them saying. Man enough to handle that all by yourself? Nuria, however, was absolutely at ease, hanging on his arm, laughing, sticking out her tongue, thumbing her nose at them.

She pulled away and paused at length in front of a display case of condoms. Let them say what they want, she said. They didn't go to Los Maños, let alone La Gran Bodega. With Nuria, Raúl preferred to visit the sophisticated bars near Las Ramblas, the jazz caverns, the flamenco venues. They talked about sexual prejudices, about inhibitions causing frigidity, homosexuality, and religion. Nuria admitted to believing vaguely, although she didn't practice; neither did her father, and she still remembered her mother's recent attempts to take them to 12 o'clock Mass as if to a social gathering. Why does the world have to have a creative principle distinct from itself? said Raúl. Why does God not need a creator but the world does? Nuria thought about it. Adolfo thinks the same as you, she said. He says the same thing about almost everything. One of those afternoons the three of them went out together. Nuria's mother had started the summer vacation with the little ones; Nuria stayed in Barcelona with her father and a housemaid. At most, her father might appear around lunchtime, and that afternoon, when they had already decided to stay in the house, quietly, to listen to records, Adolfo Cuadras showed up. He showed no surprise nor did he ask anything, no more reticent than on other occasions. Sitting loosely, he talked with Raúl about exams, etcetera. Nuria reappeared in a change of clothes. Let's go out, alright? she said, and they went out. Adolfo Cuadras asked about Federico, and Leo.

Leo who? said Nuria. Leopoldo?

Just Leo, said Raúl. He was born in August and they named him Leo. But officially his name is Leonardo. He's one of those babies who were baptized after the war.

Do you all study the same thing?

Not Federico; he studies mathematics.

And I'm the old man in the class, said Adolfo Cuadras.

They occupied exactly the same seats as before, with Nuria between the two of them, with her back to the bar. In the mirror facing them, behind the bar, above the lines of bottles and the commemorative photos, her light hair was highlighted by the cloudy penumbra of subtle colors. Their conversation was dry, sticking with safe, general questions, the merits of some work by

Sartre, or Pavese, the moral and intellectual asphyxia of the times they lived in, the lack of unrest demonstrated by students at the university, the mediocrity of everything. Nuria said that things were even worse in the School of Philosophy and Letters, that one single class had been enough to leave her feeling fed up with that parochial environment of priests and monks, of exhausted, pale-faced young men, of girls studying simply to find a fiancé or because they were in despair of finding one. They wandered aimlessly, walking in circles, and the winding streets turned gray in the long afternoon. But Adolfo Cuadras took them to La Venta. There were two flamenco dancers with red heels and, in a corner, a guitarist who wasn't playing, and a man selling peanuts, strips of dried codfish, and hard-boiled eggs. The guitarist was a gypsy—fat, serious, gray-haired, with hands like small toads. There were also customers, leaning against the bar, drawing the sluttish waitresses with their witty conversation. And one of the drag queens passed by in front of their table, haughty, twitching her tight black pear-shaped ass, looking at them rudely as she broke out in a hoarse verse of fandango. It smelled like a urinal, like a basement. There was a false parapet and a false window with iron grillwork, with paper flowers, and the walls were covered by a latticework frame of green lath, simulating an outdoor patio, all of it quite shabby, in the low light of dim bulbs.

It's too early, said Adolfo Cuadras. This place gets lively at night, very late, when the bars close.

We can come back another day. Any other night we're out around here.

Yes, we'll have to come back.

They were sitting on the terrace, in the shade of the heather-covered trellis. Nuria played one record after another; she said that the maid's room was right below them, that she knew for a fact the maid sat by her open window to eavesdrop on them.

I love him very much, she said. But sometimes he exasperates me. He stares and stares at me, and his eyes get big like a sheep's. Poor Adolfo.

She explained that he'd been in love with her forever, almost since she was a little girl, when they spent their summers in the same town. And he had never dared to tell her explicitly nor tried to touch her. He was fairly attractive with his shadowy, angular face, and there had been a time during which, if he'd been more daring, he might've gotten her to pay attention to him. He'd been very ill for quite some time, with tuberculosis, and she thought he'd get over her. But no, with the illness he only missed a year of his studies. He lent her books and wrote poems.

And who hasn't written some at one age or another? said Raúl.

Well, the thing is that his were really good. If he studies law it's only to justify himself in his family's eyes, to do something, anything, because being a writer is something you can't just declare ahead of time. But now he writes stories, and I'm sure that sooner or later, he'll decide to dedicate himself entirely to writing.

She turned to face him, hesitant, disturbed. And I'd like to do the same, she added. And from the edge of her chair, her elbows on her knees together, she revealed to him all her plans, all her doubts. She'd forgotten her cigarette in the ashtray and she uttered her words hastily, nervously. Drop out of the university? Work as a secretary for her father? Open a bookstore specializing in art books? Her father had proposed to finance the venture. Go to England to study languages, and so have more time there to write? They talked it out. Raúl made her see that working as a secretary for her father would always be a phantom job, and that books, from the point of view of the bookseller, were, definitively, units of merchandise like any other. If I could go to England, he said, I wouldn't think twice. To England or anywhere. And he confessed that he didn't have the least interest in pursuing a career in law, that he was only studying it because he wanted to be a diplomat.

I hear that's a tremendous career, said Nuria. Travel, see other countries.

And above all, it leaves you time to write, study, or do whatever you feel like.

By the way, let's see if you'll show me what you write.

Oh, no, laughed Nuria. I don't plan on doing that until I've got something that's really worth the trouble.

They realized that it was late. A light, refreshing breeze was blowing. Nuria, seated next to him, opened her arms across the backrest, as if stretching. It's fine to talk that way, about these things, once in a while, she said. The day had been hot and, after lunch, Raúl walked up to the bone-dry hillsides, while the sun went down, distorted by the dusty haze. He arrived all sweaty, and Nuria asked him if he didn't want to shower. He heard her singing lightly and then she passed him a bath towel through the door that was slightly ajar. Raúl had given her a trinket he'd bought at a booth on the street, a tiny cardboard elephant, pink and squat, with a vaguely obscene nakedness. They sat on the terrace, side by side, and he made quite sure to not touch her.

Intrigued, they tried to get him to spill the beans. But Raúl wouldn't let himself be caught off guard.

How's it going with the little lady? asked Leo.

What little lady?

Well, I already know who it is: one of Count Adolfo's disciples.

They argued again. Raúl said that Adolfo Cuadras wasn't such a bad guy, that he was smart and worth knowing.

And if this coming year we want to do something in the university, of course we'll have to include him. If there were only more like him.

He's a metaphysic and a dandy, said Federico. Come on, he's a hollow stiff, a bore. You only have to take one look at him, dammit. A dandy.

And you think you look like a worker. Well, it's not enough to just remove your tie to stop looking like a rich boy.

They heard a siren, coming closer, penetrating, and the traffic was interrupted by whistle blasts. Two or three onlookers emerged from the cafeteria, and a few customers on the patio stood up to watch the red fire trucks flashing past along the suddenly empty avenue. When it was over, Leo drew their attention to a clutch of old men at a neighboring table who were listening wearily to their conversation. It was in the Nebraska or the Arkansas or some similar joint, next to Federico's house.

It's our lot to live in a somber time, Leo began.

He pretended to sound pensive even as they furtively exchanged malicious glances.

Bad times, yes. One might say that we're on the threshold of a new Middle Ages. For the last several years, the West has been doing nothing but going from surrender to surrender: first the Asians, then the Africans, and even the Papuans. In the end, you'll see, it'll be those people who will end up sticking their noses right in our own business here at home.

Well, the fact is, from that point of view, the decadence of the West, thanks to its loss of position and influence, is not even worth discussing. I was referring to its own internal decomposition, to the social upheavals that are corroding it like a cancer.

Right. To the triumph of the masses, to that society of robots toward which we're moving slowly but surely.

Exactly. One way or the other, come hell or high water, that's where we're headed. A world of equality where there won't be any room for private enterprise, a world without stimulating benefits or incentives of any kind.

Neither spirituality nor religion serves to impede human instincts, to slow even the most basic passions.

A vulgar and materialistic world.

And it's logical. What else can you expect when the upper classes disappear and the lower classes end up in power? Especially when they're people without culture, without ideals, without any notion of a fatherland or any other interests than their pitiful wages.

It was agreeable to be able to understand one another with a simple glance, with half-uttered words or, even, with no words at all. Leo had come back quite tanned, fortified, with even greater vitality. One of these mornings they were going to Barceloneta to take a swim, or maybe late in the day, when the beach emptied of families and the whores started showing up. The sand was a little bit powdery, and where the swells broke there was almost always a scummy line of people's trash. But they dove in and swam a long ways out, to the clean blue waters. Then they stripped off, splashed around, and let themselves drift with bathing trunks in hand. They sunbathed and entertained themselves contemplating the well-toned athletes who strutted in public, arrogant, muscles tense, their tight bulging bikini briefs well-packed, with a packet of blonde tobacco sticking halfway out of the waistband just above the thigh, and a small gold medallion between their hairy pectorals. And at the pool, the exhibitionists on the diving board and the creepy faggots waiting to pounce. Afterward they drank a beer in the bar, under the shade of the thatched awning. One Sunday, Floreal accompanied them and they asked him once again about the general strike in '51, the streetcar boycott, the cars burned, the direct action, the mass demonstrations. There was a climate of true exasperation and we managed to create a pre-revolutionary situation. He explained his job at the bank, the employees' loss of conscience, so out of touch, earning the same as a laborer they thought themselves better than simply for wearing a necktie. They talked about the shop assistants and grocers' boys, the worst of them all.

When I was young, I had sketched out a plan for robbing my father's bank, said Federico. He's been a big shot for so long you can't even imagine how much I'm uninterested in finance. But of course I tell him I am. For my part, the revolution would be worthwhile if it were only to see how he'd take refuge in any boat docked in the harbor flying a foreign flag, just to see him hobble up the gangway disguised as a whore.

They made the trip back uptown on the streetcars, squeezed in among hot, sweaty passengers, wet canvas bags, encrusted with coarse sand. The line was long and Raúl had suggested taking a taxi but Floreal said it wasn't worth the trouble. Leo didn't seem to care either; he laughed and joked, separated from them by the crush of passengers, imitating the girls. Every morning he took a sandwich and he ate in the bar, along with a beer. That's what Raúl preferred, the everyday calm, when the beach wasn't excessively crowded and the bar never lacked an open table. And there were two girls sipping Coca-Cola from a straw and Leo began to act silly and say things to them, and Raúl the same, and they ended up picking them up. Federico kept quiet, remaining on the outside, and had to wait for them. Leo came out smiling. Raúl's girl, however, while they were changing in a double-sized changing room, only let him touch her and, when they kissed, some residual food, perhaps some meat fiber or strands of orange pith, slipped from her mouth into his. Her breath smelled bad.

He spoke with Nuria on the phone and they agreed to meet up as always. When he arrived, she opened the door for him herself, in one swift pull, and she looked at him significantly. Come up, come up, Adolfo's here, she said. On the terrace, Adolfo Cuadras was listening to some poem from *Les Fleurs du Mal* sung by Ferré. He smiled pleasantly.

I thought I'd come by in case you two felt like taking a walk, he said.

Whatever you like, said Nuria. You two go out. I prefer to stay home.

She complained that nothing had gone exactly right for her all day, one of those days when everything goes backward. She listed the advantages of being a woman, an object so respected that she couldn't permit herself any of the liberties that came so free and easily to men. She expressed herself mockingly, mixing in here and there the requisite shits and fucks and goddammits with the greatest aplomb. Raúl asked Adolfo about some book, and they exchanged impressions about their classmates, about the monotonous and languid university life. Nuria drew herself apart, dragged a large cushion to the railing, and sat sideways against the balusters, in silence, almost turning her back on them. She was wearing a light, pastel dress, and it made Raúl think she was going without a bra. I think I'll end up hating Baudelaire, they heard her say after a little while, without turning around, with her face dejectedly leaning on the railing. They put on another record, and it was then when Raúl noticed that she was looking at him over Adolfo Cuadras. The conversation started stretching out, with increasingly longer pauses between one sentence and the next. Raúl responded with vagaries; he had to make an effort to say something, and even more to pay attention to what was being said. It began to grow dark, but nobody got up to turn on the light. Then Adolfo Cuadras gathered up his tobacco, his lighter.

Well, he said. I'll leave you two alone.

Nuria didn't move.

Ciao, Adolfo, she said. I won't see you out, alright?

Nevertheless, she stood up immediately and moved the cushion over by the record player. She took a drink of gin, lit a cigarette. He's such a bore sometimes, the poor guy, she said. She had sat at his feet, and thanks to the plunging neckline Raúl confirmed that she actually wasn't wearing a bra. They were almost there in the dark and there was a silence. Then, Raúl slid down to the floor. I feel sorry for him, he said. They kissed, deeply, she clinging to his neck, intertwined, twisted around, and between his hands appeared her breasts, very white in the faint light. They found themselves inside, atop the bed, and everything happened in a way that was, perhaps, rushed. It was in the second half of July, a Thursday, possibly a Sunday, and they were alone in the house, the maid had gone out. He stayed lying down in bed, naked, and she returned wrapped in a bath towel and said: looks to me like you got what you were after, Raúl. That night, of course, they spoke again on the phone. A long conversation.

Sometimes they forgot the record player and then Nuria had to get up and go out to the terrace in a rush, barely covered, to load it up again with LPs. They joked, they played, they experimented, and the time went quickly by, experimenting, testing the effects of lifting up a leg until folding it over her tits, or of lifting up both of them, stretching them out, or of sitting face to face, rocking back and forth in an embrace, or of doing it from behind, on all fours, hooked together like dogs, problems of angulation, of inclination, of twisted desires, a demonstrated taste for difficult positions. Those games and those experiments which suddenly turned into something different, that sudden seriousness which swallowed their laughter as in a mute struggle, that tickling sensation and the rolling over to a squeezing and tremulous embrace while, with the record player stopped again, from outside came voices and cries, the sounds of little children. A sudden bias, the brusque change of tone when he was inside her and, as if in spite of herself, all sarcasm abandoned, her poise was broken and, with a pained expression, her head rolled upon her tousled hair, closing her eyes as her breathing came faster, tighter, then grunting and gasping madly, her rising spasm proudly achieved. Afterward they smoked, lying very close, and she exposed her worries to him. She leaned up on her bent elbow.

What do you think, Pipo?

That you're wrong, *hombrecilla.*

Don't call me "little man." And tell me, why am I wrong? What about you, why do you call me Pipo?

And she: because I feel like it, dammit.

And then she turned over, and he held her down, immobile, and they recommenced the game, warmly sweaty. But the hours were always short and they had to get dressed all in a hurry. Nuria fixed her hair, masked her flushed face with powder. She also remade the bed and washed the towel, and put it out to dry on the terrace. She said she didn't trust the maid, that little young woman, who when she opened the door for Raúl, smiled like an accomplice and moved so silently.

They'll end up catching us, she said.

She spoke about her family relations, about her father, a man of an extraordinarily youthful and open character, of good instinctive taste, capable of juggling the paper factory and tennis, and tennis with a true passion for art and books, gallery shows, concerts. The night before they had gone out together, she said, her father took her to have dinner and then to an open-air cabaret, happy—she assured Raúl—as a twenty-year-old boy. My mother is different, she said.

Señor Rivas seemed to feel sympathy for Raúl and never asked what they had done. He received them cordially, without formalities, when they arrived at the house, and he drew Nuria to him, hugging her against him, saying that his Nuri was the most lovely and intelligent woman in the world. They chatted about hunting, and Señor Rivas showed him some photos of the spaniels that he had at their country house, for duck hunting. Raúl had to promise him that next winter they would go hunting together some weekend.

By then they knew that they were going to be apart for two weeks, the first half of August; that her father was taking some vacation and Nuria had to accompany him. Now they hardly went out to the bars, and they even seemed tired of the Plaza

Real. They didn't go out much at all, at most to have a drink
in some café in the upper part of the city. One day he took her
home to his house, the day she gave him the tiny turtle, and
they went to set it loose in the garden. They sat for a while on
the steps, contemplating the turtle's cautious exploration. They
discussed which sex it might be, agreeing that it was most likely
a male. Nuria proposed that they call him *Camarlengo*, meaning
Chamberlain. But given that it was a turtle and, above all, for
the splendidly designed shield that was his shell, they agreed to
call him Achilles. Eloísa had received them with suspicion, seemingly stunned, and disappeared immediately; but, when they
went back out, Raúl perceived the delicate click of the slats of a
Persian blind and, like an almost physical sensation, the weight
of her gaze which followed them out onto the street.

The evening before she left it was he who gave her a new
present: a big ugly bird. All his money was spent and he had to
sell more books, dusty leather-bound volumes which a secondhand bookshop bought from him: *Ascent of Mount Carmel*, *The
Sinner's Guide*, *The Mansions*, an illustrated edition of *Paradise
Lost*, etcetera. But the ugly bird seduced him the moment he saw
it, as he passed by the shop window, a ceramic piece in dark,
gloomy tones, an amalgam of friar and hookbill bird, something
a schizophrenic might design.

I hope it doesn't bring bad luck, said Nuria. Depending how
you hold it, it looks sort of like a crow.

No. It's a beneficent being. Ugly, but good.

It was not an afternoon like the others. She seemed somewhat withdrawn, lying on her side staring at the ceiling. All of a
sudden she rolled over onto Raúl and he caressed her back, her
small hard buttocks.

But do you love me? said Nuria.

Of course, silly, said Raúl.

She looked at him, her pupils inscrutable from so close; then
he felt her slide off, hugging him. They got dressed sooner than
usual and, seated on the terrace, they listened to some song, *le
rouge pour naître à Barcelone, le noir pour mourir à Paris*.

Maybe I could just not go to England, said Nuria. Maybe I

can learn languages from here.

But why? Seems absurd to me. If I could go, I wouldn't think twice.

Nuria didn't respond. She smoked, the Siamese cat asleep on her knees. In the street outside, the open windows of summertime were alive, illuminated with voices and people. They said goodbye, and then she put a sealed envelope into his hand and squeezed his fingers. Don't read it until tomorrow, she said. Promise me. And she closed the door without waiting for him to step into the elevator.

He read it standing against a streetlamp, all in a rush, and walked back home, a song in his heart. There he read it again, and only the next day did he try to decide if it was better to answer right away or better to wait, if his response should be brief, or if he should write at length. He'd planned to go out with Leo, but beforehand he shut himself in his room and wrote his letter over and over again, until he managed to get the right tone all the way through.

They were having an argument, and the canary's pecking at the fine wires of the cage was getting quite annoying. The revolution has got to be peaceful, her father repeated to make himself heard. And the sister ended up joining in, from where she was ironing, leaning over the white swirls of steam. Let's see if you can't talk quieter, my goodness, the whole neighborhood is going to hear you. Then her father took the opportunity to insist that violence doesn't achieve anything, proved perfectly by the Civil War. Back then, they stood up to power empty-handed.

But you've got to look for some way to get people fired up, goddammit! shouted the brother-in-law. Or do you think the same thing didn't happen before? And how were the strikes broken? With guns! With bombs! You've got to wake people up. Now they don't think about anything besides soccer. You've got to give them a good shock to wake them the hell up.

The others just listened from the sidelines. Leo, Federico, and Floreal all appeared to be amused. Teresa listened and kept quiet. Raúl had seated himself on the sofa and, inevitably, his eyes wandered to the big color picture in front of him, a reproduction

of some academic painting, no doubt, which showed Nero
stroking a lyre and watching Rome burn to the ground. Her
father talked about how it was necessary to educate people, about
people being prepared, and the brother-in-law interrupted him
again, saying that the true revolutionary was the one who lived
like a dog, that you shouldn't trust anyone else. When the worm
turns, then we'll settle the scores, he said.

There was a moment of tension, and her father looked at Raúl
and at Federico over the top of his glasses, as if embarrassed.
But the brother-in-law continued his harangue, saying that not
even the workers were organizing, not even when they really
had nothing to lose, just their miserable salaries or a ticket to
the soccer match. He shook his index finger, struck the table
with his fist. If not, come to the factory and you'll see. I'm an
optical technician, and I've seen how people change when they
reach my level.

Before leaving they looked into the little windowless inner
bedroom, where, under the bed, in a suitcase, her father kept
the remains of his library, works by Marx and Engels, Lenin,
Bakunin, in old editions from before the war. These days, this
is a treasure, said his father. And Leo let them borrow another
book. Floreal went out with them.

I like your brother-in-law, said Federico.

He's a good guy, said Leo. But he talks too much.

And Floreal: all bark and no bite.

He said he still had the mentality of the same people who'd
caused the war, that he was still an anarchist at heart. He doesn't
understand that the basis of everything lies in mass action, and
that the only possible tactic is to attract the petite bourgeoisie,
and even the non-monopolistic bourgeoisie oppressed by the
oligarchy. There's your true enemy, right there: capital, in the
hands of the big feudal landowners. He left them at the Metro
entrance, cocking his chin at them, heading down the steps with
a cigarette stuck to his lips, hands in his pockets.

Well, said Federico. But this Floreal, is he a communist or
is he not a communist? I mean, if he's a member of the party.

Of course, you idiot, said Raúl. You just figured that out?

Leo started laughing. A Kremlin agent, he said. Thick as a brick, this was the bad part about him; too dogmatic and simplistic, maybe because they'd sent his father to the firing squad. And he had grown up in an atmosphere of such politicization that he went around as if his ideology were the most natural thing in the world, something that the people, oppressed by a powerful few, should necessarily share, without any qualms or doubts whatsoever. In this way he allows himself to be alienated, the same as my father or my brother-in-law. Otherwise, he's the only one in my family you can talk to. And he used to like going out, having some fun. If I know the Barrio Chino from one end to the other, it's thanks to him. Not anymore, now he's married and his wife won't let him, she's a kind of puritan leftist. And when they do go out around there it's to go to the movies or to take their little boy for a walk. That's all, he only goes to soccer matches.

Federico had become meditative. He said that his interest in Marxism was purely philosophical, lacking any sentimentality. Workers, individually, don't concern me. What interests me is their historical role, the fact that, for being the only ones with nothing to lose, they are destined to herald the revolution.

It's just that if you try to solve their personal problems then you're talking about charity.

Right. In reality, what it's all about is class solutions, not individual solutions.

And, of course, the worst are le petite bourgeoisie.

Exactly. Their historical role is always objectively reactionary. In a certain way, one could almost say that monopoly capital is more revolutionary.

They argued about whether the revolution was really a historical necessity, as Leo said, or whether it was not and, precisely for that reason, had to occur. That was Federico's theory. They agreed that the goal was to liberate mankind from all types of alienation; not simply to improve the living conditions of the working class, whose objective situation converted them into a potential subject of the revolution: de-alienation.

They wandered, and they found their rapport, their unity of ideas, their camaraderie of shared concerns to be stimulating.

The complicity created by their conversations was exciting, the discovery of a secret world of relationships and activities, clandestine, underlying, imperceptible in appearance, as if camouflaged by the life of the city, by the most quotidian realities. The first contacts, the first meetings with Marsal, with Escala, the first meetings of the cell in nondescript outdoor locations.

They went back to their usual haunts. They offered them joints of marijuana for five pesetas, and there was a whore who strolled back and forth along the bar, more stoned than drunk, shouting *eso, eso, a lo loco*—yes, that's right, get crazy—and she yawned and shook out her hair and fanned herself with a magazine and flirted her skirt and roared with laughter. She looked at them; I'm dying for something to refresh my mouth, she said. Neither Raúl nor Leo had any money and they invited themselves to a drink on Federico. Federico always had a little extra, but he didn't usually buy drinks and he paid for his share almost furtively, as if he was embarrassed. He asked Raúl about his girl. He seemed to be in a good mood and he told them they were playing with fire.

And your little sweetheart?

Just fine, thanks.

And Teresa? he asked Leo. I don't understand why you all don't go out together. The four of you. Raúl with his little baby doll, and you with Teresa. Are you biased because she works for your father? If not, why don't you go out with her?

Why don't you take her out? I already told you I'd let you have her.

I prefer Santa Luisa; she's more prissy. The three of us could get married together: Raúl with his girl, you with Teresa, and me with Santa Luisa. Why don't we do it? You've got to play with fire.

They rambled on about women, about marriage. Leo said they thought too much about it, that he preferred a wide playing field, a broad landscape. Women only interest me on Saturday night. They all agreed that the important thing was to not get married.

A country landscape? said Federico. I've never been out in the country. Well, just driving, seeing it that way, on a trip.

He was noticeably distracted from their conversation, chatting at the same time with one of the bar girls, attentive to her coming and going as the customers flagged her down. They were in a bar that had recently reopened, now transformed into a café. Federico drank several glasses of gin and ended up agreeing to meet the girl at closing time. Looks like this is my Saturday night, he said. And there was a guy with the face of an overripe sodomite with oily jet-black hair forming a big wave across his forehead, another guy with mustaches and long curly sideburns, nicotine teeth and Moorish eyes, a black shirt and tight denim jeans, very low in the waist, with his stomach and ass showing as he walked across the room to feed money into the jukebox, walking with his bowed legs, and with each step, above his shoes, sharp as rooster spurs, his red socks flashing out like fire, dominant, euphoric. With his elbows resting on the bar, he leaned over toward Federico.

Go find yourself something a little fresher, kid, he said, expertly, with an aguardiente voice. That slut's already screwed every guy around here.

Exactly, said Federico. That's why I like her.

He stuck around, and Leo kept Raúl company a while. They talked about the countryside, about Vallfosca, about Leo's town. When they split up, Raúl kept walking, back uptown, considering if maybe the time hadn't come for breaking up with Nuria, to get some distance from each other, little by little.

But one afternoon, as he walked through the half-empty city, he felt that he missed her, and he resolved to stay with her at least for a while longer. It was a complex mood, a mixture of placidity and nostalgia. The calm heat wave had something enchanting about it, above all on Sundays, when his neighborhood was almost totally deserted with only some isolated passerby and some car, some motorbike, unexpected, out of place. They went for a walk, and then he heard again only the breath of air among the plane trees with their fibrous leaves, their rustling more dry each day.

He wandered about indolently, overcome by the sensation that the street belonged to him, that he could walk anywhere he felt like, sit down on the curb or against the trunk of a tree and

savor that amplitude and that silence. In the bowling alley on
Paseo de la Bonanova, some youngsters, just a few, were trying
to kill time and compensate for their loneliness by making as
much noise as possible. The patios outside the bars were mostly
empty, at most some loyal customer sitting reading the newspaper, looking for company, to have a conversation. Only Las
Ramblas remained as lively as ever.

There was one particularly agreeable day, very likely the same
fifteenth of August. Public transit was barely running and the
buses and streetcars circulated like ghosts past the leisurely city
dwellers. The metal shutters in front of the shop windows were
rolled down, with their signs saying closed for, closed until, etcetera, and the doormen brought chairs out onto the sidewalks, and
gathered to gossip. The windows remained sealed shut and in
the street one glimpsed, at most, a maid in white walking the
dog, some solitary man in mourning, sweating and morbid, boys
swarming about on bicycles, and on La Avenida Diagonal, some
anxious drag queen, some miserable whore. It was then when Raúl
remembered Nuria, when he thought about her imminent return.

Then, the weekend was over, everything changed again, and
toward mid-afternoon the streetcars passed by packed full, there
were no taxis to be had, and the sidewalks were an interminable
procession of sunburned, sand-encrusted beachgoers, in bathing
suits, with floppy canvas bags, a torrent of overheated young
people, families, little kids. And the main access roads turned
into a chaos of automobiles loaded with items for the beach,
motorcyclists with their wives riding behind, family-sized sidecars with bundles, paellas, fishing rods, all passing by, overtaking
each other, zigzagging in and out, insulting, splitting off, rushing
headlong in a sudden invasion.

And the rash of fires continued; many of them forest fires.
One morning, Raúl noticed a great billowing cascade of smoke
blotting out the flanks of Tibidabo, and the next day he could
see the track of the fire blackening a still smoking valley floor, as
if it had been burned on the grill. He went walking and skirted
those hillsides and when he got back home put on records in
the sitting room, at top volume, and with the window open

he listened to them from the garden, under the plum tree. He talked with Papa, who brought news from Vallfosca, about Aunt Paquita, and Ramona. Ramona was engaged, she'd found an excellent match, a fellow quite a bit older than her, twelve or fourteen years older, one Jacinto Bonet, very involved in the business world, with a promising future. Apart from his personal fortune, he had studied in Madrid, was very well connected, and moved among influential people. Poor Paquita, however, had the whole family worried. Her migraines, her constant pains, perhaps only worries, but the truth is she had certainly hit a real slump. Besides, she had now devoted herself to the task of securing the beatification of a prematurely dead seminarist, a young man from a good family, skinny and big-eared, with oligophrenic characteristics, judging by his face in the pictures; and, beyond that, to founding a new religious order, too. Look, maybe deep down it does her good. It takes her mind off things.

Raúl had not seen her since the previous summer, the few days that he spent in Vallfosca, the minimum amount of time possible. It was when Estrella had a litter of pups and nobody knew where she'd hidden them. She was exhausted and flighty, coming and going every which way, slithering around like an otter. But she guided him through the woods, with a hurried pace, turning her head—almost smiling—as if to make sure he was following her, and so she led him to a small hollow formed by some rocks, and went inside to lie down by her puppies that scrambled around in search of her rosy pink dugs, on a bed of moss and clawed-up soil, while she looked at him from within, her luminous, topaz-colored eyes shining green in the gloom. He and Polit brought the puppies up to the hayloft, although there, she still wouldn't let anyone else come near, drawing up her lips to bare her teeth, growling.

The family was gathered on the verandah, around Aunt Paquita's chaise longue, and they discussed Felipe's unexpected vocation for the priesthood, his sudden enrollment in a seminary of the Opus Dei order. They repeated ad infinitum that, as Felipe was the oldest son, it was sad for the father, but that if he felt a true calling, etcetera. Uncle Gregorio opined that it was already going well with Felipe, and Papa said that while it was a shock that didn't stop it being a consolation, too, having brought a pastor of souls into the world. It's a sacrifice, no doubt about it, but if God calls him, what greater honor for a father than to offer God his first fruits. Everyone nodded, highlighting the fact that it could not be considered some whim or heedless decision, given that Felipe already knew the world, he was a professional man, a lawyer, and he'd also done his military service. With all that experience, he'll surely be ordained right away. That's one way the Jesuits haven't changed; they still want people who are prepared. There was some disagreement about the real characteristics of Opus Dei; someone said that being a normal, everyday parish priest, in continuous contact with the parishioners, with the problems of modern life, was most meritorious. For Aunt Paquita, going to Vallfosca was now nothing more than swapping one chaise longue for another, one verandah for another, that porch behind her house was just suffocating, the way it heated up like a greenhouse in the afternoon sun.

They talked in Papa's room, Papa lying atop his bed, dressed, his hands folded behind his neck, his little suitcase like an old-fashioned doctor's kit bag on the chair and his overcoat folded across the backrest. He said that he was tired of Barcelona, that he was going to return to Vallfosca as soon as he could; he'd only come back to town to take care of a few business obligations. The Company, his retirement, human ingratitude, the usual. When I left, I did it with my head held very high: healthy assets and fresh possibilities. And now they go and deny me my retirement, as if the founder and manager of a company had fewer rights than a typist. And I was stupid selling my stocks before taking up this matter. That was my big mistake. Now they have the control and they'll do what they want. But, look, I was feeling old and tired, and they abused my trust. Then they were all smiles. I don't know; nowadays people have lost all sense of morality, and now I'm the first to point out to you that if you want to avoid big headaches, don't get mixed up in the business world. He said that earlier, including during the years of the Republic, a man could trust in his friends and relatives. By contrast, in recent years, a whole breed of nouveau riche had appeared, people with fortunes made after the war, a bunch of Don Nobodies, those kinds of guys who, with powerful patrons, lots of financial backing, linked to the big banks and finding protection in the public powers, commit all kinds of outrages.

There's no more morality, son, no morality or confidence, and the only law respected is the law of the jungle. And look, the Company was a business that I started with all my hopes and dreams, for you all, so that someday you could all succeed me. But with your legal studies, what you should do is specialize in something. Maritime Law, for example. Have you thought about that? Maritime Law is a nice specialized field that still has a lot of open possibilities.

Yes, of course. But I think I'd rather be a diplomat.

That's not bad either. Nowadays, everything that's about getting connected, depending on the State, is a secure life. And if that's your vocation, follow it. You already know that I've never wanted to encroach on your desires.

He was wearing a well-cut alpaca suit; but seen close-up it was full of wrinkles and stains. And beneath, a yellow shirt, cheap fabric, and sandals with socks on his feet. He asked Raúl when he was going to go up to Vallfosca.

Maybe in September, when Uncle Gregorio is there. He just sent me a postcard from the spa asking me to specify some dates.

I'd prefer that you come with me. I feel a little lonely, you know.

He became fond of the garden, watering the parched plants, stimulated in a certain way by Eloísa's example, who had planted geraniums, daisies, and marigolds. At first it was just a simple distraction, dig, prune, water, but he ended up taking a real interest in it. He pulled out some acacia saplings and pittosporum that had grown outside the beds, in the thin gravel, and he replanted the flowerpots. The wind rang light and clear among the acacias, shaking the dry seedpods. In the back part of the garden was a great creeping vine, stretching out along the ground, luxuriant with sickly leaves and wild grapes that never ripened, small blackish beads. He repainted the garden chairs green, and in the morning sat down to read in the shade of the plum tree where the sun was like a blinking gash among the leaves. He chatted with Eloísa, while she, talkative and frisky, moved around the garden, showing him the new sprouts and buds. She even seemed to be reconciled with Achilles and she entertained herself pampering him, praising his graces. *¡Animalito!* she cried. Atop the walls of the neighboring gardens crept rosebush feelers, long and limp, and explosive boughs of red oleander with a mellifluous odor. Jasmine floated on the air.

Nuria returned at the end of August. Her hair was even lighter, and her eyelashes; her skin, brown and freckled, almost rough. She opened the door for him herself and she seemed to him shy and awkward, as if they were two strangers. Then it passed, in bed, as they made love like crazy, and everything returned to the way it was before. The Siamese cat had slipped into the room and playfully tried to join in; they had to throw it out. He stared at her stretched out on the bed, her slender thighs and pointy breasts, her mouth determined and stubborn, her golden eyes, eyebrows darker than her hair. See how the ugly bird didn't bring us bad luck? he told her. And just like before, they listened to songs by Leo Ferré on the terrace.

Nuria asked him about his previous erotic experiences. Raúl became mysterious. Santa Luisa, said Nuria, as if annoyed. Evasive, Raúl refused to say either yes or no. He did say that what he'd never liked was visiting whores, not only because as an institution it struck him as degrading, but also because it humiliated him to have to pay to make love. But that wasn't what bothered Nuria. If sometime you like some other girl more than me, you have to tell me, she said. Promise?

One afternoon they returned to Raúl's house, walking without hurry. Nuria with her camera. They were planning some getaway for around the end of summer, without their families knowing, a few days in some town on the Costa Brava, Rosas, for example, or some other. In the neighborhood, from Paseo de la Bonanova heading downhill toward the city center, every time you looked there were more new buildings, half-constructed lots, tall cranes, gray structures, and more than one old villa had been replaced by heavy blocks of flats. And they criticized the ugliness of the new buildings, peering through the fences into the shadowy old gardens. Raúl stopped before the outer wall of a convent, a sunny wall, eroded, with cracks and weeds, crowned with glittering shards of broken glass; a few steps away, spying through the cracks in the wall, a motionless boy, aiming his air rifle.

I also used to come this way, to this wall, he said. To hunt lizards.

Poor things, said Nuria. Only a really bad person does that.

Don't worry, I'm increasingly tenderhearted about stuff like that. Lately, I'm even starting to feel sorry for rabbits.

Work had stopped at the construction sites and the streets stretched out, peaceful, lonely. They walked along, hip to hip, their arms around each other, and the afternoon was lovely. A clear western sky, rainbow hues in the distance.

Later that Sunday, when they went out at night to hit their regular bars, they ran into Floreal and Leo. Raúl greeted them without introducing Nuria, as if they were on the move, and they observed her with amused eyes. And your wife? he asked Floreal then, and Floreal answered him with a wink. They had a drink at the Plaza Real, under the arches, still lit by the sunset, and they also went barhopping along Escudillers, now lively and bright in the nighttime. They crossed over Las Ramblas into the streets on the south side: Conde del Asalto, San Ramón, San Rafael, San Olegario, Tapias, on toward Paralelo. From there the mass of Montjuich was visible, looming near, as if surging up out of the blocks of houses, on fire, volcanic. From the bars came songs sung in chorus and there were characters hanging out on the corners, looking for action. It was then they ran into them and Raúl told them that she was Swedish, a fresh pickup.

How do you understand each other?

Really lousy; in English. But that's the least important thing.

She wanted to know who they were, and Raúl said that, along with Federico, they were his best friends. Federico was out of town at the moment, he said, in Sitges, with his family.

I like these guys better, said Nuria. Federico is, I don't know, a little strange.

Strange? Why?

I don't know. Just strange.

They ran into them again in the next bar, and in the next. And also out in the street, always going in the opposite direction. They must have gone on ahead of them and gone all the way round the block, running, and when they crossed paths again they greeted them by bowing their heads gravely. They retraced their steps, along Arco del Teatro, and at a newsstand on Las Ramblas they bought a Swedish newspaper. The air was still and the plane trees seemed peppered with sparrows, as if petrified. They went back along Escudillers. At last, in La Venta, they struck up a conversation.

What's happening in Sweden? they asked.

Nuria folded the newspaper and, to maintain the charade, answered them in English.

What do you want?

He is a friend of mine and this is your cousin.

Oh, they are very nice.

Leo looked back and forth at them.

So, this is the famous little lady? he said.

And she turned right around and laid into him.

What do you mean little lady? My name's Nuria, hotshot.

They joked, Raúl a little uncomfortable, but the others only stayed a short while, long enough to have one more drink; they said it was late, tomorrow was Monday. Raúl felt relieved, more relaxed now. Seated in their corner, they ordered another half carafe of dry sherry. The bar had filled up with some well-known queens and the frowsy flamenco dancers and singers stamped their heels and clapped their hands and sang a chorus of obscene songs.

You're gonna turn me into a little drunkard, Pipo, said Nuria, leaning her head back. But I feel really good, like I'm floating.

After closing time they found their way to a bakery and ate some fresh *ensaimadas*, hot out of the oven, to pick themselves up. The bakery was long and deep inside, red and black like a forge, full of the late-night crowd. As they went up Las Ramblas, the halos of the street lamps were growing faint in the dawn, and in a newly opened bar in La Boqueria they were able to have coffee. Then they kept on walking back uptown, with their heads together. The streetcars running were overcrowded and in the alleys and side streets the tricycle carts and delivery vans were making their rounds. All the lighted signs and advertisements and neon were switched off, and the long cross-streets stretching into the distance suddenly bespoke misery, the filthy paving stones and the gray dilapidated facades. The narrow sidewalks were crowded with workers and laborers trudging off to their jobs, and dowdy women loaded with baskets, all of them silent and withdrawn. And up above, over the cornices and rooftops, over the whole city, a mauve-colored halo.

And when, the same day, after a few hours of sleep, they went up to the top of Tibidabo, they visited the deliciously outdated rides and attractions, and Nuria clutched his arm, the two of them standing before the metal railing, thrashed by the wind, taking in the view of the whole city at their feet, temptress, open, generous, inviting, stretching out until lost in a misty horizon, *omnia tibi dabo*. In the distance, starting at the port, one could make out the Gothic belfries of the old city, intricate and crowded, and encircling it, the grid of the Ensanche with the spiky towers of the Sagrada Familia in its heart, the Ensanche narrowing uptown, reaching into the residential neighborhoods, San Gervasio, Bonanova, Sarriá, Pedralbes, now on the dry flanks of the hills, and on either side of the city blocked in by the working class townships and districts, Barceloneta, Pueblo Nuevo, San Adrián, San Martín, La Sagrera, Santa Coloma, El Clot, San Andrés, Horta, Collblanch, Sants, Hostafranchs, Hospitalet, El Port, Casa Antúnez, blue-collar districts surrounded by the red belt of swirling industrial fumes. Nuria took photographs of the city, her hair flying on the wind, a squat, ugly city, quadrangular, compartmentalized, juxtaposed, superimposed, anarchic, unstructured, immense, submerged in a low sun-soaked sea mist, extending to the foot of the hills, Turó de la Peira, Montaña Pelada, Mount Carmel, naked hills running in a line, like spurs jutting from Tibidabo toward the Besós River on the left, and to the right, Vallvidrera, San Pedro Mártir, hills descending toward the plain of the Llobregat River, and directly facing them, standing out above the port, rising above the shining saline fog, Montjuich, butting into the city like a sheer rugged cape. Montjuich with its Morrot, with its peaks and yawning fissures, there, mount of the Jews, with its quarries and slabs, moats and fosses, its parks and open spaces, its tin shanties and ersatz palaces, a mountain now silhouetted flat against the sun, thrust forth like a bruised black snout.

V

LOOSEN THE GUY LINES SOME MORE, man, my rainfly is starting to soak through.

Well, go fuck off. I don't feel like it.

But you're closer to the door, you cunt.

Sure. Tomorrow you can shave me.

You can do it no problem, asshole.

And so what the fuck? This week it's Ferracollons's turn.

Hell, he's on leave.

Ah, well, loosen them yourself. It's not leaking on me.

This Ferracollons is a cheapskate. He didn't sweep up, didn't fill the water jug, nothing.

We've gotta do something to fuck with him good.

Right, man, but if someone doesn't adjust those ropes quick, we're gonna get more water in here than the other night.

I don't care, man, let it leak. I'll wrap myself in plastic and go to sleep.

They all raised their heads and looked at the tent pole in silence, the dull brown canvas darkened by the moisture. Around the base of the pole, in the gun rack, there were rifles standing vertically. There was also a water jug and a broom and, halfway up, tied with wire, two extinguished candles. They remained motionless on their worn-out sleeping mats, atop their flimsy cots, in their thin, ineffective jackets, wrapped in dirty blankets. Raúl closed his eyes again; he smoked sitting up, sideways, resting his muddy boots on the neighboring mat.

What's a real pain is that the rifles will get all fucked up. Whoever's gotta go on parade tomorrow can do something about it.

Goddamn, man, the thing is the weather on this mountain is worse than monkey shit.

95

Fuck, this is the asshole of the world, fucking dead-end street to nowhere. It can be raining here and down at the beach maybe they're lying in the sun. And when it doesn't rain, the wind blows you away, or the sun peels the skin off your nose. And the fog, man. I've never seen the way it is with the fog here, that everything is dry except under the trees, the exact opposite of what happens with the rain.

But, why do you think they chose this spot? The camps are always in places like this.

And now, since there's firing practice tomorrow, you'll see how the weather's nice. Here it only rains on Sundays.

There's just no fucking place to go, man. There's no room in the canteen, and outside the tent you get soaking wet.

Aw, fuck, inside the tent, too.

You can't even go from one place to the other, man. Why don't they let us have umbrellas. They just want us to get wet.

And why did you have to spend your money in the canteen, dammit? Could've eaten in the tent. For half the money you eat much better. Me and these other two prepared a fucking good meal. Right, man?

Well, you know what I'm telling you? The best thing to do on Sundays is to eat chow in the mess hall. There's almost nobody there and you can eat almost like in the canteen.

No way, man. I'll take anything before having to go stand in line. The best thing is eating in the canteen, which is the closest thing to actually eating like a real person, you know, quit talking shit.

The best thing is to go find some whores in Tarragona, man, and get a really good blow job.

There was a wave of laughter. Now, insistent, there was a dripping sound increasingly watery, perhaps against the bottom of a small jar or pot.

Well, for me these passes to go on leave are worth less and less every time, you know what I mean. Between traveling and everything, you end up with less than twenty-four hours, and then, when you find yourself back up here, it's even worse.

Yeah, man, it's true. The only pass worth getting is the pledge of allegiance pass.

That's why everyone without a pass was Catalan.

Well if you don't like going on leave, you can all let me have your pass. I would've been in the whorehouse, I would've been on the beach, found some place with good romesco sauce, and right now I'd be headed for the dance, dressed like a normal person.

Oh, man, but with the pledge pass, it makes sense that they give preference to the Aragonese. Some of them live way far away, and weekend passes don't do them any good.

No, fuck, no. They do them the same good as they do us, that theoretically for the same reason we can't go to Barcelona. What happens is that the Aragonese have got it made. All the connections are for them, quartermaster, postmaster, everything.

Oh, man, do they ever. But it's not that they get preference because they're Aragonese, it's that they fucking hate us because we're Catalan.

Yes, sir, now you're talking. This is what it is, we Catalans don't like the army and they know it and so they fucking hate us.

On the other hand, most of the officers have gone through the military academy in Zaragoza, and all the Aragonese get recommended to them. Whichever way you slice it, in Zaragoza everybody knows someone in the army.

Swell guys these Aragonese, man. Lucky that there's none in this tent. Do you know any of them who shower? I've never seen guys who are filthier or cause more trouble.

When I think about that bastard who five minutes before the bell for formation goes and asks me to borrow my rifle and on parade they give him an extended pass because I had the thing so clean, man, and when I tell him I deserve the pass, he answers me, yeah, in a pig's ass. That's exactly what he said, man. That's it, I'm not lending it to anybody for a long time. Fuck.

That's what happens for being too nice. I swear he wouldn't do that to me.

No, man, really, the guy's got no right. We're always working, sweating it out, way overloaded, and they're always slacking off, ducking out of work all day long. But in the end, no worries, no Aragonese gets in trouble. And if one of them makes colonel it's only because I'm not exaggerating.

And always stirring up shit. Saying Catalan is just a dialect and all that. Them, they're all veterinarians, think they've got a right to mouth their opinions, man. Calling the language of Ramón Llull a dialect, the language of Ausias March, Joanot Martorell, Verdaguer, and Maragall, a dialect!

Joanot Martorell? Well I don't know who that is either, man. Joanot? That's a fucking joke of a name.

No, man, the one who wrote *Tirant lo Blanch*.

Ah, right, of course. You had me confused there, man.

You think they'll ever not be respected? A language is a language when it has a dictionary, a grammar, and a literary tradition, dammit, and Catalan has all three.

Well, if you want to piss them off, tell them that Agustina de Aragón was Catalan, man, which is the truth. She was the daughter of Fulleda and she was married to Commander Roca, another Catalan, doomed to die in Zaragoza.

And Jaime Primero ended the Reconquest before Castile, and Catalonia was one of the principal powers of the Mediterranean. And the Almogávars conquered Italy and North Africa and half of Turkey, and they were Catalans, man, the Aragonese did nothing. And when the Castilians tried to take Barcelona they had to besiege it for eleven years, and we gave the French more shit than anybody. It's just the truth, for fuck's sake. We don't like the army, but when it's time to fight we've got more balls than anybody. They saw that in the Civil War, man; the Montserrat Third Regiment was the best there was, and all of them volunteers. The thing is we like to work better than lie around, and that's why they've got it in for us.

Sí señor. Before the army, or anything else, man, better to break rocks. Being a soldier is spending your life in the shit, working nonstop. Pure bureaucracy, goddammit, and that's a no go for us Catalans. But then, when they let us be, there's nobody'll beat us. Not in sports or anything, man. And right here, it's the fucking truth; the Catalans always get the highest marks in company. They don't like to acknowledge it, but it's true, man, no one's got bigger balls.

Well, that seems pretty fucking stupid to me, man. The best

thing is to go unnoticed. If you stand out for being good, you look like a volunteer and then you never stop working. And if you stand out as a slacker or for being a good little ass-kisser, you're fucked. Look at Pluto Farreras; he ended up without an extended pass, without even leave for today, and I'll bet you what you like, just for the failing grades he's received, they'll kick him out. But with me, I sleep through theory class, I copy on the tests, I don't even try hard, but I'll pass. You have to be as invisible as possible, man. The captain doesn't even know me.

But the lieutenant does, and he says that you're a lazy ass.

So what, man? He's even lazier. If you meant the second lieutenant, fine. But the lieutenant's a joke.

The one guy who's not bad is Captain Mauriño. Really, man. He's not here to fuck around and he's a little bit stiff, really, but he's incapable of fucking you over. And I prefer a guy like that over one like Cantillo, from la Primera, who jokes around a lot, but later on he fucks you. And another one I like is Sánchez Clavijo; he'll never ask you to do something he's not capable of doing himself.

Strict? I'd say he's oligophrenic.

And what the hell does *oligophrenic* mean?

Well the second lieutenant is worse, he's also a son of a bitch, and doesn't even crack a joke. That's something I can't fucking understand. A guy who went to university like us and has also been a cadet and a sergeant and that, during the months of training, has been a bigger bastard than the guys who are career officers. I swear that I'd like to run into him someday when the two of us are discharged, in the street, man to man. I swear.

What the fuck for? What good would it do? When I make second lieutenant I'll also put all the little lambs to work, make them eat shit. When you're a fucking cadet they all screw you over, right? Good, well wait until I'm second lieutenant and you'll see how I'll be the one who'll give all the other ones hell. Around here, man, the only law is fuck with 'em first before they fuck with you. And that's all there is to it, man.

Goddamn, poor regimentals. Now that's a shitty time. At least with us, they don't smack us around or cut our hair short and we don't have to clean latrines, man.

Well, that's really fucked. At least regimentals are good for something.

All right, that's enough, eh? That's enough. How many times do I have to tell you I don't want anybody sitting on my mat?

He waited by the door and the one who was on his mat stood up. Shut up. Fuck, they told him, you sound like a broken record. Why don't you start by being a little more polite, dammit, he said. He removed his cap, and from underneath his rain poncho produced a compact package. He shook out the folds of the blankets and knelt on the seat. Turning his back on them, he began to stow the contents of the package in his suitcase. You guys have mixed up all my stuff. Who used my little stove? He looked again at the other guy who, now seated again, went on eating cookies, quietly, as if minding his own business.

It was Fofo. He also swiped himself something to eat.

Cookies?

Fuck, what a stupid ass you are, man. Yeah, we used the stove to make some food for ourselves, but we used our own canned heat.

Well, gosh, at least ask permission. I've already told you all that I don't want anybody touching anything in my suitcase.

Don't be stingy, you dickhead. Did you get a visitor? Hey, what are these novels? Lend me one, man.

No, fuck it. I'll do whatever I feel like with my own things. And I'm sick of sleeping near the entrance, and how you all sit on my stuff. Which I suppose you did just to piss me off.

Well, fuck, of course.

Man, looks like it's stopping.

Come on, lend me that Wild West one. You're not gonna read both at the same time.

No, dammit, I already told you no.

Yeah, man, it's stopping. I'm gonna take the opportunity to take a dump.

Raúl also stood up; he put on his heavy cape, his cap. He pulled out the letter from between the pages of a book, the envelope stuck slightly to a page by the postage stamp moistened maybe too much, and he tucked it into a pocket of his military jacket. He buttoned his cape. From all the nearby tents soldiers were looking out, crowding around, shouting to each other back and forth.

Lemme have it, dammit.

Go fuck a duck.

An immense fluid flotilla of dirty clouds loomed very low, and the camp appeared isolated in the countryside, only that multitude of brown cones sticking up above the small bare scrubby trees, fences, and boundary lines of whitewashed stones wavering away across the undulating terrain, among more tents, more trees. They were pines with round tops, now glazed, glistening sharply with rain, the needles still dripping quietly, and a few soldiers playing at getting wet with raindrops by means of shaking the most flexible trunks, ramming into and chasing each other with the impetuous vitality of young bulls. The company had become populated with voices, soldiers sprinting, and in a few moments a tumult formed around the fountain spouts, bodies gathered with water jugs, aluminum pots. Raúl discovered Federico waiting for him at the edge of the next company; he wasn't wearing his Sunday best but coveralls instead, with a machete hanging from his equipment belt. He was smiling, his thumbs hooked in his belt, and one foot resting on the white track of aligned stones.

What's up? he asked.

Nothing, man, pretty fucked, said Raúl. I think I'm gonna head over to the post office again in case there's a telegram. Why don't you come?

Fuck no, I'm on barracks duty and it pisses me off to ask permission from the bastard of the week.

He'll never fucking notice. Just put your poncho on and tell any guy to stand in for you.

Nope, follow through, you've got to follow through. Discipline before all else. You've got to follow through to the very end.

Well, the end comes sooner or later, no matter what.

All the more reason, all the more. What you could do is pass by the Co-op and bring me a bottle of gin.

I don't know, man. I'm suspicious that Nuria hasn't come, and we don't even have more news.

Maybe she's had some problems. But, hey, don't forget about the gin.

I won't forget, dammit, don't be a drag. The most logical thing, really, is that nothing has happened to her. They'd catch us first.

Do you think so, man? If they catch us we won't get out of the castle for the rest of our fucking life. Together till death do us part.

Leo won't say anything. Besides, the logical thing would be that any arrest comes through Floreal, and Floreal hasn't been bothered... Alright, dammit, I don't want to think more about it. The best thing is to wait until Fortuny tells us what's happening. It could just be something unimportant, some little scare.

Or maybe it's something so important that even poor Fortuny's already been nabbed.

They read the telegram over again, the gray letters grouped in strips, between bluish creases: *León grave primo bien Nuria*: León serious cousin fine Nuria. Sure, said Raúl, if she means Floreal it's to make us understand that, although he's fine, that's the path they'll follow to us. A soft drop fell on the paper and brightened the blue.

Or that Floreal is the only one who hasn't been nabbed, said Federico. Listen, that's good, about the castle. The prisoners of the little Castle of If.

Drizzling, not drizzling, and the mud meandering away in brown streams. Raúl moved along the row of latrines; one by one, he inspected the small compartments lined up facing the wall, some occupied by squatting soldiers, clutching the doorway, their coveralls wadded up between their knees. It smelled bad and the flies covered the brick walls, the clogged drains deliquescent. On the extreme opposite side of the row appeared a prissy gentleman cadet in his Sunday best. Taking a stand, he began to unbutton his belt with a moronic smile. Fuck, sounds and smells like a livestock auction, he said, and there were several audible grunts, most likely from annoyance.

He opted out. He had to skirt the last companies, penetrate the woods for a few hundred yards, into deep shadows. The pine trees grew tall, thick, and black, in intricate patterns; then the forest opened out, as the ground gave way to a shallow depression, a flat, spongy terrain with a mossy oozing humus. The declivity was slight, brusquely interrupted by a low precipice, forming a natural barrier that isolated the spot from the noise from the army camp. There, in the shelter of the rocks, one could glimpse the residue of other visits, soggy papers, dissolved by the rain. He chose a new spot, fresh and clean, without flies, facing the empty space invaded by the fog, and distracted himself contemplating the bare track of his footsteps. The river churned somewhere down below, surging more forcefully into the ravine, and occasionally some dark crow glided silently out of sight. A few steps further on was a flat spot between the rocky crags, above the sudden cliff, a perfect spot to read peacefully during free hours or, simply, to reflect, something just as important as showering or shaving every day. He was facing north, above a landscape now only sensed, a quiet landscape, inhabited, enclosed in the distance by that bulky mountainous massif that stretched across the sky like a horizon unto itself. Flat, mesa-like, sparsely vegetated, a massive mountain wall, which occasionally seemed suddenly to loom over him, always startling him with equal intensity, as if he were seeing it for the first time.

Walking back, the camp offered a vast and surreal panorama, one saturated with imprecise sounds, like sonorous anthills, just barely emerging from among the camouflage of those rough scraggly boughs, like a forest on the march. They were in the magazine tent, playing poker, seated in a circle around a folding cot, covered with a blanket; the canvas flap was drawn closed across the doorway, and the halo from the candle enlarged their oscillating shadows, blending into the tightly wrapped boxes and bundles. In the background, someone was tuning the strings of a guitar. They raised their heads, and Pluto, taking a carbine down from the gun rack, pointed at him in challenge.

Who goes there! he shouted.

¡España!

¡Santiago!

White Horse!

Yeah, boy, wish I had a bottle of that. Have you eaten in the canteen?

They were talking about Captain Cantillo's latest dirty trick, yesterday, in the first company, when he ordered a surprise weapons inspection, and one of the guys who was already set to go on leave had to stay behind because they had swiped the rear sights from his rifle and he had no time to go and borrow some from another company. They said that the poor guy was in the cantina totally shitfaced drunk. But, can we say that this guy is really having a fucking bad time? asked Pluto. Because, here, what matters most is that you have a shitty time, a really shitty time.

The others called his attention, and Raúl studied Pluto's hand. The only saint that interests me is Saint George, said Pluto, as he studied the discard. Hunt dragons, that's what they all must have done. He poured himself some more cognac; they drank from a motley assortment of plastic cups stolen from the canteen. The bottle with the candle, the cigarettes, the piles of coins, the cards face up; he'd lost. Raúl asked how it was going.

Fucking great, man. If only they hadn't swindled me out of my pass, right now I'd be with my girlfriend in Sitges; or with the English girl in Tossa. But forget it, I'm here and they're cheating on me with any old son of a bitch. This is what you call plucked and fucked; I'm beaten and she's cheatin'. Goddamn it to hell. And all because of one lousy button, fuck.

He paid out carelessly, like one stubbing out a cigarette. This happened to you for letting yourself get caught by a cliché at the beginning, they told him. When the captain said to him, Farreras, what do you think, you're in an Ursuline girls' school here? And he said yes.

It's the captain, he's such a nitpicker. What's wrong with an Ursuline girls' school?

Cut it and shut it, dammit.

You cut it, man, instead of yanking it, 'cause it's showing. Fuck, this place is full of ascetic jack-offs having fun with Miss Rosy Palm. What are you all laughing at? Well, next Sunday you can all have some fun giving yourselves a good one thinking about how I've got my girder in good hands, meaning not my own, because I'm outta here whether I have a pass or not, I swear.

He spoke and swore at the same time, ceaselessly, replying,

quarreling with someone who was starting to tell about how, the last time he was on leave, with some skinny little chick, etcetera. Sure, man, you got lucky. They saw you together, and everybody was saying how you had a plan and then you fucked her and all that. Alright already, we know. He was betting borrowed money and said he'd lost more than three hundred. Fuck, it's just that I'm nervous. Today was my day for carnal exercises and they screwed it up for me. And after I've been stuffing myself all week ... What's the matter with you all? Haven't you ever heard of the path toward perfection? You're all a bunch of illiterates. Above all things, love, that's what it says in the Bible. Not divine love or human love, no sir; feminine love. That's what nobody understands. Not Kempis, not anybody. My bedside reading is the Kama Sutra, or the Pinchatwattie or the Pentateuch or the Brahmapudenda or whatever you call it. It's the book that describes the 69 elementary positions. Of course some of them are pure bullshit. Besides you'd need to be hung like a horse. The others were getting flustered, there was laughter, protests, and that medical student ended up getting really pissed off.

C'mon, c'mon, no need to be an animal. Show a little respect, for Christ's sake.

What's the matter? Have you read it? Then don't talk. I almost joined the Jesuits, and I know what I'm talking about. What do you think you learn in the Seminary?

You wanna shut up already? Seems to me that although you don't believe, the least you can do is not offend other people's feelings with your bestiality.

Fuck, who's offending whom? Did anyone this morning consider asking me if going to Mass might offend my feelings?

They argued with increasing anger, their sweaty foreheads shining brightly in the candlelight, and at some point two or three miserable fucking cadets came in, also very heated up. They were talking about getting a jam session going in their tent and they needed the guy with the guitar to come. You come, too, Gaminde. And fucking Pluto Farreras. They said they had bottles to spare, they were going to have more fun than playing cards but except for Pluto, the others from the card game weren't sure.

The one with the harmonica patted Pluto on the neck. Come on, Pluto, shit. Pluto looked at him over his five cards.

Man, I don't give a shit.

He'd lost again. He threw his cards onto the cot and stood up violently; he shouted that he was going out to piss, but that the game was still on and if anyone quit he'd knock him out with his rifle. He was sweating, and everyone went quiet. C'mon, Raúl, he said. He turned around, moving away, pulled back the tent flap to reveal the bleak, cloudy brightness, and let Raúl exit first while inside behind him arose, with growing clamor, a booing, woah, woah, easy, man, slow down, that'll make one less. They walked toward the latrines, heads down and hands in pockets, skirting puddles.

If you don't put on a bit of a show these sons of bitches will never take you seriously, said Pluto. But now I'm going to skin them all. I plan to leave them broke. It's not exactly a trick, y'know; it can backfire on you. Of course then I don't pay them. That's why I always play with borrowed money. Shit, I mean in this fucking place, you can't ever tell who you're really dealing with, not even the guys who aren't out to get you, even though you can keep your eyes on them, can't be trusted. Besides, I plan on swiping some rubbers and ramrods from them. Have something in store for emergencies. Fuck, so many thieves. I'm so pissed off… I think I'm going to lay low for a few days. But it won't make up for losing my pass.

He emerged from the latrines buttoning his pants. At the fountain they had a drink of water. They talked about Leo.

I was waiting for a telegram, said Raúl. Now I don't think it'll come.

Poor guy. Do you think they've made him squeal?

Fuck, I know about as much as you do. I suppose Fortuny will bring some news.

If you need me for anything at all, you already know where to find me. I'll be playing cards with these assholes all afternoon.

That was a fantastic avenue, running past the fountain and the latrines, a fantastic avenue that, rising gradually toward the Parade Ground—la Plaza de Armas—divided the camp into two, a large open area, laid out on the terrain as if on a blueprint, on a one-to-one scale, with its boundaries of whitewashed stones, with its symmetrical crossings, laid out perpendicularly—also of whitewashed stones—and its ornamental motifs, some truncated arc, some isolated column, of brick, and the officers' little huts, diminutive, almost like models, and the partitions of more latrines, of more shower stalls, and the shelves of more fountains, and the tips of the tents among the pines and the tall posts and the spectral cables, of phantom urbanization. A city traced in lines and squares on the gentle flat plain of rickety trees, a quadrangle of companies, of avenues counterposed to transversal streets which led to the service areas, Mess Halls, First Aid and Sick Bay Stations, Co-op, Infirmary, Post Office, etcetera, while the three avenues, the main one in the center, el Paseo de Gracia, as they called it, opened out into the vast parade ground, seat of the officers' headquarters, and public buildings, the Major's headquarters, the church, Central Command, etcetera and, as if to give it a happy air, off to one side, the canteen.

The men from artillery lined up in front, four by four, at ease, nervous, those who had permission for leave particularly nervous, with their gear all packed and ready to go, adjusting their caps, checking every minute the smallest details of their uniforms. Companies kept arriving and falling into formation behind them, as soon as each sergeant delivered his report to the lieutenant, each lieutenant to the captain, and each captain to the Week Commander's assistant. The Commander was from the artillery division, and he began the inspection with his own battalion. His voice rose sharply—Battaaaaaaalion! Attennnnnn-shun!—the lines tightened up crisply and stood facing the sun, as if nailed into place, while up there, at the head of the avenue, a sharp-edged silhouette was outlined against the sky above the Parade Ground. Another figure was visible, too, surely the assistant captain, and he ran to meet the commander, to give him the report. The commander was sickly-looking, short of stature, and he wore smoked glasses. Clamped under his arm was a baton of heather wood. Flanked by scrutinizing officers, he noiselessly passed through row after row, between restrained breathing and

fixed eyes staring straight ahead as if blind. Hardly had he passed
by when Raúl could already glimpse, out of the very corner of
his eye, the expressions of joyful pleasure among the formation,
although the baton had already pointed at Pluto's jacket, signaling, with a solemn pause, the poorly disguised flaw, the broken
symmetry, the empty buttonhole, an irrefutable sign of the missing golden button. They moved on, and Lieutenant Noguero,
on noticing, said between clenched teeth, *esta vez te va a caer el
pelo*—this time your hair is going to fall out—smiling, perhaps
amused, by the man's bad luck, for the fact that the pardon
meted out as punishment for the negligent loss of his rifle sights,
granted by Captain Mauriño at his request, had turned out to
be so much in vain, in the same way that his previous sworn
prediction—the one about how they are going to skin you alive,
Farreras, meaning that, from his perspective, Pluto was destined
to end up without a pass—was fatefully fulfilled when, upon
rehearsing the very same exercises, the commander singled out
Pluto in front of the entire battalion, asking him which company
he belonged to, telling him, very possibly without even listening
to the response, well you're putting your captain in a perfectly
outstanding situation, *muchachito*, really outstanding, you know.
That lieutenant from the theory classes under the pines, if the
captain was absent, made Pluto go to the chalkboard, for everyone's amusement, and stand before him, when, for example,
he discovered him urinating on a bush and called him with his
deep voice, let go of that thing and come over here, Farreras,
indolent, well-built, and ruddy, always appearing to be sleepy,
good for spending time with, for killing time, getting caught up
in one of those arguments that made the morning more entertaining, wherein Pluto knew so well how to loosen his tongue
and respond with agility and precise indolence, skirting the very
limits of what was publicly tolerable.

The start of class was delayed and Captain Mauriño, behind
his field table, silently contemplated them all growing more
restless by the moment. Captain Mauriño, his pauses, his empty
silences, taking refuge behind his black glasses, his inhospitable
eyes, feigning a forceful furrowing of the brow, on the point

of remembering, of seizing the thread, of specifying what he meant to say, and especially, what he meant it was supposed to mean. Lieutenant Noguero chewed out the one responsible for not assigning someone to bring the chalkboard. So what's the colonel supposed to do, graze on the grass? he said. And Captain Mauriño made a vague gesture, the gentle valley, the quiet pines limned with splendid radiance, in the direction of the camp. C'mon, move, go and bring it. Go that way, through the fog.

Captain Mauriño spoke about logistics, and Lieutenant Noguero went to pester Pluto, furtively. He approached him during formation; that morning, when, after reveille, happy and Spanish, he appeared with his sleepy cat face, and they marched in step, maneuvering toward the mess tents, crossing the central avenue and the Artillery groups, in search of the obligatory Sunday morning breakfast, with the queues forming up before any one of the three boilers ready to ladle out the steaming slops. Pluto went ahead of Raúl, his head down, dejected, clinking his tin cup, and Lieutenant Noguero, puffed up like a big cunt, said to him, pretty little view, eh, Farreras? And Pluto answered, sure, splendid. The mess tents were lined up perpendicular to the cliff, a sheer precipice that plunged straight down to the terraced skirts of the sun-soaked barrens. From there one could see clear out over the dark plain below, stretching out into the distance, and, beyond, the sea, the sea and the clouds that, like an explosive crater, enclosed first the sun, the endless sea, an endless bronzed smoothness, with metallic reflections, auric, steely, stained with gloomy continents, with terraqueous globes, submerged, an endless surface finished in low saline flashes, in caverns of light, covered with stratified clouds, piled high in the shape of a lofty city, like a mountain, an embattled city, with high walls, with towers and cupolas and celestial banners, a city with its own radiant light and its own cloudy marine horizon, generator of suns and planets, of days and nights, rotations, periodic cycles. Past the mess tents, also backed up to the cliff, there remained the quartermaster's warehouse and the commissary and, on the other side of the parade ground, the first-aid hut and the infirmary, and, on the corner of the parade ground, the post office barracks.

He asked the soldier at the counter, a distracted regimental officer, who sat reading a Wild West novel under the spotlight of a desk lamp. Back outside again, he dropped the letter into the mailbox; he barely glimpsed the sentry at the motor pool passing by in the fog, rifle shouldered, bayonet sharpened, sparkling, and also like an angel, another crow appeared, gliding languidly by. At the head of the road, as if hanging above the void, the outlines of the first-aid hut and the infirmary, the path of lazy cunning devils and humiliated men which, as it led straight to the abyss below, served as a definitive warning. There from the parapet, on clear days, the panoramic view was splendid, now that the late dawn coincided with reveille, joyful and Spanish, the aura of the aurora refreshing the face, pleasant smells of pine woods and dew. He squatted down, and while he waited in the door of the first-aid tent, out of the wind, he saw the companies dispersing from the parade ground, marching in-step, singing. They moaned their complaints, shrunken, huddling, curled up, convincing themselves of their own misery, and Raúl leaned his elbows on the parapet. The sun turned the fields and the flatlands rosy pink, the tender stands of pine, the violet-colored gorges, the dewy steaming grass of the valleys, thin mists belonging more to the coming equinoctial September. Then the mist began to dissipate and little by little one could clearly see the populated plain, the flat beaches from which the white sails of the conqueror of Mallorca had departed, and the sea widened and widened in lucid blue. Closer, above towns and cultivated fields, rose the first foothills of the sunny lands, a stepped mountain of successive planes and spurs perpendicular to the plain and parallel to one another, steep craggy precipices, masses of overwhelming presence, difficult to climb, a jagged wasteland of a mountain of ancient abandoned terraces, of knolls overgrown with brambles, rising to the flat summit, without any animals, possibly some overflying crow, rotating in flight, on the lookout for garbage heaps. And facing away from the parapet, above the camp, inland, more terraces, heights even higher and further back, flat-topped pillars of rock, a brittle progression of notched heights broken by steep narrow canyons and deep forests, more flat peaks, rising higher and higher, from which one might see, standing out sharp, clear, and unmistakable, Montsant, Scala Dei, rocky and stepped, to the west, perpendicular to the Ebro Valley. It was a clear morning, and the cold harsh wastrel wind out of the southwest raised whirling dust devils across the Parade Ground. Then the orderly came out, with his insecticide halo, reporting that the captain doctor had said that they either shut up immediately or he was sending them all back to their respective companies. He knew him from before, from when he'd been in the infirmary several days—how many?—at the start of the summer, and the orderly ran errands in exchange for tips and he rented out gunfighter novels. That infirmary where you were admitted with a broken leg and discharged with colitis, or you went in with the flu and came out with furuncles. That hot, whitewashed room, with white beds in a row, and that toilet where you had to throw the paper in a wastepaper basket, and the prodigious bitter pill as the single remedy for every malady, and the insecticide smell, and the convalescents' conversations, hours and hours chatting about any old thing, planning ways to fool the captain doctor. They put him between some softly-worn and still-warm sheets, and the guy in the next bed whom he started to get to know pretty well as his fever came down was Fortuny. Federico came by with Pluto and they brought him cigarettes and his mail, letters from Nuria and a postcard from Papa with a painting by Velázquez on the other side, a Venus with a sinuous derriere that caused a sensation. Nuria informed him that she had definitively decided to abandon her studies, and instead of taking a vacation, she was starting immediately to work for her father, as a secretary. Nuria? The perfect tachy-mechanostenomagnodactylotyphonographic secretary, cliclick, cliclick, click? *Pajarraco.* Slyboots. Big ugly bird.

The Parade Ground spread out like a marsh, miry and exhaling, evaporating, and the fog seemed to burn off and different shapes took shape successively in depth and detail, the mass of the water tower, square and heavy, crenellated, stone by stone like a fortress, with its gargoyles in the form of tiny cannons

and the ramrod flagpole which clashed so much with the clock
that was better-suited to a parish belfry, tiny little castle that
might… Yes, it was clearing up, the mist vanishing from the
parade ground, its wide expanse now visible, the whole face
of the camp clearer and clearer, a rectangular plaza, enclosed
on three sides, with the water tower and the officers' barracks
dominating the first stretch of the longest side, before reaching
the central avenue that, branching off from there, symmetrically
divided the base, facing—also symmetrically—the main guard
house, on the opposite side, open to the countryside, to the highway; and past the avenue, now in the second stretch, the chapel
and the command post, and toward the back, directly opposite
the post office, face to face, the porches of the cantina, the sharp
rooftops of the grocery, the tobacco shop, the barbershop, and
the savings bank. A harsh, unpleasant place, yes, and the fucking
brown slimy mud sticking to your boots, weighing them down,
thicker and lumpier with every step. He heard a few undefined
rhythms on a harmonica, and to one side of the water tower he
spotted a couple kissing, she wrapped tightly inside the soldier's
poncho, the pair suddenly revealed by the thin, lifting fog, a fog
just like in the morning, not dense enough to skip outdoor Mass
celebrated in the presence of the three battalions in formation
there, between trumpet calls, all standing at attention, immobile
before the brightly-colored chasuble visible even from the back
rows, green for the umpteenth Sunday after Pentecost. They had
the second lieutenant behind them, but toward the end, when
the *ite misa est* was pronounced, Pluto could whisper to Raúl,
that's one less, man.

The canteen was still packed, overflowing with families
stuffed full with Sunday paella, drinking coffee, tables covered
with dirty plates, with bits of rice and chicken bones sucked
clean, fathers in a good mood, satisfied to see their sons healthier
and more manly, remembering their own youth, better times,
times past, and one mother, perhaps a widow, who tried to win
over an easy, affable sergeant major in the name of common
acquaintances, recommending to the embarrassed young fellow,
a fucking cadet with a technician's lanyard, to get him some

preferential treatment, some privilege. Behind, on the smoothly sloping meadow, prudently close to the cantina's protective eaves, more visitors, relatives, fiancées, small groups here and there on the grass, with their scotch plaid blankets, their thermoses and their baskets of food, as if on a picnic. Raúl ran into the day patrol, three or four miserable fucking cadets following the lieutenant on a boring round, and now outside of the enclosure, he looked for a rock beyond the families, past the armory clearing. The time Nuria came up to visit him, they had gone as far away as possible, and in a bright clearing she laid out the contents of her basket, the most traditional sort of wicker basket. She behaved as if the situation were still so very amusing, but she no longer had the natural ease as when she'd jumped out of the car, radiant, dressed with those lizard colors which looked so good against her complexion and her sunny hair, and she kissed him in front of everybody, not even when they left the cantina behind, she holding his arm, her hand resting upon the stiff sleeve of his army jacket. Raúl made an effort to ask questions, and as she seemed to relax, as if she'd caught his mood, he put his arm round her waist. They even had to make an effort to make love and, afterward, to laugh at what a disaster it had all been. He wrote her the same day, almost immediately after she left, and they agreed that she should not come up to visit again. When he had a weekend pass things were different, quick lustful trips to Sitges or to Tarragona, out of uniform: on Saturday night and on Sunday morning everything went well but, after midday, the two of them started to fall quiet once again.

The big rock was flat-topped, with bright, spongy moss; it was wet and slippery, and he had to sit down, spreading out the folds of his cape. The armory, sunk into the terrain, appeared to have become a quagmire, and the artillery pieces, wrapped in tarps, looked monstrous in the pale puddles as if drinking from them. To his left was the camp and to his right, toward the west, the black gloomy forests, the gorges, the heights covered by the fog that had lifted, stony, castle-like, crowned by Montsant, of the which, on a clear day, from that rock, you could, at most, discern its smooth peak, distant and diaphanous, a rough mountain elongated like a ruined wall running toward the Valley of the Ebro. In the parking lot, below the canteen, there was a lot of movement, and two or three cars drove slowly along the barely visible stretch of the muddy, rutted road. On the parade ground, at the main sentry post, there was a changing of the guards. That was a bad spot, too close, with officers passing by constantly and you had to salute and count their stars and announce, Guards, attention! Then he reached the cover of the shale rocks, for example, or the arsenal, which was even further away, and he could smoke in peace. Before the pledge to the flag, the only ones to stand guard were the regimentals, and they, gentlemen cadets, not sworn soldiers, were on alert, kept watch, drilled, had four straight hours of instruction, practiced, and during free time, scaled the rocks on the perimeter, to water the wheat sown along the fence line by the tents so that it would sprout as couch grass, to inspire their decorative motivation, any frivolous gaudy doo-dad with an inscription, with a touch of spicy humor, borderline naughty, demonstrating, to the eyes of future family visitors, their youthful spirit and virile joy. They worked the whole afternoon, first each company on its own, executing the same movements over and over again, timed by the whistle blast, Captain Mauriño screaming himself hoarse, Pre-seeeeeeeent… Arms! Rest… Arms! And they opened ranks and spread out, making a tight formation, all the companies of the battalion now joined, facing the commander, wrapped in a cloud of brown dust, literally scared shitless by the chance of turning to the left instead of the right, or skipping a beat, or falling out of step, a misstep that would cost them their extended leave pass, of that ceremony so many times rehearsed before the battalions finally paraded one after another past the colonel along the length of the parade ground. A perfect parade, memorable parade, the parade which culminated with the brilliant display, the parade ground—la Plaza de Armas—adorned, shining, awash in flammiferous reflections, the air aglow, the sun floating in a golden halo that twenty-fifth of July, the day of Santiago, Saint James, the knight on his white charger, savior of the Christian *Patria Hispana*, the Spanish Fatherland, when the horse cadets, in the presence of a large public, were solemnly made soldiers, deacon militants of the war. They waved the flags in an explosion of red and yellow, and the band played military marches uninterrupted, on swearing to the flag I kissed it and my kiss was a prayer, *madre mía, madre mía*, the kiss that I would give you with my heart. And the brief but emotive allocution, not of an orator but rather of a soldier, sounding distant and indistinct on the esplanade of petrified formations, Spain, glorious warrior nation, sacrosanct fatherland, our longing and our pride is your greatness, that you be noble and strong, and by seeing you feared and honored your children will go happy to their death. And also, from the presidential viewing stand, the homily of the august cardinal in purple or red, the same difference, his invocations to God and to Caesar, today the feast day of Santiago, lord of the armies, the proto-apostle proto-patron of the proto-patria, lightning bolt of the war that has so often intervened providentially, saving Spain from the international enemy, from conspiracies, intrigues, and hatreds of the which traditionally, gentlemen cadets, our father-land, and its interests has been the victim, or better, exhortations about how the earthly peace of the fatherland must be called a celestial peace; saying how the social peace is tranquility through order, a harmonic disposition of similar things or similar people, each one in their proper place; saying how when the earthly city disturbs the peace, the children of the City of God resort to war, a just war because its objective is peace, the restoration of the destroyed order, and then it is God who conquers through his children, who gives them victory; saying how this is the way of human history, how while the earthly City endures there will be children of the saber and rifle. And, to conclude, a final call, here above, near to the bright stars, on this mountain of battle-hardened ruggedness, propitious to meditation and repentance, to firm resolutions, wrathful domain of thunder and lightning.

A little boy was exploring the muddy arsenal ground, wan-dering in zigzags between the artillery pieces sheathed in canvas, stopping here and there to look, head held high, eyes raised, the menacing inclination of the cannons, at the ready below their covers as if for some forgotten salvo. Hardly any visiting families remained, and the first fine drops of rain hastened their dispersal in a few seconds. All voices gone, the invisible river was audible again, far below, plunging down through the gorge, the white cascade wildly pouring onto the calm water, a dark quiet pool, with small fine bubbles, and eerie semicircles spreading out, diminishing. The rain came, slanting down, running through the woods like a chilly shiver, and in the opposite direction, toward the west, the fog seemed to descend again, to invade the ravines of raw rock, light and soft, ghostly. The last cars drove out in procession, very close together, and now departed, coursing the tight curves, moving ahead with caution, wheels almost to the gutter, to allow an old passenger bus that was arriving to slip by, doubtless bringing back the first ones returning from leave. Raúl buried his face between the upturned flaps of his poncho and made a skittering run to the parking lot behind the canteen. No more than half a dozen got down out of the bus, all of them miserable fucking cadets, with their backpacks, and they ran off quickly, splashing in the mud, splattered by the rain. In their place the few visitors that still remained climbed aboard, and only one couple lingered before the open bus door, still embracing, the girl pressing up against his poncho. Hands waved in the small windows and one heard words of farewell, messages, orders, errands, advice, *adiós, adiós, mi lindo marinero*, my handsome sailor. Raúl went back up the hill of the canteen with his face to the diminishing rain, a passing spell of weather, now reduced to brown drizzle. The atmosphere inside the canteen had changed, the airy porch now half empty, the benches and tables spattered by the rain all along the railing, below the dripping uralite eaves, limpid, vitreous shining drops falling rhythmically from one end to the other, now no one there from outside the camp, only sergeants and miserable fucking cadets and a small group of officers midway along the bar. They served him a hot cognac. Someone was arguing about whether soccer was spectacle or sport, and separated by a dribbling leak from the roof, several sergeants were listening, doubled over with laughter, man, and he said, hut orderly? he said, fuck that's the first time I see a sergeant being a hut orderly, just like that, man. They doubled over, clutching each other by the shoulders in a rowdy chorus. Goddammit, man, that was shocking. And before he told him, and this gentleman, what does this mean? And the captain had had it, man. And two sergeants were arguing, each insisting on paying, alongside the officers, don't fuck with me, dammit. The officers were also in the mood for screwing around, Lieutenant Noguero and Captain Cantillo and the captain-major and the sub-captains, more than one ass-licking second lieutenant who, taking advantage of the momentary suspension of all hierarchy, laughed along with them sympathetically, as if among his regular drinking buddies. And the captain-major ended up going round to the other side of the bar and started serving them personally, filling glasses, making fun of the colonel, oh, I was saying, aw shit. But the one who had the singing voice was Captain Cantillo, with his voice like burnt silk and his dramatic, heated, slightly crazed gestures, red-faced, his heavily-veined neck, like a boxer, and the others joining in the chorus, all of them singing gleefully together, a real laugh riot. And then the Aragonese joined in, *what I really like is to drinkalildrink, from the bota take a drink*, and Captain Cantillo talked about the female soldiers when there was the war, not just girls but real good time broads, that the only thing they were looking for was good treatment with the ramrod, that's right, syphilis guaranteed, the secret weapon that the Reds never hit on using because Durruti didn't have half a brain; he let everyone surrender to us instead of shooting them. Or all that business with the whore from Tetouan, with her little shoobedoobedomedaddy, Captain Cantillo, with a fleck of grape on his tongue, big drinker, stiffer than a rifle or a 133 caliber mortar, with bigger balls than a bull. Well, you shouldn't dip your wick in any old shit in Africa, either. Fuck, you can't tell, catch the clap and anything else. Fuck. Fuuuck. Hah. You can't tell. Worthless shit the ones from Africa. That's right, they suck it harder than a kif pipe. Fuuuck. Hah. And the worthless whores there, begging till I agree and I tell her, strip it all off right now or you can fuck off. And she climbs on the table and takes her clothes off, the fucking whore, when she's bare ass, she squats down and starts pissing. And I tell her, I am gonna stick it up your ass, girl, and she tells me, let's see if you really mean it. Fuuuck. Fuuuck. Hah. What're you drinking, goddammit. Raúl ordered another cognac.

The canteen barmaid. She croons in a lilting voice.

La, la, la-la, la-la, la, la
La, la, la-la, la-la, la, la
La, la, la-la, la, la
La, la, la-la, la, la

The beer-barrel polka. Captain Cantillo.

He breakfasted on churros and thick, hot chocolate while the loudspeakers blared out popular paso dobles from scratched records and, like at a religious festival, visitors continued flowing in, a crowd of families and fiancées, and seemed to celebrate the fiesta, the brash carnivalesque joy, right up to the time before the imminent official ceremony; he ate breakfast sitting there, in the cantina, hung all around with rippling flags and banners, next to his chaste, brown-skinned spouse, chaste and in mourning, busty and chaste, her hair in a bun, *olé, olé*, you're the envy of the flowers, María Dolores, Spanish wife, both of them silent, him, covered with shining golden decorations, proud warrior, victorious crusader, blue divisional commander Captain Cantillo, with grizzled mustache and vacant gaze, distant eyes that seemed to contemplate the growing pandemonium of the dust clouds, spiraling rebelliously above the parade ground as if a white horse had just gone galloping across it, meditating perhaps on the promotion ladder or perhaps, simply, enjoying the leisure of being there, killing time, while in the wink of an eye, with a Major's commission the bonus pay for July doubled almost automatically, with its credits and meals, in memory of the glorious victory. Or even, for example, Captain Cantillo in the city, in conversation, a conversation with comrades in arms accompanied by their respective spouses, all in civilian dress, with their sober and well-cared-for Sunday suits, gathered together surely in some room at the Casino Militar or in some formerly renowned locale, now with neon where there were once chandeliers, the seats reupholstered in plastic, an old *cervecería*, yes, but still socially acceptable and, what's even more important, with moderate prices. They

chatted, they conversed using the most stale Spanish courtesy
and liberality of sentiments, manliness, courtesy, stately deport-
ment, with elegance and authentic wit and bonhomie, and their
respective wives corresponded with cunning modesty, nodding
their heads, studying one another, their lacquered permanents,
their tight Astrakhan cuffs and necks, fake pearls, smiling, jealously hiding their most intimate thoughts; nice tranquil evenings out. And, suddenly, once again in a field uniform, now
departed in the train amid crammed goodbyes—*sag mir wo die
Blumen sind*—now in the camp, with a company under his command, a company of miserable fucking cadets in coveralls, and
with their hair cropped short, provisioned now with folding
cots and straw for their mattresses, with marmite, tin cup, water
cooler, and blankets, everything necessary, once there, far from
the world of daily life, on that mountain of flat peaks, abruptly
terraced, stepping up and up like the promotion ladder itself,
when with the first formations, as if starting from zero, he began
a new life, the brusque transformation; damn it!, you can go
now, like a bat out of hell, get your cap, for fuck's sake. And
Lieutenant Noguero asked him, how's it going, Gaminde. He
turned to the others, this one's turned into a lazy hooligan, too,
but he's a silent killer. Captain Cantillo fixed his eyes on him,
very black and penetrating beneath his hairy eyebrows, with a
penetration that immediately seemed to dissipate, as if cloud-
ing over, perhaps from incapacity for persistence, perhaps for
lack of interest toward such an accidental reality. Well, fuck,
let Gaminde's son have a drink, he said, and the captain major
served him, solicitous. For you, boy. Lieutenant Noguero asked
him again how things were going and Raúl started to say they
were alright, but no one was listening to him, everybody attentive to Captain Cantillo, who was talking about how things used
to be, except for exceptions, the recruit, the soldier, the little
lamb, the young replacement, the common soldier, the small
fry, with neither spirit nor heroism nor balls enough, country
bumpkins, uncivilized yokels not worth wasting time trying to
train, or inculcate in them feelings they didn't have, or treat them
humanely, in any other way that wasn't at the point of a rifle,

or a good clean slap across the face. And the second lieutenant, a malicious affected little dandy from Andalusia, with smoked glasses, listened smiling, entertained himself twirling the little chain of his whistle, coiling and uncoiling it round his index finger. And in the war, all that stuff about having to be at the front of the troop is just stories. Behind, at the rear, and with the pistol, and for the one who tries to retreat you just give me a clear aim at him and you avoid getting shot in the back, fuck, I've been in Russia, said Captain Cantillo, methods probably not shared by Captain Sánchez Clavijo, who arrived too late to participate in the Civil War, in the Eastern Campaign, and in the fight against the Maquis; he, who in the academy—he recalled again and again—had his hands turn bloody from handling the rifle so long when the cry came—Attention!, conscious of the formative character of that oh-so-apparently mechanical train- ing, first phase of the road leading to the long awaited battlefield. Fuck, man, Clavijo, come over here, they said. Really good to see you, goddammit. C'mon, man, don't fuck with me. Whose idea is it to get started at this hour? They offered him a glass and Captain Sánchez didn't say no, barely resisting, corpulent, with a guileless face, with his red cheeks, and his mustache like a tin soldier, clumsy and astonished until he'd had a few drinks and then he proved to be one of those shy guys that let loose and turn out to be funny as hell. Mauriño, Mauriño, *no tengas morriña*, don't you start yawning, he suddenly shouted on seeing Captain Mauriño in the back, all by himself. Watch out, you'll turn Gallego, all their wordiños endiño in iño. They shouted to be understood above the vociferous choruses, above the verses sung monotonously within the shelter of the bar, rhyming vir- ile consonance, *coño y moño*; *cojones y purgaciones*—fucked but outta luck; balls, balls, the clap calls—vulgarities repeated over and over again, from one soldier to another, from class to class, year after year applauded in the canteen, on Sunday afternoons, like a drug that summons memories or evasions appropriate to one who, like Captain Cantillo, knows that he'll never rise above lieutenant colonel.

The air blew in chilly and gray from the parade ground, the

parade ground framed between the brick pillars and the still dripping eaves, vast, swampy, the puddles shining like blind pupils.
Another captain came along and, for a moment, the group broke
apart into two or three small knots, a good moment to bid farewell to Lieutenant Noguero with some witty, impudent remark
which he tried in vain to summon up, offering instead a brief
explanation about the fact that it was getting time to rejoin his
company, or his plan to buy a bottle in the co-op, saying goodbye to take advantage of the moment to get out of the way, to
be forgotten, to transform into one more of the cloaked forms
wandering about the parade ground, where, little by little, the
canteen bar, elbows and glasses and caps and cigarettes would
be getting mixed up as in a vague struggle, the songs and noises
increasingly dampened, and Lieutenant Noguero's see if you save
a slug for me.

Not like Captain Cantillo, nor like Captain Mauriño, serious,
yes, but already very worn out, with a lesion, the consequence
of an old wound, which incapacitated him, in fact, from
greater responsibilities than commanding a company. No,
Captain Sánchez Clavijo had neither Cantillo's voice nor his
manners, nor, above all, his vision of the military life, which
showed rather plainly when Captain Mauriño had the flu and
Captain Sánchez Clavijo, without abandoning his company,
took charge, as well, of the instruction and theory classes for
the Third Company. He supervised Lieutenant Noguero's work
and, at times, took command directly. He spoke to them about
the war, and everyone, seated in a loose semicircle under the
pines, made themselves comfortable, placidly disposed to listen,
and even those who were reading westerns on the sly put them
aside. But instead of sharing with them some anecdotes or life
experiences, he unreeled disquisitions about war as a natural
and, simultaneously, social phenomenon, and soon nobody was
listening, beginning with Lieutenant Noguero himself, who
was leaning against a tree trunk, chewing on a stalk of oregano,
whispering under his breath to Pluto; they started reading
again, they studied the movements of the insects among the
grass, they half closed their eyes, sleepy from the sun and the

aroma of warm sap. To live is to fight and life is combat. War is the normal stuff of daily life; peace is an illusion, abnormal. The war between peoples, as history so well demonstrates, will always endure, and the word peace is nothing but a cover which nations like to use and abuse to cover up their will to dominate. His concluding words turned out to be embarrassing, a sudden and tense pause which seemed to make them wake up while he looked at them in silence from his folding table, heavy and taciturn, embittered—people said—because his wife had cheated on him and they'd had to separate. Only during drill did he fly off the handle, screaming himself hoarse—one, two—when at last, as the afternoon drew to a close, they paraded before the colonel across this vast and swampy parade ground, clotted with puddled footprints. He looked at the sky, the low dome of cruelly flattened clouds, the barracks' rooftops made thin, sharp, and steely, burnished by the fallen rain, and, as he approached the stony bulk of the water tower there sounded again, now with greater clarity, the sad harmonica rhythms. It was then, more or less, when he observed the presence of a small group of trumpets and drums gathered before the water tower, belfry or scaffolding, now too late to turn and run and, turning to the left, to take refuge in the co-op before, outside, the weather seemed to stop and everyone froze, as if paralyzed, while the consecutive drum and bugle calls for flag and prayer lasted, a ceremony repeated day after day, an ancient summons resounding when, each afternoon, the companies lined up on the parade ground, first facing the east while they lowered the flag, and then, facing about, toward the west, standing at attention until the last long trumpet call ceased, their gaze fixed on the low dying sun, white and tenuous as a sacred host, veiled by a fluid, yellow mist, the landscape populated by barely visible hills, calm pine stands, and rough, rocky crags, evocative of the approaching equinox, of the summer in the throes of vanishing, the same as those increasingly early sunsets. He stood stock-still, therefore, among other scattered figures equally immobilized wherever they had been surprised by the bugle call, in that hour of nostalgia and recollection, suited to contemplating the visits received, those beloved absent beings and their daily life down there, while there at the camp, above the clock upon the embattled tower, the enormous flagpole stood naked, erect, out of service. And at the same time, mingled with such sentiments and longings, a comforting expectation based on the irreversible character of the passing of time, on the evidence that one day more was one day less, that with the approaching autumn there also approached the moment in which, like the veterans who would graduate in July, they would retrace, one by one, but in reverse, the various stages of their arrival. They rolled by packed into trucks, everything now fulfilled and purged, singing, shouting, waving with their caps, enveloped in the violent liberated dust, little Spanish soldier, brave little soldier, the pride of the sun is to kiss your forehead. They sang, they shouted, *adiós, muchachos, adiós cantina, adiós* retreats and all the goddamned silly imaginary things, all the mechanical jobs completed, cleaning latrines and scrubbing pots. For them there would be no more corporals nor thrashings, nor crewcuts, and there would be others than them, equally unknown and close-cropped, the ones who now would be wandering around the companies of the miserable fucking cadets in search of some leftovers or scrounging a tip, offering to shine boots, clean rifles, wash clothes. There would be others in their place because they would no longer have to go scurrying along carrying their bundles, furtive like spirits or malefactors, stinking, slinking, scheming, snooping, swiping; for them, that was all over now.

But he would keep on as always, following a route opposite the sun's direction, opposite the company's at the canteen, in a northwest direction, his face to the shadowy gorges, to the forests, and the cliffs and escarpments of that mountain range which, like a staircase, ascended in a brusque succession of buttresses and mesas, spurs, precipices, above whose heights stood out, far away, the smooth peak of Montsant and the Carthusian monastery of Scala Dei, toward the Ebro Valley, and then, crossing the parade ground, from the canteen to the co-op in a southwest direction, as if threading the parapet of the camp, the steep pitch of the sunny spot tumbling in craggy masses toward the flat plain of subtly shaded farms and fields, with the high sea in the distance, in order to return at last to the point of departure through the clustered artillery, in a north-south direction, the shadow lying ahead, twisted toward the right, tiny, flattened. Only occasionally, with some concrete purpose, looking into the post office, for example, would he take a north-south-west roundabout path to reach the canteen and from there, now returning, retrace his steps, crossing again the parade ground and, now facing the post office, turn to the left and after making any purchase in the co-op, fruit, a quarter pound of ham, a bottle of gin, waiting patiently in line, like in some small-town grocery, then walking through the artillery cluster once more, toward the central avenue, his company's road. And the next day, at the firing range, down below, on a steep slope of the desolate sunny ground. They descended along a rough, rocky trail loaded with their full field equipment, one by one, an interminable trail, and from the fellow ahead, owing as much to an excessive abundance of legumes in the daily diet as to the uneven ground, a continuous ether of stinking fluted sonorities burped from the depths of his trousers. I don't understand how you still have the desire to climb a mountain, said Pluto. The only thing you'll see from up there is other mountains. And after work, when they were resting in the shadow of an outcropping, he still insisted. I don't give a shit about the mountains. Everything in view but nothing at hand. Fortuny was there, too, and Federico didn't take long to find them. They talked about the first thing they would do when they got back to Barcelona, when they were all done. Well, this whole experience out here in the country, here at the camp, seems to me an interesting one, said Federico. Look, just like a spa treatment where they bathe you, make you swallow purgative waters or depuratives or whatever you call them, and you come out fresh as new. Well, here, it's the same. Living together with other people, discipline, brutal treatment, giving them the most hellish time possible. And all to end up naming you an officer, linking you to the hierarchy, turning you into one of them. And Pluto: fuck, just like vampires.

More than a spa, it makes me think of jail, said Fortuny.

What the fuck do you mean a jail? A girls' convent. I already told the captain. The only difference is that here people cuss.

Well, tell me what difference you see between a prison and an army camp. At least there you're in for something you've done. Here, however, just because you're a certain age and you're more or less normal. And lemme tell you, for sure, for the same amount of time, I'd prefer prison. At least in jail you know that once you're there they can't do anything more to you.

Fuck, don't be so dramatic. This place is a school, nothing more. Where else could you learn about playing war if not here? Playing war at our age, fuck, a bunch of adults playing war.

He turned to Raúl. Why don't you write something about this, since you like novels? And Federico: this is a job for Count Adolfo, our official chronicler. He'd take the job more seriously, like Hemingway, bitter people, hard drinkers, and the protagonist has to desert and all that.

With eyes half-closed they contemplated, at the feet of those steep flats topped with a dry crust, the fields on the plain, olive groves, locust tree groves, vineyards, symmetrical hazelnut groves, the toasted fields in the colorless midday quiet, the wide open towns, the chalky vapor, from the sea and the sky, the beaches from which the conquistadors' victorious ships had set sail, the blessed standards which they planted like a wildfire on the sweet island in the serene sea. They had set up tents and, upon going to fill the water cooler, they discovered a long, blood-chilling, verdigris snake, resting between the clear pebbles in the spring. It turned and reared up at them, hissing, fork-tongued, then slithered out of sight, disappearing in an almost imperceptible way. Or instead of the firing range, guard duty; it was his turn in the main guardhouse and Captain Cantillo was the one reviewing parade. Hope nothing goes wrong for you, they told him. But he managed to get out of it by complaining he wasn't feeling well, and while the others marched, he remained in the tent, pacing back and forth like a tiger until it was time to present himself in the infirmary. He awaited his turn leaning on the window sill, from where he could still make out the last columns descending, torturous files of soldiers and mules disappearing from sight in the imprecise panorama of little groves, rosy pink flats, violet-colored gorges, vast valleys seemingly forged even as the fog burned off, and when they called for him he complained it was colitis, a sham formality, sufficient for them to dose him with medicine and send him back to his company. Then he prepared himself calmly, his uniform, boots, buckles, belts, rifle, machete, and, without any mishap, managed to survive that parade inspection in which Captain Cantillo managed to punish almost all of them, not by checking how they held their rifles but by checking to see if there was any dust in the joint groove of their machetes. The rest of the time, it was even agreeable to stand guard; in front of the slate-roofed shed, for example, thoughtfully smoking, the lonely hours spent in those pine groves softened by the breeze, silky green, as if water-streaked, sounds on the air, like an organ playing lightly. And the magazine on a blazing hot afternoon, there, so isolated and dominating, within the shelter of the sentry house, the hazy plain, the waxy mountains, the pocked and whitewashed plain, and the mountain seeming to flatten itself from peak to peak, tumbling down step by step, and the quiet canyons of stratified rock in curved depressions, and the muted brightness of the rocky crags and outcroppings, and the few trees, blackened lattice, just as if they'd been burnt to a crisp upon the airless sunny barrens, and that light droning of cicadas arising from the lower mountain, below a sky of hot steel. And even the guardhouse graffiti, inside that dumpy little cavern of reverie, the detailed drawings as inside a urinal, the declarations: In this place, your father solemnly whacked himself off in celebration of his final guard duty, an encouraging inscription, perfect to awaken the imagination, to think about what his daily life would be when all that had concluded. And the other scribblings, more reflective, inciting one to ponder the ephemeral character of such dreams, the miserable reality of their real situation: Fucking cadet, don't you dare celebrate your last guard duty without first thinking that you still have another summer to go. A summer wearing sergeant's stripes, but definitely another summer, a passing stay, limited time, but not, for that reason, wasting a single minute, time no less real and irremissible for one who, no mere visitor, does his time up there and endures it. The same mornings spent in theory classes, the same afternoons drilling, and above all the same imperfect variation in formation which so exasperated Captain Mauriño; in response, Lieutenant Noguero organized a quintet in which each man had to follow the nightly rotation, to present himself a certain number of times, in the course of the night, now with full field gear, now in his Sunday suit, now in workout clothes. And, especially, after the flag pledge, exercises in open order, the so-called tactics, the marches, and the maneuvers. And at the end of the day, the return, the songs, the hymns along the road, long columns flowing in triumphantly from all parts, streaming onto the parade ground to the martial rhythm of the drums and the ta-ta-ta of the trumpets, singing, tired but proud, yes, fired up deep down inside, virile machos, their shirtsleeves rolled up and the hair on their chests puffed out gallantly, singing to Lily, the phenomenal blonde, or rather to the dark-haired Madelón, not too bad-looking either; singing to Margarita Rodríguez Garcés, a bing-bang girl, a solid .50 caliber; singing to Sole, Sole, Soledad, *oirí, oirá, oirí, oirá a la española una y nada más*; singing and carrying the rifle the same as all the others; and the three battalions all congregating, the showy ceremony of striking the colors from the crenellated water tower, a true little castle, steadfast in formation, facing the east, and turning round, facing west, absolutely motionless while the ancient trumpet notes hung in the air, and then, in a tremendous final procession, again singing thunderously, company after company, the descent along the fantastic avenue toward their respective barracks.

He took a shortcut, on the diagonal, through a battery of sergeants, between the tents, and there witnessed a fight. Songs drifting out from under some dark tent, songs sung in chorus, accompanied by guitars and ukuleles, in some sad and lonely tent, boys from the student music group perhaps, students nostalgic for another time and place, for bygone university days, no longer able to be nostalgic for that naughty and unworried— namely sane—university life about which old settled men only remember the good bad times they went through, young love with many girlfriends, whoring with the whores, and the books they pawned, etcetera. And two men emerged to fight, slipping in the mud, beating the living shit out of each other, egged on by the onlookers they attracted, until the day watch arrived, and the lieutenant cut through the crowd and stopped the fight. Come on, with machetes, goddammit! You fight with machetes, like in the Foreign Legion. What? Now you don't feel like it? Idiots! Well with the report I'll write on you you'll be under guard for at least a week. And what are the rest of you all looking at, goddammit? Who else wants a boot up his ass? There was an uproarious general dispersal, hasty flights, tumult, shouting. Among the tenebrous tree trunks, the rigid pines, without relief, the camp appeared populated by shadows, by faint radiances, forms in movement, peals of laughter, songs. The tents looked morbid, pale puffy canvas, with deep folds like the mouth of a furnace, smoking, aflame.

Inside, the candles wired to the tent pole dripped thick grease upon the edge of the gun rack. We've made one hell of a dinner, man, they told him. A real fancy spread. They ate dinner seated on their cots, face to face while, on a little stove, the water for coffee heated up, calmly debating the fact or fiction of the rumor that the next day on the firing range there might be hand grenade practice. They chatted easily, enjoying themselves, and as they watched him cut a slice of stale bread to make himself a ham sandwich they asked him if it was good. However, they started picking on Fofo when he speared an olive from the salad; they'd had work detail and Fofo came in to fetch his silverware.

Listen, you ugly bastard, you mind telling me who invited you?

Fuck, man, Fofo is one of those guys who never misses a meal.

Aw, fuck, he can go fuck himself, for fuck's sake.

Raúl went to look for Federico in the neighboring company. He was drinking with some others, by the door of the tent, and they invited him to come in.

Come in, come in, a man with a bottle is always welcome.

I'll pay you for it tomorrow, man, my money order's supposed to arrive, Federico said. Today I'm broke.

Spent all the money you never had, man, said Raúl.

Huh? Federico grunted. Ah, right. What's in store for us?
Twenty years? They'll lock us up together, in a castle. And Raúl:
quit talking bullshit. They spoke apart. Federico with his eyes
smiling and lazy, as if thinking about something else. Nothing,
nothing, the Castle of If is what I meant. And he asked him if
he knew how to compile an inventory. Outside, someone called
barracks corporal! barracks corporal! inspection! and then everyone in the tent started shouting, that corporal, c'mon, that
corporal, he's turned into a mean bastard. Federico put on his
cap in a hurry. Fuck, the inventory, he said. I have to go to the
major's post. Then he reappeared in the armory tent in search
of a second-year cadet who, once located, explained to him, in
detail and with paternal seniority, the proper way to write up an
inventory. And the one shuffling the deck said: damn it, man,
this thing's a mess. And Federico: yeah, man, I'm fucking it all
up. They argued about whether, to become a second lieutenant,
it helped at all to learn how to compile an inventory, and Pluto
said yes, that it was fundamental, and expounded his theory of
the inventory as the prime mover or breath of life in the army. In
the beginning there was the inventory. And the inventory didn't
add up. And the inventory had to add up, and then there was
the army. He was winning a lot of money, around five hundred
pesetas, and in a certain moment he winked his eye at Raúl and
slyly showed him a set of rear sights from a rifle in the palm
of his hand. The other three, however, seemed to be in a bad
mood. C'mon, play, and quit screwing around, said the medical
student. And Pluto: yeah, man, I don't mind taking you guys to
the cleaners. The cognac was finished, and between games, they
passed the bota from hand to hand, a thick, bitter wine, a tense
black stream which, the throat pulsing and gulping it down,
stained the seams of the lips, the chin. And a heavy guy came
in with his uniform covered in mud, as if he had slipped and
fallen, and he said that in the canteen there was a scary fucking
sight and that the officers were making toasts and giving the
communist salute, raising their fists in the air. Shit, man, I'm so
loaded, he repeated, laughing, and he let himself fall onto the
canvas that covered the supplies, getting it all muddy. Listen,

you oughta hit the sack, they told him. They talked still about how different everything was going to be when they were second lieutenants, how they would treat the troops. You'll say that, well, of course, there's a difference, said Pluto. A huge difference. Like when someone gets hit by a car; it's better to be the driver than the guy who gets hit. The uproar from the jam session in the other tent became deafening, harmonicas, guitars, and a drum set made of tin pots, so loud that the only way they knew the bugle call for curfew had been sounded was because someone stuck his head outside to pass the word with a shout. They went out relaxed, unhurriedly, until the rumor started that the second lieutenant was making the rounds and then they stepped it up noisily, jostling one another, piling up at the end of the formation, clinging to the one ahead to avoid being pushed still further back, to the last positions. But it wasn't the second lieutenant's voice, it was Lieutenant Noguero's, deeper, which they heard while the sergeant focused the flashlight on them, to be rewarded with the come on, let's go, that line. I'm going to take names on the last six men, screamed the sergeant, and in the white light, after one final spasm, the lines finally stabilized.

Hey, Ferreras, how's that going, said the lieutenant, his face seemingly haloed by the shine of the flashlight. How'd the poker game go?

Nothin' special, Lieutenant, sir, said Pluto. I only won a thousand pesetas.

There was some naughty laughter, which turned into wild shrieks when the lieutenant said, you see, man, how much fun you would have missed if you hadn't stayed here. They were still moving, covering ground, furtively, and in other companies they were already counting off. Ten, eleven, twelve, shouted from various points, like an echo, four, five, like an echo repeated from different distances, resounding deeply across the now quiet camp. Well, enough joking around, said the lieutenant. And when it turned out that the numbers didn't square, the sergeant made them reform the lines and began to recount them by threes to see if they were out of formation, the lieutenant said that was alright already, that each time it would come out worse, and he signed the tally. Then, supplied with light by the barracks corporal, the sergeant read the report and the list of guards and of reserve guards and, on breaking ranks, there was a violent ovation which bit by bit decayed into a hullabaloo, as they dispersed into the darkness, everyone repeating that the lieutenant was one hell of a great guy.

He'd pulled second reserve guard. They walked in a group, straggling along, as if groping along, blinded by those walking ahead of them, agitated forms, confusedly standing out against the faint light from the tents.

Did you hear? said Pluto. They're saying tomorrow we're practicing with live grenades. If it's not just some rumor, of course I'm getting out of it. They scare the shit out of me, fuck it.

No, it's not a rumor. They heard them telling that prick captain about it.

Well, it's dangerous, man. There's some guys might kill four or five. Imagine that Ferracollons throwing grenades, for example. I'm sure one'll slip out of his hand when he throws it, and it'll land right on our heads.

Fuck, he's the least of your worries, said Pluto. What happens is with the noise I end up deaf for a few days. It's a question of having balls.

Balls? What the fuck, balls! Cock! What you've got to have is a big cock. And the bigger the better.

Later, now alone, he tried to get news about Leo. Nothing new? he asked. Look, it's just that I've thought that we might have to do something, man. These people are animals, and they might just beat the shit out of the poor guy and, if you don't do something, they'll give him twenty years on top of it, y'know. My father knows some retired colonel, but he was a military judge or I don't know what and he has quite a lot of influence. He's a guy who owes him favors and stuff and, if my dad asks him for it, he'll do what he can. He also knows a police commissioner. What do you think if I write to him so he can talk to them? Do you think it'll do any good? And, at the fountain, two or three miserable fucking cadets from some neighboring company were holding up some slack body, shining a light on the spewing mouth, eyes closed, mouth hanging sloppily half-open. C'mon, you stinking carcass, they were saying, and another stood by waiting, cleaning his eyeglasses on his sleeve, timid and serious, blinking. There was a sudden rush toward the latrines with their off-white walls, a coming and going as if on a carousel, boots sounding adhesive, sticky, on the muddy pavement of the corridors. They followed one another in silence, occupied the shadowy compartments, and, without talking deeply, exchanged lazy words, humming between their teeth, more or less absorbed in their own difficulties of urinating, as the feeble sputtering stream did little more than splash and spatter upon soggy papers, upon stagnant backed-up waters, until, with a brusque pull of trouser bottom, they laboriously stuffed their pricks back into their pants and vacated the stalls. Micromacromundi, that panorama of drifting green-black ordures, floating collard greens, sulfurous brussels sprouts, viscous heads of garlic, broccoli trunks, phosphoric onions, explosive radishes, powder dry mushrooms, dark eggs and gelatinous toadstools, mucilaginous seas, densities, abyssal liquids with reflected firmaments, close quiescent constellations, swampy stars, vaporous moons, snorting extrusions from convulsive craters, streams of stars, revolting evacuations, burning, a profound series of warm infernal dumpings, cataclysms and transmutations, cosmogenic semblances and images.

Soon the last ones would arrive to close the canteen, a quick drink before they closed, or perhaps, at the grocery, a yogurt to settle the stomach, and in the tents everyone would begin to open their cots, to prepare their mattress, the sleeping bag, disputing whether this, that, or the other thing left no room for the rest, about whose turn it was to do the cleaning and fill the water cooler that week, commenting on the day's most outstanding events, the scuttlebutt, the shitty luck, still singing, drinking the last swallow, arguing, commenting, retelling, swilling, disputing, a diffuse rowdy clamor of voices that would only stop when, after the bell for silence, the night watch began its round.

He ran into Emilio and they said hello briefly, as if in a hurry. He'd thought that he'd glimpsed him during the first days in the camp, in the canteen, with sunglasses and a mustache, and then,

one Sunday, he definitely recognized him strolling by, accompanied by his parents, also greatly changed. And even on leave, in
Tarragona, also around the beginning of summer, one Saturday
when he was out with Nuria, he spied Emilio in the middle of
a group, all of them sporting their uniforms, walking behind
some girls. But they didn't speak until a different night, some
days later, when coming out from the latrines Raúl lit a cigarette
and then, a few centimeters away, appeared that smiling face,
of diffuse outlines, the tiny tongue of fire shining brightly in
his pupils, highlighting the fuzz around his trumpet mouth,
that of a spoiled, unweaned crybaby. Don't salute, man, he said,
and it was the same voice. Don't salute. He asked him what he
was studying and if that girl was his girlfriend; he said that he
was studying medicine and that everything was going well, and
it turned out that he was in the same company as Federico.
What? he said. Do you still remember how to throw the bolas?
And inevitably he ended up mentioning the death of Mallolet.
Tuberculosis. For us, specific bilateral transmission with hema-
tological origin. They had done one of the first marches of the
season and the company was on the verge of getting lost in the
fog. They camped out in some fallow fields, next to the small
village, a tiny hamlet of abandoned orchards, abandoned streets,
abandoned houses, a lovely ruin where, judging by the bed of
straw and flattened cow pies covering the floor of one room,
cattle sometimes sheltered. After eating he searched through the
intricate and narrow interiors with Pluto and Fortuny, the floor
barely paved with rough stones, worn by the centuries, a labyrinth of dark stairs, blackened ovens, nooks like grottoes, rotted,
worm-eaten beams, gaping gray walls, open to the fog, and that
odor of manure, of burnt stone. They entered the bare church,
with its echoing vaults, and outside someone from another group
rang the bell in the tower by throwing stones at it. Behind, in
the little cemetery choked with nettles, they examined the niches
with their illegible inscriptions, the iron crosses nailed into the
earth, twisted, rusted; the graves marked by a border of pebbles,
and only after a few minutes did they notice that the spongy
ground, among the damp weeds, was sown with bones, orange

vertebrae, shards of skull, jawbones with teeth, spindly ribs. And further on, to the northeast, on the other side of that mountainous massif which stretched out like a horizon, flat, plateau, stark, barren, a mountainous massif now only sensed, swallowed up by the fog, on the other side, within the shelter of the wooded gloom, at the foot of the steep slopes of pine stands, the monastery of Poblet dominating the clear open hills of la Conca, a sober isolated compound, with its towers and high walls, dark sepulchers, a calm golden ruin, Gothic naves, cold and resonant, damp flagstones, recumbent statues, bas-reliefs, lost slag heap of conquests, of glories and victories, splendid epitaph of trophies, Mallorca, Valencia, Murcia, Sardinia, Sicily, Tunis, Algiers, Athens, Constantinople. And the walk one could make, solitary, through the half-collapsed Romanesque cloister, and through the Gothic cloister, with its serene fountain, and the cypresses and laurels, and the rose bushes, and a delirium of swallows in headlong flight.

He found the first reserve guard, his tent. He was sitting on his duffel already packed while his companions, as if in a chaotic dance, got theirs ready stooping, asses in the air, or squatting down, or undressing in a hurry, hopping about on one foot in floating shirttails, hairy legs in socks, in worn-out underwear, meaty buttocks, some going to sleep in their coveralls, joking, the candle flames fluttering from their stirring about, capering shadows on the canvas. And when Raúl offered to take his place as reserve guard, the other one glared at him angrily, raising his voice as if to attract attention.

Right, smart ass! Then I do the second shift, eh? No way, wise guy.

Fuck, I wasn't talking about switching, said Raúl. I'm just saying, if you want, I'll do your shift, too.

La, la, la-la, la-la, la, la.

He packed his duffel bag, he opened his cot, the thin mattress, the sleeping bag, blankets; he removed his suit and put on clean coveralls. There was the same racket as in the other tent and, as he crossed off one more day on the calendar traced in chalk on the canvas, the raucous shout in unison: one day less, one day less, one day less of being here. And, while they undressed in a no less chaotic and extravagant dance, they talked about the joking that went down in the canteen, whether or not it was a rumor about the grenades, about the ones who'd died during maneuvers the year before, of the inferiority complex and the rancor because of them, because of the miserable fucking cadets, inside they felt grateful for the commissioned captains who'd been promoted from the ranks, thanks to the fact of them being career soldiers with superior training, as compared to the ones who in six short months were promoted to be officers; about if Captain Cantillo would have at least made commander if they hadn't found out about a little side business he was running out of the quartermaster corps; about how fucked a soldier's life really was, to spend your whole life as they were doing now, always working your ass off; about what a terrible fucking climate there was in this place they'd chosen for the camp; about how little all of this would matter to them in the coming weeks, faced with the tantalizing perspective of the imminent end of their sorrowful stay; of what they would do first upon getting back to Barcelona; of the hazings they'd inflict the next summer, when they were sergeants, on the new batch of miserable fucking cadets; about how no way in hell would they ever again spend a week as fucked as the first one from this summer, in a stupor all day long, without understanding anything, forever running at the ringing of the bells; about who was in charge of the cleanup and filling the water cooler that week; about what a bunch of animals the Aragonese were; about the evident superiority of Catalonia above all other lands, etcetera. The candles consumed, reduced to short dripping stubs, hardly shedding any light on anything but the conical peak of the tent, they argued about whose turn it was to replace them and each one ended up lighting one of his own atop his duffle bag; they passed round the bota and picked on el Fofo, who was busy examining his hemorrhoids with the help of a little mirror and a flashlight. C'mon, finish, fuck, this would turn anybody on. They considered the dirty tricks they could play on the ones who were on leave.

Sew their sleeping bags shut, man.

No, fuck, then they'll wake us all up.

Leave Fortuny a note saying he's pulled guard duty.

Exactly, man, 'cuz tomorrow he's on parade.

Or dissolve some laxative in their water cooler.

Yeah, man, Ferracollons has got colitis.

That's doing them a favor, man. Then they'll be out sick and won't have to do target practice.

Right, a good purging.

Fuck no, man.

Raúl searched for his machete and flashlight; he buttoned up his cape. Federico wasn't around and, when he asked where he was, the other guys in the tent, now all in bed, began shrieking in women's voices. Oh! A man! He's from another company! Come in, come right in, and we'll fuck you, I'm a Virgo, really crazy, and he had to step out, and wait outside. Federico appeared with his shaving kit and a towel draped round his neck.

Monte Cristo! he said. The condemned count.

Quit talking shit, dumbass. You know well enough the only one who'll get caught is Leo. Au contraire. I think we're all screwed. Except Count Adolfo, he's one of those guys who comes through without a scratch.

Well, yeah. What I wanted to tell you is that I'm doing the first two reserve watches, which means I can talk with Fortuny the moment he arrives.

That's good: solidarity, moral support, symbolic expiation, that's really good.

Fuck, Federico, you're such a pain in the ass. Would you please quit fucking around? If there's any news, I'll wake you up.

Right, wake me up. I want you to wake me every hour. You can give me the news.

Every fifteen minutes, if you want.

Even better, every fifteen. But please just admit that we're screwed. Admit it.

Alright, fine. We're screwed.

And the bell for quiet rang, when every solider's mother is praying for him. Quiet! they were saying in the neighboring companies, and the reserve guards tapping on the canvas, tense strokes, flashing flashlights. Fuck, these lights. The patrol will be coming around. Coughs, laughter, complaints, quarrels, interrupted songs, left hanging as if in suspense, on a clear night, of white stars, my lover's sweet complaints, my sorrows. Raúl sat down next to the tent, against a tree trunk, sunk down within his poncho; a trunk almost too slender, a bit uncomfortable. The wind gusted, spluttering their words, voices like echoes in the ominous forest, the empty, sterile wind, the dark sound of branches, and the oppressive premonitory passing of the dense, heavy clouds, opaque, moving away in closed masses.

Give me that photo, man. Let's see if I still have time to jerk off.

Turn off the light and let me sleep, for fuck's sake.

Fuck, here he goes with his cough again.

You're fucking screwed, you're tubercular.

It's the humidity, man; what do want me to do?

Well, hold it in.

The first one who snores, I slice his dick off.

Shut the fuck up all of you.

Go scratch your balls.

And you, go suck your schlong.

Really wish I could, man.

Did you loosen the guy lines?

Don't be a jerk.

I don't give a shit, man, I'm wrapped in plastic…

I hope it does rain and we don't have to go to target practice.

Shut up, faggot.

You shut up, the way you snore.

Go fuck yourself.

In your dreams.

Voices separating little by little, quieting down, falling off, and then only the wind, emptiness, nocturnal abysms, dark night, serene and starless night, calm, clear, quiet, a night transfigured, burning, opaque, pitch-black, placid, dark, black night black as a crow's wing hovering overhead, menacing, and so, clamor of complaints or perhaps wild laughter, and so, and so, so falling and rising and fading away, and so, and so, in slow inquisitive semicircles. So?

VI

CLOUDS, BRILLIANCES, TRANSPARENCIES, neither red nor topaz nor celestial, an unstable sunset. It was dazzling, this way, looking at it straight on, at the end of the street, above the perspective of two rows of foliage shrinking, vanishing in confluence.

Down below, no. Gazes, flashes, reflections in the windshield, in car windows, in streetcars, in the mirrors of shop windows, in the glass of front doors, superimposed images, fragmentary, in motion, the too-slow march of the passersby, hindering, exasperating. He slapped his sunglasses back on.

They walked along very close together, arm in arm, perhaps too quickly. There was a newsstand or, at least, people standing around a newspaper seller, and the stand was selling chestnuts. Also there were people standing outside an appliance store window, watching television. And further on, in front of the trolley stop, all waiting in expectation, crowded together in undecided assault toward the step not yet come to a stop, already too many of them while the screeching grew louder and the glass became filled with flashes of light. He noticed that Aurora was looking over her shoulder.

The fuzz, he heard her saying.

They were on the broad chamfered corner, the snub nose of a patrol car sticking out past the parked cars, and the machine guns were clearly visible, carbine barrels, peaked caps tipped down, boots, hands gathering up the leaflets scattered on the sidewalk upon which, suddenly, a space had opened out among the pedestrians. Don't turn around, Raúl said. They weren't far from the corner, two or three doorways. He quickened the pace, squeezed the sheaf of leaflets against his thighs, in the pocket of his overcoat. They turned the corner to the right, the facade of the Sagrada Familia rising up sharply across the street, a hollow structure expanding broadly in the empty air. There, the traffic was much lighter than on Calle Mallorca and the sidewalks stretched out, bordered by straight walls of brick, under the auspices of the dazzling, rapid sunset, peaceful, only a few people looking upward.

Federico's car was half a block away, across from the entrance to the church construction site, the motor running, not so much parked as already pulling away from the curb, softly shifting into gear to head off up the street, accelerating, until turning to the left, at the first cross street. But what's this imbecile doing, said Raúl. Look, said Aurora, and it was as if in obedience to her cocking her chin that the pair of cops appeared coming down the middle of the sidewalk toward them, their slow uniform stride, their stiff guns standing out in parallel fashion. Wait, said Raúl. He put his arm around Aurora's shoulder and kissed her on the cheek, his left hand sunk in his pocket, against the leaflets, as if gathering in his overcoat. They crossed with their heads together toward the entrance to the enclosure around the Sagrada Familia, a small hut open in the wall which, functioning as a vestibule, plastered with postcards, brochures, pennants, and bulletins, gave access to the interior of the lot, to the staircase leading up to the temple. From the first steps it was now possible to take in the whole street in all its width and breadth, from over the wall, and they could watch the police patrol, slow, vigilant.

On the stairs and landings there was a certain number of visitors, couples, families, tourists taking pictures of themselves before the portico, people seated on the parapets. They contemplated the high, bristling towers, the smaller cupolas, and the porticoes of the facade, a rough triptych gouged out from the beveled wall at the doors; the Facade of the Nativity, of the east, of the dawn, destined to express the mysterious pleasures which surround the coming of the Redeemer, the beginnings of his life. The Door of Charity, for example, in the center, limned by great arboreal columns with their bases carved as tortoises and open capitals in the manner of palms, boughs of welcome, trumpets of angels announcing the good news, a door divided by a wooden interarch linked to the earth by a coiled serpent, tree of paradise lost, remote cause of all that, of that classic Nativity

Scene situated at the base of the tympanum, with the ox and the mule standing out beneath the empty frame of the stained-glass window and the great rose window, the Child adored by Joseph and Mary, and, from the beveled cantilevers and reliefs in the walls, by kings and shepherds, gray flocks gathered, roosters, capons, Christmas turkeys, and, higher up, the archivolt of the portico, magnificent curvature which, from on high, vainly invited one to cross the threshold, to penetrate it, a growing avalanche of lobed, dripping, frond-like forms, like secretions and adherences of flower or bivalve, like ice floes and flower petals, stars configuring the zodiacal plane of the sky in that dark night of Bethlehem, of messianic destiny, Gaudian delight, a pleasure that so soon disappears and once gone gives pain, for no rose grows without thorns. And higher yet, the archangelic scene of the Annunciation, crowned in the apex of the archivolt by a great cupola, root of the finialed gable piñon which, sharply erect, rising, now between the four towers, takes the form of a bushy ceramic cypress, eucharistic canticles, Sanctus, Sanctus, Hosanna, Alleluia, a heart bleeding love, bread loaves, an amphora, the pelican, delight, country of wonders. And on each side, symmetrically flanking that conglomeration, two other doors of smaller proportions, and the not-yet-visible Portico of the Rosary, with its Virgin wreathed by a rosary of pink roses, rose of epiphany, a large vaulted doorway to the nonexistent cloister which, by means of amniotic isolation, should envelop the temple, isolate it from the daily roar of the city. Thus, to the left, the Portico of Hope, with its floral corbels and its friezes in the bevels, the massacre of the innocents, the flight into Egypt, providential detours along the path of Redemption, and scenes of Nazareth on the tympanum, the tender baby reappearing, with saws, hooks, chisels, and hammers sculpted on the lintel, the protean archivolt curling as if in eruption, up to the cupola crowned with a grotto, from whence, among rocky crags, emerges the saving ship piloted by Saint Joseph and the dove, tongue of fire, crowded pyramidal crags on the pinnacle, abrupt crests, harp-shaped summits of Montserrat, crown of rocks, stone scepter rising high with mystic emphasis, dominant.

And to the right, the Portico of Faith, enraptured altarpiece centered on the presentation of Jesus in the temple, with an outline
of images now solemn and impassive, now violent, like the one
of John the Baptist preaching in the desert, foretelling the coming of the Messiah, all that upon an embroidered background
of wretchedness and suffering, of an interwoven framework
of thorns and flowers, buds, corollas, thalamus, sepals, petals,
stigmata, honeybees drawn to pollen, and superimposed on the
bramble-crag crenellations, the lantern, a three-peaked oil lamp,
eternal triangle, base of the Immaculate Conception, dogmatic
effigy rising in ecstasy, like an ejaculatory prayer from within a
large cascade of sprigs and grape clusters, all those details one
can spot carefully from any one of the points of the belfry towers, as you climb the airy spiral staircases, from the doorways,
from the enclosed balconies sinuously integrated on the projections of the architraves and cornices of the frontispiece, balconies
with bulbous wrought iron railings, small contorted galleries,
catwalks, small steps, intestinal cavities, twisted corridors of
irregular relief, passages conjoined in a coming and going from
the belfries to the facade, four intercommunicating bell towers, harmonically erect, which, if near their bases appear rather
strangely compounded with the parameters of the porticoes, as
they separate, each acquiring its own shape, they become curving vertical parabolic cones, the two outer pairs equal in height,
the two center towers taller. The ascent can begin with the one
situated furthest south, on the extreme left-hand side of the
facade. There one confirms that the two plinths which serve as
the starting point for the archivolts are quadrangular sections
evolving toward the circle. This cylindrical part, with apertures
that spiral upward, is followed in each bell tower by another
form of parabolic silhouette, developed in twelve perpendicular
striations which, higher up, become reduced to six, resulting in
a prismatic volume of triangular section and polyhedric facets
concluding in a finial in the shape of a mitre, a ring, and a cro-
zier all fitted together, four bud-like crests, mosaics, shining, of
Ferruginous qualities, carbonaceous, vitreous, porcelain, polychromatic in carmine, incarnadine, pontifical gold and white,

bottle green, mauve, crepuscular rose. Passing from one bell tower to another, negotiating a series of narrow catwalks, hyperbolic arches, cramped twisting galleries, small steps, irregular corridors, intestinal cavities, passageways stinking of urine scrawled over with inscriptions and drawings, the large window openings formed by overlapping spirals, enable contemplation of both the foreshortened reliefs of the facade, its cupolas, canopies, vaulted niches, groups of sculpted figures, and the ruinous amphitheater of the empty interior curving toward the north by the vertebral sweep of the temple's central apse, from which we see, as the towers rise, the city spreading out in ever-greater breadth. An exuberant locale, in the heart of the Ensanche's grid, that neighborhood dominated by the spiny shell of the apse, an airy skeleton with specters of empty frames awaiting their stained-glass windows, open to the air and undulating molded waterspouts, gargoyles imprinted on snails, reptiles, lizards, braided serpents, sylvan crenellations of finialed gables and brambly pinnacles, a frenzy of tight rosebuds, of sprigs and thorns, bunches of grapes, rose corolas, of pure lily, wild leaves, virgins, violent deflowering, stems, calyxes, petals, stigmata of passion or pleasure, fossilized faunal flora, curling tension, sprouting stonework sheltering the desolate central esplanade, with its numbered ashlars among weeds leveled by the dust, stones cut from Montjuich, laborious work, an anthill of laborers, wheelbarrows and pulleys, planking, wooden platforms and scaffolds, hammer blows, all done very much according to traditional handicraft, as churches are forever built, stone upon stone. There was the sound of a whistle and the workers called it quits. They turned toward the barracks, gathered around a spigot, scrubbed themselves clean, combed their hair, changed their clothes. Meanwhile, high above, the stonework structure appeared carved from brilliant flashes, doorways opened onto thin air, entrances which led to nowhere, bright flashes rising higher and higher from that splendid sunset, the sun sinking down to the west of the city, heavenly corolla, carmines, purples, garnets, ambers, corals, vermilions, tonalities of flame perhaps degraded, perhaps somewhat altered by the dark lenses of his sunglasses.

Why don't we just drop them all from up here? said Aurora. That would be spectacular, right? said Raúl. A kind of socialist miracle.

They took all the leaflets out of the bag and the pockets of his overcoat, and Raúl made them disappear, dropping them into the dark round mouth encircled by a wooden handrail, which opened in the center of the slender rotunda, the base of the final section of the belfry, a well blinded with debris, rubble, plaster fragments. The rotunda stank of urine and, above their heads, the tower rose in a tensile hollow, striated with lights and resonances. Exclamations could be heard at varying distances, disjointed commentaries, calls of imprecise origin while down the stairs, a fading echo of heels. I'll keep the map, said Raúl. What harm is there in a map? He opened the map in successive folds, and with his ballpoint pen started randomly adding new marks, notations relative to the city's parks and museums, underlinings, improvised indicators, monuments marked out with a traced circle, a line like those already drawn around the Obelisk of Victory at the intersection of Avenida Diagonal and Paseo de Gracia with its black inscription stone with the eagle clutching a yoke and arrows in its talons, or around the Columbus monument at the Puerta de la Paz, overlooking the port, a stepped circular base with lions guarding the raised bronze column crowned by an observation deck in the form of a terraqueous globe, a golden pedestal for the statue of Columbus discovering America with his index finger, a lordly gesture unfolding against that sky of flashing leaflets fluttering down in soft flight, falling slowly upon the traffic below, in the vast plaza open to the dockside, crossroads of governmental buildings, Customs, Military Headquarters, Naval Administration, the Royal Shipyards Museum, with enough time to take the elevator back down and exit through the underground passage before the employees notice what happened and, blending in with the crowd, to watch the arrival of the police minutes later, pushing through the crowd, cordoning off the area, watching them from the sidewalk like killers who return to the scene of the crime. There were also other marks more difficult to conceal, all in the northeast sector of the city, through the slums of San Martín, San Andrés y Horta, locations of the principal industries, Hispano Olivetti, Enasa, Fabra y Coats, La Maquinista, etcetera, working class neighborhoods, housing projects like Verdún, La Prosperidad, La Trinidad or el Buen Pastor, including the bridge of Santa Coloma along the banks of the Besós River, now outside the city limits.

A city with its back to the sea? Not entirely, not always. Not the old city. The medieval town stretched from watchful Montjuich to the seaside district of Barceloneta, with its moorings and its small anchorage, without sea walls or docks or wharfs, right up tight against the sandy flats, a Barcelona centered around the Mons Taber, built outward around the slight grade of its lower slopes, a prominence now buried, almost imperceptible beneath this crowded nucleus of broken alleys delimited by Las Rondas, surrounding avenues laid out along the perimeter of the demolished walls, a polygon crossed perpendicularly by Las Ramblas, starting from the Columbus monument at the wharves, a protonaut in the attitude of discovering America, still decked out a few days earlier in flags and pennants, floral anniversary offerings, a river of plane trees flowing with gentle undulations, as along a fertile plain, prematurely withered and faded by the persistent storms of September, shining tobacco-colored in the subtle atmosphere of October, dividing the Barrio Chino on the left from the Barrio Gótico on the right, the backbone of an enclave so full of enchanting romantic spots like la Plaza Real or la Plaza Medinaceli, peaceful patios like the former Hospital de la Santa Cruz or el patio de los Naranjos, cloisters, bell towers, here Romanesque like San Pablo del Campo, there Gothic like Santa María del Mar or Plaza del Pino, San Justo y Pastor, Baroque facades, Belén, San Severo, San Felipe Neri, La Merced, temples and palaces, the Neoclassical restraint of el Palacio de la Virreina or La Lonja, the medieval commodities exchange, regal buildings, public edifices, el Ayuntamiento, previously el Consell de Cent, opposite la Diputación, the former seat of the Generalitat, the two of them facing off, the space between them forming la Plaza de San Jaime, of Santiago, of Saint James, white knight, defender of the Spanish fatherland, and the el Palacio

Episcopal and the Civic Government, the old Customs House, and the Military Government and Headquarters, construction executed upon what was the central office of the Mercedarian Order, and the Comandancia de Marina, strategic points like the Telefonica office or the Post Office, at the foot of Vía Layetana, a street choking with traffic which splits the old quarter wide open, a defile of offices and agencies, shipping companies, insurance companies, delegations of governmental organizations, the sinister Superior Police Headquarters, a fosse of overwhelming rectangularity barbarously drawn with a ruling pen amid that glowering mass of towers and dark corners from other times, smoke-darkened stone beneath industrial city vapors which turn the jumbled declining streets gray, mansions converted into flophouses, shops, taverns, hooker bars. The belt of Las Rondas, laid out around the perimeter of the walls demolished in the nineteenth century to allow expansion beyond the confines of the old city, linking a series of important urban junctions like Plaza Urquinaona or Plaza de la Universidad and, above all, at the top of Las Ramblas, Plaza de Cataluña, a hideous commercial epicenter formed by God's perversity between the arched portals of banks and hulking department stores, dislocated masses, discordant compositions, lumpy buildings from which, shortly before closing time, the scattered leaflets fluttered down, white like doves of freedom winging out in a loose whirlwind upon the gawkers clustered together before the shop windows, those bustling avenues tracing the circuit of Las Rondas in the form of an irregular hexagon, with one of its longest sides perpendicular to the line of the sea, a polygon forming the borders of the old city and bounded by all the rest of the city, an outline whose eastern side offers proud nineteenth-century perspectives, delimited by the Ciudadela Park and its Modern Art Museum, which so ephemerally housed the Parliament of Catalunya, while the western side borders the Paralelo Boulevard and its faded accents of the roaring twenties, its gunmen and cabaret singers, striking cartoon facades, footlights, nocturnal lights, la Calle del Marqués del Duero today a mere scarecrow of its former self, a hard bleak chugging artery of heavy traffic, the main

axis of the Pueblo Seco district and its slums, now within the
limits of Montjuich Park. Enveloping the old city and on an
inclined plane toward the amphitheater of surrounding hills, the
Ensanche, the work of Ildefonso Cerdà, prophet in the desert
cast out from his own land, a monotonous close-knit grid of
perpendicular and transversal streets laid out in modules of
chamfered intersections, like at Avenida José Antonio, previously
la Calle Cortes or, simply, Gran Vía, and el Paseo de Gracia,
before reaching los Campos Eliseos, luminous commercial focal
point and stock exchange with its ostentatious shop windows
and its cafés, hotels, concert halls, splendid flowing rivers of
tobacco-colored plane trees, an oasis in that endless succession
of straight streets, exactly identical, those parallel to the sea:
Aragón, Valencia, Mallorca, Provenza, Rosellón, Córcega; those
perpendicular: Nápoles, Calabria, Sicilia, Cerdeña, a whole well-
archived empire, a clairvoyant plan of realization, systematically
pre-destroyed, uglified, adulterated, Phoenician greed, mean
poverty, blind bourgeois incapacity, a snub-nosed grid crucified
on a crooked cross, radially, from the point of intersection
of the Plaza de las Glorias Catalanas, an unfulfilled center of
activity for greater Barcelona, along Avenida Meridiana, city axis
running north-south, and along the Avenida del Generalísimo
Franco, once called—and still—before the fourteenth of April,
Avenida Alfonso XIII—vulgarly dubbed La Diagonal—running
east-west. El Ensanche, a district whose name means enlargement, an already narrowed expansion, latticework fenced off
in turn by new ramparts of towns once peripheral, old towns
annexed by the expansive inertia, populated areas difficult to
assimilate, still characterized by their old, small-town atmosphere, working-class districts like Gracia, and Las Corts with its
immense stadium el Camp Nou, more leaflets fluttering down
upon bleachers and grandstands, before one-hundred and fifty
thousand spectators, residential neighborhoods like San Gervasio
and Bonanova, of graceful and subtly variegated villas, harmonies
of times gone by, Sarrià, Tres Torres, Pedralbes, sunny gardens,
peaceful roads cut into the gentle slopes rising up to the foot of
the mountainous neighborhood, again with a view looking out

to sea, over the city, and the working class suburbs to the south
and west, the gypsy neighborhood of Casa Antúnez butting up
against the Montjuich Cemetery, El Port, Hostafranchs, Sants,
Collblanch, La Torrassa, Hospitalet, and now along the banks
of the Llobregat River, San Feliu, Esplugas, Cornellà, and to the
east and north, the poor industrial districts of Pueblo Nuevo,
San Martín, El Clot, La Sagrera, Campo del Arpa, Horta, San
Andrés, and on the far side of the Besós River, toward Badalona,
Santa Coloma, San Adrián, chemical factories, iron and steel
foundries, textile mills, streets and streets caked in soot, smoking chimneys, flames from furnaces, cement-colored walls, gray
warehouses, rust, square housing projects like blocks of funeral
niches, between vacant lots and garbage dumps and a stalled
conglomeration of basic brick buildings, a chaotic development
of muddy sidewalks, streets broken by erosion and neglect, of
undulating pavement, with puddles, places without automo-
bile traffic, appropriate for driving at top speed. Federico at the
wheel and Aurora and Raúl in the backseat, tossing out leaflets
in a white trail, at dusk, before the patrol cars on duty doubled
in number, when people were coming out of work, throngs and
throngs on their dark march.

   They ran out of gas on a side street in San Andrés, a few
hundred meters from the Buen Pastor neighborhood, and they
were stuck. They had to go and look for the nearest service
station and they had to ask to borrow a watering can to carry
the gas back to the car. Can you imagine how absurd this would
be if this had happened to us five minutes earlier, right in the
middle of scattering these things about? said Federico. They
also went out at daybreak, and the workers gathered on the
sidewalks, before the heavy doors of the factories, picked up
the leaflets, naked arms, naked proletarian hands, Catalan or
not, immigrants from elsewhere in Spain called *charnegos*, workers from the south, Murcians, Andalusians, emigrants from the
countryside, people with bodies bent and curved like sickles,
from reaping and harvesting olives, labor lured to the big city,
reserve army of capitalism, lumpenproletariat, now workers
like the rest, like those who had always been, like the workers

who were sons of workers and grandsons of workers, each one united to the others by common class interests, and during the rest break at noon they argued collectively and, now by night, under the kitchen lamp, around the pinewood table, drinks and black tobacco, ideals, a dawning of consciences, of notions and grievances, catchwords shared, the seed of clandestine organization, cells and committees, picket lines, Red October, leaves withering away and cold in emergent crisis, naked arms, fists raised, pumping, pupils like ruffling cedars, wrathful, stand up! famished legion of workers! sons of the people, on your feet, to the barricades!

Look, Daniel, said Escala. What distinguishes us from any other political party, apart from the structural differences of apparatus and organization, is the fact that we possess a totally scientific method of analyzing reality. Which means that we are capable of appreciating reality just as it is, with its laws and its dialectic, without letting ourselves get disoriented by phenomena, by appearances and veils which can obscure it, by its partial or static aspects which don't let you see the forest for the trees. Evidently there is room for errors of interpretation or application but, the same as in any other scientific terrain, subjective errors, it's the person not the method which fails; the method is sound, as objective as reality itself. So, why tell you all this? Well, because, before an action like the one we've got planned, we're obligated more than ever to study reality like an equation or a theorem, without letting ourselves be swayed by ideals, mysticism, or metaphysics, which can lead us to opportunistic or adventurous attitudes. So, yes, if we calmly examine the present situation, what typical traits do we find in the foreground? How do we formulate them and apply them correctly within the frame of our political line? Overall, the unquestionable reality is that the first part of the battle is won. Three short weeks after the start of the academic year we have succeeded in making the strike triumph in every school and department and have effectively shut down the university. The initial phase of our agitation campaign culminated when the police, in order to suppress our attempt to demonstrate, and in an attempt to avoid repeating the events of last February, invaded the university campus and environs

and arrested dozens of students. We presented them with the
alternative of either trampling their own laws underfoot once
more or respecting them, and once more they made a mockery
of them. The student committee's response was to plant an explosive device on the Obelisk of Victory, an act which, fortunately,
caused no real damage and which, not being claimed by the
party, did not compromise our political line either. Although,
let's say it directly, it could have had grave consequences. It was
an action only partly justified by the student committee's confused state following the arrests and, to a greater extent—the
paradox is justified—by its proven inefficiency, but, and this is
perfectly clear, under no circumstances should such an action be
repeated. Because what we now intend is that the action not stop
here, that it continue, elevating it to a level that is quantitatively
and qualitatively distinct. From the university we have moved to
the street, and we hope that our appeals to the citizenry's opinion
and, primarily, to the working class, uniting with other economic
demands of a purely political character, that they might crystallize next Thursday in a general strike and a boycott of public
transportation. Our comrades in the metalworking industries,
textile workers, construction workers, militants in all cells, are
all working in the same direction, but for basic security reasons
our activities must not be interfered with. Besides, given the
situation, it is precisely we, with our departments closed and
our students arrested, who should act as a kind of spur to provoke an outburst comprising a series of chain reactions which,
as experience shows, if they triumph in Barcelona are likely to
spread to the other industrial centers of the region. With only
five days to go, the prospects are, quite frankly, good, exceeding
all our predictions, permitting us to be optimistic even supposing we fail in our attempt to extend the strike, given that,
when a struggle for demands is not in decline but rather in full
development, as in our case, any frustrated attempt is not a step
backwards, but one forward, a simple phase of the process which
leads to subsequent actions with positive outcomes. And if from
the examination of the current situation and its possibilities we
move to a much broader, all-encompassing examination, if we

examine the present moment integrating it into the general process of the struggle against the dictatorship, if we compare it, for
example, with the situation as it existed in February, what differences can we notice? What conclusions can we reach? For us,
the most appreciable change in the objective conditions resides
in the evidence of a growing collective awareness, in the distance
that goes from a more or less irrational outbreak of rebellion to
a massive, rigorously planned action, one charged with political implications previously non-existent, likely to develop into
a social context with an increasingly broad base. I refer to the
new qualitative fact that our ideology, the communist ideology,
can take hold, as it has in various levels of bourgeois society,
through their own children, the youth, the Spain of tomorrow,
a phenomenon which is obviously the fruit, the evidence of the
level of decadence to which the Regime has fallen, and of the
now insoluble conflict which exists between the forces of production and the oligarchical regime controlling production. And
I also mean the prospects which this new fact opens up to us,
in agreement with the postulates and objectives of our political
line, and, more concretely, the possibility of finally uniting the
diverse parties and opposition political parties, representatives
of all the social classes, including the non-monopolist bourgeois
and the working class and, why not, certain factions of the clergy
and even of the army itself, against their common antithesis and
the fascist forms of the government. Which means, the same
line of alliance with all classes and social levels who are victims
of the oligarchy, which is showing such good results all across
Europe, now adapted to Spain's particular situation. The October
Revolution, the great Chinese Revolution, were the product of
some very concrete circumstances, of a situation assisted by
the European war on one hand, and by the World War on the
other, circumstances, although not unrepeatable, it's true, at least
imponderable, facts that don't have to be counted on, because
none of them have to do with the present Spanish political situation. It's for this reason, Daniel, precisely because the objective
now in the foreground is unity, for which reason we cannot
permit ourselves the slightest false step, nothing which deviates

from our aim of national reconciliation and peaceful overthrow of the dictatorship, now that, as was so well demonstrated during the time of the Maquis resistance, the country is fed up with violence, and any type of direct action would be exploited by the enemy in order to separate us from our possible allies. This, alongside deeper theoretical considerations, such as to what point, in the current circumstances, the recourse to violence does not presuppose a certain lack of confidence in mass actions and in the combative capacity of the working class. So let's put aside all those dreams of sabotage and assault against radio stations until the objective conditions are different.

They moved on to the study of practical methods, how to distribute the work, the writing and printing of leaflets, distribution on foot and by car, dividing up the city according to the official map, marking key points, streets, plazas, buildings, heavily visited spots, hubs of communication, metro stations. They also decided to agree with the remaining university opposition groups to, in a single night, emblazon the walls of the city with calls for the strike, and finally, they discussed the security measures to be taken in case statements made by arrested students gave the police any clues.

Escala: his predilection for museums as the perfect place to speak quietly and furtively. Thus, the Romanesque galleries in the National Art Museum of Catalonia, on Montjuich; or the Royal Shipyards factory museum with its Gothic naves, the present headquarters of the Maritime Museum; or the Museum of Modern Art in Ciudadela Park, inside the old armory which had seen so many different uses before it became the museum, inhabited successively as a royal residence and the ephemeral Parliament of Catalonia; or the Diocesan Museum, installed in the old Seminary, set ablaze in 1936, or the Marés Museum, located within the main building of the Grand Royal Palace, or the City History Museum in the former Casa Padellás, always changing locations, of course, without insisting on anything other than caution. The most important thing: to always have more imagination than the enemy.

It seems like all that business about torture and electrical currents is pure mythomania, said Federico. They've beaten others much less than Leo and almost all of them have spilled the little information they knew.

But it's not the same thing either, said Raúl. Leo had a responsibility that these guys don't have. After all, they're just a few poor bastards picked up randomly.

It's nothing, nothing at all, a slap on the wrist.

There were rumors of new arrests, in which a student wound up dead, that the Falangists were making a blacklist, rumors of searches, of people followed, their telephones bugged. And before they visited Leo's family they'd called on the phone, to see if Floreal was there, and he didn't think it was safe to meet them. Floreal was there, but, more than wanting to leave he seemed desirous of exchanging impressions.

They'd not seen him since before the vacation, at the end of the spring, when he set up an interview for them with Cayetano, a middle-aged textile worker who'd fallen in with Marsal, the same as Leo, and he brought them regards and encouragement from Leo. A man who'd spent seven months in jail, until the court martial, and as he'd neither said nor admitted anything, he was released, acquitted. The mythic Cayetano, who in the course of the interrogations was black and blue from the blows, and they shocked him with electrical currents right in front of his wife, dislocating one of his kidneys and almost ripping off his scalp, while he was hanging from a heating pipe, with several ribs broken and his feet so swollen they wouldn't fit into his shoes. And he stayed that way for around three weeks, and several more in the hospital, constantly under guard, but neither he nor she had talked, and they were acquitted. Floreal received them happy and excited, showing off a little, saying that Leo was a great kid, that he'd earned the sympathy of them all. Six years? He'll be out again and back in the breach in less than three, dammit. And he told them about Maruja, a connection that had turned out the same as him because she also kept her mouth shut. She's a woman, but I swear to you she's got more balls than most men. And that matters more than the teeth she got knocked out in the police headquarters. She didn't say anything about

Marsal, although, he said, you've got to keep in mind that she was tortured for almost a whole month and she's still got no feeling in her thumbs from the days she spent hanging from some handcuffs. And he told them about the comrade who was on the point of committing suicide by making a kind of noose with his handkerchief. About Leo he said that he wasn't having an especially hard time, a few truncheon blows and several hours handcuffed squatting down, until his wrists swelled up like clubs. He was lucky; he was one of the last ones to be caught, and the police were already tired and by then they'd learned enough.

And Floreal: I think it's going to be a success, he said. The working classes are with us. At the bank it's the only thing they talk about and I understand that in the factories there's a tremendous desire to resist. The very use of force and provocation by the police does nothing more than backfire against them and popularize the strike. And it's just that the people won't put up with more, they're not willing to tolerate the dictatorship any longer, starvation wages, and unemployment. Everywhere there's nothing but business failures and bankruptcies, suspension of pay, unpaid bills; and the discontent which the government's political economy awakens is so great that the non-monopolizing bourgeoisie has definitively turned its back on the dictatorship. There are even industrialists who are willing to help, to back the strike. They're for the workers, for a minimum living wage with a sliding scale, for the right to strike, and for democratic liberties.

Let them help, let them help, said Leo's brother-in-law. Then later we can work things out with them.

Floreal smiled, sure, superior, without taking him seriously. There'll be no need, man. Let their own contradictions destroy them. The politics of communism is no trick, simply this: let things run their course. In the very heart of the monopolist oligarchy lie ever greater contradictions, contradictions natural to the imperial phase of capitalism, and this economic crisis has no solution of any kind. Because you've got to keep in mind that there are two kinds of contradictions: the antagonistic ones, meaning those of Spain, and the non-antagonistic ones, meaning the ones from the socialist camp, and peace-loving countries.

These are surmountable problems, sibling rivalries, as it were; the others are overwhelming. And the petite bourgeoisie and the middle class are beginning to understand it and to realize that the only solution is socialism. And, listen, man, what I'm telling you, they'll end up accepting it voluntarily.

Voluntarily? The only way is with a pistol pointed at their heart... I don't know about theories or about the cosmopolitan bourgeoisie, but I do know how you achieve power, because that's not a question of theories, it's about having balls. I was there when things were going seriously and I know that the one who convinces others and calls the shots is the one who's got the upper hand.

Leo's father intervened, smoothing ruffled feathers. There was something, he said, that he'd seen with his own eyes: Mane, Tecel, Fares, hurriedly scrawled in chalk by some impetuous graffitist along the corridors of the Metro, in the Plaza de Cataluña, on the ad posters. The thing is, it's all just like the grand feast of Belshazzar, like the last days of Pompeii. Capitalism knows that its days are numbered and, while the people suffer, it indulges itself in all kinds of debauchery. He tacked the cloth together as he talked, his glasses slipped down to the tip of his nose, and Teresa listened from the ironing table, serious and working carefully at the same time. The canary in the cage, the dining room table strewn with patterns, the sofa bed and worn-out chairs, the sideboard, the vividly colorful picture of Rome burning, the radio atop a side table covered by a shawl with a fringe of yellow beads. He commented that on Sunday they'd gone to see *Don Juan Tenorio*, the immortal play by the great Zorrilla. A work which, although inspired by religion, never stops being a denunciation against the mentality of the powerful and privileged. What pride! What contempt for their fellow human beings! And the thing is that Zorrilla, a man of the people as he was, could not stop criticizing those who believed that their wealth and position entitled them to have everything, that their life need be nothing more than a succession of wasteful carousing. For wherever I went, I trampled reason, I scoffed at virtue, and mocked justice, and I sold women. He looked at them from above his glasses.

That's the idea! said Juan. And why? Well, because he's got the strength, and whoever has strength can only be conquered by force.

And Leo's father: one way or another, socialism will triumph, that's inevitable. But we all have to do what's possible for the change to be peaceful, because it's the people who suffer the most from violence. Faced with the despotism and outrages of the repressive forces, our peaceful position makes it possible for socialism to garner the sympathies and respect of all, Catholics or agnostics, democrats or bourgeoisie. Bit by bit, each one will be won over to the cause of socialism.

No, sir! No, sir! If one day you convince the bourgeoisie and the priests, it will be because you'll have stopped being a revolutionary. We live in a military theocracy and all the evils of Spain come from the clergy. And that's it.

Now this is another topic. The only religious thinker who has been, at the same time, a humanist was Confucius. And there's no doubt that Christ, as a man, was a great man, but the Catholic Church, however, has always been against progress and liberties, oppressing the true forms of Spanish life, which come from the people, in society. Long before the Romans, the Arevaci, and I don't remember which other early inhabitants of the peninsula, already had a kind of communism. And, if you go looking, throughout the course of all history you'll see how the people have been rebelling, rebelling, here with the peasants purchasing redemption charters, there with the *comuneros*, the men of the Castilian townships who rose up against Charles I, the Revolt of the Brotherhoods in Valencia and Mallorca, and on the other side the Catalan Reapers' War and the viticulturists' revolt and, more recently, the revolutionary impulse of the Catalan and Basque working classes, of the Asturian miners, and the Andalusian farmworkers. It's taken many inquisitions and exactions to subdue these natural impulses of the people, many, mind you. And there lies your role, that of the intellectual humanists: to give culture back its true popular character.

The brother-in-law said that he, too, was for the people's culture, but that of a people in power, exercising revolutionary vigilance. Culture without power only serves to carry you before the rabble, like with Ferrer Guardia. For the people, there can be no culture without power. Of course, then, once their liberties are crushed, yes, then, yes, you might then talk about the spread of culture, spiritual as well as physical. The conversation moved toward the heart of scientific truth contained in popular knowledge and natural medicine, so despised by the bourgeoisie, a class of people who live on the backs of nature, so slandered by the selfish interests of doctors. They spoke about the benefits of a more natural life, one opposed to clerical obscurantism, of rational nutrition, of physical exercise. The father nodded: *mens sana in corpore sano*, he said. And he began to talk about a curandero, a faith healer, who'd relieved his pain when, after having visited who knows how many expensive doctors... But the other one didn't let him continue: he explained the necessity of doing away with the family, and liberating sex, the healthy effects of nudism, of exposing the genitals to the sun and the air, that part of the body most usually hidden when it is precisely the one most in need of natural conditions. Sex must be liberated and the family done away with, he repeated.

Lucky that Antonia can't hear you, said Floreal. And I'd like to see you if she decided, I mean, c'mon, to strip it off, and start liberating sex.

But that's got nothing to do with it! It's that nudity is not a vice! Nudism is in no way indecent. It's a serious and scientific thing. Very simply, what's natural.

Floreal smiled, but one noted a certain embarrassment, and he conspicuously insisted on changing the subject; he folded his hands together between his parted knees, looking at the floor, and, now and then, at Raúl and Federico, as if nervous. They talked about Leo. They explained to them again the last visit they'd paid him, in Burgos, and how Teresa was able to see him by passing herself off as his sister. Teresa said that when they saw him, his morale was outstanding and that, apparently, all his companions in jail respected him greatly. Even the guards, said his father. There was one who approached me and asked me if I was his father. I told him, yes sir, and mighty proud, too. And he told me, well you've got yourself a smart one there, you can sure count on him, you can be satisfied. Teresa said: he's got prestige everywhere. And she told how everyone in the neighborhood asked about Leo, how was Leo doing, when was Leo getting out, even people who barely knew him. That was an outrage, that one, said his father. When they came to take him away, if you'd seen them. They behaved in such a way, turning the place upside down, threatening, saying they might just haul us all downtown, that we Reds didn't even have a right to live. And their faces, the hatred. He stopped talking and there was a silence. Then he pointed to the color illustration of Rome burning, under the watchful gaze of Nero, in the foreground, strumming a lyre. We're like the early Christians who suffered as many as ten persecutions, he said. They spoke about Leo's future when the Regime would fall and how he'd have all the doors open to him, about the possibility that he might be pardoned, as they'd been told by a general's chauffeur, and be released in September. If the Regime lasts until then, they said. The people, they said, weren't willing to suffer the consequences of the crisis, hunger, unemployment, and would not tolerate again what they'd already been through after the war, that terror and that humiliation, some in living conditions more appropriate to the Middle Ages.

Each morning, in the marketplace there is a real protest about the high cost of living. All the women complain. Fact is, they can't make it, the money doesn't pay for their groceries.

It's just that after the war people put up with rationing, smuggled goods, abuses, everything, they put up with everything, because their morale was defeated. Now, however, people are filled with the spirit of victory.

I remember eating that rationed chocolate, said Raúl. It was pure carob.

Well, if that's how it was for you, imagine what it must have been like for the worker, said the brother-in-law.

At home we had everything, said Federico.

On leaving, in the car, they talked about how those visits were beginning to feel painful.

Poor Leo, if he could hear them, said Raúl. But, how can you contradict them? Even Floreal himself seems a bit out of touch.

The thing with Floreal, he's just like that, y'know, the guy's a few cards short of a full deck.

Stupid? No way, man. Floreal's a good guy. But he's so engrossed in his discussions and political readings that he's losing sight of reality. He sees everything so clear that if you told him that things are not so easy as all that, that the Regime might still last for quite a while, that it might just take a few years for it to fall, he'd think that you were the one who'd lost sight of reality. And it's for this reason, because he must only talk to people who think just like him; and if someone disagrees with him, he won't even listen to them.

With Adolfo Cuadras it was different, with Fortuny himself, so moderate, no love for passing judgment, for talking too much. With them you could argue, really get into things, they shared many common assumptions, although there might be differences, like when Adolfo Cuadras questioned whether the actions set for Thursday would be successful.

In '51 and including last year, too, the strikes and the boycott of the trolley cars started in the street. Which means, from the ground up, and not the other way around, like now. Then there was no need for appeals or leaflets. At least, I don't remember seeing any.

Because you weren't involved in the matter, said Raúl. But behind things like the strike in '51 there's always some organization. I remember perfectly how the word strike was written everywhere, in chalk, or with whatever was at hand.

That's what I mean, that in every case the initiative started with the masses, it was something in the air. But not now.

Well, then, what good is political activity? If there are no favorable, existing conditions, then someone has to make them.

Excuse me, the ones possible to create get created, although it seems a trite thing to say.

Fine, if the workers don't answer the call it's because they're sons of bitches and they deserve everything that happens to them, said Federico.

Besides, if there were strikes last year in the textile industry, impromptu shutdowns on the factory line, trolley car boycotts, and all that, why not have them now, when the economic crisis is so much worse?

They were in the bar of some big hotel, relaxed and comfortable, with its light odor of blonde tobacco, Chez Adolfo, as they said on the phone to arrange a meeting. Aurora said, look, she's going to lose her slip, and their eyes all swiveled to follow a showy jeweled woman, tinkling, resplendent. They laughed, and Aurora looked at them meekly, quiet, as if waiting to participate. But she also started laughing when nobody was laughing, while they chatted about any old thing, without any specific comic intention. Then she went back to her gentle silences, her hand on her cheek, her eyes looking down, focused on the floor. She stayed on the edge of the conversation, and if they asked her opinion, she just said it was fine, or she came out with some marginal observations, questions about the details expressed in a deep voice, barely audible, leaving her sentences unfinished, hanging in the air, seeming to say something more out of courtesy than for being interested in the subject. She was quiet, somewhat withdrawn, and only sometimes, when they'd most forgotten her, did she then raise her eyes, and Raúl felt her gaze, almost sensing her, furtive, penetrating. He looked at her, too, and then she turned her eyes away, looked back again at the floor. When did that start? And when did she stop avoiding his gaze and, like joining one's reflection in the mirror, finally meet the challenge in his eyes and hold his gaze? Not many days had passed since the moment when, the strike in full swing and them planning to spread the protest from the Law School patio to all the university departments, Federico appeared at the meeting accompanied by Aurora, smiling and silent, limiting himself to introducing her as their connection to the Faculty of Medicine. Afterward they gave her a lift to her house and Raúl asked her if she also studied medicine so she could dedicate herself to helping children. Aurora said no, that she didn't like children, that she was majoring in medicine because it was what a cousin of hers was studying, and well, look. Now he's got a fiancée and he's going to get married, she said. She spoke with that deep voice, without turning around, seated next to Federico, but her serious face was reflected in the rearview mirror, her lips very carefully painted, her black eyes looking straight ahead, her hair short and very black. They dropped her off across from the street door, on the sidewalk opposite, and she crossed the street running.

Hey, where did you find her? asked Raúl.

It's a mystery, said Federico.

You brought her along because you like her. C'mon, because if not, I don't get what she's doing here.

The medical students. The medical students have picked her as their liaison. It's their deal.

Fine, but you like her.

Why do I have to like her? She looks like a drag queen. You're the one who likes her. C'mon, I noticed it right away. You like her, tell the truth. She looks like Nefertiti.

She's not bad, man.

Better than Nuria? Who do you like better, for example, Nuria or this one?

What kind of question is that? They're not a bit alike.

Nuria suits you better. She's the right kind of girl, more active, more independent, with her own life and job; y'know, what you might call a partner, a female partner. Look, she'll become an interpreter at the UN. The two of you could work at the UN together. Like that, together, but you each do your own thing. When does she come back?

Well, in June, I suppose. Maybe she'll come for Christmas. Or for Easter. And if she doesn't come, we'll meet up in Paris.

And then you'll get married? In secret? You could choose someone important from the party to be the godfather. Mr. H himself. Mr. H would be fine.

And who's telling you we're planning to get married?

Then, what? You'll be one of these model progressive couples? The ones who don't get married, but it's like they were married and they try not to cheat on each other and everything?

But what the fuck are you saying about cheating and all this bullshit? I couldn't care less about cheating.

Ah, so you don't care if Nuria sleeps with other guys?

Of course not. Y'know, I mean it's a question we've never

even brought up. If she's got to spend two years in England and I'm here, it seems like the logical thing to me.

That's good. You're mature people, evolved, that's very good. So then, what you've got to do is sleep with Aurora. I knew that you'd like her, I was sure.

A pale and fragile girl, seeming to lack vitality and yet, so subtly variable, that pale nakedness of full, clean, burnished breasts and tight, lean midriff, the delicate outlines of her lithe, flexible body, the points of her breasts, dark like her lips, like her sex that opened below the soft trim arrowhead of hair, Aurora, now walking ahead, leading him along a series of steps and narrow footbridges, winding along within the forms and projections of the facade, interlinked with the inner hollows, twisted corridors, small rotundas stinking of piss, the contents of bulging bladders aerated upon the columnar bases. She answered him that she wasn't tired. You're agile, said Raúl. And Aurora: well, it's because I have a classical dance class every day. They stopped in some hidden corner and examined the graffiti, names, dates, initials. Nice spot for poor lovers, said Raúl. Through the sinuous aperture one could make out the expanse of the city spreading out toward the setting sun, crepuscular, sonorous as a seashell, the Ensanche extended toward the west in mechanical repetition of the now aging grid of streets, a formula planned more than one hundred years before, Cerdà's plan, an enterprise born under the most auspicious auguries of the oh-so-energetic and driven 19th-century bourgeoisie in those years of grace and disgrace, of good fortune and misfortune, of pain and pleasure, of revolutions and restorations, of barricades, repressions, assaults, and communes, when a phantom ran through Europe, an enterprise destined to transfigure the city, predestined, an expansion still being carried out, only now a bit meaner and cheaper, square as an inventory, only on the map, atherosclerotic grid, without parks interspersed nor open blocks with tidy central gardens, but instead blocks closed in around garages, warehouses, small workshops, tight edifications mechanically repeated, windows facing windows, balconies facing balconies, terraces facing terraces, with an ample panorama of more terraces, balconies, and windows, plus some highly coveted attics and penthouses, all facade, artificial stone, dwelling places now no longer homes nor containing the highly-prized symbolic hearth, now simply points of family concentration, mechanically conventional with respect to some forms of life too quickly fluctuating, flats now lacking the spacious 19th-century comfort, no proper parlor, the dining room and bedrooms rigidly planned, without dark vestibules or sunny galleries, a sitting room and nothing more, and a stingy profusion of dividing walls, interior patios, flimsy partition walls, calculated inventories of interior height, square footage, cubic footage, palms, handspans, narrownesses, ruinous streets crossed by a degraded extension of a network once previously projected as liberating, cellular excrescence, gray railings, bars, grates and grillwork, the phantasmal outline of those verticalities, four towers like prongs rising up in the dusk. The Sagrada Familia, unfinished temple of rare perspectives, four belfries, an apse and a facade of exuberant imagery, stars, blood, children, flocks of sheep and kings, sculptural groups, ecstatic altarpieces, a precursor or prophet of burning word made flesh incarnate in rapturous effigy, colorations of the sunset, unfinished work, simple anticipation of the promised future, prophetic structure of presumptuous forms, elegant, mere initial phase of what someday was going to be an ambitious shape, the form of a great enterprise realized and raised upon the sacrifices of generations, dogmatic protoplasmic form raised upon what was once only a shadowy wasteland of spectral profiles. Superhuman project, that temple of ardent mystic outer body, the interior wrought like a celestial Jerusalem of leafy branching cedars, a city bound for destruction, that future factory with its unfinished porticoes of the Nativity, Passion uninitiated, Glory unfulfilled, rosary of mysteries in the respective facades east, west, and south, where the sun is born and then vanishes after touching the zenith, with its mass of towers, a serrated mountain of towering summits, craggy thorn stalactite bell towers, Christ's conical ciborium swelling higher than all else, flanked by four evangelical obeliskoid peaks, eagle and child, lion and ox, of the twelve apostolic bell towers, the immaculate cupola of the apse, the dome of the ciborium, the

four ovals of the sacristies, slender cusps, pinnacles, pompous
pinnacles, lofty aggregate shaped by the dark valley of a cloister,
expiatory temple, burning redemption, haughty iron sconce of
purification, sharp flames, crested, spiked, and thrusting, shaping a sonorous organ or radiant beacon, all light and harmony,
prodigal precursor of most highly purified forms, discoverers in
radial forms, ascendant, ovoid arrangements, angular, sloping,
waves of undulating lines, vibrant, brambled, elliptical figures,
parabolic, hyperboloid, fan-shaped, serrated, sagittal, bulbous,
gravid volumes, potbellied, stones set with drafty chinks, chaotic
masonry, finials with vertical limits, hypertrophic forms, protean,
eruptive, delirious, frothy, rough vegetable luxuriance, bone-dry
mosaic, madrepore, crustacean, fruit. Strange edifice, structured
from fragmentary elements, indistinct, joining them in a shifting whole, evolving, full of contradictions and coherences, of
asymmetrical symmetries, contrasts, resonances, repetitions,
gyres and ellipses, allusions and elisions, meticulous concretions,
abstractions, forms derived and derivative, in fugue, like a helix
which ascends and turns, vanishing in the void. Above the city,
the clouds lost their pink tints and turned pale, limp roses of
autumn, and the bells rang mildly, like an angelus announcing
midday, sonorous city, stretched out toward the west.

Beautiful russet sunset contemplated from that vantage,
from the south slope of Montjuich, its back to the city, from
the cemetery on the southwest flank, when the glittering sun
slid down from the highest part of the columbaria, sunk behind
the lowlands around the Llobregat River, fading distances,
skies oozing mother-of-pearl slowly losing color, fading to
gray. Serene clarity, before a distant terminus of mountains,
one glimpsed quiescent shorelines and plains, the incipient
intermittencies of the airport, hazy mudflats, smokestacks, and
chimneys, quiet smoke unfurling from the industrial outskirts,
and closer, almost confused with the cemetery, cubic forms
of whitewashed shanties, and further, now along the edge of
the waterfront, the Campsa company oil and gas tanks, silvery
masses planted around the foot of the Morrot, the promontory of Montjuich brusquely plunging into the sea, blocking

the port, leaving only long wharves sticking out, the lines of the
breakwaters and counterdikes, the faint beams spinning from the
lighthouse. At its arrival, the sun dyed the dusty dividing hedges
yellow, low, beneath the swollen foliage of the avenue among the
long lines of trees. They left the car and walked on foot up the
streets and tilting pavements flanked by Monk's Pepper, gnarled
lobed cypresses, clouds of sparrows blowing away, multiplying.
The initial nucleus, developed in a gentle slope from the wide
avenues, stood out ostentatiously with its solemn mausoleums,
human vanities, privileged zone of pantheons crammed together
among the luxuriant foliage, cupolas, towers, needles, obelisks,
a silent succession of clasped wrought iron gates, locks, grilles,
wrought iron, bordered in chains, wrought iron gates spun
around pavilions and chapels, Neo-Romanesque structures,
Neo-Gothic, Neo-Plateresque, Neoclassic, Neo-Mudejar, Neo-
pharaonic, sculpted cyclopean slabs, truncated columns, tombs,
crosses, some hieratic bust, an adolescent with a wilting stalk, a
little girl with tousled curls, wings and drooping bugles, flaming
swords, fallen pageboys and sleeping beauties, epitaphs, crowns,
pale withered flowers and black ribbons, dry nosegays of everlastings. Further up, as the slope grows steeper, surrounding the
sector of pantheons, a wide area of hypogea set into the earth,
one avenue atop another, a varied network of facades of modernist flavor, a series of successive doorways, airily curved corbels,
dark stained-glass windows, mosaics, floral overlays, wrought
iron garlands and grape clusters, an open iron gate, the echoing
voices of washerwomen, the stink of bleach. And the sound of
hammer blows, a cortege of cars swiftly rounding the turn. And
still further up, more visible every moment, between increasingly
steep slopes and longer stretches of stairways, the first blocks of
niches monotonously repeated, a grid of columbaria and trapezia
rising up like skyscrapers, glass gleaming in the sun, reflections
interweaving, blocks increasingly bare and vertical, sepulchers
now not even whitewashed near the flat crest of the hill, designed
like a hypocritical application of the evangelical principle, in a
way that while the privileged classes were buried in the lowest
areas of the cemetery, the humble people were raised up, the

inverse of earthly life, even to the most high, a purely utilitarian, bureaucratic arrangement, final dwelling place or passport, the final number, outskirts with ashen scullery women preparing and cleaning, borrowing the ladder to climb to the top, cleaning the earthenware flower urns and the opaline vases, pouring in water, bouquets, plastic flowers, dusting off portraits and relics, brightening up the inscriptions for their own eyes already set on the soon-to-come All Souls' Day, when along the paths, among the sepulchers, a mournful multitude in a line like ants would heed their call: Barcelonans, in memory of those who fought to give us a more dignified life, in memory of those for whom you fought to provide them with a more dignified life, Barcelonans!... They'd set a date to meet at Chez Federico, a nondescript barbodega near his house, and Raúl was the only one to arrive on time. The radio was broadcasting the twelve chimes of midday and a brief prayer in Latin. The bells announcing the angelus, the good news which would be fructified in the joyous nativity nine months hence. Before long, the place filled up with construction workers, mostly *charnegos*—non-Catalans—Andalusians, dingy, threadbare, road-weary. They talked, loudly and excited, how the new trolley cars were so badly inspected, about a soccer pool with thirteen correct guesses on the card, about a woman standing outside the construction site. Women can go fuck off, goddammit. Here, smoke a real man's cigarette, dammit. *Ideales*? Sure, fella, they don't kill anybody. This time I got a good pack. Sí, señor, these are the good ones, this batch got properly inspected, they've got the right amount of tobacco in them. I bought them yesterday, no, the day before, when I got off work. And the moment I walked out, I see it's a good pack, I go back in and buy another pack. I get home and I say, goddamn, for once finally, and yesterday, yeah, yesterday, I go back and buy myself thirty. Yeah, you can tell they've been properly inspected. Good, but what the hell do you mean inspected? Look at this gal, look at those pants. Psst, psst, hey baby. I'd give you such a fucking. Hey baby, right here, baby, let's see you loosen that tight ass and shake it more. Baby, baby. She'd come sniffing right around my zipper... In short, the typical lumpen conversation, *charnegos* from the countryside without class consciousness or the spirit of making demands for themselves, monotonous chatter about their monotonous work and the monotonous holiday distractions, using leisure time with the leftover fruits of their labor, soccer and cinema, dancing, the bars, whores, girlfriends, wives and children, family meals, Sunday strolls along the streets filled with people out walking, like everybody else, consequences of a life made of empty spaces filled in with too immediate necessities. Joyfully getting comfortable in the new apartment finally granted to them, for example, any old flat on any old block of workers' apartments, feeling pleasantly at home among those four walls after so many years of moving from one crowded house to the next, of sublets, of shanties, now the whole family reunited, a joy identical to that of knowing how to read comics and censored, government-approved publications, or of being able to listen to whatever the radio was broadcasting, or watching, in the bar, the television programs, until, perhaps a word or phrase from some companion, maybe a brief conversation or even reading a leaflet, would unleash in them the unalterable process of becoming aware, the conviction that they'd left their hometown behind for something more than a plate of lentils, no longer the necessity of a greater salary, but rather of a different social structure, other ways of living.

When Aurora came in, the *charnegos* in the doorway stopped whistling and there was an uncomfortable silence while she advanced toward Raúl between smiles and muttered comments. Federico made them wait a little while more and didn't even sit down, leaning toward them, his hands tensely clutching the edge of the table. We'll have to leave the thing with the cemetery for the evening, he said. He explained that there was danger of new searches and arrests, that he'd had to change the location of the Gestetner machine, move it to another, safer place. He had it outside, in the car.

But, what's going on?

Nothing really, I suppose, collective panic. The only sure thing is that those guys have squealed themselves hoarse. But it's in case they end up saying something they don't even really know but it turns out to be correct.

Fortuny watched them from the backseat, covering the cyclostyle with a folded overcoat. We've thought about Pluto's studio, they said. It was a clear morning, transparent, of limpid autumnal clarities.

Goddammit! shouted Pluto. I was afraid of some shitty luck like this. What, don't you have any better place than my pad? Just let you print all your papers here, man, like it's nothing. You guys are crazy! Crazy!

I warn you that if they catch us you're going to be in trouble, said Federico. The owner of the house always catches the worst of it.

Ah, well, I'm warning you guys that I'll sing, alright? Come the first shakedown, I'm spilling all the beans. Besides, you guys aren't serious about anything. To start with, why do all four of you need to be here, like some committee meeting? Wasn't it enough for the one guy to come who had to take care of this piece of junk? That's what I think, at least. And now, there'll be guys trooping in and out. The lady at the front door is going to think I've turned queer.

Pluto's studio was on the terrace roof, with a view down into the center of the block. It consisted of a single room with a large loft, barely furnished, a bed with oversize pillows like a sofa, an electric heater, glasses and bottles, a record player on the floor, set on a colorful striped blanket, the walls with clippings, most of them reproductions of nudes. On the roof, the door of the toilet banged now and then, flimsy. Pluto watched, seemingly astonished, as they placed the cyclostyle in the center of the room. At other times he would be relaxing on the sofa, spinning his brilliant disquisitions, for example, about the need to officially resurrect the phallic cult, starting with the basic idea that all human beings naturally tend to seek maximum pleasure, now physical, now spiritual, also called mystical, only achievable by the overcoming of the individual ego, only achievable through the complete physical union with another being or mutual understanding, a pleasure which no one achieves by themselves alone, since no one can be united with themself, also demonstrating the always frustrated character of the pretended self-unions or masturbatory practices, owing to the impossibility of being, at the same time and in the same sense, each one of the two parts or determinate objects of the union. Therefore, the pleasure results from the performance or penetration of one exterior agent in action, in the same way that the kinetic energy of active heat, which is the fire, causes the log, which is potential heat, to become kinetic energy as well, and thus modifies it. Just as a cane doesn't move if it is not moved by the hand which clutches it, it is therefore essential to make reference to the said modifying agent, the penetrating subject or phallus, necessarily adequate to the task, the efficient cause or creative act par excellence, and to accept the cult, now unofficial, its function almost furtively described as being consubstantial with human nature, converting it, consequently, into the official cult of humanity. And he offered an examination of the singularly rich vocabulary that popular language uses in naming the aforementioned phallus, generally allusive expressions, owing perhaps to its external apparatus, perhaps to its driving power, expressions of every kind, feminine, ambiguous, neutral, epicene, exploring the attributes of omnipotence and omnipresence which have always been traditionally applied to such a venerated tool. But now he was in no mood for jokes.

At least take it up to the loft, he said.

The others, however, as if suddenly exalted, rushed back down the stairwell in a whirlwind, pushing, reckless, a staircase with kitchen odors, voices, radio music, echoes gathered from floor to floor, beneath the dim central skylight, and now in the doorway, they laughed uncontrollably when Aurora, straggling behind them down the last flight, asked them to explain the precise meaning of the word *carajo*. Splendid noonday, yes, all in the full sun and a lovely feathering of cumulus clouds. And in the car they started arguing again about whether the time had come for direct action. Federico said that, the risk being more or less the same, they might as well do things seriously.

I find it absurd that they'd shoot you simply for planting a purely symbolic explosive, he said. This is playing Prometheus.

Well, but the explosive's already gone off, all right? said Raúl.

Even if the police picked us up now, it's not like they're catching us red-handed, so I don't see why they have to know that we set it.

Oh sure, like they're just some thumb-sucking idiots. They'll know perfectly well it has to be the same people who were dropping the leaflets. What's funny is that Pluto thought he was just joking when he said they'd beat us black and blue if they caught us. He thought he was teasing me. But the police don't sit around sucking their thumbs. They wouldn't treat us like the ones they caught at the university.

Alright, alright, don't get on my case, a small explosive is one thing, a real bomb is another, said Fortuny.

I know that. Except for the police it's the same. That's why I say it's ridiculous, man. We might as well plant bombs. Why don't we? Why was Mr. H chewing your ass?

No señor, no, because then you'll change the subject away from the peaceful tactic of mass action, said Raúl, which is the only thing possible right now. Look at what happened with the guerillas. Apart from the fact that Escala does nothing more than toe the party line, which is exactly what we've got to do.

Not to mention how much it costs just to get a simple strike going, said Fortuny. Well, let's be a little reasonable, dammit. Who's likely to follow us if we use violence?

We've got to get them to follow us, that's irrefutable, said Raúl. Revolutions have never been carried out with peaceful means. But first we've to go manage to create some objective conditions of a pre-revolutionary system.

Mr. H. dixit, said Federico. The boss has convinced you. The boss is the boss and you've let yourselves be handled.

Boss, my ass, said Fortuny. It's just the way it is, man. Violence is always the last resort.

The other way around, the last resort is what we've got right here and now, something symbolic. They're willing to shoot us and we're contenting ourselves with symbols like the Obelisk. If there's no real direct action it's because we're incapable of carrying it out and then we console ourselves by saying that a peaceful strike is more effective. Is that why we learned to throw bombs? See, they're more realistic in the army.

C'mon, c'mon, don't say stupid things, Escala's totally right, said Fortuny. What do you think, a few bombs are going to topple the Regime? Arguing about this is like continuing to worry about Budapest when our situation is precisely the opposite. Just nonsense.

And, in any case, Escala doesn't say so because he's Escala, but because you've got to think that Escala knows the objective conditions better than we do. He has a broader vision, less partial, in fact, and knows things we don't know which serve as a basis for the analysis that the leadership is making. We always move in the same circles. Besides, if we belong to the party it's not to make war on our own account. By ourselves, we're not going anywhere.

That's perfectly clear. And think of the repression that would follow any real bombing.

Better. That way things will really heat up. Everyone knows that. The weird thing would be if there were no repression, seems to me.

C'mon, c'mon, don't talk like an irresponsible fool, dammit, said Fortuny.

He seemed annoyed, and Federico insisted on pestering them with his descriptions of arrests and torture. They'll accuse us of setting every bomb in recent years, he said. And Raúl just joined up. And then, the firing squad. Accomplices like Pluto will get thirty years. Firing squad? said Federico. If we survive that long. After the electric shocks, after they rip out your fingernails, after they cook your feet over a brazier. Can you imagine? And Aurora said *qué horror*, the same as when she said *qué susto*—what a fright—without intonation, without emotion, more as if she would like to feel the horror than as if she really felt it. They dropped her off in front of her house, on the opposite side, and she crossed the street at a run. So long, Epaminondas, said Federico. Upon entering the doorway, Aurora turned briefly and waved. Raúl had moved up to take her seat, in the front.

And to you, Pelopidas, said Federico. I'm going to call the two of you Pelopidas and Epaminondas.

What's that supposed to mean? said Fortuny.

But Federico didn't answer, his eyes amused, deliberately fixed on the steering wheel, with the same expression of days before, when he asked Raúl what was going on with Aurora. Are you lovers? he'd said. At that moment they'd also been in the car, except without Fortuny. What nonsense. Why do we have to be? Raúl had said. And Federico had said: because, that's why, because you look at each other, the expected observation, expected since, a few days earlier, sitting in a creamery, Raúl noticed that Federico had noticed the looks he'd exchanged with Aurora. Just the looks but nothing more, not that contact beneath the table, the foot sought out, the foot not withdrawn, in mid-discussion, when he said, it seems very good to me, and she said, me, too. And Fortuny said, the what? Chez Fortuny, a neighborhood creamery, and of course Adolfo Cuadras was absent. They talked about Adolfo Cuadras and his opinions about the convenience of balancing political action with—if not subordinating it to—professional training. I don't mean to be nosy with Count Adolfo, said Federico. It seems fine to me that he devotes himself to his novels and all that. I also switched from Pure Math and now I study Economics, which is what interests me. The only thing I have to say is that, objectively, political activity is more important. Now alone together, Federico tried to get him to talk as he drove him home. When they got there, he shut off the motor and they kept chatting for a while.

You're sleeping together, he said. I know it for sure. C'mon, it was obvious right away. And it's fine, totally fine. Perfect revolutionaries. Clandestine behavior must be organized just so, by couples. Then there would always be this thing of emulation, of trying to look good in front of each other, I mean. Like the Sacred Band of Thebes.

The university now closed down, as they were leaving the meeting where it had been decided to take the demonstration to the street, it was Aurora, the liaison to the Medical School, who offered to help them. If you want, I can help you, she told them. Federico made fun of the precautions they were taking, of the meetings on the patio in front of the Central Library, at Chez Adolfo or Chez Raúl, of their sunglasses and synchronized watches. Seems like we're just playing at being spies, he said. But when the time came, his hands and forehead were sweating. When in the translucent, colorless dawn, the city

streets, el Paseo de Gracia, frozen, inert, Raúl walked with Aurora
toward the steps around the Obelisk of Victory, arms around
their waists, and he passed her a cigarette, the fuse sticking out
of her open purse, she said I don't know how to smoke, blowing
in an attempt to fan the cigarette tip that didn't ignite the fuse,
and because of the delay, Federico drove by to pick them up at
the exact time without them having finished, his face frozen
in the frame of the car window, the motor in first gear, while
Raúl was still busy placing the explosive at the foot of the black
plaque with the imperial eagle. They pulled away, driving up
Avenida del Generalísimo Franco, the three of them in silence,
until, a few blocks further on, the liberating explosion sounded
from behind them, their emotions running no higher, really,
than when simply scattering leaflets, the same wait, the same
slow series of dizzying seconds of vacillation, as if desiring to
suddenly pull back from the now-arrived present moment, the
leaflets dropped from atop the Columbus Monument, from
a rooftop, from any random street corner, in the magnificent
sunset. And then the handoffs in cars, at twilight. Did they
really think a mishap was possible? They were seized with an
excited euphoria or delight, and even the little blunders made
them laugh, when they ran out of gas after just finishing that
drop-off, for example, after visiting the Montjuich Cemetery,
through the industrial neighborhoods, which shortly thereafter,
now at night, would be a glowering no man's land, with their
strings of street lamps and spotlights illuminating empty streets,
of extended uncertainty, boxed in between endless walls, squat
masses, silhouetted chimneys, whitenesses like skylights.

Shining city, there below, windows, shop windows, symmetrical streetlights, weak like early morning stars, and the sky,
the clouds dissipated, not wild, but smooth, neither carmine
nor purple, nor scarlet, nor vermillion, nor flame-colored, nor
pink, now only mauve, lilac, distant blues, livid distances, vast
finale to the sunset, empty skies, finally pacified, pearly paleness
increasingly higher or further away, crystallized, forged from
cold stars. A broad expanse overflowing from sea to mountain
and from river to river, open on the west to the flats of the

Llobregat and on the east to the Besós and Maresme, a city without rivers, between rivers, of shining arteries traced upon the boulevards, built upon the now buried sandy loam, alluvion deposited in the shadow of Montjuich, great hulk tumbling down above the sea like a cape or promontory, solitary, quarried, with its pergolas and lookouts, shanties and palaces, museums, its Pueblo Español, and its cemetery, its prison and its fun fair, Tierra Negra, like a wolf's ass, where the whores gathered, its park, its autumnal avenues, woodsy avenues scoured by the crisp October wind, boughs stripped bare, and at the end, at the far opposite end of the city, the outline of the chain of hills, San Pedro Mártir rising before Puig de l'Ossa, Vallvidrera, Tibidabo formerly called the Sierra de Collcerola, with its funicular and its rides and attractions crowned by the Church of the Sacred Heart, expiatory temple, new Acropolis from which, on a clear day, it was possible to glimpse, standing out far in the distance, the massif of Montserrat, ogival rocks, a monumental group like an arrangement of miters or scepters, Tibidabo and its foothills, Carmel, Güell Park hosting elegant waltzes, subtle wit, art of ingenuity, lucid Gaudian delight, el Turó de la Peira, nicknamed la Pelada—bald mountain—a relief of hills closing in like a fortress wall, opacities rising higher as one descended, almost gropingly to the dim window apertures formed of overlapping helixes, reflections from the streets snuffed out the dark foundational stones. They had discovered Federico's car parked in the same spot as before, in front of the building, illuminated by a street lamp. At the foot of the bell tower, in the interior esplanade, two or three figures were moving beneath the dim glow of a few lightbulbs, and someone said to them in French that they'd need to leave by the other gate, on the Calle Cerdeña, where someday they were going to erect the Facade of the Passion, to cross that desolate spot surrounded by dimensions magnified by the gloom. Sacred institution, enterprise born beneath the best auguries of the oh-so-influential 19th-century bourgeoisie in those years of the Lord, of disgrace or delight, of revolutions and restorations, or barricades, shrapnel, repressions, attacks, uprisings, pronouncements, revolts, communes, when a

phantom ran through Europe, flower of the east, temple raised
like an immense spiky flower, amazed at having sprouted up
there in this restless, turbulent city, among mischievous, violent,
and incendiary people, an enterprise destined to transfigure the
city, predestined, Gaudian proto-project, prophet in the desert,
superhuman work, temple of hopes and certainty, of glory and
passion, of resurrection and death, of redemption and fall, an
eminence of towers and towers like summits gathered in a ring,
sum of obelisks, Sardana of giants, Corpus Christi, flowering
broom, striated sierra, streaked red and yellow like the Catalan
flag—la senyera, mountain of the brown-skinned Virgin, pointy,
like scepters or miters, crown of thorns, Catalan rose of flowering
April, angelic organ, mosaic, tall and slender, immense expiatory iron sconce of sharp flames, monumental future. But now,
now along Calle Mallorca, where someday they would raise the
Facade of Glory, only a brick wall which barely permitted one
to see the rough, incongruous back side of the four bell towers
and the curve of the apse, the empty inner area, all facade, the
Facade of the Nativity, appreciable in all its details as one turned
the corner on Calle Marina, altarpiece dedicated to the rosy
epiphany, to the joyful coming of the beloved bonny baby boy,
offspring of non-parents perplexed and joyous, not conceived,
hosanna, alleluia, come to the world to fulfill his historic role so
many times prophesied, to suffer, redeem, and be glorified, Star
of Nazareth, of Mount Zion, Jerusalem of branching cedars,
celestial city, chosen people, captive people, liberated, led, and
driven to a new homeland by that messianic pre-messiah born
of the waters, visionary who, by the favor of the powerful ones
among whom he had been raised, preferred the cause of the
oppressed and fought for them, although in spite of them and
of their own weaknesses, knowing that he would never set foot
in the promised land. Unfulfilled destiny, ruin or mountain or
rose of four holy thorns, four traces of blood upon a background
of gold, lost colors, neither crepuscular gold nor blood, starry
sky, bright lights and sparkles from the street.

Sagrado Aborto—Holy Abortion—a work which merely
seems something wherein the Barcelona bourgeoisie might have

wanted to see its own reflection, but, above all, to perpetuate, project, and give itself permanence, to embody its future in stone, like in an open book situating the family at the center of all social organization, a family that if, on one hand, reproduces the scheme of the most Holy Trinity or the unity of the three—three persons in one single nature—on the other it is conceived in the image and likeness of its own family ideal, with a father that is more, much more than the man equal to any other who pretends to be, a father who is really the creator, the founder, the generative force par excellence, and a mother of immaculate purity and, above all, a beloved son who, satisfying the expectations placed on him, after overcoming, one after another, the trials life holds in store for him, will definitively consolidate the paternal enterprise, converting it into a true empire. Except that this enterprise might very well not flow along the expected channels. It might well be overwhelmed or crushed by an enterprise no longer distinct from it but even opposed to it, and it fit that that Dies Irae, Dies Illa was not the long-awaited one, and while that empire fell, a new one was constructed from its ruins, in its place, a temple sporting distinct facades, the Facade of the Popular Uprising, with its stony reliefs of the masses taking the streets and barricades with weapons like raised fists and explosions and fires, fire at will, a people on the march against the repressive charges and discharges, advancing, overwhelming, crushing, with a red deployment of flags, a final flourish, proclaiming their triumph. And the Facade of the Revolution, depicting the construction of socialism per se, where hammers and sickles would cease to be weapons in order to become tools, where the machine would not be used to contend against muscular strength but would augment it, in that singular representation of a construction which constructs itself, soberly but harmonically, in the light, with the strength of intelligence, like a sun soaring high in the sky. And in the center, flanked by the other two, the Facade of the New Society, for some reason, like the *Divine Comedy*, more abstract, more difficult to express or perhaps, to imagine. An enterprise not metaphysical but materialistic, not mechanical but dialectical, critical of criticism. What sense would any other task, or any other problem, have in the face of this one, the most intimate reasons for living, writing, setting down, like a line of ants, one word after another, one paragraph after another? What importance could the rest have? What might be comparable? Gaudeamus! Gaudeamus igitur!

Did they think it possible? Any mishap? They chatted on happily, without any excess emotion, Raúl leaning on the back of the front seat, his head between Aurora and Federico, and Federico, attentive to the traffic, talking about what happened. Then it's turned out well, he said. Young people willing and with initiative. It's turned out very well. And he told them he'd gotten rid of the remaining leaflets, tossing them out at several intersections, over near Horta. I didn't see any cops around there. They must have all been around here, trailing us. He spoke to Raúl, looking at him at intervals in the rearview mirror, his eyes bright, smiling. I thought they were coming for me. Suddenly I had the feeling that I was driving the only red Renault in Barcelona. And I thought, now they're going to shoot and they'd shoot holes through the cans of paint. Can you imagine if they shot up the trunk and I started leaving a trail behind like Tom Thumb and they ended up catching me? Man, no matter how fast I drove, I'd be leaving a trail and they'd nab me. I'd have no way out. Just like some wounded rat, like common vermin. And they talked about that night, when the police caught them painting slogans and, now at police headquarters, they started to ask them about the names of those who, in the other sectors of the city, would be also emblazoning the walls with a call to strike. Now Aurora was quiet, still, looking straight ahead. Hasta luego, Epaminondas, said Federico on dropping her off, and she crossed the street and waved. Raúl took her seat, wondering, without saying it, whether or not now was the time to sever ties. They agreed that Federico would come by to pick him up at a quarter to twelve on the dot. The car stopped in front of the shadowy garden wall. Federico cut the engine and leaned on the steering wheel, turned partly sideways. They'll stick us in there together, he said. In the same cell.

The family was gathered in the study, Papa, Felipe, Uncle Gregorio, and Felipe would lead them in praying a rosary. The litanies echoed darkly. What are they doing, he asked Eloísa. Well, they're praying the rosary, said Eloísa in a low voice. She told him about Uncle Gregorio and about Leonor, how every day, shopping, she came up to her to confide her frustration about Uncle Gregorio. It seems the poor man is a mess. He forgets everything, loses everything, his overcoat, his hat, everything. If it weren't for Leonor, he might well have walked out naked into the street. And she's desperate. She always tells me that if this happens, that if that… She is such a talker. And ugly. She's got a face like a lumberjack. But look, it seems she takes good care of him. Since she's been with him so many years. Besides, each to his own. And people talk so much that I don't listen to anyone anymore. She turned back to her pots and pans, evasive, seemingly eager to change the subject.

Felipe: the sense of strangeness which increasingly, inevitably, his brother's aspect aroused in him, perhaps because of how infrequently they now saw each other, that soutane fitted to the waist and, then below, open in well-cut pleats which he gathered as he sat down, those skirts which, when he walked, offered quick glimpses of his light shoes, his hands, white and nervous, searching in his pockets, and his seemingly weightless fluttering black cape. An attire which, as if by contrast, seemed to alter his figure, and even his physiognomy, more than the passing of the years, his cheeks seemingly dislocated, his curly eyelashes around his close-set eyes, with soft dark bags under them, and his mouth affable and slack, and his slight prognathism; his whole aspect, in short, suggesting something of Velazquez's young monarch.

Uncle Gregorio leafed through magazines from a jumbled pile next to the lamp, reading them very close to his face with one eye open, the other covered with the palm of his hand. The lamp glowed like a distant planet and sat in a corner of the table, that table with legs carved like a beast's claws, with its escritoire and table cover, its bronze paperweights, and the tall glassed-in mahogany bookcase to one side, and the cubistic armchairs crowding the too-small room. They chatted about the strike, and the closing of the university.

This is what they call nowadays hooliganism, said Papa. In my time the same thing happened with the business about Maura yes, Maura no.

Well, from the looks of it, the students who were arrested have been beaten terribly, said Raúl. They're saying, too, that they've been tortured with electrical shocks.

Just gossip, said Papa. In this country, anything that will make the authorities look bad is sure to get plenty of attention.

He said that what young people needed to do was study more and protest less, that with these things you only played right into the hands of politicians and troublemakers. Look at Ramona's husband, this Bonet boy. And Pedro himself. They sure know what they're doing. How are you going to compare a Jacinto Bonet, an Arcadio Catarineu, responsible, organized, well-educated people with good reputations with this bunch of sinister characters who talk about fixing the world, who promise the world and heaven to come after a revolution when we all know already how it will turn out? How can you conceive of a world without lawyers, notaries, property records, administrative agencies, protocols, registries, and all those things which are the reality of everyday life, the things that make the country run? Very nice all this thinking that everything belongs to everyone. But theory is one thing and the realities of a practical society are something quite different. The magazines slipped off of Uncle Gregorio's seat. He'd stood up and they accompanied him to the door.

Eh, let them protest, he said. They're young. I'd protest, too. Never a lack of motives, never will be.

C'mon, Gregorio, don't talk gibberish. My son studies, he does well, he pays his expenses doing some translation work he found, and that's what counts. At our age, for pensioners like us, the main thing is peace and quiet. And may God keep it that way.

Felipe said grace and Raúl, sitting across from him, had to pretend to cough in order to not join in on the Amen at the end. Papa took their hands, Felipe's left, Raúl's right. Tonight my happiness is complete, he said. The two of you here, with me. One son a priest, dedicated to God, and the other who will succeed me in the business of this world, Raúl, who is already like a consolation, a support in my old age. He'll get married and he'll be a great lawyer. What more can a father ask of God? Felipe in turn squeezed his hand and made some joke, he said that, besides, with soups like the ones Eloísa makes the happiness was even greater. He spoke excitedly and with a certain haste, anecdotes from his life in Jerez, of the mentality of Andalusian women, so distinct from Catalan women, always thinking about parties and balls, bullfights and hunting parties, charming women and well-meaning at heart, yes, but predisposed, by the upbringing they received and what they might say, to persist in their anachronistic customs of pomp and ostentation, and of the enormous work that could be performed from the confessional correcting, inexorably, their weaknesses, awakening a sense of charity deeper than mere holiday fundraising, stimulating their moral responsibilities to help those in need, the masses of people without work and without any true spiritual formation. He didn't want coffee with dessert but he asked Raúl for a cigarette. Now he said that given that Raúl surely saw social problems from a different angle, someday the two of them had to talk at length, with complete frankness. And he was concerned about the poor priests, generally older men, who didn't give social questions the importance they deserved, who kept spending all their good intentions fighting against modern dance styles and women's fashions, as if there existed nothing more than the Sixth Commandment. Prudish sanctimony. I find it absurd that those priests want to invent problems when there are so many real, urgent ones. What's the problem with this rock music or whatever they call it? It's physical exercise like any other. They were alone in the small sitting room, in the armchairs of the three-piece sofa, and Felipe looked at him smiling, those pleats hanging over his pointed shoes; a stranger, a stranger evocative of distant memories, no more familiar to Raúl than when, still a seminarian, during some Christmas vacation, he spoke to him of his sudden vocation upon reading *The Way*, his journey to Damascus. The Way is Jesus Christ and to find our way is to find Christ. It was after dinner, before Felipe retired to his room, and there was a silence. Then he'd said, you must think, oh man, everybody knows I've got a brother studying to be a priest, and he laughed sitting across from him, in the other armchair by the three-piece sofa, next to the record player with the built-in radio. It was that same night, later on, when Raúl discovered a forgotten hair shirt in the bathroom, next to the sink.

He closed the door and put a record on the turntable, at low volume, one selected at random. The seat Felipe had occupied was still warm and he moved to the other one. He glanced at the northeast sector of the map, the city unfolding toward the east in successive creases, from left to right, toward the Besós, toward San Andrés and the ancient town of San Martín. Folded up again, he left the map on the small Moroccan table. He looked again at his watch. Footsteps sounded upstairs, the rattling cascade of a toilet flushing, and in some nearby street, rhythmically moving away, the sound of the night watchman's staff. He settled down in the armchair, sideways, his legs hanging over one side. The sitting room was to the left of the vestibule, opposite the office, and it communicated with the dining room through a glass door that always stood open. Dining room in what style? By the light of the sitting room it was possible to make out, among four chairs, the square table, thick spindle-shaped legs, ringed, symmetrically striated, the chairs studded, with initials in repoussé on the black leather backrest and, in the shadows behind them, the solid dimensions of the sideboard and trencher, with its small brass shields and its gray marbles. The sitting room offered a more homogeneous aspect, the haughty Imperial table pushed up against the wall with its non-functioning bronzed clock, an allegorical cluster of agricultural figures and tools, and its alabaster lamp, the wood carved like palm trees and opaline globes, the small glass table with tubular framework, the Dutch vase, the glass cabinet with porcelains and silver, crystal, cups for drinking chocolate, ivories, Chinese knickknacks, tiny baskets of zinc flowers, presents from Papa's wedding or perhaps from Grandpa Jorge's or Grandpa Francisco's, and the photo of Mama in Port de la Selva, and the painting, that garden scene in a golden frame with a rose bed in the foreground. The three-piece suite had no specific style, simply overstuffed, upholstered in caramel-colored plush, slightly worn, the sofa sunken down at one end, next to the floor lamp, the whole set centered around the Moroccan table, which had come from the old chalet on Calle Mallorca, a small marquetry table with arabesques, geometric patterns, heavy and low, with closed horseshoe arches, very inviting for a child, easy for them to imagine that it was a castle or a fortress.

VII

THEY'RE NOT GOING TO let you eat in peace, Eloísa said. All your food's going to get cold.

Who was it? Papa asked.

Uncle Gregorio, said Raúl, he's coming over for coffee.

Above all don't forget about Arcadio Catarineu, Papa said. You should thank him for the interest he's shown: good manners cost nothing. He's a wonderful person and I'm sure that he must've moved heaven and earth. He's a very close friend of mine.

When I get back from school, Papa, said Raúl. Right now I've got a pounding headache.

You should rest a little, Papa said. Why don't you take a little nap?

You're going to go to school today, too? Eloísa said.

Of course, said Raúl. Just like every day.

Right, just like every day, Eloísa said.

She smiled again through her tears, her face in shambles, her features momentarily smudged. She stayed standing, behind Papa's chair.

And Achilles? Raúl asked. What's he up to?

Achilles? Eloísa said. He's doing really well. He still hasn't gone and hidden away. Since the weather's been good this morning, really, he went and took a walk in the sun.

She tucked her handkerchief inside her sweater cuff, now composed, though her voice was still rough from sobbing.

He's a smart turtle.

Sheesh, it seems unbelievable how smart that lil' creature is, Eloíisa said. Everything, he understands everything. The same as a person.

More, said Raúl. More than many people.

More, more, said Eloísa. Can it be possible, so small? But have some more cauliflower, help yourself. It's no good cold. Here, eat, eat.

She wanted to know if it tasted good, with so many delays she was worried that it might have turned out bad, that she might've overcooked it. She couldn't keep any eye on the oven like that, with the telephone ringing all morning. Really, hasn't it gone all mushy? she said. Ah, and also that girl with the man's voice called, twice. And that young lady who sounds like a foreigner. And that tall, handsome boy, the one dressed in brown. Well, he didn't say who it was, really, but I figure it was him. He said that he'd call back. And look... She lowered her eyes, as if embarrassed, as if embarrassed with satisfaction.

Well, yes, yes, Papa said. Everybody has shown maximum interest in you. And it's those moments when you find out who are your real friends and who aren't. They've all offered to help me, unconditionally.

All of them, really, you hear? Eloísa said. The telephone hasn't stopped ringing all morning. How was it possible these bandits weren't going to release you right away? Look how they wanted to keep you prisoner.

She cleared away the dirty plates, put the dish of cauliflower in the oven.

Well, as you've seen, they haven't been able to, Raúl said.

Right, that's it, they haven't been able to, they heard Eloísa saying from the hallway.

But, damn it, son, you've given us such a scare, Papa said. Such a scare.

He explained that when they gave them the news, Eloísa almost had a nervous breakdown. And he began making calls immediately, to seek out influential people, Jacinto Bonet, a Jesuit father, Arcadio Catarineu, Montserrat. Montserrat has performed magnificently, he said. And that morning when the inspector showed up to request information, Eloísa looked at him as if she was going to claw out his eyes. I served him some coffee and told him, come on now, this is all absurd, the fact that you ended up locked inside the university didn't mean that you were one of the troublemakers, after all, you're a good student and a good son. And this perfect animal goes and says to me that they're not so concerned with all that as with what's behind it all, because it's always the communists who are behind these things. Can you imagine! He was the typical sort, the very lowest kind. And then I explained to him, see, what our family stands for, that we've always been Catholics, right-wing, and I'd belonged to the Maurist Youth, what we endured in the war, how persecuted we were, how your cousin died and the posthumous medal they conferred on him for his heroism. And Eloísa, when she served him coffee, looked and looked at him in that way, and didn't even seem to hear me. I was finally able to send her out to go shopping and then he asked me if she was nuts, or I don't know what kind of rude thing he said. A real beast, what you call an animal. Only when we were done, as he was leaving, did it occur to him to tell me that it really wasn't a very important matter, just a pure formality; after the whole time having me on the edge of my seat. A real animal.

Eloísa served Papa a ground chicken breast patty and Raúl a sirloin steak with green peppers. Papa added a few spoonfuls of his preserves to the ground meat and then licked the spoon. Eloísa had returned to her spot behind Papa's chair, watching Raúl eat. Raúl raised his eyes, their glances met, and once again she scrunched up her features around her eyes.

That man, she said.

But you see now, they acted ridiculous, Raúl said.

My boy, my boy, Papa said. Thank God it was no more than a scare, but you've put us through a real trial. Why didn't it occur to you to get out of there in time? To have to tolerate questions about you from a man like that, especially about what you do and what you don't do, the same as if you were a criminal. I told him that you weren't mixed up in politics: your father, your studies, and nothing else. That when one is young there's always the danger of bad friends, of falling in with the wrong crowd that takes advantage of your good disposition, like this Leo, whom I've never liked. But I told him that you hadn't let yourself be fooled.

You talked to him about Leo? Raúl said.

Yes, of course, but I told him that he was already in jail, Papa said. He asked me all kinds of questions, about your friends, what you read, if you attend Mass on Sundays, if you play some sport, and God knows how many other things. And by the way, this fellow Quintana. They've caught him, too? Goodness, my boy, look what fools you're all turning into; to let yourselves get caught in this trap ... Then the communists come along and take advantage of it to make propaganda. Such an awful situation, my boy.

The telephone rang and Raúl stood up again. Leave it, I'll get it, he said to Eloísa. It was Aurora's voice. Hola, he heard her saying, her deep Hola, followed by a pregnant pause filled with expectation, with meaning, her voice exasperatingly unalterable, the way she said Raúl stretching it out, softly accentuating both vowels, as caressingly as ever, as if nothing had happened. Would it be possible to go back, to recover what was lost with the same naturalness that he had always managed to maintain, without explanations or any type of scenes, to turn into a mere passing accident how much had happened since he began to notice the glances Aurora and Adolfo Cuadras exchanged, the soft, gentle eyes suddenly raised, staring silent and steadily while the others talked, feet touching underneath the table and brusquely separated when, at last, midway through dinner, Raúl bent down to pick up the napkin that he'd previously let slide off his lap? They met alone one afternoon, before he stopped calling her, save for questions strictly about political activity, and they kissed. Tongues sliding back and forth, twisting, just like at first, when they took advantage of any pretext to lag behind, to embrace with violence or fury and then rejoin the others in the most imperceptible way. Good fellow, Adolfo Cuadras, right? he'd said. Since he's like that, rather cold and reserved, at first he's sort of inconspicuous. But the more you know him, the more you appreciate him. And she said: I find him fascinating. He walked with his arm around her shoulder a little longer. They'd met on the way out from classes and they went walking casually along the unkempt curving streets of Vallcarca, among stepped gardens, gallant noucentist towers, peaceful atmosphere of yellow facades, as if the sap lost by the leaves as they withered, dried, crackling, curling inwards, colored the very calm air, perfumed by the smoke of autumnal bonfires. Then Raúl said that deep down inside he didn't care for anything or anyone, not even his own skin. Only to destroy, to contribute however possible to the disappearance of the society they lived in, of himself, if it were necessary, to put an end, once and for all, and at any price, to this monstrous farce.

Sometimes I'd like to be a bomb, he said.

And he scrutinized that light, those transparencies, losing himself inside her pupils, eyes tranquil, elusive, shifting gaze. Thinking what? Wanting what? The sensation that he had just admired a landscape that was not only impossible to embrace but one whose beauty was impossible to evoke.

Everything is so strange, Aurora said.

They seemed to be searching for the stairs which linked the cross streets in brusque openings, offering unexpected views. From the top, leaning against the hard iron railings, Aurora contemplated the city, and Raúl, giving her a light, also lit his own cigarette, two glowing coals from the same flame. Now returning, Aurora stopped halfway across the viaduct. Down below, framed by the populated striations of El Putxet and Mount Carmel, their confluence in the foreground, they glimpsed the buildings at the port, cranes, metallic towers, ships anchored and tied up alongside the most distant wharves, the line of the seawall and, as if surging from the hazy horizon, the steam from a reactor penetrating the sky above, drifting, in a light arc. It's like one of those illustrations in a children's book, Raúl said. He watched her look, raise her glance, her face like a projection of her neck, as if emerging from the loose straight hair, gleams of light from jet and black patent leather, nocturnal suns, mercurial reflections, raising her glance and slowly dropping it, as she continued, features slanted, marbled lines and something like the shadow of a wing upon her face, impenetrable augury. He walked her home and at the door kissed her lightly, hardly brushing her with his lips; he crossed the street without turning around. Ciao, he'd said, and smiled, and she followed him with her eyes while he walked away or perhaps not, or perhaps she was on the verge

of calling him or she called him perhaps too late, uncertainties
imagined beforehand, as he tried to imagine her attitude, and
now recalled, now that he wouldn't go to meet her coming out
from school. He contemplated them, given over to a giddy
excitement increasingly less dissimulated, unsettled, audacious,
playful, affectedly naughty, turning with insolence toward their
companion, the hypocritical countenance, crafty movements,
the eye lively and greedy. He rapped his knuckles on the table,
and as the calm spread among deliberate shhh-shhhs and the
final comments of the slowest ones, the final winks of pleasant
guiltiness, noise of chairs and impudent coughs, the conjugation
yo fui, tú fuiste, él fue became more and more pronounced,
chanted in a chorus in the class downstairs. The classroom was
spacious, surely an old dormitory superficially remodeled: the
balcony, open to the canopies of the trees, centered between tall
wainscoting of greenish plastic paint; and a row of coat hooks
hung with small jackets, and a chalkboard which at these hours
always gleamed and made it necessary to turn on the florescent
lights, and the emery-polished glass door, distorting, and the
pattern on the floor turned gray by the scrapes and scratches
made by the legs of the tables and chairs. They were arranged
by order of height on the staircase in the entryway, very straight
and tidy, very close together, in their new suits, short pants or
golf trousers, neckties straightened, hair impeccably combed,
slick with pomade, affable, goofy expressions, lightly squinting
against the light, smiles, mouths slightly open, some eyelid half
closed in brutish stupefaction, in vacant gaze; in the first rows,
the freckled face of Ángel Gómez, the dead naughty boy, who
knows if unconfessed, run over by a streetcar coming back from
the beach, in Barceloneta.

You can consult the book. It doesn't help you at all either if
you copy from your neighbor because I'll notice it right away.
The theme I am going to set you is general, it does not correspond to any specific question. I'll not be satisfied with names,
dates, and battles. What I am interested in is the concept.

The concept? He looked over those rows of crossed arms
upon the table, in candid, astonished attitudes. Was it possible

there might not be anything more behind those faces, apart from the habitual solitary double life, smug secrets shared by all, that there might not be anybody with even some imprecise discomfort, some incipient unease, or a need to rebel, though not manifest, or exteriorized, something that might emerge instead of the conventional mischief and pranks, someone with an indocility more insane than mischievous, more horrific than applauded by his elders? Not five nor three nor even one? The class downstairs had fallen silent, and now, from the balcony, came the dry rattling of the foliage, the golden brown plane trees pattering like the rain. Behind and above, the fan-shaped fronds of a tensely slender palm tree opened to the sun, a pompous projection from the dark scanty garden, without plants, crushed by all the footsteps, with a delicate filigree of iron fence over which the boys climbed wearily during recess. He had the luck, just upon leaving, of spotting a taxi coming slowly down the street, solitary, and now in Via Laietana, as they drove past the main police headquarters—la Jefatura Superior de Policía—while the taxi driver spun out his ideas to resolve the increasingly urgent traffic problem, he stared meditatively at the balconies' thick iron bars, the police standing guard on the sidewalks. He got out at Plaza Ramón Berenguer, a bronze equestrian statue of the gallant count standing tall before the fosse of green grassy spaces which extended to the foot of the old Roman wall, cornered blocks of stone crowned by the bell tower and the buttresses of the Santa Agata's chapel and, rising behind, King Martin's Watchtower, with its rounded arches, the towers and spires of the cathedral, a strict composition of ogival heights and arrogances. On the lawn were old stones, cippi, head-stones, columns, Roman remains, carefully arranged, and black ivy crawling up the walls, and some cypress airily elegantly erect, rough, with gnarled burls. There were still a few minutes remaining and he felt the serenity of walking into those streets from other times, without cars, without the din of traffic, vertical narrows and reliefs, towers, cornices, sober facings, sliced buttresses, gargoyles, reliefs animated by the wingbeats of pigeons, stained-glass windows, long windows, blazoned arches, a deep

portal open to a patio with porticoes, with flights of steps, a
tranquility made almost oppressive as one plunged into the
subterranean passages of the City History Museum, upon
descending to the level of the Roman and Visigoth buildings
excavated from the subsoil of the Gothic Quarter, either from the
entry in the Casa Padellás, in the Plaza del Rey, or more probably
entering from the area around the ancient Palau Reial Major on
the Calle de los Condes de Barcelona. He wandered through
the vast rooms of coffered ceilings, like clear skies, low and
white with the dull buzzing of the air extractors and the insect-
like squalling from some sputtering fluorescent light, women's
heels striking the wooden floor, walkways edged with cord
stretching along between foundations of bulwarks and ruined
walls, disinterred remains, dolios, pools, drains, sewer culverts,
fragments of mosaic floors, columns, mutilated sculptures, funeral amphorae and tombstones engraved with epitaphs, display cases holding ceramics, oil lamps, earthenware
vessels, domestic utensils, a wheel rim, and almost exactly at five
o'clock, without any more delay than the time needed to arrive
at their meeting, he saw him appear from the opposite direction, approaching casually, eyeglasses sparkling, satchel hanging
perpendicular, barely swinging. And they continued the museum
visit together, following the outlines of the ruins spread out in
the quiet light, terreous walls, hollows, fragmentary pavements,
pausing before the display cases, sarcophaguses, models, marble
busts, talking without looking at one another, looking without
seeing those neatly labeled objects.

The analysis of what we might be able to call momentary
logistical factors, by the light of a panorama characterized, on
one side, by the undoubtedly generalized development of the
protest movement and, on the other, by the progressive isolation
and increasingly evident weakness of the inner circle wedded to
power, offers us a somewhat paradoxical balance of appearances.
But the paradox, Daniel, is nothing more than a problem superficially raised or resolved, in such a way that, if we probe a bit
deeper into reality, the apparent dissonances will begin harmonizing until they finally coalesce through distinct phases of an

absolutely logical process. For example, there's nothing casual about us seeing ourselves bound to a situation in which, with respect to the preceding phase, the relationship between forces and possibilities is, in fact, found to be inverted. While the leaders of the principal labor sectors were ruined as a consequence of the arrests caused by the repressive spread of the dictatorship, and from that point on it proved impossible to push the masses of people toward a general strike, currently, the party apparatus is not only being reconstructed cell by cell but also the number of new militants—the vast majority of them young people—has multiplied exponentially, giving us a much wider foundation than any other postwar movement. Furthermore, as the economy is presently in crisis, with no long-term stability, and the emigration of manual labor abroad serves to conjure up the ghost of unemployment, the opportunities for action in the industrial centers are much more favorable, now that the workers don't feel threatened as before with massive reprisals, when there was the constant risk hanging over their heads of being fired from the company and going on to swell the ranks of the army of reserve labor. However more stable the situation of the proletariat, however higher its standard of living, the greater is its ideological maturity and, consequently greater, too, is its willingness to confront and combat both economic grievances and, no less aggressively, political ones. That's why, precisely, they should be the Asturian miners, and the Catalan and Basque working classes—not the lumpen Andalusians—the most traditional and dependable redoubts of all truly revolutionary action, those workers capable of moving beyond blind, sporadic violence, albeit the recent awakening of the southern farm workers denotes a degree of political awareness heretofore unseen and very worthy of being considered in the future, especially because all reports we've received seem to confirm that their movement is somehow related to our own. The situation in the university, however, is found to be characterized, perhaps, by some less positive traits, the fruit, nevertheless, of the considerable degree of development we have achieved. The active opposition minorities are notoriously more numerous than in years past and are more politicized, their organization better aligned with the diverse interests that they represent; but due precisely to this process of radicalization, they are similarly and on the whole more disconnected from the collective student mass and, at this time, can boast of fewer possibilities of converting the university into a true spur of genuine political uprising. It's appropriate to elucidate this point to the maximum, not in order to resign ourselves to the possible failure of the strikes and student demonstrations in solidarity with the Asturian miners we are planning to develop starting Friday but rather in order to take the opportune measures leading to reducing the negative potential of this situation and, in any case, to face realities, in order to comprehend that the simple labor of agitation which we have deployed in summoning people to these demonstrations, distributing pamphlets, gathering signatures and, above all, the fact that the university departments have joined the debate, and one of them, the Faculty of Economics, has approved a motion of support for the striking miners and against police repression, is now, in itself, a giant step forward in the current objective conditions. Moreover, the fact that for the first time the students have let their voice be heard, no longer solely in clandestine newspapers but directly, through their university departments, is such clear proof of the fertility of our tactic of making use of the legal possibilities that I almost dare to say that the role of the remaining anticipated actions, demonstrations, and strikes, need be no other than that of further enhancing and amplifying the political triumph already achieved. Which does not prevent—quite the contrary, it's one more argument in its favor—considering the matter of Friday as vitally important whether we frame it within the actual university protest itself—a fire which must be kept burning at all costs—or if we situate it within the entirety of our politics of national reconciliation against the dictatorship, with its demands for constant, growing, aggressive challenges at all levels and in all areas, in light of the fact that what matters least is whether we meet those demands or not, that the final objective is different, so much more so when the capitalist system, torn by its inherent contradictions, is naturally incapable of satisfying them in any real and definitive way, of applying another politics—not stop-gap solutions, not hot compresses. Our fight progresses in a field where, strictly speaking, it is not fitting to speak of isolated successes and failures without referring continually to the political context considered in its internal dialectic, to the general sense of the work undertaken. And at the present time, given the gap which exists not only between one local sector and another, but also between the different environments of each local sector, our line of strategy is that of stimulating all the partial actions possible, however small they be, as an inevitable prelude to vaster actions that will end up culminating in the anticipated strike on a national scale—precisely, the national political strike—and the subsequent outcome, the overthrow of the dictatorship. For this reason, our primary foreground objective before actions like what's coming on Friday, an objective which must not be confused with our principal objective, is no other than that of preventing the pre-existing rift between politicized minorities and the student movement from becoming dangerously accentuated. It's essential to not lose this contact with the mass of students although it might be a momentary lessening of the political level of the actions already begun; we have the obligation to establish closer ties with the student masses, making their challenges our own, joining with them in mutual understanding, galvanizing them with an aggressive program of protest capable of helping to precipitate the surrounding potential energies. As a vanguard organization, our role consists of this, to be attentive and to know how to put into play all the elements capable of consolidating people's willpower and to widen the operative base, so that our final objectives will appear framed in a more general panorama of demands, such as those specific to the university and, above all, those proceeding from the specific history of Catalonia. This is the direction our work must take. Meaning, aside from the fact that in university circles we find ourselves avoiding an impasse, perhaps the one which precedes the final assault, our principal effort in this phase of consolidation and reorganization—of biding our time in winter quarters, as it were—must be to move toward emphasizing more than ever problems such as Catalan nationalism and the Catalan people's politico-cultural aspirations for national independence. In other words, from this point on, to raise the most appropriate challenges so they take root and develop in the present, and in the future, to unify, around our axioms, the overwhelming majority of this youth of bourgeois extraction which fills the lecture halls of the University of Barcelona. It's about a question already present, in the street, not created by us, but now our duty, if we want to prevent the forces of the bourgeoisie and the anti-Francoist petite bourgeoisie from distorting our traditional position in this regard, the position of a working-class party, from raising our flag as their own, as some exclusive standard of bourgeois nationalism. If we wish to avoid this, our duty is to assume the vanguard of legitimate popular aspirations and channel them, and give them a correct and revolutionary solution according to the Marxist-Leninist postulates of the national problem. Let's recap.

Escala, a fascinating personality, all logic and realism, rigor and method, implacable and precise like a machine as well as in his theoretical analyses, in his expositions expressed in dialectical terms, beyond operations only formally true, like in the practical verification of such analyses, in their modifying application of an objective reality of whose examination they were, at the same time, a product. A man of action, equally fast and reflective in decisions, serious, inflexible, meticulous, resolute, cautious to the maximum, with his notes hidden in the false bottom of a matchbox, in his packets of cigarette papers, on a candy wrapper, his codes, his security methods for attending meetings, his system of making the telephone numbers which he wrote down unrecognizable by removing from them some previously determined digit, his habit of not leaving behind even a single cigarette butt.

What should reality be called? said Fortuny.

They were wondering if he might live in secrecy like other members of the leadership or if, as seemed most likely, he concealed his true activities under a completely legal situation. In that case, given his education and abilities, how could he not be some well-known person, at least in intellectual circles, especially because nothing in that world, as likely as not, followed any deliberate purpose of Escala's, of avoiding public life, of being completely devoted to the revolutionary fight, a complete dedication full of stimuli and suggestions, an impassioned perspective indicated by the clarity of his conduct and his objectives, by his necessary withdrawals, an enterprise which made any other task, by comparison, diminished, contingent, ephemeral, and absurdly marginal. And they considered the attractions and risks that, in contrast to the monotonous and insignificant exercise of practicing the law, could offer them this double life, an anodyne exterior hiding a pseudonym popularized through clandestine writings, a subversive action quite dangerous enough to keep all the police in the country in a state of anxiety, a political responsibility which grew in secret and, in the decisive moment, to appear at the front of the revolutionary forces which like a phantom army would sprout up in the street, raised against the established powers, in an uncertain fight. Fortuny insisted, however, on the convenience of creating for himself a solid academic position, not now as a personal future but rather, above all, as a political platform for the future; a professorship, for example, he said. With Federico, however, it wasn't possible to talk seriously about these things, always with his little smiles and reservations when he found out that they'd attended some committee meeting. What, what does this boss of yours matter, he'd say, or simply, what does Mr. H. matter, with reticence and sarcasm ringing in his voice directed especially at Fortuny, and Fortuny, catching his drift, accepting the game, patiently began to defend the theoretical principles or practical details called into question, while Raúl rarely joined in. But when he did, as if, in Federico's presence, he couldn't resist pestering Fortuny, he contradicted him and recanted himself to take Federico's side, in order to back him up with some obvious sophism or joke.

Saint Lucas is right, said Federico. If we manage to raise enough hell for them to close the university, now that will be accomplishing a lot. We've dedicated so much just to play at conspirators, to organize committees, liaison committees, and committees of committees, that we're no longer capable of

organizing anything else. And this business of taking advantage
of the legal opportunities seems to me a Machiavellian folly.
Why make demands through channels that we never tire of
denouncing as antidemocratic? What kind of revolution is this
that makes use of the same legality it claims it wants to destroy?
What you'd have to do, instead of wasting time infiltrating it,
is to create a new and parallel power, a real power, which will
turn the official legality into fiction. This is playing their game
and Saint Lucas says that he's fed up with games, and he's right.

Alright, alright, let's not kid around, said Fortuny. I respect
Cuadras as much as you do and I consider him to be a valuable person, he writes very good material. Or put it this way, as
a friend and as a writer, he's very good, but when it comes to
politics, forget it, man, he understands nothing. And not because
what he says isn't true, but rather because, although it's true, he's
politically incorrect. Those are two very distinct points of view,
and Cuadras, for however much he does, will never know how
to see reality in terms of a political perspective.

They let Federico drive them to Miramar, to stretch their
legs, he said, to get a bit of fresh air, and the car sat parked
underneath a streetlamp's cone of light, and they wandered along
the deserted sidewalk, stopping here and there, leaning on the
parapet. Below them the glassy reflections of the port looked
deeper and deeper. Speak: also like a reflection in the water,
not yet like a footprint in the sand, still looking at the present
and not the past, formulating oneself while formulating what
one believes, explaining to yourself in the act of explaining it,
meaning, creating what you believe or wish to believe or what
you wish would seem that you believe. They'd spent the afternoon
at Adolfo's house, arguing the whole time. Adolfo hadn't
intervened, nor Aurora, seated at his feet, next to the record
player, taking no notice as if she were part of some group of
sculptures, the record spinning round and round, tiny inexorable
singers, hybrid tendernesses again and again, infinitely, barbarous
ire or delirium, exalted triumph of death. And Adolfo ended up
interrupting them with his listening, this is the best thing in the
world, directed at Raúl, as if they hadn't heard it enough already,

and turning up the volume on the record player he made them be quiet, whether they were listening or not, *quantus tremor est futurus*, the choirs interrupting, uninterrupted torrent of madness, cries, bugles, *liber scriptus proferetur*, and then we will see in the lower part, underground, the black fire and the claws, naked, contorted, clawed open and burnt, the serpent sent to strike at a friar's sinful sex, condemnation into which the reprobates are hurled, right and left, from the tombs broke open by the tumult, chaos of those abducted and stolen away, angels and demons, reptilian bats, dragons, Capricorns, celestial wings, and there above, in glory, above meeknesses of beatitudes, a rupturing of roaring vermillion, rent asunder in a full cataclysm of blues, the Incarnate, the Born, the Suffered, the Dead, the Entombed, the Resurrected, with his arms extended as a discoverer or navigator now come to demand accounts, open wounds on his hands, descending at the vanguard of a whirling headlong rush of exterminators just as implacably just as justly implacable, final judgment, a grandiose miniature belonging to the so-called Missal of Santa Eulalia, on display in the Chapterhouse Room of the Cathedral, masterpiece of the master Destorrents, the very image, at the same time, of the cathedral which serves it as refuge, this cathedral of lugubrious sepulchers and cryptical darknesses, stone beneath stone beneath the which there is nothing more but necrosis and folded layers of ash, and on high, the glorious light, stained-glass and rose windows projecting themselves in a circumference one could easily imagine eternally crossed by reflections, by polychromatic incidences refracted upon the gold of the altarpieces. Raúl drank in silence, careful not to look at Aurora, seemingly lost in thought and meditative, feigning not listening more than to be polite, or at least trying his best to look like what he was pretending, as if, at heart, disinterested, as if for the sake of pure respect and deference toward Adolfo, as if especially so many personal questions could separate them, noble, decently.

It was the night before, at most the night before the night before. Federico came by to pick him up after dinner, and they had coffee together. Raúl talked to him about Aurora, said that he was beginning to question her sincerity. Federico asked him about what, in what way.

I don't know, in everything. Politically, for example.

Of course. What did you think? C'mon, man, it's obvious that Nefertiti doesn't, as they say, give a flying fuck about politics. Ana María, yes, she does, you see. Ana María is sincere. Besides, the fact that her face looks exactly like a squid puts her in an objective situation comparable to that of the proletariat: she's got nothing to lose.

But the thing is, Nefertiti's case is very curious. She's the daughter of exiles and it seems that her father was one of those men who wouldn't listen to any talk about coming back to Spain as long as Franco was in power. I mean, she grew up in the most politicized environment possible.

That's why, that's why she's already immune. She's a communist because she fell in with our group. She could just as well have hooked up with some Carlist bunch, and now she'd be a Carlist.

Sitting by the windows, either careless or sleepy, he rambled on between yawns about the advantages of having received the most reactionary kind of upbringing imaginable, despite however much conditioning that might imply, because being raised in such a way awoke, in those capable of overcoming it, an inevitable predisposition for radicalism and intolerance. In that way I'm an old-fashioned kind of man, he said. The best saying is that one about spare the rod and spoil the child. It's what normally allows a sour-tempered person to become most broadly developed. And there's nothing that makes one quite so stupid as these modern pedagogical methods, with classes designed to seem like games, just inane, without any challenges. Old-fashioned, I'm an old-fashioned man. He looked at him cheerfully, and as the conversation drifted toward the dangerous waters of raising the child to be a sociable being, in conformity with contemporary society, Raúl had to redirect the focus to Nefertiti.

Well, of course, in the case of Nefertiti you can't talk about intolerance. On the contrary, she's one of the freest people I know. And I warn you that this, too, has its advantages. Our

relationship, for example, has been totally open, without the
exclusiveness or fidelity that all women demand. In that way, at
least, she's like me, very independent. She's always done just what
she feels like, and I do the same, and it's never occurred to either
one of us to ask the other one what they're doing or to make
scenes or anything. We've never really felt tied to each other,
not ever. This has got nothing to do with politics, of course,
but what I mean is that meeting a woman like Aurora is a nice
break. When it runs its course, we can go our separate ways and
still be friends. At least she's got this going for her: she knows
how to behave herself.

She was among the first ones caught, under the porticoes
swept by the water cannons, among the students who had
remained on the periphery of the crushing crowd throttled
by the narrow doors and interior staircases, a stumbling staggering avalanche toward the garden and the patios that had
happened when, as the explosives were set off, the police charged,
a compact mass bristling with billy clubs that poured in through
the vestibule over the broken glass and fallen sopping placards,
and Raúl saw a policeman point him out with his finger, then
he felt a strong blow on his arm, next to his neck, while he
stood there as if blocked, against a military jacket, and they
pinned his arms behind his back, lifting up on them, pulling
him along doubled over, shoving him, into the lecture hall, and
they locked him in with others, a few of them all soaking wet
and everyone battered and bruised to one degree or another. And
then they made them come out one by one, at gunpoint, and
started putting them into vans, the plaza completely cordoned
off, full of cops on foot and horseback who chased away groups
of onlookers, rerouted traffic. As he looked around vainly trying
to spot Aurora he saw two or three policemen bring Federico out,
almost dragging him, handcuffed, struggling in his jacket, and
at police headquarters he caught a glimpse of him again from
the peephole in the underground cells, after they'd booked and
fingerprinted him they searched his pockets, *tamquam reus*, a
cell where there was already some stranger who asked him what
he knew about it all, with whom he had nothing in common,

and the cell started filling up, all of them looking at the stranger, all somewhat disoriented, some stranger who didn't look like a student, and so many detainees kept arriving that they had to move the whores somewhere else to make room, or maybe the drag queens, or at least this is what they understood the guard was giving orders about, let's see, move the girls, and in one cell they started to sing *Gaudeamus Igitur* but they made them shut up immediately before anybody else got the urge to join them, and as the first names were called to make their statements the place started to go quiet, and when he saw Federico through the peephole he asked the guard to open the door and tried to meet him at the urinal, and Federico said, Daniel in the lions' den, and they immediately separated them, move it, move it, Federico toward a cell further away from the stairs, and he ended up reappearing partially visible in his field of vision, below the peephole, when they called him to make a statement without him coming back down after a short while, like the others, who came back downstairs saying that they'd heard shouts, saying that the police had discovered a mimeograph machine, saying that somebody had squealed, saying that they were beating the shit out of some student from Sciences, that they were searching everybody's house, that they'd made a film of the demonstration, talking about it, more and more frightened, and he stayed there glued to the peephole and then he heard his name, Raúl Ferrer. Badly lit stairs, iron bars, the guardroom, more stairs, blind corridors, doors, skylights, inner offices, interconnected offices, cold throughout the whole way, his hands in his pockets, preceded and followed by two sad-faced cops, and the inspector invited him to have a seat. There was a calendar with a high mountain landscape in colors, and the inspector made small talk; he wanted to know if he was there because of what happened at the university and he talked about how when he was a student, too, before the war, and about his admiration for Ortega and the poetry of Juan Ramón, and when the voices that reached them through the skylight increased in violence and those inarticulate sounds became clearly defined as a kind of cry or whining he smiled at him, his eyes luminous, before, naturally, they took him into the

adjoining office, which had a window with translucent panes
and that neon light so annoying, buzzing and chirping like an
insect, and he entertained himself contemplating how the glass
turned clear in the light of dawn until a man dressed all in
black appeared who shouted at him to stand up. Are you tired?
Well, look kid, I'm even more so, just look how things stand.
Two or three others had come in, staring at him in silence, and
when they removed the Coca-Cola-style wall calendar, showing
a picture of a girl with long blond hair and big showy tits, in the
little window frame he caught a quick glimpse of some shining
pupils. They left him alone again and, after a short while, in
the office where they took down his statement, the cop in black
offered him a cigarette as the interrogation started, questions
and routine answers which he dictated laboriously to the typist,
questions intoned with sarcasm and a certain lack of enthusiasm,
assuming the answer to be yes, no doubt, no reply necessary,
he'd learned about the demonstration by reading a handbill, if
he didn't know, of course it's clear, who were the ones responsible for destroying the portraits of Franco, and for setting off
the explosives, if he didn't maintain relations or contact with
some clandestine organization, if he hadn't incited his friends
to cause a disturbance, if he hadn't shouted subversive slogans,
if he didn't know one Francisco Guillén, student of economics
and, once the statement was signed, personal questions, if he
was happy, for example, or what were his political ideas and
his religious feelings, questions offered an equally concise and
negative response: I'm not a strong supporter of Franco, I'm not
interested in politics, I have no religious beliefs, etcetera but not,
for that reason, accepted with any less friendliness. We don't persecute anyone for ideas, out there each person is free to believe
what they think, they said. What we do persecute is when those
ideas are demonstrated with subversive motives. And they took
him out into the hallway, and he saw that Federico was sitting a
little further down the hall, his expression alert and expectant,
and as soon as the cop in black stuck his head out a door and
shouted, Jenaro, get these guys out of here, another one of the
cops who was there said to Federico, alright, and tell your family

that next time there's no need to move heaven and earth, it's not the end of the world. Nothing happens to the guy who's done nothing wrong. And here you've seen we're not cannibals eating human flesh. The same inspector who'd accused him of being Federico Quintana, the one who'd knocked down the portraits of Franco, and who had given him three minutes to talk if he didn't want them to tune him up, because he wasn't saying a word, like a communist, three minutes which Federico watched closely on the clock until it ran out, and then he said, time's up, and the policeman knocked him down with the first backhand, this one's a cocky stuck-up little son of a bitch.

But they didn't touch me again.

They must have noticed you're a masochist.

No way, the flesh must be tamed, subdued, disciplined. This is what's called an experience. Getting arrested, I mean. Mr. H. will help you see its positive aspects right away. It's a forge, a school, etcetera.

They ate breakfast on a café patio, euphoric and haggard, their faces seemingly illuminated by the early morning sun reflected off the sidewalks. They'd gone inside to the telephone in the back, on the right, through the sordid interior sown with wet sawdust, to call their respective houses, Federico saying, it's always back and to the right, and Raúl, this reminds me of the police headquarters, and on the way they cleaned up in the men's room, lightly, hurriedly, without stopping their chatter, exchanging conjectures, reconstructing the events. They suddenly changed their behavior, said Federico. It must have been when my parents started using their influence. It seems that they showed up at the Headquarters and, since they wouldn't let them see me, they got the governor to intervene or I don't know what. Like a gentleman, I've come out like a gentleman. From the looks of it, going into my house, the police shit their pants. And Raúl: my father also just told me that he got in touch with I don't know how many people. And Federico: it's the police who started all the trouble with their searches. The only thing that pisses me off is that they haven't returned my address book. Did the guy with the mustache question you, too? And Raúl:

with the mustache? Yes, but not your guy. That one dressed all in black. Listen, and Nefertiti? Do you know if they released her? And Federico: Nefertiti? Of course. She was wonderful. And Federico explained how he'd been in the next room when they questioned her and he'd listened to it through the skylight. She stammered a lot, and I heard them saying: this girl is an idiot, he said. They released her right away. I think they let all the girls go. They asked what she was doing in the very front line and she said that she'd wanted to get out of there, right away, but that, when she saw so many billy clubs in front of her, it scared her. A truly great performance. They'd ordered another café con leche and more ensaimadas and, as the waiter brought their coffee and was clearing away the other cups, they sat back in their chairs, as if lost in their thoughts.

Then Raúl said: the one who I'm sure I didn't see, not even a hair, is Adolfo Cuadras.

He leaned on the table again and watched the coffee-soaked sugar lump on his spoon slowly dissolve, without raising his eyes, but Federico's sarcastic tone as he said that guy, that guy, made it easy to imagine him shaking his head like one who wants to feign annoyance, laughing with his eyes.

That guy, that guy. He's our evangelist but he lets himself miss an episode like this one. Bad, very bad for a writer. I always tell him that, as a writer, he's got to try everything, seek new experiences. Everything, you've got to try everything.

Go on, keep cracking jokes, one day you'll find yourself in the shit without knowing how it happened.

They talked about Guillén. Federico said that the one who'd squealed was Puigbó, that they'd found him with a packet of propaganda and then the guy spilled the beans. I don't think they caught Guillén. He must be hiding out. What's going on is that Puigbó must have said that he was the one who passed him the propaganda, and now they'll charge him for the explosives and the pictures of Franco. He'll have to run up to France. And Raúl: and García Moll? Nothing, said Federico. If his name hasn't come up yet, that means it won't. They also talked about the advisability that some comrades should hide out for a few days no matter what, and they studied the precautions they should take for themselves, starting with the supposition, more than probable, that they were going to be followed and that they would have to be very careful using the telephone, how to reorganize themselves as soon as possible, of recontacting Fortuny, Fortuny, who, at these hours, would be out walking with Escala around the sunny cloisters of the cathedral, spacious corridors, their floors worn smooth, with sepulchral stones interlaid among the flagstones, inscriptions, emblems seemingly filed down, barely decipherable, around the patio enclosed by iron gates, framed by the spare, meticulous openwork of the transept arches, the patio, the quiet mass of palms and magnolias, the Well of the Geese, the shrine of the lavatorium, cold stone, fountain of clear bubbles and oozing mossy excrescences, with the sparkling spout which seems to center the attention on the keystone of the shadowy vault, in its high, jutting relief, Saint George battling the dragon, brambly vertigo, the flight of feints and claw strokes which precedes the decisive blow, the final victory, triumph and transmutation, Saint George, rival of Perseus and Siegfried, rescuer of captive princesses, destroyer of chimeras, of the mythic griffin which, once dead, becomes a rosebush or a maiden no longer spellbound, Riquilda, mystic rose of April. He'd entered through the portico of Saint Ivo, on the Calle Condes de Barcelona, one more visitor among those wandering beneath the lofty naves, like leafy palms or cedars, lightly visible above, vaults deepened by the tenebrous transparency of the stained-glass windows, enhanced by their Gothic ribs, ribs which, as they meet in tight knots, at the bottom of the column, turn shadowy and join together, rising black heights, uncertain emptiness, a penumbra in which irradiations and golds took shape bit by bit, the thorny darkness of the choir stalls emerging in the center, penumbra gradually populated by concrete presences, columns with bases worn smooth by passing hands, shiny contours, pews worn thin from use, golden images, patinas, fulgencies, smokes, odor of wax, forms of worshippers facing the iron bars of the side chapels, gazing upon inspirational effigies of special devotion, arrayed before the polychromatic altar of the Virgin of the Rosary, for example, or before that of Saint Severus, facing the altarpiece of the Transfiguration, before the soberly sculpted sarcophagus of San Raimundo of Penyafort, or, above all, in the Chapel of the Holy Sacrament, kneeling before the Christ of Lepanto, Corpus Christi, brown and contorted, defender of the faith, protector of poor shameful men and whores, Ecce Homo of dusty carnal blackness elevated above the flickering altar lamp, ephemeral flames one puff away from extinction, undulating in a single tension or fusion, waxen ex-votos, humility and decorum, genuflections, mantillas, figures kneeling, seated, kerchiefs poorly placed over long curly manes, hands clasped on laps, hats resting on knees, reverent bald heads, canes or crutches, deformities, a child wailing, mourning clothes, grilles and confessionals, mutterings, sacramental discretion. Like one visitor more of those that were praying contemplating the polychromatic carvings, the gilded curling crests, lingering before the ambulatory side chapels, forming the apse in the sad light of the stained-glass windows, toward the coming and going in and out through the cloister doorway, the cloister obfuscated by the palm trees' crowns, of the magnolia leaves lustrous from the rain, the spacious corridors, with their flagstones worn smooth, viscous stone, gargoyles spouting cascades, deliquescent colors of the leaded stained-glass windows.

A coffee bar rebel. That's what Lucas is. He takes himself for a writer and it disgusts him to collaborate on such anonymous tasks as writing for *Realidad*, just a simple underground university newspaper. He must think it's beneath him, he must think that it's a lot to ask of a professional like him, that it's a job for some nobody, anybody, you, me: that it means nothing to him. A typical reaction from a pure intellectual. No, your observation doesn't surprise me at all. After all, you mustn't forget, his father is one of those lawyers who works as a bloodhound for financial groups, one of those persons who came up after the war, taking advantage of their condition as ex-combatants, a rich little dandy from a family fallen on hard times that, if not for the war, would never have been anything more than some no-name shyster, the most immoral kind of individual, with a sweetheart who knows everyone in Barcelona. And that's how the son turned out. Like in the case of Esteva, he's a product of his family's connections, and don't start defending Esteva simply because he's a friend of yours. Judge his attitude dispassionately, put aside the appreciation you might have for him and other subjective motivations, separate them from the strict consideration of Esteva as one militant more. Judge him impartially and you'll find no more than a slight degree of difference between his attitude and Lucas's, and then only outwardly, not any deep internal difference. No, Daniel, let's be serious; Esteva is a very similar case, just as their respective family circles are similar, although to tell you the truth, the comparison will put Lucas in a bad light because his father is a paid defense attorney for the interests of the monopolist oligarchy, meanwhile Esteva's father, as far as being a bank director and, above all, as a member of a dynasty of financiers, is fully integrated into that oligarchy, something always preferable, now that his position has at least greater solidity, more sociological coherence. And there's only one thing worse than the capitalists themselves: their lackeys. But, don't fool yourself, Esteva's joining the party is, more than anything, the product of a temporary crisis of conscience, including the well-known reaction against family and social circles. Meaning, the search for a solution to personal problems, not to objective problems. A defect, unfortunately, very typical of the pure intellectual. Of course, there are exceptions, like you, like Ferrán, but, lamentably, the intellectual who plays at being a revolutionary is frequently moved to do so by hidden anger, by idealized arguments, often concealing a hypercritical and antisocial personality, one that is most definitely ill. Those are not the sane, healthy principles of the proletariat, class interests, factors based on economics—all nonexistent in the case before us. No, such individuals do not make firm and steadfast companions, nor can they, because their roots are neither firm nor sure. We're not talking here about true, devoted comrades; in these kinds of people there is almost always some artifice which, if they don't make a great effort to overcome, always, unfailingly, ends up creating complications for us. So, the best thing to do is think it over calmly and consider it carefully, from the beginning, the elements in question, accepting how much good they can do for our struggle, without allowing yourself to be deceived. It's the only way to avoid future disillusionment and fatal consequences. And when their class conditioning ends up dominating them and they turn out to be the creatures of their class that they really are, so much the worse for them. The history of revolutionary movements is full of these inevitable desertions that, as we already know, usually lead to the individual's total frustration, to his ruin, not only moral, but also professional, and I would almost dare to say physical. It is they, not the party, who come out on the losing end. Fortunately, for the revolution, there is no one who is irreplaceable. Let Lucas continue, let him go on with his stories which, on the other hand, apparently don't get censored, which could already be an explanation, a manifestation of unconfessed impotence. If not, why not take advantage of the legal possibilities that censorship offers, however thin they might be, and thus be able to reach the people, making censorship, in consequence, a useless instrument? Is it that the people, the Spanish people precisely, are too deaf to hear what truly interests them? Does he think that people can't understand him, which would be bad enough, or rather that they have no interest in what he might be able to tell them, which would be worse, although perhaps more accurate? Be that as it may, however, doesn't there exist here an evident aristocratic attitude, an indubitable undervaluation of the popular taste, of the tastes and the interests which, in the end, should constitute the touchstone of the true, legitimate intellectual revolutionary? Let Lucas continue with his stories and Esteva with his professional doubts. Also these indecisions, Esteva hesitating between mathematics and economics, Lucas between law and his fondness for the pen, ultimately demonstrate that they are hardly serious. The thing is, with this type of people there's always something of the spoiled boy lurking in the background. Well fine, first let them grow up and then we'll see. A writer… Who's he writing for, then, if he doesn't publish what he writes and then shirks his duties when it comes to collaborating on *Realidad* and some other underground publications? It's clear as far as I can see: he doesn't write for anybody. His contempt for praxis is one of the chief characteristics of the pure intellectual. Given over to his subjective speculations, the pure intellectual frequently seems to forget that we, the truly intellectual revolutionaries, unlike bourgeois thinkers, may not limit ourselves to theorizing about reality, we must transform it. We don't pretend that the truth and exemplification of our arguments are manifest only in books, but rather also in praxis, a praxis which even as it sanctions those arguments, also creates, by virtue of its own dialect, a new analysis. And what are the regime's recent and various concessions made in response to, if not to the latest urgent demands of the working class, an application in the field of praxis of the theoretical analyses of the objective reality carried out first and foremost by the vanguard of the proletariat, the communist party? Let Lucas write his stories. That won't alter in any way, shape, or form the fact that the true history is written by the masses.

The smashing rain shredded the patio gray, thrashed the pond and the black ivy, the ever-fluttering geese, shattered into turbulent mercury stars, poured off the long shadowy leaves, spattered the stone, and everything became a great cascade from gargoyles and shimmering liquid cornices, slippery viscous stained-glass windows in that cloister of sharp arches and worn flagstones, framed by the parameters of the cathedral and the Romanesque chapel of Santa Lucía and, in its outer wings, along the Calle del Obispo and the Calle de la Piedad, an exterior of severe reliefs, the sharp-edged prismatic buttresses, the symmetrical facade and its enormous windows, austere iron grilles, rows of finials, water-spitting figures spouting down from high above, fantastic knights, riders with extravagant mounts, hounds, serpents, unicorns, gryphons and Tarasques with gaping empty mouths standing out in this crowded group of naked horizontal masses of stone, with the bell towers, steeples, and spires striking the note of verticality, dominant cathedral, raised on the summit of Mount Taber, above the city, above the town stretched out before the sea, a domineering town, haughty, airy arrogances all across the area from the northeast flank of Monjuí, Montjuich,

with a knight dallying with a lady in the foreground, at the
foot of a tree, and, now on the luxuriant verdure of the rolling
plain, a variegated composition of orchards and gardens, a
farmer plowing with four oxen outside the city walls, before
the Almerian walls, a double ring of fortifications encircling the
city, the belfries, the clustered high-rises, and beyond, a fertile
distance of hills and cultivated fields populated by small towns
and, along the coastline, between promontories and shoals, the
port, the shipyards, the suitable and sandy beach, perfect for
tourneys and jousts, and a full arcing rainbow touching down in
the east, over the coast, in a meticulously feathered sky, exalting
the fallen rain, the merry laughing sea and the jocund earth, the
long and spacious sea, more full than the lagoons of Ruidera.
There were argosies, galleys strung with pennants and streamers
waving and fluttering in the wind, and they swept the placid
waters, and from within sounded bugles, trumpets, and oboes
with soft bellicose accents, while in the city, upon lovely horses
and to the sound of many oboes and kettledrums and the noise
of hawk bells, out rode an endless train of knights bedecked
in dazzling livery, and all the people seemed infused with sudden delight, the joy of San Juan, radiant solstices of summer,
and from the galleys the soldiers fired their guns into the wind
in festive salvos and those atop the city's walls and ramparts
responded in kind, and with a dreadful thunder the heavy artillery broke the air, turbid with intoxicating clouds of gunpowder.
A great expanse of sky and, like every summer, a pattering burst
of trilling swallows grazing the towers, vertigo, flight reiterated,
enthralling phoenix, the city transfigured, rebuilt upon its own
ruins, reconstructed, superimposed, juxtaposed, implicated,
interlined, expanded, raised up, enclosed, locked away, compartmentalized, fragmented, cornered, bees bottled up in cork
hives, deconstructed, demolished, buried, resuscitated from its
own ashes, cryptic dilapidated landscape, ruins, roofless walls
beneath cloudless, transparent skies, quiet light and the smell
of dead earth, coppery necropolis, historic mausoleum of splendors, glories, and apogees, an entire past petrified, simple earthy
vestiges, roughness and crudity of those that once were, oh the

pain, the sorrow, delicacies and urbanities, harmonious symmetries, classic severities of the Roman metropolis, suffocated
panorama, its length and breadth spanned by the creaking rope
footbridges, beneath the humming air extractors and locust-shrill
neon radiance, vast rooms of coffered ceilings, a white succession of low planes suspended over an itinerary of sliced-up, sec-
tioned buildings, fragments of wall, shards of mosaics, remains of
pavement, baths and cisterns, drains, sewers, truncated columns,
funerary amphorae, sarcophaguses, pedestals, torsos and heads,
busts, mutilated statues. The visitor will now have to undo and
retrace the route he has followed, passing by the ticket counter
at the entryway, and he shall discover in Hall D, and at his feet,
some Roman silos or dolia, and some plinths placed back in the
same spot where they were discovered. In Hall E, dedicated to
the sculptures found in the excavations, the visitor will be able
to admire: a mutilated statue of Diana, along with the torso of
a young man and various marble heads, awaiting identification.
By contrast, some outstanding pieces, the heads of the Empress
Agrippina and the Emperor Antoninus Pius.

A bust, supposedly of the Empress Faustina, daughter of the
former and the wife of Marcus Aurelius.

A model of the Temple of Augustus.

A relief sculpture with a lithe dancer, worked from Montjuich
stone.

A bronze statuette known as The Venus of Barcelona.

Because, if it is indeed true that we defend the unquestionable political and cultural personality of Catalonia, we do so as
communists, meaning, as the vanguard of the Catalan working
classes, for them and representing them and without, on the other
hand, prejudice against the interests of our fellow workers in the
other towns and cities of Spain. We reject the old Catalanism,
the traditional bourgeois nationalism, which foundered during
the Civil War, more bourgeois than truly national, and its selfish class interests camouflaged in folklore and sentimentalism.
And if before the Civil War, the upper-crust Catalan bourgeoisie,
already driven by its fear of the proletariat on the march, was the
first to betray its own cause when, with Cambó and company, it

abandoned the ship of nationalism and its crew of petite bourgeoisie and middling hands, upon repeating, with the help of Primo de Rivera, the Paviada—the coup d'etat led by General Manuel Pavía y Rodríguez de Alburquerque—which so effectively helped put an end to the First Republic, since then, in the postwar period, it has done nothing more than ratify its betrayal by completely and definitively joining the Spanish monopolist oligarchy, thus bringing its expansionist interests into a phase of sharp conflict not only with the interests of working-class factions but also with those of their old separatist allies. But in the same way that it failed in its role as the leading class, in the same way that it failed in its political management, it will fail, it is already failing, in its economic management, and now it is the turn of the Catalan working classes who, raising their old flags charged with revolutionary tradition, must build, alongside their remaining brothers in Spain, Euskadi, and Galicia, a community of socialist nations. Meanwhile, our party, the Catalan communist party, though rather well and intimately integrated with the Spanish communist party of Spain, still remains an outside organization, and this reality already, not coincidentally, constitutes in itself the badge of complete political authenticity. The fact that a significant portion of the Catalan proletariat, the greater part, I would venture to say, is comprised of non-Catalan workers—a result of Andalusian and Castilian emigration—is important merely from a systematic and economic point of view, given that Catalonia's assimilative capacity is a fact well-known to all. It was finely demonstrated in the Civil War, when the Murcians, so-called at that time, acted in defense of their class rights, in solidarity with their own Catalan companions, meaning, as a Catalan working class, without any evidence of competing interests. Their class rights, not the interests and privileges of the Catalan bourgeoisie camouflaged as national rights, this middle class which, after failing in its attempts to enrich itself with the political monopoly of Spanish capitalism in its incipient imperialist stage, ventured forth on the roads of separatism in order to then utilize the rebirth of the old national dreams as an element of negotiation with the central power, with whose most reactionary sectors it eventually allied itself.

Glimpses of display cases, vestiges of the primitive settlements of the Barcelona plain, corroded wagon-wheel rims, pottery shards, Campanian, Iberian, Greek ceramics, remains of the diverse pre-Roman cultures who settled within the geographical region of the present-day city. A display case on the mezzanine floor of the Casa Padellás, at the patio level, between the steps leading down to the excavations and the staircase to the upper floors, a historic itinerary commencing on the underground level of the ancient Palacio Real Mayor, from the ruins in the Roman forum, a progression of subterranean spaces, a series of enclosed ceilings above a panorama of columns and pedestals, mosaic floors, pilasters, columns and capitals, bases of equestrian statues, sculptures, togaed torsos, marble hands, reliefs, votive stones, altar stones and vaulted niches, epigraphs, funerary inscriptions, archeological pieces belonging to the opulent city of the Augustan age, the majority of them unearthed in the course of excavations carried out along the foundations of the city's outer wall, Barcino's protective belt rebuilt in the third century with the rubble of Augustan Barcino, razed by the first barbarian invasions, defensive works to whose construction the new city consecrated—literally, you might say—all its resources, perhaps in expiation of its impious past, its paganism, its dissolute customs, the Christianizing city of the Early Roman Empire, with such a thoroughly monumental wall, its imposing presence completely enclosing a poor and diminished urban nucleus, without any luxury whatsoever nor any trace of earlier splendors, to judge by the visible remains in Rooms G and H, the latter excavated right underneath the Casa Padellás itself, the museum's central location, as a way of extending the underground hall from the Plaza del Rey, the wall's inner face dominating an area of ruinous rooms and masonry walls, outlines of streets and sewers, drains, cisterns, modest constructions with all their domestic elements, fornax, silos, millstones, useful objects, utensils now displayed in glass cases, glasses and glass jars, loom weights, lamps, punches and pins, personal effects labeled, all that situated at a lower level than what the Visigoth necropolis occupied, centuries later, now all covered over with earth, buried

beneath the sepulchers of tiles and urns now set out next to the
foundations of the wall, a stony perimeter embedded in earlier
constructions, digested by the city in its development, residue
of residue, prevailing wall upon which so many others were built,
to serve as protection for the new medieval towns, outlying
suburbs developed successively beyond the walls, la Ribera, el
Arrabal, San Pedro de las Puellas, expansions tightly enclosed by
the new fortified Gothic walls of Jaume the Conqueror and
Pedro the Ceremonious, expansions slowly erected and fortified,
modernized until well into the eighteenth century and finally,
with romantic impetus, demolished by need of expansion, for
the sake of the urban demands of the age, the city's limits and
buffer zones now surpassed by the Ensanche, the nineteenth-
century quadrangle staked out and developed along the entire
width of the so-called Barcelona plain, absorbing the ancient
towns, invading the fields planted long ago, extending to the
shadow of stout, delicately curved walls, Gothic crenellations,
watchful battlements, gates and portcullises, escarpments,
posterns, bridges reflected in moats, in the virtual oscillating
skies, fascinating image, sublimated, evaporated, vanished, forms
prefigured and survived by these others, so long buried and
blended into the earth and, at last, flourishing anew, period to
period, from the entrails of the old quarter, its outline excavated,
cleared, patiently rediscovered by the municipal pickaxe,
progressively cleaned and free from adherences, residual traces
of the concealing edifices now demolished, panels of tiles, floral
wallpapers, plaster moldings, vanished staircases, black chimney
stains. The Roman wall, irregular nine-sided polygon with a
current measurement of just over one kilometer around the
perimeter, according to the plan on display on the ground floor
of the Casa Padellás, Room Number One, at the terminus of the
route through the museum's subterranean section, a wall not
hard to imagine defying the air with its seventy towers and
seventy-times-seven battlements enclosing Barcino, a populace
of urban structures still recognizable today, centered around the
current Plaça de San Jaume, situated at the approximate location
of the ancient forum, the intersection of the Cardus Maximus

with the Decumanus, meaning, the current intersection of Calle Fernando and Calle Jaime I, crossing the current intersection of Calle Obispo and Calle de la Ciudad, the city of Mons Taber, a colony established by the legions of the Republic on an isolated promontory, surrounded by marshlands that safeguard it from the pre-existing nearby towns, Barkeno, or Laye of the Iberians, a people probably Etruscanized, a nuclei preceded in turn by earlier elements in the region, as it seems, from the expansion of diverse peoples, Celtic, Illyrian or Pre-Celtic, Almerian or Proto-Iberian, etcetera, invasions crossing over a more ancient background, amalgam of vestiges of cultures by then already completely extinguished, Pyrenean culture, cave culture, dolmenic culture, beaker culture, etcetera, migrations and meanderings which, doubtless, knew the nearby surroundings of that promontory jutting out at the sea's edge like a natural fortress, shelter of sailors and colonizers, beaches where Heracles or Hercules, as his ninth ship arrived, the others scattered by the storm, must have founded Barcanona, a city, in this case, of maritime origin, though its roots could just as well be Punic, a small factory of Carthaginian making founded by Hamilcar or by Hannibal, from whose common patronymic, Barca or Barcino, that in both cases means a flash of light, would thus proceed the city's denomination, which could therefore, on another hand, also be called, in memory of its namesake of Cyrenaica, or as a derivation of Barschem, a Hittite or Phoenician name for the planet Saturn, a possibility that must not be discarded and that, precisely in this case, one might suppose, without a doubt, that Barcino was a colony of Tyre, a theory seemingly confirmed by the discovery of clues that would prove the existence of a local cult devoted to Astarte—the moon—and to Tanit, a manifestation of the starry heavens, as well as the sun, Baal, the latter identifiable, even, in the opinion of Don Salvador Sampere i Miquel, with the Egyptian Amon, although there are also those who insist on attributing Greek origins to the city, without managing to trace them back to Heracles, who offer hypotheses no less conclusive in favor of the presumed existence of a colony under the command of either Pelasgians and

Tyrrhenians, or of Carians who came from Bargylia, a place near
Mileto, or better yet, as in the case of Empúries, of a Phocian
colony radiating from Marsilia (Marseilles), Greeks from the
diaspora established, why not, at what must have been the head
of a natural bridge, attractive to the maritime power on duty, a
point destined to pass from the control of one group to another,
from the hands of the descendants of Dido—extreme beyond
controversy—to the hands of the descendants of Aeneas and,
more concretely, from the hosts of Gnaeus Cornelius Scipio, who
might have added the cognomen of Favencia to his conquest,
just as Caesar would, perhaps, add that of Julia, and Augustus
himself that of Augusta, upon officially proclaiming a Roman
colony the delightful Punic seat of government known until then
generally as Barcino, despite the fact that in ancient times there
was no shortage of other names for the city: Barcenone,
Barcinona, Barcilo, Barcelona, Barcelona la Pía, Paterna, or
Patricia, noble titles, epigraphs established over the years,
petrified epithets, now as epitaphs from that city whose full and
complete name probably was Colonia Favenica Julia Augusta
Paterna Barcino, parvus oppidus, the small town, dominating
the whole area between the rivers Betulón and Rubricatus and
between the massif of Collserola and the peninsula of Mons Jovis
or Jupiter, that lofty lord of lightning and thunder. Small port
of Hispania Citerior, subsequently called Provincia Tarraconense,
a great city whose expansion was cut short by the first barbarian
attacks and which resurged afterward boasting perhaps the most
solid walls in the Empire, the Pax Romana uncertain, cornered,
subverted, rich in popular martyrs, like Santa Eulalia or San
Severo, victims of persecutions and repressions, bloody centuries,
palm fronds and crosses, daggers, poisons, assassinations,
betrayals, conspiracies, vile deeds, daily disasters in Arian
Barchinona or Barcino of Ataulf, ephemeral capital of the
Visigoth monarchy in those times of conversions, of dark
metamorphosis, a city under full medieval shadows would appear
transformed into Saracen, or more precisely, Mozarabic,
Barschaluna, temporarily infidel, unfaithfully lost and recovered,
now allied with the enemy, now an enemy of the ally, scabrous

terrain, of frank uncertainty, preponderant center of Afranc, no man's land, the frontier overrun indistinctly by Franks, by Arabs, by Normans, land of incursions, exoduses, blights, sackings, pillaging, atrocities, a land where, between rapine and forays, there began to form the cloudy embryo of a homeland, among the mists, at the intersection of the Pyrenees and the Mediterranean, from the rude mountain refuges of Otgar de Cataló and his nine famous barons, Otgar or Otger Catalón, Kathasolt, Gazlantes, Gotlantes, or Gotlán, strong fortunate man, enterprising forerunner of the celebrated Catalonia or Catalonya, land of castles, conquests financed by Vifredo I el Velloso, also known as Wilfred I the Hairy, although there was, perhaps, an earlier Vifredo, in which case he would be the second one, Vifredo or Seniofre, Wilfred, Guifred, Gifré, Xifré, Jofre or Guifré, better known as Almondir, that is, El Bravo, by the Muslims, first virtual sovereign of the County of Barcelona, although, according to the feudal hierarchy, known as Marquis of Gothia or Marca Hispánica, belonging still to the Dukedom of Septimania of the Kingdom of Aquitaine, vassal of the Carolingian Empire, a prince with whose blood Carlos the Bald personally traced the four bars across the shield of gold, which became from that moment forth the very blazon of the city which still remained to be overrun by Almanzor and reconquered for the Cross by Christian arms, with Saint George leading the knights, brandishing a bolt of lightning, the dead and resurrected head of an incipient state, fatherland of fratricides and excommunicants, merchants and crusaders, troubadours and navigators, Catalunya, crown on horseback of the Pyrenees, its authority extended to Provence under the scepter of Ramón Berenguer el Grande, bi-member state, Crown of Aragón, monarchy of poly-member development impelled by James the Conqueror, man of deeds, cofounder, along with Saint Pedro Nolasco and Saint Raimundo de Penyafort, de la Merced, Order of White Knights, redeemers of captives and capturers of infidels, re-conqueror of Valencia, as well as Mallorca, *dolça illa daurada*, the sweet golden isle, the most esteemed of his conquests, the neighing of horses and sound of arms, a trail of sails and flashing steel covering the sea in white, the island running red, and the Donjuanesque Don Jaume shouting, an asp on the crest of his helmet, a bat unfolded, wings spread to frighten, terrifying, sending men to their grave, shouting Victoria soldats! Victory, soldiers, victory, victory and glory imposed by the forceful blow of swords, ¡desperta ferro! swords awaken! mors stupebit et natura, death and nature will be astounded, a Mediterranean confederation in expansive apogee, Sicily, Corsica, Sardinia, Naples, Calabria, Malta, Jerba, Morea, Gallipoli, Athens, and Neopatria, trophies secured after great difficulty by the Almogavars and their valiant swordsmen, saviors of empires, usurpers and destroyers, rampagers, vengeful Catalans, mercenaries, soldiers of fortune earned in countless combats with Moors and Turks, Greeks and Bulgarians, French and Genoese, when not even a single fish could swim across the seas without the emblem of the four bars and the Parthenon was called the Seo de Santamaría, empire on horseback of the Mediterranean, from island to island, from peninsula to peninsula, golden isles on the horizon, scattered crown, poured out, spilled, blood, bars of gold, greed, and evil uses, land of farmers and highwaymen, warriors and artisans, mystics and cartographers, lords and servants, redeemers and redeemed, revolts, repressions, uncivil and revolutionary society of the fifteenth century, aborted Humanism, Renaissance of adversities, with its bitter repertoire of misfortunes, plagues and famine, crisis, calamities, time of decline, implacable perigee with antagonisms instead of harmony and dreams instead of realities, the Cataluña of Ferran or Fernando forging Catalan national unity almost without realizing it, a monarch too ambitious for a people too self-absorbed, unconscious of the fact that upon enmeshing itself with a flourishing Castile, strengthened and enterprising, it had agreed to form part, the lesser part, of a superior entity, the Spain where Isabel counts for as much as Fernando and even more, the Catholic Kings in the act of welcoming Columbus upon his triumphant return from the Indies, the beginning of a grandiose colonizing labor, of the creation or destruction of an empire, a question of perspective or rather of color, of the color of the skin with which one

watches, royal offering in any case, a new world at their feet, as
if served up on a platter, a world already become village, discoveries and gifts of all kinds, birds, fruits, precious stones, plumed
redskins alongside pages and heralds, prelates, men-at-arms,
cuirasses, mantles, red damasks, ermine pelts, feathers, pennants,
pikes, trumpets, miters, and scepters gathered presumably in the
Saló del Tinell, below those arches like palm trees spread wide,
vast throne room of the Palacio Real Mayor, with a view, from
the adjoining antechamber, constructed atop the Roman wall,
of the plaza of Ramón Berenguer the Great, favorite son-in-law
of El Mío Cid, the old warrior on his bronze horse, helmet
heightened by the beating wings of a dove alighting on it, fine
sprightly warrior seeming to direct the traffic along the Vía
Layetana, a trench brutally plowed across the width of the Old
City, directing or simply witnessing, his back turned away from
the rear windows of the Palacio Real Mayor and the rear facades
of the adjoining edifices, the Chapel of Santa Agata, also
constructed upon the towers of the wall, the royal chapel and,
later, over the course of the years, school, warehouse holding
decorations from the Gran Teatro del Liceo, printing house and
workshop, presently restored, after so many vicissitudes, with its
polychrome coffered ceiling intact and its altarpieces of the
Epiphany and Pentecost, Calvary and the Resurrection, single
inner pointed nave which communicates thus with the antechamber of the Saló del Tinell as with the upper floors of the
Casa Padellás, conjoined edifices, all encircling the Plaza del Rey,
intercommunicating spaces which, along with the network of
subterranean excavations, form the current City History
Museum, a grouping of zones and enclosures with its central
headquarters in the Casa Padellás, a Gothic construction organized around a patio with corridors where an open staircase leads,
in a single flight, up to the main floor, a palace vacated, due to
urban necessities, from its earlier site and moved here, rebuilt
stone by stone the way churches are, like the Temple of Mount
Zion, for example, now on the Rambla de Cataluña, or Santa
María de Junqueras, now the Parish of La Concepción, on the
corner of Calle Aragón and Roger de Llúria.

Which means, said Escala. In three quarters of an hour, at
six. On the patio in the Faculty of Humanities. A gathering of
students from all the university departments with the goal of
compensating for the individual defections they expect from
each department. To form a protest line intended to prevent
from entering those who, by belonging to departments situated
in la Ciudad Universitaria, might lack the excuse for showing
up at the university's main campus downtown, la Universidad
Central. The motion approved by the Economics Committee
in support of the Asturian miners and against the repression in
Asturias will be read aloud, and all present will be invited to join
in solidarity, also gathering as many professional and political
demands as emerge from the masses gathered together. Banners
will be unfurled and displayed, the portraits of Franco will be
thrown down on the patio, and, taking advantage of the fact
that at that hour the streets are filled with people coming home
from work, we'll try to march out in demonstration toward
the Civil Government following the planned route, Gran Vía,
Plaza de Cataluña, Las Ramblas, and the Paseo Colón. We've
got to use any means necessary to get the authorities to close
the main campus. That accomplished, we call for a strike in
protest of the holdout university departments refusing to join
us, and make sure that there is a general suspension of classes
throughout all the university campuses in the district. That way,
the Catalanistas' light explosives can have some positive effect:
to force the authorities to intervene, precipitating the events;
in a word, to catalyze the situation. Although such acts deviate
from our political line, perhaps it's not a bad idea, under the
present circumstances, that they be carried out by others. The
socialists promise they'll do the same, but it's surely just one of
their characteristic bluffs. Your role consists of resolving, along
the way, however many questions that come up, always keeping in mind that you must remain embedded in and identified
with the mass of student protestors. Make the opportune decisions without it seeming like you are the ones who make them.
Centralize the picket line activity. Order the unfurling of the
banners. Channel the demonstration toward the bishopric, just

as the Catholics wish, instead of toward the civil government, if that seems to be the predominant opinion. Counteract the police's dispersive actions. Avoid clashes, except when the police try to make arrests. Let me emphasize that those of you in positions of responsibility must not draw attention to yourselves, at no time should you stand out from the mass of students. It would be a grave mistake for the organization to reveal the one secretly responsible instead of the one who appears to be the real leader. That's what people like Ros, Martinell, and Guillén are for. As for Ferrán, it doesn't seem prudent to risk exposing him to the investigations he'd arouse, were he arrested, being as he is the son of an old, well-documented militant. He shouldn't even get close to the fray, especially because no one has recognized him yet, and by staying on the sidelines he's the perfect person to maintain the security connection. If you run into some delay or feel that you were being watched, he can go in your place to the meeting. Tomorrow at eleven, in the cloisters. The only thing necessary is that he not receive your call, that you don't call him tonight from a pay phone saying you want to go to the movies or something. And then he'll show up. Cover your asses and cover me. Be especially careful with telephones. And get rid of any compromising papers. No notes.

Keep in mind what the last ones who got arrested went through, the new surveillance techniques used by the police. When they follow someone, various agents do it at the same time, relieving each other continually to avoid attracting attention, communicating with each other by radio. They use cars and motorcycles. As a rule, you should mistrust men wearing typical, dull, everyday uniforms, soldiers, tram drivers, street sweepers, etcetera. Don't forget either that women also participate in surveillance operations. Take every kind of precaution. Catch the Metro at the second to last station on the line, for example, where it's easy to spot if you're being followed. In case you notice anything out of the ordinary at the meeting place, take out your handkerchief to blow your nose. You always meet by crossing paths, planning each person's route ahead of time. You appear to run into each other by accident and then each person goes their own way. One goes toward the exit at the Plaza del Rey and the other toward the exit for Calle de los Condes de Barcelona. Or rather, whoever enters via Plaza del Rey must leave by way of Calle de los Condes de Barcelona. Or rather, at the Cathedral, entering by Calle San Ivo, also called Calle Inquisición, and coming out on Calle Piedad or Santa Eulalia, both at the cloisters. Or entering through the Chapel of Santa Lucía, a Romanesque structure integrated into the structure of the cathedral, and leaving from any other door, onto Calle de la Piedad, Calle del Obispo, right at the front steps, leave and get lost in the convoluted violet side streets of the Old City, take Calle Puertaferrisa or Calle Canuda toward Las Ramblas, Calle Pelayo and Plaza de la Universidad or, crossing Avenida de la Catedral, take Calle dels Arcs toward Puerta del Ángel, Plaza de Cataluña, Las Rondas, and Plaza de la Universidad, wide plazas and streets, thick with traffic, the city's shopping district, monotonous alignments, grandiose buildings with ground-floor windows, banks, cafés, enormous department stores, leaving behind that nucleus of rancid narrow streets and damp stone, wafting odors, belonging to the streets surrounding the cathedral, businesses and crafts developed within the shelter of the Church, an always-attractive temple for the sale of goods, fleeting effluvia, wax, crammed antiques, books passed through umpteen hands, rough matting and wrought iron, odors successively diffused upon a more general background of choking industrial vapors, contrasting morning atmosphere of yellow light penetrating the shadows, transversal and turbid, metalized sunlight, as if infused with metal filings, revealing the eroded palaces now become neighborhood houses, corroded facades, gray rough cast, disfigured by touch-ups, bricked-in doorways, poky windows clumsily open in the thick stone walls, balconies sporting potted plants, clothes hanging between Romanesque, Gothic, Renaissance, Baroque, Neoclassical, and Isabeline architectural elements, gargoyles and cornices, *ajimez* windows, large doorways and staircases with little boys, tourists photographing arches no longer triumphant, battered doorways for horse and carriage, now bodega or antique shop, grocery store, herbalist, tobacco shop, secondhand bookshops selling souvenirs and postcards, the workshop of, the warehouse of, etcetera. Or even on any block of the Ensanche, a quadrangle repeated to labyrinthine extremes, on the block formed, for example, by the following streets: Diputación, Sicilia, Consejo de Ciento, and Cerdeña, turning circles counterclockwise or vice versa, until you run into Escala or, on occasions, directly with Obregón, each time on a different block, apart from the meetings, also with Obregón, at Park Güell, in the mornings, Obregón with another outfit and dark glasses, contacts so much more precious because so less frequent, notified previously by Escala in the course of a meeting conducted on some block: Córcega-Nápoles-Rosellón-Roger de Flor, for example, turning clockwise, or again at the City History Museum, entering through the ancient Palacio Real Mayor, which later became the very seat of the Inquisition, the shield of the blazing cross above the portico visible even today, on Calle de los Condes de Barcelona, and leaving through the Casa Padellás, in the Plaza del Rey, after having met, perhaps, in the basement passages, perhaps at any point of the itinerary which, including the Salón del Tinell and Santa Agata's Chapel, both places approximately at the second-story level, leads toward the upper rooms of the Casa Padellás, on the third floor, rooms decorated in the styles of successive centuries, with corresponding relics, histories and events set in stone, sculptures, carvings, portraits, shields, weapons, flags and standards, cannonballs, furniture, glass cases with ceramics and fabrics, antiques and reproductions, models, explanatory charts and maps, classical resemblances, typically gorgeous eighteenth-century pieces, illuminated illustrations, cavalry marching away, the horses' prominent hindquarters, modernist flourishes, dioramas, illustrations of sieges and expositions, receptions and revolts, fiestas and solstices, trophies and disappointments, days of ire and delight, images of war and peace in Barcelona, an engraving in simple colors, of aged yellows, the city seen from Montjuïc or Montjuich or Monycich or Montjony or Montjoin, etcetera, fortified and guarded seawall previously called Mons Jovis or Mons Judeorum, Barcelona of the sixteenth century, mirror, lamppost, star and north of the knights errant, school of hidalgos and archive of courtesies, Barcelona the rich, fertile, and plentiful that made the young Carlos say I prefer to be Count of Barcelona more than Emperor of the Romans, Carlos I of Spain or Carlos V, Emperor of Austria, heir of kingdoms and principalities, dukedoms, counties, scepters and crowns, the Crown of Aragón and its stele of Mediterranean domains, the German states and Castile, Burgundy and Granada, Luxembourg and Navarre, Flanders, Artois, Brabant, Holland, Zealand, etcetera, plus the North African possessions and the growing Viceroys of the Indies, the inheritance of four grandfathers all grouped together, extended throughout the four cardinal points radiating out from Barcelona, temporary Imperial court thanks to his telling preference for its optimal residential qualities, appropriate, on the other hand, to a progressively provincial city, one given over to the petty consolations of a marginal, vegetative life, the simple capital of an exhausted and decadent principate, too impotent to prevail, striving too hard to be eclipsed, *aurea mediocritas* of a noble city, all facade, lovely crenellated walls, polygonal towers, gates and moats, portcullises and escarpments, battlements, roofs, belfries, patios and gardens, a select orchard of pomegranate trees, lemons, oranges, palms, pines, grape vines grown close to the walls, palaces, churches, belfries floating on high, the cathedral where the emperor convoked the Conclave of the Knights of the Order of the Golden Fleece, amid incense and purple, brocade, velvet, angelic songs, emblems unfolded, stepping forward to receive the collar, under the emblazoned Lion of Spain, Cristerno of Denmark and Segismundo of Poland, arrogant kings, dreamers, heading the list of knights, their names detailed minutely *et in saecula saeculorum* in the choir stalls, neither gold nor purple in this oil sketch painted from behind at the radiant high altar, shadowy chiaroscuro of stained-glass windows and luminaria, organ pipes, sconces, skylights, and ogival windows like an echo of songs, no more crimson mantles nor entourages, no moments of splendor, only past glories, venerated victories, el Cristo Negro, the Black Christ, ensign of Lepanto, champion of Christianity and defender of the Faith, the bolt of the Sublime Door, fourth quarter of the Half Moon, unprecedented confrontation of argosies and galleys, apocalyptic butchery with its all-too-famous consequence of scars and mutilations, hands lost for the plume and for the sword. Decisive battle, apogee or zenith of an empire where the sun never managed to set, galloping across three oceans and five continents, from Sicily to Chile, from Florida to Oran, from the Philippines to Flanders, unfolded omnipotence of the eagle, black wings, black legends, penitential robes, sentences hung from the defendant's neck, bonfires and gibbets, *rex tremenda majestatis*, Philip II in his isolated Escorial, pantheon and cradle, first and last residence of so many monarchs, king of kings, lord of the armies until then undefeated in all kinds of fights, regiments and armadas ultimately vincible, sunset of Flanders, lances so long raised erect now broken and folded, turned against themselves, internal wars of a decaying empire, hegemony called into question, absolutism relativized, uprisings, separatist and centrifugal movements, as on a sinking ship, fleeing from the shipwreck, Netherlands, Portugal, Italy, Catalonia, land or terroir on the political periphery because it is neither economic nor spiritual, with its industrious towns and its cultivated fields, wrought with brute strength from the naturally rough and wild landscape, hermitic mountains, apt for the contemplation of the supernatural, shelter of ascetics and destination of pilgrims and palmers, crags afire with broom. The Black Virgin of Montserrat, to whom Saint James offered his sword, Montserrat, sanctuary of retreats and meditations, inspirations, visions, determinations, heart of a principality weary with costly but effective discriminatory favoritisms, raised against the bureaucracy with its affected elegance and purity of style, developed in the shadow of the royal sclerosis, true dynastic decadence, a despotic void of power throughout the whole government, capital problem of a country where life is a dream, court of miracles, country of monks and Don Juans, of court jesters and maids of honor, rogues, adventurers, ruined hidalgos, the empty purse of Don Dinero, powerful knight, unpaid soldiers' salaries dispatched only to quell unrest, the cause of sackings and anarchy, rioting by the soldiery, the cause of revolts against the soldiery, a vicious circle enclosing the turbulent Barcelona of the seventeenth century, true threat to the Spanish monarchy, virtually felt to be strange and foreign by a city jealous of its privileges and customs, exasperated by the subjugation of its traditions, capable of both begging to God and asking for help from the very devil himself, a rebellious land, insurgent, sickles, black veils, and severed Castilian heads in the Bloody Corpus riot: reapers turned butchers, a people up in arms, a city of fearless defenders, a city assaulted by sea and land, as much by the Spanish as by their occasional allies, French, English, Germans, by the Marqués de los Vélez, or by the Duke of Vendôme, or by the Duke of Anjou, or by the Admiral Lord Peterborough or by the Duke of Berwick, images of siege from a bird's eye view, with a description of the positions and camps of the besieging forces and of the disposition of the blockading ships, as well as the fortifications and defenses of the plaza, bastions and batteries, the shield of the city in an angle of the engraving, escutcheon in four quarters, as can also be appreciated in the various reproductions displayed in the vestibule, war themes, patriotic motives, causa belli, a shield with the cross of Saint George in the first and fourth quarters upon a silver field, and four bars en gules in the second and third upon a field of gold, gold and blood of an outlaw nation, rich in bandits, popular heroes, defenders of lost causes, successions and secessions, Catalonia with its castles shattered and razed, like a battered warrior with broken ribs, cast out from Castile, muted by having its tongue cut out, minimized, reduced by force, centralized, meaning isolated from all central power, distanced from its own destinies, dispossessed of privileges and autonomies, its university moved away and traditional laws suppressed by royal decree, *la Nueva Planta*, unwelcome weed of a land still fertile in spite of all, lush and flourishing, precisely, in proportion to its distance from imperial life, stripped of its avatars, consequent grandeurs and subsequent decadences, a land soon flourishing anew in the frame of a Spain drained of blood that did not cease to decline, a region soon adapted to hard reality, times of capitulation and recapitulation, times of integration and work, of enlightened progress, lights of the century, eighteenth-century allegories, just counterpart of an integration that, if it closed some doors, opened others, those of America, to the new full-fledged Spaniards, commerce delayed but no less decisive for the Principality, and which, together with its inhabitants' natural virtues of industry and good common sense, would create an incipient process of capitalization, a base of industrialization developed without pause from then on, notwithstanding the mishaps of time, wars and guerrilla fighters, invasions, independence defended, hardly in any unanimous way, by all the peoples of the peninsula, all indisputably tied together against their common oppressor or liberator, the Catalan people confronting Napoleon as they had once long before confronted Hannibal, Caesar, or Almanzor, crusading spirit enveloped in wrath, war proclaimed by the priest, a call to arms from altars and pulpits, plebiscite tribunes, together declaiming themselves against the Revolution or the Empire, uncertain cut-throat struggle, executions by firing squad, by impaling, Goyaesque horrors of war forever engraved, their hybrid seed perhaps also forever rooted, hybrid, prolific, fecund nursery of fervors equally apostolic and liberal, revolutionary or absolutist, the hundred thousand sons of San Luis marching openly, unconstitutional paths, holy alliances, secret societies, terrorism, military uprisings, declarations, rebellions and restorations, monarchists, Isabelines and Carlists, bands opposed, irreducible, warlike, passing the time exterminating one another, a Spanish crossword puzzle, Iberian circle of asses, witches, and apes gathered in an orgiastic dance, ferocious nineteenth-century witches' sabbath of that renascent Principate, impeller of progress and democracy alongside a lawless traditionalism, impeller of republican, federalist, cantonalist, anarchist movements, all the while reformist, protectionist, colonialist, imperialist, festering acrimonious contradictions of a Catalonia both working-class and bourgeois, antagonies spreading at the same time as the rising smoke of its industrial centers, between riotous turbid revolts and punishing cannonades, Barcelona under falling bombs, explosions of violence and unrest, the riot on Las Ramblas, for example, when the rioters assaulted the

Governor's Palace and murdered General Bassa, a romantic scene of workers, farmers, and intellectuals joined in brotherhood, and who knows if not students, too, frock coats and striped blouses, dark top hats and red caps as if they were Phrygian caps, sabers and pistols, rifles bristling around some defenestrated body, broken, burned in a bonfire kindled with the papers thrown from the balconies of the Police Delegation, fluttering down upon the exultant mobs, fists thrust on high, wrath, a dog sniffing at the debris, recriminations, choleric expressions, physiognomies altered by wrath, strange factions, irreconcilable positions, class warfare, anarchist furor, attacks, lethal exterminating explosions, Orsini bombs hurled at the audience in the Gran Teatro del Liceo opera house, one of them, which did not explode, exhibited alongside the pictures showing the fear which filled that tragic November night, while Rossini's *William Tell* was being performed, people fainting and weeping in the lounge, the big wheel spinning, and an agitated image of the streets with carriage horses rearing, kicking, whinnying, shouts, running, livid flashing of eyes, the anarchic flip-side of the coin of a society in full expansion at a tremendous rate, a Catalonia of an increasingly greater weight in the public life of the Spanish nation, presence incarnate, without going further, through General Prim, kingmaker, persons with redeeming frailties and whims, rapidly rising career, from Reus to Castillejos, from Castillejos to Barcelona, from Barcelona to Madrid, from Madrid to heaven through the sublime Puerta del Turco, amid the stench of a regicide, transported by a carriage possibly similar to the one he had used in Barcelona in order to make his entrance in the Plaza San Jaime or the Plaza de la Constitución, at his victorious return from the Moroccan campaign, a tremendous reception offered by the city to the man whose meteoric ascension seemed but a prefiguration and omen of a collective providential destiny, victories, triumphal arches, flags and pennants, streamers, red and yellow striped flags fluttering in the wind. Also in this room of the Casa Padellás, a model of the equestrian statue of President Prim, a horseman of haughty presence and military bearing, who presides over the elegant eighteenth-century perspectives of the

Ciudadela Park, a monument erected by a Barcelonan society that converted into gardens what had been a fortress executed by Vauban, with its parade ground, its dungeons and its gallows, the impetuous steamroller of a society on the move, forms of life in transformation impelled by a bourgeoisie that was going to outstrip the limits of the past with its new initiatives, to smash down walls, to project a new city in its own image and likeness, the effort of visionary clairvoyance or, more simply, a question of vision, with a good nose and refined calculation, the Barcelona whose expansion only appeared eccentric, its plans only partially extemporaneous, a city of colossal enterprises, of modernist extravagances, the Barcelona of the Universal Exposition, romantic and delirious expansions of grandiosity, days of euphoria and jubilation, not even dampened or overshadowed by the miseries of 1898, the gradual degeneration of a Spain at the heart of which, and in the name of a reality, Barcelona now reclaimed the power or the authority, with so much nineteenth-century bourgeois Catalan impetus, and without beating about the bush; the renaissance of a Catalonia equally traditional and innovative, capable of initiating the monumental work of the Expiatory Temple of the Holy Family and, simultaneously, restoring the facade of the cathedral, that Gothic museum of past splendors, petrified histories and legends, resonant naves, murky penumbra, the organ and the choir, the crypt, spectral forms, incense-bearing angels, recumbent images, sepulchers, Santa Eulalia's for example, or the sepulcher of San Raimundo de Penyafort, and by the door that communicates with the cloister, the sarcophagi of Ramón Berenguer the Old and his wife Almodis, founders of the cathedral which predated the present one, the vanished Romanesque cathedral, built, in turn, upon the ruins of an even older one, the early paleo-Christian basilica of uncertain fate, re-consecrated after having been a Muslim mosque and, previously, in a no-less-episodic manner, the seat of an Arian episcopal see, a temple whose foundation is attributed to Saint James, all that in the immediate area where stood the pagan temple dedicated to Augustus, superimposed constructions of which now only remain vestiges in the subsoil of the current stonework.

An interior pierced by sunlight, a relief vault aureoled by the early morning lights, iridescent beams from the stained-glass windows, oblique transparencies coloring the ribs of the columns, ashlars, flagstones, chromatic stains increasingly lower down, increasingly conspicuous in the depths of the transept, grave symmetries, gloom thickened by the sheen of old gold, yellowishness from days gone by, carvings, Baroque sculptures, altarpieces, paintings veiled by a bright reflection, veiled and unveiled according to how one advanced under the radiance of the multicolored corollas of the apse, toward the dazzling opening and closing of the door that offered flashing glimpses outside, the cloister, a corner of serenity and even traditional solace, pointing to the oil painting painted from that very same angle, an eighteenth-century family in the foreground, next to the shrine of the spout, the father with walking stick and top hat, the mother in the attitude of turning to her little boy who appears stuck to her skirts, as if she was telling him something, who knows if something about the dancing egg, *l'ou com balla*, or about Saint George and the Dragon, an enchanting traditional image with the patio's vegetation in the background, flowerbeds, young trees, just barely flowering, all framed by archways without bars, arches repeated, the geometry of their fretwork projecting itself oblately on the flagstone pavement, progressively diminished by the perspective, luminosity similar to that of today, no less today in spite of the vegetation's growth, the patio's gated thickness, tall palms with their hearts like pollen, great magnolias splashed with iridescences, solar sparkles, and the honking of the geese, and the mossy bubbling of the waterspout, ivies, shady stone, odor and light of undergrowth in the corridors of that enclosure open to Calle de la Piedad through the door of the same name, and to Calle del Obispo through Santa Eulalia's door, facing the monument to the martyrs of Bonapartist tyranny expressed on the exterior adornments of the Church of San Severo, a sculptural group flanked by panels of tiles with explanatory texts and illustrations about the event, an expressive vocation of the diverse events befallen which followed from the horrifying scene, or rather, following the execution of five patriots on the glacis of the Citadel, when meanwhile the sentence was carried out against the five Heroes, three more valiant men of Barcelona, namely Don Ramón Mas, Don Julián Portet, and Don Pedro Lastortras, who sounded the alarm bells in the cathedral tower to call together the People and liberate their brothers. The Napoleonic troops raced there and, locking the church, mounted the most careful search. Desperate after not finding them, they offered to pardon them, shouting it so at such frequent intervals that the three aforementioned men finally emerged from beneath the organ bellows after having gone more than seventy-two hours without eating or drinking anything. They managed to reanimate them with generous draughts of wine, thus fanning the promise to pardon them, the same soldiers who then, breaking their word, pressed for their death, which sentence was executed the twenty-seventh day of that same month of June in which they died gloriously, the remarkable composure and exemplary bravery of some men who, for faithful devotion to their cause, for loyalty and abnegation, for requisite nobleness, for solidarity with their comrades, risked and lost their own lives in the attempt to sound the alarm with a useless outburst, all for nothing, Barcelonans with their ears shut tight, for whom the bells toll, for whom they toll and toll again from these towers, preeminent cathedral, rising high, surrounded by churches and palaces, raised up like a raised projection of what was once Mount Taber upon a sinuous contour of edifices from other times, mixed styles, superimposed elements, all set at different levels. Thus, without going further, taking a simple turn around the outside of the cathedral, starting from the portico of Santa Eulalia, for example, on the northwest slope of this prominence of intercrossing side streets, and turning always in a clockwise direction, we will find, at the foot of Calle del Obispo, the Episcopal Palace, of Romanesque origin, and turning the corner, along Calle Santa Lucía, La Casa del Arcediano, a building of plateresque design jammed against a residual section of the Roman wall, a compact building that, next to la Casa de la Pia Almoina, erected in the fifteenth century with remains of earlier buildings, frames la Plaza de la Catedral or la Plaza de Cristo

Rey, spread out between both buildings, the steps that enhance the facade's nineteenth-century pastiche, and turning again to the right, skirting a ring of visitors listening to their jabbering tour guide, we head into the Calle de los Condes de Barcelona, where we happen upon the worn stones of the ancient Palacio Real Mayor and the Archive of the Crown of Aragón, previously el Palacio del Lugarteniente, and after turning again to the right, along Calle de la Piedad, torturously clinging to the line of the apse and to a wing of the cloister, las Casas Canonicales, a group of buildings lovingly restored which runs as far as Calle del Obispo in its confluence with Calle de la Piedad, before the Gothic side of the old Consejo de Ciento, a bifurcation that, turning right, will lead us back again to our starting point, and to the left, following Calle del Obispo in its downward slope toward the southeast, all along the Gothic side of the old Consejo de Ciento, currently called the Diputación, leads to Plaza de San Jaime, formerly Plaza de la Constitución and, also periodically, Plaza de la República, the city's administrative center, location of both the City Hall and the Catalan Diputación or Provincial Council, the two facades with their rigorous lines facing off; San Jaime, Jacobo, or Santiago, patron saint of Spain and battering ram of Christianity, captain of the armies, champion of battles, son of the thunder, knight on his white charger, who, reaching Barcino, ascended to the summit of Mons Taber and, after contemplating the city, founded the cathedral there on high, core chthonic cornerstone, touchstone, like a transformative philosopher's stone, like a talisman or enchantment, transubstantiation of the Acropolis, consecration of the temple, prevalent tabernacle, exalted, Mont Taber or Mont Miracle, Mountain of the Disappearance, neither Moses nor Elijah nor shining lights, mountain transfigured, flattened by the very growth of the city, buried, up in smoke forever et in saecula saeculorum, centuries of history contemplating, phantasmagoric vision, spectral procession of empires and dominations, a city condemned to relive, to survive itself, Rome engendered by lost Troy, vertex of a fatherland built bit by bit over the course of the years, with the passing of the states and sovereignties, a rhetorical train of titles, exiled

names, flatus vous, Aquitania, Septimania, Occitania, Marca
Hispánica, the Crown of Aragón, poly-member monarchy,
Mediterranean empire on horseback, vapor trail of golden islands
of an archaic empire, meaning, precocious and, in every case,
outdated, short-lived, an empire soon dismembered, unhorsed,
riderless steed, wagon enmired, a kink in the rope, a litany of
misfortunes, banners flagging, lowered, dreams of greatness dissipated, agonic delirium of an inconclusive destiny, aborted,
failed, the rose of April topped, crown of thorns, crown of
flowers, its sole court the crenellated complex of Poblet, slag heap
of triumphs and splendors, buried conquests, remote relaxing
isolated retreat, monastery of gilded stones, with its towers
inhabited by soft solitary owls and the sluggish swallows flitting
round the cloisters, while in the high vaults the shadows deepen
ever more absolute, alabaster monarchs in repose, empty pupils,
one last look, self-absorbed center bitten the dust, returned to
dust, and blown away, anonymous earth, mixed, crucible and
crossroads of the old world, classic route of invasions, occupied
country, fatherland unrepentant, thirsty for freedom, famished
for independence, hunger and epidemics, endemic ills, ill-fated
days, of displeasure and disgrace, of discouragement, Dantesque
times, of fury and cholera, of plague, of oppression, of racial
abysses, moats and declivities, rotund walls, a fortified city,
enclosed and surrounded, city of Numantian sieges, assaulted,
conquered, re-conquered, conqueror, impeller of expeditions and
occupations, city of traded fortunes, liberator and captive,
subdued and reborn, recalcitrant and fractious, uncivil, city of
rebellions and restorations, of uprisings, riots, attacks, bombs,
barricades, massacres, lynchings, charges, discharges, machine
guns, bombs, festive bonfires, city of flaming bright colors,
yellow, red, yellow, red, yellow, red, yellow, red, yellow broom
flowers, pure smokeless flame, inextinguishable fire, phoenix of
April, re-flowering on the wind, flag praised in song and hoisted
high, *la senyera*, dominant, singular flag, the red and yellow
Catalan flag, golden shield with bars of blood and, upon a silver
field, the white cross of Saint George, chivalrous patron saint,
providential and decisive rider, savior and martyr, killer of

spiders, oh fable of time, city of nonexistent patron saints, ubiquitous Virgin of Mercy, Eulalia flayed, despised maiden, her breasts hacked off, neither virgin nor martyr of Barcelona, rather, pious splitting of her namesake from Mérida, a phenomenon similar in its development to that of San Severo, whose feast day is celebrated today, the sixth of November, Severo de Rávena, bishop and martyr, fallen in the course of some persecution and later brought here with his life and miracles, including the one with the fava beans, mysteries of history, *aucas, aleluyas*, funny faces, jocular mouths, shocking giant heads, the king and queen of golden coins, as depicted on *la baraja*, the Spanish deck of cards, spinning on their tiny feet, their features ecstatic, gestures modest, Catholic kings of cardboard and cloth, ceremoniously lording over the street, retinues, popular festivities, flags unfurled and streamers fluttering in the sun, pennants, tremulous oriflammes, tall standards flowing gracefully, ecclesiastical standards, banners, damask and purple, draperies, tapestries, bands of musicians, cornets, drums, kettledrums, horns, cymbals shimmering like suns, wind and brass in rhythm, riders, white horses, glittering plumed helmets, dress uniforms, the Guardia Civil, waists girded in red sashes, Catalan caps, shimmering confetti, streets threaded with streamers, a procession emerging from the cathedral, large, calm, moving deliberately, hieratic steps, guards, canopies presided over by prelates and dignitaries, gregarious swaying procession, multitudes on the march toward Calle de los Arcos, Puerta del Ángel, and Plaza Cataluña, sidewalks crowded, streets cordoned off, congregated masses, concentrated in Plaza de San Jaime, given over to the most beautiful dance, the pulsating Sardana, circles forming and breaking apart, carpets of flowers, sketches of petals, broom, carnations, the ground colored red for Corpus Christi, cardboard heads, carnivalesque masks, carnal assaults, Bacchic promiscuity, generalized debauchery, grape vines and laurels, palm fronds of welcome, religious feast day celebrations, joyous carefree city, smiling, foppish, handy, Barcelona good and malevolent, with its New Year's Eves and its ancient celebrations of Midsummer's Eve, summer saturnalias, cakes and champagne, paper fringe, foil paper, sequins,

lanterns, fireworks displays, nighttime bonfires, fires deliberately
set, convents burned down, smoke of gunpowder and gasoline,
civitas diaboli, rude, crude, and cowardly Barcelona, always quick
to break its word, to besmirch all that is human, all that is divine,
whore disguised as nun, nun disguised as whore, humiliated
countess, princess sans principles, queen of drag queens, *res pub-
lica*, archive of courtesans, second Rome, traitorous Barcelona,
quick to applaud and acclaim, to offer an ovation, to receive
warlords and drag bodies drawn and quartered along Las
Ramblas, to celebrate downfalls and liberations, dominations
and thrones, dethronements and executions, disjointed conjunc-
tures, tortures, dislocations, inquisitorial judgments, rigorous
sentences, exemplary punishments, torture turned fiesta, duels
become norm, anniversary become commemorative exaltation,
divergent perspectives, different aspects belonging to one place,
simultaneously the cradle of honored citizens and bandits, capital
of   a   coarse,   untamed   land,   fields   sown   and
fertilized with violence, a coastal region raised upon one accom-
plishment after another, from century to century, turbulent,
rebellious serfs and freemen, *cadells* and *nyerros*—sixteenth-cen-
tury civil-military factions defending landed interests—puppies
and piglets, head-hunting reapers, using sickles to cut off
Castilian heads, bandits and indentured grape growers, repressive
squads, *mossos d'esquadra*, mobs, conflicting parties of soldiers,
emphatic interferences, wounds inflicted thanks to ancestral
rivalries, a situation prolonged over the course of centuries,
tolerably passable, passably unsustainable, forever knee-deep in
adversity, wading in it, evading it, falling into it, unlucky land
of castles destroyed and counties condemned, Count Arnau,
unrepentant lord of abuses, extorter of servants and violator of
abbesses, condemned soul with tenebrous retinue, nighttime
rides like steel scorpions, sparks, galloping echoes, a country
accursed, land of blasphemies and sacrileges, of ransacked sanc-
tuaries, Friar Garí or Garin, outrageous violator and murderer
of Riquilda, daughter of Wilfred the Hairy, maiden returned to
life fresh as a rose when, seven years later, perhaps nine, the
despised hermit, changed into an unrecognizable wild beast, was

captured on the crags of Montserrat by a group of hunters and taken back to Barcelona in a cage. There, all hair and nails, he confessed his crime to the astonished court, a carving by an unknown artist placed in a landing of the staircase, exposed to the people's curiosity, people disposed to render tribute and acclaim, to praise even upon the scaffold, unhappy star of Juan Sala, alias Serrallonga, native son of Viladrau, prototype of the good thief, knight-errant to the poor, to the needy, cunning knave of the Guilleries mountains, like Robin Hood, bandit immortalized like Tallaferro y Trucafort, like Perot lo Lladre, meaning, the Quixotic Pere Rocaguinarda, better known as Roque Guinart, popular heroes, gunslingers of the people, race of illustrious libertarian inclinations, Ferrer Guardia, victim of injustice, the Sugar Boy—*El Noi de Sucre*—Quico Sabater, laureled martyrs, done to death, start all over again, reset accounts, a race of iconoclasts and image makers, saints and criminals, mystics and forerunners, transporters and navigators, saviors, poets, visionaries, fratricides, conquistadors, Phoenicians, Philistines, merchants, a bastard history of transactions and conspiracies, activities secularly centered in Barcelona, prostituted city, city of leisure pursuits and occupations, of political ambitions and courtesan hopes, prisons and gallows, lost glories and abandoned empresses, miracles and revolts, perverse and versatile city, twisted, malicious, pharisaical, Manichaean, sweet-talking, dissimulating, keen, dissolute, insolvent, anarchic, separatist, fundamentalist, reactionary, plutocratic, rich loafing laborious city, libidinous, lascivious, insane, profaner of sepulchers, incendiary, blood-streaked city, caked in blood, underworld of hoodlums and crooked cops, bullies and bombers, employer of bodyguards and syndicate gunmen, terrorists and shock troops, assault experts, policemen, civilians, Civil Guards, esprit de corps cloaked in wrath, organizations polarized just as the *cadells* and *nyerros* once were long ago, a beam sought in another's eye, eye for an eye, tooth for a tooth, a cocktail of violence, a mixture of explosive Chicago and camorrista Naples, a chronicle fundamentally marked off by black events and bloody days, tragicomic weeks in a city accustomed to settling questions in

public, to liquidating them around the corner or along the streets
stretching away into the distance, if not in the no-less-expedi-
tious revolts of Montjuich or La Rabassada casino, the gutter
become law, law of the loophole, a people oppressed, a people
persecuted, a people held captive, a messianic people, always in
exodus toward itself, quicksand promised land, city built on
sand, below Las Ramblas, from mountain to sea, from river to
river, soil born from the waters, terrain sprouted from the receding salt marshes, sprung up between alluvium and sandbank,
islands and peninsulas gradually enlarged and extended until
forming one single misty bubbling plain of sedimentary clay, of
algae and fungi, drifting viscosities settled gradually into a pasty
green germination, accumulated herbaceous vegetation, woody
entanglements, gigantic branches, roots securing the earth,
climbing stems enveloping it in tangled hangings, reverting to
earth, decomposing, fermenting in slow vital cycles, laying down
the bases of the fertile plain, of future Barcelonas, a fleeting
succession of flowerings and desolations, phoenix deceased and
revived, reborn from its prostrate ashen wingspan, a city today
unfolded within the arms of the encircling mountainous amphitheater, from Tibidabo to the port, from the Llobregat to the
Besós, boundaries overflowed each day by the Mediterranean's
greatest human concentration, peripheries woven from posts and
cables, chimneys, irons interwoven beneath low-hanging layers
of industrial vapors, factories upon factories, railways, arteries of
ingress, labyrinthine slums, suburbs more and more dense
around the city center proper, pleasant seat as much with very
lively centers of activity as well as outlying residential zones, calm
and quiet beneath other skies, lighter airs, tremulous foliage
along peaceful avenues and boulevards, delightful quiet flowering
orchard, cultivated land of poetry contests and spiritual exercises,
a city traditionally open to progress, preserver and restorer,
archiver of past splendors, words and gestures made myth,
fantasies in stone, a profitable archeological past unearthed by
the city government for the benefit of all, stimulating, ennobling,
valuable profundities, fecund excavations, arches and aqueducts,
truncated columns, facings cleared, left open to view, urbanized

ruins, recomposed perspectives, limpid green lawns sprouting
long thin lampposts, ivy-crowned heights, classic cypresses, myr-
tles, fructified stone, and triumphal laurels, Barcelona, city of
trade fairs and conventions, as that great sign planted in the
green grass proclaimed, before the old city walls, perchance since
the equinoctial festivals last September of La Mercè, the Virgin
of Mercy, before the walls of the exterior circuit of this involuted
labyrinth of back alleys and side streets, crossed slantwise by the
declining afternoon sun, populated by anonymous footsteps,
little children's clamor heard amid a natural rumor from the
unexpected small plazas and open spaces, winding turns and
hidden corners, patios, staircases, gates and porches of run-down
houses, overshadowed by the dark gray edges of the cornices, by
the iron rust run down the wall to the low graffiti, large old
doorways standing open to dark interior workshops, small
businesses, antique shops, artisans, image makers, ornate estab-
lishments crammed with goods, narrow shop windows, secondhand bookshop, bodega, souvenir and costume jewelry shop,
postcards on display outside, diverse views of the cathedral and
its surroundings, Plaza San Jaime, Plaza del Rey photographed
from the Casa Padellás, Plaza Ramón Berenguer el Grande seen
from above, at dusk, against the acid yellow of the dusk and the
nitid crosswise cirrus clouds, views from Calle Obispo, from
Calle de los Condes de Barcelona, from Calle de la Piedad,
following the outline of the cathedral apse, detailed views of the
cloisters, the medallion of San Jorge, for example, in the keystone
of the temple, carved stone, archivolts and capitals, the door of
Santa Eulalia, the door of San Ivo, the portico, and more standard architectural compositions, the facade in the background,
and a projecting section of the Roman wall in the foreground,
the entire cathedral head on, the nucleus of what was once Mons
Taber taken in its entirety, a structure of rooftops, of ochre reliefs
with interspersed green spaces, aerial panoramas from the commercial center, from the wharves, from the Ensanche, a partial
view of the city from Tibidabo, with the amusement park rides
at the very top of the mountain hanging out over the void, or
from Montjuich, the castle parapets silhouetted before distances

tightly packed with buildings and in the hazy distance a terminus
of hills like clouds, partial views, sunsets and backlit western
skies, glowing nocturnal blues, typical images of Barcelona, the
Columbus monument streaming with pennants, Columbus
against the heavens, the terraqueous globe like a pedestal,
Columbus in the spotlights, pointing to the darkness, Columbus
hanging on the rigging of the caravel Santa María anchored in
the port, as if mounting the heavens on his terraqueous globe,
the Arco de Triunfo, triumphal arch, the Obelisk of Victory, the
Sagrada Familia spectrally illuminated, the stadium in Las Corts
filled to capacity with spectators, the fountains of the 1929
Exposition, the Ciudadela Park thick with amazing lucent April
yellows, Park Güell and its quiet paths, perfect for morning
trysts, petrified paths and passages, trees of rock, rough and
writhing, Park Güell and its oblique columns, its airy serpent of
multicolored mosaic, flowers formed from fragments of flowered
tiles, snapshots of the streets, bustling drudgery and pleasures of
daily life, Las Ramblas, polled plane trees with naked boughs,
with spring shoots, dry leaves, tobacco-colored, hanging on edge
above the passersby, a variegated coming and going between
kiosks selling books and magazines, pictures and postcards of
the city, among flower stands, bouquets and plants and freshness
like dew, chrysanthemums, nosegays of everlasting, stiff wreaths
of golden Butcher's Broom, funeral offerings, sad Novembrists
in memory of those who shall nevermore, of those who no longer
come and go nor even stop nor will stop before the kiosks on
Las Ramblas, before the flower stands, in anonymous coincidence, the instant fixed forever, in a corner of the postcard, from
behind, a painter before his easel colorful with sketches, everything picturesque, local color, movement, Las Ramblas and El
Liceo, La Plaza de Cataluña seen from Las Ramblas, Plaza
Cataluña overflown by pigeons, La Plaza de la Universidad
spinning with traffic, various currents turning and branching,
trams, family cars, taxis, buses, a plaza congested, presided over
by a facade of sober symmetries, twenty minutes to six on the
clock tower when he entered the building through the main gate
with determined step, after confirming the presence of police

detachments stationed at all the surrounding side streets, jeeps, horses, police forces prepared to intervene at the first symptom of agitation, to cordon off the plaza, redirect traffic, break up the groups of spectators, keep the pedestrians back while the water-wagons moved into action, while they blasted the porticoes of the entrance hall, clearing the way for the police on foot, opening a path for them through the broken glass and the fallen sopping banners. At first, except for the very small number of students gathered, fewer than even the most pessimistic predictions projected, everything proceeded according to plan, even too closely for the final result to proceed according to plan, for it to create an inflammatory climate of confrontation capable of liberating energies, of empowering and spreading, of spontaneously unchaining a process of sweeping, uncontainable galvanizing actions. But the morally decisive factor in the later march of events, more than a mere question of number, was, perhaps, the crude confirmation of the unquestionable inefficacy, by circumstances not so imponderable as mysterious, of all their appeals to the conscience of the university, an immediate and manifest cause, in the long run, of the situation they now found themselves in. They were few, the usual suspects as they say, those directly responsible, the committed few, and their fervent activity proved insufficient to compensate for the absence of the masses summoned, insufficient even to silence an increasingly less precise conviction of having embarked on an enterprise headed straight for disaster. Two hundred, perhaps? At least one hundred eighty? Some spoke out from atop the patio benches, encouraging their companions, but next when they read, without even a breath of improvisation, their declaration of solidarity with the Asturian strikers, it all came out rushed and confused, almost unintelligible. The signs and banners also appeared too suddenly, without seeming very natural, unexpectedly small and isolated, and the shouts sounded almost furtive, like asides, a feeble chorus. They burned a few newspapers that had published the official reports on the strikes in Asturias, and the portraits of Franco and José Antonio, tumultuously pulled down from the lecture halls, were soon lying shattered on the ground, and their voices seemed lost in the rounded strophes of the *Gaudeamus Igitur.* The movement toward the street started with certain indecision, without it being completely clear to everyone where they were headed, which route to take, along which streets they planned to carry out their demonstration, maybe because no one really believed that they could make it past the front doors, the doors where they usually congregated, unsure, confused, confronted by the police phalanxes, by the water wagons spraying, now shouting *Libertad! Libertad!* while struggling against the pounding water until, when the explosions went off, one after another, too powerful, the police responded, charging them in a tight formation of boots and billy clubs and steel helmets. It must have been just after six in the afternoon.

I went because I was curious, to see what was happening.

Curiosity, nothing, said Montserrat. You can drop your stories with me, I'm not the police. You went because you had to do it.

Well, but out of solidarity with my friends, I mean. Nowadays all you do is ask for freedom and they instantly call you a communist.

Now? They'd even call José Antonio a communist.

Eloísa cleared the table and, from the sitting room, through the open glass door of the cabinet, they saw her run with her plates toward the kitchen, her face suddenly contorted, clouded with tears, just as when Raúl had arrived home and Papa hugged him and she heard him saying to him my son, my son. Montserrat interrogated him with her glance. They were alone. Papa had left the room, probably gone to the toilet, moments before Montserrat appeared, who stopped just in the doorway, emphatic and triumphant, and without answering his greeting, she was upon him throwing her arms wide to squeeze him tight between repeated kisses, pulling him, her purse and gloves against the back of his neck, holding him at arm's length to see him better, holding him by his shoulders while she kept repeating *machote, machote,* you're such a big boy now. Raúl refilled the coffee cups, poured more cognac in Montserrat's; his own, however, remained untasted, not very appetizing as tired as he was and, especially, so amazed, tension resulting

from the unusual events of the last hours, of the condensation
of events, of the absorbing character of the accumulated emotions leaving him dry and rough, as if hungover, his head thick
with somnolence, soft haze, deforming his perception, words
sounding against open spaces, echoing against incoherencies,
the binding thread of the phrase, questions difficult to formulate
and even more difficult to answer. An even greater difficulty
given that Montserrat's conversation was now in itself rather
incoherent, scattered ideas, fleeting, expressed with exaltation
and haste, changing themes too brusquely, José Antonio's personality, young people of an earlier generation, ideals. The real
José Antonio: a sublime character, irreducible, the poetical and
manly qualities of his style, and his speech. She had met him in a
meeting, during the days of the Republic, when Jaime was
one of the Falangist leaders of the university. People with an
immeasurable capacity for sacrifice, contagious, people totally
and passionately devoted to the cause, above and beyond selfish
interests, devoid of all pettiness. The unforgettable magnetism of
an era, of a way of being, men who mattered, who knew how to
shake things up, real men, like José Ramón and José Pedro, like
Florentino, like Vittorio, like Ernst himself, who, at least in this
aspect, regarding manliness and bravery, had no reason to envy
anyone else. A generation of heroes, something unimaginable
to those who had not lived through it, that attitude of bravery
and sacrifice, of disregard for life, always betting against death,
living as if for a brief moment, squeezing out every last minute
of their short leave from guard duty, just as happy as naughty
boys. Such temerity! Bold features and bold gestures! Arrests,
disdain, fierceness, arrogances, contempt, exploits... Impossible
to express what that time was. The best died and, now, the
others, the deserters who never fired a shot, string us along like
we don't matter. Because we didn't fight a war for these leeches,
for that gang of the Opus Dei, for today's Falangists, for those
who run the show and take their cut first, and look out for their
own interests while they talk about stability. Their money, that's
what they want to keep stable. Do you think anyone would have
given, let alone risked, their life for the pretty faces of these black

marketeers, the insiders, the nouveau riche, for these bankers and financiers who've taken control of the country's economy? *Tocinaires*, as we called them back then, pork butchers, scoundrels, scumbags who didn't even have anywhere to lie down and die before the war and then made a killing on the black market. They sure helped themselves. In the worst way. Even disappearing while there was danger. If only José Antonio could rise from the dead! There are so few remaining, the faithful, those dedicated to the true cause. But it's a consolation knowing that you can count on them for whatever you need, that they'll answer you unconditionally, that they'll move heaven and earth if necessary. When I heard about your situation, I only had to call Madrid, to speak with Florentino, a dear friend, the one who recommended you when you were an ensign. Montserrat, he told me, I'm going to put in a good word for the lad as if he were my own son. That he was misinformed; wrong about the facts. Or at least he had some distorted idea of things. But, for God's sake, Florentino, don't you realize that with the way things are now an honest young man these days can't possibly adopt a different attitude? Or that his attitude, deep down, and even though perhaps not even he himself knows it, is that of a truly committed person, given his basic, fundamental loyalty, if not to the letter then definitely to the spirit of the same principles which inspired us? Have you forgotten about when we were his age? Do you think, confronted with a situation like the one nowadays, we would've behaved any differently? And I've made him see that for us you even represent an obligation to encourage, support, and direct, as we can, as many of you as we can, in these times of confusion and sinking values, you all appear morally healthy, with concerns and courage, with ideals, with altruism. And Florentino told me that, well, of course he was going to show the same interest as if you were his own son. He's a perfect gentleman, completely true and proper, incorruptible. She was quiet for a moment, shaking her head, arching the faint outline of her plucked eyebrows, nostalgic. There were moments when her face seemed a mask, that slightly swollen smoothness of features in a cluster of folds pasty with makeup, her face powdered and white, her hair clear and stiff, straightened, and her bulging eyes in the middle of her face; it seemed to make her lean forward in her seat, her elbows on her knees, as if on the attack, and then leaning back against the chair, her legs stretched out, her glass of cognac resting on her bulging belly. She asked him about his life and his projects, about Nuria, about his studies.

And your girlfriend? Is she still in England?

Nuria? Yes, in England. But she's not my girlfriend.

Girlfriend or whatever you want to call her, you understand me, we're not going to start beating around the bush, you and I. Did you let her get away?

Well, the truth is we've never really been a steady couple. And now not even that.

Ah, well, you see my question was completely innocent, I didn't know anything. You know I'm not one to try to rub you the wrong way. That's for everybody to figure out on their own. But if you want me to tell you the truth, I think you did the right thing. I'm sure that you're a ladies' man, and the last thing you want is to get married. Well and good. You're still very young to be forming serious attachments. For that matter, I'll tell you the truth, if I were a man, I'd certainly never get married. And I don't say so for the sake of the freedom that you'd surely sacrifice, but rather for the lack of trade-off, for the disappointments that you have to bear, for jokes and misunderstandings. Believe me, there's no more thankless responsibility than marriage. And how it weighs everything down. I don't know exactly what you plan to do with your life, but I'd bet my neck that it won't be something ordinary, but rather, the opposite, something very unconventional, that demands independence and personality. Writing, for example; because I don't know exactly what it is you write, but I'm sure you do write, you can't fool me, I've got a sixth sense for these things. Well, imagine that now, what a problem. Monsina, because she's a girl, and for a girl things are different, because a girl always has everything to lose and you've got to be careful, but I swear to you that if I'd had a boy instead of a girl ... Especially, forget about falling in love, above all. You do what you want, but don't fall in love, I'd say. Set things up so that you

don't make a mess of things and, if you do, fix things so they
don't drag you down. And if someday you really feel like getting
married, get married, but don't fall in love, because then you're
lost... Of course, the girls today aren't the best ones to inspire
lofty sentiments. The girls, and the boys who are really no better.
These arrogant little pups, they seem like they were raised in a
nursery. From the looks of it, it's a worldwide problem. You've
traveled so you'll know if it's true. What I can assure you is that,
at least here, these little stillborn puppies these days, the ones
who come by the house when Monsina throws a party, are really
the last straw. At least I can't figure them out. It's like they have
chocolate milk in their veins instead of blood, no passions and, at
the same time, no principles, no problems, no remorse, no struggles, neither here nor there, I don't know, they're just insipid. I'm
sure you must think differently, but for me it's essential to have
religion, to have principles. You must have other convictions,
but at least you have this, convictions, and don't think, I've also
been down in the dumps and faced doubt. But the truth is that
I wouldn't know how to live with myself or get along without
Sunday Mass, for example. Without Mass, Sunday would be
for me a kind of crippled day. The thing is, I believe it brings
me luck. On the other hand, not for them, you don't see any
contention in them, no compunctions, no convictions. It's as if
they had nothing inside them, nothing to contain. On one side,
they know it all; but on the other, nothing interests them. And if
I, who am almost an old woman, feel young compared to them!
But them, nothing, they've got no ideals, no worries, they're just
indifferent to everything, they only talk about nonsense... You
don't see them with something, what you call character, mettle.
I don't even think they're interested in girls. They only talk about
clothes, just like girls. Anything that's not their clothes, their
records, their guitars... Does that strike you as normal? Only a
few years ago, four, five at the most, this didn't happen. You, for
example, at their age, you were different. And the thing is, kids
like you, although you didn't experience the war, you remember
it, you're part of a different generation, no doubt about it. And
it shows. At the same age, you all had more nerve, more drive,

you were always searching, you chased girls, all perfectly normal, of course. It was more like in my day, the way it's always been. And I think it's for that reason, because of the war; you saw it, even though you were kids, you touched it, you grew up within the struggle, and so you know that the reality of life is just that, struggle and fight, no feather bed. On the other hand, talking about our war to these youngsters coming up now is like talking to them about the Stone Age.

He held Montserrat's gaze, but without looking straight into her eyes, without establishing a reciprocal relationship and, as if inert, he let himself drift through that stare, nodding. It was like stubbornly continuing to read when distracted by something, getting only partial intuitions of the sense of the text, isolated flashes that instantly vanish, forcing yourself to make connections between them, to reconstruct their continuity. So then he heard her say: recollections, contrasts, contrapositions, evidences. Then: volunteers dead at seventeen, sixteen, even fifteen; Jaime, at twenty-two. He watched her search through her purse, root around in her purse while she talked, and carefully pull out the photo that she finally handed him, a face with very pronounced features, a full warm youthful smile, hazy and retouched around the edges, as if haloed, cardboard with dirty, worn edges, smelling old and handled, like a wallet. Now, however, now: where will it end? Boys increasingly effeminate, girls ever less female. Toward a complete confusion of the sexes? She asked him again about his projects. Would he try to earn a teaching position via competitive examination? Sociology? That's what we need, teachers, leaders, brains. People to look out for society. Competent, well-trained people, with vision, with authority. People who govern, not for the benefit of a few, but for all. With social sensibility. Who expend no energy on private interests or granting favors. The common good. Inflexibly. A difficult road, full of misfortune and bitterness, so many people failing, giving up. Sad, a recent disappointment suffered with someone who was a very close friend. I considered him true and uncorrupted but he turned out to be what we call here in Catalonia *un torracollons*, someone who stabs you in the back and roasts your balls over the fire. Believe me when I say I admire you. But I couldn't, by now I've forever lost my confidence in other people, I've taken too many blows in life. She had finished her cognac and now refilled their glasses, ignoring Raul's negatory gesture, his hand trying to cover his glass. Too many, she said. And then right away: c'mon, let's get smashed. She dipped her fingers into a packet of blonde cigarettes and rummaged around distractedly, without success, and ended up crushing the empty pack over an ashtray. She silently accepted a cigarette of black tobacco, and Raúl, as he gave her a light, noticed that she was looking above him, toward the door, and he saw her stand up, releasing a mouthful of smoke, smoothing her skirt. Uncle Jorge, darling. Stubbornly reading and re-reading, words superimposed, simultaneous sensations, impressions unfolding, turning the pages again, searching the newspaper unsuccessfully for some reference to the incidents at the university. Look, thank God, just a scare. Maybe it taught him a lesson at least. Folding the paper, gulping down his coffee, checking the time, the cup on the small table, the newspaper folded on the chair, to his side, images reiterated; going to school, teaching class, catching a taxi, the appointment with Escala or Santiago or with some connection, or a strategic planning committee meeting, or a meeting with Fortuny and Federico, at Adolfo's house, theoretically to discuss some practical questions, if it was the right time to approach Marius Cots and ask him directly about joining the party, to see if he still harbored any residual feelings of his earlier petit bourgeois *Catalanismo*. And when there were no practical questions to discuss, they met anyway and, in fact, went over the same themes again, rehashing perpetual problems, theoretical disquisitions, the circumstances that fostered Stalinism, Budapest, socialist countries and proletarian internationalism, the possibility, probability, or certainty that the Spanish communist party, accepting the parliamentary gambit just like so many fellow parties, would end up becoming institutionalized in perpetual opposition, problems and distinctions which, impelled by Federico's designs, drifted easily toward personal territory, here, in Catalonia, communism has always belonged to the petite bourgeoisie, Cots will

become fast friends with Fortuny, I told him that if Catalonia is
not an independent nation there must be some reason, etcetera,
going round in circles, fluctuations of tone and even
arguments around an unalterable nucleus, the attitude or, if you
prefer, each person's role, personal positions dressed in variable
and derivative concepts, as words, for example, lead the singer
in a patriotic hymn, with all their residual debris, as they develop
into specific ideological expositions or some story of apologetic
nature, with its hypotheses and interpretations so frequently
articulated by rhetoric, an exegesis likely to become lost in the
course of a sentence, in the roundabout language and commentary of the period, conclusions seemingly created by the very
dynamic of the oration, by the magnetic attraction that some
words seem to exercise with respect to others, independently of
what is appropriate to their application, in agreement with a
fundamental development not so much in the objective data to
which one believes it to refer as in the words employed, words,
words, who knows if with a certain awareness of what the only
thing that remains certain in the end might be. Montserrat said,
you can be proud of him, and the telephone began to ring, and
Papa looked at her with suspicious eyes, and Raúl said I'll get it,
and he went ahead of Eloísa, and Fortuny, surely calling from
some pay phone, said that no one was seriously ill, that everyone
was recovering, that he'd not lost the ignition key, diaphanous
codewords, due to the telephone being bugged, explanations
almost more incriminating than if spoken in a normal way even
as Papa was saying Oh, c'mon, c'mon, the authorities thoroughly
bungled the situation, what more proof do you want than that
they had to release him, and Raúl asked if he knew whether there
had been any classes held at the university, if anything else had
happened, and Fortuny said no, that classes had taken place as
usual, that he would be calling him, but that afternoon he could
not meet in the usual place. But no one can say I've been negligent raising my children! said Papa. Meeting at Adolfo's house,
arguing, digressing, playing records, drinking gin, simultaneous
images, reiterated. Adolfo with Aurora at his feet, as it were,
Aurora listening or seeming to listen, fascinating sentences, some

cataclysm repeated perhaps until daybreak, irreparable drunkenness, *dies irae, dies illa, illa daurada*, lost golden isle, vanished
intonations, abortive youthful Mozartian madnesses, requiem
for youth and life, Teste David cum Sybilla, dolorous awakening,
Michelangelo beauty, reclining and naked, enigmatic, marble
Aurora. And Adolfo, serene, *pensieroso*, the left hand grasping
the smoking pipe between his teeth, for as long as he didn't topple from the pedestal, as long as the myth didn't crumble to
pieces; for that long. Why respected? Why fascinating?
Fascinating for whom? Fascinating for all? Respected by all? By
all. Including Federico, and perhaps respected by everyone just
as long as he remained respected by Federico, respected to the
point that not even Pluto would dare to crack jokes at his
expense. Or well respected because everyone agreed that he was
a very intelligent guy although, in truth, since he hardly ever said
a word, there was hardly any way of knowing if he really was
intelligent or not. Or because everyone said that he was writing
a great novel, a great work which, on the other hand, no one had
seen, except for fragments, and which, consequently, might just
as well turn out to be a disaster, in the safe supposition, just like
with everything else bound to happen, that he'd manage to finish
it someday. And so much more respected because, who knows
if for a priori reasons or as a result of their own collective attitude, all of them, Raúl first, implicitly granted him a certain
measure of authority or acquiescence, quieting down as soon as
Adolfo asked them, ending up in discussions from which Adolfo
refrained, letting him impose his voice when, having listened to
anyone else besides Adolfo, they wouldn't have managed to even
hear him. They all clammed up, Raúl first, and they drank their
gin without listening to the music or listening to it in spite of
themselves, acknowledging, one by one, what Adolfo might have
said, not so much because they agreed as because, on the verge
of agreeing or disagreeing, they discarded beforehand the opportunity to cast doubt on him, in accordance with a kind of deference imposed by the mood, a mood most certainly established
by themselves. Where might they locate the root of such deference, of such respect? Or rather: what quality did Adolfo have

that no one else had, neither Federico nor himself nor any other person no less intelligent, no less sharp or brilliant? Fascination? What was the exact sense Aurora imparted to the word? Something definitive, of total value, absolute, coming before anything else? He tasted his cognac.

Quite frankly, what I don't understand is how you can listen to Juanito, man. Don't you see that Juanito is what's called, speaking realistically and calling a spade a spade, a real shithead?

Because I'm a lawyer and I know what "apathy" means. And what he's accusing me of is gross negligence.

But don't you see that he's the one who really doesn't know what apathy means? If he knew the meaning of what he's saying, then he'd instantly cease to be Juanito.

Man, oh, man, for the love of God. Look what he's saying, that I, who've got a son who's nothing less than a priest, that I've been a negligent father, precisely when the family environment they've been raised in couldn't be more Christian, when I've given all my loving care for them to attend the best religious schools, and I've never hesitated to make any sacrifice regarding their education. What fault is it of mine about what my sons do later, if I've done everything I could? Besides, this thing with Raúl is nothing more than a mistake of which he's been a victim, just the same as could have happened to anyone else. The proof is they had to release him. It's these people working for the police who want to discover shortcomings in the very people who pay for their dinner, no matter what. He was attending classes, like any other day, and he got caught up in all this craziness. That's his big crime.

You can be proud of Raúl, that's all I have to say. He's made of the same stuff as Jaime. None of his other cousins is good enough to shine his shoes.

Well, for heaven's sake, let your brother mind what he's saying a little. You can't criticize people that way, without rhyme or reason, without having sufficient elements for judgment. Not even having them, c'mon, because things are not as simple as they seem. Judge not and you won't be judged, much less launch an attack that way, like hurling a stone. When you don't know what you're talking about, the best thing is to keep quiet. What does Raúl have in common with your poor brother dying like a hero, fighting against the Reds? Because he was a hero.

What do you mean "poor"? The only poor fellow here is Juanito. Poor for lacking spirit. Jaime was anything but poor-spirited, he was the personification of courage and generosity, he was greatness itself. Neither in his life nor his death is there anything that deserves to be called poor. God help us from wishing some misfortune on Juanito, but God always takes away the best. I promise you that's true.

Well, you see what he's going around saying. That he wants nothing to do with the people who killed his brother. That's exactly how he said it. To Gregorio, just this morning.

Two of a kind. Gregorio has also turned into some big gossip. I'm sure he wasted no time coming to tell you about it. Now, regarding Juanito, why do we need to talk? Lots of badges and so much of his highness up and his highness down, but in the hour of need, he wouldn't be capable of risking even one of his dyed hairs for Don Juan, not one. And, apart from this, don't pull him away from his Equestrian Circle, from the ultraviolet lights, and from his little whores at the Bolero, that's where all his ideals crawled away to die. Ah, and from the Association of Friends of Model Railroading, where they've named him spokesman or something like that.

That's what I'm complaining about. That someone like him, who's suffered no wear and tear, who doesn't even know what it means to work, who's always been dedicated to chasing the good life, now dares to criticize me, who, apart from being his father's brother, from the respect he owes me, I'm a man who's fought, a man who's given himself to his work, who's consecrated all his efforts to give his children a Christian education. After being destroyed by life, after the grief of losing Eulalia, I suddenly found myself with two sons in the world and no wife, eh, and hounded by the Reds, and that in spite of everything I've managed to give them a steady, healthy upbringing. No, nobody knows the things I've had to suffer.

For God's sake, uncle, of course I know it all too well. But Gregorius also made a mistake telling you something that, coming from whom it comes, has no importance. He's an incorrigible gossip, now and always, for the rest of his life.

I wish you could hear him. You'd see how I've not invented anything.

But for God's sake, uncle.

I'd just like you to hear him. He should be here right now. He was with me this morning, in the garden. And he said that he'd come right back after lunch. I don't understand how he takes so long. He knows I always take a little nap afterward.

He must have forgotten. He'd forget his head if it wasn't attached. He forgets everything, he falls asleep everywhere.

I think it's because he takes too many pills. All that crap for insomnia leaves you wrecked. But if you have a healthy routine, then you're ready to go. And besides they're really expensive, a real drain on finances. He also says that he's got anxiety. I think he's full of manias. Sometimes he seems, I don't know, kind of crazy.

He must be crazy with love.

Well, the thing is no one would say so, but I'm six years older. And Paquita herself, half-disabled and everything, the way she is, the poor thing is eleven years older, and her head is much clearer. Gregorio is senile, he's not in his right mind, honestly.

It's what I'm telling you, love. You only have to see him out on the town, with Leonor. They walk arm in arm like two young people in love, like a couple little turtledoves. I ran into them one day, months ago.

It must have been when he was going through that depression. Poor Leonor, well, she's a good woman. She's like Eloísa, she's been so many years in the house. He's lucky to have her, that he's not so worn out yet. I don't know what he'd do otherwise. He's like a little boy, he needs them looking after him all day long.

You can be sure I'm not criticizing them. On the contrary. The idea that she's a nursemaid doesn't count for me. As if she were the queen of England. Gregorius is perfectly free to get involved with whomever he wants. The thing is that she's not precisely what you'd call a paragon of charm. That's the only problem I see with his Leonor.

Montserrat, Montserrat, you know I don't like you talking so freely. You say things in jest, but someone who doesn't know you can take them seriously and, well, it creates a bad impression. And then things get repeated, people are terrible. You mustn't make rash judgments, Montserrat. You're quite the one to make them and it's not right. At least not in front of me. And I'm telling you seriously, honestly.

But uncle, you know well enough I don't say it against him. I don't mean to criticize him. I love Gregorius very much, with his strange qualities and everything, and I know perfectly well that he'd be lost without her. He's completely absentminded. It's enough to tell you that some years ago, when Monsina was nine or ten, I had to forbid him from taking her to the park. You know that Gregorius is crazy about Monsina, well, about all kids, perhaps more about Monsina, and that children always love him, who knows why, but Gregorius is a kind of institution for the children. Well, then, I had to tell him that I wouldn't let them go alone to the park anymore, that if they didn't go with Leonor or some responsible person, then no. And the thing is, you know how crazy he is, playing with her, seems they were struggling, he was lifting up her skirts, that he was playing that he was going to paddle her, and so one day a circle of people gathered around, and a policeman even appeared and started to ask him questions. A real spectacle. And he was lucky that there were some people there who knew him from other times. They must have taken him for one of those crazy perverts who chase after children. Why am I telling you all this? Ah, yes, well nothing, because the little girl is all grown up now, a young woman, he keeps on with the same jokes. And, of course, people who don't know how he really is will just think that he's just some dirty old man. But he doesn't even realize that he makes Monsina miserable; she blushes red as a tomato and one time she started crying and everything. And I said, but, for God's sake, Gregorius, don't you realize that you can't touch a fifteen-year-old girl on the ass?

Of course, Gregorio is really the last straw. And what do you think about that time they stole his overcoat in the park? He says some young fellow asked him what time it was and before he knew it, his overcoat had disappeared off the backrest on the bench. I think he must have fallen asleep.

Nothing surprises me. He falls asleep, he forgets things, and then he thinks that he's been robbed. He even falls asleep in the cinema. Seems that one time he scared the hell out of the ushers, they thought that everyone had left the theater, and there he was in his seat like a dead man.

Right, right. He acts like someone deranged. I think he's out in the sun too much, and the sun cooks his brain and leaves him stupefied. So much sun can't be good. He falls asleep like a dormouse and then, of course, at night he's wide awake and can't get to sleep and so he takes sleeping pills. That's just a vicious circle and he doesn't know how to break out of it. Paquita's head is much more clear, I tell you.

Aunt Paquita? What do you want me to tell you? I think that if she were in her right mind she would never have swallowed all these stories about the ancient history of the Ferrers and the family crest that these genealogy swindlers use to rip her off. Of course it's Juanito's fault, he's such an idiot, and he filled her head with all these ideas; but only a few years ago, she would've paid him no mind. We've all got our own little manias; she's got hers, like praying to saints, and religious observances. Well, as I recall, I'd never before heard her talk about family histories and coats of arms. And now she sounds like a broken record, she only talks about how in 1963 or whenever it's the family's thousand-year anniversary and if for some reason she's not around anymore, we mustn't forget to celebrate it. Poor thing. Imagine, how are these disgraceful heraldic investigation people going to know things about our family that we don't know? But they stir up people's vanity with noble coats of arms and family trees that they simply invent, and they actually make a living from it. The only one who takes them seriously is Juanito, who ordered a seal for his ring and goes around bragging about it, telling everyone that the first Ferrers were lords of the Ampurdán who went south to establish themselves in I don't know what lands in Tarragona province. And I tell him, don't you see, you stupid idiot, that Ferrer is one of the most common names anywhere?

Look, everybody has their little manias. It's perfectly harmless.

It does no harm, but it makes him look ridiculous. His monarchist friends must be the first ones to joke about him the second he's out of earshot. Of course they don't have much reason to be proud either, newly minted titles for most of them, awards for civic virtues and good business, no real glorious origin stories there. Everybody knows that in Catalonia there have never been nobles in the conventional sense. Nor have we ever needed them, by the way. There have been counts, that's true, and the rest were lords and that's all. And where did all these marquesses come from now? But if any of these pseudo-titles now looks so ridiculous alongside the Duke of Alba or Medinaceli, you can be double sure how foolish Juanito looks pretending to have noble blood.

So what, woman, so what. Besides, who knows if there isn't some truth at the bottom of all this.

For goodness' sake, uncle, honestly, we never heard such nonsense at home until Juanito ran into these swindlers. What's happening is that, you know perfectly well they've got Aunt Paquita hooked on that ancient history business, and that's where we're at.

Poor Paquita, she's also got quite a cross to bear with her bad health. Life hasn't given her much more than difficulties and misfortunes. She's got it like with me, that apart from seeing her children well set up ... First she loses her oldest child, then her husband, and now she's sick, slowly eating away at her for years and years. And so many other beloved people just disappearing, your parents, the two of them in full health, eh, in the prime of life. You might say God wanted to put us to the test. For my part, I've always accepted it all with resignation, but sometimes I think why, my God, why. Eulalia's death was a terrible blow to me, you can't imagine, I don't know what kept me from losing my mind. Without faith, without religion, I believe I would've done something drastic. Lucky also to have my children, who obliged me to react, to keep fighting to make a life for them. Apart from them, I had no other dreams, I'd lost my desire to fight, completely. And I'd barely recovered, the war, the persecutions, and once again starting all over, one blow after another. But losing Eulalia marked the start of my misfortunes, it was the true tragedy of my life. If I'd had her by my side, I would've never

retired from the company the way I did, tired of life and everything. But without her I felt old before my time, without strength,
and once my kids were on their way, one of them a priest and the
other completing his studies, I lacked incentives to stay on as the
head of the company. Of course a man of frugal habits like myself,
who has no needs, lives with nothing, and our income covers all
the household expenses, thank God. But it's not the money, not
the desire for money, no. It's the moral aspect. I had skills and
drive, and I could've managed to become, let me tell you, a man
like Jacinto Bonet, a real somebody in the business world.

Jacinto? Well the truth is that I don't know what you see in
him, apart from him being filthy rich. To me he seems like nothing special. I don't know, pretty ordinary, I'd say.

Jacinto? Ordinary? For the love of God, Montserrat, don't
tell me that. Jacinto is a good fellow, everyone knows it. At his
age, the connections he has, and the position he's made for himself. I, for one, think he's amazing. He's a man who's had, well,
great success. What more do you want?

He's just one more out of so many who suck on the public tit.
And that way they can have fancy cars and servants and always
be traveling around from here to there. Besides, a man who goes
to America by ship and to Madrid by car because he's afraid to
fly, excuse me, but he's not my type.

But look, woman, you've got to see beyond those things, they
don't mean anything. Ask whomever you like in Barcelona about
Jacinto Bonet, go ahead, and if it's someone in the know, someone who's really involved in the business world, they'll tell you to
show some respect. Jacinto Bonet is a man of recognized worth.
So he's got enemies? Like any important person. In this world
it's all envy and slander, that's well known. But the ones who
criticize him are the people who help themselves to what's really
yours. And they sure help themselves, alright. The bottom line is,
the secret in the business world is this: knowing how to make the
most of situations. If people had no desire to make money there
would be no economic activity. As long as you don't infringe
upon the laws … And this Regime might have many defects, but
the Stabilization Plan was a necessary measure. I'm speaking to

you as a businessman. A medicine that had to be administered to the country, and the Regime has done it and, believe me, time will show that it was the correct response, although right now it might be hard for everyone to swallow. As people already know, you've got to take the good times with the bad. And even with all the defects this Regime might have, anything is better than returning to the past. That insecurity, always on the edge of our seats, expecting to be shot down in any ditch, that they'd kill you for no other reason than being someone of standing or because you'd voted for the right wing. Or simply because they caught you wearing a scapular. Those criminal bands on the loose, riffraff unleashed, secret police, raids. They stole our jewels, silver, everything they could. There's not even a proper name for everything they did. And now we're going to complain about stabilization? Come on, come on. As if stability wasn't what was precisely needed, stability and more stability. The thing is that we Spanish are never content. Do you want any greater misfortune than a revolution, social and economic chaos, reprisals, the loss of so many loved ones?

So tell me then, uncle. And this is what I'm complaining about, that Jaime didn't die for what we have now. This all might be a lesser evil, but he didn't die for this.

Yes, look, things never turn out the way we want them to. Poor kid, he was a hero, a true idealist. In these matters the just men always pay the price for the sinners. And precisely him, so young, so full of life and energy. He had such bad luck. Certainly, and you, for your part. It seems that destiny wanted to fatten us up for the kill. Deaths, infirmities, wars, economic disasters, every kind of calamity. Misfortunes never come just one at a time. Who was going to tell your father, for example, when we were young and we were playing in the big house on Calle Mallorca, that he was going to be the first? Of course he was the oldest brother, but at his age, in the prime of life, it seemed impossible. Now, the oldest is Paquita. And then, me. Do you remember the big house on Calle Mallorca?

But, how could I remember, uncle? I think I wasn't even born then. I'm old, but not that old.

Well, it was something worth seeing. One of the best little palaces of its time. Now it would be worth millions. And it was sold, I don't know, for some ridiculous price, for a song.

That's how we all are now, the crippled leading the blind. None of us has any real chance of buying Vallfosca from the rest of the family. It's still an indivisible property. Save Jacinto, of course, who'll end up owning the whole thing.

Ah, no. I've already told Gregorio, no. From a legal point of view, there's nothing to prevent him from doing it, but as the oldest sibling and with the moral force that gives me, I'm roundly opposed. I've already told him.

So what do you want to do? One by one we're leaving it behind, and that house is more and more abandoned. And now I don't know what's going to happen. Poor Polit, what with everything, being a shameless scoundrel, you can't deny he's managed it well. But the fact is that a country house that belongs to many different people can never be kept up in good shape. And at this rate, in the next generation, it will have fifty different proprietors. But Gregorius will sell his share and, in the long run, it'll be the Bonets and their children who'll end up enjoying it. By the way, it seems that Ramona is expecting again.

No, really, I promise you otherwise. I've spoken with Gregorius and I'm confident that I've been able to get him to forget the idea. That place is like the family manor of the Ferrer Gaminde family and it must stay that way. I've not tired of repeating it to him. But isn't Gregorius something. To side with them now. Who would imagine it?

Excuse me, uncle, but it makes sense up to a certain point. If you're the first one to declare Jacinto some kind of prodigy, as the pride of the family, and Jacinto goes and says to him that he'll buy his share from him, and Gregorius agrees and it seems like a good price to him, well, then it all makes sense.

Not true, not true. It was Gregorius who made the offer to Jacinto, not the other way around; it was Gregorius. And Jacinto accepted, naturally, because he's got vision and knows that in the future, that place is going to be worth a fortune. And this is what Gregorius doesn't see. But it's all his fault for offering it to him. I've told him a thousand times. Don't be a blockhead, it's crazy, really crazy. Who would think of making such a proposal to Jacinto? Don't you understand that Vallfosca is, has been, and must continue to be the Ferrer Gaminde family heritage?

Oh brother, what do you have to tell me about inheritances and entailed estates. To start with, if we'd applied it in our case, by now we wouldn't be arguing because neither you nor I would have our share. Everything would have passed on to Raúl's children, to Juanito, more precisely.

If you don't want to understand me, then don't understand me. It's not for the material interest, it's because of what it represents for the family. That place is linked to our family name, it's our family estate, not just any old property.

His hat was tilted over his nose and he looked at Uncle Gregorio from the shadow of the drooping brim, stretching his neck in a haughty show of bulging Adam's apple, protruding chin, hooked nose, and eyes staring from behind. Inquisitive and still like an old bird. And Uncle Gregorio, seated sideways in his chair, almost with his back turned to him, protected himself from the sunlight flaring round the plum tree with a folded newspaper. Eloísa listened from the steps, pretending to be shelling peas.

But what're you telling me? I've got no descendants. And I don't know what good I'd be doing my nephews leaving it to them when I die if the state will just seize almost everything. Besides, Ramona is just as much my niece as any of the others. They'll settle things between themselves then, don't you worry. And meanwhile, well, I'll make a few pesetas. That's the problem. What good is it for me to keep my share? What do I want it for? On the other hand, if I invest its worth in stocks, in paper, it produces something for me, brings me income.

You're unbelievable Gregorio, stubborn as only you can be. When you talk like this, I don't know what to do with you, you drive me insane. You're a perfect idiot. Isn't there any way to make you understand that the property you're now willing to sell for peanuts will someday be worth a small fortune? Now that everybody is starting to own their own car, if you subdivide it for development, people will line up to take the lots off your hands. And figure how many houses that could fit there. The only thing needed is to promote it.

Sure, exactly right there. They've got all Catalonia to choose from, but they'll drive their nice little cars right straight up to Vallfosca. Or maybe the rest of Catalonia will end up selling itself off by the yard, too?

And why not? It's happening everywhere. With cars, people will now all want to have their own chalet, and it's such a lovely place. The beaches will become impossible. You only need to see the photos in the magazines, the hordes of people. They're so full that sooner or later people will start to return to the countryside. They look like canned sardines, the way they're packed so tightly together. Besides, with a car, that property will be, as they say, just steps away from Barcelona. And it's got millions and millions of yards.

Look, Jorge, don't make me laugh. By then, we'll all be bald old men.

Gregorio, you don't know what you're saying, you're just raving. Don't you see that the only thing needed is to promote it, find some capital to set things in motion? There are so many places that don't have all the good qualities of Vallfosca, and yet they're already in fashion. For God's sake, don't be shortsighted.

Well, let's see if you find the money. For my part, I'm delighted. Now, if it's such a good deal as you say, what I don't understand is why you don't just buy out my share among the lot of you. I'll sell it to you really cheap and then everybody's happy.

I don't know what's the matter with you, Gregorio. It makes me so angry to hear you talk that way, I'd like to box your ears. You seem like a cold ingrate. So little attachment to your family name, your house, your own people? Because you know perfectly well, at the moment, none of us is in any condition to do that, to buy out your share.

Of course I know. I'm just talking. But really I don't know what you want me to do. Life is ever more expensive but income stays the same. That's why it seemed the best thing to do was to sell my share to Jacinto.

Well, it was a lousy idea, honestly. It's like selling your

inheritance for a plate of beans. Jacinto might promote that for his own benefit, as an interested party, but he can never be the titleholder of our family inheritance. That place is the future of our family.

Well, I can't tell what difference you see between me selling my part to my niece's husband and selling off parcels to strangers.

Well, it was just a lousy idea.

El Polit, sucking in one of his cheeks, clucked his tongue, said that it was all ready. During the war, then, back then. And afterward, when there was rationing, when the people came from the city and bought potatoes and greens at any price, eggs, flour, fresh meat. And the hands worked for low wages and they kept the farm as tidy as a garden. Now, no; now, just me, one single worker, doing everything was too much, I could barely keep it weeded. And when you take your potatoes to market, now they don't give you anything. Not for wheat either, or corn, even less for vegetables, tomatoes, fava beans, peas, green beans. And grapes aren't even worth harvesting. Ever since they started farming down south in Almería, and it seems they harvest sooner. Seems they grow vegetables all year round. And here you go to market and what you take for sale isn't worth anything now. And on top of it, before the harvest, they still import from abroad and they lower the prices on you. Seems like they only want to give farmers a hard time. Now, nothing but the trees, poplars, plane trees, everybody's switched to planting trees. And, at least, after a few years, and without worries, it's easy money. I told his lordship Jacinto myself: trees. He raised his head and turned it slowly, as if taking in the luminous afternoon sky and hills, the golden stubble field, barren expanses, fallow fields, overgrown cabbages among the weeds. A light now without swallows, of autumn, in the quietude the stark arcing flight of the wood pigeons. El Polit. Neither on the stone bench nor in the bulrush chair: seated on a wicker chair, swollen, purplish, with some dark glasses planted before his eyes. He said that those who came afterward would eat the figs without even knowing that it had been he who planted the fig trees. In the Hospital de San Pablo he also came out to the vestibule in the pavilion and sat on the stairs. He contemplated the poor withered garden, the clouds flowing over the buildings. He smiled as if self-conscious. A stroke, you see. He asked him for a cigarette, said they'd taken away his tobacco since he became ill, but that the nun on duty in the morning didn't say anything, she was alright. And now they wanted to give him a job as a doorman, here in Barcelona. It was surely his wife's doing, his wife who'd asked Señorita Ramona. Or Señorita Montserrat. She can't fool me with her little stories. He turned to the nurse. Well, ma'am. When do I get to go home? His peasant coloring contrasted with the paleness of the other patients, and his large knuckly feet, gnarled like wood, shod in sandals soled with tire scraps. And upon returning to Vallfosca, no sooner than getting out of the taxi, the first thing he did was sit down there, under the plane trees by the threshing ground, facing the fields, at the foot of woods and hills. In his house there were no armchairs and they had to bring him one down from their house. He sat rigid, elbows stuck to the creaking wicker armrests. Calella, they would go to Calella with their daughter. They said there was a lot of activity there, all along the coast, foreigners, meaning tourists. There would always be something to do there, and it wasn't like the city. Mercè had always enjoyed the city, but, in this case, he preferred Calella. His gaze followed a flock of wood pigeons, his eyelids squinting behind the dark lenses. He'd already sold the animals, he said. The chickens, ducks, rabbits, cows, pigs; and tomorrow they were coming for the horse. He still had the dogs. And the cats. No matter where he ended up, he couldn't take them with him. The scratching, sniffing, howling dogs, the whole pack gamboling playfully, growling, snapping their teeth, tails wagging, flirting. They seemed restless, watchful, or perhaps unaccustomed to the silence of the corrals and stables, to the calm yards not yet pecked over by the hens, unscratched, unexamined, roosters crested and cackling, pecking at the tomatoes, chicks, egg layers, hens in motion, startled eyes, staring, necks cocked to one side, suddenly running, escaping, flapping wings giving bursts of speed, heads pointing forward, taking big steps, the feet covered in loose yellow skin shooting out like springs. No chickens, no ducks, no rabbits, no cows, no pigs, no horse.

He took a taxi to reach Llinás, right from the station, and along the way he arranged with the driver to come back for him first thing in the morning. Outside of the house, in the transparent shade of the autumnal plane trees, a small multitude of neighbors and relatives had already gathered, serious and expectant people, dark, silent farmers making way for him with circumspection when the car departed. Inside the house the women held sway and it was hot, stuffy rather, from lack of air, and the sweaty expressions of affliction and mourning were heavy, overwhelming, cries of grief accentuated to the maximum in the moment of bringing out the coffin. The procession followed a lengthy route, and the widow and daughter followed the cortege in a trap, squeezed in among other women, almost unidentifiable beneath their black veils. The greater part of the attendants bid farewell in the town, leaving the church; only a few chose to make the climb up to the cemetery. The road flowed, twisting and slanting through the vineyards, steepening, ruined and rutted, and the priest climbing up into the cab of the black and golden hearse, alongside the driver, awkwardly silhouetted against the afternoon skies, heights still frequented by flashing pigeons. It was a difficult slope and, besides, the hearse left behind a redolent stench, perhaps from the grease caked around the axles. Raúl had walked in the company of the son-in-law and they explained to him some family mess, one of Polit's sisters with whom they didn't get along and who had now shown up, full of reproaches, daring to bring up some old differences with Mercè. He walked among the poor crosses of the tombs, between funeral niches grouped together, along the sandy paths bordered by cypresses, past unpleasant hedges with birds taking shelter; hammer blows rang in the air.

On the way back, the people began to split off into small groups, as their paths took them, and some farmers loosened their collars along the way, after a while, removing their jackets and even their shoes, while they chatted between yawns, loquacious and unrestrained, once again familiar, with the relief produced by returning to the world of daily life. Isolated in the

calm, soft as dissipating smoke, their voices drifted away from
the diminishing clarity, shortcuts, evasive paths of that landscape so well trodden, solitary, filled with wildlife, so thickly
sown with rocks and pebbles, with movement, muted, grapevines
and stubble, interwoven boughs, and only the soft sound of
the wind through the pines after the gunshot, the pigeon fallen
like a fluttering angel, in a feathery tumult, the same hills now
opaque, now that the turning of the sun is lower each day and
the dawn of the night that comes earlier, the lights cut off, the
valley growing dark, reliefs vanishing, fields almost extinguish-
ing themselves in the austere nocturnal emptiness. The trap had
driven on ahead of them and, when they arrived, the women
were already working away in the kitchen, letting Mercè do
anything. Her daughter, however, was cleaning greens, to keep
her mind off things. Mercè, by contrast, said nothing, staring
into the fire, and suddenly she began to pout again. A sigh, and
they all continued their tasks in silence, cousins, sisters-in-law,
relatives come from other towns. The men talking in the dining room, killing time, vague phrases, at odd intervals, general
sorts of observations; they passed round the porrón, tobacco.
They ate dinner together there, taciturn, Mercè wanted nothing
to eat and ended up scrubbing her plate, far removed from the
talk, anguished. The dogs prowled about infuriatingly, startling
them with their sudden howls, all rushing out together, and
the son-in-law had to go out and tie them up. One remained,
curled up next to Raúl's chair, awake and sniffing about, its
eye edged with fright. The doorway illuminated, the fresco of
the threshing grounds, the road to the house, a smooth curved
slope penetrating the threatening bough-thick, storm-clouded
sky, the garden strewn with leaves, toward the building as if
sheltering against the sky, the blind windows, the dark eaves.
And then, inside, the sitting room, the portraits of the grandparents, and of the great-grandfather, an oil portrait painted, by
all appearances, from a photograph and, very possibly, after his
death, in reverent memory. And the framed photographs lining
the hallway, hard, yellowed cardboard, Cuba, the uncle's factories and their products, his house, his lands, his sugar harvest,

his livestock, his blacks, estates and heirs, children, daughters-in-law, sons-in-law, distant relatives, anonymous family faces, ocher poses, astounded, an instant frozen in time, backgrounds showing balustrades, gardens, parlors with portraits and mirrors, belonging, perhaps, to the chalet on Calle Mallorca, in this dimly lit hallway, gloom, exemplary shades, funeral memories. Muted night, of unease, of insomnia and imaginary figures, until the white dawn lit up the sky, opaline. And the black birds fluting and flittering about.

Ancient faces. He faced her, haloed by bouffant hair, re-dyed blonde, alcoholic breath, burning, firewater, her words more and more fiery. Quit telling stories; for me, the Ferrers begin with our great-grandfather. I wouldn't search any farther on, I always tell Juanito, maybe you'll find one who was a church canon. That's why, when I talk about our ancestors, I refer exclusively to our great-grandfather's generation and those that follow. Namely: great-grandfather Jorge and his brother Jaime, who appears to have participated in the African campaign with General Prim. He's included in the Gallery of Illustrious Catalans, and it seems he participated in the Battle of Tetouan or the Battle of Castillejos, a feat immortalized by Fortuny in a grandiose tableau visible everyday from 10:00 am to 2:00 pm, holidays included, in the Museum of Modern Art in the Ciudadela Park. There is a very interesting letter which makes reference to the embarkation of volunteers in the port of Barcelona, la Ciudad Condal, a true historical document. There is also a mention of a Ferrer who fought as a lieutenant under Cabrera in the Carlist factions; but of all this, in relation to the family, nothing is certain. And the same can be said of another Ferrer who figures in the chronicle of the anti-Napoleonic wars in Tarragona province. We know from great-grandfather Jorge, however, that he emigrated to Cuba in his youth, to Matanzas, and that in only a few years' time he amassed an immense fortune. He married María Ignacia Gaminde, of pure Basque stock, belonging to an old Guipuzcoan family, from Rentería, a family name that stands out among the lords who gathered around the tree of Guernica. It's also known that great-grandfather Jorge,

although the uncles and aunts don't like it to be mentioned or
recalled, sowed the island full with mulatto bastards. Well, he
was what you call a *machote*, a vigorous man. With him, with
him begins the history of the family that, like the history of
nations, has its periods of ascendence and its periods of decadence. Grandfather Raúl, for example, a perfect gentleman; he
installed himself in Barcelona shortly before the loss of Cuba,
built the chalet on Calle Mallorca, and invested his money,
which was a lot, in stocks and some other properties. It was he
who added his mother's family name, Gaminde, to the Ferrer
family name, intending to prevent it from disappearing, at least
within our family, now that, from the looks of it, he had no male
descendants. That's where the name Ferrer Gaminde comes from,
properly speaking. It seems that Raúl's grandfather was a very
pious person. They even managed to offer him a Pontifical title
in return for his charitable works but he refused it, because he
wasn't seeking any social compensation, nor is nobleness a mere
question of a title. What we were saying before, authentic nobility, the genuine kind, is something different; nothing one merely
inherits : a person is either noble or they're not. For this reason
I prefer to speak of the nobility instead of the aristocracy, because
not every aristocrat is, strictly speaking, noble. And even less so
here in Catalonia, where, like in the Basque Country, the lords
have always been simply lords. A more legitimate conception
and, above all, a higher one, not dependent on a title : nobility
not of blood, but of spirit, something that people nowadays call
coming from a good family, having a good name, really nothing
more than rich bourgeoisie, people who will never have power,
with their cowardice and mean characteristics, enclosed in a narrow world, without greatness. A proud style, a broad outlook, a
gallant attitude, this is what distinguishes the wellborn. And
grandfather Raúl, even without having his father's ambition, was
such a person. The grandmother's family was something else,
liberal bourgeoisie from here, a dynasty of lawyers and notaries,
like your mother's family. What I call Calle Fernando people.
People with everything, completely respectable, but without the
personality of the Ferrers, of the grandfather, without that special

something, that *je ne sais quoi* which grandfather possessed. And his siblings: Felipe, who with the loss of Cuba moved to North America, and Cecilia, married one Andechaga, of Basque origin, in Santiago, where there are still descendants today, the Andechagas of Santiago, who continue feeling very Spanish. Juanito still corresponds with them occasionally, as well as with the Ferrers in North America, who, I believe, live in California and are also extremely proud of their Spanish and—more concretely—Catalan ancestry. And their children, Cecilia—who died when she was a little girl—Papa, Aunt Paquita, Uncle Jorge, Gregorius. Gregorius has always been something special, but the others, in their youth, hobnobbed with the best of Barcelona. And it's not for nothing, but it seems that Papa was really a person endowed with superb mettle and intelligence. And don't think that it's just a matter of my personal memories which, naturally, have little value for third parties, but rather of the testimony of so many people that had the opportunity to know him, that still truly adore him. For some reason he was named after grandfather. Just like you were, by the way. And both your father as well as Aunt Paquita herself, here where you see them, it seems that they were some real pampered angels, their whole life laid out nicely before them. Now they're well along in years with all the typical quirks of the Ferrers, because, you've got to admit, we Ferrers are an odd bunch. But your father, well, it seems that he was a very fine fellow. It was after the Republic, more or less, when we started having a real hard time, when all kinds of misfortunes began to rain down on us, like blows in the darkness. After Papa died, and Mama, Aunt Eulalia, who was so close to Mama, Jaime, all of them gone, one after the other, in such a short time, with hardly any time between them. I think that only a general tragedy like the war, a massacre like that, could distract us, as much as possible, from our own family tragedy. The war and then this inflation and the constant devaluation of everything, which has ruined the country while a handful of well-connected people got filthy rich from the black market, just like now with the Stabilization. It's the whole big-fish-eats-little-fish double standard. Because Gregorius always says that if Uncle Jorge had had a sweetheart instead of going into business, he wouldn't have lost so much money. Of course, that's easy for someone like him to say, he's spent his whole life living off a fixed income. But I'll say this, and in defense of your father, I've had to fight to make my own way to get ahead in the cardboard manufacturing business, which keeps my daughter alive. I guarantee you, life has gotten very difficult, and nowadays it's almost impossible to stay afloat this way, surrounded by big hungry sharks. Besides, let me tell you, Gregorius has always played it safe, and if he hasn't lost money it's because he's never risked any, but he's also starting to think twice before spending a single peseta. And it's not that it makes me happy, but it's good for him. Inflation spares no one, much less people like him or Juanito, who think that only idiots like us actually work. In their hearts that's what they really believe. And the thing with Gregorius, with all his talk about how if he were young again he'd go to America and do God knows what, you can be sure that in reality he'd still turn out to be exactly the same, that he'd never go off to America or anything and that, now that your father's not around, he'd end up marrying that skinny bitch, which is how he'll end up, for sure, in time. You'll see. He isn't the typical sort who, because he always goes his own way, taking the easy way, never manages to get anywhere. And look, I love him very much, but the truth, the real truth, is that Gregorius is a loafer, and selfish as only he can be. And among us cousins, as you see, there's not too much good hardwood, as we say. It's not for the sake of flattering you, but really the only one in the family I see who has pride, real pride, is you, the way Jaime was, who was cut from the same cloth as great-grandfather. Even physically he couldn't have turned out to be more of a Ferrer. Give him a mustache and beard and tell me if he doesn't remind you of our great-grandfather. Because what all the others are is soft, soft and lazy. Ramona married this man, who must have made a huge fortune and everything else, but I consider him to be basically dishonest, and I'm smart enough to be able to affirm it. Pedro, rather unsubstantial, small potatoes; Juanito. That's it, period. Well, and me, I'm the worst off of all, since I'm no longer good for anything. Ah, and Felipe, who by the way is increasingly worthless. He hasn't always been that way; he used to be, I don't know, a pretty normal fellow. Seems it's this stuff with the Opus, busybodies can't leave well enough alone. The last time he goes and comes out with this nonsense about how he doesn't want to sit next to me in the car. He must have been scared that people would think he was driving around with some floozy or I don't know what, and so there I am in the front with him in the back seat and me driving him around like I was his chauffeur. Does that seem normal to you? I just can't understand people nowadays. Some turned into posh snobs, others are prudes, and we're all in a real mess. When I compare young people today with the ones from my time. None now like Jaime, who was just exceptional, one of a kind, you had to see him in the months before the uprising, in the meetings, serene and proud, gallant, undaunted, the very picture of fierceness, calmly facing the hordes of people that had it in for him. Not with Jaime but with anyone else. Someone like Florentino, like Abelardo, fellows who, without being anything out of this world, had this manliness, this decisiveness of those days, things that seem to have been swallowed up by the earth, characteristics, qualities almost extinguished, practically withdrawn from civilization. Or maybe it was my lot to live in a privileged time, a generation of heroes who blossom young, and what happens is that I'm just spoiled for the world now. But for someone who lived through it, it's something that marks you, something unforgettable. You'd have to have lived through it to understand what it really was. The Montserrat Regiment—el Tercio de Montserrat—la crème de la crème of Catalonia, young men in the prime of life who risked everything for the sake of everything in order to be able to slip across the border into France and take up their duties for all of Spain and there continue risking everything for the sake of everything. And the provisional ensigns enlisted in the shock troops, in the Legion, in the Regulars, in the anti-tank troops, like Jaime. And the captains of the warships, and the pilots like José Ramón, a flying ace, who flew one hundred battles and received a special award, he died so absurdly, during an aerial exhibition of acro-

batic flying. That's the way things go. Perhaps if he'd
survived, I might have married him instead of Ernst, and my life
would have taken a very different turn. But that's what life is, a
roll of the dice. I met Ernst and look; we had a three-week relationship, what they call a war marriage. The typical story of those
days; I was his wartime godmother, and we wrote to each other
and I mailed him packages, until one day I met him in person,
when he was on leave, in San Sebastián, and it was the craziest
kind of love affair. With Vittorio I had a relationship in the
hospital while he was recovering from an injury. What a man.
One of the few truly manly Italians I've met, not a bit cowardly
or effeminate. I mean that he wasn't like one of those men from
Guadalajara, one of those little gents who seemed more like
ladies, and even wore hairnets. No, Vittorio wasn't one of them,
I assure you. He seemed Spanish, well, like the Spanish men of
earlier times. I'd like to know what must have become of him.
He must have died, those kind of men never last. And the truth
is that Ernst was also a man of irresistible courage and attraction.
That's what dazzled me; while I was passionately in love with
him I was blind to everything else. And naïve as I am, because
that's what I am and what I'll be my whole life, a naïve fool and
a dummy, I only realized that he was a social climber after it was
too late. He started to get really deep into business and he ended
up, inevitably, a crook, embezzling money and running off to
South America with that nasty whore. Oh, the things I've
suffered thanks to that almighty son of a bitch. And like this one,
so many other unhappy disappointments. They say that only
scoundrels prosper, stooges, wise guys, cynics, smooth operators,
deserters, the ones who've never fired a shot and take advantage
of the time when others are doing the fighting to usurp their
places, to help themselves to key positions and get rich at our
expense and then, on top of it, leave crumbs for everyone else.
If at that moment some prophet had foretold for all of us pure-
hearted men and women that everything was going to end up
the way it did, we would have taken him for an agent provoca-
teur, for a Red propagandist. It would have seemed inconceivable
to us. It was the climate of those days, the enthusiasm. Imbeciles,

that's what we were, that's what I think now. And, nevertheless, other times I think that I'd sign up again, that despite the disappointments, that's always preferable to the inertia of young people nowadays. There was a richness of experiences, an intensity of emotions, of feelings, I don't know, such an elevated vital tone. Life had a different sense, more strength, with death like a sword always hanging over your head. And the risk, the spirit of sacrifice, the companionship, the same form of loving, of commitment. And those moments of apotheosis, of brotherhood, of entering a newly liberated town, for example, something indescribable. Things that have disappeared, that have been lost, that seem unbelievable to people nowadays when you try to explain them. And, what's worse, young people nowadays are not even interested in them. And the younger they are the more indifferent they become, the more unbearably stupid they get. And I see it each day in these spoiled little brats who follow Monsina home and who aren't interested in anything but silly things. Real good-for-nothings, not only are they pansies, spiritually they're hollow as jugs. You only have to listen to the way they talk, the vocabulary they use, which is revoltingly poor. Four vulgar expressions, pablum, and a handful of adjectives that they use for everything. Things are either shitty or awesome, and they use the word "excellent" to substitute for the thousand different shadings in our language that distinguish one word from another, beautiful, sublime, pleasant, handsome, attractive, comfortable, harmonious, and hundreds of other words that I can't even think of now. For me, that's the most symptomatic thing, given that such a loss of expressive richness is only the reflection of a general loss of values. Monsina, no, Monsina is different. And don't just take my words for a mother's doting, because if she were an idiot or a prissy I'd tell you just the same. But really she's a delightful girl, and very chic, a real doll; she seems like a little German girl. And her temper, sometimes she's got such a temper and says the wildest things; of course you know where she gets it. After all she'll be, she already is, tremendously successful. But I'm not going to let it go to her head, and I try to raise her according to some very strict moral principles, because apart from the fact that it's my duty, as a good Catholic, which is what I consider myself to be, a good Catholic, that's right, without prejudices, apart from that, I'm a thinking person, although it seems old-fashioned to say it, that religion always provides a check. I know some people here in Barcelona—it's just a tenement house of a city—they skin me alive, say I neglect my daughter's upbringing, that I do nothing more than set a bad example for her, that I'm an irresponsible mother, etcetera. People were also saying, I know, that I had a banker friend who took care of me. Oh, wouldn't I like that, poor me, nothing less than a banker. But precisely because I know how people are and what life is, I've devoted myself so much to Monsina's upbringing, because she's a girl and not a boy and, in our society, don't kid yourself, an honest woman, of good faith, a woman honest enough to trust in her own natural impulses, well, she's bought and sold already. I can assure you because this is what happened to me, and it's what I don't want to happen to her. Because, and please pardon the pun, I'll tell you that they've screwed me too many times without letting me enjoy it, I've had too many bad times and none of the good. So I'll do the impossible so that Monsina can go out into the world prudently and not have to go through the same, so that she's got some common sense and discretion. I prefer that she knows what's what right from the start, that she's not going to be fooled. Like one of my godsons, you must know I've got many godchildren, his parents were going to send him to a boarding school run by monks, and I tell him right away: watch out, they'll try to grab your pecker. And Maruja: but for God's sake, Montse, what a thing to say to the poor kid. Me: really? Well, keep your eyes open and you'll see. And well, we take him to the school and, no sooner do we arrive, than a monk comes flouncing out to greet us with such a sashay in his step, I thought, sure enough, here he comes. And sure enough, not long after, the great big scandal, that when a boy got sick the monk in the infirmary gave him abdominal massages and all that. You tell me. As if I don't know anything about monks and nuns. And it's better to warn him, so the little fellow knows what to watch out for and you avoid him having a nasty shock.

And with Monsina I do the same. I don't want to lead her astray, but at the same time I don't want her to be a prude. She needs to know how things are, simply to look out for herself and, for the rest, be a normal modern girl, so she's not a fool or one of these girls with problems. And above all, that she not marry for love, which is the most foolish mistake you can make. Let her marry some rich man, and later she can do whatever she feels like. If she were a boy and not a girl, I don't say that I would've raised her the same. But she's a girl and that fact, in our society, changes everything. A man can flirt and have affairs as he likes and nothing bad happens, but a woman, on the other hand, she's stuck dealing with her big bulging belly. Just a slight difference. Apart from that, I'll tell you that I'm almost happy that she's a woman because that means she won't get into politics. Really, at least not like men do, who are the ones who have to put their balls on the table when it all comes down to it, when the shooting starts, because that's the truth, however much you want to say that women are equal to men and all this drivel, the result has already been seen that they gave the Reds their famous female militia, those big broads that they themselves had to end up shooting, and the truth is, what cannot be cannot be, however much one tries, and, with the nonstop idiocy they keep repeating to us, we're not going anywhere. War is a man's business and that's all there is to it. And that's why I tell you that although I really do admire your rebellious spirit, really very much, I don't dare say that, as a mother, if I had a son, I'd urge him to follow your example. I've already seen too much blood and too many dead. And I've had to bear too many disappointments, too many blows. People's ephemeral memories and the ephemeral nature of friendship, so many times, in the moment of truth, they just leave you to fend for yourself as best you can. Time is a sieve, and if among all those who call themselves your friends you end up holding on to a handful of faithful ones, you can be satisfied with that. When I have occasion to meet with some of these few friends who've stayed true, with Claudio—el Claudillo, as we call him—or with Florentino, who's surely been the minister with the shortest tenure in his post, because he could neither grant favors nor could they allow him to not grant favors, because this is the truth of what happened, because we always end up gripped with sadness when we remember those times, our frustrated dreams, how our ideals were betrayed. Besides, there are fewer of us all the time. Except for Abelardo, who, as long as he was an honest man, couldn't fail, and like him so many others. And, above all, the ones who have left us, Carlitos Martí, Xènius, José Pedro, who died there, confined in the VI Region, as General Captain, when in all honesty, it was his right to be Minister of the Army. But, in spite of everything, for the few of us who remain, we've got more than enough young spirit left in us to have a good time if we go out on the town there, making the rounds in Madrid. Because, don't think any of us have lost our fire over the years, and, thank God, we're all still simple people, happy and honest, and what we really like, well, is that, good spicy tapas and Valdepeñas wine. I've enjoyed myself sometimes, life doesn't have to be all thorns and, truth be told, sometimes I've enjoyed myself, and now I only regret that it wasn't more often, that I've not done more as I pleased, which is what I would've done if not for Monsina, with my responsibility as mother. Our circle, when we were all together, was exceptional, that's the truth, select people, elite, and everyone got along so well, thick as thieves. I think I've never laughed so hard as that time we were all in the Atheneum, listening to Xènius, who was giving a lecture, the great Xènius, a great person and a great friend, and Xènius, when he saw us in the crowd, a bit tipsy, by the way, he goes and starts reciting, almost at random, that satirical romance in honor of that silly twerp the Duke of Windsor when he abdicated his throne, a romance that, truly, is so little known that I think it remains unpublished. Well, it made you want to piss yourself, the whole slate of monarchists right there, totally nonplussed. I think I've never laughed so much in my life. And Xènius wasn't just a first-rate mind, maybe the best brain Spain has seen in this century, Xènius was, besides, an extraordinarily human person and a dear friend. And each one in his own terrain, all the people in the group, people of clear competence and authority, intellectuals, politicians, military officers, financiers. And true friends all of them, the kind who show you their friendship through their deeds, the kind of people capable of moving heaven and earth for you. Always, whenever I've needed help, whenever I've had some problem with my little cardboard factory or with anything, they've known what to do, they've helped me. You'll see, you've got to live, you've got to defend yourself. And I am a single woman with a daughter to feed, and if you don't have a deft touch and, especially, good connections, then you might as well throw in the towel. When you see so much immorality everywhere, you can sure enough conclude that you'd have to be a sucker not to make use of your friends' influence. In the long run they're purely disinterested favors, pure exercise of friendship, and in this sense, something completely natural, that if there's one thing in life that you deserve, something worth the trouble to save, that's friendship. Besides, their women are their women, but in terms of the group, the fact is that I'm the only woman, and of course, the men adore me, and there's nothing on earth they can deny me, just as there's nothing that I, with my limited possibilities, could refuse them. In a certain way, I am, as we might say, a bit like their little sister, and there's neither pain nor joy which they don't share with me, nor any problem I don't share. Claudio, for example, never fails to call me when he comes to Barcelona, to find some time to share, no matter how busy he is, like the good Catalan he is, Catalan of pure stock, Catalan like Jaime, like our great-grandfather, like his brother Jaime, he has the same name as my brother, the other Jaime Ferrer, good Catalan men precisely just as they are good Spaniards, insofar as they belong to a key part of the Spanish whole, to a whole of which, secularly, they've been forerunners and proclaimers, men of military lineage, enterprising men, true conquerors. True Catalan men who, like always, traditionally hold themselves higher than petty personal interests, proven defenders of Spanish integrity, willing to invigorate the cause of national unity and of its supreme interests with their own blood so often necessary and, wherever it has been necessary, whether in Cuba or in Morocco, and in Catalonia itself, so often in the trenches and on the front lines of the motherland; Catalans of the kind by which Catalonia would perish if its personality must only be seen as an impediment to the Spanish personality; Catalans, in short, who've aligned their greatest yearnings with the task of building forever, outside any distinction of creeds and colors, a Spain for all, an enterprise of which, with all their being and all their vehemence, they are the safety and surety.

A noble people, a patrician land, rich in art and commerce alike, in pleasures as well as industries, panoply of feats and reputations, of honors and of triumphs, to the envy of the world and of the stars. Persistent homeland beyond vicissitudes, recovered under adversities, Principality or Crown, province or county, viceroyalty or Generalitat, republican experiment or libertarian hypothesis, fatherland in exodus, fatherland of exiles and incarcerations when not their sepulcher, common grave of natives and strangers, a never-completed extermination, a land of laws and atrocities, of silences and screams, reborn like the broom covering its land, inextinguishable flame of April, omnipresent from mountain to sea, from peak to peak, angelic golden mountains. A long history of splendors haloing the exploits and adventures of Barcelona, city of rancid traditions and modernist extravagances, a city charged with resonance, echoes of choirs, of scheduled dances and sonorous choral societies, eulogistic scene of festivities and popular spectacles, explosions of collective jubilation, of violence, insurrections, popular uprisings and purported low blows, blind furor, charges and discharges, fire, gunshots, shrapnel, sickles and knives, clashing broadswords, city of factions, bipartisan, consumed by internal struggles when not by conquest in the name of expansion, bifid effigy, a winged asp cresting the helmet, the very image of great deeds, champion Barcelona, a place frequented by knights, from Santiago to Don Quixote, passing through Saint George and the Knight of the White Moon, the real emulation of the no-less-white nor less-real White Knight Tirant lo Blanc, and who knows if even through Roland himself; the Barcilona of Don Remont, prisoner of Myo Cid de Vivar, errant bandits, wrongdoers, propitious place for the creation of fantastic fabulations, histories of a people, a land, and a language, the word so often made blood by the conjugation of diverse factors, always somewhere between dream and reality, between common sense and castles made of sand, between death and resurrection, city of delights and disappointments, disenchantments, desolations, disappearances, city of death throes and resurrections, uncertain trances, yearnings, raptures, annihilations, city buried and unburied, sepulchral, mummified, petrified, a city transfigured like heavenly Jerusalem *qua resurget ex favilla*, phoenix reincarnated from its own ashes, the heart of a people of contradictory impulses, of strengths discovered and eventually lost, the useless efforts of a homeland seated on a border, on the frontier between Catalonia and what is not Catalonia, apparitions and disappearances of an identity centered around Barcelona, ancient hegemonic county of an expanding Mediterranean empire, today simply an honorific escutcheon on the family tree of its Don Juan condemned, a count languishing in the golden exile of Estoril, a virtual title in the same way that, once royal, when being Count of Barcelona meant being King of Aragon, of Mallorca, of Valencia, of Naples, of Sicily, etcetera, so, too, and no less virtual were the titles of King of Hungary, or Lord of Dalmatia, of Croatia, of Serbia, of Bulgaria, just like the Duke of Athens and Neopatria or the King of Jerusalem. Unfortunate civitas. What was its unlucky star in the deep firmament? Or was it perhaps the divine enemy, violent impious nemesis? Or was its insensate lightness alone the cause of so many sorrows, of so many perditions and blows redoubled? Neither republic, nor principate, nor county, nor kingdom, nor any glimmer of a chariot of fire, dominions dismembered, sovereignty dethroned, a crown of thorns and a scepter of reeds after the four blood-red bars of the emblem, passion lampooned, time's vandalizing deterioration, history's disgrace, an intricate history, full of rough roads and mysterious difficulties, sinister dalliances, narrow ways, frequently unholy solutions, denouement of intrigue, complex city, a once-magnificent amphitheater, today mere stage machinery and footlights, unhappy scene of farces and comedies, parodic trickeries and superstitions, a lamentable relic populated by pedestals and effigies, figurations, dead kings, and supplanted myths, histrionic mausoleum, now ashes, now loneliness, no less than legendary Italica or fallen Troy, of ruined Athens, or Rome lost but not found in Rome, homeland of gods and kings. Past splendors, lights eclipsed, bloody gilded islands vanished in the distance like a shimmering sunset, inner fire, faded yearning, mere ideal lost in thought, taken refuge in the hermetic folds of Montserrat, arid heart of this poor, sad, and luckless homeland, unyielding castellated temple in its merlons of rocks and crags resonant with chants, swan song, slow substitution of one tongue for another, from above and below, from within and without, bifurcated fatherland, slowly drawn away from its primogenial image, Catallunyàna, rocky land of songs and disenchantments, land of castles, sandcastles, castles built of playing cards, châteaux in Espagne, land of holy mountains, a landscape more classically supernatural than natural, a mountain dedicated by the ancients to Venus, more sensible of the sensual, venereal nature than the ascetic implications of its reliefs, the Roman Extorcil, indecorous décor in excess for its future scatological functions, crags like hermits or phantoms, a pleasant, welcome land for pilgrim patrons and knights-errant, apostolic missions, predilections, dissipated hoaxes, processes unraveled, unknown quantities clarified, a noble land without nobility, county sans count, principality without a prince, estate without land and land without estate, decapitated capital, headless homeland, bound hand and foot once again at the feet of Spain, delivered to its mercy, the Black Spain reanimated, reanimated but not resuscitated for it never was dead, reanimated and perhaps eternal as they say, penetrating from the Ebro, flooding it all like a rising river, land captured, uncivilly conquered by Francoism, a reconquest from the past, a plot reversal, end of the adventure, the occupation and consequent unhappy ballad of penuries and heavy griefs without even the manners of other times, no longer a pleasant reaction, no longer retrograde scholastic criteria: a purely troglodytic clawing. Historic personality of characteristics not respected by fate, discontinuous errant destiny, drifting away from events, from the whims of destiny, the separatist Barcelona of 1934, the anarchist Barcelona of 1936, the communist Barcelona of 1937, the fascist Barcelona of 1939, cheering, triumphal, overlorded, symptomatic versatility, ominous spectacle, ignominy extolled in the memory to the point of volatilization, a presumed nocturnal nightmare if not a carefully mounted Potemkinesque mise en scène. The history of a people more rewritten than written, adapted to the historic necessities of the people, linked to their rebirth, a grandiose epic, epic incarnate, made reality in the ambit of the fantastic. Vicissitudes, experiences, hopes and expectations of a more-than-battered cause, Catalunya, romantic bourgeois sublimation of an erroneous collective behavior, disheartened independence without vigor or without spirit, political incapacity taken for individualism, unfortunate bloody-mindedness confused with Numantian resistance, clumsy rapacities transformed into virtuous laboriousness, obstinate meanness transmuted into common sense, avaricious poverty recounted as austere gesture, ancestral characteristics, images greatly magnified in the mirror of time, peculiarities reclaimed so much more the more outdated if not nonexistent, residues of the past converted into an excuse for present-day impotence, into dreamy contemplations of the future, after-dinner longings around the table, speculative conversations, being from here, one of the few important things that one can be in life, destiny amid the universal, best thing in the world, gift of God, messianic quality, promised entity, mythic Mediterranean motherland now made reality in decorative maps for the parlor, territories and borders, regions and frontiers in a golden frame, Catalan Countries—els Països Catalans—more than forty, extending from Alicante to Rousillon, not to mention from Murcia to Provence, materialization of Catalan spiritual identity, poly-member entelechy, pompous rapture, the smug flush of erudition, lyrical utopia of merchants or Philistines, fortunate island, a truly ideal country, peonized by *charnegos*, the shifty nightcrawling southern immigrants, and financed by tourism and foreign investments, better than civilized, urbanized, for sale by the centimeter, simultaneously loom and hostel, landscape dulled neither by the spindle, nor manufacturing

activity, nor enterprising spirit, nor private initiative, both an
idyllic corner of nature and an agile, efficient organization, eminently practical and simultaneously sublime, vision or dream of
the epigones of some hypothetical Mediterranean Netherlands,
of what might well have been a Belgium or a Holland, a Portugal
even, empire still on horseback of four continents, in spite of the
fact that nobody pays it too much attention, or possibly and
above all, a kind of sunny Switzerland, traditional haven of peace
and foreign currency, a spot of oil in a puddle of blood, privileged land and people of the Iberian arena, where the dogs were
leashed with spicy pork sausages, dreams that someday, and why
not, they would no longer be dreams, they would be realities,
only a little bit late and not in the way foreseen, less heroic, less
decisive and showy, when, at least in this part of the world, the
national problem being that, more than anything, a question of
calculations, convictions, and conveniences, more an affair of
the pocketbook than the heart. Polemical dreams, conflicting
theories, conceptions, separatisms, centralisms, Spain as sorrow,
Spain as a problem, Spain without a problem, Spain, Europe,
Catalonia, entities with their own personalities no longer historical, cultural, or geopolitical, but rather substantial, ontological,
the Mediterranean and the Meseta, the Meseta and the Periphery,
centrifugal movements and centripetal movements, decadences,
renaissances, grandiloquences, pompous words, conjectures, precisely symmetrical and reiterated mechanisms, pieces of attractive
but inexact dialectic and even stupid, pretty little nothings not,
like everything, unfeasible or non-demonstrable, unethical theses
about transcendental preeminences, the Iberian and the Roman,
the Arabic and the Germanic, dilemmas, elucidations,
Mediterranean or Atlantic vocation, American or African, folklore
and *costumbrismo*, typical subject matter, lamentable cause as well
as the effect of topics made flesh by force of being believed and
repeated, made alibis, profitable reflection, justifiable mental
restriction, lying by simply not speaking or naming, a language
not simply sclerotic: cadaverous. Rejection of Spain, proclamation
of Catalonia, forgery of a recently dead dream, of a lost empire,
supplanted by the memory of another now reverted to dust, that

of the Catalonia that would be if it were or if it had ever been. The Reality, here and now: an industrious Spanish region where labor is massively non-Catalan and, in short, the capital interest, the benefits of integration, always the preferable lesser evil. The slow reduction of an ideal, gradual materialistic penetration to even the most recondite places, a visceral anguish and intimate rending produced by the dissociation of ideals with respect to the material base upon which they rest, the inevitable corruption of an always obsolete, out-of-touch enterprise, either because of a lack of driving force in the opportune moment, or for lack of sufficient elements susceptible to being set in motion by the driving force, either, in this case, pure formal residue, hypostatic fable, or rapture. Like a gem crystallizing too slowly or a floral geometry killed by frost, an annunciation without epiphany, gestation without childbirth, promise or prophecy unfulfilled and inconclusive, for so many other people, in the conjuncture, in the romantic age of the *risorgimenti* and its irrevocable affirmations, when, having overcome the latest convulsions resulting from Catalonia's status as despised stepdaughter, now one among equals, an indiscriminate participant in the peaceful exploitation of colonial possessions, of the colonization of the possessions, of the pacification of the diminished but not negligible exploitations, Catalonia even tried to Catalanize Spain, to infuse it with a different spirit, to renovate it. Not then, but rather when the hard times arrived, the final colonies worth considering were lost, the good times were over, a problem presented doubtless as a political alternative to colonial politics, a market problem, of imported goods and foodstuffs, a domestic question, the talk in the street, spreading like wildfire capable of igniting social intercourse, of igniting the language, of fanning the flames of the past, of raising standards, of unfurling flags. Not in the opportune moment nor with due decision, vacillating always between remaking Spain in its image and likeness, with Prim and the First Republic, who gambled and lost the game, or marching for the sake of the habitually steeper path of independence, the uphill ascent of direct action, movement without fights, without true national uprisings, without heroes, a cause

that, if it had not had its Petőfi, was not going to have its mayor
of Cork; a cause, in fact, sincerely undesired by the local govern-
ing classes, something like that woman who, with her daring
attire worn to high-society gatherings, with her attitude and her
words, can well make her admirers believe they'll have no trouble
seducing her or becoming her lover, and only after the disappointment do they understand that her true intention was not
to cuckold her husband but, by offering him the solicitations
obtained, to increase her value in his eyes, more an element of
negotiation than an instrument of separation and liberty, namely,
like Manuel del Palacio's sonnet "*El Enano de la Venta*", more of
a verbal threat than anything, a wildcard to play according to
the circumstances, in response to socioeconomic vicissitudes.
Catalonia apostolic and liberal, land of bourgeois protectionists
and anarchist workers, the whole repertory cast, active players
one and all in the spectacle, eagerly devoted to the historical
mishap of the Spanish farce, a romantic comedy of comic opera
personalities, grotesque unloved monarchs and grim, funereal
warlords, simian characters, of atavistic reactions and totemic
spirituality, lamentable pullulation of witches and asses, of
Figaros and strolling cigarette vendresses, with a blood-stained
danse macabre for a backdrop, impossible to be further removed,
completely deafening mob and excremental excrescence, decrepi-
tude of an empire that was, on horseback across four continents,
perhaps the greatest power that ever existed, from Cathay to El
Dorado, with its oriental specie and its occidental mines, prized
precious metal, Age of Gold slipped away like sand in an hour-
glass, and the metropolis like a crumbling arena, its ancient
image, a prefiguration of John Bull or Uncle Sam, reduced now
to a picturesque field of exploration for curious travelers arriving
from other latitudes, from higher levels, a land held up boldly
at gunpoint, attractive only as an anachronism, rather like
Garibaldian Italy, pleasant local flavor and pugnacious operatics,
but with a touch of the cruelty and mystery of the Sublime
Ottoman Porte, intolerances, brutalities, circus tent and boxing
ring of savage pugilism, the circle squared, nineteenth-century
Spain coming apart at the seams, canton by canton, junta by

junta, interchangeable constitutions, minor military uprisings, pronouncements, the scourge of violence spreading through decorative institutions, characteristic images: the Spaniard and his honor, the Spanish woman smoldering behind her wrought iron lattice, Torquemada and El Cid, Don Quijote and Don Juan, bullfighters and priests, gypsies and guerrillas, soldiers, shameless thieves, hands outstretched to plunge the dagger or beg an offering, heads or tails, the right-hand side and the other side, one single history lived out in diverse ways, differences derived from two degrees of development, adjusted to the distance that measures between one degree and another, bourgeois vulgarity of a lofty-sounding and moirological Catalonia, land of grasping idiot magnates, predatory men, locked and loaded, ready to shoot, Phoenicians among Phoenicians, men of the world by dint of being polished by roughness and, notwithstanding, always close to the earth, with the persistent vices of one who knows the ground he walks on, peasant crudeness and coarse manners, abrupt manifestations under a certain appearance of provincial cosmopolitanism, clumsy commerce and hypocritical self-restraint on one hand, self-contradictions of an industrial society, and on another, coexisting alongside, all that is properly Spanish, meaning, Castilian, and especially, characteristically, from Madrid, the convoluted quintessence of Castile, of its fields sown thick with garbanzos, stubby mesas taken for superiority and stepped isolation understood as dignity, generic traits softened in the court by their peculiar festive animation, aberrant virtues of an existence carried like a reliquary, frugal drynesses or big-bellied silhouettes, a sad figure, Old or New Castile, plain, flat, encumbered or not, no less the one from up north or the one from down south, the high clergy, the military classes, feudal lords, idle landowners moved directly from the habitual immobility found in all absolute monarchies and consequent hierarchical rigor barely tempered by corruption, to corporations, to the councils of administration, people not given to compromise and dialogue and, much less, criticism, people with a propensity for levying coups, for maximalist solutions, for favoritism and agreements between gentlemen and only between gentlemen, colloidal pride and abysms of class, a situation maintained by direct and indirect procedures, by the one who strikes first, a practice, on the other hand, also familiar in the rest of the peninsula, in general a propitious land for retrograde movements, preemptive uprisings struck down as if by a saber blow, preemptive and curative, deep cuts, life-saving amputations, barbaric reactions, elemental, committed with shocking naturalness, rammed through with almost relaxed good humor, like slap-happy old friends playing around, and the compensatory logic of all that, progressive miseries, anarchist actions realized with rough imprecision, without rhyme or reason, and vain attempts to give them a certain coherence, to inform them with a poor dialectic, refried ideologies, abstractions brought from other meridians, simplified to the point of foolishness by the reduction implied by all transport and, in the absence of a revolutionary mentality capable of infusing them with some new originality other than their heroic impotence, reverentially sustained against wind and shrapnel and, even more painful, against all lucidity, by moderately intelligent mediocrities, progressively idiotic, a prolonged saga of mutual affronts, of bitter confrontations, of a civil war that gestated for years on end, an organ created by the very exercise of its function, a fabulous spectacle, the sleep of reason, cortege of monsters, diabolical caprices, the black and red once again, tonalities of explosion, a circumstance barely adequate to sustain now-marginalized questions about the central nucleus of the conflict due to the very dialectic of the events, hardly able to safeguard ephemeral autonomies and other fictions proclaimed by the political representatives of the local petite bourgeoisie, Sunday fishermen on a river too wild, incidences of an enterprise fatally whirled away on the fly, swallowed up in the course of the fight between centralist bourgeoisie and revolutionary proletariat, destined to lose no matter who loses, to be unrealized, at least the way it was dreamed, a motherland—which one—undiscoverable, only its ruins as unique evidence, as it crumbles and falls away from an implacably objective analysis of the events, its rubble. A distressing awakening.

A Barcelona stretching from sea to mountain peak and from
river to river, yes, but not according to what was imagined, so
much less Catalan the bigger, the more massive it gets, populated
with immigrants, converted into El Dorado for *el charnego*, the
immigrant from southern Spain, Mecca for the lumpen, reduced
now to a shadow of its former self, surrounded by its suburbs,
progressively assimilated, all within a superior and distinct unity,
officious infiltration, often overlapping, neighborhoods
frequently nonexistent on the map, of casual etymology and
nomadic toponymy, Somorrostro, Casa Valero, Casa Antúnez,
Torre Baró, Campo de la Bota, etcetera, multiplying slums and
shantytowns, tidy whitenesses, thin whitewashed walls and
flimsy roofs, warp of tin and tar mixed with sand, earthy
suburbs, ashen, breezeless, sun-beaten, out-of-the-way places,
rich in folkloric scenes, in impressionist colors, naturalist blights
sooner or later resolved one way or the other, homes and hearths
eventually well-established into compact constructions, extending as far as the eye can see, from the Besós River to the Llobregat,
from Tibidabo to Montjuich, a human agglomeration, an explosive environment naturally predisposed, like a germinating seed,
to soak up communist ideology, as tinder accepts the spark, as
sails the wind, a reserve army no longer quite so capitalistic as
socialistic, productive forces in development, a forest of spreading, climbing, frenetic industries on the move, formations of
gray blocks closely surrounding the city, interwoven antennas,
sparkling windows, sunny fluttering rags, as if advancing, looming over, closing in around the city, so splendidly planned by the
nineteenth-century bourgeoisie, the quadrangle of the Ensanche,
the perimeter of Las Rondas, the Old City divided by Las
Ramblas, Mount Taber to the right, in the heart of the Gothic
Quarter, museum of past glories, of petrified triumphs, the
Gothic Quarter composed of stately streets and plazas, Plaza de
San Jaime, Plaza del Rey presided over by King Martin's Tower,
Plaza del Rey with its Salón del Tinell and its Chapel of Santa
Agata, the Archive of the Crown of Aragon, its Casa Padellás,
principal seat of the City History Museum, the womb of that
recomposed complex of Roman city walls, of Romanesque

arches, of Gothic spires, of churches and palaces, an age marked
by belfries, from angelus to angelus, resonant spaces, hieratic
austerities, the cathedral towers above all, prevalent, overflown
every summer, by identical iterations of swifts and swallows.
Triumphal ruins! Royal grandeur! Magnificence magnified!
Fructified residue. Perdurance of the metamorphosis, of the
ruined glory in rubble, of the stone become temple, stone by
stone, discoveries disinterred, images brown and venerated,
museum become vainglory, cemetery become victory, permanence of vertigo, fugacity of stone! And now? The denouement,
the final phase of the process, the synthesis of contraries or
negation of the negation, meaning, affirmation, resolution,
dissolution of the diverse contradictions developed over the
course of history of this small town, a minor people resurged
from the spoils of the Romano-Visigothic slave-owning society,
in the High Middle Ages, a people of precocious Mediterranean
expansion and also of precocious social conflicts in the metropolis, conflicts as much between the farming class and the feudal
structure of the age, its servitudes and evil misuses, as between
aforesaid structure and the incipient bourgeois classes of artisans
and merchants that emerged under the guise of the gradual
enlargement of the empire, political forces in ascension thanks,
frequently, to the support of the monarchy and, in symbiotic
correspondence, its absolute disinterest, utilized by the monarchy
to finance royal power, the crown ceaselessly reaffirmed and
enlarged until the dawn of the Renaissance, when in the full
period of economic and demographic decadence and reemergent
social agitation, coinciding with the general tendency of the age
toward the formation of nation-states, driven toward the doubtful proposition of forming a nation, almost in spite of itself, by
virtue of its union with Castile, as a cornerstone of the modern
Spain, a new State constructed not only at the expense of the
fact that Catalonia—the weak partner in the marriage—might
fatally relinquish its ancient Mediterranean hegemony, but rather
also because, even in the same peninsula, its area of influence
would be seen to be reduced to its current regional limits, disconnected from those who were brother countries, converted by the

law of the jungle into the tail of a lion, a simple provincial principality separated from all colonizing enterprise and facing a frequent crisis of survival with the reigning absolutism and its local representation, the viceroy sent by the court, a principate encrusted in Spain more than integrated, wound round the imperial crown just as much as Flanders or Portugal or the Kingdom of Naples could possibly be, no more Spanish in practice nor with more rights nor weaknesses nor more official function nor benefit, without that being an obstacle, rather quite the contrary, for the progressive lack of involvement of the so-called flat state and of Catalan economic life in general, spared from complete insolvency by the same ostracism to which it had been subjected, development consolidated when the suppression of the restrictions that impeded commerce with America, upon opening new markets in optimum competitive conditions, permitted the incipient industrialization to be built upon sound material foundations, the basis of prosperity and the rising prosperity of the nineteenth-century Catalan bourgeoisie, in contrast to a Castile that was now eroded by decadence, in the heart of a Spain more than anachronistic, regressive, barbarously enraged, and at war with itself, a contrast that did nothing but clarify the ascensional movement of this Catalan bourgeoisie gradually identified with the ruling classes of the rest of the nation, a bourgeoisie increasingly more elevated, more and more Spanish, day after day, of patriotic sentiments grown in direct proportion to the amplitude of the new markets, Spanish to the end, to the point of attempting, and in a certain way of achieving, to make peace with the central power, of molding Spain to its image and likeness, meaning, of fomenting and realizing the bourgeois revolution in Spain, attempts reiterated and, as if the reiteration, more than riveting, caused a loss of impulse, progressively timid, the more timid the more identified, as a class in ascension, with that power, how much more unnecessary when the goals were made not undesirable, more a process of osmosis than assault, an impulse ultimately scuttled, braked, by the phantasm of social agitation, a weakness of attack or arrest that would later become widespread in proportion to the very meaning of its corresponding historic role in the imperialist phase of capitalism, always insufficiently decisive, always grave, always mortgaged by its own scarcity, grandiloquence and pompous words to cover up its lying probity, its frightened prosperity, its tendency to promulgate favorable laws and to violate unfavorable ones, its mastery in bribery and speculation, its custom of receiving a granted baker's dozen, of remaining middle of the road in all matters, the mediocrity of an attitude simultaneously attributable to the weakness of the economic structure which served as its support, namely greenhouse production and winter tourism, manufacture and commerce appropriate to a land poor in natural resources, of scanty attractiveness, in principle, for other sources of capital than the resultant accumulated labor of its inhabitants and, in consequence, more given to industrial dispersion than industrial concentration, and similarly, attributable in no lesser degree to the ambiguous character of its relations with the rest of Spain, simultaneous bureaucratic corset and market stimulant, contradictions apparently written into the fate of this regional bourgeoisie which, when it seemed launched upon the enterprise of redeeming Spain from its historical hemophilia, of establishing new constitutional formulas which would wipe the slate clean of all the monstrous inherited landowners, was pulled brusquely backward, you might say that it was frightened by the turn of events, by the consequence of the exercise of the liberty so long demanded and finally achieved, contributing to the dismantling of the First Republic in the same way it had contributed to building it, enclosing in parentheses what came to pass, unleashing the monarchical Restoration, events that, as they introduced the upper Catalan bourgeoisie to the ebb and flow of Spanish political life, severed this one from the middle classes of its own land, where the primitive federalist regionalism of some intellectual nuclei was exchanged for separatist nationalism, in accord with a phenomenon of radicalization which, somewhere between courageous and reticent, was ceaselessly promoted by the political representatives of the upper bourgeoisie, not as a real aspiration but as an instrument of negotiation with Madrid, as blackmail or as a straw man, thus

twisting an ideal previously and seamlessly interconnected into
an exclusive benefit for the interests that they represented, traf-
ficking with the popular sentiment, selling it and selling themselves, the deceptive realities of politics that could only end up
depoliticizing the only social class totally removed from the
interests at stake, the working class, the working masses of
Catalonia objectively forced toward anarchism and libertarian
maladjustment, toward all manner of violence, of direct action
as a response to public order, a singular dialectic whose crescendo
could only unchain once more the hard line of an authoritarian
regime which might deserve the confidence of the ruling classes,
a reaction or coup in which the upper Catalan—and more
concretely, Barcelona—bourgeoisie now acted in a shamelessly
self-promotional capacity constructed to defend its positions
from the sudden blows of history when this totalitarian scaffolding would inevitably collapse, and driven by the fear of the newly
liberated popular forces, set in motion in the course of the
Second Republic, wasted no time in resurrecting once more
democratic legality from the archives of Francoism, in frank,
open civil war with its own people, as well as with the remaining
peoples of Spain, a betrayal made complete once the interests of
this upper Catalan bourgeoisie became definitively integrated
with those of the Spanish monopolist oligarchy, with the which
it was going to be identified to the extent of being converted
anew, no longer an accomplice but an objectively responsible
party, following the polarization of positions and the modifica-
tion of alignments resulting from the Civil War, from the political oppression of the Catalan reality in particular, as well as the
economic exploitation or, rather, the plundering of the Spanish
people in general, an unprecedented situation, qualitatively new,
given that, upon adding to the fundamental contradiction
between monopolist bourgeoisie and Catalan national bourgeoisie, contains the seed or implication of not only the logical
alliance between proletariat and non-monopolist bourgeoisie,
but also the surmounting of the historical antithesis between
Castile and Catalonia and, in the final analysis, the fusion of
such diverse social, political, economic, and national elements

in a revolutionary synthesis, a true qualitative leap which fore-grounds the antagonism existing between Franco and his party, on the one hand, and the Spanish people as a whole, on the other. Catalonia and Castile, two peoples called to complement one another once redeemed, rescued from so many differences imposed from without, from above, that have managed to sepa-rate them, to join together in fraternal unity with Galicia and Euskadi, countries of equally problematic existence, united in the task of building a different Spain as a voluntary unified socialist entity, a unity without uniformity, a unity in diversity, decentralization compatible with democratic centralism, revolutionary nationalism understood as opposition, as unani-mous support for the politics of the Soviet Union and other countries within the socialist landscape, an enterprise in which such an important role is reserved for this Barcelona of immense working-class suburbs charged with revolutionary ferment, the first industrial center of Spain, the capital of a land traditionally shaken by liberation movements, libertarian Catalonia, Catalonia of the Generalitat, of Red October, of July 19th, reddened by fire and conquered by Franco and his mercenary legions, his Moors, his battalions of Moroccan Regulars, flags of blood and gold, thunderous troops; Catalonia treated unjustly, subjugated, Catalonia fallen and risen again, back on its feet, now in another direction, with a different designation, now decidedly on the move after the communist party, vanguard of the proletariat and final and decisive political force, appeared in the fight, root, stock, and cornerstone of a society on the verge of being newly forged, of a new fatherland, an illustrious future where there had been a mistaken past, sweeping progress, fasces of hammers, triumphal drum rolls, wings and bugles, final battle, judgment failed, now resolved by history. No Spanish Empire much less a Catalan Empire, no more specters from the past: instead, la Union de Republicas Ibericas Socialistas, URIS, the reality before which, Daniel, all the rest will be only a dream within a dream.

VIII

SADDER, YES, IF POSSIBLE, sadder, but not with the tender sadness that satisfies one deep inside nor with any selfish sentiment, not sunk in solitary daydreams, no, but rather with the depressed spirit of one who contemplates the victorious arrival of enemy armies and, in contrast to the movement and the surrounding acclamations, does not perceive his body as anything more than a grave presence, a stone irreparably fallen. Low, lower in spirit than others during those same days of nefarious pre-Christmas atmosphere, when the season's greetings of good cheer pile up in the vestibule and the shop windows are decked out in stars and the streets are garlanded with lights and tinsel and in front of the cathedral one finds the tangled alleys of the Christmas bazaar, la Feria de Santa Lucía, selling nativity scenes and yuletide boughs, mistletoe, moss, holly, flowerpots with shrubs glazed in rainwater, shining and green in direct contrast to the sadness and choking pressure and fury accumulated throughout the year. And especially greater today, thanks not only to the advance of events, nor even the omens, or at least not only them but also, no doubt, thanks to the grim looming clouds and coming rain. Like the spring, like the rain. What relationship exists between the low tonalities of the soul, the depressive levels, the inner fog, the inert emptiness, and the rain? What causes of physical order, what actuation of atmospheric factors, what influx of certain fluids upon the organism? Or of symbolic order? Such as when the shoots break out and push forward, and the buds burst open and the rosy stems and the vine tendrils stretch forth, and what at first happens one by one soon multiplies uncontrollably, extends, recovers, gains thickness, and before the fresh fronds one feels as if they also had roots, not for transmitting any impulse but for an infusion of strength, of dynamic breath, to become fixed in the earth, to mineralize it, to become conquered the same as a pagoda overgrown and swallowed up by the luxuriant jungle growth, immutability in the change, impotence in the action, appearance preserved. Thus this rain that might seem momentarily lifted as if by magic, although not enough to make the umbrellas and overcoats disappear from the street, the shimmering plastics, in some way tranquilizing the humid air, the translucent heights of December, middays like evenings, the whole day between two lights, the anodyne clarity of the neon and the worthless frippery of the Christmastime trappings against the black glare of the expanding clouds, the shifting glimmering light above the plaza, where, as if awaiting the cataclysm, the earth opened in the center of it and the sepulchers traded places with the flowerpots, *Dis Manibus Flaviae Theodote heres ex testamento.*

The peculiar sound of footsteps treading a pavement more sticky than wet, along the blind reflection, along various streets, Canuda, Vertrallans, Santa Ana, and, crossing Puerta del Ángel, along Condal, to Number 20, headquarters of the Municipal Court Number 4. Dead dull asphalt, softened by dissolved pollutants, streets of a somber tone, the city's violet-gray which, like the red of London, the black of Paris, or the golden glow of Rome, characterizes Barcelona, the color of slag or a tumor which, in the Gothic Quarter, joined to the general degradation of the facades, acquires a particular relief, however much that fact, possibly, escapes the notice of the Barcelonans, in the same way that, beyond a certain degree and by virtue of the cityscape's familiarity, its startlingly convoluted corrugations and drynesses makes people forget how old it all is. A comparison so fateful as to be exact! The baneful exterior of Municipal Court Number 4, for example, the severe patio suggesting a prison, the sinister staircases, the gloomy interiors; everything there exudes disgrace and shelters corruption and bribery. Everything, even the most common objects and implements give off a certain oppressive sensation which quickly imposes itself on the visitor, the furniture of the successive offices and departments, the desk equally ignoble and indestructible found in the most sordid offices, the chairs, the filing cabinets, the abominable small stove, the lamps that barely shed enough light to orient the citizens who wander about or wait, men and women whose expressions configure the feigned rancor, atrocious servility, or abject avidity appropriate to those who, like the inmates of an asylum, know that their situation gives them no more right than what it graciously wants to concede them. For their part, the functionaries, from the ancient female typist to the first secretary, carefully allow their attitude to make clear, as much through what they say as what they remain silent about, that it is indeed so, that once inside those hostile domains, nobody can rightfully hope for anything more. In that way, limiting ourselves in our considerations to the functionaries in charge of the Civil Registry, if the despotic conduct of one of them can give the reasonable impression that the whole place is rather more of a police station, the taciturn cynicism of the other, who with a twitch of his snout indicates that he's already noticed Raúl's presence and is considering it, makes one suppose himself in the presence of one of those men who survive in their job despite the vicissitudes of every different political and social regime, Monarchy and Republic, Catalan Generalitat and Francoism. A place, then, that a writer like Balzac would have not hesitated to qualify as *rongé, crevasse, execrable, puant, étouffant, nauséabond, lugubre, affreux*, and not without first satisfying the curiosity *du passant, du voyageur*, revealing that the building in question had once been the property and residence of the Ollet family, for instance, until the ruined family had it sold at public auction for the ridiculously cheap price of eight thousand seven hundred reals, and might have ended up pointing that out in order to show how a formerly noble mansion is now reduced to such a state, *il faudrait en faire une description qui retarderait trop l'intérêt de cette histoire et que les gens presses ne perdonneraient pas.*

I'll be right with you, said the clerk who had responded to Raúl's greeting. Catalan, peevish, efficient. The other, not Catalan: self-important, evasive, volatile, and, in consequence, more capable of softening up despite his initially tyrannical manner, of having a humanitarian expression, of being not only a bureaucrat, but also, and above all, of being human. Very human, almost paternal, as he pockets his tips. Of saying thanks, son, and pressing his elbow with an intimate gesture, in an expression of inexpressible sentiments. The Catalan clerk, by contrast, more efficient, expeditious, including when he picks up his cigar or the twenty-five pesetas left on the desk, half opening the drawer with his left hand and sweeping the coins in with his right, cleanly, as if to better highlight the proverbial, though voluntary, character of the compensation, discreet but significantly evoked by the golden ring of the Havana cigar that stuck up from the breast pocket of his suit jacket. Imperturbable, resistant to effusiveness, without even the impertinences of his colleague, verbal aggressiveness always capable, in the end, of offering a certain degree of belligerence, of giving way to dialogue; more unfriendly, more myopic, more manic, his pencils and ballpoint pens and fountain pens and nibs and stamps and ink pads and paperclips, all systematically arranged, between one tic and the next, automatic gestures. A sly old cat, his craft distilled through experience, wisely skeptical, implacably closed thus to both public protests and gratitude, insensible and deaf to the complaints of the never-ending supply of impatient waiting clients who, possibly because of a singularly irascible temperament or some inferiority complex, cannot suppress their disgust on seeing themselves passed over in favor of the managers and other professionals who gather there in the habitual performance of their duties, people naturally pushier and better connected, disgust, contrariness, and reprobation often translated into imprecations muttered in an undertone, evidently meant to extend their personal ill humor to all the others waiting, making them feel individually and collectively despised, fathers of newborns too proud to let themselves be dragged down by bitterness, widows with too many hours of experience to try to force the fatality of waiting in lines, old men too shrunken, adolescents too habituated already in their adult roles, all imperturbable to the greater resentment of the troublemaker, also Catalan, a functionary with

the look of a bricklayer become building contractor, simultaneously pissed off and melancholy, the unmistakable victim of the
headaches inherent to his social ascension—children, wives,
bills—the type with heavy eyelids, stocky, hairy, dark, reeking of
tobacco, with the rough tattered voice of a man whose throat is
ravaged by cancer, mouth ruined by cognac, and chapped from
constantly licking his lips. Insensible and deaf, as well, to the
gratitude expressed in the form of promises or future projects
that the obtaining of solicited permits and certifications usually
elicits from some people, promises fully sincere when uttered,
impelled as they are by the joy of the moment, leading to a quasi-
superstitious feeling of gratitude toward the authorizing bureaucrat, the material incarnation of the task resolved as well as of
the advantageous consequences that can result from all that, a
gratitude no less ephemeral than sincere when a few minutes,
not hours, later they will have completely forgotten that grave
and prudent man for whom they just felt so much spontaneous
appreciation, that anonymous and unselfish being who spends
his life serving the public, enormous forgetfulness, clearly,
considering the firm resolution recently adopted while dealing
with him at the edge of the bureaucratic barriers that separate or
bring together those administrating and those administrated, to
create a relationship of true friendship, always useful on the other
hand, to return another day and have a drink on the way home
from the office or even go out to have dinner some Saturday with
their respective wives, and while the ladies chat about their silly
ideas, during the after-dinner conversation, each man with a
good cigar, one tells his friend his opinions about life, his problems, thus inviting the other to share his own. All that in the
supposition that once back out in the city streets, barely
reintegrated into his typical daily drudgery, he won't start to
recapitulate, to build up little by little, each time more the
farther away from the Municipal Court, a mental summary of
all the little servilities committed and humiliations borne, and
transform his meek cooperation into rancor toward a few fellows
who, because they work as pen pushers in some shitty municipal
court, think themselves something they're not, and it seems that

they do you a favor attending to you when it's nothing more than their obligation, that's why they collect from the taxpayer, directly from oneself, if you take a look, with the goal of getting the bad taste out of your mouth and overcoming the irritating memory, in a healthy exercise of mental hygiene, he'll make long-term plans, for the day when he's somebody, a well-known and respected personality in some field, with influence, and then drop in here some morning and take pleasure in seeing this whole string of faggots all lined up to lick his ass, because in life you pay for everything and where they give they take, etcetera, interior monologue developed according to a scheme all-too-familiar, no doubt, to the Catalan bureaucrat, conclusions more than well-known in order to consider any of those initial effusions with any other attitude than reserved indifference. Sensitive, however, perspicaciously attentive and receptive when it's a question not of an occasional, informal contact but an ongoing professional one, the manager, the attorney, the lawyer, the true client, assiduous and able, confident and experienced who, as is customary, knows how to proffer a tip properly couched in phrases simultaneously witty and conventional, the deal closed between subtle shadings upon the basis of a tacit understanding, with the touch of a seducer who in each bed accommodates the rules of the erotic ritual to the particular longings of their lover, as intuition dictates, according to an experience that in the long run always turns out to be preferable. Bird in the hand, neither fathers of large families, nor disconsolate sons and other family members, nor cuckolds in the trance of separation, nor passive widows, nor stupefied servants, nor philosophical old men, nor uncultured idiots who surely know how to make money, but not how to utilize it opportunely, nor drama queens who insist on suggesting that they've already suffered enough in this life so why wait for the next life to come, factions of tricksters and troublemakers, charlatans, disgraced men, cheaters, gamblers, card sharps, crooks, blunderers, show-offs, and adulterers, an Andalusian laborer ready to work, mute and submissive, asking, almost affirming, whether or not he will also need a certificate from the parish, possibly with the goal of

showing his good disposition, unlike others, in the face of
administrative requirements, an unconditional adhesion that
leads him to comply in full with the rigorous pertinent requisites,
completing them and perfecting them with new proofs and additional documentation, an attitude fatally destined to arouse the
mistrust of the Catalan bureaucrat, for being unusually removed
from the normal and reasonable antagonism that tends to manifest itself among those who need to show any kind of certifica-
tion and those who are in charge of authorizing it, and who in
fact does grant it, but not without a tug of war equally conflictive
and fruitful; mistrust and censure exteriorized through a glance
over the top of his eyeglasses, an interrogative repetition of some
parochial term and a leafing through his papers muttering something, formulation or judgment which, by the twisted dilations
of his mouth, might well be some beastly comment, some beastly
comment or something similar. Mistrust and censure only
certain to intensify in direct proportion to the humble worker's
greater efforts to neutralize or at least mollify the bad impression
obviously produced from the start, and more insistent his determined effort to show that he was nothing if not precisely that,
a lowly worker, a laborer as ignorant as willing and eager to
please and, surely, in need of guidance, and what's more, with
the moral right to demand assistance, to have the opportunity
of making patent his obedience, he, the docile one, the laborer
with neither ideas nor learning, which for that reason I'm asking,
simply on the off-chance, and pardon the question, I asked it
because I don't understand those things, I understand that you
people here must be fed up with everyone asking you foolish
questions, but you understand these things, which I've asked in
order to facilitate your work maybe, for simply on the off-chance,
an obstinate and useless and even counterproductive remark
when addressed to the Catalan bureaucrat, hiding behind his
mutterings in a savage game of stamping papers, he would end
up turning instead, as one might suppose, to the non-Catalan
bureaucrat, more vulnerable to the purely deferential compensations of character and truly disposed toward confraternity, even
managing, obviously flattered by the allusion to the complexity

and responsibility of his job, to resolve matters with a stimulating and comforting bit of don't mention it, my good man, that's what we're here for. Thus, one could establish a correlation or equivalence between the willing worker and the non-Catalan bureaucrat, the former, as a member of the public, a replica of the latter, as a bureaucrat, in the same way that the troublemaker with the face of a bricklayer-become-building-contractor could be considered the Catalan bureaucrat's doppelgänger, all that resulting in a new and illustrative antagonistic relationship, more about the behavior of the elements considered than their different functions, a divergence or polarization not of horizontal but vertical lines, a contraposition between what might be properly considered a reverence for mere appearance and formality in the first case and, in the second, an instinctive animosity toward rules, precepts, and other strange circumlocutions when they do not run counter to what is strictly practical.

A fanatic's pupil behind his Coke-bottle lenses, the Catalan bureaucrat stood up and, with angry but stubborn step, walked decisively to the balcony as if to check on something happening outside, or some information pending confirmation, although quite possibly he simply needed to rip some unstoppable fart whose sound would be masked by the traffic noises out in the street, not a perfectly improbable explanation, especially in light of how rigidly immobile he remained as he executed the maneuver, destined by all evidence to avoid the logical loss of prestige that not exiting would have caused him in the eyes of the waiting public, faces of a quiet variety, slack expressions reflecting, as a breeze-riffled puddle, passing curiosity about the others in the room, flights of insubstantial ideas, almost on the edge of sleep, a proximity that perhaps favored the tepid closeness of that angry atmosphere made noxious by the damp clothes and shoes which, with the warm humidity, caused the body to emanate its most intimate effluvia, postures momentarily slack and distracted then suddenly again upright and intent, as if corresponding to someone in the midst of requesting something, patiently awaiting their turn, a passivity that in no case excludes their attentive observation, the search for some partiality, the struggle to get ahead of the other people, to accelerate the necessary paperwork and shorten the waiting periods by any means possible, exceptions granted, obviously, for those who come here to register a birth if, on one hand, the very nature of its management means they are exempted from coming back another day, the euphoric state that such happy events usually bring, on the other, it makes their waiting more bearable, so that they frequently reach the point where they consider themselves the center of the event, forgetting that the true protagonist of the inscription is someone else, the real newcomer to a circus where the only easy thing is getting a ticket to the main event. Like forgetting, one Sunday at noon, what it must be like to go out in the afternoon, the passersby with their heavy digestions, the lines outside the cinemas, the full stomachs, the harsh sunset; or like ignoring, once again, the no-lesser abomination of the days that follow this time period of bubbling Christmas, when all the twinkling glitter comes down, and the bustling streets outside the cathedral, particularly lively today with the excited groups of seamstresses celebrating the feast of Santa Lucía, December thirteenth, Tuesday, the Spanish day of bad luck, a date quite expressive enough to resume the black streak of recent days, the string of misfortunes, the repeated setbacks, events not foreseen or at least not foreseen as a problem capable of affecting him, the business about Pluto's girlfriend and the death of Aunt Paquita and Nuria's father's accident and the loss of his overcoat and the doors of the subway train pulling away right under his nose, small mishaps no less exasperating than the big ones, a chain of events whose examination, in an attempt to reconsider its origin, to precisely identify the starting point, would force him to accept the conclusion that Achilles's death was, without a doubt, the first bad news.

Could Raúl have ever imagined telling Florencio Rivas Fernández, when they saw each other for the last time, precisely at Aunt Paquita's burial, that only a few days later he would be holding Florencio's death certificate in his own hands, who could have imagined it, a man like Florencio, so full of life, with so little experience of the irreparable, etcetera, meditations appropriate to the difficulty of accepting the fact, that in the case of Francisca Ferrer Gaminde, widow of Giral, death had brusquely, brutally, irrevocably, and unceremoniously snatched her away. An uncontrolled tumor, no one sure exactly when it began, when her perpetual complaints and pains and her fears and her migraines all began to roll into one, to form part of the process, nor when the family learned the truth, nor if she suspects it, if her capacity for deception permits her to keep on believing it nothing more than just an accumulation of small complaints, not major ones, just complications from sciatica, rheumatism, cramping, intestinal infections, as a way to explain the progressive prostration of a body officially, supposedly, affected by a mild case of hepatitis, even though from a certain point it becomes barely believable that the truth has not dawned on her completely and that, in fact, she's doing nothing more than pretending to believe her relatives in order to spare them the necessary behavior of family members who know that she knows it, who knows the nearness of the end and the identity of her illness, that thing that it now seems they're on the verge of curing or, at least, of identifying, of discovering, which is saying a lot, and whoever does, well, it's that you've got to build them a monument, and the most curious thing is that it seems that it's not, properly speaking, some illness, not an illness like other illnesses, I mean, not just a microbe or something that comes from outside, but rather something that she carries inside, something that the body itself produces which ends up destroying the organism that produced it, a kind of disordered development of the cells which acquires powers from the ordered structure from which it proceeds and then kills it off, without it really being known why, nor what unleashes that random, unconstrained growth, the only thing known is that it's not contagious, luckily not that, some people get it, others don't, and if it gets you then you're finished, bad luck, and if not, well, no one escapes death either, and, if you're going to go, well look, it's so much the same, that thing as any other. How are you, aunt, said Raúl. And she said, very well, Raúl. He nodded his head at her comments about the bother of such an unpleasant illness like hepatitis and its truly alarming spread or frequency nowadays, although it's also possible that he didn't really pay her any attention and only nodded from habit. She looked at Raúl and asked him about Nuria, when they were getting married, and about his studies, obliging him to assume the air of a young beau confused by his elders' questions or, more precisely, of a nephew who feigns feigning a certain embarrassment, given that the questions formulated usually follow a well-recognized pattern of interest in the one interrogated, whose merits demand open declaration, to effect their future familial consecration. Well, look, said Aunt Paquita, earlier, to be precise, I had a dream about you. Well, in all of them, you were also there. We were in Vallfosca, in the garden, and there was a kind of picnic going on, and they were handing each of you a glass. She rubbed the back of one hand with the other, aching from the intravenous hookups, small burst blood vessels, black and blue and yellow, not much more immobile between the sheets than in her chaise longue in Vallfosca, nor more weightless than upon the discolored cretonne cushions, her voice no less distant than when she called them from in between sun and shade, in the corner thick with hydrangeas, vivacious irradiations, green sounds, the early smell of the steams and rivulets, sour grapes, warm straw, wasp nests between the ceramic roof tiles, the porrón that the young men carried with them out to the fields, the magpies at dawn embroidering the sky. It must have been quite a few years since he'd seen her, and when they said that she'd slipped into a coma he went to see her, more than anything so that Papa would stop reminding him each night that he should go. Why go back? What inertia or force made him say that he would return again next week, against all expectation in the moment of saying it, and indeed return, and again say that he would come back and then return again, however much each week he supposed that by then she would be dead? Was it some subjective unscientific understanding, based merely on the conviction or desire that the situation cannot worsen, but the opposite proves true, that it can indeed worsen, and what was merely a question of hours ends up being one of days and weeks, a condition between life and death showing that her prior composure and much-commented-on

serenity now mean nothing more than if they described the
behavior of a mushroom or a larva?

The decline that starts the moment when the discussion of
the patient's suffering is invalidated by a surprising recovery of
their faculties, all the nervous worry expressed by family
members and close friends changes tenor, the calls, visits, explanations, and the embarrassing fact of having to clarify for all
involved that it was only a false alarm, and so much the better,
although, of course, in reality she's weaker every day, the poor
thing, she's like a flame slowly dying out, I warn you that
sometimes it happens that in their final hours they seem to
respond to treatment and it looks like they're going to get better
and everything, but it only seems that way, of course, and you
see her head's completely clear, a true miracle, the doctor no
longer dares offer an opinion, the important thing is that she
doesn't suffer, go on in if you all like, better not to overwhelm
her now, she's resting easy, that's why, perhaps she could sleep,
words in a low voice in the next room, and inside, the odor of
Sterilair, the excessively bright lights, the way Aunt Paquita likes
them, the way she scrutinized him when she discovered him
alongside her bed, perhaps seeing that Raúl's pupils already
reflected death, and the doctor took her pulse and said there was
nothing wrong, a reckoning always awaited with a certain anxiety, such as a verdict or the exam results read aloud at the end-
of-term party, for all present to hear, even those least informed
about a disease's particular details, unlike the family members
surrounding the patient who become intimately acquainted with
its progress, their progressively shifting interest, initially centered
on the patient's personality, toward the details that characterize
the evolution of the illness from a more technical point of view,
more properly clinical, the more definitive the prognosis the
more unnecessary, the consultations following new complications, the difficulty of effecting compromised micturition, the
impossibility of ingesting solid foods, tests, medicines, injections,
punctures, sedatives, open sores, etcetera, the phenomenon of
movement or passage, or better yet of supplanting what, in the
end, only leads to the certain and gradual reduction of the person

to an elemental organism consisting of one single large tube, simultaneously mouth and anus. The cat seemed to be everywhere, rubbing itself noiselessly, relaxing, staring, eyes reduced to slits, the clear green iris, like crystallized moss, in the vestibule, in the parlor, in the small adjacent sitting room, although it's also possible that there were various cats instead of only one, and that they were exactly identical. Murmurs, heads together, exposition of similarities, exchange of impressions, if she's recognized Pedro, if now only Ramona can understand her, if it doesn't seem that she's suffering, but it appears that she's experiencing something like hallucinations, that's from the sedatives, yes, the effect of the sedatives, they go right to the poor thing's head, look, it seems that Ramona asked her if she wanted the guaiac, and she said I don't understand, it's just that the poor thing isn't aware, I think that sometimes she doesn't even know where she is, nor whether she's still here or if she's already in heaven, because with the devotion she shows to this relic, I'll put it here for you, Mama, on top of the bottle of saline solution, and the picture of Pope Pius and the scapular of the Virgin of Mount Carmel and the small medallion of the Immaculate Conception she received when she made her First Communion, and the one from Fatima and the one of Saint Francis of Assisi, and the framed benediction from Leo XIII from when Grandpa Raúl took her on a pilgrimage to Rome, and the photo of Gemma Galgani, and the rosary made of olive pits from Gethsemane, objects for which she professed a special fervor and which, linked with specific practices, orations and short prayers, signified a substantial wellspring of indulgences, one hundred, three hundred, five hundred days rescued from Purgatory, an estimable quantity, very much on the human scale, given that an immeasurable remission, fifty, one hundred thousand years, might be counterproductive, disheartening more than encouraging to the person in grace, the only possible subject of the blessing, doubtless inhibiting ahead of time any attempt at maneuvering in a realm where the operative quantities are of a similar magnitude, an uncertainty covered in every case by the plenary or total exemption resulting from exercising such

practices as observing the nine First Fridays, the cycle of nine
months fulfilled time and again by Aunt Paquita, in uninterrupted succession throughout her whole life, a fact that might
explain her now apparent disinterest for piousness, devout exercises for those who only seemed to surrender, when their condition allowed it, suggested by those trying to comfort her this
way, the Creed, the Hail Mary, the Confiteor, some mystery of
the rosary, some litany, the Viaticum, including extreme unction,
even though, in this respect, the most probable thing is that, in
that moment, her awareness of receiving a sacrament from the
living was practically null, Latin phrases muttered, as if yawning,
by a poor, miserable parish priest, with habitual abbreviated
celerity, the superficial application of the holy oils, the forehead,
the hands, the mouth, in invocation, *per istam sanctam untionem*,
of the most merciful compassion of God. We can stick our heads
in a minute, if you all want to; she'll be excited to see you, said
Ramona. Maybe she's resting a bit. She had such a bad night,
the poor thing. Better not, better not, actually. I'll tell her that
you've been here. You should certainly rest a while, you must be
wiped out. She's the one who carries all the weight and if she
doesn't take care of herself she'll end up getting sick. It just seems
that with the poor thing you have to help her with everything,
and like Ramona she's the only one who understands her. Such
tension. Ramona's a girl with a lot of spirit. She and Elvira,
they're so lucky to have Elvira. She's been in the house for so
many years it's as if she were one of the family, one of those
people you don't find anymore, not like the ones nowadays, it's
that they don't know anything about anything and they're always
thinking about something else and everything seems to matter
very little to them, with that talk of how people abroad earn so
much and how much, I don't know what we're coming to, our
maid drives me insane, she threatens to quit for any little thing
and then starts looking through the want ads and calling up her
friends and the days go by and, then, after all, she doesn't leave,
but one day this will come to an end, because I'll take her at her
word and I'll tell her, very well, you've said that you want to
leave, it's true, well go then, let's go, what are you waiting for,

let's see if you find another house like this one, and I'll just kick her out, and then you'll see how she backs down and asks me if she can stay, but by then I'll already have found someone else and I'll tell her no, that in this world no one is indispensable, and it'll be her loss, because besides she's grown really fond of the kids, which is lucky, they grow really fond of the kids and then it's hard for them to leave, so if she hadn't already walked out on me when I least expected it, with the guests all seated at the table, and look she's a good girl, that when she wants to she knows how to do things, but it's just that this can't go on and can't go on, with her blackmail she really gets on my nerves, and all because you treat them with too much consideration and then they abuse it, they take you for a fool, you've got to treat them like maids, because that's what they are and it's the only language they understand, being talked to like maids, maids who live in a world of maids, their friends, they're like a gang, the boyfriend, the dates, the telephone, family relations, the foolish things they say, the gossip, the affairs, the tantrums. Not Elvira, no. And it's not because she's not a grumbler or doesn't have a temper; when she's in a really bad mood she's capable of tongue-lashing the morning star. A tremendous Navarran, one of those who's a real force to be reckoned with. You see, those Navarrans, splendid people, folks, I don't know, sort of whole, sort of real. Look, they liberated Barcelona. The Navarran brigades from Solchaga. As if I'm going to forget, that emotion, that enthusiasm. I remember, in Calle Cortés. The Navarrans. Praise for the Navarran: a real man, from head to toe, loyal and brave, hard-working, of sound constitution, big heart, noble sentiments and virile religiosity; traditionally traditionalist and jealous of his customs; at the same time, he's a very hospitable host, a friend of the good table and, of course, likes to booze it up a bit, but in no way corrupt or womanizing, prone rather to healthy recreation, fighting rams, betting, and other pastimes he shares with the Basques, the brethren of his race, those whom he resembles so much thanks to what they have in common, only without separatisms or social problems. Nevertheless, Jacinto expresses the classic Catalan pessimism, appropriate to one who's already seen too many things

in life, which, nevertheless, will of course break down, he hopes
that the Basque Country is going to be industrialized and you'll
see how they break down. Navarra already is an industrial region
these days, it's changed a lot and more change is coming, and
then all that will be lost and Navarra will stop being what it is,
body and soul of tradition, stronghold of pugnacity, people who
rise to the occasion without a second thought and deliver themselves to the cause hand and foot and defend it tooth and nail,
capable of having their throats slit for God and country and, in
the end, and in virtue of what we represent, by ourselves, those
here gathered to the sad awaiting of the last breath, fainting, dead
breath, omega of life. Go in, go in. Won't she be tired? If she's
not resting, we'll just stick our heads in for a moment. Come in,
come in, for Heaven's sake, the poor thing doesn't rest for more
than five minutes at a time. Just a quick minute: come in and
then out you go. Listen, listen, although I don't know if she'll
recognize you, come close, this bright light is unpleasant, but
she asked for it, maybe when she could no longer see more than
silhouettes and colors and movement, faces suddenly up close,
though not, like the voices that arose and faded out, any less
disconcerting. The tall stand with the hanging bottles of saline
solution at the foot of the bed, a small table with the instruments
for curing her, gauze, syringes, ointments, cotton, cologne,
adhesive tape, and the nun with the fisherman's face muttered
something to him in such a low voice that Raúl responded to
her with a prudently affirmative cough, as if absorbed, his attention focused on those eyes that did not seem to see anything
specific, watery, with an increasingly superficial shine, her tresses
like those of a little girl who braided them herself, an ashen
contrast to the puffy whiteness of the bed. The adjacent room
appeared illuminated by the television screen, clarity without
sound, and as if silhouetted on the horizon against the dawn sky,
the whispering figures, the teacups, the teapot, the ladyfingers.
There were quite a few people in the room, and the talking was
inevitably too loud. Ramona moved from one group to another,
attending them with mundane aplomb and responding to their
shows of interest and moral support, and a maid was offering

drinks. The balcony doors were halfway open and, like a tulle fog, the light animated by the cigarette smoke escaped toward the darkness outside. Discreet conversation, without stridencies, branches of the old trunk distanced one from another by unequal luck or fortune, relatives and relatives' relatives who only now meet up on solemn occasions, obligatory appearances, weddings or funerals, and they fulfill their obligations, expressing interest, offering polite responses to courteous questions exchanged again and again, your health, your mother, the little ones, how things are going, the latest problems, housemaids, financial difficulties, some imminent ministerial reassignment, how everything is getting to be so screwed up, problems without solution, always expressed with that mix of indignant surprise and fateful certainty, points of view, generalizations, sharp positions reiterated more than anything as a character trait or affirmation of personality, family anecdotes, Gregorius, who's a disaster; Merceditas, who is expecting again; Pedro, who's become a ne'er-do-well crackpot; Montserrat, who is a daring, carefree woman; Jacinto and his obtuse Francoism; Juanito and his ideas, everything treated with an exquisite respect by the family lines that over time have stereotyped each other's social images, with tact, affability, and tolerance, in a tacit search for what harmonizes and unites, including when the conversation ends up focusing on the hottest controversy, on what all Barcelona's buzzing about, what invariably interests us all because it refers to our own environs, by what it implies for everyone in terms of indirect retaliation, either exemplary retribution or identification with the triumph, some transparent gold digger in an obvious marriage for money, for example, or, better yet, an especially scandalous separation, here discussed while carefully avoiding all delicate or scabrous detail, saving for a more opportune moment, with more intimate friends, the retelling of a conjugal crisis that began with a civilized agreement between both spouses to live and let live, and ended with judicial summons, private detectives, public notaries, compromising photographs, witnesses, disappearances, abandonment of family, and the argument that she was the first one to actually take a lover, notoriously consented, and the counter-argument asking why wouldn't she since he could only reach orgasm by means of a warm enema administered by four masked naked women.

From any balcony in the Ensanche, the city offers the stranger—always more attentive to general impressions than details—a view approximately identical to any other view from any other balcony, from any balcony around this busy intersection on the corner of Calle Mallorca and Pau Claris, for example, on the monotonous facade of the six-story building erected on the lot after the grandfather died, a property that until then had been occupied by the Ferrer Gaminde family's chalet, according to the now classic Barcelona custom of demolishing old buildings with the greatest possible frequency in order to replace them with new, and invariably uglier ones, a practice that, for whatever speculative benefits it might bring, might also be considered consubstantial of all bourgeoisie, and in this specific case, of Barcelona only tacking its vulgarity, bad taste, and aberrant modesty onto its frustration over what was a grandiose nineteenth-century project. Of the excitement and geniality that once attended it, there now only remain adulterated glimpses, sufficient, nevertheless, to give an idea that such a vision could be realized with such a high degree of mediocrity, a sign of the vast distance between one generalization and those that follow it, an extensive mediocrity seen throughout the very same early embellishments and grotesque dreams of an upper-class bourgeoisie converted into an aristocracy by the force of imagination, by the power of pontifical titles and provincial cosmopolitanism, a mimetic fascination for the Castilian nobility, for its virtues and its shortcomings, a collective attitude that, in the economic field, perhaps explains the development of a marked, heartfelt proclivity for absentee land ownership and speculation, stock exchange, insurance policies, finance companies, real estate, land, concessions for public services, namely, legitimate business, and the same for the situation of privilege, for exclusivity and protectionism, just like its allergic reaction against any frugal, coupon-clipping concept of industry, seeing it instead as an enterprise to be directed and, consequently, its distaste for the rest of the Catalan bourgeoisie, those industrialists and merchants with whom a good family must only relate as a last resort, if the hard mandate of necessity demands it, through canonical connections, people who, for having reinvested their fortunes, generally of identical overseas origin, into industrial activities, and for having inculcated in their descendancy a strict identification with family name, product, family tradition, and factory continuity for the sake of a constant competitive growth and improvement, turn out to be perpetually assimilated into the social image of the nouveau riche, the newly moneyed business-man, a being easy to identify by his undisguisable lack of class, lineage, and nobility, his eagerness to insinuate himself and make social relationships, his disgusting manners, his strong Catalan accent, his strident laugh, there's nothing about them undeserving of scorn, both his splendid love of showing off as well as his spectacular flukes of luck, the same for the money earned in circumstances which, thanks to their immediacy, necessarily turn out to be murky, and his shameful ruin, frequently as sudden and rapid as his accumulation of wealth and assets, suspension of payments, fraudulent bankruptcies, foreclosures, what doubt can there be about the unapologetic reprobation of those who, in the worst cases, by selling their luxurious properties, are able to spread out their general decline over the course of several generations, their pronunciation ever more snuffling and nasal, their presence evermore pompous and affected, their minds evermore cretinous, evermore hare-brained, block-headed, thick-lipped, and lisping, following the natural course of such things that come, the declining arc from the ancestral heights to the current levels of mental retardation. Forms of decadence which their haughtiest and most quick-witted prolongers acclaim before denying, converting them into their opposite, distancing and distinguishing them from those who now hold economic power, converting them into conjectures about how different everything would be if things had gone differently—unassailable in their nostalgia over what never came to pass, in their capitulations and recapitulations, lamenting only that the ancient feudal lords of Catalonia, perhaps from excessive confidence in the

rights and merits of their own lineage or from a hierarchical itch
that could only inhibit all exuberant noble dignity where the
highest aristocratic rank was a mere count, but in any case with
an unspeakable lack of foresight, without a precise awareness that
family names come and go while dignity remains—they might
not have worried about giving objective immanence and validity
to their concrete prerogatives, about sanctioning and qualifying
their generic lordly status with the usual hereditary titles, or
about arranging and articulating those titles in a formally immu-
table body, thus arranging how many had to succeed them as the
leaders of Catalan society, to the natural aristocracy of future
centuries, languishing in a state of notorious and lamentable
inferiority relative to the nobility of the rest of Spain and Europe,
trying to justify it, submitting it to prolix and vexing explanations, particularly in those times when nobody has too much
time, condemning them to the recourse, humiliating at bottom
because of the messy quality and consolation they imply, of
sporting a fin-de-siècle title, if not something even more recent
or pontifical, the only means of overcoming the pedestrian, and
highly uncertain, notion of a mere good name; or lamenting
that, perhaps owing to the polymember development of the
Crown and its precocious apogee, prior to any conception of the
city more civil than military, what could be a continued enrich-
ment of the Barcelona court and harmonic accumulation resulted
in a vast dispersion of efforts, always insufficient achievements:
Palma, Valencia, Zaragoza, achieved at the cost of the monumental density of Barcelona, a city devoid of the tradition of
street as art or the small plazas characteristic of so many small
Italian towns of incomparably minor significance and rank. We
are not speaking now of a Campidoglio, of a Lido, of a Piazza
del Duomo, altars where before the eyes of the whole world a
city is consecrated and the privileged inhabitants of such a splendorous past are ennobled, an aristocracy for which the problem
of remaining in their ancestral residences is, mostly, a problem
of taxes, unlike in our own palaces, whose primitive sobriety and
poor magnificence excuse to a certain point Barcelonans' general
disengagement with respect to their good luck, the consideration

that it's the business of the municipal government to rescue from abandonment and demolition some mansions that they have just turned into *conventillos*, tenement houses, insofar as they are incapable of compensating with prestige the lack of comfort common to all medieval construction; or lamenting the fact that Felipe V's indiscriminate rancor against Catalonia—however just his intention to punish those who opposed his installation of the Bourbon dynasty—impelled him to no less a retribution than ordering the destruction of all the castles of the Principality, almost half of those extant in Spain, reducing to now-eroded ruins what would today be the glory and splendor of the landscape, the scenery and symbol of social elevation; or lamenting that the exclusion of their ancestors, for whatever reasons, from all participation in the conquest of America during close to three hundred years had deprived Catalonia of the importance and influence that other Spanish regions had indelibly inscribed in the history of the new continent, great feats and discoveries, foundations, honors, fortunes, vice-royalties, as well as the logical reflux of riches toward the metropolis, which instead, unfortunately, shows an almost complete dearth of Baroque sumptuousness; or lamenting the fact that some people in Catalonia, with incomprehensible stubbornness, still insisted on expressing themselves in Catalan, thus establishing, in relation to the rest of Spain, a wall of misunderstanding, suspicion, and automatic antipathy that forces those of us who express ourselves in Castilian Spanish, a tongue whose turns and accents unmistakably indicate its origin, to firmly remember that, thanks to the grace of God, not everyone in Catalonia is automatically reduced and relegated to be traveling salesmen and textile manufacturers, and above all, that it's one thing to be Catalan and another, but very distinct, to be a Catalan nationalist, a minority individual whose small, narrow-minded mentality we are the first to denounce and scorn, now that all the nations in the world are speaking about joining together, they come out with these separatist notions, you've got to look up higher, see beyond the simple provincial image of the little house with its tiny toolshed and garden plot promoted by such figures as Maciá and Companys,

seek objectives less minimal and narrow, ideals worth defending
with something more than the Virolai and the Sardana; or
lamenting the Catalan's political incapacity, understanding as
such his ineptitude for reaching the peak of power, as well as the
less-vaunted and even frequently ignored economic incapacity,
understanding as such not his lack of skill in making money, but
rather his instinctive rejection of how much is required to com-
bine efforts and to fuse capital resources, no longer capable of
creating true industrial complexes, in accord with the gigantism
that is nowadays a question of survival, but rather including,
unlike the Basques, some major bank that, by backing projects
of a certain importance, would contribute at least to the remodeling of an economic landscape characterized by industrial
smallholdings and de-capitalization, all that fruit of our radical
individualism and long-term suicide. The fact is, that's how we
are and we have no remedy, being individualists among the individualists, and in the same way that what was here during the
communist era was not communism but anarchism, so too in
businesses and in everything, so that that might not work against
us but rather in our favor, we're too gentlemanly, too lordly, too
lacking in honorable mercantile qualities that distinguish us
from so much new money and so many vulgar, grasping, bloodsucking parvenus, that exonerate and purify us of all confusion
with the surrounding and so grossly adulterated atmosphere,
capable as we would be, like Samson, of pulling down the
Temple upon our heads and perishing before compromising—in
the matter of principles—with the times and the upstarts, criteria
and considerations that if in a general way propitiate skepticism
and desperation, the idea that history, for example, does not
seem to make coherent sense and perhaps does not have to,
much less provide an obligatory happy ending, they also propitiate a unified disdain toward innovation, in the bitter confrontation about what's being lost, in the form of closing ranks against
what's transcendent, here and now, everyone, like always when
the bells toll for someone's death and everyone else comes and
gathers round, a comfort in time of pain, consolation for affliction, united, joined together, unanimous, marching along one

after another conscious of the support that represents, not only for the relatives, but also for each one of those of us who march, made fervent by the way in which those present mutually empower one another and by the depth that the circumstances confer upon the act of clutching and pressing a hand, signing the book of condolences or placing yourself entirely at their disposition, sincerely moved, no doubt sincerely moved, as we offer ourselves to the relatives of the deceased, a great lady with whose disappearance disappears for all a little bit of our own past, of what we usually understand to be our times. Around two in the morning, in the sitting room there now only remained men, relatives of varying degree, friendships particularly attached to the family or especially trustworthy gentlemen, and Pedro, as if to correspond to what was doubtless expected of him, became the focus of the attention of some of those present with his anecdotes about whores, skirting, through precise, ingenious circumlocutions, every crude or scathing word, a deference ostensibly directed either at the maid who brought more coffee and emptied the ashtrays, or at Ramona, who sometimes drew near to light a cigarette in his company. But, do they do it for pleasure or for money? asked Ramona, snug against the arm of the sofa, while not even the naturalness of the tone employed nor the simultaneously serene and objective and confident gesture were sufficient to prevent even a stranger, or a person unfamiliar with the economic power that Jacinto Bonet repre- sented in Barcelona, from understanding everything immedi- ately, his wedding, his impossible desires, the reasons for that impossibility, and under any appearance of mere curious interest, would not guess the fascination that was evidently produced by everything relating to the matter and, more concretely, the key to the erotic mechanism, the mystery of a forceful penetration; amorous affections. They also told political jokes, not without criticizing that oh-so-very Spanish custom of always criticizing the one who governs, inverse to how the English consider it incorrect to simply raise the subject of politics during gatherings, and they talked about the superiority of the Anglo-Saxon edu- cational system, of our team's chances for the Davis Cup, about the striptease shows one can see in London, more outrageous than the shows at Crazy Horse, various topics, adequate for a situation in which the night is still young and it's better to chat about entertaining things in order to ward off the tension produced by the presence of a body lying in some adjacent room, the waxen gloom of the burial mound. When Raúl said good-night they were talking about the terrorist sentenced to death, coinciding besides, in essence, with the criterion that had prevailed in Leo's house in what's referred to as the causal act for the sentence, the work of a madman, now dramatically reassessed due to the news of the sentence having appeared in the afternoon paper, even though here the assessment of madness was based on the conviction that only a madman could attempt to effect change and bring about the progressive economic development of the country with bombs at the very moment when the fruits of Stabilization were beginning to reach the most humble classes. Meanwhile, at Leo's house, a similar recourse to some methods already mentioned in "*The Bakuninists at Work*", almost one hundred years before, had been rejected as counterproductive, only … it could be considered as one more example of the exas-peration of the popular masses, without the negative and even provocative aspects of the action being an obstacle, nevertheless, so that all the pronouncements of solidarity with the victims of repression were formulated and, more concretely, the victims of police brutality, whatever their political creed might be, the same as in cases like those of Marsal or Obregón, in the case of this poor boy, surely so full of generosity as to be misguided, that if he'd not already been executed by firing squad, after an even more hasty, summary trial, the reason was, without a doubt, because his physical condition had prevented him from testifying before the court-martial with greater urgency; extreme theses, or conjectures, too far removed from the daily life of those gathered at Aunt Paquita's wake—raised as they were by some unsuspect-ing spirit and with little sense of the situation—for basic sensitivity or etiquette to have prevented them from expressing support for the idea that, for admonitory purposes, the execution be carried out in the public plaza, as with Juan Sala, alias

Serrallonga, or any other villain of old. Serrallonga, who on the eighth of January, 1634, according to the chronicles, was lashed, had his ears cut off, was paraded about on a wagon, his flesh pierced with red hot pincers, then drawn and quartered, and his severed head displayed on one of the towers of the Gate of San Antonio of the present city. *Anima eius requiescat in pace.* Amen.

When will the martyrology end! said Leo's father, and like in a picture from the Baroque era where the supernatural plane is imposed triumphantly upon the overwhelmed witnesses to an apparition, thus, in the meditative pause that followed his words, such an implicit and respectful homage of silence, the image of Obregón hung by his arms from a water pipe became almost palpable, his wrists skinned, his feet crushed, his skin marked by cigar burns, or the image of Marsal handcuffed to an iron bed frame transformed by electric shocks into a screaming abyss, or Leo himself, felled by a round of blows, scenes always with something unreal about them, perhaps due to the sordid familiarity of the surrounding circumstances: offices that could belong to a notary public, fellows that could be insurance agents, all quite vulgar, devoid of the plasticity and mythical weight of a Sebastian pierced with arrows or a Savonarola on the pyre, but not for that reason any less realistic and immediate, something like what happened to Obregón could have become reality for Floreal if he'd not hidden in time, something that no one stopped imagining was already really happening to Escala when the rumor circulated about his arrest, in the same way that the sheer luck of having beaten the police to the flat where the fellows from the student committee kept the mimeograph machine had prevented it from becoming a reality as well for Raúl and Federico. This is like the last days of Pompeii, said Leo's father. The volcano will soon erupt. Already, back in the days of Hegel, the great German philosopher whose thoughts, although he was an idealist, served as a basis, perhaps, for those of Marx, Barcelona was already then a world-class city that counted among its history more fights at the barricades than any other, and now the final battle draws near. On one side will be the powerful people, with their luxuries, their vices, their profligacy; on the other, the people with their hunger and misery. While the rich are increasingly rich, the poor grow ever more poor, and the millionaires and plutocrats see their enormous profits and their personal dividends constantly grow larger, and at the expense of workers' salaries. That's why the revolution is the worker's task. The worker is the only one who has nothing to lose, except his chains. But it's foreseen that the same progression of events goes on demonstrating its truth and then, in their fight, the working class will receive the support of other classes and social levels, democratic students, progressive intellectuals, small liberal bourgeoisie and non-monopolistic bourgeoisie, as well as ample sectors of the clergy and even the army, meaning, from all the people of goodwill who, before the disaster of capitalism and the perspectives that socialism offers to resolve the problem in Spain, are beginning to see things clearly. We believe that the land belongs to those who work it, and for that reason the farmer, as he makes this principle his own, is converted into the natural ally of the working class. This does not mean, however, that we need to be against private property, just the opposite, we even defend it from those who would attempt to monopolize it to the detriment of the community. The proof is that, in socialist countries, even nowadays various kinds of private property continue to exist. And with the question of the Church, the same thing happens, that we've got nothing against the fact that the good and faithful Catholic practices his religion. Here Teresa intervened: it seems that in Poland, for example, she said, the people attend Mass much more than in Spain. And Leo: besides, he said, in reality now it's not about making a revolution, but about restoring parliamentary democracy to Spain, a transitional regime in which all democratic forces and tendencies in the country are represented. And I can assure you all that, when the moment arrives, not only the soldiers recruited in the heart of the town, but the very members of the repressive forces—armed police and civil guard, as well as a great number of sub-officials and heads of the army and even some public officials and bosses—will all join the peaceful national strike. You cannot fathom the discontent voiced in the flag halls, about the ridiculous salaries that Francoist agents collect for doing a job that disgusts them, about how shabby the prison workers' uniforms get. I was talking quite a bit with one fellow from my building, and I assure you all that we can count on many of them not only when it comes to overthrowing the dictatorship but also in the transitional phase toward socialism. And the same with the Church, said Leo's father; the lower clergy, who see the workers' problems up close, will end up playing their part and pulling their weight, and the hierarchy will have no other choice than to do the same. The first thing that priests would have to do is go with women, said Juan. Now, with them having to do it secretly, they all turn into faggots. The Development Plan will fail, said Leo. Only recently they nailed one there up on Montjuich, in the Tierra Negra, said Juan. And that stuff about the parish priest from Pueblo Seco, who fondled the little boys in the parish, if the police hadn't intervened they would've lynched him. The only thing the Development Plan will do is create contradictions, said Leo. There are too many rifts and too many antagonizing interests and forces in conflict for it to make progress. Inflation, unemployment, depression, a deficit in the balance of payments, when it's not one thing it's another. And that's owing, apart from the fact that the country is on full sit-down strike, as that one guy says, since the Civil War ended and that's why production is so low, a real boycott on a national scale, that's owing to the fact that the Regime has already decayed to such a degree that now the same groups and factions that make up the Francoist party are the first ones to jam a spoke in the wheels. From what it seems, even Franco's inner circle itself is willing to support your national peaceful strike against the dictatorship, Federico said as he was leaving. And Raúl: maybe, Leo could tell you. Well it's a bad affair, said Juan. If they have so many allies, it must be for some reason. Here the same thing happens like with that business about winning the war before making a revolution. For what and for whom? Well, the same thing happens here. Talking about overthrowing the regime alongside the bourgeoisie is deceiving the people. If it took a world war to bring down Hitler and Mussolini, what the fuck do you think you'll achieve with peaceful strikes? And they know it all too well. That's why they shot that poor kid who set off the bombs. Arming the people

is what's needed, arming the people. And Leo: the fact that they
shot him is one more proof of the Regime's weakness, he said; the
cat turns dangerous when it's cornered.

Obligatory question: can a fellow like Leo turn stupid, meaning, behave as if he were, or was it more about an appearance
appropriate to the state of disorientation that he doubtless
experienced upon coming out of prison after everything he had
experienced in there for more than three years, or perhaps he was
already an idiot before and they had simply never noticed? But
this was not the only change in his behavior they observed: a
certain instability, too, like uneasiness or apprehension, nervous
manners, his laugh a bit strained, or coming too soon or too late,
after a sort of stupefied reaction, symptomatic, perhaps, of a
relative absence or alienation from what he was saying. The
impatience that showed plainly through his silence while the
father was saying, no, it's because we are men, Fortuny, and it's
human that for a father the first thing is his son, but Leo has
already paid his debt, and what he has to do now is to dedicate
himself to his own business and wait, be reserved, keep things
to himself, look how well he served his time and these people
are judging him. Finish his studies, earn a living, get married,
start a family; and although he didn't mention Teresa at all, it
was as if Teresa began to grow like an inner tube being pumped
up, how it swells out and stiffens and takes shape, getting larger
until it becomes noticeable even for one not watching it, in the
same way that, although it might have fallen outside of our visual
field, a spark becomes perceptible to us. Impatient, uncomfortable, self-conscious, as if controlling himself so as to avoid letting
fly some inconvenient remark or uttering some incongruous
phrase, with the exasperated impotence of the one who only
keeps quiet because any word he pronounces will only become
redundant in the thorough explanation of a theme whose mere
mention he would have preferred to avoid, so that it were better
to feign absent-mindedness, as if Leo did not seem affected or
as if at least Raúl did not notice that he seemed that way, forcing
the conversation, unfolding it, for example, with any phrase
directed at Leo when the father was asking Fortuny, isn't that

right, Raimon? and Fortuny said yes, it was, that an attorney now plays an important political role simply by pursuing his career, limiting himself strictly to taking advantage of the legal possibilities, at the margin of all clandestine activity, and Federico was saying, well it's true, to defend the humble man from the abuses of the powerful one. And then Raúl asked Leo and they talked about sleeping pills, or about some specific tranquilizer, a surefire maneuver to change the subject, one of the few topics about which they could extend themselves without tension or reticence, once they'd mutually identified themselves as people who took pills, meaning—without it having to be said—that they each presented, although distinctly characterized, a neurotic portrait, more properly depressive in Leo, more nervous anxiety or anguish in Raúl, with insomnia in both cases, and to compare reactions experienced and secondary effects of the medication, always disregarding, as if by tacit agreement, all reference to motivations, to the cause of their need to take pills, always a very personal theme and, at bottom, no less removed from the realms of consciousness than the realms of willpower, regardless that in any given moment, for perfectly obvious reasons, it might sharpen the need. Obregón's arrest, for example, in Leo's case, and more concretely the responsibility, just as involuntary as effective, that doubtless corresponded to him for the fact of having contributed to swelling Obregón's police record, the charges which Obregón now had to answer, thanks to his declaration from three years ago, when Marsal was arrested, when he, Leo, knowing that Obregón was safe, hoping to limit the interrogations as much as possible, had admitted belonging to the communist party and maintaining contacts with Obregón, and later with Marsal trying, so far unsuccessfully, to create a university committee, a statement not only coherent and credible, given that there was no other student's telephone number in the coded notes found in Marsal's possession, but possibly even clever, in the supposition that Leo would have been quite sure that Obregón would never fall into the hands of the police, a more than questionable presumption, as the events had just demonstrated with abundant emphasis, for it had been, precisely,

Obregón, and, among the sectors affected, precisely the university, so that it would not be risky to suppose, regarding Leo, that
where they had to seek the immediate conflictive nucleus was in
the mental reconstruction of his own arrest, more than Obregón's
arrest, in the same way that it could not be said that for Leo the
problem was properly one of fear when he sent Raúl the final
order from Escala, received via Floreal only hours before he
would also, in turn, disappear from circulation, as if to better
underscore the gravity and urgency of the events, of an arrest
that deeply affected the metalworking industry, university
students and administrators, sectors that, apparently, between
people arrested and in hiding, had led to a total collapse, without
organic contacts of any kind, a situation, more than uncertain,
more alarming by the moment, a chain-reaction breakdown to
which someone had to react, in some way, however possible, to
prevent it from becoming a true catastrophe. With no time to
lose, he had to remove any compromising papers from the apartment where the student committee printed its propaganda and,
if possible, save the mimeograph, get everything out of there
before the police arrived, if they had not already, a risk that had
to be undertaken that very night, as soon as they closed the
building's main entrance, load it all in Federico's car, you and
him, the two of you will be more than enough, it would be
counterproductive for me to come along with you, they're surely
following me, the Social Investigation Brigade all know me,
considerations taken not exactly out of fear, not, at least, from
fear of a new arrest, or not only that, from the fear of a new and
more painful interrogation, of the physical pain, of more years
in jail, the fear that he might end up talking if apprehended
again, like his fear, above all, about what he might have ended
up saying if the interrogation had lasted a bit longer, if the detective, overcoming his carelessness or his fatigue or his routine, had
insisted a little more, the eyelid contracted so as to better dominate his twitching pupil as he looked at Raúl, his lips pressed
tightly together as if to say if you haven't been through it don't
talk, if you haven't been through it you can't even imagine what
that is, his attitude thus referring to an experience that he seemed

to consider nontransferable, very mistakenly, no doubt, given the fact that Raúl's reaction, like that of the apprehensive man who, thanks to his own familiarity with disaster, ends up being capable of facing it serenely, it could be well determined, for having already imagined it too many times and, including lately, almost desiring it, arriving at the flat to find the police there, for example, the interruption to his current situation it would have meant, to his problems, who knows, perhaps even to himself, and so, in passing, teach a lesson to Nuria, who was so good at repeating, when something needed to be done, well, then you just do it, the only thing you need is balls, equally clear and determined in her judgments as Teresa and much more free in her expressions, a lexicon that to Teresa, in all certainty, must seem just as inconvenient in a woman as improper to a self-restrained revolutionary, strikes, scattering leaflets, police repression, demonstrations, tortures, acts of heroism, phrases that on Teresa's lips had the potency of an incantation, the gift of summoning the heroism of the people more than just simply witnessing it, when, examined closely, she would do better speaking less, that after all, Escala said, Leo's conduct has not been precisely that of a Dimitrov. That's the most that can be said in his favor: that he behaved with weakness. Raised in a semi-proletarian environment, Serra has been able to study, however, thanks to his parents's effort, like any other child of the bourgeoisie, permitting himself as well, also like any child of the bourgeoisie, to be a lousy student when the prestige of his political activity demands the exact opposite, that the communist student must also be a good student. Neither an intellectual nor a worker, Daniel, Serra has those defects that have remained in him halfway along, without the ideological rigor of a Ferran, for example, nor the characteristic solidity of our militant workers. An ambiguity that perforce had to be made clear in an extreme situation, which is exactly what an arrest is. Of course in an arrest the comrade responsible crumbles, just as Marsal crumbled, the demoralization is usually contagious to the other ones who've been picked up, and that's precisely what happened then; but that doesn't erase the objective fact that Serra's comportment was incorrect. Nobody was arrested on his account, that's true, but his comportment as a good militant communist leaves much to be desired. If he wasn't expelled from the party, like Marsal, it was only because he didn't bear the same responsibility to the party as Marsal did. After all, what did Marsal do? Turn into a traitor, into a police informer, deliver the organization he was responsible for into the hands of the police? Of course not. He gave an address: the one where he was living. And there were notes there, telephone numbers. And one of the numbers was repeated: in code, like the others, but also not coded. And with that the police decipher the rest, foil all of Marsal's contacts with the different party cells, arrest the connections who've not had time to get to safety. Serra among them. One of those connections, the textile worker, caves in and tells the police what he knows and part of what he doesn't know. The result? Almost fifty arrests and the need to rebuild the organization from top to bottom. And Serra? What does Serra do? Turn us all in, his university pals? Not that either. Serra is alone, he's the only student arrested so far and knows that he has to stay the only one. But he doesn't feel strong enough to take the bull by the horns, so he looks the police right in the eye, to tell them, in effect, gentlemen, I belong to the communist party, for which reason, it is my pleasure to tell you that you're not going to get a single word out of me, the statutes of my organization prohibit me from revealing anything to you. That way, face to face. He doesn't feel strong enough and instead is opting to try to fool them, to make the police believe that he's giving in, that he's ready to squeal. He talks about Obregón, about how he met him in Paris, through a Spanish student, the son of exiles; about the contacts that he later maintained here with Obregón to study a plan to infiltrate the university; about how Obregón introduced him to Marsal before leaving again. An ingenious declaration; talk but without telling the police anything useful, even shortcutting the police's guesses with respect to the university by confessing himself the only one responsible for the party activities in that sector. But what's ingenious is not the same as what's correct. There is a question of principle, an attitude when facing the police, that was not, shall we say, what Serra displayed. But there's even more. Does Serra really believe that he didn't tell the police anything useful to them, that he didn't compromise anyone with his statement? Does he imagine the police don't remember? That they won't use his signed statement against Obregón, if someday they manage to catch him? Reflections that, at this stage, everyone, except Teresa, now seems to have made, as if she'd ignored or might have forgotten all the details relating to Leo's arrest when she added her voice to Nuria's, both of them emulating each other with impetuous fervor in declaring their militant integrity, a political fidelity in which, perhaps, given its inappropriate insistence, they saw the depersonalized symbol of a desirable nuptial fidelity, with which Nuria and Teresa identified completely, however much separately they did not waste a chance to criticize each other, to create some distance, Teresa presumably lamenting that Nuria had ended up trapping Raúl, in the same way that Nuria lamented that Leo, who's really handsome, had ended up falling into Teresa's net; Leo deserved something better than this girl who's been waiting three years to get him into bed when he got out of jail, to really sink her claws into him and marry him and get him away from his friends as soon as possible, which is what she's trying to do by whatever means possible. An insidious campaign by Nuria, a contagious phenomenon or a coincidental reaction, the hostile climate Teresa experienced among their friends since they released Leo was something nobody could pretend to overlook, especially Leo, sensitized to the very smallest allusion, the smallest sign, getting lost in his own thoughts, drifting in the clouds, not antagonistic contradictions, but certainly aspects of the daily usury that in some way could contribute to his psychic stability, a stability put abundantly to the test recently by the transit supposed in moving from ideological discussions about the Spanish reality, in prison, to direct contact with that reality, or rather, with its appearance, so irritatingly plagued by oblique particularities, scattered incidents, disorienting exceptions, and parasitic excrescences, that the mere effort of keeping his ideas clear, to keep perceiving within such a tangle the key aspects of the true reality, was something that had its price, that was paid in some way, a sudden sensation of tiredness or somnolence, for example, a downy muffling of the intellect, manifestations of prostration that Raúl was capable of recognizing insofar as they fit his own experience, although, regarding what concerned him, unlike what could be presumed about Leo, every attempt to define the cause, the active principle of that kind of discomfort, of isolating the concrete fact, the word, the thought it had provoked, ended up leading him, more than to a shock from the depressing personal circumstances in which it was debated, generators not so much of a slack tension as of petrification, not so much a sensation as a state, more than to that, to a run-of-the-mill ideological discussion, to the debate about the praxis of some theoretical principle, to the abstract formulation, argumentations which, in the way a toxin infiltrates the bloodstream and infiltrates all the body's members one by one, seemed to spread out inside him, and like a fever, distanced him from what was being said, marginalized him from the conversation, isolated him, a progressive absence that with much difficulty he managed to assume as a thoughtful silence, sometimes with the impression of already having experienced that moment, of knowing exactly what was going to happen and then, the trembling of the feathers against the wires, the old man with a kerchief knotted around his head moved across the landscape of empty rooftop terraces, what Federico said upon breaking contact and turning halfway around, leaning on the steering wheel, Aurora bringing ice, the sidewalks of any block in the Ensanche, the terrace of a bar, pigeons fluttering their wings, suddenly meeting Escala, two friends running into each other in the street and walking together a while, the most normal thing in the world, self-criticism, Daniel, the need for self-criticism, errors derived from an overly penetrating analysis, of overestimating the enemy's intelligence, their danger, because the fact that the Stabilization Plan has not been a complete disaster does not mean, not by a long shot, that the Development Plan must necessarily constitute a success; we're not going to be the kind of people who surrender our plans to the enemy beforehand. The reality is that the precise

conditions necessary for the triumph of a peaceful national strike
do exist. But even if the conditions were not optimal we weren't
going to play into the enemy's hands by proclaiming it out loud,
nor simply cross our arms waiting for better times. There are
occasions when a certain dose of subjectivity is not only healthy,
but also absolutely indispensable. What would have become of
the party if the comrades in charge of it had not let themselves
be guided by that healthy subjectivity when, at the end of the
Civil War, they found that it was necessary to start again, almost
from the very beginning, if they hadn't believed that the hour of
revenge was near, if they'd known it was going to take so long,
and that at this point, more than twenty years later, they were
still going to be in the underground opposition? Wouldn't they
have been defeated by discouragement, by compromising and
defeatist attitudes? How can you doubt the fact that without the
constant and enthusiastic action of that subjectivity on Spanish
political reality it would not have been possible to cover, as has
been covered, the distance between the situation then and the
way things are now, between the installation of the Franco dictatorship and its overthrow by means of a peaceful national strike
in which all the anti-oligarchical forces will convene without
exception, conscious of the fact that their political future depends
on them demonstrating in the street? That's right, we must
stimulate the formation of various groups: Catholics, socialists,
pro-Catalan factions, or simply democratic groups, help them
to become aware of the interests they represent, of the historical
role awaiting them as spokesmen for the different social classes
and strata, make them know our democratic alternative. The
democratic alternative: topple the dictatorship; the immediate
formation of a provisional government without institutional
trappings and with communist participation that organizes free
and democratic elections, the party's role in the new resultant
regime, a transitional regime characterized by the party's acceptance of the parliamentary game, the triumph of socialism by a
peaceful path; the flash of those lenses, more substantial, you
might say, than adjectival, as if the glasses' true function was not
to sharpen his vision as much as to hide, behind the reflections,

his look, his thoughts, his personal secret. It seems that when he was a student he created the first postwar communist cell in the university, right during the time of the Maquis, said Fortuny. Don't mention it to Federico. Seems that it didn't take root, someone was arrested, but nothing happened to him personally. By contrast, during the general strike in '51, when he was already a lawyer, someone squealed and he was fully implicated and he had to flee his house over the terraces and rooftops; he was the person responsible for propaganda and they'd even managed to set up a little print shop in a basement. Ever since then he's been underground. He knows almost all the socialist countries. The People's Republic of China, the most wonderful country after the Soviet Union. I'll tell you Daniel, personally, despite my unlimited admiration for the Soviet Union, I've always thought that everything would have been easier if, as Marx expected, communism had not been born in Russia but in Germany. More rigor, without a doubt. Notwithstanding, although on the global level dogmatism indisputably represents a great danger, revisionism continues to be the greatest danger on the national level. And in Catalonia, especially, Titoism, because of how it flatters the spirit of petit bourgeois nationalism. And Trotskyism or leftist deviationism. Regarding Cuba, Castroism is only a passing phenomenon; Castro is to Cuba what Kerensky was to the USSR. As a spectacle, perhaps impressive to someone like Lucas or a crazy fool like Esteve. And Federico: or rather, an adventurer, a romantic. And Floreal: the very same; the proof is that when he wants to do something serious he's got to turn to the party cadres. And Juan: well, if you ask me, the guy's a fascist. And Leo: a positive phenomenon that will be overcome by the very dialectic of the revolution. And Federico, at Adolfo's house, or perhaps in the car: Abstractions! Madness! Have you noticed? This shows just how dangerous the police are. If when they nab guys like Obregón or Zorro they're capable of beating them to death it's because they're just as crazy as them. Mass actions in which you only see cops and a vanguard of the proletariat but upon closer inspection it seems to be formed mostly of students, children of the bourgeoisie, spoiled brats like you and me. And

Juan: isn't that the truth? Shitty little brats, yes, sir. And the father: let's not generalize. Just like everywhere, there's a bit of everything. But I find that the worker tends to be best understood precisely by the student. And why? Well, because the student is a cultured person. The thing is that the lessons of culture, which until now have been the privilege of a few, need to be channeled to all people. Give the people culture, that's what needs to be done. That's why we've made sacrifices, so that Leo can study. And the sister: Leo is different. Leo is, how shall we say, a worker. And Juan: you be quiet. Don't talk about what you don't know. Do you think that workers nowadays are like ones before? I'd let the workers nowadays have it myself. Now, if their salary isn't enough, they take overtime and sit around talking about soccer. But wait until the Republic returns and you'll see how then, it'll be legal to go on strike, and then they'll go on strike for any damn thing. I'd let these sissies nowadays have it with the machine gun right in the face. And Floreal: and what's so wrong with young people liking sports? I'm sure young people in '31 liked sports, too, and who would have said, a week before April 14th, that there would be a Republic? The thing is that you're stuck on the war years and you think everything's got to be handled through violence. But the world has changed in many ways, and even Lenin himself, if he were alive now, would be on the side of peaceful protest. And Juan: the one who really brought about the Russian revolution was Magnus, and then Lenin had him killed. And Leo: the problem is not that the intellectual cannot be a revolutionary. The problem is that, though he be a revolutionary, he doesn't truly know the working class. He's not in contact with the masses, not integrated with the people, and his vision is partial, theoretical, only seeing the working class from outside. He doesn't know the true reality. And Floreal: the intellectual revolutionary, thanks to his greater preparation, currently has before him a great task to carry out in lecture halls, discussion circles, social groups, and associations of a cultural character, choral societies, sports clubs, parish centers, etcetera. And the father: Leo cannot get mixed up in trouble. He's really worn out and they've got it in for him. And Floreal:

that's how we'll all be soon enough, the word will be that we've managed to convince them all, but we'll be eating our words a few days later, like in an empty cell, sarcastic echoes for whomever succeeds in remembering them, for although no one gave much importance to the first news, to the first signs of an arrest, a comrade's arrest, an administrative employee of a pharmaceutical laboratory, not necessarily proof of anything, one swallow not making a summer, one tumbling rock doesn't automatically make an avalanche, in the same way that nobody worries about the porter's ironic smile as they leave the building, although one does start to get uneasy if they run into the same look wherever they go; from the typists in the office, the waiter at some café, passengers in the metro, staff in your section at work or in the notary's office, students in your department at the university, mourners at a burial, how everyone started to get uneasy while the alarming information proliferated and occurred at such a rhythm that, for a moment, they began to fear that Marsal's arrest had only been like a rehearsal for the one now, whose true dimensions were concentric circles spreading out from the starting point, the presence of the police in the home of the person arrested, the search, the agent boasting about how the detainee had been tailed for quite some time, that they'd caught him red-handed with one of the big shots, with a member of the communist party leadership, the confirmation that said big shot was Obregón, rumors of more arrests, in the metalworking sector, among office workers and bank employees, that, through a comrade from the savings bank who studied economics on his own, the arrest had spread to take in the whole university group, tales of tortures, of a suicide attempt, searching houses to nab the ones who had to hide out, the news that Fortuny wouldn't return from Paris until the situation became more clear, Escala's disappearance, at first thought to be an arrest, Floreal's flight only a few hours before the police showed up to look for him, his last instructions, waiting in Federico's car watching the door of the building, going up to the apartment with two empty suitcases, the moment it took to open them, getting the typewriters and filling the suitcases with all the

writings and stencils they could find, now without even thinking
that the police, like a spider on its web, could be there waiting
inside, waiting for them, for Federico, for Raúl, could also be
waiting for them outside, in the street, to catch us with our
hands in the cookie jar, carrying all kinds of stupid shit, look,
look, pamphlets and handwritten drafts, copies of *Realidad* and
personal letters, little love letters, look, Dear Mireya, I'll bet she's
really ugly, little love letters between comrades, a nest of love and
revolution, imbeciles, thanks to the fault of these imbeciles
they're going to catch us as if we were communists. Or do you
think that you're still one? What're we doing here? Why've we
come? For love of Leo? For moral support? Excessive sweat,
characteristic of a physical effort greater than carrying all that,
eyes spinning like a whirlwind of frightened pigeons, the same
irrepressible laugh from when he found out about Pluto's girlfriend, a contagious laugh, product, probably, not so much from
the desire to annoy that Fortuny might attribute to him, as much
as an exaggerated sense of the ridiculous, joined with the habit,
not precisely new, of situating himself in the center of the imagined situation, converted into an object of general derision,
making Raúl out to be some common criminal, for example, a
militant communist finally jailed for his complicity in an aborted
attempt, don't you see that Pluto, just by making a joke, is capable of spilling the beans until they bust you all? It'd be funny to
end up in jail, not with the politicians but with the thugs. And
he added: in any case, I'm sure it's better with them than with
the politicians, a sure guess, absolutely, as if Fortuny weren't
waiting in Paris for the smoke to clear, but rather with them, in
Adolfo's house, with Nuria and Aurora and Pluto and Mariconcha
talking about going out for a stroll on Las Ramblas, just like
months before, when Leo got out of prison, before he started
going out with Teresa and, if he got a little drunk, he still got
euphoric, too, almost like the old days, mingling with people,
loquacious and incisive, although with a painful tendency, perhaps not completely new, perhaps for that very reason necessarily
painful, to offer a political interpretation to what could just be
a mere alcoholic manifestation, of teasing, for example, some

poor tacky person without class consciousness or fraternizing to
excess with some presumed proletarian in search of a scapegoat,
following any astute suggestion, possibly as insincere as intuitive,
the affirmation that he didn't kiss anybody's ass, or some similar
sign of politicization, a natural attitude, despite everything he'd
been through, just like the old Leo, not cowed, not inhibited,
without hardly drinking, like on the increasingly less frequent
occasions when he'd still accompanied them since he started
going out with Teresa, his circumspection increasing the growing
distance between his old life and his new one, between his old
friends and his new relationship with Teresa, conscious of that
distance, just as they were equally conscious, and for the same
reason, with all evidence, closer and closer to Fortuny, now that
they'd almost stopped seeing him too, without which Raúl's progress toward the intellectual cell and the fact that Fortuny had
become the organizational secretary for the student committee
were sufficient to explain by themselves the change, the narrow
relationship created between Fortuny and Leo, the growing
distance of both from the group, a reticent posture to which, no
doubt, certain observations by Escala were not irrelevant where,
under the explicit references to Federico and Adolfo, any wise
person could discover a clear warning directed at Raúl. The
working class is not one worker, Daniel, but rather the proletariat
considered as a whole, a whole that is different from the sum of
its parts, and therefore not simply theoretical data, but, similarly,
eminently operative in the terrain of praxis. The working class
is not one of those workers whom you can just happen to run
into some Saturday night in any bar in the Barrio Chino, the
working class is something more than that, and if there is an
ideal symbol for it, it's that worker who works his eight, ten,
twelve, and even fourteen hours in factories and construction
sites, who goes from his house to the job and from the job to his
house on mass transit, metro, streetcars, buses, from point to
point in the city, a trajectory frequently more tiring than the job
itself, that worker who lives in apartment buildings like beehives,
if not in shacks and slums with fathers, children, brothers, sisters,
and sister-in-law and brothers-in-law all crowded promiscuously

together; that worker with a wife who, like a true companion, does housework and errands, extra hours, whatever it takes, because they've got to help their kids get ahead and the daily wage just doesn't cut it, this, this is the working class, Daniel, hardship amidst opulence and not the personal and atypical image that Esteve or Lucas might have formed as a consequence of their nighttime incursions as rebellious little rich boys, especially Lucas; to judge from what he writes, one would say that the workers's job means sitting in the bar, in any old bar that he might slide into on one of his nights out, exploring life in the gutter, his encounters with drugs and alcohol, homosexuality and delinquency, prostitution and the lumpen—all examples, in short, of what a worker is not, of what has got nothing to do with the rigid morals and fine political instincts that characterize the worker—the only kind of people you can find in the company of Adolfo and Federico, on a Saturday night, for example, with Aurora, with Nuria, with Pluto, with Mariconcha, with Manolo Moragas, on an insane hunt for the filth necessary to justify filth itself, the lasciviousness to justify lasciviousness itself, the inebriation to justify inebriation itself, meeting up once more at any old altar of their ritual pilgrimage, before a bar swabbed off with a wet rag and some glasses not even dried off, and who knows if they were even washed, again running into the two oddball regulars, the two proletarians given over to wild Saturday night revelry, the two of them a little more drunk than the last time, the *charnego* from the south clapping his hands and striking his heels, goofing, reveling in his dark suit, his necktie flashy though loosened, his pointy shoes, and the other guy, the Catalan—possibly a mechanic, judging by the lustrous grime underneath his fingernails—now still singing his companion's praises, repeating his most amusing expressions, urging him to show off even more, apparently resigned to his role as a sidekick, accompanying and inciting him, now seemingly absent or absorbed, as if sunk in his thoughts, perhaps really admiring the guy—an Andalusian, or a Murcian, or an Extremaduran—and envying his nice dark suit, with its flashy tie and his pointy shoes, in humiliating contrast to his checkered flannel shirt and duffel coat clashing with his pants, surely rescued from some old suit, also envying the other one's diabolical talent for making friends with people, of amusing everyone with his witticisms, of seducing women with just a few silly words, remarks that would never occur to him, not even when drinking, other words and, above all, another way of saying them, not in a rush or furiously, like when he drinks and he blurts out everything like a machine gun and nobody can shut him up and then the women end up sending him out to take a walk when the guys get pissed off with him and he ends up getting in an argument with anyone, frustrated, misunderstood, maybe from his incapacity to express himself, maybe for the lack of an audience to whom he could be funny speaking in Catalan, more sardonic, more rural and down to earth, based, for example, on the interlocutor's exaggerated praise, counterpoised to an equally exaggerated minimization of oneself, a humor that in order to be completely effective requires the listeners to know who is one and who is the other, in a way that the respective situations of the one and the other in the community become objective and unanswerable support for the irony, but where nobody knows anybody and when it's not even sure that they understand what one is saying, it becomes just as impossible as imitating the other one successfully, the Andalusian, who's graced with a more parodic sense of humor, founded in metaphor or burlesque classification, essentially formal and descriptive, a kind of humor for which the Catalan simply lacks the language, the accent, the sarcastic edge and, above all, the facility, coarse, low approximations which, far from fooling anybody, are evidence of the joker's clumsiness and evil shadow, marginalizing him, at the level of a personal relationship, in any circumstance requiring a vital display of wit, rejected as a valid partner in the conversation, excluded from the dominant mood as long as the mood of the language dominates, limited to his improbably appreciated jokes in Catalan, returning to his exaggerated praise for the other fellow and to his self-vituperation, a contrast that, upon not being duly understood and celebrated, neither by his antagonist nor by the people gathered there, can make him seem a touch menacing, even to force a more explicit inversion of terms, making the conversation swerve toward dangerous extremes, put up your dukes, out in the street, man to man. And it's then when the Extremaduran has got to intervene and make peace and clear things up and put the matter to rest by buying everyone a round, the Extremaduran once more the polarizing force of the general attention, with the disdainful security of the potter who, as if deaf to the exclamatory astonishment of the onlookers, strives more and more in the portentous conjugation of rotative movement and digital sorcery that turns the clay into perfect forms, lording over the situation without more authority than the emanation of his natural elegance, complying perhaps not without reservations nor rancor for the Catalan, but compliant, one of those Catalans whom he admires for always knowing where they're going and, especially, that they go, stubborn, tenacious, always capable of distinguishing what's essential from the merely accessory and of going after something and messing it up completely in the end out of the pure cussedness that they have, a people who don't know how to drink nor have facility with words nor any grace, with that ability to start laughing by themselves, in excess and ahead of the punchline when they make a joke no one finds funny, and that because they're always thinking, because their head is always somewhere else, about what they have to do and to stop doing, not in the fact that today is Saturday, but that the day after tomorrow is Monday. But today is Saturday and there is no reason at all to be thinking about Monday morning, not even about getting home at dawn, nodding off on the first metro if—as is most likely—he's not got enough left in his pocket for a taxi, nor his wife who's waiting for him in a bad mood, nor his children, nor how they're going to manage to pay next month's rent, nor the excuses he'll make to the landlady when she comes to ask for the back rent they still owe, nor when his brother starts reproaching him about how he hasn't tried hard enough, what face to put on so he won't make any reproaches, that at this rate he won't be able to get married nor ever have his own flat, about how many back in the village dream of it, and when they bring the mother, and if when he gets married, and when his wife says she should

never have married him, and his mother will ask why did God
ever have to punish her by making her bear such a cross of a son,
and the little children will cry, and the people in the shack in the
lot next door will scream for them to be quiet, and the people
in the flat downstairs will bang on the ceiling, so you might as
well order another Cuba Libre and forget that you can't continue
that way, without saving, without a flat, without getting married,
living in a sublet and going out on Saturday nights, spending
like people who really have some money, he, who has nothing,
who is nobody, who is a disgrace, with a selfless woman he
doesn't deserve, with some beautiful children he doesn't deserve,
with a beloved mother he doesn't deserve, who is old and worn,
who will surely die without the peace of mind of seeing him
well-settled, because time passes by and he's not getting ahead,
and he can't get ahead as long as he doesn't change his way of
living, as long as he lives from day to day, trudging on until he's
no longer any good for anything, that is if he doesn't have an
accident first and end up totally disabled, living this way is no
life, what you've got to do is forget, not think, think that you've
got to forget, that life is a tango, a puff of air, a roulette wheel,
failing and failing, don't gamble again, not with your heart, I'll
tell you, not with your soul in your hand, not that way for the
world, you're one of those people who would give it all away and
so then they take advantage of you, the world is full of false
friends, of bad friends, of sons of bitches, your brother, your
sister, your wife, your brother-in-law, your girlfriend, your
mother, all of them bitches and bastards, all except your friend,
and you've got to tell him to let him know, put your arm round
his shoulder, sing for him alone, so that he knows, that's a real
friend, one and only, and all the rest are just sons of bitches, all
except that one, a true friend, there, that Catalan, a person with
a heart so big, despite him being a bit abrupt on the outside and
the natural differences in character, a man who doesn't laugh so
easily, less voluble and communicative, usually rather frowning,
with the look of a person who thinks, who turns things over, a
guy with ideas, with ambitions, who knows where he's going and
what he's after, this gal, that motorcycle, I'll be damned if I don't

have one before the year's out even if it's secondhand, man, she's
gonna sleep with me no matter what, they don't know how good
they've got it, if I was a woman fucking hell, drinking all day,
night classes, correspondence classes, a tool maker, some kind of
technician, specialist, and then they rip you off, and you, yes
you, you say, not you, you pussy, I'm going to this company that
pays me more, and if they don't pay me more I'm going to
Germany, fuck you, you already know, man, that's life, like in
the army, man, and then everybody respects you and you're
somebody and then all the neighbors can fuck off, goddamn,
he's got a motorcycle, shit, he's screwing all the girls, fucking hell,
he's buying an apartment and getting married, and you move
out of the building and they can all fuck off, they all smile
politely and come around to butter you up, but they can all get
fucked, and you man, drink that down, drink and drink and
drink, and they can all fuck off, they'll all see then, when they
see you've got rooms of your own, that you're getting ahead,
married and with your own home and watch your wife just as
you would your neighbor, the one who doesn't keep his eyes
open better that he gives up, man, in this you've got to have your
ideas clear, it's the asphalt jungle, man, and the guy who doesn't
get wise will never be more than a tacky, low-class charnego
disgrace, and people will just piss on him, meditations, without
doubt, of a distinctly different content than the Murcian's, but
of very similar value from an ideological point of view, probably
because of his churlish manners, his passion only tempered by
the mistrust of the fact that he's not sure of the ground he walks
on, the colors of his complexion, including, they pointed out
that it couldn't be any other way, the same as his companion, a
classic example of domestic migration, of south-to-north movement, of country-to-city exodus, the farmhand absorbed into
the industrial workforce, into the reserve army that the capitalist
economy demands for its development, cheap manual labor, to
the extent that, for his very misery and rootlessness, devoid of
class consciousness—he also came from the country, from some
backward part of Catalonia, some interior district mired in economic depression, in such a way that, although being Catalan

and finding himself in Barcelona, his belonging to a proletarian
flood composed almost exclusively of Spanish-speaking people
places him in the uncomfortable and ambiguous situation of
being a stranger in his own land, a case just as sad—if not more
so—than that of the typical emigrant, the one from southern
Spain, and of course no less conflictive, a circumstance that
results in his lack of integration, despite being Catalan and a
worker, into the Barcelona working class, a traditionally revolutionary proletariat, born from the decomposition of the last
guild-based structures, the residues of the hierarchizing and
negotiating spirit of other times put early to the test by the
industrial revolution and its compulsory suburban decoration,
cobblestones and smoke, distress and shifty rascals, overcrowd-
ing, tuberculosis, hungry legions aware early on of exactly what
kind of progress the steam engine meant for them, ready to take
justice in their own hands, which the bourgeoisie did not delay
in proclaiming an ominous international hand, dangerously
skillful in handling pistols and bombs, a reincarnation of the
Anti-Spain, secular enemy of Spain and of the secular values that
Spain represents, something that comes in from outside like a
microbe and which, like a microbe, must be treated or, even
better, prevented, with the traditional reactions, with a strong
right hook, for example, the hard right of the right wing, thus
verifying itself as a phenomenon, more than of approximation,
of identification between the great Catalan bourgeoisie and the
Spanish oligarchy and its healthy antidotal and therapeutic
values, a parallel phenomenon of inverse logic to proletarian
internationalism, a reality, as a matter of fact, more dialectical
than real, except for what might result from refusing to get
involved with the Catalan national problem, relegated over time
between one group and another, like the ground-floor seats at
the Liceo, for exclusive use of the middle classes, a meaningful
indication of the elevated political level of a proletariat that,
thanks not so much to its economic development as to its
demanding combativeness, has managed to reach a fairly free
and unencumbered, if not brazen, position, of a proletariat that
not for finding itself, owing to its high technical qualifications

and the fact of having been replaced by the southern immigrant in the very hardest jobs, on the very fringes of the working class, where the worker becomes a technician, and must renounce his sensitized class consciousness, relative prosperity which, doubtless, does nothing but accentuate, by contrast, our mechanic's bitter thoughts, the lumpen Catalan, the oddball regular, pushing him to seek the compensations that the capitalist system offers the people, cheap vice, the saturnine Saturday night rounds of cognac and whores, anxiously on the lookout from one bar to the next, propping up the bar, given over to the operation of selecting the right piece of meat, of adding her, even if only mentally, to his delirium of colliding bodies, of rearing ejaculations, a pursuit capable, although independently of the final result, of making him forget for even a few hours the reality of his situation, Catalan and poor, or better yet, an unprosperous Catalan, with a bad temper completely similar to the bad temper which is to a certain point inherent in the condition of the prosperous Catalan, but without any of the satisfactions that for the prosperous Catalan undoubtedly derive from a greater respectability, the logical sour temper of a Catalan who has had to emigrate to Barcelona, like some southern Spanish charnego, and to live in Barcelona among charnegos, without help, without relations, without significant figures close by, some family member, some person from the same town who has been successful and will now offer a hand to his fellow countrymen who followed in his footsteps, or something like that, nothing, everyone in a situation similar to his own, leaving the town behind like him, with one hand stretched out forward and another behind him, a town of unfortunate people offering misfortune to anyone unfortunate enough to be born there, a town without lands worth the trouble to cultivate nor sufficient natural pastures, nor industry nor tourism, nobody went there and if anyone did they drove him away with stones or nearly so, bumfuck nowhere, some mountain town, that's right, very healthy, mountain air, mountain water, mountain cooking, long-lived people, good complexions and thick blood, ardors that light the eyes with passion and make your eyes misty and fire the veins bursting

with desire, your member swollen to extreme sizes with unbelievable frequency, just like that, from the slightest stimulation
whatsoever, his cock like a fencepost, totally stiff, just like that,
looking at those girls, especially the one with all the long hair, if
they knew it, if they knew what he was capable of doing, how
they came round to jump in bed with him, the way he slams it
home, bang her and bang her and bang her, he drove them wild,
if he had the chance with one of those girls with rooms of her
own, like the one with the big hair, one of those rich dolls, and
if she couldn't forget him, and if she took him with her to see
the world, in her car; give me the world and I'll raise it up with
my cock. The pause that refreshes. Maestro, two more Cuba
Libres. A generous gesture from the other oddball regular, from
the charnego, trying hard once more to light his incombustible
Farias cigar with a certain lassitude, as if sleeping momentarily
on his well-earned laurels, the glittering fixedness of his stare, his
mouth slack after such a flight of merry chatter, a touch of triumph and a dash of scorn in his expression, scorn for all those
who could not share his triumph, the triumph of being from a
land that even though he had to leave it behind to make a living
and which, like all those who had emigrated, like all those who
would have to emigrate, a place he wouldn't return to for the
whole world, but it was, doubtless, a unique land, boy, flamenco,
manzanilla, the deep-fried gobies they call *chanquetes*, bulls,
smooth clams, the impervious randiness of the women, the grace
and flair of the people, truly unique, truly true, the astonishment
of foreigners, the attraction of tourists from all parts of the
world, something grand, boy, the white towns, the sun, boy,
something the whole world envies, and he was from there, boy,
he, fortunate among the fortunate, Andalusian, receptacle of that
joyous beatitude only comparable, in terms of self-contempla-
tion, to what another Andalusian might harbor, whether
landowner or peasant, whether laborer or the owner of a large
estate, uniquely separated from one another, definitively, by a
few thousand hectares, the farmhouse and the Baroque palace,
but each one possessed of the same conviction of existential
privilege and the same rakishly goodnatured and elemental

ignorance with respect to all that is not Andalusia, affinities
cemented upon a singular coincidence of tastes and identity of
interests, whose enjoyment, for the large estate owner, will be
understood as the natural wonder of a harmonic universe, the
spontaneous gift of a domain where each thing is in its place,
while for the laborer, it can only signify something much more
immaterial, a state of being more than anything else, a state
which you can always inhabit again, similar to that weightless
repose attainable through the practice of various yoga exercises,
the exact location almost doesn't matter when one comes from
there, all that's needed is a favorable disposition of the spirit and
a little company and a little singing and a few small drinks, even
if they're just Cuba Libres, at arm's length as they say, saying there
I go and, as if conjuring up the atmosphere in the room, rhythmically fluttering a palm atop the bar, suddenly reactivated, eh,
boy, viva Málaga, back downtown once again, he was also looking at Nuria, doubtless provoked by the way she shook out her
hair, for a moment his exultant eyes insistent, willful, as if saying
to her, don't pretend, little girl, I know for a fact that you like it
when they eat out your pussy. The call of the *taconeo*—the
stamping heel—hands clapping with redoubled intensity, now
impossible to pay attention to anything else, propitiating the
precise unction and reverence in order to step out now for fan-
dangos or cachondeos, the lively Malagueño, a night of making
the rounds and carousing, *un tangáy del caráy, ay que me mu con
el guirigay, que al Uruguay no me voy, guay guay, con el marabú,
con el ay, sal y pimienta y guindilla y aguardiente, la que se arma,*
ululations one might interpret to mean, *a crazy goddamned mess,
I'm struck dumb by all the chaos, but I won't run away, won't fly to
Uruguay with the stork, oh woe, oh woe is me, won't flee that hungry
plague of ants, just give me salt, black pepper, spicy chile, and firewater, or whatever you've got on hand.* But the other guy, Mr.
Stickhisdickinit, Mr. Tittieslurper, was in no mood for stories,
waiting there with his arms crossed for the lively Malagueño to
conclude, like someone agonizing over his florid coplas, and on
seeing that those three whores were getting up with their johns,
he immediately began, his eyes like burning coals, as the saying

goes, and his nervous hands in his pockets, to scan the remaining females present, to size them up, to consider the possibilities, firm in his brutal resolution of fucking, of getting his hands on some girl, and finishing off his wild Saturday night in bed, both of them naked, going at it, tongue and groove, unwilling as yet to accept the end of each week, or the habitual conclusion of his desire in some unhappy transaction, with hookers, on Calle Tapias, one of those women with a macabre mouth, belly scrawled with stretch marks, sphincter broken in, used, and yielding, without giving up his hope yet, with the dogged perseverance with which a mentally handicapped person with homosexual propensities—fierce longings, if not impossible, indiscernible—guarding his stubborn intention of someday sodomizing the admirable citizen on the corner, whom he glimpses in the mornings from his balcony. Without renouncing the possibility of fucking some girl, too, of prying her open and slipping her the handle, of laying her, banging her, shagging her, humping her, screwing her. Without renouncing anything, the night is young, life takes many twists and turns, and it's a small world, as is demonstrated, without going further, by the fact that our two irregular oddball regulars cross paths with them again, now in the final phase of the habitual Saturday night Stations of the Cross, as Pluto would say, attending one of the last stations, a dive bar with flamenco and wild women, Mr. Stickhisdickinit or Mr. Tittieslurper working like the devil to get under the barmaid's dress, the Lively Malagueño screaming himself hoarse for a person with the look of a foreman or manager and his coterie of guests, seated around half a dozen bottles of manzanilla, a kind of petty Ottoman despot, severe and sarcastic, the typical Andalusian with a silhouette like a cracked and damaged tree, spongy, sallow, with a pudgy snout and lisping speech, hyposexual, without any room for doubt. They went to the Jamboree and the Venta, at that slightly lugubrious hour when the bars start closing up, the waiters winding down, turning off the lamps, the metal shutters rattling down, while the people regroup, frustrated, hesitant, as if disoriented, taking something like two hours to find some other bar with music, dancing,

cabaret, some cavernous locale with flamenco. They walked in
behind the albino, just in time to make sure that it was him and
to walk back out again, just as the haggard faggot at the door
finished rudely hawking his invitations to come in, all hope lost.
At the Jamboree they hadn't done anything more than step in
for a moment then leave in a hurry, as soon as their eyes adjusted
to the gloom and the smoke, too many familiar faces for it to be
attractive to stay there, unless of course their purpose had been
to gather in a free assembly and move to approve some moral
revolutionary manifesto in erotically charged solidarity to the
blues of Gloria Steward. It was then that they saw the albino,
walking just ahead of them, the memorable albino, apparently,
from the first or one of the first nights that Leo went out with
them, after getting out of prison, a purblind albino, so very
drunk that, with the elevated lightness of the music lover, singing
tangoes in that bar ennobled with horns and banderillas and
autographed photos of supposed bullfighters, and the barman
said to him, listen señor, show some taste. And the albino: listen,
I haven't insulted anybody. And the barman: well, you tell me,
if you think it's correct to come and get sloshed in my place, I'll
have to put it to you another way. Wounded dignity. The albino
tried to stand up and gather himself together, clutching the bar
for support, with the rigor of one who might well be an authority, a person of influence, an important functionary whose
services we might need someday and who, as an enemy, can cost
us dearly: listen you, you don't know who you're talking to, you.
And the barman: with who? well, with an albino, for fuck's sake.
Ignominious expulsion, an incident that must have tested Leo's
peculiar sense of humor: to celebrate the triumph of superior
wit over the ridiculous presence of the exploiter, roles, in this
case, difficult to precisely identify, to somehow connect with
historical reason. In reality, that's all quite sad, said Leo, the night
now hopeless, the disappointment and dejection ineluctable, no
matter if they left one bar and immediately started arguing about
what would be the next place, as if the happiness of their night
out depended so much on whether they went to one place or
another, as if the effort itself of trying to make things turn out

like the old days wouldn't sharpen in them the awareness of how
time had passed them by, Pluto's jokes, for example, useless,
extemporaneous, if not counterproductive, like when he said
that if he'd never gotten into the party it was only because he'd
never smeared its reputation, and Federico's laugh became so
hysterical that it could only end up provoking, in both Pluto as
well as Leo, an unease similar to that which a misunderstood
joke usually creates at any worldly gathering, as it forces a certain
faction of those present to recognize that its laughter obeys different and even opposing motives than those of the others
present, a muggy sensation of being hoisted by your own petard,
a sense of fractured time, the introduction in their friendship of
an element of uncertainty that could only infuse them all with
an acerbic memory, as it betrays Pluto's attitude, now that with
the business about Mariconcha they started to see each other
again with a certain frequency, her anguished determination to
make herself seem conventional at any cost, his nervous bewilderment as he kept trying too hard to top his own jokes, fluid,
euphoric, absurd, the stuff of the Pluto of old, and that,
evidently, not because the self-parody pleased him nor because
he still believed that it was going to please anybody, but rather,
more than anything, for fear of the void that might well be
opened between them if, although only for an instant, he flagged
in his attempt to maintain the tone at any price, of not giving a
margin to the discontinuity under any circumstances, even at
the risk of enraging Mariconcha or perhaps with the deliberate
purpose of exciting her wrath, of exploiting the value of the
spectacle that usually surrounds all scenes between a couple, an
effect likely to result from any obscene or simply impudent
expression, as you all well know, her lack of mental brilliance is
more than made up for by her sexual brilliance, her scintillating
orgasms. And she: you want to shut up now, you clown? And
he: the fact is that, at least in bed, we thrash as wild as a couple
of crocodiles, right Mariquim? And she: that's enough, alright?
lowering her voice, with the blushing restraint of one who really
means to say: what are your friends going to think of me? And
if she doesn't say so it's only for fear of ridicule. And he: that's

why we screwed up and got knocked up, because of our excessive love of pleasure, interrupting the coitus interruptus, also known as *el salto del payés*, literally the farmer's trick, the peasant's geyser, a home remedy which some have dubbed splitting before the eucharist, not because it's abominably disgusting or bad for the nervous system, but because it's sanctioned by tradition. By having attended to what's prescribed, we wouldn't be talking about this, dammit. Meaning, if we'd rhymed our method with the rhythm method, if we'd followed her period, period, without trying to force it. But our problem is what we might call overzealous rutting, just like dogs. Saint Augustine said let the member be vigorous, and, well, you see what we get for listening to him. This one, I mean Mariclam's clapper, or Marifluke's flapper, or Maripain's pussy, is no jaded performer, it still gets a thrill from each performance, ending up in ecstasy. Maripain hurled a retort he could easily dodge, with a roguish annoyance, as if amused at heart, that barely concealed her real irritation, the ease with which her laughter could dissolve into tears. Really, I think your friend Pluto's name suits him perfectly, said Manolo Moragas. He's just like a big friendly yokel. A guitarist and four crazy flamenco musicians, two fat women with birthmarks, and some kind of old woman, a queer midget stamping his heels center stage, thump, thud, a horrendous blockhead, from Mount Porón, then out came a little Nordic amateur, straight hair and starry-eyed, the tails of her shirt knotted below her tits, and the lesbians urged her on, tossing money to the guitarist so he wouldn't stop, shrieking like a redskin, her nails sharp, the indignation with which the house dancer finished up, stalking off stage, furious, scorned. And there was a sailor stiff as wood, lizard eyes, offering Federico a drink, looking to hook up. They talked about Santa Luisa. Santa Luisa? Luisa Valls, do you all remember her? Well, seems she's a lesbian. And Carbonell, that guy from the Sindicato Español Universitario, el SEU, who turned out to be queer. Like me? said Federico. And Nuria: nothing would surprise me less. What I don't understand is that there's any woman who's not a lesbian, said Adolfo. Or any man who's not a queer, said Federico, evidently for Nuria's benefit. See, you're

not a man, you're a shemale, said Pluto, but Nuria paid him no
attention; following the direction of her gaze, Raúl glimpsed
Marislit or Marislut or Maributch or Maricunt at a corner table,
alone, holding her face in her hands. I'm sick of this hysterical
hyrax he heard Pluto say. Nuria was partially crouched down
next to Maripain's chair and was talking to her, and Maripain
shook her head without taking her hands from her face. And the
Nordic woman seemed to be tied to the post, naked, hair
disheveled, wide-eyed, the lesbians dancing all around her. I
don't want you to cheer me up, said Marifuck. I don't want to
cheer you up, Nuria said: what I want is that your mascara
doesn't go running down your face: look at yourself. She pulled
a little mirror out of her purse and, taking her by the chin, forced
her to stare at her reflection, her eyes blurry, horrified. Marigrief
pointed at Raúl. And him? Is he a good person? This guy? said
Nuria. This guy is a prick. Well, get lost, said Mariache. Make
him go away. I don't want to see him. Not you either. Not anybody, I want them to get rid of it. What I want is for them to
take it out of me. She covered her face with her hands again. It's
not even four more days, said Raúl. Well, I just can't wait
anymore, said Maripang. I can feel it growing. It's like a tumor
that eats away at you from inside. I'm not gonna be able to stand
it until then. And Nuria: yes, you can, you'll see. And Raúl: she
better not drink any more, don't you think? And Nuria: why?
Better she sleep. Did she get a little dizzy? asked one of the
witches with the birthmarks. She died, said Nuria. Raúl helped
her take Maripiss to the ladies' room; Marithrob's hands were
wet from sweat, appropriate to a person tormented by anguish,
to the nymphomaniac or politician. Raúl was in the men's room,
half done pissing, and a guy stumbled in, puking, barely giving
him enough time to avoid being splashed. Back in the barroom
a fight was about to break out, chairs knocked over, and the
hunchback selling peanuts—simply a tottering cripple,
perhaps—was complaining about people's lack of charity, that
someone had spat on him. Everything, the cackling of the
women, Adolfo's unusual loquacity, the ingenious displays of
Manolo Moragas, the sticky shine of Aurora's eyes, Federico's

euphoria, Pluto's collapse, green, mute, everything pointed to
the end, the definitive close, their final gathering in the Plaza del
Teatro, under the watchful eyes of the monument to Pitarra, a
Saturnian culmination; ritual apogee, the last date, the last
opportunity to hook up, to find there among those gathered
together a fraternal breast or a complimentary sex, in that blind
bend along Las Ramblas, in that tenebrous sphincter of the dark
before dawn, eyes, smiles, approaches, anxious observation
beneath that stony excrescence seemingly humid and erectile,
seemingly lingual or clitoral, a point of confluence for the swirling nocturnal crowds, habitual noctambulists or Saturday night
owls, congregating from all points, flowing en masse through
the shadowy streets, in a turbulent procession, with the progressive indiscrimination which is established along the course of a
mass pilgrimage and that ends up triumphing as the diverse
groups of pilgrims come arriving at the sanctuary, the different
forces present slowly intermingled, while they advanced in showy
deployment from their diverse departure points, from the
Avenida Paralelo, Calle Tapias, and Calle Robadors, for example,
on the left side of Las Ramblas, along Arco del Teatro, Conde
del Asalto, Calle Unión, and Calle San Pablo, the filthy dregs of
prostitution along with the dykes in the singing cafés, the dope
peddlers and thugs, as well as other addicts to the many different
kinds of dildos available for sale; on the right-hand, north-side
of Las Ramblas, along Calle Escudillers, from Calle Códols,
Calle Serra, Calle Nueva de San Francisco and Plaza Real, the
whores there relatively expensive and, in general, the streets of
town with a more sophisticated tone, more bourgeois in terms
of clientele, less popular, invested in exploiting both sexes, jazz
aficionados, progressive-leaning students, daughters of families
who are theoretically spending the weekend in the country
invited by a friend; along the lower part of Las Ramblas, from
the upper part of the city, like lazy outdated types with an
aversion to working, the well-moneyed homosexuals, attracted
by the tug of war with the zipper, when the prices go down, like
in all markets, with the change brought on by a sale; and the rich
boys and girls at the Liceo, also along the lower Ramblas, barely

risking to show off their etiquette beyond the avenue's central promenade, sufficiently stimulated, on the other hand, in their viscous erotic progression, by the simple intuition of sin; and, who knows from where, the crippled beggars, the retards, the frightening oddballs, all of them coming out, like tributaries, to increase the river's flow, the multitudes already gathered around the stone monument, where, in the way of fanatical worshippers of some obscene deity, apart from the curious passersby and the inevitable presence of the fuzz, they came together, seeking some kind of satisfaction, the active representatives of all kinds of vices and deviance, wastrels, fags, drug addicts, sadomasochists, alcoholics, coprophagists, viragoes, hermaphrodites, a tumultuous concentration that a superficial observer or a person unfamiliar with the city's customs might well take for a demonstration or a public meeting.

We should try to make an effort to go out less, said Nuria. I used to handle it better, but now, the next day, I feel like shit. And Raúl: you're the one who always ends up suggesting we go out for a stroll. And Nuria: naturally. Or do you think I'm amused by your plan of going to Adolfo's house, we get drunk talking about stupid stuff, always the same gossip and the same lame jokes. What I don't understand is the need to see people every night. Is it so difficult that just you and I go out around there alone, peacefully? And Raúl: you know well enough that's worse. What you could do is not get so drunk and the next day you wouldn't feel like shit. And Nuria: and how do you want me to stand it then? Besides, the worst thing isn't the alcohol, it's the tobacco. Drinking, you smoke twice as much, and I think that's what gets me the most wasted. But without a glass of something and a cigarette, I can't stand it for even five minutes; it's almost a problem of expression, of what face to put on while you're getting fed up hearing the same thing every day, Federico's little jokes, those witty little boasts from that idiot Moragas, how Aurora puts on such airs. I don't know how you stand her. And, above all, that habit of criticizing people who aren't there, which is what makes me most nervous. Oh, Jesus, all night talking about Maripain, the poor thing is so stupid, it's

a provocative stupidity, as Federico would say, similar to those
people in the movie theater who do nothing but talk to their
friend next to them, but what's happening now? Is she cheating
on him? And it drives us to the point of physical aggression.
Or talking about Pluto, about how fucked up he was, or all
about Leo again, about Fortuny, or who knows, maybe about
themselves too, when they weren't present, in the same way that
they started making cracks about Moragas, he'd just barely left,
that night when he'd assured Federico that the king was gauche.
At any rate, said Adolfo, better a bourgeois snob than a bourgeois who's not a snob. Don't let Moragas hear you, said Nuria:
I've practically memorized his whole spiel about the difference
between the bourgeoisie and the aristocracy. The one who's really
odd is Ana Moragas, said Federico; she's one of those people who
seem really fun at first and then it turns out that what they are
is really stupid. Aurora challenged Federico: and that girl you're
going out with? Why don't you bring her along some night?
That's what you'd like, said Federico. Besides, she's a completely
different case. Less stupid than Mariconcha, but much prissier.
And Aurora: almost perfect, right? She spoke with aplomb,
almost with indifference, hardly looking at her interlocutor, as
if she were directing her words to someone else. I wouldn't call
it aplomb, Nuria was saying on her way out. The only thing
she's got is that unction of an already well-settled woman, a little
bourgeois who's going to get married and who's closing ranks,
her Adolfo, her penthouse apartment all decorated, a conversation piece. Just because they're living together without being
married is nothing more than a front for them trying to be hip,
it's got nothing to do with the other thing. If it weren't because
in reality she might perfectly well be a lesbian, I'd consider her
incapable of all those wild stories she tells about Adolfo and her.
Considering how boring she is, you tell me. But it only took
Aurora's presence, to see her moving through the living room,
to hear her rather infrequent remarks, for all the conjectures and
presumptions spoken in her absence to vanish as if before some
evidence to the contrary, neither could Aurora's almost insolent
serenity be confused with the placid satisfaction of the socially

well-positioned woman, nor did her relationship with Adolfo have anything in common with a wife's contented renunciation of an independent life in exchange for the material security and morality implied in marriage, but rather with something much more mortifying; the natural dependence on love with respect to the beloved one, the unconscious tendency to be at every moment attentive to their desires, the conscious desire of carrying, as much as possible, such servitude beyond the limit of their own strength. Equally impossible to try to remember her in less fortunate moments, to revive her image from the past summer, for example, when her broken ankle coincided with some kind of condition which produced sores in her mouth, and she followed them everywhere with her foot encased in plaster, unable to go swimming, pale, clumsy, excluded; he was able to remember the facts, the events, but not her image, the way she looked now, superimposed, was stronger, her beauty implacably reaffirmed by the changes in her way of dressing and fixing herself up, progressively introduced by Adolfo, she seemed thoroughly more complete and also more sophisticated, with a decadent touch so suggestive as to have been heretofore unsuspected. Except for the terrace, where Aurora cared for her plants as if they were puppies, the entire top floor also showed Adolfo's influence, that quality of an apartment as yet uninhabited, almost finished, white, nude, without any kind of personalized details, the built-in stucco shelves and benches in the sitting room, the cushions, fitted carpet, the curtains, the enormous bed that would look abandoned in an empty room, facing a mirror, the worktable completely clear, like brand new, pipe and books arrayed as if to add verisimilitude to the setting, including the music, Italian compositions from the Baroque, operas by Mozart, cantatas by Bach. And the *Requiem*? asked Raúl. Don't you play it anymore? I save it for when I'm working, said Adolfo.

Federico went out with them. In the car they talked about Adolfo's novel. Do you think it will win the Nadal? said Federico. I'd be happy for him, said Nuria. But, even though I've only read bits and pieces, I think Raúl's right, you can't write about reality without compromising yourself, without being fully committed to your party, without having put it all on the line. And Raúl: well, I don't mean political commitment: what I mean is that nobody can write a novel about us, which is, in fact, what his novel is, a *roman à clef*, limiting himself to give testimony to a partial version of our acts, without going deeper, without at least giving things some meaning—whatever that might be—that make it literarily valid. Lacking all that, the tale is pale, darling. The simple objective transcription of our comportment, of our drunken sprees, of our affairs, no matter how well written it is, couldn't possibly interest anybody who knows us. And Nuria: besides, it seems to me, I don't know, sort of immoral, to submit an unfinished novel to be judged for a prize. And Federico: but if the judges decide it's good. I agree, said Nuria. But isn't that, like Raúl says, sort of an excuse? Isn't it more about how he doesn't know how to finish it? No, no, it's not that, said Raúl. And Federico: the thing is, it would be a lot to expect, don't you think? And Nuria: apart from whether or not the protagonist's rebellion consists in going to live in a penthouse apartment with Aurora, it's a great idea. Why, instead of rebelling against society doesn't he seriously try to change it? Moving into a penthouse with Aurora, it's practically a joke! And Federico: fuck, that's real bad luck. And only then Nuria seemed to understand the game, as she noticed Federico's amused smile. Indignant, and too aggressively, she pointed out that she did not like pretending; that if she had something to say about someone, that person would be the first to know it, that she didn't say anything about someone that she wouldn't say to their face, and Raúl stopped talking, somewhere between irritated and worn out or sleepy. Once back at home the telephone would ring and Nuria would carry on talking about the same topic, she'd repeat from beginning to end exactly what she was saying now, blaming everything on Federico, and he'd let her talk and then tell her that Federico had only made an observation about her way of talking about people, about her verbal violence, about her expressive crudity, and that, substantially, Federico was right, that you can't talk trash about everybody to everybody without everybody ending up finding out, and she would protest, the thing is that I'm not a hypocrite and I don't know how to be nice to people who, the moment you turn your back, start flaying you alive, which is exactly what they do; and he, having a sense of humor doesn't mean flaying anybody alive; and she, well, then I don't have a sense of humor; and he, and I don't feel like arguing about nonsense at this hour, and he'd hang up, and she'd immediately call back, mollified, Raúl, please, let's not fight; we're just going through a bad time, but let's not make things worse, and who's the one who's making things worse? I am, I know, it's just that I'm really nervous, don't get angry with me, Raúl, and the next morning, if not that same night, her first call would be, doubtless, to Nuria Oller, and she'd unload, telling her everything for an hour, Federico's meanness, Aurora's feebleness, Adolfo's equivocation and, above all, how cruelly, even worse, how brutally Raúl treated her. Verbal violence and expressive crudity that, undoubtedly, were not far from the sort of provocative talk people usually expected from her in bars and public places in general, nor from the fact that most taxi drivers ended up making her propositions when she caught a cab by herself, a kind of talk that Raúl had at first considered part of her passionate, uninhibited charm, but that now—for some reason that he would do well to specify with greater exactitude: adolescent vivacity transmuted into bitter aggression, perhaps—seemed to constitute a personality trait that was not only unflattering, but also downright unpleasant. And that was increased by the depressing situation in which she now found herself, her father's death, the sordid circumstances surrounding it, the new presence that her mother's relationship with Amadeo had acquired within the family; more depressing even than the chaotic economic situation created by the sudden death of Señor Rivas, the suspension of payments that threatened to become bankruptcy, that seizure of assets and freezing of accounts that ruins one only momentarily but ruins nonetheless, actual poverty, a less traumatic factor than the accident itself and the sudden solution of continuity created with respect to the past, but no less capable of eroding morale with its persistent presence, not so much for the change of plans this might mean for Nuria in the future, an obligatory renunciation of certain projects, the need to work, to deal with things, being the older sister, her family responsibilities, as much as for the limitation it would impose on her present life, a constant reminder, like placing a ring on a different finger than the habitual one, of the disgrace befallen her, the limitation of having to make a budget, of having to calculate, of suddenly having to be conscious, for example, of the fact that taxis cost more than the metro, or that a glass of gin is ten times cheaper than a glass of whiskey, of seeing herself in need of pawning her watches and jewelry not just to get some spending money but from the need to pay for daily expenses, a particularly hard situation for a person like her, for whom it had previously been almost impossible to go out in the city without buying something: books, records, some article of clothing, half a pound of marrón glace, doubtless not from some zeal for collecting or accumulating, since she hardly ever tried the candy, forgot about the books, never got around to listening to the records, and gave away the clothes she bought before she even tried them out, but rather more for an unexpressed tendency to maintain as much as possible the external circumstances that had informed her childhood. So much pride, so many luxuries, and now look, said Eloísa, serious, almost serene, not exactly with delight, of course, but yes, in a certain way, with the relief of one who witnesses, once again, the final triumph of justice in the world, the implacable oscillation of a colossal scale, its two sides seeking the point of balance. Seated on the edge of an armchair, hands in her lap, she watched him eat breakfast, everything, the shady sitting room, the sun barely touching the middle wall of the garden, the newspaper open to the light of the lamp, the headlines whose contents she tried in vain to make out, everything exactly the same as days before, as if it was the same conversation or as if the similitude of formal elements might propitiate or prefigure the similitude of thematic elements, when meekly overwhelmed, shocked, Eloísa had brought him up to date on the death of Achilles. Look, Raúl. Do you know what's happened? Achilles. Achilles? Yes, Achilles. The garden at nightfall, the pile of dry leaves, the bonfire and, that morning, gathering up the ashes, the turtle's blackened body, stiff, cold, burnt to a crisp, poor little animal, the little animal must have suffered so much, details and reflexions that she might have well omitted, however much that not even by omitting would have spared Raúl the recurrence of his own reflexions and details, nor changed the basic fact of them being a dreadful omen. Yes, a dreadful omen, introduced into the panorama of his oh-so-obstinately rejected, but no longer concealable, private superstitions and maniacal rituals, flowering like an inexorable spring in the most diverse environments of his daily life, a panorama of obligatory gestures and systematic rep-etitions, directed to neutralize, as much as possible, the ominous signal, the adverse prophecy: the rigorous succession of acts that constituted his morning toilet or proceeded his nighttime repose, for example; the complexity of operations apparently as simple as washing hands or brushing teeth, the need to rinse exactly seven times, taking into account that in the not-entirely-infre-quent case, of losing count, the surest thing was to begin the count again, including for the purpose of computing, the inde-terminate number of previous rinses in the first of the rectifying series, and breaking down the last into seven more, with the goal of making sure to not end up on the number thirteen; or rather, the convenience of clearing the three garden steps in a single leap and with his feet together, or of picking up the mail on the way out of the house, never when returning home; or of centering the mat outside the front door of every flat he was about to enter and only then to ring the bell; or of always choosing, from a series of identical objects, the one in the center, and in the case of there being only two, always the one on the right-hand side; or use his pipes or shirts in a series of inflexible rotations; or to lay out his books and papers on his work table in a pattern no less rigorous than that of the crockery on the breakfast tray, disciplines only observable, it's clear, thanks to the implicit knowledge and even complicity of Eloísa, an assistance both invaluable and discreet in the work of counteracting the threat derived not so much from the fateful value of an objective fact or of a subjective projection—no less valid in practice—as, more properly, from the failure to comply—forced or voluntary—with the rituals necessary to avert them ahead of time, an operation destined to infuse his conscience with the moral strength proper to one who attends to his duties and obligations, an instrument more precisely defensive than expiatory, just as with the other weapons in his panoply, like the mediation of propitiatory elements, people, or things, an article of clothing, for example, or his recourse to invocative formulas, humming some specific song to himself, capable, occasionally, of firing the spirit's protective mechanisms, of provoking a change of mood, of making us soar, like some wondrous liquor, of annihilation, into that anguished post-coital state, when something in the heart seems to have burst and overflowed at the same instant as his sperm. All useless, nevertheless, when like now, after a night of sleepless agitation, a sweaty and shrunken subject of nightmares impossible to reconstruct, one mishap after another, slipping in the shower, spilling his *café con leche* at breakfast, breaking the worn-out mouthpiece on the current pipe in his rotation, nothing in the mail but a few odd bills and some hateful advertising circulars, heading out just when it started raining again, missing the bus by a matter of seconds, on the next bus buying a ticket whose number was only five digits past being a palindrome, also missing the metro, unmistakable warnings that today, December thirteenth, Tuesday, Santa Lucía's Day, the day of the blind, of Catalan literature and the modistes, everything was going to turn out ineffective if not counterproductive, the sterile emptinesses argued in the sociology seminar, the impossibility—one would say—of ever finding someone at home when you called them, the fruitless attempt to get a fresh advance on future translations, his request foreseeably denied, although the literary director at the publishing house didn't know that he'd not yet even started the last translation he'd been paid for, as foreseeable at least as the uselessness of his appointment with Curial in the Atheneum library, thus what stood out as the morning's only positive outcome, as the only significant success, was obtaining a death certificate on the spot, so it seemed better to just return home and not move until tomorrow instead of walking around there with his hands in the empty pockets of his overcoat, the same

shapeless blue overcoat he'd worn in his last years at school,
rescued from the mothballs by Eloísa with embarrassing altera-
tions done by Señor Vericat, as a substitute for the one he'd lost
weeks before, forgotten in the taxi or perhaps in the brothel
itself, right as the cold weather set in, a substitution which if,
from the start, was a little embarrassing, would not be long in
proving to be, besides regressive, literally regressive, in terms of
experience, returning after several years to Señor Vericat's house,
a prestigious tailor solidly rooted in the family circle, the best
tailor in Barcelona, people said, the most classic, even, curiously
though, outside the family, his name didn't seem to ring a bell
with anyone, a fact that Raúl perhaps would have never recon-
sidered if he'd not seen himself, forced by necessity, in the
situation of having to enter once more that silent and shadowy
apartment, where in any moment he might expect to see the
apparition of a grandfather between the curtains, to face once
again, only with another attitude, produced by distance, more
critical, Señor Vericat's jovial surprise upon recognizing him, his
mechanical way of speaking, absorbed, like that of a teacher
become childlike from dealing with children, his trembling
fingers, the stench of torturous digestions that emanated from
his half-opened mouth while he took his measurements and the
models and figurines from the deserted waiting room, indica-
tions that, more than classic, the more proper expression for all
that was that he was out of fashion, the setting proper to a person
who, peacefully settled into the immobility of the postwar years,
has rejected as ephemeral the latest mutations in fashion, hoping
that things will go back to what they always were, and who
continues waiting, and only the identification of criteria and
chance, joined with a relative stability in price, is capable of
explaining the loyalty of those, doubtless few, who continue to
be his customers; and regressive, besides, as a symbol, a compromise that doubtless failed to fool anybody, but that even
independently of whether it was noticed or not, made him feel
himself, in certain circumstances, like the soldier known to have
launched an attack without the necessary artillery support,
diminished beforehand and with his morale undermined, such

as at the burial of Nuria's father, before the appraising eyes, like
a jeweler's, of so many manufacturers from Terrassa, before the
watchful eyes of so many present who only waited for the last
floral wreath to be laid down to become a pack of creditors,
people who would not fail to notice the detail and, what's more,
with increased sarcasm, the fact that in the first interviews he
had with them he was still wearing the same shabby overcoat,
just as neither the notary nor his classmates failed to notice it,
in the sociology seminar, however much he carried it under his
arm as much as possible, or even just for that reason, alerted by
his incriminatingly self-conscious manner, and even less invisible, at school, to the rapacious penetrating gaze of his students,
the satisfaction it must have given them to see him arrive, hasty
and crazy, completely distracted, seating himself in front of them
as if in front of a jury, with the happy row of their small, plush
coats as a backdrop, an embarrassing and disturbing situation
not so much for how keenly aware the children might be of the
contrast as for them identifying his own awareness of the fact
that he'd also come in wearing his own school overcoat, only ten
years later, the sensation of a lack of progress implied, that in
reality, nothing had really changed so much, uncomfortable mistakes and parodic impersonations, Papa asking him if he could
pay for the gas or the pharmacy, for example, more than for a
true lack of resources, doubtless, although the cost of living goes
up so much, son, and we have less income than before our big
setback, and now the company's booming, I should never have
left it, but losing Eulalia left me disillusioned, son, not so much
for that reason as, obviously, for the moral satisfaction of being
able to depend on a son who's already bringing money home,
who writes translations or I don't know what, who teaches, who's
a lawyer, who's training to be a professor, so it turned out to be
preferable to take the bill and pay it although it came at the cost
of selling some books or an old suit or borrowing the money
from Federico until he could collect another advance, all that
before breaking it to Papa that he had no intention of becoming
a professor or, much less, of practicing the law, nor did he intend
to explain to Federico what Federico, like Adolfo, could only

think was some stock phrase, that his own case wasn't like theirs when they said pay for my coffee, man, I don't even have five pesetas, and they bought just fifty pesetas' worth of gasoline at a time and they didn't mind eating any old thing at any cheap dive bar, something that for them could almost qualify as exciting, for the impression it gives them of connecting with reality, but which does not correspond in any way with his actual situation, although it might be difficult to pinpoint that subtle difference, for the same reason that now in the high school it was difficult for the rich kid to notice the difference that separates him from one who only appears to be, economic straits too little dramatic to get anybody excited but keen enough to make one fed up even more so on days like today, now, once again beneath the street's brilliant lascivious shine, without knowing exactly where he was directing his steps, without feeling like doing anything or seeing anybody, in that state of mind capable of making any interlocutor into the typical gypsy woman trying hard to cast some good luck on a young fellow, picked out from among all the passersby due to his innate shyness, and to the one who will fatefully end up imposing herself thanks to her ability to catch people off guard, so that the unhappy young man will pay her whatever it takes to get her to cease with the show, now only anxious to escape, to get away, to evade the matter, flee up into the air carried by a pigeon, toward the gloomy ridges of the wet cornices overflown by the pigeons, the air an exaggeration of dimnesses and scattered metallic glimpses. He retraced his steps, toward Puerta del Ángel, not without first having discretely dribbled a bit of saliva into his handkerchief, as he did each time leaving Aunt Paquita's house or, in a more general way, from stuffy places, with cloying atmosphere, metro stations, cinemas, buses, etcetera, heading toward Puerta del Ángel, and from there, as if carried by the minor effort required to head down instead of up the gently sloping street, toward Calle dels Arcs and Avenida de la Catedral, the weight of inertia, the weight of money in inverse relation to its value, in the same way that nothing lighter nor more stimulating, including from an erotic point of view, than feeling against one's breast the pressure of an encouraging hand, the check waiting to be cashed palpitating inside his wallet, especially for that one who, trapped between adversity and his own despondency, sees himself impelled—his capacity for action, as well as for decision, blocked—toward the burnout of repetitions and recurrences, toward the maneuvers of compensation, a self-imposed behavior in order to be obliged, one might say, to not do what one should do, his libido inhibited like his creative faculties, no more brilliant when staring at the target of the blank white page than in the target of the white bed, yesterday, with Nuria, nor in fact in any other terrain, from thence his lapses, his forgetfulness, and, above all, his apparent unpremeditated renunciation of punctuality, his propensity for arriving late everywhere, indicative, with all obviousness, that his desires to go anywhere or start doing anything were really null. And his insomnia? The difficulty of getting to sleep provoked by a systematic recounting, the moment the light was out, of how many problems there might be capable of keeping him awake. And why not avoid thinking about them? Because it's really a question of not sleeping. Why? Well, to delay as much as possible the start of another day like the one before, that confronts him again with the problems keeping him awake, slow arousals drifting between what reappears oppressive and the falling weight from what is reconfigured, a sensation that from then on would not stop driving him all day long as if between two dreams, finding himself suddenly walking along Calle dels Arcs like some defeated Balzac, not piercing reality like Jupiter's bolt, not dominating it, but rather, at its mercy, injured and vexed and harassed like one of those adulterers from past centuries, exposed to the general merriment atop the back of an ass driven through the whole city, naked, sins confessed, surrounded by anonymous cackles of laughter and sudden anonymous blows, subjected to the cruelty of a multitude of every kind of vile, unhappy persons, redeemed of their frustrations by the simple opportunity of projecting their own vileness and misfortune onto someone else, of materializing them, of incarnating them in someone to sacrifice and through his torment be saved, externalizing then the jubilee and celebrating the fact through the

streets, sauntering through them like the modistes saunter
through them up and down in rowdy groups, perhaps making
fun of his overcoat, hubbub and lights and pre-Christmas sparkling brightness, the chorus of the carols returning funereally
from the loudspeakers installed who knows where, ashen
December, somber solstice of Capricorn, the season of Advent,
the announcement of Christmas and the augury of Epiphany,
the inexorable course of Adolfo's good star that on the eve of the
coming of the Three Magi was going to help him win the Premio
Nadal, gold, frankincense, and myrrh for his novel *Los Ángeles*,
a work with enough attractive qualities, no doubt, to impress
the jury, youthful rebelliousness and objective technique, formal
correlation and thematic rawness, ingredients turned into
epithets, epithets made slogans, not promise, revelation, not revelation, consecration, and while Raúl persisted in his immobility,
the kind of insensitive prostration that far exceeds what any stone
experiences, a tombstone, for example, upon which the rain falls
and which feels it falling and which feels the unstoppable
erosion, incapable of saying no longer to Fortuny, nor to Federico
either, nor to anybody, not that what he was writing was better
than however much Adolfo had written or was able to write, but
incapable as well of insisting on the simple fact that he too was
writing, Federico's attitude was too skeptical for him to insist or
offer some kind of proof in support of his pretensions, not to let
Aurora claim he was writing in reaction, out of jealousy or spite,
in the same way that Nuria's firm confidence in his creative powers, without any other basis for judgment than his personal
antagony with Aurora, the reduction of a problem of competition to a competition in bed, neither could it serve as comfort
for his undeniably sensitized self-love, to his distrustful defenses
not exempt from wise prophylaxis nor the superstitious habit of
not speaking about things not yet done, unassailable in his isolation. Better not to tell anyone and one day surprise the world,
unexpectedly, with a masterwork, and suddenly leap to the highest rank, the inverse of Adolfo, everybody talking about him as
a writer, but one whom nobody's really read more than a few
short stories or fragments of that novel that he never ended up

finishing, his self-confidence particularly grown since he got up
the courage to read Adolfo's manuscript, conquering his fear
that, given their experiences and friendships in common, Adolfo's
work, impacting his own, would have beaten him to it, a trial
by fire from which he emerged nothing but fortified, not only
because contrary to however much he was able to suppose based
on the commentaries and observations of those friends who had
read the unfinished manuscript of *Los Ángeles*, the relationship
between what the one and the other were capable of writing was
barely more than anecdotal, but above all for the resulting
conclusion, his personal conviction about the superiority of his
projects over Adolfo's accomplishments, the certainty that *Los
Ángeles* was nothing more than a sublimated mimesis of Adolfo's
personal circumstances lacking true talent, a world more like
what he would want it to be than what it really is, more intelligent, more free, almost like dolled-up pedagogical intentions
or, perhaps, as if describing it in that way, the author might find
in the work of doing it the satisfactions denied him by reality, a
work which if Raúl felt compelled to praise, it was only, putting
aside the problem of Aurora, so that he would be thought
envious of the writing when in fact he was envious of Adolfo's
luck, not so much the fame or the money, for example, but the
implications of the prize itself and the implications of the implications, the circumstance of being somehow protected from
arbitrary police despotism, the Premio Nadal would be awarded
to Adolfo Cuadras—consider it a fait accompli—for his novel
Los Ángeles, in the ballroom of the Ritz Hotel, in the longer term,
but with no less exactitude than the fact that tonight, in the
inner sanctums of the Hotel Colón, they would be announcing
the awards in Catalan literature, justly here, in a spot facing the
cathedral, when all those stalls selling nativity scenes and
Christmas wreathes would be closed up and, the sidewalks, calm
and quiet in the light of the street lamps, from the fixed reflections of the cars lined up, without gregarious joy or Christmas
carols, without those modistes dancing in a circle, hand in hand,
around an astonished solitary passerby, those groups of modistes
at large in the city on the hunt for the obese, the mourners, terror

of vicious men and exhibitionists, cruel forays from the Cathedral to the Ciudadela Park, from Canaletas on down Las Ramblas to the Port, when boarding the little pleasure boats that go around the harbor, the assault on the breakwater, defying the city from the boisterous decks, proclaiming the vigor of the construction cranes, the dead weight of the overladen ships at anchor, the panorama gaining amplitude with the distance, as the wake they carved opened and closed upon the oily water, the Puerta de la Paz and its pigeons, the monument to Columbus perched there with his imperious finger thrust out at the turbulent clouds, as if calling the city's maritime facade to order, high ranking officers, Naval Administration, Military Government, Harbor Command, Post Office, Civil Governorship, buildings taking form seemingly conjured up by Columbus's energetic gesture, and the caravel Santa María and the fortified shape of vigilant Montjuich and, within its scope, the extended sands, perfect for tournaments and racing horses, triumphant Knight of the White Moon, champion of legend, personification of myth, proclamation of the reality of the imaginary, consecration of superstition, Troy lost and reincarnated, Rome in Rome renewed, transubstantiated into Rome, like a new god laid down atop a dead god, under other species, with the same nooses, the permanence of metamorphosis.

Awakenings like dreams or fantasies. The abysses that open in the mind of a traffic guard when, in the course of one of those bottlenecks that thicken the central locations in a city at peak hours, he discovers himself blowing his whistle until he nearly chokes, and not precisely with the spirit of reestablishing the fluidity of the traffic but rather, quite the contrary, joining his whistle to the clamor of the car horns, with a sudden, violent desire to become captain of the chaos, to put himself at the head of the din, inciting with his showy gesticulations the simultaneous massive surge forward in every direction, beyond lights and signals and traffic laws; or, rather, the abysms of one's own awareness when the guardian that rules it also ends up challenging the traffic cop. Thus, with the insecurity or lack of direction that characterizes the behavior of that astonished man, perhaps not so much for the magnitude of the events as for the inner vertigo,

he turned to the right, from Calle dels Arcs, and headed down
Calle de la Paja into the neighborhood, pausing before the
secondhand bookshop windows and antique dealers, without
any other apparent motivation than preferring that street to the
agitated movement of the Avenida de la Catedral, the peaceful
winding streets of the Gothic Quarter, the medieval city, a tightly
pressed warren built stone by stone, laboriously, tenaciously, with
neither refinement nor ostentation, the sobriety of a people faithful to its austere peasant traditions, defined more by its tenacious
hard work than its natural riches, no friend of pomp and uncom-
pensated squandering, a generalized propensity that can also be
understood, as Dante called it, *l'avara povertá di Catalogna*—
Catalonia's miserly poverty—and in the same way that an unexpected fortune—inheritance, speculation, the black market—
facilitates in families an adventurous and prodigal or destructively
wasteful attitude, which usually leads to a disaster no less
expected and rapid, or, at most, to the ephemeral splendor of a
few generations, meanwhile some constant investments, be they
modest or growing, serve to stimulate the economies and, thanks
to their transcendence in other orders of life, are even more
important, causing a marked tendency toward calculation which
endures across generations. Thus, Barcelona is the result of a
patient collective savings, a city that owes its survival more to its
own obstinacy than to any geopolitical element, a city which, if
it cannot boast of Rome's golden halo or the absolute geometrical
monarchy of Paris or the accumulated capital of an empire like
London, can boast, at least, of a positive quality: solidity. A
common characteristic, in effect, as much in the Gothic Quarter,
image and likeness of Barcelona's medieval society, as in modern
Barcelona, the nineteenth-century Ensanche and the new urbanized areas, whose spirit of frustration is a reflection of its
citizenry's frustration, of its prudish prejudices, bourgeois rectitude, demure appearance, all facade, steady indicators, after all,
as much in the Gothic palaces as in the nineteenth-century
mansions or in the residential villas of the postwar era, of the
fact that the rich people here were always less rich than the rich
from other places, however much the myth that the passage of

time—yellowed photos, family anecdotes, social histories, paintings of the age—arises and flows from this alone, making
possible in the young generations, as the years turn round, the
illusory identification of the provincial and underprivileged
world of their ancestors with something similar like the world
of Guermantes, which does not exactly mean that the world of
Guermantes was not underprivileged and provincial as much as,
perhaps, that modernist Barcelona never discovered its Marcel
Proust, with no greater luck than in previous eras, a city without
mention and news of better travelers than Festo Avieno and
Cosimo de Medici, without other literary references than the
purely anecdotal and circumstantial ones of a Cervantes or, in
the wider scheme, of a Genet, without more living literature than
at the level of *aucas* and *aleluyas*, a neighborhood genre, as they
say, apt, in its way, for local application or consumption. And,
notwithstanding, solid: prototypical fruit of an essentially well-
organized bourgeoisie, each thing in its own time and each time
in its place, take the wife to the Liceo, the lover to the Excelsior,
and out with friends to El Dorado or the Eden Concert music
hall, more vulgar and loutish, and by way of spiritual compensation from so much devotional social exhibition, from material
support, from economic power, undertakings like the Sagrada
Familia, expiatory temple erected in the heart of the Ensanche,
that urban expansion laid out in a vast grid for the purpose of
providing a better—and, above all, more prosperous—life, without its development there never would have been an obstacle to
thinking as well about the other life, in that other ensanche
extending uphill, along the slopes of Montjuich, the New
Cemetery—el Cementerio Nuevo—destined to immortalize this
passing life, to magnify there above the transit to the great
beyond, to another world in the image and likeness of this one,
posthumous luxury of mausoleums, tombs and obelisks and
other showy monuments which, along with good advice on fiscal
questions and timely testamentary arrangements, contribute so
much to calm the fatigued conscience in its confrontation with
the cruel questions, pantheons constructed one by one, garishly,
their structure reflecting that tormented conscience: a

neo-Gothic exterior, for example, something like a miniature
cathedral, with its spires, its gargoyles, its reliefs, its stained-glass
windows, its portico leading to the small chapel, and inside, in
the center, the foot of the altar, and the dusty golden glow of the
everlasting flowers, under the tilting marble slab, the opening to
the damp green ladder which, between niches with dates and
initials, descends to the bottom, on whose floor, as a kind of
milestone between history and prehistory, a final slab of alabaster,
smaller, square, separates us from the ossuary. The Sphinx comes
for us all, Eloísa said. You can have millions, it comes just the
same. What a fortune Ramona must have spent to save her,
between doctors and medicines. But Jacinto's millions are good
for nothing when the Sphinx says time's up, not even if he had
a hundred times as much. That's life: some live on and others
pass away and some are called up to heaven and others dragged
down below. And the one who's down today can be up tomorrow. Look at Leonor, and I'm not about to start calling her Doña
Leonor now, look how well everything has turned around for
her, and with all the right gadgets, washing machine, blender,
central heating. She wants for nothing. By contrast, everything's
going downhill in this house: a cheap oven that doesn't draw
well because the chimney is crumbling, the heating that doesn't
start up because replacing the plumbing means tearing up all the
floors, the drains clog, the lightbulbs burn out, the dampness,
the vents, the switches, nothing works here, everything's old,
everything's broken. The best thing to do with this house would
be to tear it down and build a new one in its place, completely
modern. Ah, but there's got to be the means to pay for it, and as
there looks to be none, I'm the one who pays for it, who deals
with all the extra fuss. Like a slave in olden times, without a
washing machine, with a prewar clothes iron, with an icebox the
junkman wouldn't even haul away, not even if repaired, with the
oven that starts smoking depending on which way the wind
blows, with a stove that can't handle all the pots of food the old
man wants me to cook, he thinks that fifty pesetas is enough for
all the shopping, he doesn't realize that fifty pesetas nowadays
doesn't buy what it used to, he thinks two hundred pesetas is a

normal salary, I'd like to know who he thinks he could find to
work for three hundred, anyone would be horrified just seeing
the house. Like a slave in the olden days, that's how I am; and
everything's going downhill around here. But I don't really care;
if I end up in the charity home, well, that's the end of it. Raúl
asked her about her wrist; talking about her wrist put her in a
good mood. Eloísa showed him the swath of little-red-riding-
hood-colored knitting hanging from her needles. Look, see, it's
almost done. I only need to finish the cap. Everything else is
done, the skirt, the blouse, the socks. I'll skip the bloomers. Of
course if it's wintertime, poor girl. You'll catch a cold, eh, girl,
won't you catch cold? She fluffed up the skirts: lovely, beautiful,
who loves you. And Leonor tells me, you seem crazy, she tells
me. If I don't like the cinema or even understand it, so what.
And so I prefer to make little clothes for dolls instead of for the
little girl, it makes me happier. And the neighbor who lives above
my relatives, well, above my nephew, well it seems to be true,
well at least they're saying it's true. She makes little bracelets and
she says she'll make one for her, right, my little queen? She's my
nephew's neighbor. And I might even ask her to do a little pearl
necklace. Let the little girl's mother make her clothes; if not, why
get married. And Leonor tells me, you really are strange. And
you know it's true that I am, even though I don't look it. I don't
care if I go out of the house with brown shoes and a black purse.
I'm really odd that way. I don't care if I go out looking that way.
I go on Fridays. Not Sundays. The house where I go, my nephew's, right, they were already waiting for me, right, but I realize
that it's the day when they go to the afternoon movie and I don't
want to be a pest. I prefer to be here, with my things. On the
other hand, on Thursdays we meet in the backroom of the shop
and, look, we watch TV and that's how we spend the afternoon.
Because they have a television, and nowadays people are really
rich or poor. Their little girl already knows all the programs.
Don't you think she'll really love the doll? It's her present for
Epiphany. She kept on knitting the skirt, her head tilted a bit to
the side. She'd begun to dress the doll around mid-October, just
before the bad spell began, the way an early cold snap, along with

the fallen leaves, increases the obituaries. And she'd not yet finished: the slips, the scarf, a tailored suit, a fine blouse, another little overcoat; the possibilities of enriching the trousseau, of completing the wardrobe, were limitless. And on Sunday, devastated, she realized that the doll had no nightgown or négligée. Look, Raúl, what am I going to do now? Raúl had returned relatively early. In the little sitting room, the only lights the radio dial and the pale blue butane flame, an aria from an opera was playing, *Le Nozze di Figaro*, probably. Eloísa was listening from the kitchen, with the door open, busy removing the lace from an old salmon-pink petticoat. I don't understand how he can fall asleep next to the radio, she said. The music grew quieter. Is that you, Raúl? Papa called. He'd turned on the lamp and was waiting in his armchair, sitting very stiffly. It's *Le Nozze di Figaro*, from The Liceo. I thought that maybe you were there. I've been with some friends, said Raúl. And Papa: who are those friends who have a box there? The Moragases? I used to know a Moragas, a doctor. But they never had a private box, not in my time anyway. I went a lot when I was young. Before I got married, especially. That's where I saw Eulalia for the first time, and I wouldn't stop until I got up the nerve to introduce myself. After that we got to sit in the best boxes. Poor Paquita and me, I mean, the older ones. The divine Mozart. Raúl went up to his room. The window offered him a shadowy reflection of his bright room, not the night outside, the back part of the garden, the ashes of the dead, raked-up leaves like the dark body of an immense bird struck down from the sky. What sex was Achilles?

The problem presented by Uncle Gregorio, how to give him the news, how to avoid telling him, given his current state of health, turned out to be, in fact, precisely because of his condition, a rather simple solution. All it took was for Leonor to remove the obituaries page from that day's newspaper. And just like the child whose mother dies when he is too young to even understand the meaning of the word death, and will only understand that she has left him, without managing, however, to comprehend the brutal motivation for such behavior, thus he will erect the same defenses against that original injustice, those which will color his progressive comprehension of the event with indifference and even disinterest, the same as old people, for the greater convenience of everyone, usually get used to, without too many questions, the disappearance of those who have formed part of their world, turning the gradual gaps in their world into comfort at being alive, while at the same time sparing their nearest relatives the unbearable daily contact with that awareness, present but unexpressed, of death at hand. The important thing, for the moment, was to spare him not only the last image of Aunt Paquita, the tomb, the four funeral candles, the gaunt sunken arms of the crucifix, the black veil, of stiff, heavy folds, snuffing out the waxen glow of the casket and that body beneath the glass, its probable banana-skin quality, limp and empty, and the smell of Sterilair not even masked by so many flowers, but similarly, let's be practical, the hard trial of a funeral sung aloud, that windy morning when the purples of Advent were swapped for black, the black wind and the golden drifting leaves outside, borne aloft, like in the songs, upon leaving the Church of la Concepción, where, in the miserly light of the shortening days, he would have had to dismiss the mourners from his chair, alongside his brother Jorge, his nephew Pedro, his step-nephew, confronting each one of those faces, both mournful and stiff with cold, filing past in endless succession, offering their respects one after another, while the most intimate friends—or those most desirous of fulfilling their duties—regrouped buttoned up against the cold and climbed into the cars, waiting to depart in an impossible cortege toward the cemetery at Montjuich and, once there, retrace the route already followed when they had to bury poor Pedro, alongside whom Paquita was now going to rest permanently, a pantheon not like that of the Ferrer Gaminde family, centrally located and of imposing presence, but situated rather higher up, further away, and if it had a rather excellent view of the mouth of the harbor, it was much simpler, a simple slab covering the opening to the crypt, flush with the ground, at the foot of an angel with a finger to its lips, as if demanding silence: the stone guest. To get there they had to follow a path between the gnarled cypresses and the dark shapes of the funerary structures, a peaceful panorama that, along with the silence, broken only by the hammers tapping ever closer, along with the hieratic marble figures and reliefs, seemed to invite an attitude of reflection, respect, and meditation, of resigned solace, *vanitas vanitatis, sic transit gloria mundi.* There is, however, on such occasions, a general tendency among people, to try to hasten things along, to consider settled matters still being settled, and so, even before reaching the cemetery, inside each comfortable car the first symptoms of change can already be observed, talking about other things, returning to the mundane, to life's small compensations, so violently interrupted by the reality of the cadaver and only gradually reestablished in full with the complicity and the relief of those who only expect someone to open fire, pressed, perhaps, by the terrible justice of the sentence, let the dead bury the dead. So, an ordinary comment about the departed person, it's curious that by the end she couldn't stand the light, for example, that she only repeated turn off the light, shut the door, although the light was out and the door was closed, a comment like that, stumbles, generally, against a sterilizing climate of emptiness, that usually makes its propagation impossible. Ramona herself, unfailingly serene and measured, was the first to set the standard, as much for her presence of mind as, in a show of class, thanks to her own attire, neither mantilla nor veil, but a stylish hat, no dolefully dyed clothes, but black furs, somber elegance in her garments and tact in her manners that made them presume and applaud a resolute decision to immediately overcome the misfortune, to return to daily life without further delay, to reestablish habitual rhythms, fully aware of breaking loose from the sudden quarantine, far removed from old-fashioned mourning, incompatible with the modern world, rigors imposed by society as a preventive measure, moreover, defensive, and not understood, evidently, as affliction and desolation, as a precaution toward debts more than as a posthumous distinction for the deceased, not so much an emblem of faithful memory as an easy distinction or external sign of betrayal; a guarantee for the community of the limitation of the interrogations that unlock the blackness in daily life, with the grave risk of altering its normal course, of interfering in one's neighbor's affairs, a sure way to distinguish and frighten away the sad and mournful, the gloom, the silent, the jinxed person, especially in those places and occasions of a necessary relaxation. It wasn't strange, therefore, that the atmosphere in the cemetery was, from the start, not very oppressive, nor that, as if contagious, as the mourners began to gather again, the mood became light and even artificial, in the way that everyone made an effort to not let the tone decay and, the brief prayer recited, the peak moment of the ceremony—the lowering of the casket—happened as discretely as possible. They were talking about a town in the mountains that someone had discovered on one of those weekends, a lovely place, unchanged since the Middle Ages, intact, with pigs and chickens and a restaurant for having lunch, like that, in the rustic style, ribs and rabbit and sausage all grilled over hot coals, everything delicious, and so cheap it was almost a joke, so look, there were six of us, and the food, the wine, the flan for dessert and eight, no, nine coffees, how much would you say? Passionate expectation, everyone awaiting the answer, under that spell that causes rich people to save money, the satisfaction they experience buying something cheap, their love for discounts, sales, bargains, not simply the fruit of avarice nor mere compensation for their obsessive idea—not entirely unfounded—that everywhere they go people raise the prices on them because they guess that they're wealthy, but something at the same time more subtle and with greater substance, the tangibility of money saved, meaning, personally earned from the seller, in a way that's totally direct and immediate, a money of much greater reality, less abstract, than that produced by the mechanism of negotiation, in accord with a psychic process similar to what makes the soldier's sadistic instincts find an infinitely more intense satisfaction from running his enemy through the guts with a bayonet than annihilating an entire city from the air. Near Rupit? Don't tell us, it'll get ruined right away, and the way everyone has a car nowadays, it's impossible to go anywhere on the weekend. No, nonsense, near la Bisbal, really close to the Costa Brava. Imagine:

people will start buying houses and remodeling them, and then it will lose all its charm. You sure have a beautiful piece of property, Vallfosca. Papa nodded. He seemed to pay little attention to those words intended to take his mind off things, refusing as much as possible the conversation offered by those faces which, as if obeying a systematic plan of relays, stood out one after the other among those present, uninterruptedly, from among that crowd busy exchanging greetings and talking with one another; neither the fluidity of movement nor the changing arrangement of the groups, constantly shifting between forming and dispersing, was an obstacle, nevertheless, as far as an attentive observer could determine, with barely any margin for error, the relationship that, in broad terms, could be established between the members of each group, or classified by their belonging or affinity to such and such a branch of the family, or in agreement with the motivations for their attendance at the funeral. The Giral family, for example, the uncomfortable ambiguity of their position, at once hosts, the center of the ceremony, as proprietors of the pantheon, as well as an excluded presence, relegated to a secondary role due to their merely collateral and political connection to the deceased; at the same time praised for the quality of the gathering, for their social and economic weight, and bitterly conscious of the fact that the actual prestige of their family name was not precisely the object of such a turnout, the true reason why people had gathered together, and also, aware that Aunt Paquita's passing also meant the dissolution of their most direct link with that part of the family, and the distance now separating them from their cousins was becoming unbridgeable, more concretely their distance from Jacinto Bonet and from how much Jacinto Bonet represented, completely aware, with the lucid pessimism of those cut out of the will, with the clairvoyance and even the relief with which a ruined human contemplates how topsy-turvy the world is in order to thus dissimulate and even justify their own ruin, given that, like that poor wretch after whose catastrophic conception of the universe, from which he can divine no other way out than self-immolation, hides nothing more than his own misfortune—professional disasters, conjugal quarrels, bounced checks—mere personal unhappiness that, through force majeure, he would like to see dissolved in a catastrophe of universal proportions, thus the imperious pessimism in families that, in one way or another, are no longer what they once were; even if, in spite of his condition as priest, Father Giral, of the Sacred Hearts, as he spoke of Aunt Paquita already watching them from heaven, with the same contrived naturalness with which a materialistic spirit speaks about death, or with which a faggot talks to another faggot when they get old together. How to not guess that for the Girals in their tormented reserve, any detail, cousin Ramona's new Astrakhans, any chance observation, any comment caught on the fly, the excellent location of cousin Pedro's office, on the corner of Gran Vía and Pau Claris, felt like a recitation of their own death warrant? For example, the feeling of inadequacy they also seemed to experience in the presence of the Ferrer Gamindes, who knows if because of Vallfosca or, more simply, as a consequence of the vertical perspective of a plunge to the lowest depths, usually the result of the very dynamic of demoralization. Papa, distant, taciturn; Raúl, now a lawyer and, as was generally accepted in the family, future professor of sociology; Montserrat, with her allusions to the Ferrer Gaminde pantheon, with her magnification of the grandfather, confused in her memory, one might say, with the image of one of those old irascible men in the movies, some retired colonel, for example, implacable conqueror of the weakness of the youth of today, authoritarian, sarcastic, and a bit mythomaniacal, what's known as a real character; Juanito himself, who even now, and with being that nullity of man who, in the emptiness of his adolescence, from some courteous and casual consideration made by some friend of the family as a deliberate compliment to his washed-up personality, seems to be English, for example, channels and settles his physical appearance, his garb, his knowledge, and his manners, with such sense, converting the jealous maintenance of that appearance into his purpose in life, even so, Juanito did not, for that reason, cease to inspire respect from those who knew him even superficially. How could the Girals see the Ferrer Gaminde family in their decadence any other way? Only the figure of Uncle Raimón, the reasons for whose presence nobody had been able to quite explain, clashed with those gathered, shy and fearful, intimidated, as if wanting to negate with his attentive and respectful attitude, betrayed only by the details, his denigrating condition as an insurance broker, the sickly sweet loquacity that comes with the job, the sonorous rumblings of his guts, the result of a difficult, high-pressure life, as difficult as his impossibly alleged honorability; nevertheless, the disgust with which Papa received his presence and the reticent distance that he maintained toward him was fully evident, in every point, as if denying him any and all right to represent the part of the Morets, a family name which, in terms of social class and recognition, was in no way less worthy, save in the case of that undesirable man, than the name of Ferrer Gaminde. It became undeniable, however, that the greater part of those gathered there were present by virtue of their connection to Jacinto Bonet, an economic power with sufficient weight in the life of the citizenry to bring together at the same time around his person—as Raúl would have to discover weeks later—both Nuria's father and Amadeo García Fornells, or spontaneously bring together busy people visiting Barcelona on business, like that friend from Madrid, such a Madrileño, with that admiration for everything that's happening in Catalonia only comparable to the enthusiasm of the Catalan for everything that manages to get done outside of Catalonia, all meaty and full-throated, duly provided with the typical little mustache and burgeoning double chin, that, in general, distinguish the members of the Madrid monopolistic oligarchy. The rest of the people there belonged to that class of people whose cultural orbit was harder to define, distant relatives or relatives of relatives, or family friends or relatives of friends of the family, cordial and respectful gentlemen, subjected to a pitiless process of going bald and getting paunchy, people hard to place, the same as the señoras, a tad uniform due to their common bourgeois pomp and their precocious resemblance to the Sun King, even though only formally and at first glance, without the halo, with a touch of Louis XIV, in effect, but more reserved in their impertinent and foolish self-assurance, more stuffed-full, with that invertebrate and definitive inert quality of the calamari which, along with some other features, characterizes them, the sphincter-like mouth, prudishly pursed between flaccid hungry jowls, eyes only dully alive, eminently stingy, and those powdery little wrinkles formed from smiling so much at young ones, and the rigid blond hair teased into a solemn tower, and the small pearl earring set discretely in each earlobe, and above all, when smiling, the teeth, now almost like those of a skull; and then, the questions from that gentleman we don't recognize, but who recognizes us, you're Jorge's son, more assertive than informative, all wisdom and sharp perspicacity between his contracted saurian folds, with his singular knowledge of the human soul which, apart from an old man, only an attorney can have, thanks to his daily contact with the reality of life and death, of bequests and inheritances, ins and outs and hidden snags. And so what do you do for a living, he asked. Montserrat was talking about Gregorius's wedding, the trip to Teruel, Leonor's family from Aragon, they're splendid people and quite well-positioned, from the country, but people of position, with land, and as they are so many—the siblings even have grandchildren—and all of them determined to flatter us with gifts, and what with Teruel being the land of *jamón serrano* and since I more or less represented the groom's family, I've never seen people eat so much, the least of it was the wedding reception itself, which was outrageous, but it was just one big party after another, and with the wine from that area, it hits you like a hammer, like wine from Cariñena, and on top of it all, after the wedding, one of the brothers-in-law, who lives in Vinarós and he owns a shipping agency, who insists on inviting us to Vinarós, to eat prawns, exactly what Gregorius needed, considering how much he loves prawns. I left them there, I wasn't going to act like some chaperone on a honeymoon, and it looks like they made it all the way to Valencia; I'm not saying that business about the infection he got from the injection didn't contribute to causing his collapse, but what I can assure you is that all the big dinner parties those days were enough to raise the cholesterol of a whole army regiment. Look, the lucky thing is that it was no more than a scare. And, above all, Leonor de Aragón's luck, she's a really good woman, with her character, with her spirit, like everybody, but with a heart this big. It's her luck, she couldn't have found a better companion. She bathes him, tidies him up, helps him get dressed and looking smart, she looks after him, she takes him out for a walk, and when the weather's bad, she takes him to shows, to the big department stores, to the Corte Inglés, once I think she even took him to the grand opening of a new metro station, she arranges everything to entertain him any way possible and, look, she looks out for him and she's got the patience of a saint, considering how peculiar and careless Gregorius is, and how he was hooked on barbiturates, there was a moment when he was fit to be tied, when I thought he wasn't going to come out of it, that's how things would be for us, and look how I, unfortunately, have experience in seeing how things can go belly up. What would a disastrous bachelor like him have done, who would have taken care of him like she has, however much we all love him, if they'd not gotten married? The truth is, I like seeing them walking arm in arm through the park, like two lovebirds. I call them the lovers of Teruel. Scabrous point, right at the limit of what can be aired in public, there where the slight non-antagonistic conflict, considered outside the heart of the family, could become an antagony, where the raw enunciation of the facts—he married his housemaid—deprived of the heat of their context, could not help but make the Ferrer Gaminde family close ranks, now that, at last, with the exception of Juanito—he's intolerant, I don't understand—it was the general position to consider such an outcome as a lesser evil, and now he's got better company, and besides, he had to straighten out his life some way. Papa, after the shock, had even stopped blaming Gregorius for selling his share of Vallfosca to Jacinto Bonet, almost as if he regretted having accused him previously, what do you want, if he was interested in selling his share, the only person in the family who could have bought it was Jacinto Bonet. Better him than some stranger. Of course. I think he's done well; what he needs is a steady income. Why does he want to hang onto property that generates no income if he's neither

got nor going to have any children? So that the State can just
take more than half of it when he dies? I wouldn't be surprised
if Leonor pushed him into doing it, that between leaving
something to her nieces and nephews or Gregorius's, she must
certainly prefer to bequeath something to her own family,
something that can be easily liquidated, something easier to hand
out than a portion of an undivided bequest. Well, I think that,
more than anything, he's done this because it must have been
embarrassing for him to go there with her, playing the role of his
wife. Don't think, in fact for years he's barely made ends meet,
and the truth is that lately he's not been so buoyant either, eco-
nomically I mean, the same amount that used to let you live like
a prince is now barely enough to survive on. I'll let you know we
also go up there very infrequently; Pedro goes the most, some
weekend now and again, with his bunch, half a dozen cars. The
only one who really keeps going there is Uncle Jorge. I don't
know, it seems a shame to me, especially since Polit died, he was
a scoundrel, a sly fox, a smooth operator, you name it, but, look,
he had a big heart; in Vallfosca he was practically an institution.
Now, look, with those Andalusians who don't take care of anything, that what's happening, I think, is that they've not made
things clear with each other, I mean, they're not *payeses*, not real
farmers, not from there. No, it's not that, the problem is that the
land just doesn't produce anymore. And, besides all that, there
aren't any more real peasants, no real farmers like years ago.
Exactly, because now the land doesn't produce. And where it does
produce they buy a tractor and they work it themselves; what
they don't want to do is work for someone else. Oh, that business
of sharecropping is history now; nowadays, if you find a husband
and wife from Andalusia who want to care for your property a
little, charging only whatever occurs to them to ask you for, you
can consider yourself satisfied. Let me tell you that some of them
are very fussy and tidy in their work. Unfortunately, that's not
the case with the one taking care of Vallfosca. Paco, Pepe, or
whatever his name is, I never remember, just one rough
Extremaduran like him. Well, with things the way they are, it's
almost better that Gregorius doesn't even go near the place, now

that everything is so abandoned. Gregorius? The last time he was there Polit was still alive. Abandoned, yes, that was the word, abandoned more than untended, the crops, the terraced fields, the grape vines overgrown with grass, the forest growing in around the clearings, paths lost, roads that no longer lead anywhere, rutted, eroded, what were cart tracks now turned into dry washes, the garden choked with brambles, the ivy spreading, the weeds and undergrowth hardly cleared back from the house. As far as the inside of the house, only a superficial impression could make you suppose that it was kept up the same, not smelling, not noticing the deterioration that comes from use just as much as from disuse, from the lack of life-giving contact for objects, which means using them, inhabiting them. The vestibule, the stairs, the dining room, the parlor, the verandah, the bedrooms, especially the bedrooms, progressively emptied of furniture, untouched, as if tied to the destiny of their titular occupants, assigned to them for life. Gregorius's room, for example, with less disorder than Papa's room, but in far worse shape, almost stripped of personal elements, as if it really belonged to a pension in town, with that aroma like a crushed-out cigar that impregnated it instead of that drugstore smell that dominated Papa's room, without the chaotic accumulation of Papa's room, without his leftover medications, nor his collections of insects, nor his books of botany filled with dried, pressed leaves, nor his law textbooks from when he was a student, nor his walking sticks, nor his binoculars, nor the collection of materials for his little inventions that always made it impossible to close the bureau. And between both of them, Aunt Paquita's room, closed, but intact, exactly the same in appearance as the last summer that she spent there—ten? twelve years ago?—so much exactly the same that, doubtless, it must turn out to be surprising to not see the gloom, her pupils looking up from the pillow, her soft eyelids, her sickly sweet breath, the bed warmed by her intimate emanations. Everything so identical, but only in appearance. Because just as in nations, so it goes in the patriarchal home—*la casa pairal*; like in those nations subject to the inevitable phases of splendor, decadence, and rebirth, like in that nation that after

a period of dissolution and absentee landownership, of abnegation of all responsibility toward public concerns, of general
surrender to the corruption of private enterprise, there arises a
patent need for someone to put an end to the dissolution and
laxity and, with a firm hand, take the reins of power and wield
them in an absolute and totalitarian way, like in that nation, in
las casas pairales, following a whole period of undivided atomiza-
tion and necrosis of the family ties, families also end up imposing
the condition that the property in the end reverts to a sole
responsible proprietor.

Let's see: Raúl Ferrer Gaminde i Moret, son of Jorge and
Eulalia. That's right, his name was Jorge. I knew your father,
just as good as he was crazy. Is he still alive? Drawn up February
6, 1960. So you're a lawyer too, eh? Or rather, you represent
the widow Rivas, according to the powers that Doña Dulce
authorized in my presence last December, general powers in
favor of, indirectly, Señor Bellido and yourself.

Why do lawyers' offices always have that vague resemblance
to police headquarters or, more certainly, the atmosphere of a
grandfather's apartment? Perhaps owing to their dark, heavy
decorative elements? That's right, with a placidity and prosperity not frequently seen in mere offices, public and private alike,
for however long and uncomfortable the wait in the anteroom
might be, in the reception area, in the hallways and even among
the stacks of files and the typewriters, alongside the desk of a
graying official—superior in knowledge, doubtless, as well as in
dedication, to the lawyer himself—where even the words of his
dictation and the secretary typing, far from bewildering, produce in the client a rather more soothing and invigorating effect,
the way the spring rain does to the farmer, words that are heard
the way one inside the house hears the rain pattering outside,
comfortably, the encouraging mystery of the juridical formulas,
the ritual rigor of the terminology employed, sounding almost
like a prayer, psychologically supporting the confidence the client places in the mechanism of the profession, in its incorruptible probity, a secular defender of the individual's interest in the
face of the Administration and, more specifically, when facing

the Treasury, according to tradition—especially in Catalonia—
of singular antiquity and deep roots, *et propter enmendacionem
ipsius culpe per hanc scripturam donations nostre damus vobis
ipsum Castrum quod dicunt Portus quod est in territorio barchi-
nonensi a parte occidentali predicte urbis ad calcem montis cuius-
adam qui vocatur iudaicus in marinis litoribus*. All that, joined
to the character, more desired than merely voluntary, of the
agreements normally contracted in lawyers' offices, as well as
the habitual happy ending of the events, contributes to the fact
that inner peace shines through the features of so many who
otherwise remain self-absorbed there, who, standing at the
ticket window in a station, so parsimoniously gather their
change after buying their ticket, conscious that they, unlike
most of the people waiting impatiently behind them, will take
the next train without racing to catch it; and that the chatting
from more garrulous clients with any one of those aged amanu-
enses has that tone somewhere between conciliatory and
viciously crafty belonging to the general ideas that tend, in such
cases, to be imposed as a conversational theme, the advantages
created by the State granting concessions to private capital for
Telefonica or railroads, for example, how rapidly the result
would be achieved, how quickly service would be improved,
because the State can't, not if there's no stimulus, not if there's
no initiative, because stealing from the State is no sin, it's for
the good of the individual, because taking your complaints to
the bureaucracy is a waste of time, because the bureaucracy is
just a crooked free-for-all, blame the blacks, blame the Chinese,
because with a half-dozen atom bombs, because Chinese cooking, let's be honest, I think we understand each other, Chinese
cooking can't hold a candle to a good plate of *butifarra con
judías*. Thence the animation and good humor and that man's
crafty eyes, undoubtedly a minor industrialist, who invited the
graying official to have a smoke while he took a final glance at
the key clauses of some document awaiting a signature,
enriching the contractual aridity with vivid commentaries about
the development of the negotiations whose culmination and
synthesis were the present contract, without ceasing to point

with his winks toward the waiting room, where, it seems, the
other party was waiting, the buyer, a foreign investor, a German,
representative, from the looks of it, of a firm interested in the
industrial sites for sale, interested and it's not risky to suppose—
given that he bought them—even satisfied with the conditions
of acquisition, conditions that he probably judged advantageous, without ever suspecting that the minor industrialist
Bertrán judged them to be even more advantageous for himself,
Bertrán, as he called himself, or Beltrán, happy liquidator of an
industry amortized a hundred times, of equipment never renovated so as to not lessen the benefits, everything always ready
for when the moment arrives—as it had doubtless arrived—in
which prospects seem to worsen, and he could then convert,
without further ado, his company into a ruined enterprise,
resort to filing an official statement of financial difficulties and
shake off the death with maximum celerity and neatness; and
then, money in hand, on to something new, public works contracts, plastics, suburban developments, what most represents
what is called an occasion, an opportunity, what turns out the
best, the same as a soldier of fortune goes wherever they pay the
best, just like his glorious medieval ancestors, the Almogavars,
who trooped to Sicily, Tunisia, Greece, Turkey. Yes, like the
Almogavars, like them that Bertrán or Beltrán and so many like
him, small-time and middling businessmen, who constitute the
vanguard of the Catalan industrial collective; and as with the
Almogavars, the first impression you can have of them being
rather negative or unfavorable, due to their mere presence, only
serves to facilitate the later inversion of that first pejorative
image in favor of one of admiration and astonishment when
faced with their innate fighting mettle, speed, and fearlessness.
People with clear ideas, who laugh at those who don't know how
important it is to laugh first, to get off to a good start, and to
get the last word. Woe betide the one who underestimates their
reactions and resourcefulness or downplays their mobility and
business sense, their killer instinct, true Almogavars of our time,
hardened, pugnacious men skilled in schemes and stratagems,
as Josep Sol i Padrís, the great poet of Valencian Romanticism,

sang of their resolution, especially when their swords shone anew as they cried *Desperta, ferro!*—Iron, Awake!—yes, that's how jealously they defend their enterprises. Let's not despise, then, the small Catalan industrialists nor underestimate their positive attributes in the name of abstract principles, nor let us ignore their capacity for maneuvering because of, for example, their assumed individualism or a presumed absence of associative mentality which impedes them from joining with others in the task of creating the true industrial empire, the gigantic enterprise demanded by the economy of today; nothing more deceitful than letting yourself be carried away by theoretical schemes or by prejudices relating to ancillary matters, their gross tastes, their ostentations, their delusions of tycoon grandeur, their heavy-handed manners, characteristics explainable in the long run by virtue of the mimetic relationship that tends to become established between the man and his business, in such a way that, as it isn't difficult to suss out in the herdsman attitudes and even traits of his livestock, similarly there exists an evident correlation between a mechanism's repetitious function and the social comportment of a representative of small-time and mid-level industries. To our understanding, there is only one single proper and pertinent yardstick to measure the worth of those small and mid-level businessmen, of that industrial collective: their undeniable, better yet, their extraordinary talent for making money; any other basis of judgment would not be more adequate; for example, estimating the Almogavars not for their excellent fighting skills but for their rough aspect or their rudimentary arms. It was precisely this error, and none other, that cost Gulaterio de Brionne and his French horsemen their lives, when they saw that ragged infantry, without understanding that the troops' lack of a shield was its best shield, that its light tunic was its best mount, that its predilection for stones among all weapons fired, flung, or hurled was its best source of arming itself and, above all, that that miserable appearance was, precisely, its great secret weapon: the surprise factor. The ermine's counterpart: the dog that hunts it; the same for the collective industrial enterprise, perfectly knowledgeable that, like the French cavalry, there are few things more vulnerable than an industry *comme il faut*, where, in general, its Achilles heel is usually nothing more than its own prestige.

Trompas, tabors, senheras e penos et entresenhs e chavals blanc e niers veirem en brieu.

E no pot enser remasut, contra cel no volen tronzo, e que cendat e cisclato e samit no.i sian romput, cordas, tendas, bechas, paisso e trap e pavilho tendut.

Adoncs veirem aur et argen despendre, peirieiras far destrapar e destendre, murs esfondrar, tors baissar e deissandre e.ls enemics enchadenar e prendre.

Tan grans colps los ferrem nos drut.

Lo perdr'er grans e.l grazanhs er sobriers.

Anz sera tics qui tobra volontiers.

Trumpets, drums, banners and pennants, ensigns and horses, white and black, we'll see them all go flashing past.

And no strength will stop the splendid glittering lances as they fly through the sky, nothing prevent the vestments of sendal, golden cloth and richly embroidered silks being shredded, rent to tatters, nor the ropes, tents, stakes, canvas cloth and lofty pavilions from being wrenched and torn asunder.

Then we'll see gold and silver squandered, catapults winding up, taut, hurling, walls collapsing, towers broken, torn down, enemy ranks captured and clapped in irons.

And we'll punish them with such blunt and brutal blows.

Great will be the loss, but much greater the gain.

Or rather, rich will be the man who plunders as he pleases.

Charlatans and braggarts to a certain extent, perhaps, but it would simply be suicide to mistake their vehemence for bluster or to consider the activity they develop to be anti-economical. Quite the contrary: generally gathered around big industry, the industry we could call structural, those mid-level and small-time businessmen, the collective industrialists, are truly the very tip of the lance and, simultaneously, the rearguard of all industrial development; lighter, more fluid and dynamic forces, but in some way useless, negligible, and to a far lesser degree, condemned to disappear, as some disgusted materialist might prematurely conclude, now that, far from being the small fish destined to be swallowed up by the big fish, they more closely resemble those delicate little birds that clean and sharpen the crocodile's teeth in a tacit symbiotic relationship and, thus, the strategist would be mistaken, thanks to overconfidence in the penetrating and demolishing efficacy of his armor-plated divisions, forgetting in his logical plans the decisive role played by the infantry that advance behind the wagons, scouring the terrain, making it entirely their own; equally mistaken would be the economic planner who discards the role that the mid-level and small-time businessmen play in every process of development, and the efficacy and other practical virtues of those men with whom we are concerned.

In contrast to the collective industrial activity we can now typify the figure of the structural industrialist or major industrialist, attending preferably not to his belonging to this or that sector of industry, but to his company's volume of production, as well as its longevity—centuries, frequently—factors which, on the other hand, given the kind of life they are obliged to lead, usually affect the individual's personality, vigorously differentiating him from the other members of the upper bourgeoisie, components of Barcelona's mercantile, financial, or professional bourgeoisie, against whom, even currently, one might say, the structural industrialist, for motives equally futile and sophisticated, enjoys less consideration and audience, socially speaking. Flagrant injustice, it need not be repeated, not only toward one of the firmest bulwarks of Catalan progress, but also toward the same human quality of the representatives of a preeminent social class, of a designated social class, according to the most faithful interpretations most authorized by the very members of that class, meaning, closer to the criteria with which a family tree is reconstructed, more sensitive to the magnifying sentiments that are appropriate to attribute to all clients of a genealogical research bureau, described, as mentioned, in archetypal terms, like captains or conquistadors, men fundamentally sound in both body and soul, conscious of the advantages, both in the moral order as well as in the energetic one, of a prudent excess of weight, the hard, innocent eyes of the one most purely convinced of the rectitude and universality of his principles, his concept of the economic benefit not only as a right or privilege as much as an obligation, his militant social paternalism—or rather, patriarchalism, his inflexible righteous will to cheat taxes, his scant appetite for outside signs—more than for purely fiscal motives, for his intimate belief that only a peseta saved is really a peseta earned. In short, a life drawn in the image and likeness of a Sunday newspaper, morning copulation, and Mass, a sunny stroll with the kids, and the long, slow conversation after the midday meal, the visit to the grandparents, a little television, a frugal supper, the theater, an exemplary image that, by banner blazon and licit behavior, in the way that a book of etiquette must serve not only for the young generations to match their steps to their elders' steps but, especially, to offer a model to the titleholders of the new fortunes, riding the crest of the rising and falling tide of history, of its choppy waters, its tumultuous and episodic fortunes, that will only settle and solidify if their economic consolidation matches their moral integration along the way. Meaning: a mentality whose most adequate historical antecedent we could find precisely in the Catalan expansion throughout the Mediterranean, an expansion of eminently familiar and patrimonial character, conquests made to acquire lands for one's offspring, as property or wedding gift, fortunes that will perhaps be dissipated with the parents' deaths, if the heirs turn out to be prodigal or inept, meaning, something that no longer has anything in common with the traditional concept of Empire but rather, simply, with that of the modern State, a fact that although it cannot contain any moral judgment, neither favorable nor adverse, according to the mentality of the age, still shapes the character of a people who, thanks to the avatars of history, never surpassed such a state, nor have known the successive phases of development and decadence common to the other peoples of western Europe. All things considered, and having excluded from our exposition any suspicious element of partiality, any notion that the members of the elite Catalan industrial bourgeoisie show a propensity for encomium more than objectivity, in order to present as a collective enterprise and public utility what is, overall, a business for personal profit, to convert the industrialist's family name into a myth, to involve it in cultivating the arts and sciences by means of petty patronage and rapacious collecting, to understand social coexistence like a social game, all, perhaps, excessively sublimated for the reticent contemporary retina, in the same way that, gazing upon the portraits arranged in the Gallery of Illustrious Catalans, a critical-minded spectator will probably relate those venerable hoary beards not so much with Captain Ahab as with the protagonist of *Don Mendo's Revenge*. Thus we are conscious, in all things, of the limitations of the essentially literary image sketched by us, of its defects, from a scientific point of view, of the provisional character of our conclusions, valid, at the most, there being no more definitive and satisfactory interpretation established, an interpretation not idealistic but rather materialistic, not metaphysical but rather dialectical, meaning, an interpretation which, unlike the present one, must be the fruit of something more than simple intuitions and anecdotal observations, superficial and insufficient, however much they might be based on facts that are just as certain as they are, on the other hand, truly shocking. Thus, Florencio Rivas Fernández: a self-made man, alert, dynamic, insightful, a born winner, and, notwithstanding, barely integrated into Barcelona's upper-class bourgeoisie, his natural social environment. And this not due to any lack of economic heft, nor less so for his particular lifestyle, almost exaggeratedly high, nor again for his rather attractive personal conditions, his friendliness, his natural elegance, and— if not natural, adopted with extraordinary aptitude—his apparent good taste and, as far as it goes, even his relatively cultivated spirit. Or better yet: not for economic, professional, or personal motives but surely for something in some way related—especially formal—with all that, in how it relates to the antagonic, the way in which any sagacious interlocutor glimpsed in him, against all expectations of an industrial impresario who had come as far as

he had, his ultimate indifference to money, the gambler's special
indifference, for whose passion money is only a means while the
game remains the true goal, or the way in which, even without
ostentatious bad taste, his carefree refusal to link professional
reputation and private life was evident, or to not consider, not
even for the sake of protocol, private life as an extension or
complement to professional reputation. Obviously, a man like
that could never be fully integrated, especially given his own
resistance to being integrated, not least because, in principle, the
non-integration was lacking—or must have been lacking—repercussions in the normal development of his activities, in the
mechanics of the business world and its laws of credit and
solvency. Least important were his origins, or better yet, his
record, his career: from failed publisher of popular editions of
the classics to manager and majority shareholder of one of the
most important graphic design companies in the city, meaning,
in the whole country, altogether something obscure, during the
obscure years of the forties; really the least important thing.
What was important was the other thing, well-demonstrated by
the commentaries raised by the circumstances of his death:
something that in any other case, in relation to any other person,
might not have been considered so much an accident as something casual and fortuitous, was here generally judged to be the
inevitable consequence of a moral attitude, of a line of conduct;
temerity, contempt for form, scandal. It had to end that way:
early one morning, crashing into a lamppost, doubtless drunk,
in company not remotely dubious. What would be most difficult to precisely determine is if, just as when a man joins his life
to a woman who's had a great deal of experience, the aloof and
impartial observer won't know how to say with exactitude if she
was the one who chose, if she preferred that man to her lovers
up to that point or, on the contrary, if he was the first in the
series to be honest enough to cope with her, to make up the
difference, i.e., the final victim of the catch; thus in the case of
Florencio Rivas Fernández, the doubt—essentially sterile—
resided in knowing if his way of life, especially in recent times,
was what drove him to that fatal accident, or if the accident was

the a posteriori cause of his later lifestyle becoming public domain, a lifestyle that if it hadn't ended in tragedy could have gone on indefinitely.

The telephone. One Saturday night. They'd gone out with Federico, Moragas, and the Adolfos, and upon dropping off Nuria, in front of the entrance to her building, they'd argued with that irritability that alcohol sometimes causes, but when he got home he found out that she'd already called, telling him to wait for her, that she'd swing by to pick him up. Papa scrutinized him with his eyes wide open, somewhere between suspicious and apprehensive. Looks like her father has had some kind of an accident, Raúl said. In the taxi Nuria told him that the maids had met her at the door in tears, saying that they'd called from the clinic; her mother and brothers and sisters had gone to spend the weekend in the country. The nurse in the emergency room said, yes, a car accident; are you family members? And Nuria: but how is he? And the nurse: hold on, woman, I first need to find out where he is. And he consulted a directory and appeared to write down a telephone number, and taking advantage of Nuria's distraction as she lit a cigarette, showed the paper discretely to Raúl: dead. And he said, come this way, you'll speak with the doctor. It was the same nurse who later said to Nuria, do you want me to remove it? Remove what? His ring; with a little soap it'll slide right off. Rigor mortis.

Nevertheless, despite the telephone ringing, the telegrams piling up, and the succession of visitors offering their condolences, there was an upheaval of time as well as of space in the Rivases' invaded house, where one quickly observed, along with everything else, a certain improper undercurrent in the climate which usually develops around a death in the family. Beneath the familiar expressions of grief, and the exaltations of the departed, and the vacuous topics relating to the dangers of driving, everyone recalling cases, telling about careless close calls, horrors, everyone a little like that widow fishing around in others' lives to see if she can discover some drama in the other person and can thus establish a nexus of affinity and mutual comprehension based on their respective misfortunes, beneath all that, one could intuit more and more the tenebrous theme of conjectures and suspicions, it was enough to take into consideration the same absence of questions about the circumstances of the accident and, above all, the disquieting silence that followed one of so many anodyne utterances: you see, nowadays, just getting in the car is suicide itself. The well-intentioned but useless remark from the joker on hand: pretty soon you won't even be able to have an accident in peace. Raúl slipped away to hide out in the bathroom, to smoke a cigarette; the enamel on the edges of the toilet bowl was cracked in two places, one almost in the middle and the other on the outside, residual signs that, although carefully cleaned, indicated the habit of one or several family members to squat above the bowl, perhaps one of the boys or Señor Rivas himself. Señor Rivas's house occupied the top floor and penthouse of a relatively recent, multi-story addition constructed atop a modernist building on the Rambla de Cataluña, a building with a horribly mutilated exterior, with the cupola lopped off and the group of sculptures above the portal torn down, no doubt to disguise, in a flush of rationalism—and profitability—that horrid blob of artificial stone, very 1950's, placed atop a facade of erstwhile asymmetrical harmony.

If the generalized presumption of a suicide was the first notice of the reigning atmosphere, a rumor probably founded on the fact that Señor Rivas had taken out a very valuable life insurance policy, completely out of character for a man in his position, who logically needed to trust more in the good progress of his business than in the benefits of his death, when it came to thinking about the children, it was Bellido, stunned, nearly whimpering, to whom the very development of the events, by virtue of his position as family attorney, became a fledgling herald of catastrophe: the firm's most delicate economic situation, the banks' more-than-reticent attitude, the household employees' possible infidelity, and the intransigence of the creditors, monolithic, maximalist, orchestrated, perhaps, by the same brain that had provoked the banks' negative reaction to Señor Rivas's death as well as the defection of those personnel until then considered discreet and trustworthy; in short, the need of enacting an immediate suspension of payments that might gloss over, for the moment, what might well end in real bankruptcy. And with the same anxiety and anguish with which, as during an earthquake, a nation's government, legally constituted or simply installed into power, receives the initial and confusing news of something more than a mere riot turning out to be a coup d'etat: a statement from the military academy, support for activating garrisons both on the border and abroad, as well as several bodies of special forces, ambiguous conduct from the air force and the police themselves, the radio stations and presidential palace fallen into the hands of rebel factions, the radio broadcasting problems, press communiqués, contradictory news relating to supposed petitions for political asylum, arrests, summary judgments, executions, H-Hour in which everything is surreal to the degree that it remains uncertain, although not so much, of course, to make it impossible not to conclude that something grave and even irremediable is unfolding. Thus, the Rivas family saw the events happening quickly, with the fatalistic impotence with which those developing or, frankly, under-developed, national governments contemplate the violent finale of their mandate, far, very far, from the serene and solemn ritual succession that, as in the death of Aunt Paquita, is foreseen by the constitutions of Western-style democracies, whether the naming of the head of state be elective or hereditary, following the death of the queen of some Nordic country, for example. And then, treachery, the low blow, the evidence that only one person who in theory enjoyed sufficient confidence with Señor Rivas as to have direct access to his desk in his office could have placed in circulation that sheaf of photographs found in a drawer—so they said— while organizing files, those photos whose existence, on the abstract plane of vicious rumor, finally took shape when deposited, with hypocritical solicitude, in Bellido's law firm, confronting him, no doubt with all premeditation, with what a man like Bellido, like the rope around the neck of a condemned man, felt incapable of confronting: scandal. Not least because the identity of that beady-eyed little slut joyously posing in vari-ous fornicating positions—on all fours, head on, with her tits hanging down like goat's udders, on all fours from behind, her head cocked round facing the camera, smiling, on all fours from the side, raised up on one elbow in bed, her backside attractively displayed, etcetera—it was rapidly established, and her relations with Señor Rivas were revealed like an open secret among the household staff, Mary, the very same woman, no doubt, appearing up close and personal in the photographs, recognizable by her anatomical details despite the closeness of the lens and the arrangement of the photographic elements, a mouth, that mouth, in the throes of slurping two erect male members, one of them darker, one of them apparently a negro's; a woman—her hair covering her eyes—engaged in the same operation but sucking only one cock while being penetrated by the other; or what is more striking and curious, the woman, the same woman, apparently being penetrated by a man, and penetrated at the same time, unmistakably, by another male member, the dark one. Mary and the black man. But who snapped the photos? All things considered, more significant than the personality of the members of the trio was the clarification of the personality of who now was moving the threads of how much was happening and of the motivations that they had for moving them, to create such a dramatic situation for the Rivas family: a name, Plans, the paper manufacturer, a fact quite concrete enough to give footing not to heated conjectures but to hopeless conclusions. And then another clarification: the kind of relationship existing between Señor Rivas and his wife, beyond suspicion for those people closest to them due to their very proximity, in the same way that frequently the most immediate family members of a homosexual man are the last ones to realize his habits; unsuspected more than unsuspicious, in fact, something very simple, the classic conjugal arrangement for when it's too late and, although better late than never, turns out to be obvious, for however little lucidity one has, that it's no longer possible to remake nor straighten anything out, to save yourself in the end from the abject matrimonial gratification, from their merciless fulfillment, from their licenses that are increasingly sordid with the passing of time as bodies grow creakier, hair turns gray, wrinkles, loose teeth and loose sphincters, varicose veins, hernias, hemorrhoids, but, above all, mutual hatred and repugnance and aggression that one tries to bury, as much as possible with this kind of arrangement. And the blow, the low blow, consists of the simple fact of that private arrangement becoming public news, and that not only Bellido but also Doña Dulce and Nuria, not to mention the little ones, found out about it: that it had become news, with all the charm of a historical record. How dare they talk about it? said Nuria. What do they know about my father much less my mother and what do they care what kind of relations they had? These men, cuckolds frequenting the whore-house, how dare they cast the first stone? My father did what he wanted and he did well. My mother also had a lover: Amadeo García Fornells, everyone in Barcelona knew it, my father was the first to know. Everything was clear between my parents, without hypocrisy, without bullshit. And that's all they're interested in? What do they know about him, about what he was like, about his capacity to love? The efficacy of the low blow, mission accomplished: undermine the morale of the Rivas family, destroy their security, make them focus their attention on the problem of maintaining a good reputation with the goal of distracting them from the root problem, doubtless essentially economic, and more than seeking the root of this problem and its possible solutions, to ensure that the family worry about the surrounding reactions, that they feel wounded and exasperated, for example, by all the inconsistencies of people's rumors, on the one hand, that the accident seemed to be a suicide and, on the other, that Señor Rivas, when the accident happened, was accompanied by unmentionable acquaintances, whose presence had been hushed up. Raúl guessed it the same day as the burial: for one of those present, all that was nothing more than an interval, the pause that precedes the gesture of turning the cards face up; let them finish burying the dead, that's why they had come. And, if he wasn't just guessing, the widow Rivas must certainly have had some sense of foreboding during the ceremony, serene and weeping, sincere and insincere, unharmed and despondent, with the confusion and distress that can result as much from the deepest sorrow as from that type of stunned guilt—features clouded, flaccid—that in the wife usually follows, dilatorily, after several hours of intense carnal pleasure, confusion, dumbfounded, in her role as widow, more than pallid, almost translucent among her black veils, with sufficient residual intuition, notwithstanding, to sense something, even though, like the spendthrift overwhelmed by his bills, letters, expiring contracts, payments coming due, still strives to find a better explanation for his lack of money—a mistake, misplaced funds, some swindle, bad luck—resisting accepting the naked fact that he's spent more than he could afford, with the same innocence Doña Dulce failed to guess correctly to be able to explain to herself the basis of that presentiment. Impossible to really specify anything with her, neither then nor in the following days, as events unfolded, too vacant to offer any more ideas or clarifications, let alone an opinion, about Bellido's catastrophic predictions. Bellido was a competent attorney, perhaps, for routine matters and paperwork but not for facing up to a situation like the present one, characterized by the celerity and forcefulness with which the events unfold in these cases: the banks blocking all kinds of credit and discount following the death of Señor Rivas by using the firm's eminently personal character as a pretext; the declaration of a suspension of payments; the disappearance or, at least, inability to locate important documents along with the evasive role, almost a bald-faced boycott, assumed by more than one high-ranking household employee; the report of bankruptcy, that the company's debts were greater than its assets, the announcement of meetings and assemblies intended to create a council of creditors; the involvement of Plans, the paper manufacturer, behind all that, his evident determination, in his condition as minority shareholder and principal creditor, to acquire the company for a song and build it back up once he had it under his absolute control. And Bellido, knowing himself outclassed, also knew, doubtless beforehand, like the sergeant who in the thick of battle loses all his commanding officers, who could expect no outside help, that her babbling and clumsy suggestion—too dramatic to be natural—of resorting to Amadeo for help, as if somehow deprived of good sense, that suggestion pregnant with so much significant expectation of being accepted, as if desperate that it should turn out that way, that it be grasped differently than it was grasped, with Doña Dulce's silence and Nuria's complete refusal. Nobody there seemed capable of proposing any intermediate solution between the halting negotiation and the heroic, last-ditch struggle that, by adjusting itself to the terrain chosen by the paper manufacturer Plans, meant, by any reckoning, playing the game according to his rules.

The facility with which the businessman, throughout the course of a fierce argument, can become a gangster or policeman, especially when there are various people participating in the verbal harassment and the attacks from the opposing side grow stronger, a morose debtor, for example, or a casual creditor or any other person which the nature of the commercial relationship places in a lesser role, in a way that only the lack of the proper channel or legal support—due to negligence or scruples from the legislator—prevents them, working together, from moving directly to applying the third degree; yes, for poor Bellido, the first skirmishes with Plans's people must have been a tough test. However, when Raúl began to accompany him to the meetings with the creditors' legal team, more for moral support than from really considering himself useful, the tone of these meetings no longer had the character that, if he could believe Bellido, they'd had initially, when he found himself inside those same offices, among a series of individuals gathered together with the tough determination one usually feels from part of the crowd exiting a boxing match, like hired thugs on the way to teach someone a lesson, spurring each other on with brutal sarcasm. Either because they must have made quite an impression on Bellido, or because they considered that time was on their side and they judged their own position to be increasingly strong, what's true is that now they seemed to be in agreement about adopting the relieved attitude and affable calm of the man who knows himself to be in possession of the exact key needed to close the deal and, in consequence, exempted, if he so please, from keeping up appearances, of being friendly, free to be a gentleman or a swine. In the process, on the other hand, Bellido's true measure was even more on display, his scant qualification for such confrontations; the sort who prefers to wait for a taxi on a lonely corner than fight it out with others waiting for one at the intersection of two major avenues, so Bellido seemed to prefer to deal with the creditors' proposals—better yet, conditions—as if they formed part of a normal although not entirely favorable business deal, than to have to consider it like a suicide maneuver, as—pure and simply—a filthy rotten mess, something that obliged him to behave in a way unnatural to him, he, Bellido, a meticulous and well-ordered person, very hard working, known and commonly appreciated in the national Treasury office, the courts, civil registry, notaries, and public offices in general, but always among the ushers, secretaries, interns, the type of person least likely to be measured against predatory men like those working for Plans, habituated to act according not to the idea of who strikes the first blow but rather who strikes the last. Raúl, in his turn, so brusquely turned into a practicing attorney, felt no more secure than a construction worker who, returning home, crosses through a residential neighborhood in the city, feeling disturbed, or what's more, overwhelmed, by that sumptuous and relaxed atmosphere and, especially, by the elastic and confident stride of some women who seemed to neither expect nor fear the obscene expressions that he, in any case, would not have dared direct at them. Thus, despite all his experience, not judicial but intellectual, Raúl felt inept among such people. His overcoat was only one more element, a detail—a quick fix—that could not have escaped the notice of any of those present. Had it dawned on him in time, Raúl could have shown up without an overcoat and simply made some passing allusion to his supposedly capricious hatred for overcoats, even though, to avoid being even more conspicuous, he should have also prepared some excuse—nearby errands to run, a visit, another meeting—so that when the meeting was over they wouldn't have caught him off guard, asking him the way they did, where, given the harsh weather, he'd parked his car, obliging him to admit that he didn't own a car, that he was going to catch a taxi, thereby giving Plans's people an opening to triumphantly offer him a ride home. But that wasn't really the most important thing, rather something much more general, his lack of conviction about his role in that whole affair, his scant confidence in the efficacy of his performance and even in the mere impression he might make on Plans's people during each meeting, each time, as they wrapped things up, with the nervousness of a person who, when relating some incident, conversation, or argument, becomes self-conscious of his own words, and doesn't recount what he really said as much as, in retrospect, with everything said and done, meditated and reconstructed, the thing unsaid which would have been better to say, some quick retort, expressed with measured transparency, the brilliant response that the situation required which he never managed to utter. And nevertheless it would almost be possible to guarantee that, in the long run, Raúl's interventions, if they had some significance, were more positive than negative, by reason of the surprise, confusion, and even uneasiness, that they produced in Plans's people, due to how unusual they appeared to be in the kinds of deals so familiar to these men: his courtesy, for example, in a certain way improper given the circumstances, or his tendency to ask questions, the answers to which, in reality, really didn't interest him, more appropriate to a train compartment than a business meeting, the result, no doubt, of being a natural stranger to such business, of an unformulated rejection of the problem that made him delay actually starting the discussion as much as possible, not so much from cowardice as from repugnance or embarrassment, not like the criminal in chapel who avoids thinking about the blue gleam of the rifles but rather more like that man who suppresses the memory of a steamy sexual experience; hence the reaction of Plans's men, impatient—the impatience that the conduct of the young man who shadows her time and time again without talking about more than the cinema or novels can provoke in a young woman—at the same time mistrustful, the same type of mistrust aroused by the sangfroid of the unknown gambler as he coolly accepts his first round of losses at a gaming table, the fear of the others upon finding themselves in the presence of a professional who after stringing them along, completely fleeces them all, a reaction that very possibly contributed decisively to hastening events. It was as if, from inconvenience more than haste, they had decided that the matter was already ripe enough so that it was necessary to continue interweaving proposals and counterproposals, that they had reached the most delicate point of the entire negotiation, the moment of specifically defining and revising, of properly dealing with the thing once and for all when, apart from what's being said or no longer being said, each party knows already what to be attentive to with respect to the other party, there's no other solution, handsome, it's not true that they've made you another offer and you know that I know, and the other guy knows it and only hopes that his opponent doesn't also know that, although being some tougher conditions than the ones he initially believed he would manage to get, he would sign even though they were even less favorable on the condition that they be done with it once and for all, of finally breaking the tension produced by what's about to fall out; and with everything, even knowing what's coming—the same as when, in trench warfare, to move beyond the impasse of the stabilized lines, a sudden concentration of fire announces the imminence of the bayonet charge—fearing the decisive instant, of the slump, the mouth half-open, eyes staring, guessing by the other's apparently indifferent expression what he was going to say even before he said it, what he would pronounce: the ultimatum. The fair amount, meaning, just enough, given the circumstances, for it to be accepted, now that, however much is lost, more would be lost by not accepting and, in every case, no need to say, you, as legal advisor, and you, young man, as intermediary, representative, or whatever you are, you will also have your piece of the pie, no need to worry about that, that in the end this is about a sale and when there is a sale there is a commission. That's right, we're interested in knowing your response before next Tuesday, Señor Rodriguez (wasn't he the bad guy before?) has managed to get Señor Vilá (wasn't he the good guy before?) to convince Señor Plans to wait until then; it seems that Señor Plans is increasingly less interested in dealing with a matter like this one, so messy, we might say, so uncongenial, but Señor Vilá has been able to convince him that it won't take more than a week, although Señor Plans says that he would prefer to invest in a different venture that's become available to him, a real opportunity apparently, and let the bankruptcy run its legal course, given that Señor Plans has already wasted quite enough time and money on this matter with Gráficas Rivas. Well, hell's bells, that's it. Accept the terms, like it or not. Just like in Goya's capricho, *Trágala, perro: Swallow it, dog*, depicting some raving monks with a giant syringe about to forcibly administer an enema to a trembling man in the presence of his veiled wife. And Bellido, attempting to gain more time, to justify, at least formally, the fact of not formally rejecting a proposal that was, according to its minimum requirements, thoroughly unpalatable, to grease the business with a little bit of vaseline, so, we'll look it over, Señora Rivas, well, the Widow Rivas—a touch of melodrama—has the final word, and in her situation, a widow; and the others, Plans's men, of course, of course—more vaseline—but you realize of course, a bird in the hand is worth two in the bush, you know, no amount of vaseline will make this any easier. The double error committed by Plans's men: on one side, their haste, tightening the screws too tight and too soon, like kidnappers who, once they've collected the ransom, come back smiling toward the little body of their victim, bound and gagged and roped to a chair, saying, now, let's do him! without having previously made sure that their hideout isn't surrounded by the police; on the other side, lack of resolution or perhaps of calculation, not striking in the heat of the moment once their game was discovered, giving a week's time to consider instead of just twenty-four hours, not thinking that the opposing side could use that time to start playing a different game of their own; in a word, dozing off, falling asleep like the seducer who promises his young victim a life of happiness in his company and, having stolen her virtue, while she trembles in his embrace, smokes a cigarette thinking about the most expeditious way of ending the already tiresome story, still far from imagining that the most likely conclusion to that story will be a wedding. Thus even

Bellido himself would dare to insist again on the need to see about resorting to other weapons and even Nuria herself would accept the advisability of consulting Amadeo, of bringing him up to date on the situation.

The meeting was short and polite, almost formal, given that if something now seemed evident it was that Amadeo didn't really need to be brought up to date on anything, however much he listened to Bellido's explanations and more than once asked Raúl's opinion about some detail; but the ambiguity lay especially with the person not named: Doña Dulce. And also, perchance, in the not quite sufficiently concealed curiosity with which Amadeo seemed to be weighing Raúl, a curiosity logical enough to a certain point, as Raúl was his lover's eldest daughter's lover, and perhaps increased by the red communist halo that the Rivas family must have seen floating over Raúl's head; in fact it was to him and not Bellido to whom he spoke when he said: call me tomorrow. I'm one of those people who never make a decision without sleeping on it first; the best kind of divination, believe me. More intellectually, and even physically agile, than Raúl had imagined; younger, more alert, more cynical as well. It only took one interview like that one to understand that Bellido's efforts were not misguided, that if anyone could yet save the Rivas family from ruin, that someone was precisely Amadeo García Fornells; however, only later, once he was out in the street, thanks to the change of mood brought on by all feelings of relief, he could begin to be amused by the idea that he was starting to make inroads into the domains of monopolistic oligarchy in a real way and not from a purely theoretical and speculative plane. On the phone, Amadeo's voice was, if possible, even more convincing: I've been weighing the various aspects of the problem, he said. And if we're looking for some professional capable of handling the matter with the highest guarantee of responsibility, I think it's worthwhile to choose the best specialist in the field, Espada, to my understanding, a superb attorney, besides being an excellent person and a great friend, an ace negotiator, a master swordsman, if you will, a real ace of spades. So I've taken the liberty of arranging for you a meeting for tomorrow. Operation

Counterstrike: make initial contact with Ace of Spades, offer a fresh summary of the situation, whether or not Ace of Spades even worries about trying to disguise to what degree he was already informed, too busy, doubtless, to beat around the bush. Ace of Spades agrees to take on the case or, rather, doesn't conceal what he had accepted beforehand—Señor García Fornells need only ask me. Raúl and Bellido arrange new meetings with Ace of Spades, not so much because their direct collaboration is needed as much as to be up to date on the progress of the anti-Plans plan, the beleaguered Bellido increasingly less beleaguered, again feeling at home in his secondary role, in his modest position of auxiliary or conscientious manager. Working hypothesis: Plans has undermined the banks' confidence in the future of Gráficas Rivas, S.A., in order to provoke suspension of payments and to take over the company's assets and liabilities at bargain basement rates. Ace of Spades' strategy: act in a parallel manner and move quickly, without allowing time for matters to reach the judicial level, making the board of creditors abort their efforts before they officially partner up. Method: first, get the banks to grant a new line of credit to Gráficas Ricas, S.A.; if necessary, by means of an increase in capital which, I'm convinced, we'd have no trouble covering; next, simultaneously—I've done my research about this—make Plans see that the situation with his paper company is not entirely without complications if it's found, for his part, that the banks limit his discount, not to mention credit restrictions, as long as, of course, we all believe it advisable. So, all in all: we want Plans to understand that he's in no position to take over anything. A stratagem truly worthy of an ace negotiator, although admitting that his strength lay not so much in his own skill as in the tutelary shadow of Amadeo, without whose backing all skill would have been for nought. However: for Raúl, all that could not fail to leave him somewhat rattled; despite his ideological foundation, despite his perfect comprehension of the fact that Amadeo's probable triumph over Plans represented once again, in the most basic scheme, a highly illustrative example of the triumph of the oligarchy over the non-monopolistic bourgeoisie, it was inevitable that Raúl would become aware that, similar to the floating, displaced image of his high-school overcoat in a cloakroom, was the fact that someone might have to deal with cases like the present one with no other prior experience than having studied historic examples and test cases at University, in the same way that the housemaid who decides to turn to prostitution, however unfamiliar she might be with the legendary qualities of a dowsing wand or with the different ways of getting a male member to sit up straight, becomes familiar, not without awkwardness, with the slang of her fellow water witches and the demands of their clientele—beatings, whippings, rear penetration—by virtue, above all, of the time it takes to adjust to the new codes and revelations, to the apparent reality in which, until then, her life has unfolded, the environment to which she was accustomed, the house where she served, the owners, the friends who frequently visited, whose habits and behavior acquire a totally new significance in light of her own current experiences.

At the cemetery, after the prayer for the dead, before concluding the ceremony, the priest wished to direct some words to those gathered, an old clergyman, friend of the family who, as he stammered to explain, in a strong Catalan accent, had baptized Florencio with the same hands with which he now blessed his coffin, and he spoke of the Enemy, the crusade against Satan, that Tempter, who, due to the fall of our first parents, managed to plunge humankind into sin, expose them to the threat of eternal punishment, to the true death, the death of the soul, compared to which the death of the body was only a pallid reflection, this that has so violently struck the body but not the soul of God's servant Señor Florencio Rivas Fernández, dear friend and exemplary Christian, the same as if, from spite, the Demon must have been pleased to make him die on the eve, as it were, of the birth of the Baby Jesus and of his glorious Epiphany, depriving him of the joy of the feast days with which all humanity celebrates and commemorates the appearance of that small star in the heavens above Bethlehem which shone to proclaim man's Redemption. That old clergyman was also responsible, with two other no-less-ancient priests—days

later—for saying the solemn funeral mass, officiating that endless
ceremony, pronounced by some deacon through a microphone,
hands extended, bodies curved forward, eyes fixed on heaven,
their lips kiss the altar, Christ's bed, a kiss of adoration; etymo-
logically, adore means to raise to the mouth something that is
venerated and, in Greek, to venerate—*proskunien*—is to kiss while
bowing down. Various people took communion, Papa among
them, and Raúl remained seated on the pew the same as when, in
high school, he had to let pass by those who stood up to receive
or who were returning with their eyes half-closed and their hands
together, the same odor as then, like paper money, the smell of
the kneelers, of the prayer books, of the boarders' little prayer
rugs, while he thought, I've got seventeen masses left to go,
ten masses left, seven left. You shall receive communion with
your eyes lowered, your hands folded together or crossed over
your breast, with devotion and modesty, making acts of faith, of
sorrow, of hope, etcetera. When receiving communion keep your
head straight and, the tip of your tongue upon your lower lip,
you will receive the Holy Form with modesty and devotion, you
will try to swallow it as soon as possible. Finally, return to your
place, kneel down, think, meditate, reflect, what you have done,
Whom you have received, how you can thank Him for such a
great boon. Regarding eucharistic fasting, the rule is three hours
for solid nourishment and one hour for liquids. Water does not
break the fast, but it is preferable to abstain from it as well.
And Gomis, with hypocritical perfectionism and a spoiled boy's
hunger for attention, perfect for one who, more than interested
in the strict enforcement of the rules, wants to make everyone
aware of his pious conduct, raised his hand and asked: What
about saliva? Is it alright to swallow that?

He returned home with Papa, by bus; he'd not taken the bus
in some time, far longer—years—since he'd ridden it with his
father. The breeze was blowing, black, fearsome. Why do you
want a taxi? asked Papa. The bus is more convenient. He counted
his change parsimoniously, perfectly poised on the raised platform at the rear of the bus, in spite of the relative roughness of
the ride; before sitting down, and removing his hat, he said hello

to the wife of an acquaintance. Seated just ahead of him was
another one of those acquaintances, vaguely neighbors, people
who for years had taken the bus at approximately the same time
and gotten off at the same stop; during the ride, Papa and the
other man, half-turned toward one another, spoke about that,
about the years spent riding the same line, first the streetcar and
now the bus, before the city was so built up, when the neighborhood was only individual houses and the passengers who rode
to the final stops knew each other by sight, there was no pushing and people were more polite, although, despite everything,
the bus was still the best way to go, without the problems and
worries of a car, with so much traffic, and dangers, always getting
worse, exactly, you see, we're just coming back from burying a
close friend who was killed in a car accident. A new neighborhood had been growing from the Paseo de la Bonanova downhill
toward the sea, densely built up, all in tune with that enterprising
and optimistic air of the young couples living there, and what
had once been an open landscape of fields and empty lots, was
now simply a classic middle-class composition, as decorous as
it was monotonous, smooth wide sidewalks, small businesses,
utility vehicles, maids doing the shopping, mothers with their
little ones and strollers and bulging pregnant bellies; the streets
above Bonanova hadn't been saved either from a progressive
transformation, even while conserving its garden-like ambience
amid reforms and demolitions, renovated villas turned into
clinics, high schools, kindergartens, remodeled houses, enlarged
in area and height to the very limit authorized by the municipal
ordinances, compartmentalized, subdivided into apartments,
but this is a mistake, it's better to hold on until they change the
municipal ordinances—sooner or later they have to change—
and you'll be able to build on the entire property, and then, with
no problems from tenants, think about it; I won't live to see it
but you will, and although we don't have much garden around
the house, the lot is just about eleven hundred square meters
with fifteen meters of facade, figure that they'll pay you a little
over five thousand pesetas per square meter and, look, that's a
tidy sum of money. The rusty creaking iron gate, the anarchically

overgrown garden, all a mess, the few flowers all intermixed, like
in a slum, the faded blinds, the delicate wrought ironwork of
the balconies, its rust stains running down the facade, coming
loose from the airy moldings of the cornices, from the garlands
and festoons and floral copings, almost down to the base of the
facade, swollen and breaking off from the damp. Papa waited
by the gate while Raúl pulled it closed and then followed him
through the garden, lagging behind a bit. A man in full possession of his faculties, he said. Poor Paquita, on the other hand;
for her it was almost a liberation. She was the oldest child. Now
I am. As if isolated in the opaque, overcast sky, the hammer
blows from some nearby construction reached their ears. He
carefully wiped his shoes clean on the doormat. It seems that
his company had financial difficulties and now everybody's
going after the poor widow. Human ingratitude; I know it all
too well since the disaster with the firm. The static repetition
of his shoes scuffing the mat, the molten amber of his eyes that
seemed to be interrogating him, stunned, innocent, resigned,
with the fatalism, for example, with which the customer receives,
once again, the sorrowful confirmation that he is only worth any
respect before paying, when, purchase completed, he turns to the
salesman, till that moment entirely at his disposal and now
devoted to some other customer, wanting to ask some final
question about his purchase, in order to only run up against
cool replies and sardonic manners, whose meaning, as implicit
as ostensible, is nothing more than to say: if you want more
courtesy make another purchase.

Evidently, the Rivases' economic situation worried Papa not
only because of the family itself, for the affection and sympathy that he might have had for Nuria, but rather, above all,
for Raúl, now that, since he had never asked questions about
the nature of Raúl and Nuria's relationship, perhaps because,
although still unannounced, their engagement seemed obvious
and, by consequence, for more than reasons of tact, he judged
it preferable to not bring up the matter, it was clear he couldn't
help worrying about Raúl's future with a woman who, contrary
to expectations, would perhaps not be able to bring anything to

the marriage. But he seemed unaware of the other circumstances surrounding the death of Señor Rivas, very probably because, like with a child who must be kept in the dark about certain things, nobody would have dared to involve him in the current gossip. So, how are things looking? he asked Nuria on Sunday, during lunch. And Raúl: what do you expect? deliberately, as if the Ace of Spades' plan had not already been set in motion, or at least established, the night before. He was in a sour mood, and had been since waking up, with a hangover, feeling bad, and neither the turn of fortune that the Gráficas Rivas, S.A. affair had taken the previous afternoon, with the simple exposition of the Ace Spades' anti-Plans plan, a turn by whose light the decisive meeting set for next Tuesday with the people from the paper company seemed like something very different from what the other party must be imagining, which only intensified the satisfaction of flatly rejecting, with measured indifference, not only their ultimatum but also the need to prolong the conversations, leaving them perplexed, incredulous, incapable of reacting, possibly, to what could only seem to them the result of the other side's madness, if not their own; neither that turnabout nor the subsequent night out on the town with Adolfo and Aurora and Federico and Pluto and Marichone, their euphoric ramble through the Barrio Chino until dawn, nor then, the time— how much?—he spent with Nuria, given over completely to their erotic distillation, to the liquifying pleasure, none of that now seemed to him sufficient motive for feeling, not necessarily content with himself but simply content, futile facts and even out of place before the dark panorama of the day, lunch with Papa and Nuria, the visit to Leo's house, the somber desolation of a Sunday afternoon and above all and in a more general way, before the cruel entity of the unquestionable: he was more and more bound to a woman whom he didn't love, he was a lawyer and disgusted by being one, he wanted to write and he couldn't write, and he had no money, and he couldn't talk about any of that with anybody, not with Nuria, or Federico, or Aurora, or Adolfo, or Leo, or Fortuny, he couldn't, or better yet, he didn't want to, he was tired of them all, they bored and depressed him and he had nothing to say to them. But as with Papa, his worry about the Rivas family's economic future and its possible consequences in no way affected how warmly he treated Nuria or, if it did affect it in some way, the result was nothing more than an increase in attention for her, but with Eloísa, on the contrary, as if in the spate of adversity that had fallen upon the Rivas family she had found a kind of official sanction for hostility against Nuria, the events of recent weeks had accentuated, if possible, her irrepressible recourse to slights, goads, and rude remarks. After lunch, while Papa went to take his siesta, Nuria, in one of her repeated attempts to gain Eloísa's goodwill, counterproductive to the degree that they instead stimulated in her the awareness of power of the one who knows themself solicited, went to have a chat with her, to ask about how she was coming along with the clothes for the doll she was making for her nephew's daughter, etcetera, and Eloísa, with radiant malice, had to show her, knowing perfectly well that Nuria could not at all have failed to notice that, on the contrary, the doll that she had so uselessly given to Eloísa some time before, was still perfectly intact in its box, exactly where Nuria had left it, atop a small console in the sitting room. What? Raúl heard. Bad weather? Well, the sun was out bright and early this morning. People who sleep in late miss everything, you know. Eloísa, tyrannical, triumphant over things as simple as pretending to not understand someone else's words and make them repeat themselves, thus scuttling, implacably, their spontaneity, or rather forcing them to specifically explain the meanings of obvious expressions, or even, ultimately, adopting a purely negative position, slamming the door on however many assertions the other made, however indisputable they might be. And all that, according to a reaction which it would be very mistaken to interpret as simply a desire to wound, given that it was fundamentally about clearly establishing a position of primacy, similar to how in a child, the act of tipping over an ashtray a second time, for example, must be understood, not so much as an act of defiance, a purely contrary spirit, or swinish stubbornness, as much as, in a more abstract manner, a manifestation of clarifying whether the adults' punitive response is strictly in answer to the act of spilling the ashtray or if it's the result of a more sporadic and arbitrary nature.

Supposing that Nuria's obstinacy toward Eloísa was simply an attempt to improve her position, by dint of perseverance, among the people who in one way or another formed part of Raúl's life, her already established habit of paying a visit now and then to Leo's house responded, however, more probably, to an effort—although one more modest but no less useful—to strengthen, to secure her past, to remain loyal to the people, places, and customs from the times when she and Raúl first met, to keep alive as many elements as possible that might represent a nexus of union between the both of them, of turning them into allies, even at the cost of denying the damage and artificiality of some visits identical to themselves, like going to Sunday Mass and, like this, painful in their recurrence. Leo and his girlfriend and his sister and the old man with his soliloquy and Juan with his outbursts, interruptions which, as a form of counterpoint, the old man seemed to incorporate throughout his monologue, absorbed in the exposition of his concepts about that man who although slogging through life—family, business, competition, thoroughly harried—sometimes glimpses something great in the world, in the sky that cleared up over the city after the rain, for example, or in an eighteenth-century Dutch seascape, or in a book that he doesn't understand, but which doubtless contains some magnificent idea, something great that he would like to express and in fact tries to express, to express to his friends all that he glimpses, to his clients, to his colleagues and his workers, words that elude him, conceptual clarities that become cloudy in the very moment of trying to grasp them, stammers, gesticulations, emphatic hoarseness that—with eyes popping out, mouth gasping—little by little, irreparably come to define him, in the increasingly wider circles of his world, like the classic bore you've got to flee from at any cost, the drip, the drag, the pest, the nag. But if Nuria was right in saying that, all in all, Leo's father had always essentially been known for being a tedious talker, pigeonholed as such by everyone, it was still unacceptable, however, to have to keep tolerating the cumulative effect of his oppressively concentric digressions, ever more reduced as the years went by, like a sauce thickened by endless stirring. And, still more objectionable, the utility of putting to the test in such unfavorable circumstances her uncomfortable relationship with Leo, of updating each time his increasing distance, much greater—and of different significance—than when he was still an inmate at the Modelo prison, before the trial, and Raúl and Nuria went to visit him once a week, going in, preceded by the guards, through that succession of hallways and doors that shut behind them, everything smelling like the inside of a high school, like a cafeteria, like a refrigerator, and in the visiting room, on the other side of the double grating, Leo would appear, and they talked almost without knowing what they were saying, self-conscious like on the platform at a train station; an ever-greater distance between them, as if it had to come up each time, since he was released from prison in Burgos, when, out of touch due to the time he'd been away or perhaps not yet adapted to being free, they could talk, however, almost the same way they'd talked before, nobody afraid of being misunderstood, like that morning when, precisely, he talked to them about his father, a little congested from drinking vermouth, the sun shining on the terrace outside the bar, I don't know what's the matter with him, he's become unbearable, I come home and I find him slumped in an armchair, and he says so many times that he's tired that it starts rubbing off on me. He makes me sick, he only talks about retiring, that he's now old enough to retire, that a son's first duty is to his father, that he sees me just as little as when I was in jail, that he feels lonely, that now that he's old he finds himself without a happy home. And before prison he wanted to get me a clerk's job in the firm of some fourth-rate lawyer friend of his, a sort of crook, some lifelong communist who—as he says—has been forced by life's circumstances to abandon the struggle; now he's talking to me about some other friend of his who owns a mussel farm. I suppose he'd like me to work with him, that I marry some industrious wife, have children. Me, not my sister; my sister's kids don't have his family name, and besides he says that my sister looks like my mother

and I look like him. I think that's why he never paid her much
attention, because she must remind him of my mother, and he
never paid any attention to my mother. And I never see my
sister's kids more than a few times a year, and he doesn't want
my sister to come and clean or tidy up during the week, he says
Teresa does a better job. And it's not really that, she doesn't do
a better job, she does everything; my father takes the customers's
measurements and then he goes and sits in his chair, and she's
the one who cuts, sews, and irons the clothes, and makes the
deliveries, while he talks and talks about the revolution, about
socialism. You understand what I mean, Ferrer? And the socialists get treated the same as the Arabs, people think they were
savages but in reality they had more culture than us. The
Almogavars, the Almohads, the Beni-Merins, they all left us
immortal monuments that attest to their culture. The real savages
were the Christians who, with the obscurantism of the
Inquisition, persecuted wise humanists like Fray Luis de León,
who said that God had made the world for all, but that kings
subjugated people. The same as today, the way capitalism treats
men of good will, like the Rosenbergs, a crime of lèse majesté.
But hell or high water, everything comes together, it all turns out
the same, the world rushes ever faster toward socialism. And the
thing is, as long as there's no exploitation, the human being feels
more responsible and surrenders more and puts socialism before
everything else. You can see this even in the Olympics, where
socialist athletes continuously break their own records. And man
will conquer space in the same way, and explore the depths of
the oceans, descend to the center of the earth. With the help of
socialism there's nothing that man cannot achieve. You see, in
the socialist world everything has a different meaning, work,
sports, human relations, and this is because human exploitation
has evolved into the administration of things. And all that this
is, we might say, is only the prelude. Because as socialist society
becomes communist society all man's problems must necessarily
disappear, except, obviously, the ones that are natural phenomena, like death, earthquakes, etcetera. Then there will be no need
for armies, or police, or jails, because if someone's against it, it

means that they're crazy, because only a madman can be against it, and this is a matter for doctors, who are the ones who have to cure them. And everyone will have time to devote themselves to culture, we'll all be poets and musicians, we'll all paint, and art and literature will be things made by everyone. Churches, for example, could be converted into true temples of culture. Without prohibiting worship, of course, as long as there continue to be religious people; but, outside the hours for worship, they are places that already exist, we've already got them and should use them to bring culture to the people, to give them ideals and save the young generation from this wave of sexuality and pornography that's corrupting capitalist countries. Because although I'm personally agnostic, I think that we must respect the beliefs of Catholics of good faith, who are in many cases the first people to be scandalized that the Church, contrary to the teachings of Jesus Christ, has put itself at the service of the rich. We saw *Fabiola* the other day. Now that's a moral film, and although it's about early Christians, it's perfectly applicable to socialists nowadays. And the audience understands that what Fabiola presents about the Christians then is still true of us today. And the thing is, Christ was not God, but he was a great man and a great revolutionary. The same with Confucius. What happened is that, over time, the Church stopped worrying about the poor, and it preached one thing and then did the opposite of what it preached. But there are still Catholics of good faith, and priests of good faith too, even today. Well, then they should do something and not sit idly by, said Juan. With workers you've got to take the bad with the good. And, winking an eye at Raúl, mimed jabbing his elbow. He seemed cheerful; upon sitting down he slapped Leo on the knee, as if to strike away the somber look on the other's face. Teresa brought out some pastries and, while she prepared more coffee, insisted they pour themselves some more brandy, more anise. And Leo's sister said that they just might be moving to Germany, to work in an optical plant in some city or other, where they'd heard from some people who were already there that a good technician like Juan could earn a fortune. Juan interrupted, as if annoyed by the way she'd announced the news, or as if he feared that her explanations might be misinterpreted, without the proper political context; he pointed out that they hadn't really decided yet, but the current situation was unbearable and nobody was making a move or doing anything; and the bad thing is that this is precisely what the capitalists want, that the worker who thinks for himself a little gets tired and leaves the country. I warn you that it's a double-edged sword, said Leo; it's been shown that workers who emigrate come home more politicized than before. And with money in the bank, said Raúl. That's right, said Leo's sister. A lot of them save everything they can and when they come home they open a business, said Raúl. And the sister, Antonia: that's what I tell Juan: start something, a business, something. I know some folks who opened an electrical shop and now they've got an appliance store and a company that installs electrical systems. Others start with a restaurant. Or with a bar. And Raúl: whatever it is, the important thing is to have some foresight. He caught a flashing glimpse of the wrathful look Nuria shot him, eyes like a wild horse glaring through her heavy bangs, and Leo's more ambiguous face, somewhere between disoriented, almost pained, and critically composed, like the face of one who finds themselves caught in a lie, more or less guilty, while, with forced humor, toying with some related idea that, of course, it might well happen that they return home transformed into some greedy capitalists or something like that. And, now that the old man had taken him aside to speak one on one, it was likely that Raúl's eyes would also give him away, as the old man was saying, because I accept what's natural, hot and cold weather, earthquakes, what I don't accept are the things men are guilty of, what's natural can't be bad; it's simply natural, but men, perhaps, divorced from nature, are the ones who do evil, look, Ferrer, I believe, and while he said it and expounded his thoughts it was likely, it wouldn't be at all unusual, that the others present—except the old man—saw equally in Raúl's eyes his desire to get out of there, to tell Leo' father, I don't give a flying fuck what you believe, and beat it the hell out of there.

If the old man's endless spiels didn't seem to drive Nuria as

crazy as they did Raúl—his unflappable oratory, his uncomfortable tendency to identify himself with whomever he was talking
to, to talk about religion, for example, as if Raúl were some
young vicar with social concerns, offering concessions, criticizing himself, considering the problems of the church almost as
if from within, finding only a few formal problems to argue
against, celibacy, money squandered on liturgies, and a few other
damned little things, provided that, being fair and reasonable, his
goodwill also be taken for granted, so that, all misunderstanding cleared up, they might both, the old socialist and the young
ecclesiastic, agree to a common base of understanding, as well
as goals, which, as they talked and talked, seemed to become
something not only feasible but also real. If Nuria didn't get
exasperated, or at least not as much as Raúl, perhaps it was
because, infected by the atmosphere of sincerity and conciliation
reigning in the house, she herself, when offering an opinion,
frequently spoke in a similar manner, when, as if to slip away
from the small circle of the women, she firmly reclaimed the
general attention toward her remarks, contentious issues that
might have some value discussed in a family setting, for example,
as an affirmation of one's own independence from parents, but
which in the present context turned out at least extemporaneous, subjects like the immorality of canonical marriage being
annulled as a cover for rich people being granted divorces, an
undeniable immorality even from a Catholic point of view;
tiresome, out-of-place questions from a real bore, even considering Nuria's mental instability, that oscillation, for weeks now,
between oppressive anxiety and irritated excitement, nerves like
lit fuses sputtering toward an explosion that never happened, a
truly propitious state for any neurotic reaction, to the exhaus-
tive review of as much traumatic information as she could
possibly gather, her father's death, her critical relationships with
her mother and with Amadeo, her difficulties with Raúl, financial
problems and more, with a marked tendency to seek a common
denominator, a general cause, a single person responsible for
all that, some elusive subject in whose absence Nuria's accumulated rancor and vengeful—and contagious—wrath were usually

discharged on someone else, usually Raúl. I don't see what's funny joking about these poor people by being cynical like Federico. Honestly, I don't see what's so funny. You seem like Delacroix's Liberty leading the people with her tits pointing them the way to freedom. See? That's exactly like something Federico would say. I wouldn't be surprised if you two were lovers; I don't know what you'd do without each other. We wouldn't know how to survive. As far as Federico goes, I'm telling you it wouldn't surprise me one bit. He's more of a mental faggot than most I've seen. And he's the one responsible, with his mean jokes, for you growing apart from Leo, from politics and everything. I think he must be jealous. If not, then I can't understand why he just rips into these people who'll never be intellectuals or geniuses or anything like that, but at least they're good people, which is saying a lot, and a very close family and no one's got the right to go after them. And you think you're such a communist and all that; well you don't seem to me to act like a communist, not you or any of your friends. And that's why, with Leo, who's the only sincere one among you, you're all trying to get under his skin. Well, no señor, I'm not kidding about this, and Leo's right. Art that's not accessible to everyone, art that's not meant for the people, I've got no use for it. The problem with you all is that you've got all the typical intellectual deformities, but workers aren't intellectuals. Unfortunately. Look, in England I also met some communists and I can promise you they weren't like you guys; there they're the real thing. And Raúl: apart from you, I don't think that anybody in the world is worried about what English communists are like or not like.

Louis. Nuria's little pal, her London adventure. A childlike figure, an affectionate presence, uninhibited, available, a presence that, like in the case of that fiery revolutionary in residence at university, whose abstract radical demands usually reveal, however, the viscous imperiousness of his more crude desires—that they rub it, that they take it out, that they do whatever he says to make him orgasm—thus, with Louis, in a similar way, the exterior appearance offered no obstacle, doubtless, to his inner self harboring the most sordidly camouflaged designs, appropriate to the behavior of one who, accustomed to the lethargic sex of the Anglo-Saxons, feels simultaneously attracted to and daunted by Nuria's spontaneity, so that, incapable of seducing her directly, or simply taking her to bed, acts cunningly, disguising his intentions with oblique propositions, political or moral arguments. The erotic Chinese pillow book, for example, that Nuria had brought back from England. A gift from Louis, surely. A program of common experiences? An attempt to use this kind of reading material to compensate for his instinctive capabilities, undoubtedly scarce, well proven by the fact that, after all, it was not him but Raúl whom Nuria latched onto?

They kept on walking without talking, without any determined destination, although, like with the inert force of a tropism, they unconsciously drifted toward Las Ramblas, to have a drink in some bar, withdrawn, hateful, diminished, without anything else to do or anywhere to go, without money and, as a consequence, without any desire to do anything or go anywhere, with all the oppressive feelings that the people out strolling in the streets on a Sunday afternoon can exercise on the spirit, the crowds, the patient lines outside the cinemas, under the misty drizzle with the reflections of neon signs and the lights of the traffic, and especially, that hasty atmosphere of young people rushing to get to their planned destination—a party, a dance, into bed—groups, couples, cars passing by honking merrily, and which, like the contrast between certain lively avenues and their deserted cross streets, or, for example, the even greater gloominess in someone already numb from anxiety, typically aroused by the contrast between themself and the contemptuous displays of vitality from the male whores strolling the avenue, which could only increase the sordidness of their own inane wandering. Or the annoyance of having to adjust your stride to the steps of others until finding an opening and being able to zigzag ahead threading your way through various ranks of pedestrians, controlling the irresistible impulse to push people aside and run them down and open a path by any means possible, leaving behind once and for all the vast example of that whole family, or the pained faces of that young married couple, their small, frugal steps, the wife in an ostentatiously interesting condition, trapezoidal and grave—her water predestined, you might say, to break on Christmas Eve—the husband holding her firmly by the arm, possessive, defiant, holding his head up high against any possible affront, to the least sign of someone noticing his ignominy, that he was clearly and notoriously caught; especially as they passed the Church of Our Lady of Bethlehem, where, due to the narrow sidewalks, they reduced their pace to a particularly slow, careful walk, and it was also particularly disheartening to walk beneath the triumphal arches of lightbulbs strung across the street between the naked boughs of the plane trees and the luminous hanging street lamps, and the loudspeakers with their enervating Christmas carols, proclaiming the apotheosis of the hopeful expectation, the imminent Nativity and the Epiphany, the adoration of the Child in Bethlehem, a Catalan sort of town, with its large old stone farmhouses not far from the famous stable, and its meadows and its small bridge over the stream and—if we overlook the exotic touch added by the Three Wise Men and their caravan of camels—the delicious images of the farmers and the sheep and the pigs and poultry and the hunter with his shotgun and the parish priest with his umbrella and—the most suspicious of all for being so incomparably more popular—the crèche figure of the *caganer* squatting down to shit behind a bush. And the sharp needles of the fir tree glowing with raindrops and the moss and the mistletoe.

O vos omnes qui transitis per viam atendite et videte si est dolor sicut dolor meus. Waning moon spirit, sun slipping away, time of waiting. For what? Killing time, walking along with hands in empty pockets, as if he'd never done any other thing, just as indifferent to sorrow as to beauty, the shake of a gorgeous mane of hair, for example, that young woman coming out of one of so many different antique stores, shaking out her hair as she adjusted her coat, her profile barely glimpsed before she turned away and with a firm step gained some distance on him, leaving him behind, further away with every step, no less deaf to the splendid cascade of that golden hair than to the ringing of the bells still sounding as he shut the door, the beauty of that hair

disappearing among the people on the street just as useless as her
naked body gracing the bedsheets, indifferent, indifferent, Calle
de la Paja just up ahead, shiny cobblestones, polished smooth by
the slippery water, dim, almost a mere reflection, obsessive as the
certainty of what awaited him that afternoon, Tuesday, December
13, the decisive meeting with the men from the paper company,
more distasteful the closer it came, despite all the sweetness of
revenge, given the inevitable hardness of the meeting, while
approximately at the same time, around five o'clock, the midwife
was preparing Maripain for the second and last time, now on
the eve of the abortion, of the unwelcome visit they would pay
her when everything was over, now in Adolfo's house, without
the completely unlikely prospect of having to handle afterward
a hysterical crying jag worse than the one yesterday. The recollection of not having been and the pain of continuing to not be
it, with the rootlessness of one who not only feels distant, but
also without any desire whatsoever of being close, lifelessly,
absently, scrutinizing the engravings and books displayed in the
windows, beyond the blind reflection, forcing himself to assimilate the meaning of what he was contemplating, trying to feel
interested, fascinating windows certainly, even lacking sufficient
morale or money to buy anything, or the self-confidence to go
in and browse around and end up saying that he'd return soon,
even though, in the last place, it wasn't so much the effort of
going in and returning the bookseller's greeting and saying
clearly that he was only there to have a look around, without
other explanations or justifications of any kind, almost
aggressive, and stay there looking around until closing time,
barely half an hour, without the bookseller having any reason to
object, on the contrary, there's always something new, you know,
make yourself at home, tacitly offering, no room for doubt—like
on the screen, eyes closed, nostrils dilated, she parts her lips
slightly—the access to his inner sanctum, the small backroom
where, with the seductive power of prohibition, the books kept
out of immediate view display their titles, mostly old editions
from the years of the Spanish Republic or newer translations
printed in Argentina or Mexico, a relief from all kinds of

anxieties, given their thematic variety, from *Das Kapital* to the
Kama Sutra, by way of *The Treasures of Magda*, Lenin's *Two
Tactics*, and Engel's *Anti-Dühring*, appropriate materials for students interested in pursuing such thinking, as well as people
interested in sex, as is normal when the male sex juts out like a
challenge, in those schoolboys desirous of knowing what sex
holds in store for them, or to try to figure out, when it goes soft
later, what might have awaited them, but really did not nor will
not await them, with the typical defects of everyone close to old
age, people who, if not comforted, will find ample ground for
some fantasies when they learn that the women of Maharashtra
enjoy practicing the seventy-four arts of pleasure, speaking words
in a low voice during intercourse and desiring the men to speak
to them in the same tone, or that the women of Pataliputra are
of a similar temperament, but only express their desires in secret,
or that the women of Uda suffer an interminable tickling in their
Yoni that can only be satisfied by a rock-solid Lingam, or that
the Punjabi woman is driven wild by Auparishtaka or cunnilin-
gus, the sort of clientele easily identifiable the moment they enter
the shop, with the tense naturalness of the couple that slips into
a private room. The simplest thing to do being not to accept the
implicit invitation, Raúl went back to leafing through items
closer to hand, folios of prints and lithographs, without the
bookseller paying him further attention, more interested, obviously, in the interrupted chatter, a conversation initiated between
two customers, under his auspices, one might say, insofar as they
did not know each other personally, while the bookseller, on the
contrary, as if deliberately, seemed to know enough about them
both, their refined or complimentary features, in the manner of
an equally experienced and disinterested procuress, without
other options or proposals than that of establishing contact,
thanks to their good service, between two people who would
thank him for doing it, although if only for the pleasure
procured by that improvised conversation, although the conversation had no regular continuation, nor did it grow progressively
into a kind of milestone or institution, like the milestones of
other times in Barcelona's cultural life, nor would this moment

establish henceforth some permanent bond of friendship, under the bookseller's somber tutelage, respectfully withdrawn now to a secondary position, silent and contemplative, essentially like a beneficent gargoyle, similar to that individual—obstetrician, staff member of the Civil Registry—whose ogreish appearance conceals the spirit of a refined thinker or sensitive poet, woefully unacknowledged. What else could have generated the spark between the noted sculptor smoking a Peterson's pipe filled with mellow, fine-cut tobacco, interested in any kind of print bearing a viticultural theme, and the bibliophile with the crazy glittering eyeglasses and bald pate beaded with sweat, a collector of books about gastronomy and the proprietor and the owner of a restaurant serving typical regional fare, specializing in cuisine from Tarragona? How, between these two strangers, without the bookseller's propitiation? However, as much as the match must be rubbed across the striker for the head to burst into flame, it's no less necessary that the quality of the striking surface be adequate to the quality of the match head, meaning, apart from the bookseller's mediation, the two conversationalists shared a common idiosyncrasy, a common desire not so much for discussing as for corresponding, cultured people with whom one can speak, predisposed to understanding, to offer mutual support and agreement, people who know that their own tastes are shared by the other, who each see their own reflection mirrored in the other. And what's more important: an intelligence based on a material more subtle than the match's flame, which is the tongue, in this case the Catalan tongue, intelligence established from some phonetic, syntactic, or morphological nuance present in the first words the bookseller invites them to exchange, starting with the correct meaning of some expression or word, in contrast to the degraded Castilianisms that have slowly infiltrated colloquial Barcelona speech, centering on the linguistic terrain, by way of countersign, the basis of approximation and, even more so, of identification, between the two conversationalists, in the same way that a certain adhesive quality in the look or a laugh loosed in excess or a simple impertinent intonation are always present in the beginning of the adventure which, in the loneliness of walking the street, drags homosexuals down toward the lower reaches of the Ramblas after nightfall. Thus, in a similar way, must have occurred the conversationalists' mutual recognition, thanks to a fluid interchange equally rich in suppositions as in prospects, terrain which is a gift to survey and which, as usually happens in great moments, the morning of the wedding in the bride's house, for example, when they give the final touches to her dress and resolve then and there the little mishaps that always arise, and the people come and go and wait in an atmosphere of high tension and joy, of bewilderment and efficiency, tending to create a general atmosphere not only of trust and mutual understanding but also of exaltation and euphoria, the relief of having been found, the anxiety of exploring, of explaining oneself to each other, of externalizing their desire for understanding, the firmness of their convictions, and not only on a theoretical level, everyone mobilizing, sympathetic and solicitous, when the taxi driver burst in, a thickset Catalan man, of pachydermic pleasures, not missing from his calm sardonic haste, and requested a copy of the *Calendario del Payés*—the farmers' almanac—for the coming year, I buy it every year he said, his car parked right outside the bookshop door with the motor running, and everyone took charge of the situation—traffic cop!—and while the bookseller hurriedly took care of him, and the noted sculptor stepped outside to keep an eye out, the gastronome offered him oral moral support voicing his scorn for traffic tickets, taxes, and bureaucracy, until the taxi driver sped off victorious, not even hastened by a honking horn, everything executed perfectly like a sleight of hand, and the conversationalists, overcome with happiness resulting from fulfilling one's duty, met again in the peace of the bookshop, even more at home if possible, complicit, twinned, the bookseller, the gastronome, and the noted sculptor, and even that young man with an educated look, Catalan probably or, at least, someone who enjoyed the bookseller's confidence, and if he didn't join in the conversation, it was for youthful shyness or for commendable respect for his elders, he seemed at least an aficionado for prints and lithographs, considering the youth of today that says a lot, *Le Cap de*

Quierz, Plan de la Ville de Roses en Catalogne asiegée le 2 d'Avril par les Armées du Roy très Chrès Commandées par le Marêchal du Pléis, and *A General View of Barcelona from Montjuich,* and *Interior of the Cathedral of Barcelona,* view from the choir, with the high altar highlighted against the clear light from the dome, stained-glass windows, and rose windows projecting into the depths of a world one could well imagine flooded with color, radiances, and polychromatic incidences scattered about by the gold of the altarpieces.

Like the cook who does not begin his work until having gathered all the ingredients required by the recipe, so, only after the first exploratory sallies to delineate positions and define themes, the conversationalists applied themselves to the manipulation itself of the elements under consideration, a job of alternately glossing and breaking down the material in question, with the goal of configuring, like a sculptor, their clay, the desired image, ready to receive the breath of life: Catalonia: the Catalan character, its most distinctive traits: realism, laboriousness, sensuality, individualism, an indissoluble individualism united with a strong sense of fraternity, an ironical spirit, civilized, wisely skeptical, almost pagan, sensitive to natural beauty, to the pleasures of the senses, devoted to his traditions, gifted with instinctive mercantile attitudes, inclined, in case of dilemma, to the most reasonable solution, to the transaction, removed from all unshakeable dogma, from all fanatical furor, traits quite expressive enough to define the reasons for Catalonia's superiority, in the most diverse fields, about how many different peoples surround it, economy and art, sports and culture, landscape, even, a landscape that is the fruit of the perfect conjunction of nature and human labor, a superiority that is, in the final estimation, that of a richer, livelier, more open way of life, if we might permit ourselves the redundancy, because on the one hand, through work and tenacity, the Catalan has been able to make prosperous a land scarce in rich resources, he lacks neither vitality nor joy, and on the other hand, when it comes to celebrating that effort, in order to surrender himself to the feast of the senses and, especially, to the most exciting of pleasures, the

flesh, spectacularly successful even in that, far from the funereal
repressions or alcoholic intoxication of other peoples, a total
superiority that explains so much the impotent animosity that
the central power has always manifested toward Catalonia, like
the attraction that it exercises upon the inhabitants of other less-
gifted lands on the Iberian peninsula, upon the emigrant, the
now so-called *charnego*, assimilated today as well as yesterday, at
the turn of a generation, through the vigor of Catalan society, in
a manner similar to how, in the past, Catalonia roundly imposed
its own personality upon the heart of the Confederation, always
ahead of Aragonese, Majorcans, Valencians, and Neapolitans,
James the Fornicator, Peter the Glans, the rapacious ferocity
of the Almogavars, the phallic aggression of a naturally peaceful people, but who, when consumed with wrath, are terrible;
I understand that currently, in Greece, Bulgaria, and Turkey,
they still remember the Catalan vengeance, like a raging hard-
on whose historical resonance, thanks to the general ignorance
of nations and to the administrative silence with which Spanish
centralism traditionally misplaces the glories of the peoples
it oppresses, can end up reduced, in the eyes of the younger
generations, to little more than the boastings of a sexagenarian
who recalls chasing skirts when he was young or the fantasies
of one who permits himself the liberty of bragging about sexual
exploits, despite his shrill voice, his bean-fattened paunch, and
his presumably ridiculous little shriveled pecker. Empty your
mind, play dumb, a premeditated centralist attitude taken to
such extremes as forgetting that Agustina de Aragón was really
Catalan, born in Fulleda, married to Corporal Roca, also
Catalan, accidentally identified as a Zaragozan, not to mention
the most scandalous mix-up of them all, Christopher Columbus,
Cristóbal Colón or Colom, about whom the experts, Porter, in
fact, offer evidence, increasingly more conclusive, that he was
neither Genovese nor Mallorcan but rather Catalan, possibly of
Sephardic origin. Castilian antipathy, the envy that all things
Catalan have always inspired. An envy founded, typically, on
fear. Fear of Catalonia. Logical, to a degree, considering all that
Catalonia could have become! What it might still become, if

the old virtues weren't lost and replaced by new ones, if different peoples could coexist, the old temperament, characterized
by savagery, like today's smug potbellied pomposity, a product
no doubt of industrialization, of the sedentary habit that in
the long run supposes using machines, especially when run by
foreign operators; what it would be: lucubrations, astonishment,
lamentations and, above any other consideration, the zeal to
set itself apart from the brutal Iberian peninsula to which it is
historically and geographically anchored, from its grim and fitful
development, equally distant from French splendors and Italian
harmonies, a peninsula where even the art might be called more
nomadic than settled, Romanesque here, Gothic there, Baroque
and Neoclassical over there, but always separated, exclusionary,
as if cultivating the one demanded the confinement, if not the
demolition, of the others, a problematic distinction, on the other
hand, if in order to excel at something one must first elucidate
one's own boundaries without really knowing what ours are,
since who knows where this Troy upon Troy begins and ends,
this buried land, whose presence, however, we still sense, the
way pigs sniff out buried truffles, a perfume that sprouts from
the earth making a fading impression, a rhythm to which we
try to match our own and which gets away from us, perhaps
for being too accelerated, not like the Barcelona of times past,
with its rhythm of life like a Swiss or Bavarian city, one of those
populations structured by the centuries, inhabited by hardwork-
ing citizens, meticulous, patient, punctual, unhurried, precise,
of equally elevated financial and technical levels, one of those
cities of old stones and stout bellies, cities where craftsmanship
is an art, where progress is perseverance, where perfectionism is
the only objective and high quality the reward, virtues that were,
and which could continue being, our own, if only the city were
not becoming so virtueless, if only it were not growing so fast
until it is no longer our own, centralism, immigration from the
south, basic urban expansion, distances that demand ever greater
velocity to cover and, what's most dangerous, the inner velocity that inevitably ends up possessing the inhabitant of a large
city, destroying all moderation and moral hierarchy, disquieting

symptoms already evident in the streets and for which, perhaps, like a cancer, the only treatment is the diagnosis itself, a clinical picture before which only remains to us lucid withdrawal and the pleasures of nostalgia. *O trist de mi! Quin fet pot ser aquet? De cuant en ça esta axi Barselona? ¡Catalunya la vella! La yaya! La tieta! Oh, woe is me! What can this be? How long has Barcelona been this way? Old Catalonia! Our nana! Our aunt!*

Catalonia of old, Barcelona of days gone by, its festivals, its markets, its bacchanals, its religious ceremonies, its wonders, the Holy Christ of Lepanto in the cathedral, who grants one of the three solicited graces, the sanctuary of Santa Rita on Calle del Carmen, she who resolves impossibilities, San Nicolás on Pasaje de los Campos Elíseos, who offers help to all who come seeking it, who, with all due modesty, touch his knees, all three centers of attraction only comparable, although in a different way, to those who, then as now, in so many spots in the lower part of the city, gathered each night, according to the erotic specialty of the establishment, a true multitude, joined in fervent fraternity for the gunslinger and the loose cannon, for the lumpen and the bohemian, a city with cultural anxieties no less intense than its mercantile or social concerns, a city of intellectual conversations, of artistic movements, the Barcelona of Els Quatre Gats, of Rusiñol's *L'Auca del Senyor Esteve*, the days when any Barcelonan could recite from memory the most obscene rhymes of Pitarra, the Barcelona of El Patufet and Pere Fi along with, simultaneously, *El Be Negre* and *L'Esquella de la Torratxa*, magazines coveted by collectors just like everything that is now only a memory, like these *aucas* and *aleluyas*, the most faithful chronicles of Barcelona's customs and traditions, a permanent calendar of how much that is endearing is lost and forgotten, institutions like the Nativity Scene and el Rei de la Fava, belonging to the Feast of the Epiphany; the blessing of the sea on the feast day of San Raimundo de Penyafort, patron of sailors first before he became the patron of lawyers; the processions on horseback of Els Tres Tombs on the feast day of San Antonio Abad; the pig sale on the Paseo de San Juan followed by the slaughter right in the middle of the street with the help of an expert butcher, in front of each house, a good excuse for a family party and some enjoyment with neighbors and passersby; and, on the feast of Saint Agatha of Sicily, the traditional distribution of candles called La Candelaria, as well as special loaves of bread, which had the power to keep a woman free from any ailments in her breasts for the whole year; the carnal license of Carnival, Carnestolendas, or Carnestoltes, and its immediate expiation, Lent, allegorically represented by a fishwife with seven feet sticking out from under her skirt, the very number of weeks of mandatory abstinence; parades and religious processions for the Feast of San Medín, in memory of miraculous fava beans which saved San Severo; the pilgrimage of Santa Madrona, martyred in Thessaloniki, in proper observance of the saint's unspoken will that her mortal remains, carried to Barcelona by a tempest, remain in Barcelona; the dessert called Crema Catalana served in celebration of the feast of Saint Joseph, whose carpenter's plane, preserved in the cathedral, was drawn across the chest of young women who wanted their breasts to grow bigger; the feast of palmas and paletones, sweets to be blessed on Palm Sunday, and the Seven Churches Visitation on Holy Thursday, and the devotional Caramellas sung in choir on Holy Saturday, and the roast lamb and special pastries on Easter Sunday, the folk processions and dancing of sardanas on Easter Monday, the jousting tournaments on the Feast of Saint George, replaced over the years by the Festival of Lovers, with books and roses for sale in the streets around the present site of the Barcelona Provisional Council, and Arbor Day on May 1; the blessing of the whole municipality of Barcelona from atop the cathedral roof, in commemoration of the Invention of the Holy Cross; the Fair of Sant Ponç with its open-air market along Calle Hospital featuring candied fruits and herbs and homemade liqueurs, the Corpus Christi procession upon carpets of flowers, with its trumpets and drums, enormous papier-mâché figures: the dragon, the eagle, both symbols of St. John the Evangelist and the herald of Barcelona itself, the giant king, a Goliath who came to represent Charlemagne, founder of the historical county of Barcelona, the giant queen, angels, demons, the grotesque *cabezudos*—human

figures with enormous heads—and the scenes mounted under
the direction of the ancient guilds, farcical interludes and floats
depicting the Creation of the World, Hell, Adam and Eve,
Moses and Aaron, the Prophet Daniel, the Three Wise Kings,
the Phoenix, the Martyrdom of Santa Eulalia, Saint George on
Horseback, the Maiden of Saint George and her parents the King
and Queen Mother, all in slow procession with their retinue,
following a predetermined route along the streets and through
the plazas, and the wondrous sight of *l'ou com balla*, an egg
dancing and spinning in perfect equilibrium atop the spurt-
ing fountain jet in the cathedral cloisters; the summer solstice,
celebrations on the eves of the Feasts of Saint John and Saint
Peter, bonfires, fireworks, all of it beguiling people into drunkenness and lechery; the melon market of Saint James, in the
eponymous Plaza San Jaime, the saint who procures a husband
for many single women, James, Jaime, Iago, or Santiago, the
white knight who converted the Barcelonans with his preaching from atop Mount Taber, the traditional clay and ceramics
fair in Puerta del Ángel, based on the old custom of inaugurat-
ing new clay water jugs with the blessed healing water of Saint
Dominic, in memory of his stay in Barcelona, where he introduced the cult of the Blessed Rosary; the sweltering feast days
of the Ascension of the Virgin in mid-August and the rainy feast
days of La Mercè—Our Lady of Mercy—around the autumnal
equinox; and the marzipan *panellets* on All Saints' Day and the
flower markets set up at cemetery entrances on All Souls' Day;
and the students' petitional processions on December 6 celebrating the Feast of Saint Nicholas Bari, their patron saint before
he was supplanted by Saint Thomas Aquinas; and Saint Lucy,
patroness of the blind and of seamstresses, who today, December
13, as in days gone by, throng and mill about in front of the
cathedral, which encloses the chapel dedicated to their cult of
worship; and the festivals of Saint Thomas, on the 21st, coinciding with the winter solstice, the little booths that sprang up along
the city sidewalks, grouped together according to the kinds of
products they sold, butter and lard, garments, dish cloths, and
tea towels in the Boquería, silk, embroidery, and lacework in

Calle del Call, pastries and confections in Calle Petrixol, jewelry in Calle Argentería, ceramics in Plaza San Jaime, blocks of hard nougat candy—*turrones*—in Plaza Real, second-hand books on Las Ramblas, and so on in so many other places, but the three big fairs that remain only preserve a trace of that old spirit, the toy fair on Gran Vía, the poultry fair on La Rambla de Cataluña, and the advent fair of Santa Lucía in front of the cathedral, with its crèches and wreaths and greenery, as always a prelude to the Nativity, with its ritual of the hollow Christmas log filled with presents, and its gastronomical apotheosis, followed by the Feast of Saint Stephen to finish the feasting, and the Feast of the Holy Innocents so that we might have some good cheer as we approach the witches' coven of New Year's Eve, the single step that separates one year from the next, a step that the Barcelonan of times past—unlike today—tried to start off on a good foot, convinced that the first day of the new year would be a reflection or a prefiguration of the whole year awaiting him.

A moment to take stock, to make a reckoning of the past year: of what the new year might hold in store for us; what will be Catalonia's destiny, based on what we are, in the months to come; what luck awaits us based on the past months and years, and centuries. Because, for example, as in modern-day Italy, where the passing of millennia of radiant culture—the optimum breeding ground for natural good taste—along with, no doubt, the secular exercise of political, economic, and moral chicanery—established now and forever—as an inevitably human complement to the gilded stones of empire, weighs upon the daily habits of the Roman people and their descendants; so too and no less, the sediments of the past weigh heavily upon modern Catalonia, traits like the Catalan's tenacious application of the concrete and tangible and his instinctive mistrust of any superior organization, however more abstract or more broad, that could not be glimpsed from any of his mountains, as they say; a logical reaction, to a certain degree, in the inhabitants of a land that, passageway and causeway par excellence, has seen the rise and fall and even extinction of the political structures of the many different peoples who have invaded it. A frontier land,

a natural route for invasions, overrun time and again from the
four points of the compass, its comportment is not, in effect, less
conditioned by the past than is the behavior of that man who,
as a boy, was a frequent eyewitness to his mother's infidelities,
and who will show himself powerless to lead a stable erotic life,
incapable of preventing, every time, his every love affair from
sliding into disaster, disappointments that will inevitably be
blamed on some incompatibility in the lover, without ever realizing, perhaps, that his deep, unconfessed, unformulated desire
was, precisely, that the affair would collapse; meaning: a personality prone to oft-repeated incriminating slips and failures,
desires and aspirations developed on an oneiric and frequently
nightmarish plane, by virtue of his own unconscious repressions.
In other words: a clear example of historical hysteria, of collective neurosis, with periodic crises that tend to be repeated, to
suppress the initial trauma each time that similar circumstances
reoccur, the impossibility of assuming one's own personality and
acting accordingly, of renouncing their consubstantial maso-
chism, humiliated, beaten down, stepped on, like one of those
women forever complaining about the cruelty and mistreatment
they suffer at the hands of their lover, too often complaining to
not eventually conclude that the mistreatment and cruelty are
her only ties to her lover: departure. Stretching the terms, in the
same way that, on a metaphysical plane, if God were Spanish,
Satan would be Catalan, in the same way, moving from neurosis
to psychosis, we could even come to categorize the two terms of
the Catalonia-Spain counterpoint as entities with schizophrenic
and paranoid traits, respectively; Catalonia, sunk in auto-libid-
inous sentiments that lead it to bitterly contemplate the
destruction of the beloved, meaning, of itself; the other, Spain,
completely given over, without any kind of limitations, to its
mythomania, its delusions of grandeur, its persecution complex;
traits which, in both cases, do nothing except, possibly, conceal,
like a mask, a latent homosexuality. In consequence, as if in some
way we had to qualify the historical attitude of the one as well
as the other, we would have to conclude that Spain's role is typically sadistic, while Catalonia's is essentially masochistic; a type

of personality that, if it were possible to cast a people's horoscope just as one casts an individual's, the only possible conclusion would be to consider, in light of its historical profile, that it was born under the masochistic and self-destructive sign of Scorpio, with the bi-member sign Gemini in the ascendant, at its most unformed or immature, and clearly subject to the nefarious influence of the planet Saturn. Thus, for example, a succinct examination of traditional Catalan cuisine, in its most characteristic features, defines it for us as imprinted with a marked infantilism, by reason of its nature, at once elemental and spontaneous, rough and robust; a style of cooking that knows few spices, far from elaborate, vegetables raw or parboiled, meats barely grilled, lamb ribs, chicken, rabbit, all the meat somewhere between bloody and burnt to a crisp; the Catalan's love for applying his own condiments directly to his favorite dishes, as well as for gathering or capturing mussels, limpets, urchins, all kinds of shellfish eaten raw, wild mushrooms, snails, small game; his marked preference for those foods which he considers especially vitalizing, frugal, and flatulent, all those nasty popular inside jokes about the properties of beans, take, for example, the idea about their special nutritive and energetic power, derived from the sponginess and fermentation that their consumption produces within the digestive system, followed by compression of the diaphragm and subsequent expansion of gases, that is, the fart, tacitly considered, in diverse social milieu, as a manifestation of dynamism, vitality, and being good with people; their worship of foodstuffs with phallic or excremental shapes, *botifarra*, *bisbe*, and other typical sausages, fava beans, turnips, peppers and eggplants, garlic, onions; his obsession that the wine be fresh and unchilled, a strong variety, drunk from a bota, from the countryside, the kind that makes a man get good and hard, and spring water, with recognized therapeutic and revitalizing qualities; his tendency to celebrate with such foodstuffs, out in the open air, taking advantage of holidays, long weekends, and vacations, as many banquets as possible, by the streams and meadows of the forest, a propensity for which one need not be Sigmund Freud to make the connection with ritual practices of

sexual initiation, individual or collective. Generally possessed of
an excellent stomach, the Catalan man is capable of assimilating,
as Catalan society absorbs southern immigrants, the most undi-
gestible foods, and of defending Catalan gastronomy with a total
conviction in the universal value of its appetites, in the same way
that the greedy man who exposes or relates his savings operations
attributes to his listeners a pleasure similar to what he experiences
as he contemplates accumulative phenomena. Good proof of
that is the Christmastime tradition of the Tió, not Santa Claus
nor Papá Noel, not even the green Christmas tree itself, but
rather, more elementally, an old, dry, hollow log charged with
providing each family with the adequate holiday sweets when
conjured by a chorus of the children in the house loudly singing
the "Our Father of the Trunk"—¡ *Caga Tió, caga turrons i pixa vi
bo!*—"Oh, Christmas log, shit nougat candy and piss white
wine!"—as the log is beaten with a stick, blow after blow delivered as punishment, a luckless scapegoat that purges beforehand,
with its coveted droppings, the brutally shocking indigestion
that comes with the day, apart from emphasizing the symbolic
aspect of the obscure excremental origins of the most sweetly
savored things and, on a more conceptual plane, of the dialectical
relationship existing between the natural processes of ingestion
and defecation, a fact so much more interesting and revealing
when considering that, in Catalonia, food at Christmastime is
the very finest, the best food of the year, a ceremonial culmination that opens and concludes the gastronomic year with its
grueling menu: chicken soup, stew, crudités, stuffed golden
capon, melon and pineapple and pearly bunches of grapes in a
decorative arrangement, and nougat candy and rolled wafer
cookies, all of it accompanied by generous quantities of table
wine, champagne, malmsey, and spirits, the bottles in the
background, a plastic composition, a still life, always appearing
in holiday pictures, as well as, suggestively haloed, on old-fashioned Christmas greeting cards dropped in the mailbox by the
neighborhood watchman or garbage collector, to brighten things
up for the holidays, inscribed on the back with some bland stock
verse praising their services rendered, thus justifying their

expected tip, and offering wishes for a prosperous new year, elements evocative of the joyous popular climate and the impatient excitement surrounding these holidays, a matter somehow far removed, on the other hand, from those poets writing the best vernacular verse, who have traditionally found Christmas to be an endless source of inspiration. The reason being, apart from gastronomy, poetry is the other last bastion of Catalan culture. A poetry that notwithstanding the unfavorable initial impression that the phonetic contact with the tongue in which it's written might produce in the curious traveler, a crudely onomatopoeic language apt for composing puns and tongue twisters like *setze metges mengen jutges,* which declares that "sixteen doctors devour the judges"—or something like that, and that one about *en Pinxo va dir a en Panxo vols que et punxi amb un punxo?*—"Pincho asked Pancho: want me to puncture you with a punch?"—and so on, a language that's been capable of reaching the highest heights of contemporary poetic orography, works like *Els Carquinyolis de Sarrià,* its timeless verses of pure everyday speech, classic by reason of their exact human measure, universal by their Mediterranean concretion; or the lucid desolation of *El Triomf del Minotaure*; or the magical realism of *Me la va desfer Monna Lisa.* A living, up-to-date, poetry, which this very night, in the tutelary shadow of Santa Lucía, will see its storied past enriched with one title more, which, along with the titles of the other award-winning works, belongs to several other literary genres, making it absolutely clear once more that poetry is really nothing less than the only living form of expression in Catalan literature, and that Catalan literature is not the only integral element of Catalan culture, and that Catalan culture and its material support, the Catalan language, are not the only foundational elements of the authentic entity of the Catalan Countries. A literary lottery awarded in the grand rooms of the Hotel Colón, at No. 7 Avenida de la Catedral, by means of a patient alternating or rotating mechanism, not so much—as one might judge lightly and with bad intentions—so that the jurors and various prizewinners are announced in as judicious a manner as possible, as because materially the result can be no different, by reason of the very abundance and variety of prizes for a limited number of cultivators of a language enjoying a numerically modest public, modest to the point that any of its mandarins—author, reader, jury, prize, prologue writer, anthologist—upon confirming the watchful attendance each year of the secret police, proud, at bottom, of the relative restlessness that such events seemed to inspire in the authorities, and especially proud of the unanimous and reiterated fortitude, as well as of the punctual regularity with which, each year, the attendees of the event offered a measured challenge to those authorities, proud, almost happy, one could say: if a bomb exploded now, that's the end of Catalonia, a somewhat disgraceful utterance for whomever might understand it without any lofty thoughts, ignorant of the true reach of the problem, ignorant of its character, or what's worse, indifferent to the losses that the inexorable human condition, meaning death, infringes upon those assiduous faithful in so many of their spiritual leaders, fewer and fewer every year, although we still have figures like Uirpse, known to the world as Salvador Espiru, and Quart de Pere or Pere Quart, not to mention less-well-known but no-less-estimable figures, Moll, Coll i Alentorn, Aramon, and the somewhat compensatory uncertain appearance of promising young writers, though their almost complete lack of reputation doesn't prevent them from bringing new sap to the old trunk nor of counteracting with their presence the implacable annihilation that takes pleasure in attacking, perhaps, those enterprises most targeted by misfortune, the only explication of the perseverant circumstances that have always shadowed our culture since the origins of the development of Catalan literature. Because it's true, yes, that its appearance on the landscape of the literatures of the Romance languages came rather late, due to a purely oral existence, in stiff competition with Provençal and Latin, until then exclusively written, and which, having barely consolidated their independence, including before, including while, their different and defining features were taking shape, it already had a parallel process of dialectalization and fragmentation, according to the particularisms of the various reigns of the Crown of Aragon, unhappily being the Principality of Catalonia, least wondrous in achievements among them all; and it's also true that after the first flowering of Catalan literature, whose merits are still, on the other hand, insufficiently recognized, perhaps because its diffusion and influence were of a more moderate character, perhaps because it had premeditatively tried to marginalize them and even ignore them or silence them, a phase of the eclipse begins, an interval of almost four centuries during which Catalan literature ceases to be, literarily and literally speaking, for reasons that at first glance can seem mysterious, especially to the naive reader's blinking eyes, merits not in reality difficult to figure out through a correct analysis of the very structures of Catalan society during that period; a lacuna or void that lasts until well into the nineteenth century, when the resurrection of Catalan literature begins with the appearance of the poem in the vernacular—though written in Madrid—"La Patria"—a progressively accelerated reflowering, as if propelled, you might say, by a steam engine, a progress inevitably linked to the political, social, and, especially, economic avatars of the age, progress that must necessarily culminate with the scientific re-elaboration of that progress, codifying the language's grammar, in 1913, concretely, when everything seemed to indicate that the economic structure of that homeland in revival and its much desired political superstructure, were going to find their most natural flowering in poetry, cultivated, as in times past, preferably, by scholars and clergymen. Yes, all that is true, yes, *la Renaixença*—the Catalan cultural revival and its historical disaster; and was that disaster due to excessive confidence in the language, and a prudent fear of resorting to other kinds of weapons, equally certain and tangible as the last splendors of that poetry, which surface, like the fortune that comes to one's hands when they are too old to enjoy it, or how bodies tormented by agony usually look more beautiful after death, or to put it more crudely, like the swan's song? But it's no less certain either that everything might have been different, that the weight of the literature would have been able to reach far enough to set history aright, that even politics would have had to bow down before some literary events of greater significance, if the history of

Catalan literature had been different, if from its origins it had experienced an archaic but definitive development, the equivalent, let's say, of the Provençal lyric, or if at the right moment its own Dante had appeared, capable of making the language coalesce around his work, or with a normative Renaissance like the one in France, or something like Elizabethan drama, or with a Baroque Counterreformation like the Castilian one, or from a wider perspective, if Catalan literature, although discontinuous, might have had at least, in the course of its history, just one single figure of indisputable universal worth. Therefore: isn't its late arrival proof of the cosmopolitan and elevated degree of culture of a people who wrote in Latin and composed verses in Provençal while speaking in Catalan? And is its ready dialectical modulation not a demonstration of expressive richness and subtle nuance? And isn't its rebirth after almost four centuries of silence proof of its vigor? Of producing a poetry like its contemporary forms, whose surreal omegas have no reason to envy the best poetry written in Spanish or in any other language in this century? Is it nothing more than the product of a sick and wasted culture? No! Ridiculous! Is there any doubt that such a literature cannot die, that like in olden times, as always, Catalan literature will know how to overcome the unfavorable circumstances in which it is currently unfolding: its reduced human base, the increasing difficulty of absorbing some largely non-Catalan popular classes, the lack of support and collaboration—if not disrespectful misunderstanding—in the heart of the properly-called Catalan society, on the part of its ruling classes, of its driving leaders, of its most representative personalities, politically mortgaged to the central power, diverse kinds of human agents who mutually empower one another in a sickly vicious circle, agents who if they socially circumscribe the use of that literature to the field of bourgeois media, from an internal, strictly literary point of view, seem to slowly move toward the alternative—in its dramatic struggle at a level of linguistic survival, with the consumption of energy that the defense of a problematic existence supposes—of choosing between triviality and localism, something in every case minor or quotidian, marginal things if not alien to the interests of any person not directly implicated in the problem, situated beyond its diminished limits; what room for doubt that in spite of so many obstacles, such as the centralist administrative obstacles which victimize us, obstacles that our enemies, gaily celebrating their habitual ill will and malicious spirit, will not hesitate to classify as excuses? What doubt that Catalan literature will endure, that it has seen and has survived worse times? What doubt, personal convictions, of inner sanctum or chancel, difficult to hold onto out in the city streets, where the atmospheric element, demoralizingly de-Catalanized, capable of dissolving the firmest resolution, makes its clumsy embarrassing defense, that lack of popular support, that indifference so much worse than the violent enemy, that fear of feeling, that lack of necessary lung power, extemporaneous, ridiculously outlandish, in a city that is ours, in our Barcelona, a city whose most traditional features seem to be disassembled day by day? But, and from a Marxist point of view, in light of historical materialism, what future can await a literature initially written with apostolic ends, pious babble masquerading as homilies and sermons, with the goal of making them accessible to the public, to reach the people who, over the centuries, had ceased to understand Latin, a language more and more removed from its own rough formative language, when now, with equally apostolic ends in mind, to reach the proletariat, with the great pain and sadness and despair of Fortuny, one must abandon writing all political propaganda in Catalan, if one plans to have the people in the working-class neighborhoods manage to understand the significance of the pamphlets distributed? What future, considering that if the birth of Catalan letters must be attributed to the inadequate character of Latin and Provençal and the new realities of the age? Must you not then consequently recognize the ineluctable character of the progressive inadequacy of Catalan letters to address the new realities of Catalonia? And another new fact: the appearance of writers born in Catalonia who write in Spanish, an occurrence at least as new or unusual as the fact that one hundred years earlier, for the first time in four centuries, it was simply that writers appeared, a phenomenon which, contemplated from a Marxist perspective, seeking some material, structural, or economic reason, could be attributed to the conversion of Barcelona, immediately after the war, into the primary center of the Spanish publishing industry; or considering for ourselves other criteria, entertaining other perspectives, a kind of sociological analysis, for example, the advantages those writers had for having been born, as a rule, in the heart of bourgeois Barcelona, meaning, in a city, Barcelona, particularly open, restless, and reformist, among all the cities in Spain, and into a social class, the middle class, objectively more progressive than the sclerotic Castilian feudalism; or attributed to the decline of Spain, or to the decline of Catalonia, none of that discovering any great explanation at the heart of the matter, nor, on the other hand, the explanation, any explanation, being too interesting, not even our purpose in examining it. In short, taking good note and drawing the attention of the sociologist, or the scholar, or the simple aficionado, to a fact that, for being common to the greater part of that new generation of writers, can facilitate the description of the phenomenon, not only its interpretation: they are not ours, they are not integrated into Catalan life proper nor do they cooperate in its maintenance, generally foreign to the privileged classes, belonging to those families which, although Barcelonan by name and birth, are culturally Castilian, or for their foreign ties, or for a question of principle, meaning, for what the national unity of Spain, firmly safeguarded by the armed forces, represents for them as a guarantee of stability and order, families who are unconditional supporters of Francoism who, after the turn of only a single generation, are thus purged of their browbeaten renunciation of Catalanism, their cowardly and corrupt defection from the Catalan cause, with some children whose uneasiness—not only literary—seems to lead them to no longer renounce only Catalonia but Spain as well, their fatherland, their religion, their ilk, their class, their blood, adding apostasy to their treachery and political subversion to moral terrorism, communists, nihilist anarchists, a reaction equally unforeseeable and widespread, unfortunate in that we are all, to a certain extent, responsible, we who fought and won a war for them, for them and for the political, moral, and territorial integrity of Spain, a Spain that we wanted to hand over to them exactly the same as we had received it, or if possible, even more pure, even more purged, more identical to itself, and nevertheless, given that it's not conceivable to speak of just punishment in relation to a cause both just and victorious, we committed some error, some mistake whose nature we have not yet fully understood, so that spurious throng nests in our own guts, that new and negative generation of writers who by their conduct make all purely literary sanity secondary and accessory, given that their personal circumstance, just like any other element from the rest of the peninsula, frequently rubs shoulders with common crime, depraved drug addicts, alcoholics, homosexuals, and, who knows, maybe even parricides. Ineradicable moral cancers! Lear, oh Lear, old and blind and crazy and abandoned! What would the men of Barcelona from the turn of the twentieth century say? Men like Don Eusebio, Don Manuel, Don Juan, Don Antonio, Don José, Don Augusto, Don Francisco, what would they say now if they could rise from their graves? The loss of values, the dissolution of customs, and what's worse: the extent of evil, of which the reprehensible creations of a handful of writers and artists are only one of so many symptoms, the simple material of an intellectual conversation for people with common obsessions. A classic generational conflict brought up when one is young, and forgotten and resurrected again, only on the inverse of the equation, with roles reversed, when one is old? Is it all a result of Barcelona's social structure when, even though it's got nothing in particular that is manifested in the son of the southern immigrant who lives on the city's industrial periphery, according to his class interests, an attitude of defiance and rebellion, the same as in the world of people like the Tarrés family, of technicians and specialists, self-employed workers and administrators, and even, with the irritation and bitterness that defeat usually brings, in certain sectors of the Catalan petite bourgeoisie, the big victim, along with the proletariat, of the Civil War, cases like those of Aurora's family and the Fortuny family, for example, the argument is not quite so satisfactory and

turns out to be more than incomplete, when such an attitude
can occur in homes like those of a person like Rivas Fernández,
typical representative, no less than the paper manufacturer Plans,
of the non-monopolistic bourgeoisie, or in family names like
Ferrer Gaminde, not for being families in decline, after various
generations of absenteeism, completely deprived of social consideration, or in the heart of families like the financier Quintana,
a relevant figure of the Castilian aristocracy, linked by marriage
to the upper-class Barcelona bourgeoisie, or the attorney
Cuadras, an eminent member of that bourgeoisie, an attitude
that would doubtless be exaggerated to consider as genuinely
revolutionary, but which, although if only for its true disinterest
in class interests, in his class, seems to us frankly atypical, a
product of something deeper than a logic and a passing antagonism between parents and children, because what's certain is that
before, or more exactly, until now, all this, what's going on now,
never happened? Jacinto Bonet, incidentally, a relatively young
man although he doesn't quite look it, however, barely forty years
old, oligarch par excellence, no mere technocrat in the service of
the oligarchy like Amadeo García Fornells, but an oligarch in
the strictest sense, an involvement that Jacinto Bonet, father,
simple lucky black-marketeer, member of the postwar nouveau
riche, with everything and having amassed a solid fortune, would
never have dreamed of, inhibited perhaps by his somewhat
clumsy or primitive manners, or perhaps for the Catalan businessman's instinctive reserve—founded in reasons essentially
fiscal—regarding all excessive gravitation toward the upper circles of administration; a spirit forged in the happy postwar years,
on the other hand, our oligarch has not had experiences different
from those of so many other young people of his time and of his
class who, like him, have known how to respond to their
upbringing and education, a greater show of richness perhaps,
stronger family ties, a more optimistic vision of the opportunities
that life offers, a mentality nowadays in short supply, constrained
to disguise its nostalgia for those times and mold itself to the
present moment, obliged to feel sincere desires to forget the
origins of all that, the last blood and the first gold, to cast earth

and even mud over the memory of such mythic times, over the
so-poorly-understood ostentation of the nouveau riche, a
Thomist need to touch in order to believe, to see in order to
experience the miracle of transubstantiation of bread into gold,
of the tin into gold, of the quotas of anything into gold, of living
to see the incredible reality of money, a technicolor life like in
their contemporary American films, high-rises with swimming
pools, big luxury cars, beloved wives and darling children and
beloved beloveds, and more than anything, the wild, giddy sensation of impunity that comes, in a system of generalized corruption and coercion, of economic power unleashed, without
conflicts, neither labor-related, nor fiscal, nor social, nor even
domestic, with the most absolute liberty of abusing everything,
of knowing that there is a way to fix absolutely everything; a
nostalgia just as comprehensible, unfortunately, just as inadmis-
sible, a sad necessity, a sadness sadly sad from denying not only
any relationship with all that but also of convincing themselves
of the convenience of leaving all that behind, just a caprice of
history, the versatility of time, which makes young people starting out now, unlike those who started in the hard-but-fascinating
forties, and who, shaped by the positive principles that informed
Spanish life of those times, are now responsible men, unlike
them, the young people now, whose loving upbringing and the
family harmony and social peace in which their lives developed
from earliest infancy, contained the expectation of maximum
integration into the environment, everything seems to turn out
less clear for them—life, the world—more imprecise, if not
contradictory and even crazy—everything rolls along in such
confusion! Moral metastasis. The inconsistency and lack of consideration from today's young people is simply inconceivable;
their pastimes, pleasures, and habits so different from those of
our days, going to the Liceo, flirting in the boxes, and Sunday
mornings, on Avenida Diagonal, strolling the sunny sidewalks,
up and down the street until reaching Plaza Calvo Sotelo, up
and down, with the ebb and flow of the crowd, and the festivals
and booths along the street, and those old time dances, slow-
dancing, cheek to cheek, mouth to ear, things that meant so

much then and nothing now, as if nothing from those days means anything to young people now, and not for lack of desire—although at the same time you can't discard a possible loss of vigor in the generation as a whole—as much as for considering it little more than a waste of time, something puerile or too formal or insufficiently exciting, at the same time exceeding the norm, the detours and evasions that years before regulated the relations between boys and girls, and the exception, the veteran pride of some girls, heroic fornicators of the forties, their secret passions, their licentious memories, scandalizing them, worse, decanting them, cornering them, with how easy everything has now become, the hard-earned privileges, from house to house, family by family, almost without the parents themselves managing to understand how, their parties, their meetings, their amusements about which so little is known and so much is rumored, that elusive and famous dolce vita that so obsesses people who are no longer quite so young, questions—what do they do, where do they do it, who's doing it—which everyone—which everyone supports with their own private erotic frustrations, orgies that a feverish mind might well situate, for example, in an apartment like Adolfo's, or even right in the family house, the Cuadrases' place on the weekend and the house in the hands of Adolfo and all his friends, everyone looking for costumes, petticoats, and formal dinner jackets, top hats, suspenders, garters, liveries and corsets, furs, liturgical ornaments from the family chapel, albs and chasubles, cinctures, the dusty smell of the lace dominated by the camphor smell of the cloth, no less fatally destined, in spite of the loving care with which the parents conserve the grandparents' clothes up in the clothes attics, to the solace of the grandchildren, to give some spicy flavor and hot temperature to the new generations' parties, and adequate environment—as the poet says—to their impossible propensities, in their progressive search for times gone by, in their journey through the past, from garment to garment, until the final culmination, everyone with their original, old-time outfit, the pure and simple, collective and promiscuous nudity, in the half-light, music playing softly, glasses half-full, cigarettes—maybe marijuana, who knows—scenes to which the aforementioned feverish imagination might well add a Sistine jumble of intertwined bodies. Seems there's girls getting it on together and everything else, whatever you like, said Nuria. People always exaggerate, said Raúl. Has anything ever happened right in front of us? Nothing has happened and nothing ever will happen because Aurora knows I've got more guts than her and she's afraid of me. She knows I'm capable of going way farther than her in everything. And as for her, if she's not the center of attention, she's not interested. Well, you know the one I can't imagine in the middle of these things is that wimp Adolfo. Adolfo? I can assure you that if she gets into such things it's only for his sake, because she knows that's the way to keep him hooked, only for that, to please him. Considering what a phony manipulative little bitch she is, she'll do anything, whether she likes it or not, just to keep her claws in him. Well it seems fine to me; I've got nothing against a good, old-fashioned orgy. Me neither. What's happening is that in Spain people are too uncivilized for these things; here everybody just goes their own way, and with things that way, it just can't happen.

Uncivilized? Was that supposed to mean England was civilized? A place where it was possible to practice all thirty fornicatory positions envisioned by the sexual rituals of Taoist eroticism, including Autumn Dog? The same stupid discussion, the same stupid conjectures and suspicions that in the morning, in that bar on Plaza San Jaime, after going to pay the gas and electricity bills and after she pawned her jewelry, not yesterday, yes, yesterday, Monday, but not the morning, in the afternoon, after accompanying the Plutos to their appointment with the midwife, everybody in Adolfo's car, while they waited in a bar, and Adolfo looked for a parking spot and the assistant must already be ushering the Plutos into that cold white echoing room softened by shadows, where they would soon hear the midwife's husband's ringing voice, a sudden fright not attributable to the discord between the timbre of his voice and the loving words she would doubtless use to receive Maripain, nor to how easily he spoke while getting ready, as if instead of proceeding to dilate

her cervix he was doing her nails, but rather to something at the
same time more superficial and disquieting, by virtue of its very
unreality, the sensation that might provoke in us, for example,
the apparition of a peasant farmer with bulging cheeks, his
mouth painted with bright-red lipstick; an argument brought
up again in this case, by way of recourse, as a means of distraction, some polemical thing that would console them or put them
at ease even if only for a few moments, the time they had to wait,
at a table disagreeably close to the opening and closing door, for
Adolfo to pick them up and, in his company, wait for the Plutos
to return, in a kind of dress rehearsal for what had to happen the
day after tomorrow, everyone awaiting the joyful advent of what
must not be born, a malign algebra made flesh incognito, neither
X nor Y, definitively dismissed, an epiphanic abortion. This
chick, just a touch of her big dyke fingers and you see stars. She's
a lesbian and she was crazy about you, didn't you notice,
Maricunt? asked Pluto. And Maricunt: well, kiddo, must be that
I don't like dykes. And Pluto: I always said you were a prude.
And Maricunt: I hope the doctor's got better hands and that it's
true they use anesthesia, though I swear, in the long run, the
pain is the least of it, I swear, Nuria. Just figure it's going to be
awful for a little while and then you go through it and that's it,
she was saying, then it's all over, more cheerfully, of course, and
also more relaxed than Nuria, a Nuria totally incapable of lending her the moral support which, in principle, one might
suppose was appropriate to her role in all that, strained, gloomy,
almost lugubrious, slumped down out of sight in the back of the
car, as if exhausted by their brief run in the pouring rain, from
the door of the bar, or even confused by the furious drumming
of the rain on the useless umbrella, or feeling swamped already
by the redundant voice of the windshield wipers sweeping back
and forth the whole way, clearing away the gray with their endlessly repeated no, no, no, more dejected than in the morning,
when Raúl arrived in such a hurry as if late to the meeting place,
a bar in Plaza de la Villa de Madrid, to find that she hadn't
arrived either, and he, for not having stopped along the way after
leaving home, had no cigarettes, and was still hesitating whether

to buy a pack at the bar, where he knew they wouldn't have his brand, or walk to the tobacco shop, always a better solution, because even if his brand didn't automatically bring him good luck, it wouldn't bring him bad luck either, and that was something, and besides the tobacconist was just a few steps away and nobody, absolutely nobody, could have foreseen the horrible bother of a housewife buying Christmas gifts, her tardy thoroughness, her drivel, her coin purses, her fat cheeks, her blather, her stories, her repugnant calculations, her silly nonsense, her pasty unction of a sexually experienced and socially respectable woman, placidly taking her time choosing every single item, displaying her tastes, explaining why, not so much, evidently, for the impression that her personality might make on the tobacconist, as on the improvised public audience that her sluggish shopping was causing to grow larger by the second, and finally, for the pure and simple pleasure of stating her personal opinions and tastes out loud, no, nobody could foresee such a waste of time, so that, when he got back to the bar, Nuria was already waiting for him, still with that glazed looking of someone just awakened, it's a good thing, I thought I was late, she said. Well, you are late, said Raúl. Well, chico, you got here later than me. Don't I have time for a coffee? And Raúl: no, there's no time, and refusing any explanations, he took her by the arm and, almost running, led her along Calle Canuda toward Puerta del Ángel, letting her go breathless telling him that Mariconcha and Aurora had telephoned her, that's why she'd been late, that they had set a time to meet about the midwife, that Aurora had been strangely sympathetic, that she'd said why didn't she go to her house while the others accompanied the Plutos, I told her if it was for Mariconcha's sake, but look if your little Aurora really is a dyke and what she wants is to throw herself at me, if not, I don't understand it, frankly, she's got to know I don't really have much regard for her, wait, wait, I can't go any faster. They entered the Catalan Gas and Electric building, Puerta del Ángel 20-22, at three o'clock sharp, precisely when the porter was closing the enormous iron gate separating the cashiers' windows from the main offices, leaving barely enough room for Raúl and Nuria to

slip inside, unlike the two women coming behind them, two
friends or cousins or neighbors, in short, two women who after
hearing the lock snap shut, clinging to the iron bars like prisoners, immediately began to complain, to beg the porter to let them
through, simultaneously displaying various fairly pathetic arguments, they lived far away, their lights were going to be turned
off, he'd just let that young couple through, etcetera, at the same
time that the porter, doubtless a man of rigorous standards,
calmly withdrew his key from the lock. It was open then and
now it's closed, he said, unable to disguise the pleasure of feeling,
although only for a few brief moments, the long arm of an
implacable power, whether he grants or denies, his features waxy
and swollen, fleetingly reanimated by a despotic spark, rules are
rules, with the delectation that certain spirits find—dark revenge
for all the injuries life inflicts—in the fact of being able to
personally give bad news to the interested parties, to the closest
friends or relatives of the victim of some accident or misfortune,
that kind of pleasure experienced by one—there always is a one,
an agent of authority, eyewitness, or spontaneous messenger—
who fulfills the painful duty of participating—at first without
daring to look at the anguished face of the message's recipient—
the sad, tragic news, a fatal accident, for example, his glassy
scrutiny, later, upon accurately clarifying: burned to a crisp,
something horrifying, his sure observation of the cathartic reaction, that for once the other externalizes the pain that he carries,
emotional discharge frequently of such force that he even ends
up contaminating another, for making someone sob, meaning,
our messenger, venting his emotions in a flood of tears, looking
for relief, inner peace, feeling firm desires for remaking his life,
for improving, behavior which, in turn, usually does nothing
else but increase the intensity of the emotional response of the
others present, contributing to the general despair and stupefaction and paroxysm, a phenomenon whose origin is doubtless
similar to the greater public's love for TV series and soap operas,
crying about what one has done when they cry about what
happens on the show, to expiate one's own fault through the
propitiatory expiation represented, sins that, in general, attack

the family ties, an adultery of unfortunate and exemplary repercussions, the premeditated exclusion of the parents by the child who has prospered and is now ashamed of them, the cowardly abortion undertaken because of what people will say, etcetera, etcetera, questions of mental hygiene to those who were probably not strangers to the case which concerns us, as seems proven by the fact that when Raúl and Nuria left, the porter, always behind the bars of the gate, and who only opened it to allow those few remaining inside to go out, even continued chatting with the two women there, attentive to their problems, in the attitude of one who tries to put himself in the other's position, to adopt their points of view about life, no doubt giving them some good advice, some surefire direction for the future.

An itinerary very similar to today's schedule, with the small variations that happen in any artisanal motivation repeated to the point of obsession, because in the same way that from the Plaza de la Villa de Madrid they had reached Puerta del Ángel by way of Carrer Canuda and not by Vertrallans and Santa Ana, so, when they got to Avenida de la Catedral, at the spot known as Plaza Nueva, from Carrer dels Arcs and Puerta del Ángel, unlike today, they had continued along Calle del Obispo and Plaza San Jaime, to Number 6 Calle Jaime I, a small door leading to the section of pledges or deposits for the Caja de Ahorros y Monte de Piedad savings bank, whose central headquarters has its entrance at Calle de la Ciudad 1. Other differences: the Christmas fair selling crèches and wreaths in front of the cathedral was perhaps not yet properly inaugurated, and instead of rain, in the way of those truces that have no other objective than to undermine the enemy's morale, the air was damp and hazy, the light like a lemon-juice-colored halo that seemed to soften everything, the sounds, traffic dampened, isolated facades, spectral lamp posts, people hurrying along silently, almost feeling threatened you might say, cold and sweating at the same time, streets and plazas that, unlike the streets and squares of Dickens's London or Balzac's Paris or even, at a stretch, the Madrid of Perez Galdós, had not found and perhaps would never find a faithful chronicler for their grandeur and their misery, of their anonymous daily dramas, a Balzac who would have so thoroughly enjoyed himself witnessing the spectacle in the waiting room at the Monte de Piedad, seeing the possibility of appreciating the thousand shades that distinguish the people who come there for their appointments, from the most humble people, whatever their origin, or those fallen on hard times, but in every case people of honorable poverty and laudable honesty, self-sacrificing mothers, exemplary wives, loving daughters, to the most varied gamut of figures with a whole range of criminal faces, ruffians, pimps, swindlers, prostitutes, homosexuals, usurers, card sharks, as well as thieves in general, every kind with every speciality, each one with their own problems, each problem a complicated web, conflictive situations that, given their own individual matter, could only possibly define us in a rigorous way by resorting to the subtleties of juridical terminology, the fine distinctions which, thanks to such language, we can establish between the complex elements concurrent in a woman who goes to pawn her jewels, some mistress, for example, doubtless caught up in an emphyteutic relationship with someone who maintains her: the difference existing between ownership (in this case, her own body), possession (of the woman by emphyteusis), and dominion (the pimp's right), for whose benefit and by any reckoning she pawned her jewels, thus redefining her relationship with this man through a renewed emphyteusis, only now inverse to the first arrangement, the money obtained in the pimp's possession and her services to him consequently demanded, only under her control; lives, in short, that lend themselves to infinite conjectures and unfathomable opinions, thus gathered before the penetrating eye of the creative genius, of that climate of longings and anxieties, in that truculent atmosphere, populated by narrowness, passivity, debts, struggles, calculations, disappointments, pledges, achievements, depreciations, interest, a bank vault of misery atop a mountain of sleaze. An environment propitious, on the other hand, for dialogue as much as for confidence and even for indiscretion, according to the ties of solidarity that tend to develop between those companions who share both expectations and sorrows, such mistrust and distance resulting from jealousy or embarrassment, that of the scolding nunlike old maid, to cite one example, the old woman who while managing to avoid all contact with the woman sharing her bench—a ruined, whored-out forty-something showing the desperate degradation of a deeply beleaguered fornicatrix with the broken face of one who'll settle for being roughly stitched up— even as she huddled deeper into her dandruff-dusted overcoat, at the same time, alert, defensive, watching each and every one of those present, her features, closed tight as a clamshell, making it easy to guess at her nostalgia for a Barcelona now fallen, like herself, on hard times, the Barcelona of her youth, the good old Barcelona of streets like Calle Fernando, and Calle Petrixol, and Calle Puertaferrisa, of Calle Ancha, streets where people could and did live, and life followed a rhythm that was both as friendly and meticulous as in a haberdashery, the opposite of Barcelona today, full of strangers and inconsiderate people, full of dangers: cars, shameless people, the crush of the metro, thieves, slips, falls, gypsies, drunkards, and worst of all, the exhibitionist, that man with a satanic hard-on who stalks the lonely streets at nightfall; considerations from which, in the mind of that damned little old woman—one of those hybrid bodies, shriveled from virtue, which one always tends to consider an individual due more to periodic secretions of humors than, as when she was younger, because of her menstruation or periods as they are called—Nuria and Raúl would surely not escape, doubtless judged even more severely, if possible, by the appraiser, whose way of looking at Nuria through his blonde eyelashes, ironic, condescending, in the confessional-like intimacy of the pledge booth, evinced his conviction that the operation of pawning a handful of jewelry from a rich girl—lockets, bracelets, earrings, her watch—was nothing but the fatal invoice of evaporated extravagance and nocturnal pleasures, an impression that Nuria uselessly strove to dissipate with her chatter, from an excitement so excessive and unjustified that it could even make the appraiser presume that the girl standing in front of him found herself on the verge of prostitution, occasional prostitution, who knows if impelled by her silent companion, her boyfriend, her gigolo, surely. A wounding prefiguration and a cruel replica of the image that, soon thereafter, in the café on Plaza San Jaime, they themselves, Raúl and Nuria, might have conjured up about the infirm old couple sitting at a nearby table: she, a woman with her hair so lacquered as to appear synthetic fiber, who looked hard and affluent, a characteristic of the moral dominion that economic superiority instills in nations as well as people; he, equally mature and no less conscious than she about what the role of money means, including, in the terrain of erotic relationships, the inferiority that comes from not having it, a lucid comprehension that transpires not only from its tidy presence—that obligatory pulchritude of one who no longer has any presentable clothes to wear—but rather, above all, of the somewhat strained deference of its treatment—the numbness of the offended dignity—as well as his outdated manners, the emphasis with which he removed his sunglasses, for example, or the smirk, more smirk than smile, of his mouth, bitter tics and a correctness maintained beyond all humiliation, beyond all suffering; the desolate correctness of the man who knows how to fit in or, more simply, of the silly idiot.

They had walked into the café as if buoyed by the euphoria and comfort implied by finding themselves suddenly liberated from the most immediate economic urgencies, under that impulse of wanting to go out somewhere right away, to recap, before that very recapitulation begins to overshadow the initial and hurried bewilderment of the celebration, before an approximate reckoning of their small debts against the four thousand pesetas they had just been paid made them see that, in fact, once they'd paid back all the loans, their situation wouldn't be much more liberated than before pawning Nuria's jewels, that they'd have enough left over, so to speak, to just barely pay for the coffee they were drinking, slowly quieting down and hostile again, in sharp contrast to the lively movement of the café, its customers, in general, working in the nearby office buildings, a constant turnover and renewal of clientele, dynamic, efficient, people habituated to a different rhythm of life, to a measured and organized schedule, constantly working to accomplish real tasks; people whose mere presence usually accentuates the stifling sensation of marginalization and abnormality of one's life, uncertain, almost parasitic, although the ease and fluency of their comportment remains rooted, for any reflective spirit, in the senseless and irresponsible confidence of those who go through the world ignoring the fact that man is not a rational being composed of body and soul. How to not feel it somehow wrong—a disordered life, secrecy, problematic love affairs, economic difficulties, unrealized creative anxieties, sordid legal activities, abortions, pawning one's goods—to a certain point, or better, in a certain way, when facing the physical and moral health of a person, let's take, for example, a woman like this one, a woman around thirty years old, Catalan beyond the shadow of a doubt, who drinks her quick cup of coffee with a friend or an office coworker at the next table; wrong and minimized when faced with the multiplicity of plans with which, fully confident, one is capable of simultaneously coping? A woman with the luxuriant vivacity and serene aplomb that are the fruit of an organism in perfect working order: a perfectly regular menstrual cycle, as well as in the various phases of the digestive process, impeccable neuro-vegetative nervous system, complete psychic equilibrium; a woman of vigorous complexion and athletic aspect, tanned, with the healthy bronze skin that comes from skiing, agile gestures and a harmonious laugh, lesbian lips, an equally efficient personal secretary of some company division head, probably, as she is a housewife and helpful mother of her family at home and a punctual adulteress in her private life, without any of all that getting in the way for her—coffee finished, leaning back in her seat, enveloped in the smoke of her cigarette—to also resort on more than one occasion to the studied and lilting laugh of a woman who knows herself ogled by a libertine. Because it was on her, undoubtedly, that the crapulous man was focusing his attention, his staring eyes encircled by deep purple bags, full of libidinous designs, on her and not her friend at the table, against what one might think at first, in spite of being the friend of one of those women—not necessarily mature—who, whether it be due to a certain lassitude in her features, or her facial hue, with shades of mauve and brown, or especially, perhaps the deep shadows of her pupils, tend to suggest to us, or better, to incite us, to practice with them all kinds of perversions; with her, the Catalan woman, and not with her friend of uncertain origin and lascivious appearance, on the Catalan woman—family mother and some business manager's secretary—because at first glance you might well think the crapulous man was ogling the other woman, trying to establish between them both a fluent affinity, an understanding of depravity, it would be not only hasty but totally erroneous to exclude the possibility that it was justly her, the Catalan woman, the secretary and mother, who constituted his true objective, precisely for the reason of her fresh naturalness, of her juicy constitution, a choice that did credit to the young libertine, on the other hand, at the same time, who, as a man of discerning taste, as a penetrating connoisseur of the profundities of the feminine soul as well as their bodies, knows well what a woman like the Catalan secretary can manage to give of herself, the sweet, select words of which she is capable, the inspired expressions warmed by the cloying accent, the passionate phrases of love she manages to employ and that nobody imagines, neither in her family environment nor in her work relations; her fervent, feverish form of surrendering herself; the rough sketch of her sex with its full powerful lips. And nevertheless, our secretary and family mother would also be fooling herself if she were to believe that she was the only object of the libertine's desires, of his obsessive, wide-eyed stare; she, yes, it's true, but also and equally the ham sandwich she devoured before her *café corto* and half-smoked cigarette; what's more, it might even be affirmed, for its symbolic value, the most important thing for him in these moments was the ham sandwich, the most fully realized expression of the uncertain thoughts and feelings which seized him, of his most imperious appetites, to eat, drink, smoke, and fuck that woman with his eyes, all at the same time, domi-nating everything, devouring everything all at once, his mind flying a thousand miles a second, his calculations intermingled with lustful images and insatiable designs, the typical stamp of the person who is a prisoner of the cannibalistic reaction usually triggered by obtaining some unexpected or highly anticipated income, the product of bribery, inheritance, speculation, or mendacity, a reaction on the other hand that extended to his two companions, to their ravenous ferocity: not eating but clutching the sandwich, sinking their teeth into it, swallowing it, wolfing it down in the blink of an eye, before you could say Jesus-Christ-on-a-bicycle, just as the big fish swallows the little fish, absorbing it with all its projections and emblematic values, just as in primitive tribes the hunters devoured their prisoner's hearts, while they commented on the favorable impression—to judge by their voracity—of the interview that they just completed in some office in the City Hall or in the Administrative Council, or in the Savings Bank, an impression that, for being true, might well constitute the departure point for an excellent business deal from which everyone would benefit, gaining their percentage, their commission, the avid young libertine, his associate, the intermediary and even the one most conspicuously absent, the personality that just received them, the one bestowing the favor, all with the thought already filling their mouths, ready, willing, and able to seize their part just as they now clutch their sandwich, as if it were really two handfuls of ass, even though the projects differed according to each one's personal case, more ambitious, no doubt, in the young libertine, like in the player who wants to take advantage of the run of luck or the strategy that exploits with uninterrupted pressures the victory obtained, more ambitious and also more imaginative, illuminated by the flashes of the color polaroids that they show to one for whom money opens all doors, even more seductive women, luxury hotels, ferocious pleasures, while their associate, an older man and, especially, more broken by life, with all the look of bearing, more than anything, along with his knowledge of bureaucratic mechanisms, the experience of repeated disasters, gave himself over to obviously more modest or realistic calculations, made difficult by the effort of pretending to listen with reverent interest to the story that the third man in the group was telling, the relational element, the intermediary, for whom all that formed part of his daily routine, as very probably the same story that he was telling, about some woman, whom he almost seduced last weekend, something scarcely believable in a man his age, but that the other, the associate, the poor devil, pretended to follow as if awaiting the outcome, taking refuge in polite deference—compensating for the manifest lack of attention from their young, vicious associate—the expression of a man somewhere between amused and admiring, almost incredulous, only betrayed in his calculations by the evident vacuity or absence that veiled his gaze, considerations relating to the bills he might be able to pay and to the diverse debts no longer possible to refinance that he might be able to liquidate with the happy ending of all that, the gravy train that was at last about to come his way, under the auspices of the comfortable atmosphere of a coffee shop and the fair tone of the conversation, now centered on the singular beauty of a certain landscape, the object of the business deal in question, possibly, with that peculiar satisfaction that usually comes from the possibility of allying business and beauty, propitious for the revelation of an impetuous lyricism and of some elevated sentiments, unsuspected, even, by the very person who formulates them, the industrialist who decides to personally baptize a product ready to be launched, for example, a new shampoo, for example, that might well be called Sunbreeze, a name both poetic and catchy. Then, the conventional dispute about picking up the tab, the gestures of pulling out the wallet as if it were a revolver and, as if it really were a revolver, to silence anyone else, to beat them to it, even the youngest man, faster and more confident or with better reflexes, the eager one, the libertine, still cleaning his gums with his tongue, as he pulled out a wad of green bills in a silver money clip and peeled one off, making it crackle between his fingers and setting it on the table, sanctioning his valor with a swipe of his hand, with the characteristic imperiousness, impatience, and inclement hardness of the new generations that act so aggressively, less interested in respecting the rules of the game—for them pure formality or farcical ritual—than in hunting for their opportunity, always more combative, more contentious, more implacable, climbing the ladder no matter who topples off, surprised only by the fact that the powerful person whom they intend to supplicate in order to prosper in their shadow or overleap their corpse, perhaps for having been softened before hardened by the years of fighting, perhaps for having enjoyed the relaxation and dissipation his fortune permits him, seems to have scruples, however much of a shark he might be, about making others feel, with maximum tangibility, the true weight of his power, something incomprehensible for those who harbor some hidden aggressive feelings similar to those of that erudite young man who, upon demarcating his area of research, manages to specialize in some minor question of secondary importance, important enough to bring him a certain notoriety, but not enough to make any of his professors nervous, thus assuring himself the surprise factor when the moment arrives for him to suddenly attack one of those teachers' positions, conquering them one by one and—the luck of the dispossessed in his hands—permit himself the pleasure of personally delivering the coup de grace; some methods and a disposition which, nowadays, for being widespread, seem to flatly deny the alarmist lamentations and doomsday prophecies of so many people who blame today's youth for indulging in dissolute and hedonistic behavior even while spouting excessive idealism, forgetting that similar judgments are usually repeated in each generation when they begin to see their successors popping up on the horizon, however much, in practice, the facts are quick to demonstrate the contrary. What other image, for example, should Plans's men have formed of Raúl? What role could they attribute to him, other than the well-connected young lawyer with aptitude and ambitions, involved with fast deals and speculative insurance policies (patently exclusive, for construction, licenses, and public works projects), those types of deals in which everything is a question of perspective, determination, and helpful godfathers?

The power of words to assign, their faculty of stereotyping daily life, of interposing themselves between one and others, between one and oneself; like the shy man who, in his dealings with the man on the street, in order to mask his difficulty with communication, resorts to jokes he's heard others use on similar occasions, but when voiced by him, possibly for lack of aplomb or knack or graceful touch, perhaps for some defect of exposition or nuance, run the risk of being misinterpreted and even of gravely offending their interlocutor, thus Raúl felt inhibited and uncomfortable when he saw himself obliged to respond, even though only externally, to whichever one of the roles he might have to play as the circumstances demanded. At university, for example, the professor of some subject that did not interest him in the least, carefully watching as examinations progressed, moving kindly and silently through the lecture hall, exchanging comments in a low voice—obvious remarks—with the department chair, to give a minimum of verisimilitude to all that; bumping into his colleagues, in the hallways, on the patios, in the vestibule, the need to adopt a decisive step, without him showing any sign that he's already seen them coming toward him from an opposite direction, while preparing to offer some greeting at once original and conventional, adequate for the type of relationship uniting them, and then, almost as if he'd just noticed them, a flickering look of surprise, a smile of intelligence, his words ready all in a hurry. Or when, all at once, when Señor Rivas died, he suddenly became Nuria's fiancé, and the people who came to pay their respects at the widow's house always found the moment to ask him, between introductions and condolences and words about what a terrible thing it was, if they had been engaged for very long, and he, as if urged on by some immediate problem that required his attention, said excuse me a moment, and in the next room sidled up to any group too focused on the conversation in progress to notice his presence, or he cut short any specific question by saying something to one of the servants, or he simply locked himself in the bathroom to smoke a cigarette. The same sensation of strangeness, or better yet, of being wrong, that with no less intensity he had experienced when he still belonged to the university committee and Escala had taken him to a meeting of the labor committee, introducing him as the comrade responsible for the university sector, who's going to explain to you all in a few words some details about the struggle underway and its political prospects. What could he tell the comrades on the labor committee, not about the struggle and its prospects, but about the university itself? What could he tell them? That he had studied law only to please his father? That, from among every career, the law was the one he most detested and that this was precisely the reason why he'd chosen it, to distance himself to the maximum from university life, properly speaking? That extracurricular activities occurring in this sector, meaning political activities, were far from what Raúl had imagined when he joined the party? That the prospects for the kind of fight like the one that was unfolding were rather poor, and the possibilities for improvement within the current policy were scarce. What could he tell them without avoiding saying what was expected of him to say and, at the same time, without leaving out the truth, without either disconcerting or confounding those difficult and attentive expressions that contemplated him like something exotic, at once mistrustful—with the instinctual mistrust of any collective toward some outsider—and comforted, under the spell of the moral support which the confirmation that its principles and norms of conduct are in force, even beyond its own confines, usually gives to the members of one of those collectives? How to explain to them, in a few words and in these circumstances, the ideological conflicts under consideration in the heart of the university sector, to specify for them the doctrinal differences that split the students into diverse factions, to make them see that, with everything and against what it might seem as first glance, that situation represented progress in contrast to the university of some years ago, the university that he was still getting to know, a university defined by the uncultivated professors and the students' inane stagnation, an environment that by virtue of its total and crystal clear vacuity about the quite-obvious necessity of political compromise, of taking action, of integrating with the only organization that, precisely to the degree to which it was considered a negation of all currently active values, was revealed as the only way out, namely, the Communist Party, the Communist Party, period, without further distinctions or subtleties, something, doubtless, much more clear, more natural, more sane, from the point of view of what his audience expected to hear? The university of years past: not attending to the education of the student body; keeping it in line. Not education; blatant taming. No vocational community between teachers and those they teach; hostility, confrontation, the law of force-feeding, swallow it like a dog, only the strong survive. No guidance; spare the rod, spoil the child. No exercising of faculties; police detection of the weak spot, of the tender foot, of the Achilles tendon. No willingness to encourage; despotic imposition of farragoes selected for their capacity to inhibit, to stultify, to exhaust. No, nothing in it that could evoke the serene climate of invitation to the study of a prototypical Central European university, for example, no point of contact, either, with Anglo-Saxon education, directed not only toward the assimilation of knowledge and understanding but also, as already mentioned, forging useful members of society, and more particularly, to the United Kingdom; no, nothing in common with all that in the postwar Spanish university, expeditionary center of academic titles which students attend not so much for vocation or their own desire as because their parents' social status requires it, and where the only thing that mattered in their university career was getting the degree, especially a law degree, because, as everyone knows, the law is the career with the most opportunities for success, the one that most enables you to defend yourself, to get to know what life is like, trust, emphyteusis, usufruct, usury, a pact in any case, my son, legal concept or legal fiction. A degree that, ultimately, guarantees the gradual familiarization of one who aspires to obtain it, throughout the course of studies, with the jargon of the discipline, almost equal to how one becomes familiar with the habits inherited from the traditional student picaresque, between classes, from the patio to the bar, and some healthily roguish rigamarole, someone at the lake, for example, an old porter or some real posh snob or some real country bumpkin, and the initiation into bar crawling, learning drinking songs, books pawned for drink money, etcetera, and the episodic visits to brothels, and the always more accessible recourse to jerking off, and the timid attempts at rape on some specific female classmate, or simply a girl that I know is good for a bit of fun and whom you can be sure to get into bed, attempts generally resulting in the sacrament of matrimony, according to the most canonical rites, in the end, youthful matters, phases they must pass through that come and go, giving way to a growing sense of responsibility, of the which the formalization of the courtship is only one of its symptoms, one of so many facets of desire that our young man experiences from settling down once and for all, of getting on the right track, of forgetting the madnesses he's committed or that he was on the verge of committing, and that's how his anxieties begin to be reflected in his relationship with the reality of life, in the sudden interest he displays for the distinction existent between matrimonial property assets and extra-dotal property, or in the difference existing between legal action and court ruling, or between claim and accusation, or in the determination of concepts such as corruption or formal flaws, and even a certain sense of nostalgia—almost improper for his age—toward institutions such as censuses and rights of agnation and pre-nuptial agreements, today on the verge of disappearing, for the sake of what's practical and to the detriment of what, for its long-standing, deserves to form part of our historic patrimony, a nostalgia which, abounding in the diverse opposite extremes, confirms the continued habituation to a language, the progressive command of a cryptic and esoteric lexicon, imputable, like that of oracles, to the need to duly appraise his future emoluments. Do you remember? Fortuny asked. So different from the university these days. And what still needs to change. Imagine, when in Spain there are even only formal freedoms like in Italy or in France, imagine what prestige for the party when you're the Sociology Department chair and I'm the chair of Labor Law, for example, examples and reflections—while Raúl wondered what sociology really was—of a suspected parallelism or, more precisely, coincidence, regarding Escala's allusions about the role of the true revolutionary intellectual, approximately around the same dates when Raúl moved from the university committee to the intellectual cell, meaning, from being a leader of the former to a low man in the latter, and Escala accompanied him to the first meeting of the cell, and in his statement—without any apparent justification, with the irritated aggression with which the forty-something man usually receives young initiates, whatever their background, directly proportional, in general, to the degree of weakness belonging to the sex—criticized the posture of those who considered militancy something similar to the military, a moral obligation which one fulfills for a determined period of time and then leaves in the hands of younger followers, as if political activity and the risks it brings had something to do with age, or as if its mission would be concluded when the dictatorship was defeated, as if in a transitional regime to a parliamentary democracy—ideal conditions for the struggle, according to Lenin—there might no longer be any reason to keep fighting, as if precisely when they came to power they weren't more necessary than ever, as much for the effort that the construction of socialism represents because it would be very naive to suppose that the enemy will give up, that it won't still be there, watching, waiting to take revenge, and you'll have to remain vigilant and our ranks will demand, more than in any other moment, leaders willing to occupy their positions of maximum responsibility, political leaders borne not by personal ambitions, like bourgeois politicians, but by the legitimate aspiration to contribute to the socialist cause according to each person's exact capacity. Previously, while walking to the meeting place, rather, he had touched on some practical considerations: the convenience of Raúl changing his current code name—Daniel—for some other—Luis?—in order to sever any organic ties between university students and intellectuals, to erase all tracks that might establish connections to the past, so that the police might never be able to relate the former Daniel to the present Luis, the Luis who was going to form part of the propaganda arm of the intellectual committee, in direct connection with Blanch, secretary of the cell and the comrade responsible for the committee's propaganda. There was no drawback, however, to the fact that the cell members utilized among themselves their own names, because there's nothing less suspicious than what's natural, and nothing more natural than a doctor, a lawyer, and a graduate student of philosophy being friends and getting together for some conversation now and then. But for any other member of the various cells composing the intellectual committee, for any other kind of contact, stick to the new name, forget the old one, and do not involve under any circumstances any of his old university comrades in his current activities and, much less, guys like Lucas, Esteve, all those who, luckily, have been getting off the bus, so that none of these pseudo-intellectuals would even imagine that you're now part of the secretariat of propaganda of the intellectuals' committee of Barcelona, where there really are some serious leaders, scientists, researchers, economists, professionals, artists, prestigious people recognized in their respective fields, whose membership in the party is only kept secret for basic reasons of security. Of your companions in the cell, Ruiz is perhaps the one with the most penetrating analytical powers, but Blanch has a greater capacity for synthesis.

They met at Blanch's apartment on Saturday afternoons and his wife served them sherry and pastries. They had agreed to first dispatch with the practical problems: to reorganize the system of courier-houses in anticipation of receiving suitcases with false-bottoms containing printed matter; buying a typewriter that would be used exclusively to bang out the clichés for the mimeograph; to assign to each cell in the group a specific number of names and addresses of the people to whom to send propaganda through the mail, with the goal of diversifying as much as possible the characteristics of the envelopes to be used and—still more important—the mailboxes and the hours of distribution; the darkroom materials necessary to be able to send to Paris the negatives of the photocopied reports and documents in place of the originals; quotas and economic support from sympathizers, etcetera. Later, time permitting, a period of ideological discussion, starting with the party's latest publications or some classic text: Raúl proposed *The Holy Family*, but Blanch said the *Manifesto* was preferable because, in fact, it had it all. Ruiz said very little, at times distracted, perhaps, choosing some pastry from the tray, that he ended up choosing almost furtively; also, his hands were sweating, and he was skinny, keen, myopic, with a miserly smirk on his face like a witch. In general, however, when they finished with the practical questions, they limited themselves to discussing current national or international politics, and Blanch complained loudly about how poorly the Spanish National Welfare Institute organized medical care throughout the country. Look, these people are starting to have a lot of nerve, he was saying, and he stroked his mustache. He pulled out a copy of *Paris-Match* with a report about Spain. I keep it for the pictures and graphics, quite good, frankly; but the writing is so reactionary that it seems subsidized by the Ministry of Information and Tourism. They don't see—or they don't want to see—typical Spanish culture beyond what's folkloric; it's unbelievable. And the struggle of the Spanish people, what about that? What Marxism is lacking is a metaphysics, said Rois, then blushed. Tirant stroked his mustache. It's interesting, he said. He talked about his seventeen years of militancy in various places in Spain, and the eleven manhunts he'd escaped before settling in Barcelona, always escaping just in time; he spoke slowly, his gaze turned inwards, with a sort of contagious somnolence. A single careless mistake can expose and ruin the work of several years. And then, back to square one. That's why I consider that all the precautions we take are really, after all, very little work; you've got to know how to protect yourself so that, when Franco does fall, the party's future will depend on the militants who are free and operating, not the ones in jail. The fellow from Corella nodded, or maybe he'd only just swallowed a too-hastily chewed pastry. In any case, with all evidence, the objective of that exchange of opinions about political reality was really nothing more than a search for examples or theoretical proofs, to reaffirm one's own convictions, to hear each other reaffirming them and—Cheer up!—all taking heart together, without raising doubts, without quibbles or posing possible discrepancies with respect to the interpretations of the facts obviously intuited as ideologically correct and, in such a concept, approved beforehand in a climate where the critical insistence remained tacitly out of place, for reasons similar to those that in a community of neighbors, for example, social harmony would become impossible if each person did not respect the privacy of others, if they did not courteously greet one another when passing in the building vestibule, each one pretending to ignore everything he knows about the other, controlling as much as possible, depending on the case in question, the permissible experience of commiseration or joy, an implicit pact of good neighborliness, which, if not observed, would make the simple fact of living together unbearable, for having to share the same staircase, the same elevator with the other tenants of a building where everyone ends up knowing everything, everybody's shady secrets, the solutions and arrangements that life demands, that circumstances impose, the time that passes, things like Señor Sancho, at his age and with his ailments, he still overcomes them to keep the proprietress of a haberdashery happy, or how much the Valls family on the fifth floor, apartment number two, owe to the fact that she knew how to carry on an affair with the office manager at her husband's place of employment, or that Pepito, the porter lady's son, had been gang-raped, and all the way from the patio you could hear his parents wailing when they discovered the hemorrhage, matters which no one mentions in the presence of the people directly affected and which, in the supposition that, in some exceptional fit of rage or hysterical aggression, someone would dare to violate the unspoken rule, such an indiscretion would be relentlessly, unanimously, and harshly criticized by the neighbors. And just as the psychopath with a persecution complex finds that the current events alone usually offer him an especially wide base for his obsession, so Tirant and Curial found that a daily reading of the newspaper proffered sufficient proofs about the decline of capitalism in the face of the great triumphs of socialism, whose setbacks, unlike those experienced by the capitalist world, only constituted the requisite tactical rough patches along the road toward victory, in the same way that all orthographic depression is an inevitable prelude before reaching some new height, some new peak, in a way that, by extension, the internal contradictions and conflicts of the socialist camp appeared barely a fabulation or

phantasmagoria unworthy of consideration. But the fact that,
even in a wider cultural context, the relationship of forces was
equally favorable: Pavlov, the Curies, Yuri Gagarin, and, in the
novel, Gorky, Sholokhov, Asturias, and, above all, Howard Fast;
and Balzac himself, although personally reactionary, his professional honor—as well observed by Marx—made him faithfully
reflect the contradictions belonging to the society of his era; and
poets like Neruda and Nicolás Guillén and Aragon and Miguel
Hernández and Nazim Hikmet and Blas and the voice of Paul
Robeson, social and good, a kind of father figure, or the vigorous
popular strength of the Soviet choirs, or the songs of Atahualpa
Yupanqui, with more spirit, especially apt, in the university
environments, to propitiate one's erotic maneuvers when trying
to get closer to some female comrade, after all there's nothing
bad about free love between comrades, on the contrary, it's
almost a moral obligation, one more way of fighting against
bourgeois conventions, although these aspects might be out of
place here for both Tirant, prudent father and family man, and
Curial, due to his motives for precision, in this case, evidently
as laborious as unnecessary. And was this last extreme a consequence of both men's common extraction, of their undeniable
membership in the petite bourgeoisie, that social class which if
it has some predominant characteristic trait it's decency, a character trait that remains imprinted even, or more strongly,
especially, when one becomes a communist, either from family
tradition, like with Tirant, or as a reaction to an opposite reaction, like with Curial, ex-seminarian before earning his master's
degree in philosophy, a professor of French and Latin and a party
militant? A consequence of that but not the only cause, by itself
insufficient to explain any further the subconscious's complex
mechanisms, let alone the subject's mere comportment amid
life's stimuli, given that, like the young man's ostentatiously conservative attitudes, not really a reflection of any political position,
both because the respect for formulas such a position supposes
and an unwritten but customary code of behavior safeguard the
distance from people that his shy and fearful nature needs, thus
in Tirant and Curial their militancy was not only a hereditary

question nor one of family or social environment but also, and above all, a self-defense against the snares and wiles of the surrounding world. Of course, the same dynamic of their choice, of the compromise acquired, frequently led them to situations rather unlike their temperaments, and like that adolescent whose static narcissism, craftily fostered by some pederast's vulpine wiles, is seen irremediably destined to move from disquisitions on friendship, love, and beauty, on Plato and Gide, to the actual events. Thus, similarly, Tirant and Curial occasionally found themselves confronting the need to realize, in the terrain of praxis, the result of their theoretical conclusions, to participate in some pro-amnesty demonstration, for example, or at least some attempt at a public demonstration, a case which seemed to promise solidarity, that the whole thing was finally going to be something more than parading in the sanctioned zone indicated in the official announcement, in uneasy search, more than for familiar faces, for people looking like students or workers, waiting for the moment when the cohesive nucleus of shouts and movement would coalesce. But, even on the verge of such extreme situations, there were moments when the tough demands of the clandestine struggle made Tirant and Curial feel, if not fully spent then, at least definitely, overwhelmed by the responsibility of the task, activities such as gathering signatures for a document protesting academic sanctions, a document that had to be set in motion and circulated through the various intellectual circles with maximum urgency, in order that its publication serve as a sounding board for the new actions predicted by the university committee, which had to be concluded by the coming December 21, taking advantage of the traditional public laxity with which students celebrate the feast day of their patron saint, Thomas Aquinas. I'm afraid they'll have to make some decision, said Tirant. And suddenly, with Curial's complicit silence, he turned to face Raúl: Luis, would you be able to take charge of preparing the document's outline, and of writing it? I understand that you've had some practice.

One of Escala's typical initiatives was to take full advantage of the public actions organized to coincide with the Feast of

Thomas Aquinas. To this end he'd given Tirant specific instructions during a meeting also attended by a comrade from the university committee leadership; from what Raúl could deduce this comrade was Fortuny. He also guessed something more: the significance of his own absence from a meeting to which, in his former role as student committee director and current member of the group of intellectuals, he would normally be invited, especially because as a professor he remained connected to the university. The fact that he'd had to learn about the plan secondhand—as well as previous events: Obregón's arrest followed by a whole string of subsequent arrests, and Escala's and Fortuny's disappearance along with most of the university militants—all thanks to a momentary lapse by Tirant, a Tirant possessed by despair. Also, the way Escala admonished Raúl when the latter was transferred to the intellectual committee, so strongly highlighted by the fact that they'd had no contact since then, and Escala's insistence that Raúl sever all ties—organic and even nonorganic links—with his old companions acquired new shades of meaning, along with the fact that Fortuny had replaced him on the university committee without any forewarning: all symptoms, in short, that now seemed like déjà vu, like something already observed in other times, in relation to other people, an experience that permitted him to have similarly perfect awareness that the elements perceived by him constituted only a disconnected, fragmentary, and partial image of an average incident, which always turns out much worse if it is related by one of the individuals directly implicated than if it is related by some third party, an objectively-positioned spectator who contemplates it in its fullness and, above all, from outside the situation. The same process as with Federico, as with Adolfo, this repetition doubtless played an important role of developing proofs in the charges brought against Raúl, whose involvement in the present situation pointed to a previous involvement, along with the additional, and aggravating basic fact of the friendly relationship that the three had maintained between them; as in the case of Esteve and the case of Lucas, by now it probably took no more than some higher-level leader, Escala perhaps, making an incidental comment to some member of the university group, one of the worst of them is Daniel, for the censure to begin circulating, illustrating with an accumulation of different characteristic elements, less political than moral, the people he dealt with, his friends, Nuria, their various relationships, their nocturnal outings, really any fact equivalent to what, at that time, could demonstrate passion for playing games, for what the poker games, with elevated bets, revealed in Federico, or Adolfo's pet name for Aurora, his concubine, as he called her—an expression of anonymous origin which immediately, and somewhat surprisingly, caught on, based on the fact that she and Adolfo had lived together. Something like that, with full confidence, must have been enough for Garrido to begin phoning him less frequently, and the Corberó girl stopped looking for him on the patio in the School of Humanities, and it didn't take long for what Iglesias had said to reach him, and what Terrades had said, too, opinions and testimonies all the more decisive for being all the more vague and conceptual, how much the better they characterize the disaster of personality that cannot stop accompanying a chosen political position that is subjective and erroneous, a position that for whomever maintains it becomes the cause of their progressive distance from the correct line of thinking, producing at the same time around him, in the heart of the cell to which he belongs and like a corresponding logic, a climate of emptiness, which the individual's involuntary or premeditated lack of initiative and enthusiasm only accentuates and extends, meetings celebrated without his presence, in part because he doesn't ask, because he doesn't try to stay informed, in part because he is not advised, absences which, when he does finally attend, make him feel not only marginalized and estranged from the topic being discussed, but also useless and extraneous, in his ignorance of the precise new details for which his appraisals deserve to be considered, inadequate to face up to his previous responsibilities, gradually replaced by some other rising star, someone named Ferrán, for example. The first indication that the shock wave had already reached the upper levels: his final, disastrous trip to Paris, shortly before summer—his encounter with Nuria, his wish that

she had not come to meet him, that she leave him in peace for
once, and the climate of tension, of reticent reserve, of poorly
contained verbal violence, and the erotic frustration, and the rain
and the cold, unseasonal, and the goddamned proliferation of
the springtime, and the tulips in the Tuileries punished by the
downpour, and the tender and slippery fallen leaves, and the
appearance of Pírez, the typical jinxed idiot, a Canary Islander
from the Cité Universitaire who came recommended by Guillén
and who wanted to return to Spain, to Barcelona, to foment the
true revolution, and needed them to find him a job, as a laborer,
of course—when he went to the scheduled meeting at the speci-
fied address, and reaching the same house from the other times,
near Bastille, he ran into Escala and some unknown comrade,
some guy who looked halfway between a junior member and a
Russian violinist, and despite showing himself attentive and even
vigilant to the meeting's progress, Raúl almost didn't open his
lips, a trip he needn't have packed for—even the coffee they
offered them seemed, this time, made of old, used coffee grounds.
Paperwork hassles were quickly dispatched, almost by way of
preamble or a courteous, preliminary sounding-out of what it
was clearly all about, about the real reason for his presence there:
to proceed to what had brought them there: a vigorous ideological cleansing. Everyone incapable of perceiving the real
verification of our ideology in praxis, who does not perceive it
or who puts it in doubt, is so because his class conditioning
prevents it. Because our ideology's criterion for rationality is
determined by the individual's concrete place in society, by his
class conditioning. Thus a displacement, however small, of that
conditioning, a simple change in his way of life, necessarily
impacts his appreciation of our political praxis, to end in the
long run, fatally, by opening cracks in the ideological plane,
because the dialectical relationship between theory and praxis is
of such a nature that all deviation from a certain aspect of the
party line, for example, always ends up calling into question the
very essence of Marxist ideology. These are the well-known positions of so-called non-communist Marxists, of the communists
without a party, of the communists creating another communist

party, of those who think the time has come to go beyond Marx, or to revise him, or to update him, or to attend more to the letter than to the spirit of his texts, or to separate him from Lenin's ideas, his historical consequence; of those who invoke the pre-marxist Marx, of the renegades, of the defects, of the revisionists, and also of the mechanistic and dogmatic thinkers. They want to divide the indivisible, what constitutes a whole and which must be taken as such, hypercritical positions generally belonging to intellectuals who consider themselves disappointed or disillusioned for not having found in the party what they could not find: lingering traces of bourgeois idealism. And the thing is, even treating of objective realities, these things always contain, at bottom, some preexisting bias, almost a question of faith, of believing or not believing, so that for a mind that might not be dialectical and materialistic, for a mind that is metaphysical and speculative, socialist constructions will refute the practical results of our ideology, the palpable proofs that it offers the whole world, and even contradict any idea those minds had formed about the realization of communist theory. Due to their incapacity of seeing what is evident they are truly sick minds, but history shows us that such sick people can turn out to become even more dangerous elements for the party than the avowed anti-communists, given that, availing themselves of skillfully manipulated pseudo-Marxist arguments, they can sow confusion and even division within our ranks, undermine the confidence of the militants in the political line, in the leadership that has fashioned that political line of thinking, in the party's role as the vanguard of the working class and even in the role of the working class itself and, finally, in our capacity to transform the world and create the new society, the new man; all considerations in some way personal though not animated by any particular animosity against Raúl, but rather, the expression of an opinion little less than unanimous in the party base, the faithful image of what a thinker like Floreal's or Leo's father might have formulated thereon, of having relied on the ideological baggage and a command of terminology like Escala's, in line with a vision of the militant, of the party and the general march forward of the world, whose most adequate plastic representation would be one of those American musical comedies from the forties, one of those scenes in which a certain couple steps out to dance in some nondescript place, a banquet hall, the street, an ocean liner, and then another couple steps out and another, and little by little everyone present follows their lead and they all join in the dance, until stepping together in a single choreographically perfect body, similar in a way to how, according to that vision or conception of the world, they go on overcoming contradictions and harmonizing the interests of the popular forces, thus slowly but surely establishing the bases not only of the new society and the new man but also the true beginning of history.

Aristocratism? Adventurism? Petit bourgeois leftism? Well I think they're right; in fact, it's the truth. Look how I, unconsciously, instinctively, chose a field name that couldn't be more petit bourgeois: Esteve. And you chose a prophet's name, and Adolfo chose an evangelist's. On the other hand, the one that's really good is the one Penyafort picked: Ferrán, the name of a Catholic king. And Escala's is the most graphic: it suits him much better than any nickname you might hang on him, like when we called him Mr. H, or Zorro or just Z, like they call him now. What we should really do is all get psychoanalyzed, like the friars from Cuernavaca. Clarify the compulsion that drove each one to join the party. To talk about a guilty conscience is pure lyricism, and about awareness or about rational conclusions, you tell me. But it was he himself who said it when Fortuny was still sometimes coming over to Adolfo's house, and perhaps for that very reason, because Raimundo Fortuny de Penyafort was present and he without any doubt wrote down the things he said, even though only part of it, too calculated an effect to believe that it wasn't Federico's intention that they also reach Escala's ears, that bit about offering Escala concrete examples with which to illustrate his prophecies, his judgments, to be accused, for example, of having said this and that, at first as if in jest, a character soon dispensed with, not only because of what he was really saying, but even by the way of saying it, by the very rigor of the argumentation, exposed according to an almost Ciceronian

scheme of articulation, that might be summed up in the following propositions: Western communist parties, conscious of the
fact that their numbers alone are insufficient to foment the
revolution, accept the so-called democratic alternative, namely,
the parliamentary game that comes with a bourgeois democracy;
upon accepting the rules of the game of a bourgeois democracy,
Western communist parties can only defend the interests of the
working class by setting up, through labor unions, an efficient
mechanism of protest; the working class, certain economic
demands satisfied, tends to be assimilated by the system, within
whose boundaries the worker hopes to achieve individual eman-
cipation, to rise above his working-class condition; in
consequence, the wider the spread of demands satisfied thanks
to union action, the lesser the real interest of the working class
to subvert the established order through violent revolution,
respecting which, as happens in countries with a higher standard
of living, the workers can end up becoming the strongest oppo-
nents of communism. That, more or less, was what Federico said
or meant to say, almost without stammering or loosing a laugh,
calmly, although not without anguish in his shining eyes, like a
horse in full fury, and probably for that reason, for the unusual
brilliance of his exposition more than for any originality of concept, the sense of sacrilege that had doubtless been planted in
everyone's spirit grew stronger, a sacrilege that might be called
collective to the degree that an evasive silence, of guilty neutral-
ity, was the collective reaction of those present, while Fortuny,
incredulous, about to erupt, unable to detect the sophistry, if in
fact there was any, and for lack of the clamorous and scandalized
refutation he seemed to expect, searched with his eyes for help
at least from Raúl, saying, as if to gain some time, awaiting
reinforcements that were not coming, Raúl's ideological support,
of some intervention that never came, saying, alright, alright,
from a Marxist point of view it's not like that, and Federico, but
from a non-Marxist perspective, yes, and Fortuny, well, this is
all subject to debate, a Fortuny beside himself and confused like
one who thought he was going for a round of golf and, with his
clubs on his back, finds himself on a deer hunt, confused and

perhaps also intimately humiliated, sensible of the lack of prestige represented by the fact that a lawyer and a political leader
like himself did not manage to overturn Federico's argument, of
someone who, objectively considered, was nothing more than a
guy who had left the party just the same as if he had hung up
his career and who, nevertheless, had known how to drag him
into a kind of controversy—not from within, granted—not from
some commonly accepted bases, but from without, questioning
precisely the validity of these bases for which he was not prepared, a situation finally resolved by Pluto, saying that what's
more than doubtful is that stuff about how the proletariat make
better lovers, a literary topic best represented by Lady Chatterley's
love affair with her gardener. At that point, however, they still
didn't really know who Zorro was. It was a bit later, near summer's end, when Federico made his discovery. He'd recognized
his photo in one of those promotional shots, with gilt edging,
that one of the lawyers who worked with his father had hanging
in his office. Younger, but the same man; his name was Salvador
Puig and now, some years after finishing his studies, he was
working in the advertising business. Can you imagine? That's
where he must have learned his craft because it seems that
nobody knows anything about his political activities either at
university or underground. He must be one of those old foxes
who always escape just in time; a true savior always starts with
himself. At the end of the summer, yes; the start of autumn at
the latest. Louis had already left and Adolfo had decided to apply
for the award, and more or less around that time they began to
have dealings with Moragas; better to say: Moragas became a
regular visitor at Adolfo's house. *Los Ángeles*: a novel intended to
ratify Escala, in case he were ever really ostracized, in all his
criticisms and predictions, by providing him with the most conclusive documented proof—clearly an autobiographical tale,
almost a confession—of the scant confidence that he deserves in
general, insofar as political solidarity is concerned, that sector of
bourgeois youth that today, in open—and ideologically incoherent—conflict with their social environment, make the rounds
in a dissipate nighttime life with revolutionary pretensions,

whose marked radicalism only conceals, in most cases, the search for solutions to their personal problems, when not seeking to satisfy unconfessed desires or selfish ambitions, an essential duplicity not avoided, but rather, masochistically highlighted, by the work's very own narrative structure, built from a confluence of diverse thematic threads which, developed through objective technique from different points of view, contrast the insincerity and the self-deception not only in each one of the characters, but even of the novel itself as a literary form. In fact, said Moragas, it turns the reader into another character, into something like a special witness to the falsity of all involved, the characters, the author, of oneself as a reader, *tout le monde triche et tout c'est une grande tricherie.* He wrote quickly in his notebook and turned to look at Adolfo: listen, why don't we focus seriously on the possibility of a film adaptation? Cinema interests me as much as, or more than, the novel, said Adolfo. The same words, the same gestures, and even the same people as before, when they first talked about the manuscript of *Los Ángeles*, literary digressions from which Raúl, irremediably connecting them to his own work, felt completely distant, without any intention of creating an interesting argument, nor of deeply exploring the characters' psychology, nor of being a faithful reflection of society, and what seemed even more serious: without any formal apriorisms nor any kind of pretensions to technical experimentation, all questions which, apart from meaning nothing to him, were disagreeable due to the aggression implied in the no-less-painful fact that they couldn't discuss his work instead, a work which, not being finished, it made no sense to keep writing, and about which the others, in consequence, barely knew anything, an ignorance which, on the other hand, strengthened him and became his principal defense, a field of his own personal reveries, telling himself that not even one of those passersby he encountered, for example, or those regular customers at a secondhand bookshop, had the least suspicion that they were standing next to a future great writer, whose works would perhaps someday be the critical object of their spontaneous intellectual discussions. Henry James? said Moragas while he wrote down the name. I

thought, I don't know why, that he was the author of books like
Gone with the Wind. Federico looked impatient. *Io mi voglio
divertir. Io mi voglio divertir. Io mi voglio divertir.* They had to go
to the Liceo, to Moragases' private box, except the Plutos, who
said they weren't in the mood, but they agreed to meet back up
later at the theater entrance, to pop around to a few of the regular spots, surely until closing time. What was the most important
element among so many that influenced Moragases' sudden
intrusion into Adolfo and Aurora's life or, better yet, into the
dependent situation in which he had placed himself in his
relationship with them, apart from the availability and free time
a man of wealth and leisure like himself enjoyed, calling them
or seeing them every day, inviting them everywhere, invariably
accompanying them on their nighttime outings? A sincere interest on Adolfo's part? The snobbish satisfaction belonging to a
man in his position and with artistic anxieties about dealing with
a writer? The suggestion that he could exercise over him a way
of life deliberately in conflict with the ruling principles of the
social class to which they belonged? Something like all that, no
doubt, but in the first place, probably, the attraction that for
some people—among which, he, Manolo Moragas, found himself—seemed to irradiate Adolfo's personality, an attraction based
not so much on what Adolfo did or said as much as what he
didn't do or what he left unsaid, what he kept quiet about, his
well-chosen silences, a kind of attraction similar to what drives
the majority of women to prefer the indecisive or ambiguous
man over the typical macho, to the degree to which he thus
removes himself from the obligatory sexual response convention-
ally attributed to him, about which she has the intimate
conviction of not measuring up to, about which the effort to
simulate that she does becomes excessive, in order to fit into her
role of wild female, of manipulable object, of shock absorber or
wind-up toy, not so much from a secret aversion to the other sex
or instinctive repugnance, as much as for simple fatigue, so that
her awareness of the fact that the accepted man can be found no
less inhibited than she is when facing the image of satisfactory
behavior officially demanded of him, and this only serves to

make things much easier.

Zorro is the real Don Giovanni, said Federico. I identify with Donna Elvira. And you're Donna Anna, and Leo is Zerlina, and Fortuny is Leporello. From the bar they contemplated the splendorous movement of the crowd up the staircases and through the hallways, spurred by the announcement that the second act was about to begin. The people, I tell you, are the true spectacle, said Manolo Moragas. You see every kind of tacky fool; the other day, even our dairyman's oldest son. But take a good look at them: the men look like waiters and the women like dolled-up fishbones. Or theater extras playing a crowd of mingling bystanders, said Adolfo. Exactly, man, excellent observation. It would be fun to rile them up somehow, I don't know, appear in the box in blue coveralls or something. I promise you, there was a time, the life of the common people in the cheap seats, assholes and all, had its attractions. What's happening now is merely symbolic: the rise of one class and the fall of another. You think so? said Federico. People come to the opera now who never came before and most of the people who used to come don't come anymore. But that's because the Liceo is no longer an important social gathering spot. People meet in other places now, and in other ways, and the distance between the upper bourgeoisie and this bourgeoisie that's storming the Liceo is not stable, it's growing. Fine, I'm speaking as a Marxist: excuse me, excuse me. Zorro would congratulate me, but I think it's the truth. This is, precisely, the drama of the whole bumpkin bourgeoisie, of those people so eager to show off their prêt-à-porter tuxedoes and their bargain-basement gowns, the dress that by this time of the season has lost its first luster, from being starched, still carrying the fragrance of its first outings, when, newly touched up by some domestic dressmaker, it could still turn a few heads; anxious to be seen with that outfit and, above all, anxious to be seen here, in this sanctifying temple of prosperity itself, in this picture window that only displays triumphal artifacts, with the zeal of squeezing out, of ratcheting experience up to the maximum, of reducing, as much as possible, the price of a seat, the price of a private box, zeal expressed with applause, not only extemporaneous, but even excessive, not so much because the performance was to their liking or not as for the simple fact that nobody likes to be a sucker and, as with any other deal, the value of the show must correspond to the ticket price. A drama that, with tragic fatality, seems only to increase in direct proportion to the money one possesses: when the tuxedo isn't mass-produced but hand-cut by the priciest tailor in Barcelona, and the evening gown is only one more of the exclusive designs selected at the start of the season, meaning, when it's a question of the nouveau riche who are truly rich, unequivocal in their gauche trappings and in their disconcerted discouragement, particularly sensitized to the bitter reality that, as if in parallel fashion to their economic and social ascent, the good family names withdraw as they get closer, the same as in a nightmare where one walks and walks but never advances, and so too, now that they find themselves in a situation of providing for their children, relatively well-groomed thanks to an easy and comfortable upbringing, quite different from their own, the polished touch and the archetypal manners of the moneyed youth of their generation, that natural distinction from those days that they never could nor ever will reach, now that they find themselves in a situation to which at least their children will have access, into which they can at least elbow their way, now, now it turns out that kind of distinction consists of being up to date with the latest extravagance, lamentably imprecise, incomprehensibly within reach of all, at the margin of all criteria of value, as if the category had been stripped of all quality. As if, once seated on the train, they could shift the engine into reverse and retrace the route not yet traveled! And it's the same way that a bar or a dance or a prostitute becomes fashionable among young people, and with them those things mature, get old, and fade away, the same with the Liceo, born at the same time as a specific society, as some tremendously bourgeois forms of life, their own identity now lost and become something else, just as those ways of life die out so, too, that society into which they were born. Now that we believe that history repeats itself, said Federico, if someday they revive *William Tell* we've got to get seats in the thirteenth row of the orchestra section.

But, besides that, who is Manolo Moragas? A rejuvenated posh snob, a dandified little boy from the forties who now, when he's almost twice as old as he was then, seems to have found, through Adolfo's circle, a second lease on youth, incentives he'd missed the first time around, and like in one of those cases of latent homosexuality, even a satisfactory explanation of himself, of his way of being and even of his incapacity of being anything different, similar in a way to how a precocious bibliophile, wounded by his love for belles-lettres, usually reacts, a poet, for example, more astute than gifted, preempting all possible criticism, pretending that the banality and clumsiness of his youthful works of poetry are deliberate, premeditative, and even innovative, as if with banality and clumsiness he might fashion something not banal or clumsy, as if any attempt in this sense would not irremediably end with the work in question being assimilated into the genre of banal and clumsy works, and especially, as if banality and clumsiness did not constitute the essential, and irrepressible characteristics of that young poet, so, in much the same way, ran the defensive arguments of Manolo Moragas, his compensations, transforming his ignorance into a capricious disdain of all cultural information that was not essential to Adolfo's circle, and into frank scorn for the appreciation of the cultural values traditionally belonging to his milieu, with the cynical nonchalance that a high-society woman displays among her friends when one of them starts talking about how boring it is to have a husband. In fact, a past susceptible to acquiring, in light of his current attitude, a certain entity and even a certain interest, almost legendary, doubtless propitiated by that attitude of challenging conventional ideas and his social position, his fortune, his wife, his wife's fortune, the delicacy that distinguished the relationship between them both, overall too excessive to express the fact that, for both of them, everything was reduced to that, to keeping up appearances; a challenge, on the other hand, that in no way altered, naturally, the habits appropriate to their social position, from the sunny outdoor luncheons at the Real Club de Golf or the heavy all-night poker games lasting until dawn at the Círculo Ecuestre, passing through a summary inspection, though much less unconcerned than could be believed at first glance, of the progress of his business deals, activities in which his jokes, his misogynist boasts, his peevish, scathing comments, his remarks like: the only thing wrong with New York is that it's so terribly provincial, or: I only sleep with a married woman when her husband gives his full approval, or: the only way of avoiding sentimental complications is to have women fall in love with your money, not with you, etcetera; all of this conferring on him, among the people of his social sphere, a halo of originality and brilliance, of a person indispensable for any kind of get-together, for the same reasons, although considered from the opposite angle, for which his behavior could become suggestively unusual in such a circle as that of Adolfo Cuadras. And then, his anecdotes, his recollections, his bygone summers, I don't know if you've all heard about them, if you remember them, but the thing is that until after the Civil War, summer vacations continued being almost like early in the century, when Barcelona high society added, to the old family house in the country, a villa in a fashionable summer colony, with shady gardens and terraces with a view, seeking a cool place to escape the heat, the obsession of the time, fruit not only of the country's climate but also of an excess of fats and carbohydrates in the diet and, especially, of an excessive fidelity to the London or Parisian style of dressing, stubbornly ignoring the simple fact that August in Sitges or Caldetas has more in common with Alexandria than Dauville and, in consequence, a salakót would better serve the circumstances than a bow tie. Things that one could now consider not only with a certain perspective but also with longing and nostalgia to the degree that, in spite of the liberation from the customs prevalent in the twenties, blatantly strengthened at the start of the thirties, something of that world had endured in Spain, where, after the interval of the Civil War, everything seemed to be fixed and even going backward; in that Spain that was like an island in time, a paradisiacal island where, at the height of World War II and in full demoralization of the previous years of revolt, everything continued as always, a rhythm of life and a world that wouldn't have to disappear entirely until well into the fifties, those pleasantly uninterrupted three months of summer, now passed into history in the reiterated identity of their gentle course, like so many other things of the past that nostalgia and longing allowed to be sublimated due to their distance in time, the Liceo of an earlier time, horse-drawn carriages, the first automobiles, the cabaret singers' derrieres, gambling, scandals, wasteful luxury, gardens like the ones Rusiñol painted, top hats, straw boaters, frock coats, bustles, fur muffs, veiled hats, fans, the kind of elegance found in the jottings of Casas, narcissistic sublimations so much more intense than in an age like the current one, surpassed and forgotten in the good families whose origins have some philistine aspect, the constituent phase of their patrimony, the great-grandparents' obscene calculations and cogitations, in a time like the present one, with so many recent booming fortunes, the more that some nouveau riche is perfectly identified and, on some occasions—painful ones—even hunted down, the money no longer suffices to distinguish distances and differences, and the weight of the presence of the ancestors in the common social repertoire becomes a measure of caste and class distinction, like until a certain point it is also the problem of those young people today, of their inability to adapt to social conventions, of those fallen angels that appear—you might say with preference— even in the best families, a peculiarity that comes to add one more element of tribulation to the good family names of Barcelona, already so punished by the most traditional problem of frequent mental retardation, the dismal offspring of their heinous fornications. An upper-crust bourgeois more regressive, in reality, than progressive, lacking the creative spirit of his great-grandparents, of whose virtues he only preserves, perhaps, their stinginess; a high-class bourgeois with his wagon hitched more than ever to his own snobbism, about cinema and art and essays and vanguardist drama, organic architecture, serial music, informal painting and, above all, an elusive dolce vita—always next time or somewhere else—that generally doesn't suffer the typical ordinary difficulties; an upper-crust bourgeois who, notwithstanding, thanks to that snobbism and the patina conferred by the times, can permit himself all kinds of transfigurations and projections starting with the most elevated vulgarity, the sad luck of Antoñito Canals, who killed himself so absurdly, or poor Totem, a darling little girl, who married and was so disgraced and who fled and ended up so badly, etcetera, we have a good example of that in Manolo Moragas, with his remembrances and reflections, with the magnified profiles of his memory, when he talks about Alicia and Sunche, when he talks about Magdalena's grandmother as if she were the Duchess of Guermantes and as if Grandpa Augusto were the duke, and Doña America were Madame Verdurin, and that crazy Tito Coll a sort of Charlus, while he, Manolo Moragas, the narrative I, an apathetic Marcel, too skeptical to take the trouble to write anything, the only reason for him not already having withdrawn into his cork-lined cell, becomes a chronicler of Barcelonan society, the literary transcription of whose avatars, for any reader not directly implicated in that world, would awaken the same interest, probably, as the prose of one of those stylists in the Sunday edition of a provincial newspaper who've achieved a certain local notoriety by the agreeable character of their collaborations, stylists who philosophize like a sheep chewing its cud before the ruins of the Parthenon, not in service to the validity of the ideas developed, but rather, to please his readers' palates, of the originality of the focus and the graceful exposition, as well as this stylist's prose, the interest of the specific problems of that world, of the characters capable of inhabiting it, grazing and watering among the ruins of the culture, with the grace and subtlety and elegance of a bull's head that, like a Narcissus, gazes at itself in a puddle. They headed down Las Ramblas, penetrating the saturnine Saturday night atmosphere of tenebrous lights and anonymous movement, long endless hours making the rounds to the usual places, as if awaiting some small event, within the scant margin of variation, a phenomenon of perception both heightened and fleeting, growing to enormous proportions, conferring personality on the night, a drunken albino, the parallel pilgrimage of two workers working hard to have a good time, or any other spectacle that might offer an occasion for exercising one's own ingenuity to celebrate it, running into some acquaintance, joining up with some other group of pub crawlers, trading some rather sardonic jokes, laughter lubricated and faces lit up by alcohol. Like pulsing accordions: the memory of having been and the pain of already not being.

Ah, when he felt like he was cut in half, especially after drinking, with a hangover, all the next day, half-man, half-goat, the thick tuft of hair where the pastern joins the hoof with the low hanging belly as a support or a throne for the imperious serpent poised to strike, quivering with electricity, possessed of his fury, impelled by his energy, like a hunter plunging through the thick woodland after his wounded quarry. Not like now, behaving rather like a dog skittering here and there pissing along the trail, not like now, entering almost just because in the secondhand bookshop, helpless against any lovely head of hair, with the stabbing pain of memory: of not having become. Is this early and perhaps irremediable decline in his progress a transitional state or rather the price of excessive precociousness? No, yes, no, yes, no, no? Was this the cursed fruit of autumn, after a rough summer, full of tensions and long, drawn-out quarrels, hangovers, erotic gluttony, from the moment Nuria returned from London and phoned him to tell him that she wanted to see him, just to have a nice peaceful chat for a while, and he agreed, despite their definitive breakup, last spring, when they met in Paris, when she told him about Louis, and he said for quite some time now he hadn't seen any reason for them to consider themselves tied to one another, and why not let things take their course, she could do what she liked, and he could too, and she said no, she wasn't breaking up, that her fling with Louis was finished, and the one she loved was him, only him, and he, however, said no? While they ate dinner, Raúl was polite but cold, almost hard in his implacable distance despite all Nuria's maneuvers to get close to him, efforts that, like the rules of urbanity, have not so much the goal of facilitating relations between people belonging to the same privileged class as of easily distinguishing people who do not belong to that class and immediately establishing a separation from them, thus, Nuria's efforts to reactivate the old

codes of their intimacy were directed, more than to stimulate
an immediate change in Raúl's attitude, to make it possible to
discuss, between parentheses, how much might have happened
to each one of them on their own. They went back to their
old hangouts, and even the accordion music was the same, the
tango that pulls and rumples and falters, as if it had not stopped
playing since then, or better yet, as if they had never left the
place. I know it's all finished, said Nuria. But the thing is, I want
you. You'll never be able to avoid it; me neither, even if I wanted.
They were a little drunk and in the taxi she leaned back against
his shoulder, while she slowly caressed one of his thighs. Why
don't you come up? My family's out of town for the weekend.
They kissed almost without pause starting in the vestibule, and in
the elevator she unbuttoned her blouse, or maybe he did it, the
fact is that she was unbuttoned, and on the landing they stayed
there in the darkness and she fished around in her purse without finding the keys while he, with his other hand, felt around
under her light summer clothes according to the principle of
progressive reiteration, going deeper, with the satisfaction with
which a water diviner sees his spring begin to flow, toward the
areas of deliquescence, and she, against the door, felt like her
legs would give way, and they opened the door and went inside,
she almost naked, and they stopped in the living room, exploring each other with their hands, lips, tongues, warm clothing
slipping off suddenly, her soft hair below, centered around her
flush rosy harmonies, Raúl hunched over her breasts, over her
thighs raised high, gripping his torso, over her belly, twitching, thrusting, when, hair flying and eyes rolling, the growing
rhythmic violence converging even as the burning fusion recedes,
converging and receding—for a very long time—the bubbling
rush that, like the enormous relief that comes from releasing
an enema or like some calcium pill that neutralizes burning
stomach acids, would liquefy their bodies, calming them, after
such a frenzy, after that absorbed sighing silence only disturbed
by the creak of the springs and the suspicion, bright as magne-
sium flares, that one of the servants might be moving about the
house and, especially, the exasperating tapping of the back of

the sofa against the wall, which he tried to stop, placing his foot firmly on the parquet floor, like shifting gears on a motorcycle, to move the sofa, to separate it from the wall, without interrupting his principal activity, until abandoning his effort and his conscience, he plunged into the convulsive knot of their bodies. Coming back to themselves, they noticed that the sofa had carried them almost to the center of the room.

There were still a few embers in the fireplace. Raúl blew some life into them and added several logs. Nuria clicked off the lamp, and by the firelight, naked upon the thick carpet, they drank whiskey straight from the bottle. From fucking we come, keep fucking we must, said Raúl, ashes to ashes, and dust to dust. Sooner than you think, said Nuria. And, in fact, went right back to it, vigorously, on the carpet, on the sofa, on the carpet, using their time well, his cock in her hand, grasping it like a dagger, up and down, up and down, a dagger she plunged into herself or whose sweet thrust she accepted, sweetly up and down then starting again right away, before it got too late for them to couple again, in the heat of passion, without letting each other fall asleep, awake, active, efficient, up and down doing it over again and better every time, growing hot again and stoking their passion anew, and if necessary showing off her best sword-swallowing skills, I like it so much, I love you so much, I couldn't live without you, Pipo. Yes: recovered. He went out onto the terrace and contemplated the city in the glowing clarity of the dawn, the silence of the accumulated apartment houses, chaotic conglomeration of facades and rooftops and skylights and antennas and cables and sooty cement, a panorama of volumes and spaces that will soon begin to discharge, just as that plump gray pigeon flew away in a flash, an opaque mist of trepidation and traffic. It was already full daylight as he walked back toward his house and it took him a while to find a taxi; and as he went along, as if dazzled, by the pleasantly deserted streets, those mixed feelings of discouragement, disgust, and even revulsion gradually disappeared, the same as in other times, after other amorous adventures, they'd not taken long to flit away, thanks to the propitious oblivion one usually encounters when

we're bothered by the memory of our frailties committed, of the
confessions made at the insistence of others, affirmations, if not
completely false, certainly, at the least, exaggerated, sentiments
pretentiously experienced for some time now, or rather brusque
but irresistibly raised, unequivocally fictitious asseverations, for
however much in that instant one would like them to be not only
real but also definitive, and that under the insistent antagonic
stinger, and could even come to believe they are, desires exposed
as facts, facts adapted to the circumstances, love, love, word
and talisman and breath of life; an overreach of which one only
becomes completely conscious in the very moment after orgasm,
just a few seconds after, but already too late, confused awakening
like on an unlucky or sorrowful day that one knows they must
confront, the death of a loved one, an accident, something
already irreparable like the fact of having said something you've
said, repeated outbursts, one after another, affirmations that
although they might be reduced to a simple yes, leave us, in any
case, when all has passed, with the impression of having talked
too much, an impression, notwithstanding, like being subjected
to auto-inoculation therapy or to the physical principle according
to which every action generates an equal and opposite reaction,
soon giving way, as one walks home, to a healthy reaction of
cynicism, inducing one to recreate the pleasant aspects of the
affair, desires satisfied, to feel the intimate pride of having been
able to demonstrate one's own competence in matters erotic, in
a certain way now with thoughts fixed already on the next time,
at the end of the day it didn't matter if they continued to see
one another this way now and then, always provided that the
situation remained well clear, the kind of relationship that from
now on was going to be established between them both, if Nuria
accepted his conditions, absolute freedom for each one to do
what they felt like, without any sort of interference whatsoever,
not even the smallest right to call the other to account for
anything, conditions that although unconditionally accepted—
I'll do anything just to be able to keep seeing you—were no
serious obstacle to prevent Nuria, after only a few weeks, from
asking him, quite casually, if he'd had many adventures during all

that time, and with whom, and what they had done and if they'd done it well, as if with amused curiosity, playing the mysterious one, with the assurance of the one who knows something the other doesn't know, and then Raúl would ask her in turn if there had been others besides Louis, and Nuria would tell him no, though not very convincingly, and Raúl would ask her for details about her fling with Louis, and Nuria would ask about his affairs with other girls, and as if all that excited them both, they would end up, with reconcentrated application, making love again, or rather, depending on the day, getting furious with each other, having a violent argument, seeking offense, verbal aggression, and also making love, yes, but more like a married couple already worn down by the convenience of it, a man and woman still young returning home after a night out with other couples whom one always tends to consider luckier, friends from other times, men and women about whom each married couple can imagine that things might have been different with them, not like now, the evening spent, when, in the silent apartment, they give themselves over to lovemaking, possessing one another with cruel, suicidal fury, each one in a fierce battle with their own ruin, with their rancors, their frustrations, enclosed, like boxers in the ring, in the lugubrious matrimonial landscape. Because just as with the sprightly statue of Count Ramón Berenguer atop his horse, doubtless concealing under his dashing warlike image the trembling spirit of a lady, only comparable to the spirit of the Lady of Orléans in his vehement desire to conquer by giving his all, to possess by being possessed, thus the essential sadomasochistic ambiguity of Raúl and Nuria's relationship.

Nuria Oller's appearance, with her London memories, first of all, calling to mind his own orgasmic adventures with Nuria Rivas, their talk of mutual friends, the mishaps of her wedding to Peter and more, everyone well-informed of Nuria's fling with Louis, and, then, the arrival of Louis himself, doubtless introduced, on the other hand, new shades of meaning into the development of those relationships. It was one thing to imagine Louis from afar, his presence in Nuria Oller's photographs, where he appeared alongside Peter and the two Nurias and the other members of the group, a group whose members, as Nuria Oller pointed out significantly, shared everything right down to the last penny, but another thing was his physical appearance, his very real presence in Barcelona. It must have been around the first days of September when Nuria told him that Louis had written to her from Madrid, and that he was coming to Barcelona, and could they try to find him a room for a few days. That's all the letter said; they were in a bar and Raúl could confirm it by taking advantage of the fact that Nuria went to the bathroom for a minute, taking the letter from her purse and reading it before she returned. However: might she not have left that letter right there on purpose, maybe even dictated it herself, sticking out of her purse so that he would read it—just as he had read it—and, more trusting, accept that her story made sense, right in line with the image of the nice young fellow who likes jazz and plays the clarinet, of that hairless beardless fellow, one of those sneaky consolers of lonely women, whose leftist flirtations perhaps only serve to mask their sexual misery, their stupid fascination with the more-than-dubious myth of the hot-blooded Spanish woman, the seducer's oft-celebrated *mille tre* conquests? Another clue: the fact that when Louis finally arrived, Nuria slipped up and called him Pipo, and that, when she realized that Raúl had not failed to notice her lapse, Louis thought he should explain that Nuria called everyone whom she loved Pipo, an explanation that if on the one hand no one had asked for, on the other it was unexpected and not very reassuring, especially given the husband's typical disadvantage compared to the lover who, like a gambler, considers the wild card of adventure to always trump the sure-bet card of convenience, meaning transience over permanence, so, Louis or any other of those beloved people found themselves, in that respect, in a frankly privileged situation, a privilege whose weight could be decisive in the serene and thoughtful examination of how many arguments could be counterpoised—in the supposition that someone would spend time pondering the matter—about what Nuria's behavior might be in a similar situation: the apparently sincere fondness that Nuria seemed to feel for Raúl in all situations, careful to avoid, for fear of losing him, making a false step, given women's characteristically infinite capacity for deception, the tranquility, for example, with which she could say goodbye to him from the terrace, while Louis, already naked in bed, watched her. Nuria Oller had also come out to receive Louis on his arrival and at night ate dinner with them and then they all went to the Jamboree. I feel like I'm back in London, she said. Too bad Peter's not here. Your clarinet? asked Raúl. You haven't brought it with you? Louis shook his head. It's a shame; the hotels don't let them in. He danced a song with Nuria, and when they returned, Raúl said that he was leaving, that tomorrow he had to get up early. Do you mind seeing her back home? He patted him on the back and kissed Nuria lightly on the lips. And another day when the three of them had a date, Raúl called at the last minute and said that he just couldn't make it, that he had a meeting he couldn't miss; and one afternoon, at Nuria's house, he said that he had to go and, from the street below he looked up and saw her waving him goodbye from the terrace. Because how could he ever be sure? Had that beardless Armstrong really arrived the day he said and not two days earlier, during which time Raúl had barely seen Nuria? Had the two of them really spent the morning looking at the Romanesque galleries in the Museo de Montjuich or had they just stopped in there for a moment, because Mr. Strong Arm, Mr. Limp Dick, had an idea that they buy an art catalog and some postcards as proof? Why, if they had really gone there, instead of getting a room in a brothel, did they talk so much about the details, the David and Goliath by the Master of Taüll, and the Pantocrator and the Host? Why did they change the subject when he came back from the restroom? How could he know if Nuria was really going to stay at home all night, in spite of when he phoned asking for her with an English accent, they told him just a moment, and she came on the line, hello, hello, click? How could he know if Mr. Pija Floja, or Mr. Prickloose, or however they said it in English, wasn't there with her, since the one place he definitely was not was his hotel, or at least that's what they told him? Didn't Nuria rely on the servant's complicity, on the maid, surely the one who stayed in the flat when the rest of the family was away on the weekend? And why did Nuria play the prude and, as if embarrassed, pull away, let me go, hands off, people are going to see, when after she danced with Louis Prickloose, Raúl started caressing her hair while discretely starting to feel her up, as if in a feverish rush, exploring her in search of telltale wetness and dilation? And wasn't it possible that when he arrived at Nuria's house to find that Prickloose was already there, wasn't it just possible that he'd not really just arrived like he said, or that, in fact, where he'd just come from, and she, too, was the bedroom, after helping her to smooth the sheets and change the bathroom towels thinking that Raúl just might show up to snoop around? Couldn't they have also done it without a diaphragm, given that, as he had occasion to confirm, her diaphragm was in its case, like always, in her vanity, couldn't they have done it like that, maybe because she might have lied to Louis about her period saying she didn't need to use it that day, maybe because they decided to skip the diaphragm, however unpleasant it is to have to practice coitus interruptus and pull out at the last second, so that Raúl, when he spent that night with her, taking advantage of her family being away, wouldn't notice that she was already wearing it, and only the complicit maid, the procuress, was capable of appreciating from her room, with equal parts derision and discretion, the different sound of the footsteps on the stairway to the upper attic? The least of it was the image of Nuria wrapped in another's arms, her orgasms in another's embrace, her somewhat sorrowful expression that Raúl knew so well, the light—more precisely than the gaze—from her eyes. Thus in cases of sudden or violent death, emotional crises of greater intensity are experienced by those who were more intimately linked to the deceased, those who usually go on living with the small details which, once the first external displays of sorrow are past, after the burial, continue bearing witness to their unbelievable absence, the pack of cigarettes hardly smoked, the suit they bring back from the dry cleaner's, correspondence that keeps arriving, details about whose common afflictive value it would be wrong to give any other explanation than the irreparable rawness itself by which what no longer exists is manifested, thus, it would be no less mistaken to consider equivalent the lacerating lashes that a simple gesture, phrase, or specific posture of the faithless beloved can provoke in the person who is or who believes themself victim of an infidelity, even long after the events, when everything seems back to normal, or even more, the recurrent vision of that woman giving herself to the other, the imaginary reconstruction of her erotic behavior, to consider, in other words, that all those fluid representations in the memory are hardly more than the external expression of something much more abstract: betrayal in itself, the bare fact that infidelity has been possible. And more concretely yet: not so much the betrayal itself—especially when in reality one does not love that woman, when one is fed up and what they're trying to do is break things off, to get rid of her—as its verbal formation, meaning, the lie, which during the time she was consummating her infidelity, she was capable of writing, of repeating, of continuing to say, I can't live without you, you're the only person in the world I can love, just as that very night, the same as so many others, Nuria—although especially sated, Raúl being certain of his theory that when he arrived she had just been screwing Louis—surely had to say it. Why don't you ever tell me you love me, even just once in a while? said Nuria. Because you know perfectly well that I'd be lying, said Raúl. She pushed away from him, turning toward the other side of the bed. You don't understand anything, not a thing. She would cry a little, each time more softly, as if waiting, as if she knew that he was going to embrace her from behind, body against body, caressing her, holding her, penetrating her. And then she would say: you do love me even if it's only a little bit. And he would say: yeah, just a little.

Nevertheless, by then, the general deterioration of their relationship also affected, possibly, the erotic aspect, altering, depending on the day, his or her or both their libidos, diminishing it, annulling it, and it would be very difficult to determine if the posterior events—all the stuff with Achilles, Aunt Paquita, the overcoat, Señor Rivas, the Plutos, etcetera—were the final drops that caused the glass to overflow, or rather the excuse, the

justification for dejection and lack of enthusiasm that possessed
them, the not now, Raúl please, I'm too nervous, if not the I
know what's wrong, you just don't feel like it anymore. Why did
they stay together? From the inertia that keeps miserable people
together or, more simply, by a phenomenon similar to the empty
stubbornness with which a brain blocked by neurosis passes the
time playing with a word, a proper name, Paitubí, for example,
perhaps jarring, perhaps not, Paytuby, Paytobe, Paytobuy,
Buytopay, Tobepay, Tobebuy, or with a Latin declension, or with
an irregular English verb, forget, forgot, forgotten, a reflection
of who knows what sort of startling spells, what lugubrious
associations? And, apart from how many factors might have
intervened in the decline of their relationship, to what other
elements and to what level of awareness might it be possible to
attribute the fact that, like the solitary person obsessed by the
idea that drowning himself will garner not an unequivocal
response but rather a sentence, like in that song about the lost
keys—*Dónde están las llaves, materile, materile, en el fondo del
mar, materile, materile*—*Where are the keys, la la li, la la li, at the
bottom of the sea, la la li, la la li*—sung in chorus by some
children on the street, which then becomes a sinister ritornello
in his mind, thus in a similar way, the most fortuitous and insignificant event in his daily life could represent for Raúl the most
mocking reply of his fallen state of mind? What doubt, in any
case, that the person going through a phase of anguish, or perhaps of lucidity, as his self-confidence fails him, his confidence
in his intellectual and moral conditioning, in his own sexual
vigor, what doubt that in that individual a defense mechanism
of ritual and compensatory character will start up, where the
preventative and not rudely hygienic meaning of the ablutions
he practices before going to bed or upon rising, for example, will
come to be defined by the same implacable order and systematic
rigor with which he practices them, a tendency that will only
grow sharper to the degree to which the somber tone of his
thoughts that assault him is accentuated, questions, interrogations, I'll go back and walk down this street that I've never
walked down before, which of those old relatives only seen at

burials will I never see again, to what point will the end of others no longer form part of our own end, when was its beginning, when does it begin to end? There are cases, there are people, there are moments, unforeseeable of course, in which the same threatening stormy horizon seems to induce one, more than to escape, to seek refuge in another body, to integrate, to penetrate the body, to be materialized in the other, to be the other, losing oneself until disappearing in some lips, in some breasts, in some buttocks, in the roses that unfurl within the smooth nether hair, as if on each one of those parts they might be able to encounter the whole, the hidden secret, the Cave of Sesame, a process no less disintegrating, though apparently the inverse, than the bureaucratization of love, the love that over the years, between old lovers, ends up being finished off as if it were no more than some administrative file, as just as regulatory processes, by their very nature, engender prevarication and bribery, so the continuity and habit of the sexual life engender and announce betrayal, the attraction to adventure, of projecting the same desires onto another body, of repeating upon it an identical erotic ritual, the lascivious unction in the mouth, on the breasts, on the buttocks, on the sex, attributing, in general, to that other body appetites complementary to one's own appetites, given how many general ideas circulate about it, his own eyewitness experience helping spread the myth, *auparishtaka*, for example, women's fondness for taking a man's sperm in their mouth, a belief based, more than on a true confirmation, case by case, on the simple fact that they currently practice it, perfectly knowledgable of their efficiency, of the hot manifestations of recognition that its execution usually costs her; and based, especially, on the desire that they like what men like. And the counterpart to *auparishtaka*: kissing the yoni, according to the anthropomorphic concept of the fundamental feminine nymphomania, the idea that nothing drives a woman so wild as prolonged oral stimulation of her sex, something that they never forget, that forever subjects them to whomever has got them to achieve such intense pleasure in this way, a very common idea based on the concept of the *madanashastri* or clitoris as the equivalent of the penis or

lingam, and, consequently—how sad and denigrating for the
woman that a guileless mind could think them the same—on
the indisputable superiority of the clitoral orgasm over the vaginal, a superiority defended as much by those women sincerely
addicted to it, in defense of their unequivocally lesbian and
onanistic appetites as by those women who don't wish to stop
seeming so, without daring to reveal, believing them abnormally
insane, their vaginal preferences, be it for purely psychic
motives—narcissistic women, in general, sublimated through
transcendence, appreciating the pleasure their body is capable of
generating, reaching orgasm together, etcetera—be it for being
associated with a certain physical reality, deductions and deep
suspicions that in the man, according to a process similar and
no less tendentious, usually increase in direct proportion to the
lack of fulfillment of his desires, not being infrequent so that,
habituating himself to repression, that man ends up finding
greater satisfaction in imagining in detail the sexual act in all its
phases and variations, than in the sexual act itself, in exercising
it, a satisfaction that has the advantage of permitting him, on
the other hand, to attribute to the woman, with full liberty,
freely, without any possibility of being contradicted, an exact
replica of his desires, with the tendency to forget that although
in her those desires are diffuse, as diffuse as her body's eroticism,
they are for her no less concrete. Less studied, however, as an
aspect of male eroticism, is the recondite appeal that a woman's
buttocks and their mesial depths hold for a man, his compulsive
propensity to want to explore them, to penetrate them, a far
more widespread fixation than usually believed thanks to a
general resistance to discuss the subject, desires that men don't
discuss amongst themselves nor boast nor brag about, not so
much perhaps from the fear that as a clumsy analogy, through a
rough and mechanical transposition, they be interpreted as
symptomatic of some unconfessed homosexuality—a hypothesis,
however, somewhat disposable, as is the previous and larger
problem they raise: the obscure meaning such desires represent
for an individual, the esoteric substrate that vivifies them, less
easy to explain, for example, including for an analytical spirit,

than the application with which the young man, from his first
sexual experience and in a totally unconscious way, sucks on his
partner's breasts; more difficult and, above all, more surprising,
by virtue of the charge of profanation that the act comprises, in
maximum violation of the intimacy of the person who is the
object of our desires, more so, of their individuality, the will to
transcend supposed by that desire to enter—not always easy—in
the most reserved part of the other body, of fusion, of total
communion with the other organism by means of direct access
to its true center, to the point of confluence or outlet of all its
assimilative systems, something rather like the royal throne
room. Desires, it's clear, one only gets used to putting into practice—except when one resorts to the brutal example of force—
from a proven erotic understanding, from a progressive coupling
of rhythms, from a mutual physical concession, inserting its
realization, when not substituting it for the habitual final penetration, at any moment of the ritual: caresses, kisses,
sucking, ears, neck, breasts, buttocks, belly, the slow, gradual
descent centered on the new world that opens up merely by
spreading the legs.

The purpose and final end of the sexual act is conception.
Do you all remember? said Pluto. To hell with conception and
engendering: Orgasms! Orgasms! All the rest is just the desire
to impregnate. That only happens to idiots like me who for
years and years have believed in that stuff about the blessed fruit
of your womb Jesus Amen, and then they go and knock up
some idiot like that fool Marihole. They were getting drunk
and Mariconcha or Maripain or Marihole started crying again.
Aurora paid her no attention and Nuria didn't seem to hear,
absorbed and a bit withdrawn, fed up, you might say, by the
mere fact of being there, like a mother with her little children on
Sunday afternoon, stupefied, saturnine thanks to them, on the
verge of dementia, dancing as if bewitched to the sound of their
pooping and their crying and their baths and their games and
their squabbling tantrums and their baby food. She'd not said a
word since they arrived, while they established their definitive
plan: Mariconcha or Mariwhatever would tell her family that

she was going to spend two or three days at a friend's house, La
Molina, for example, to see the snow; at nine o'clock sharp the
day after tomorrow, Wednesday, the fourteenth, she and Pluto
would be at the midwife's house and Adolfo would be waiting
for them at the same bar as today and would bring them here
and here they would wait until she was in a good condition
to return home, not precisely tanned from the high mountain
climate, but rather somewhat diminished, the bad weather and,
especially, the misfortune of an especially pesky period, the periodic bleeding that would come from those shapeless swellings
and magmatic palpitations, happy and rapid conclusion to the
arrangements begun on the ninth, the day after Mariconcha's
saint's day, the Immaculate Conception, when Raúl went to see
the midwife, I don't know if you remember me, you helped my
wife it must be about four years ago, and the midwife remembered, so she received the Plutos, and they made an appointment
for the twelfth, today, she would prepare her, and the intervention would be the fourteenth. Correct, said Pluto: a question
to resolve between conception and Nativity. And the doctor?
said Adolfo. What guarantee do we have that he knows what
to do? You tell me, said Pluto. The kind of guarantee you get
from a big son of a bitch. We still haven't seen hide nor hair of
him. That very white hair and his big white mustache, in contrast to his sixty-something tanned complexion, almost like a
photographic negative; he would appear, he appeared, at just the
right moment, when everything was all ready and she was in the
correct position, well open and raised up, and he'd peer through
some glasses as he sat down before her to examine her, indelicate
and cynical like that leisurely passerby who stops to contemplate
the fruitless maneuvers of some new, clumsy driver trying to
parallel park their car, contributing nothing more with his bold
stare than to roil the development of their repeated attempts
and to intensify the beginner's feeling of haste and embarrassment, not simply for a lack of tact, doubtless, but rather, also,
premeditatedly, with insidious delectation, perfectly aware that,
after bumping repeatedly into the cars ahead and behind, his
victim would finally give up and drive off in a hurry, feverish

and muddled. Thus, the doctor, while the midwife prepared the anesthetic, would calmly slip on his gloves and conduct a rough vaginal examination, as if he enjoyed the situation or considered, perhaps, its effects to be cathartic for the patient, completely indifferent to the shame and horror she might be experiencing, sinister in his manners and his aspect, more a dungeon master inflicting torment than a surgeon, a sordid impression, a product, of course, more of the circumstances than his physique, a face, a presence, which in another context would perhaps have nothing especially disagreeable about them, like that Nazi officer in the movies who interrogates the members of the resistance, blonde and gray, snakelike, cruel, but who in another role, in another guise, might pass for a friendly queer. Then when she woke up, he would say, he said, look, it was a little girl.

They walked with the Plutos until they found a taxi. You two take it, Nuria said; Mariconcha doesn't feel well. The worst that can happen to her is that she aborts, Pluto said. Raúl and Nuria stood there, waiting for another taxi to come along. We could also walk a little further and take the Metro, Raúl said. No, said Nuria; pawning my jewelry will at least pay for a taxi. She turned to face Raúl: do you have anything you need to do in the morning? Nothing: an appointment with some idiot at eleven, in the Atheneum; and then pop round to the Registry Office. Then, why don't you spend the night? My brothers are at my grandparents' house. And your mother? Who cares? Maybe she's with Amadeo. Alright, I'll come over, but only for a while. Why not spend the night? Because of my dad, you know perfectly well. If they wake up and I'm not there, they'll think I've been arrested again or something, I don't know. In the taxi, they sat without talking, and when they reached Nuria's flat they went straight up to her room. When Raúl came out of the bathroom he found her stretched across the bed, still wearing her overcoat, and shoes, squeezing the strap of her purse, looking at the ceiling. We should have started living together before it was too late, she said. If someday has to be too late, it's not worth the trouble to start, said Raúl. But the surest way for it to be too late is to make things slow down. And the quickest way, not slow

them down. Nuria lit a cigarette. Really, I don't understand how
your affair with Aurora didn't last longer. You two are so alike;
what people call soul mates. You're a much better match for her
than Adolfo. And Raúl: what would be better for me is some
gorgeous girl with no brains. If Adolfo wants to deal with Aurora,
that's his business. I'll keep looking for the brainless beauty. And
Nuria: you mean I've got to hang around with you waiting until
you find some idiot to dump me for? And Raúl: no; I can also
take off right now. I'm already nervous enough myself without
having to handle someone else's worries. Nuria took his hand.
Forgive me, she said: I'm the idiot. Raúl removed his hand to
light another cigarette. Why has everything gone to hell? said
Nuria. We should have decided to move in together when all
that was happening. That screwed everything up and hurt us
both. You know I don't blame you for anything; I was a complete
coward. And Raúl: don't worry, that didn't change anything; I
loved you, but I wasn't in love with you. And Nuria: but what
does being in love mean for you? And Raúl: something else. And
Nuria: Why? Why? I've loved you so much since the beginning.
She took Raúl's hand again; the way his pupils changed, like the
colors of an aquarium with gaping fish staring through the glass.
Sorry. I'm an idiot. I'm sorry. So many things all at once in such
a short time. But that's not the problem, Raúl said. And she: I
know, I know, shaking her head, as if refusing to listen, extraordinarily similar to her mother in her moments of sorrow, days
before, when, shattered and exhausted, her face almost erasing
the familiar Doña Dulce of always, resolved and self-sufficient,
a sort of woman whom, although unaware of it, Raúl had never
met before, her relationship with Amadeo, it wasn't difficult to
see in her the determination and sangfroid typical of that housewife who, discovering her husband's adultery, makes the first
likely-looking taxi driver she can find drop her off at a brothel,
and there gives herself over to every kind of sexual activity,
offering the incredulous man all the pleasures she's been denying
her husband since their wedding night.

He stroked her hair, kissed away her tears, and she, as if sensing that their saltiness would excite him, let him caress her,

motionless but every moment more tense, more docile, as if
under the effect of a relaxing massage, until suddenly, tears still
wetting her cheeks, but now without holding back her crying,
she began to return his kisses, almost brutally, ravenous, as if
she'd foreseen that frantic undressing between more kisses and
more caresses and more sucking, following their ritual, lips, ears,
neck, breasts, belly, ass, sex, etcetera, besides, of course, any other
variant introduced along the way, any other spontaneous initiative, things that appear in one of those pornographic pulp novels
sold in secondhand bookshops described in this way: and he
used his powerful penis to kiss her breasts, applying it to them
like a blowtorch, and as if it were a blowtorch, she got hotter and
hotter while he continued using it to caress her neck, her ears,
her throat, and then she, trembling with pleasure, grabbed it,
kneading it furiously with both hands, her left hand around his
testicles, her right hand squeezing the base of the gland, caressing
it with her silky blonde hair before starting to suck it deep,
smooth, and eagerly, etcetera, or with a similar tone and diction;
or expressed not quite so graphically, more conceptual, resorting
to the various procedures, sanctioned by her own experience, by
which one manages to give variety and prolong the sexual act to
the maximum, given how much more easily the man reaches
orgasm than the woman (Kinsey, Stekel, Tong-Hiuan-Tsen), not
so much a question of erotic self-gratification—quite the
contrary on occasions—as an elemental norm of masculinity, a
question of prestige, as well as a progressive deference to the
satisfaction of the feminine libido, satisfaction understood as a
woman's inalienable right, discarding, of course, the case of
greater strength, the case in which one is seen specifically obliged
to delay orgasm as long as possible, whether for not being in the
right mood or not having a good body or whatever, and it takes
him time to get in the right frame of mind, and the effort of
forcing oneself to do so ends up leading one to a rapid and
undesired conclusion, even without having achieved the standard
required conditions of size and consistency, in the same way that
without the warmup exercises, cold, no athlete would reach their
desired goals; or put more poetically by Tong-Hiuan-Tsen, being

especially mindful when the woman takes the man's jade stalk or lingam, while he caresses the woman's jade gate, also called her yoni. Thus, the man will also experience the influence of the Yin, and his precious stalk will be elevated with vigor, erect as a mountain peak pointing toward the Milky Way. For her part, the woman will experience the influence of the Yang, and her cinnabar cleft will become moist with rich secretions. Next, the man will place his jade stalk near the entrance to the vagina—the yoni—that bushy region that seems a tiny pine forest surrounding a deep grotto. When the cinnabar cleft pours out its rich secretions, the lance—the lingam—penetrates the vagina, spilling secretions that mix with those of the woman to water the sacred field, above, and below, the shadowy valley. Tong-Hiuan-Tsen said: the jade stalk then plunges into the cinnabar cleft up to the Yang terrace; that jade stalk then seems a thick rocky crag that blocks a deep valley. Meaning: the way that a general cuts a swath through the enemy field or the wild horse plunges across a deep river or the seagulls play above the waves or a rock sinks into the sea or the serpent slowly slithers into his den to hibernate or the falcon swoops down upon the flitting hare or the brave boat sails into the teeth of the storm, that is the way until the woman begs for grace; thus. Tong-Hiuan-Tsen said: and when a man feels that he is about to come to orgasm he must wait for the woman to also climax so they might both enjoy the pleasure together; so then, the man will give light taps between the cords of the lyre and the grain of rice, and the taps must seem like the movements of a baby nursing. And then, let the man close his eyes, concentrate his thoughts, press his tongue against the back of his palate, curve his back, stretch out his neck, dilate his nostrils, contract his shoulders, close his mouth and hold his breath. In this way, his sperm, the Kama-salila, will move backward by itself. Or it will not go back and everything will have been for nothing. Something that can also happen, like the general or the seagulls playing above the waves or a rock plunging into the jade sea, before he has penetrated the cinnabar cleft; before: when the woman, turning her head and shaking her hair, like in a surge of ecstasy, like attacking or taking shelter, abruptly resolves matters, directly and deeply, and then the vision of the man tends to vanish, taking as a vanishing point the image of that hair that falls in a swirl, over her face, upon the juicy precipitant rhythm, that cozy suction cup pulsing like a hot gusting wind. Or even without *auparishtaka* or simple fellatio, or complemented with its inverse practice, meaning, a sixty-nine; even without that, even under the simple but persistent caress of a blonde mane. And even before the virile member had acquired its habitual proportions in such circumstances. Mistakes that can be avoided or at least mitigated, more than following the lessons prescribed by Tong-Hiaun-Tsen for such situations, more than realizing the acts advised by him, simply trying to remember them in the right order, although the key to success might very possibly reside in the mere mnemonic exercise and its material execution, might only be a skillful diversionary maneuver. Or rather, more simply, thinking about whatever might be, the most depressing thing possible, Aunt Paquita's death, for example, or the death of Señor Rivas, according to the principle of mental concentration as an inhibitor of the libido when its function is not specifically stimulating, in an attempt to distract oneself through memory, of centering the attention on something anodyne if not unwelcome or worrisome, seeking thoughts capable of interfering with the rising bubbling sensation, avoiding thinking that it's coming, thinking distract yourself, forget what you're doing, don't go on like that, don't think about that, tell her to stop, don't stoke that burning fusion, don't think, think about something else, about people, in banal expressions, the memory of having been, and Manolo Moragas who said the truth is all that sex business is just a drag, and Federico who said that Escala does everything he can for the sake of seeming what he is, and Leo who said that one cannot lose contact with the masses, and whoever fails to participate regularly in political discussions and the life of the party ends up losing it, and whoever loses it is, to the party, like a priest who hangs up his habit is to the church, worse than the one who never had faith to begin with, and Federico: Like Stalin and like Pluto? And Leo's father: Tertullian was a great man and if he

were alive today he would be a communist, communism has
always been pro-culture, Lenin enjoyed Mozart's music and
Marx liked Balzac, and Federico, the best way of assisting the
workers' petit bourgeois aspirations is to label as petit bourgeois
whomever does not share them because they don't share the
aspirations of the majority of the working class and for that
reason they are petit bourgeois, and Floreal, the true realities are
the subsistence wages and the accidents on the job and the
misery and torture, this is the reality that must serve as an inspiration to writers and artists, and Leo, the party is always right
and only one position can be right, and Floreal, I'd almost say
that sometimes it's more important to keep the party strong than
drive ourselves crazy thinking about the revolution, and Leo's
father, humility is the most difficult of all the virtues, and
Federico, what Leo's saying will happen but in reverse: the
proletariat will ally itself with the petite and middle-class bourgeoisie, with the upper class bourgeoisie and even with the
monopolist oligarchy. A popular front, only backwards. And
tomorrow, the meeting with Curial at eleven o'clock, at the
Atheneum, and then to the Registry Office. Tirant and Curial
and Rocaguinarda and Rocafort and Entenza and Roca Guinart
and Serrallonga and his men, Pixafort and Cagaferro or something like that, gentlemen and bandits or gentlemen bandits or
bandit gentlemen. The meeting with Curial and the Registry
Office. And in the afternoon, see the Plutos, to see if everything's
going well, to cheer them up, and the meeting with Plans's men,
the Rodriguezes, the Vilás, the monstrous offspring of that oh-
so-characteristically Barcelonan bourgeoisie, not very different,
however, from any other solidly established bourgeoisie in any
other European city. Another conjecture: that the intended conflict with Plans, which Amadeo seems to have so satisfactorily
and skillfully resolved, has been, after all, something much less
Machiavellian than the mental reconstruction of the events, fruit
of a widow's mistrust, an attorney's ineptitude, and a general
climate of neurotic imagination that had settled over them.
Simply: the maneuver—not conspiracy—of a living person,
Plans, to get the most out of the situation, undoubtedly difficult,

in which Gráficas Rivas found itself; or more simple still, to not get your fingers caught in the trap, to cover up any possible rupture. And, in this sense, Amadeo's intervention might well have softened the consequences for Plans as well as for the others. And his lost overcoat? And the ashes of the fallen leaves like the dark body of a bird struck down from the sky? Vertigo and whirlwind, names, things, people, occurrences, happening one after another, transforming, metamorphosing, that fantastic vortex, with the desire, in the center of the depths, of stopping and thinking, stopping and looking around and forward and, above all, behind, recounting it all, stopping anywhere, looking from anywhere, around, within, to the very bottom, above, up to where the summit ends, stop there and look around. And so like a man who exerts himself in response to the amorous stimulations of his partner and, carried by that impulse, only tempered by breathlessness, fatigue, and absence, does not delay in intuiting that he's gone too far too fast, the adequate form too forcedly acquired under that wild head of hair haloing his sex, or rather, by the time he'd penetrated the woman with that awareness of disaster, trying desperately to avoid the inevitable void, holding back sudden ejaculation, reestablishing the necessary rhythm, resisting the tensions that herald the final comfortable peace, the damp warm repose of one body atop another, united by the slippery, still-oozing, dilating rose, counteracting this end even when it comes on time, resorting to any old thing, mnemonic concentration, Chinese procedures, thinking don't think a thing, thinking don't be ashamed of the end result beforehand, don't accelerate the unavoidable abandon, lost morale and dejection and disenchantment that surrenders itself to the rising ardor, to this finish so brusquely ended.

IX

THE WORST THING IN LIFE: that it turns out exactly as we feared. A Purgatory where we are punished not specifically for offenses committed, but rather for our a priori assignment to this or that sentence, to this or that sector or field reserved beforehand for a certain kind of punishment. The rest, Paradise, Inferno, are only the two endpoints, interchangeable incidentally, of a metaphor that alludes to certain extreme or, for being analogous to everything one would like to find that is not found upon the mountain's arid heights, apparently imaginary situations; opposite perspectives from the same topographical accident. Why did Dante come to rest on the description of the tenth heaven, beyond the nine moving heavens and even the nine angelic choirs? Why did he lack the strength of his elevated fantasy to give us an image of the culmination of the Empyrean? Why is the word feeble itself too feeble a word to explain to us what he saw in the center of the light, the nature of the fire in the Third Circle, the reflection of an iris reflected in an iris? Why could he say no more than *un fante che bagni ancor la lingua alla mammella*? Because in the center of this fire he discovered the eye of the Inferno, and he understood that this last circle of Paradise was simultaneously the ninth circle of Hell or, if you prefer, the point of union between both; that, center against center, were in fact one and the same thing, like facing a mirror where you really don't know which side you're on, where the nearest thing touches the nearest thing. Meaning, what he'd long feared: having reached the vertex of the Inferno, contrary to what he could expect from his exceptional powers of observation placed at the service of a sadistic delectation, Dante announces his resistance to writing what he saw up there, higher than the deepest depth,

given that however much he said about it would be too little,
too feeble. Something that, well considered, was already obvious
to the attentive reader of Canto 34, the end of the *Inferno*, that
canto which like a wasteful excess, the same as the tenth heaven,
seems to break or contradict the poem's symmetry and ternary
structure, 3 times 33. How is it that no scholar or critic has yet
fallen into the necessity of investigating more deeply the meaning of that extra canto, that added canto, that canto that gives
the *Inferno* just one more than the *Purgatorio* or the *Paradiso* and
which perhaps, to offer a more precise correspondence, should
bear the number 100, as the nexus or bridge between Paradise
and Hell, as it closes and brings the poem full circle?

The process, the linking of events and, even more, the immediate motive that had led him there, to that situation, to that
forced attitude, solid as a rock or a militant or a sentinel with a
sharp bayonet, was in a certain way a question without importance; like a nocturnal Count Arnau with no need of the sparks
from his fiery horse, of those hooves that ring like chains, to
know himself condemned, or like the rapist Fra Garí in his errant
bloodsucking life among the crags of Montserrat, a product not
of his guilty conscience, as could be naively deduced, but of a
roundly objective sanction, or like an impious Serrallonga in his
surplice, so Raúl knew that one day or another, it was fated to
happen, just like an Al Capone, finally brought down by perjury
or tax evasion, the one as lethal as the other. Nor, in the long run,
would the predominant role which certain conflictive personality
traits of his could have played in all that carry greater interest—
the virtues or pietas of an Aeneas, his capacity for dedication
to an impersonal goal, to a collective enterprise, exercised with
the shrewdness and calculation of a Ulysses or, quite possibly,
to the inverse—without managing to explain to us previously
the why and the wherefore of that conflictive personality; no,
no greater interest than that of highlighting, for example, the
decisive role that Modesto Pírez played in his arrest, the baneful
Modesto, just the sort of stool pigeon who must have helped
bring down Al Capone, one of the first things he saw at Police
Headquarters, Modesto Pírez sitting in a chair, tied to it with

a belt, and the look on his face of an adult caught red-handed masturbating, the supplication for understanding contained in his desolate eyes, the acceptance of his guilt, the hope that everything would end happily. Some occurrence had to pull him out of that quotidian life that was the image and likeness of Purgatory, an image of which institutions like school or the military are, in their turn, images, forever awaiting the degree, the diploma, the final redemption, and then everything will be different. Granted, too, that the lover's natural element is the prison of his love, as for a mystic it's the prison of the body, which supports his trances. Thus, vivifying fire can become the real prison for the condemned man, to the point that, like for the mystic or the lover, if that prison does not exist, they invent it.

Motionless, standing at attention before the open door of his cell, like a Farinata standing upright in his burning tomb. But unlike Farinata, and although equally stung by curiosity or tedium, not by self-will, but—conveniently confronted—obliged to attend, like it or not, the ceremony that, marked by cornet blasts, is celebrated upon the circular platform of the prison's Central Tower, the very navel of those vast confines, somewhere between cathedral nave and ship's bridge; to look without seeing the distant purple flashes and the ritual of the movements, no less rigorous in their execution than his own, realized throughout the course of the day, crossing his cell diagonally, for example, counting his steps—seven in this one, four in the previous one, three in the first—stepping always on the same tiles, turning always to the same side—the right—bumping his elbows against the angled walls each time he turns, and starting again, one, two, three, four, five, six, seven. Or when he rinsed seven times after washing. Or when he ate his grub—lentils, beans, lentils, garbanzos, lentils, beans, lentils, garbanzos, lentils—in exactly seventy spoonfuls, always capable, however, of being adjusted. Or with each recounting, counting to twenty, thirty, forty, depending—although finely adjusted, risking more each time, however fast he counted—before taking his place at attention before the doorway, in the interval he measured between the arrival of the block boss passing by, opening the cells, and the incoming or outgoing officer who recounts and his entourage, the interval calculated according to the distance, each time variable, separating the boss's passing from the others as they checked the cells opposite and, especially, when they reached the end, the last cell on the other side and passed by on this side, according to their voices, 237 one, 236 one, 235 one, louder as they approached his cell, until the moment they appeared, 234 one, to find Raúl, cutting it closer each time, just in front of the cell door, standing at attention, as if whisked there more by fright than simply leaping into place, his expression tense and a current of air at his back, cowed by the silent expectation of the prisoners on the opposite side of the gallery, where the block boss, running his key the length of the balustrade, now went from cell to cell, inspecting or simply meting out punishments, according to the situation. Or in his obsessive arrangement of his belongings behind the headboard, his toiletries, his t-shirts, underpants, socks, toilet paper, tobacco, pen, matches. Or the strict order he followed for dressing and undressing. Or the regularity with which he smoked a cigarette every half-hour without the need to check the clock; miscalculating by three minutes more or less was a bad sign. Like an error in the order of putting on or taking off his various garments, or in arranging his things; or losing track when counting. And how, in general, also, the weather was bad, the cloudy skies, the rain. Clearly neurotic interpretive tendencies and rituals, of course; but not especially heightened by the circumstances. In the same way that now, without his medicine, without his sleeping pills, without his tranquilizers, without his stimulants, he slept no worse than before nor did he feel more tired or depressed. On the contrary. Although, of course, if he had his pills he'd go right back to taking them. Not only from fear of the insomnia, fatigue, and depression that might assault him, but also from the bad luck he could bring on himself by not taking them. An insomnia, however, you might almost call induced—despite the care with which he took to spread his overcoat over the bedstead of the bunk overhead, to block out the lightbulb, a lightbulb mounted on the wall, above the door, that stayed lit all night long—voluntarily provoked thanks to a methodical inspection, at bedtime, of his mind, his thoughts, his memory, his imagination. Insomnia: eyes, circles, owls.

Not only a manic ritual. No. A way, too, of marking time, a personal system superimposed upon the order of the penitentiary regimen, upon its rhythms of meals and head counts, subjecting the sequence of hours to a rhythm previously unexperienced, according to which the days passed quickly and the hours slowly and, even more slowly, the minutes. Thus, one would say that the minutes expired before the present instant had gone by more slowly, nine and nine, if his watch kept good time, than the whole week gone by since last Sunday at this same time, a Sunday that prefigured, no doubt, what this Sunday was going to be; repetitions that as they prolong the instant also warp—vertigo or immobility, acceleration or pause—the passing of time. Pauses which after brusquely breaking the course of his reflections, like an alarm clock that forces us from sleep, made him return to them with renewed penetration, with renewed distance, as if in the interval the key he'd previously sensed had come to him of its own accord, precipitating the mechanisms of conscience, enriching them, the same as other pauses into which all men drift who are subjected to isolation: exchanging the greatest number of words with the loutish men dishing out the grub; with the always more than cordial block boss, one Barquero or Botero; reading the latest issue of *Redención* from the first word to the last, the sole echo of the sublunary world; sing aloud songs that feed the spirit or bring good luck; hunt down the dust mice that floated through the cells (like landladies) on the air currents; look out the window, from the top bunk, when the prisoners went out into the yard; or, attentive to the noises from the gallery, to the footsteps, the voices, guards knocking on prisoners' doors, the voice of the cellblock boss asking their number, numble? cornet blasts and crazy laughter, the loudspeakers, keeping your eye glued to the stool pigeon like on a microscope eyepiece, trying to decipher the peculiar rhythms of daily life in prison; and the dialogues from cell to cell through the wall, with his neighbor, number 233; trying, also, to follow as much as possible the message of la Merche,

confusedly repeated over the loudspeakers, words about the coming Easter—*la Pascua*—a commemoration of the passion and
glory of the Lord, Pascua meaning crossing, passing over, and
celebrated in ancient times to commemorate the crossing of the
Red Sea, but, and what is a man's life but a crossing, a transit
toward his eternal salvation or punishment? Retracing the shapes
already discovered in the puddles on the flagstones; following
the sunlight crossing the floor of the cell, following the course
of its mutations from it first entering like a tiny crack and then
growing and taking on geometric shapes, oblique polygons,
irregular quadrilaterals, rhombuses, rectangles soon deformed,
rhombuses, in the opposite direction from the first one, growing thinner until disappearing as if through a slot, geometries
resulting from the projection of the bars upon the floor, a reticule
of shadows superimposed on the sunny grid of the flagstones
like the public bus and streetcar lines are superimposed on a city
map, laid out in a grid like the Ensanche, that Ensanche which
is home to the Cárcel Modelo—the Model Prison—in the
space delimited by four different streets: Rosellón, Provenza,
Entenza, and Nicaragua.

How many times had he not dreamed of this recently? A
detective was about to arrest him on Paseo de la Bonanova,
or in the garden at Vallfosca, or—also in Vallfosca—a truck
full of police with rifles and steel helmets, like German
soldiers, suddenly came round a small bend in the road, or
several plainclothes policemen chased him through the Galerías
Astoria department store, situated in the same location where
the Almacenes El Siglo had been located, destroyed by a fire
a few years before he was born, on the eve of the Feast of the
Magi or some similar date of equal importance. And he had
to flee or hide and, as he fired, the pistol jammed, or at least
the bullets didn't shoot. Or rather, in an office, various detectives asked him about something, something always difficult to
remember once awake; and he lied, invented alibis. The same
when he really was arrested, while he was interrogated for real,
not only in the symbolic sense of the word, not by police who
really act like repressive agents of the superego. A dream that

had stopped recurring the moment his arrest became reality. Just as he had not dreamed again, conscious that he did not know how to drive, that he was driving a car at high speed and, although he handled the controls at random, managed not to crash and burn. A rather exciting sensation, somewhat similar to when, as a boy, he rode the bumper cars with Manolo at the neighborhood carnival; a sensation he'd not experienced again in his dreams from the moment when he started practicing to get his driver's license, even before he'd passed the preliminary written exam without any trouble, that cold January morning on Montjuich, when nervous about something deeper than the simple extreme jitters accompanying an exam, perhaps the situation itself, childish and regressive because of what it had in common with other such previously experienced situations, like in school or military service. Like a presentiment that he was already being followed. Because that's how it must have been, given that the police themselves had made a detailed report of his comings and goings on the feast day of San Raimundo de Penyafort, the 23rd of January, the day before the exam. And everything seemed to indicate that it was precisely that day when they began to follow him, the feast of San Raimundo de Penyafort, illustrious jurist, transporter *super undas* and patron saint of lawyers; the reason for the mock trial held in the patio of the School of Humanities against a student dressed up as a policeman, when he spotted Modesto Pírez among the spectators and decided to get his attention, not only for the mix of irritation and unease that the Canary Islander's personality, and even mere physical presence, caused him, but rather because he'd come to confirm the apprehensions that Leo had expressed to him about Pírez only a few days before. One night when they went out to eat together, his worry about the confidence that Floreal seemed to have placed in a phony like that guy, whose behavior only seemed to increase his danger, moving as he moved, showing up at all of Guillén's friends' houses, friends, names, and addresses that Guillén could only have given him in a moment of Parisian drunkenness, or irresponsible nostalgia. He drew him aside—no doubt observed not by a student dressed as a police officer but by a policeman dressed as a student—to let him know there were secret police there, that his presence could draw attention for more than just having come with a university friend, especially if they took the trouble to find out that he wasn't a university student, that he'd recently arrived from France and was working construction. Don't worry, friend, before I talk I'll hang myself with my own belt if necessary, said the Canary Islander. A brief conversation, but one the police could not miss or the police who were already following Pírez and who from then on, probably, began following him, too. Until February 12, Santa Eulalia's Day, when, shortly after arriving home from a night out, during which time, fortunately, he'd not had too much to drink, the doorbell rang.

Because it might not have ended relatively early or relatively peacefully. One of those times, for example, which, the next morning, in the shower, with a hangover, made him promise himself not to give in anymore, to not agree anymore from pure habit, because until then he'd always said yes, to their proposal of going out for a walk at night, when around mid-afternoon Nuria, Federico, Fortuny, Pluto, the Adolfos telephoned him, evening excursions that didn't appeal to him, that bored him, the places, the people, his friends, everyone, he himself in the first place, adjusting to certain kinds of jokes, to their habitual role, a parody of themselves and of other times, scenes fraught with a terrifying reiterative quality, of a degraded attempt to go back or—almost worse—of carrying on the same way. The least of it was that only on rare occasions did they go down to Las Ramblas, whether for being naturally tired of that part of the city, whether for the comfort and quality of the alcohol that, along with the prices and the type of people, characterize the nightlife in the upper part of the city. Different locales, different crowds, but the same buffoonery. And if the simple phone call, the proposal accepted with such little conviction, was enough to spoil his work for the rest of the evening, when he was drinking as well, when despite his intention to not drink too much, things got messy and, in a given moment, after a certain point, he forgot his good intentions and what time it was, and suddenly realized that the sun was already rising and that he was drunk, and so then he lost the whole next day and, sometimes, even the next one, too, fog in his head and acid in his guts and—the most persistent thing—the oppressive exhaustion produced by everything unfinished, which only vanishes by getting back to the work abandoned because of the fateful telephone call. What might have happened if he'd been arrested coming back from one of those sprees, not around New Year's Eve? But, let's take for example, the night they stumbled into Montserrat at Las Vegas, accompanied by Monsina and some tongue-tied young fellow in a navy blue jacket with silver buttons? Raúl, hey big guy! The best of the Ferrer Gamindes: you're fucking great! She made them all sit down, almost had to force them, and ordered another bottle of whiskey. Me? Well, just as fucked as usual; in the worst sense of the word, unfortunately. She turned toward the next table, in the shadows. Claudio, goddamn, Claudio, look what a fucking great cousin I've got! Mama is an angel, said Monsina. She stepped out to dance with the fellow in the navy blue jacket with silver buttons and Montserrat grabbed Adolfo. C'mon, you, I don't want to commit a mortal sin with my first cousin. She hung on Adolfo's neck, falling down drunk, and they came back to the table right away, Montserrat tripping her way through a sort of involuntary tango. She slipped down between the chair and the table, dragging some glasses with her as she fell. Hitting the floor with a thump seemed to clear her wits, although she kept turning back and forth in her chair with a self-conscious smile, her gaze too fixed and staring. Goddamn, Raúl, when the hell are we gonna go out and have a few drinks, just you and me. By the time they finally managed to shake her, Raúl had swallowed four or five whiskeys, and didn't mind to keep going and, once every place was shuttered, end up at the flat of any old more-or-less-familiar good-time Charlie picking up stragglers along the way.

The night of his arrest, however, February 12, he was feeling too shitty from the start for drinking to make any difference. A listless Federico, who could only get more dull and lifeless. A certain M. M. more of a pain in the ass than ever. And the

women being real bitches, shooting to kill, and Mariconcha trying to make everybody listen to her, the problem with servants,
and Pluto cutting her off. The bad thing is the filthy cooks. They
spit right in the soup before serving it. They stick their fingers
up their ass when they're making meatballs. When they're on the
rag, they mix it right into the tomato sauce. It's very well known.
Like the bakers who fuck the dough while they're kneading it.
And Marihole: you're the filthy pig, you swine, worse than swine,
you've always got to say something to fuck it all up. And Nuria
Oller repeating: why don't we go up to Mount Carmel? C'mon,
man, c'mon, let's go up to Carmelo. Trying to catch Raúl's eye,
looking for some significant spark of understanding, insistently
trying to remind him of that other night, around the end of
October, when Federico proposed that they go up to Carmelo
and, split up into three cars, they chased each other around
the choppy curves up high as close to the summit as possible,
and then, amid slamming doors, through the quiet darkness,
they continued on foot, hand in hand, feeling their way along,
dazzled by the splendid brilliance that haloed the peak, and
once there, against the crest, as if isolated in space, as if halfway
between the frigid sky and the city that, like a mirror, seemed
to reflect the glimmerings and blacknesses up there, shouting,
they recited fragments of St. John of the Cross and Góngora and
Quevedo and of the *Moral Epistle to Fabian*. But it was while
they were looking at the constellations when Raúl felt Nuria's
hair caressing his cheek, a light touch that if he at first considered
accidental, its very persistence, along with the innocuous comments about the stars whispered into his ear, as if kissing him,
left no doubt in his mind. To feel her breasts, too, while she,
right behind him, right up against him, pointed upward asking
some question, was almost unnecessary.

Although unanticipated, the circumstances in which his arrest
took place could hardly have been more conventional. To what

point could Federico picking up Raúl in his car have distracted the police so much that they, afraid that he might slip through their grasp, decided to drop the bomb once and for all? It must not have been even one o'clock when Federico said he was going to sleep, and Raúl seconded him, and Nuria ended up agreeing, rather reluctantly. They dropped off Nuria first and then swung by Raúl's house. Federico parked and killed the engine right in front of the entranceway and leaned against the steering wheel but they only stopped to talk a little, neither with much enthusiasm. It was about twenty minutes later—already in pajamas and with his sleeping pill swallowed—when the doorbell rang. He put his overcoat on over his pajamas and opened the door himself: three detectives. The driver and a policeman were outside, pacing in front of the doorway. The night was very cold. While he dressed they casually searched the room, superficially, glancing at his papers. He thought they took something he'd written. Papa came out in his bathrobe. Eloísa watched them from the end of the hallway, a white shawl over a long white nightgown in the darkness. Don't worry, just a routine inquiry. And Raúl: especially, keep Nuria calm. Before leaving they let him take a piss and go back to his room to get his cigarettes, but without letting him out of their sight. They put him in the backseat of the car, between two detectives. If you want to come out on Paseo de la Bonanova, take the next street, he told the driver. This one's a dead-end. Yes, we already know you know your way around the city very well, said the detective who'd sat in the front seat, turning halfway around; you've got to stay on your toes to follow this guy. One of the men beside him patted him on the thigh. But what really interests us, more than how well you know your way around, is your knowledge of the party. And Raúl: what party? And the man sitting next to him patted him on the thigh again: you know much better than I do that there's only one party. And Raúl: I'm sorry, but I don't understand what you're talking about or what I'm doing here. And the man next to him: of course. Anybody would start off denying it, right? What were they going to think in Moscow? A deliberately unpleasant smile, a smile that placed between parentheses, sincerely and

without a doubt, the part of sincerity that could have been on
Raúl's side, the reality of his perplexity, the meaning of an arrest
occurring when he found himself practically marginalized from
all party life, how his mind raced with questions, much faster
than the car carrying them, questions that he only began to
orient correctly when, as he crossed through the offices of the
police headquarters, he came face to face with Modesto Pírez,
sitting in a chair, tied with a belt. The specific concern of the
statement immediately taken from him by a polite, almost shy,
policeman brought the question into focus, clarifying who was
working against him. Name? Age? Status? Profession? Did he
know Modesto Pírez, alias Salvador, member of the Communist
Party? The declarant says he does not, the officer repeated out
loud as he transcribed the answer; he typed with a beginner's
slowness and made no objection at all to the answers he was
receiving. University professor, he said as an aside. It must be
exciting to dedicate your life to teaching. He set the original and
the copies in front of Raúl and asked him to sign them. Now if
you'd please be so kind as to wait here, professor; now, let's see if
they like it, he said, and gave him a wink. He left him alone in
the room, a small inner office, with skylights that allowed him to
see the florescent lights in the adjacent rooms. He heard voices
and laughter coming from different directions. At one point, a
thickset, red-faced man, thoracic like a Negro, stepped in to look
him over; he went out, looking at Raúl all the while, the way a
collector admires his latest acquisition before sleep. In turn, Raúl
stuck his head out into the hallway and asked an officer walking
by if he could make a phone call home to reassure his family. I'll
go and ask, the other man said to him, and Raúl went back to
sit down and await the answer, important not only as an indication of the mood in the station, but also, in case they allowed
him to, what that would mean for both Papa and Eloísa as well
as for his friends, and after the phone call that Papa must have
made to Nuria when they took him from the house, they would
have already sounded the alarm, especially Leo, but also Fortuny
and even Federico and Adolfo, given the confused origin of all
that. Papa, who lately, as if he sensed something, while Raúl was

working, opened slightly the door of his room and looked in for a moment before closing it again, without saying a word, as if to make sure he was there, or perhaps, just like when at night, on hearing him arrive, he rattled a teaspoon in his glass of tea, making the sound to make it clear that it was he, not Raúl, but he, who was home.

I am a man who, in a continuous fight against adverse circumstances, has given himself over body and soul to the fulfillment of his Christian obligations. I have done God's will. I have fulfilled my duties as a husband and the father of my family. I have honored my neighbor, working for the country's industrial and economic progress. And I've taken so many hard knocks already in this life that I think I've pretty well eluded whatever place in Purgatory might have been reserved for me thanks to what I've already suffered in this world. First, losing Jorgito, my firstborn. Then, losing Eulalia, like a hammer blow. Then, the time of the Reds, always on edge, living like a refugee there in a town, with two children to feed and no resources. Then, my company collapsing. And now, in my old age, I won't mention my economic difficulties, but I do have to count every last cent. And with all the money I used to manage! He spoke slumped down in an armchair in the sitting room, as if overwhelmed by the ignominy of having tried to play the Philistine but failed. And Eloísa listened to him from the hallway, seated next to the door, knitting stockings. Ay, Señor, she said. Once in a while she went into the kitchen, to check on the broth for dinner. And Papa talked about the company, failing to mention not only the accusation about his supposed incompetence as head of the corporation—his disorderly management, his administrative carelessness, his whimsical projections and schemes—accusations that had provided management with a basic consensus for removing him from his position, but also omitting the fact that such a usurpation had taken place, taking for granted the official excuse of retirement, a retirement, that's right, to his understanding completely unnecessary even though he might have been of retirement age. It's human ingratitude, that's what it is. To me, the founder and majority shareholder, the man who got the

company up and running, when they start to see me old and
sick, without the energy I had when I was young or the support
and encouragement when I had Eulalia at my side, but still in
full possession of my faculties, dammit, and they go and force
me to retire, as if I was no longer good for anything, the way you
throw away some piece of trash, abandoned and forgotten by
everyone, without any of them even being good enough to wish
me well on my saint's day. That's how they thanked me for what
I did for the company. My mistake was having sold my shares.
I think now they're paying better dividends than ever. Of course
it's almost better to never see how others reap what you've sown
with your hard work, with your contacts, with your initiative,
with your legal advice. And Eloísa: don't worry, their time to
retire will come, too. And what good will what they've done or
stopped doing serve them when the Sphinx turns its eyes upon
them? And Papa: at least my conscience is clear. And what God
has taken from me on one side he's given me back on the other.
This house, for example, when I got married everybody was saying how far out of town it was. I bought it for a song and now
it's worth a fortune. And I expect that the municipal authorities
will authorize, that they'll eventually authorize it, adding floors
above, like on Paseo de la Bonanova. Imagine it then: worth
millions. Remember what I'm telling you: this house has got to
be the nest egg for my children. He fell silent, as if absorbed in
his mental calculations. And the country house, Eloísa chimed
in: what that must be worth. Imagine. The amount of land
there, and nowadays, when they're selling it by the centimeter;
however much you like. Such a stupid mistake Gregorius made,
selling his share. The poor man was no longer in his right mind.
And, look, seems they put this idea in his head. The shame
is about the poplars, no one grows them anymore, they don't
bring any money. Oh, and the potatoes from there were so good;
and the vegetables, and those chickens Polit used to raise. Do
you remember every week when the basket came? You think I'd
forget. That was good, fresh, natural food; not like nowadays,
everything chemical. There was a silence. Raúl, can you see, son?
Your eyes'll fall out. Why don't you turn on the light? Quiet,

I can't even see my knitting needles. It's not the end of the world? Put on the radio, señor, this house scares me. Well, it's foggy out, woman. Can't you hear the sirens from the port? It's all so dark. Well, the autumn's been really bad so far: fog, rain, cold. I don't know, señor, but this is like the twelve plagues. Egypt! That's right: I wouldn't like to die without first seeing Egypt.

He spoke like a person in front of a microphone rehearsing different versions of the same speech. And Eloísa, like that aging spectator who never stops going to see *Don Juan Tenorio* each November, and who knows whole speeches by heart, listened attentively, nodding, surprised, now you see, now you see. Less flexible than Papa in her judgments, when it was sunny, for example, and Papa sat in the garden and folded his paper. At any rate, Eloísa, it's our lot to live in a great period in history. In a few years we'll travel to the moon the same as we go to Vallfosca now. And man will travel through the solar system and learn the origin of life. The prospects have never been so exciting. And Eloísa: and what does the moon and the solar system matter to us or anybody, we can hardly handle a toothache. All this talk about the moon and science is like television, if you want to watch, then watch, but however much you distract yourself with it nobody can change the fact that you're here and not there, and your problems are what you've got here, and nothing else. Less versatile, yes, her mood less variable, except when Nuria came over, and then, no matter what they did, she closed up tight, leathery, incorruptible. These are not the times for spending money on flowers, she'd say if Nuria brought flowers when she came to have lunch. And if she brought bonbons and Eloísa couldn't resist the temptation: I'm not particular. I'm not one of these people who go around saying, I like this, I don't like that. I eat everything. And when Nuria brought the photograph showing them both together in the garden: I don't like photos. We should live the time allotted to us. You're young and, before you know it, you're already old. And she then complained about guests, meaning Nuria, as if I didn't have enough to do already with everyone in this house, the day they thought of buying dinner ahead of time, in addition to the dessert from the buttery, a stuffed capon, she left them all sitting there in the kitchen. Fine. Then I can go lie down and rest. I can tell when I'm not needed. For me, so much the better. If you can feed yourselves so well without me, well then, when I go to the retirement home, everyone will be happy. If it was a holiday or her day off, she left the house without saying goodbye, with her overcoat and her purse and her babushka knotted under her chin. She would still be angry when she got home, while she prepared dinner without a word, banging the pots and pans, and sometimes all the next day. And Papa's attempts to soothe her nerves only produced the opposite effect, due to an instinct similar to what spurs the boxer to hit harder when he sees blood welling up in the cuts on his opponent's brow. But Eloísa, guapa, my dear, don't you see they did this with the best intention, to save you some work? Come on, woman, for God's sake, don't be like this. Work? snapped Eloísa. Is she the one who washes the clothes without a washing machine and has to manage in a kitchen that's just an embarrassment, and do the cleaning without any appliances and prepare your little concoctions? And would she stick up for you when the pharmacy assistant or whoever delivers something here and you don't give a tip or when they come to collect some bill and you have me tell them to come back another day just because, to delay paying a few pesetas, and I don't even know what to say or how to look them in the eye, when you just as easily sign a check for those crooked door-to-door encyclopedia salesmen, and you pay whatever subscription price the first one who shows up asks for? It's fine, then, just fine that the Russians have the atomic bomb. That way we'll be finished and done with all this nonsense once and for all. With all the trouble it takes to live. Better we all fly to the moon. And Papa: But Eloísa, Eloísa, don't get so angry, they did this for you. For me? Would she do it for the wages I earn? Don't you know there are some who get paid more than twice what I'm getting? Imagine that, what a crazy idea. The world has gone completely crazy. People nowadays are almost afraid to go out in the street. Well, between not going out, and ending up in the charity home, then that's the end of it. To be here, preparing those concoctions you're always taking. And then you're always running to the bathroom. Because I'm sick, woman. Sick? How could you not be sick with all those concoctions that are killing you? And from the kitchen, while Papa initiated a prudent retreat to the sitting room, she continued exclaiming, expounding her idea of good health, of what's nourishing, of what's beneficial, of what does the body well, according to a scheme whose main points, established by comparison, would be the following: above all, whatever is good and hearty. Meaning: what's substantial over what's not. Spiced and spicy dishes over ones with no spice. Salty food over bland. Fatty and tasty cooking over unsavory, fat-free recipes. Sweet over dry. Rich, thick food over thin, weak food. Astringent, cleansing foods over laxative ones.

She came in quietly, wrapped in cold, with her overcoat, her big purse, her babushka. No grumbling or ranting. She sat in a chair in the kitchen, waiting for the vegetables to cook, as if she'd forgotten her rude remarks to Nuria, how she slammed the door that afternoon on going out. Look, Raúl, my nephew's mother-in-law has cancer. It's malignant. She doesn't know it. They've told her it's rheumatism and that's why they're giving her shock treatments. It seems that for some time now, at night, she could hear that tumor inside her, hear it and everything, it's that big, eating away at her from inside; but she never said anything. And now it seems they're telling her, no, it's rheumatism making her bones creak and crunch. But it's cancer. She sighed. And she spoke about her nephew's grief and her own grief for the two of them, for the poor woman and her nephew, still completely unaware that just as Raúl knew that her name really wasn't Eloísa, but Eulalia—she had changed her name because Papa had asked her to when she came to work at their house—he also knew equally well that her nephew was not really her nephew but her son. All the rest, the circumstances of the case, were unknown even to that son of hers. Seduction? Rape? Statutory rape? And the father? The priest in whose house she first worked as a maid? Some rich kid like in the soap operas? A family man? That riot policeman she spoke about sometimes? Something only she must know with exactitude, the subterranean part of her secret.

A secret that only weeks later she discovered was not really a secret from Raúl, and essentially hadn't been for years; although Raúl was the youngest, although he wasn't the man of the house like Papa nor a priest like Felipe. It was a result of José—Pepe— raising the question of Eloísa going to live with them. Probably, a question related to the mother-in-law's declining condition, and to the problem of when she left them—as he put it—of who was going to mind the children while the parents ran the bar; very probably, yes, although none of this was mentioned, of course. He'd called one Sunday afternoon asking for Raúl, surely taking advantage of the fact that Eloísa was minding the children, to talk personally, he said, about a confidential matter. The bar was located in the Santa Catalina Marketplace, and Pepe—José—told him that he wasn't making a fortune from it, but he did have a steady clientele, sufficient to save some money every month. Raúl hadn't seen him for some time; he didn't come by the house, more or less since he'd gotten married. He was changed. He was approximately the same age as Felipe, but he might have passed for his father, heavy—still eschewing an apron—and almost bald. They'd like his mother to come to live with them, he explained: she was getting old, and there she could help them without getting too tired out. When my wife's mother's bedroom is empty, he said. It's not really very large, but once we repaint it, it'll look real nice. Raúl told him of course they'd agree to whatever she decided; but it was he, her son, who had to speak to her. He did so at the first opportunity, the following Thursday. Eloísa returned home earlier than usual, quite out of sorts and furious, who knows if from the terms of the proposal, or from, probably, the abrupt way he explained it to her, from José's probably somewhat infelicitous words, or, more likely still, from the sudden revelation that Raúl, the youngest, also knew about her so-called secret. She said that she'd be leaving, that she was going to the charity home, that she didn't want to be a bother to anyone. And Papa followed her through the house, wait woman! wait woman! Her indignation only began to abate when she believed that it'd not been their idea but rather her son's, José's, Pepe's. He's a stupid fool. Stupid, I've always said so.

Stupid. I'll really let him have it. I'll teach him a lesson. She was still wearing her babushka, her overcoat half-open, only unbuttoned, revealing her heavy round heaving bust, her whole person smothered, her wrath, the heat of the kitchen. I'm better off here, with the people in this house. And Papa, but of course Eloísa, my dear, for God's sake, of course this is your home, you're like one of the family.

Papa urinating in the garden, his sex like a root between his hands. He turned as he heard Raúl's footsteps on the thin gravel. It's very good for the plants, he said; organic matter. Each day I pee on a different one. He buttoned up distractedly, shaking his head. Poor Eloísa. She's really upset about all this business with that blasted Pepe. Luckily she's got her head screwed on right. With a tragedy like hers or like mine one can only save themselves by keeping a level head. It's so easy to let yourself fly off the rails. Look at Gregorius. As if I didn't have temptations, too. But I knew how to resist them. It's not that I want to complain about poor Leonor, I mean that, and in every other way she's a good woman and, in a certain way, it's lucky that it was her and not a different one. But she's not the right person for him, for a man of his class, of his culture. The fact is, Gregorius has always been a disaster, a loafer, selfish, someone who only thinks about himself. He's never struggled like I have, he hasn't suffered. Now you compare : a completely different case. Completely. I still almost can't believe the day they came for lunch. It still makes me angry. Poor Leonor completely ill-at-ease sitting at our table, trying to help Eloísa, to not call attention to herself, and he, on the other hand, so cool and collected, worried about nothing but his food. It made me furious to look at him. He never took his eyes off her while she served herself. He sat there stiff, peevish, censorious, just lashing her with his eyes. But when it was his turn, he just took any old thing from the platter, myopic and indifferent. I like it fresh and I like it spicy, he said.

Leonor opened the door for him and he found Gregorius seated in the entrance hall, in a t-shirt, his gaze abstracted, staring at the bright ceiling globe. Hearing voices, he seemed astonished at the sight of Raúl, with a disbelief and an effusion that could only be explained by the fact that he had confused him with some relative or friend from his own childhood, long dead. He embraced him repeatedly, pushing aside Leonor, who was saying they should move into the living room. Enough, let me be, woman, it's nicer in here. His breath smelled bad. When Leonor heard that Raúl had come to invite them over for lunch, partially from her astonishment and partially because it really was true, she hastened to let him know that although Gregorius was quite recovered, he was still not the same as before. And as if to prove her right, while she talked, Gregorius's gaze swam back to the globe above. Look, there's just no way I can get him to put on his shirt. And this is because he sees that it's sunny and so he says that he's hot. But if he sees that it's cloudy, even though it's summertime, he insists on going out with an overcoat. And he takes pills secretly, when I'm not looking, he eats and drinks and smokes and does everything the doctor's forbidden him, and there's no way to control him, he always manages to outsmart me. I've even caught him smoking sitting on the toilet. During the week, I take him out to the Corte Inglés or Sears or to some museum, and that's how we spend the afternoon. Or to the Barraquer Clinic, to the waiting room, and he sits there and reads the magazines. But Sundays, after Mass, where can I take him except the park? Sometimes, now that the weather's good, I'll take him to sit on the terrace at some bar, but then he orders a vermouth or a coffee with Anís del Mono, and if I say no, he gets furious and really throws a fit, until everyone is staring at us and he ends up getting his way. I can't leave him alone. I still don't know how he manages to buy cigarettes and sausages. And when he goes into the bathroom to sneak a cigarette he's crafty enough to open the windows to get rid of the smoke. Quiet, said Gregorius. He took Raúl by the arm, subjecting him again to his penetrating halitosis. Hey, are you planning to go to Vallfosca this summer? I'm really ready to go. It's much cooler there. And if we go together it's more fun. You let Polit know to wait for us at the station in his cart.

Early November, all saints departed. They arrived after dark. They were riding with Federico and Nuria Oller was following, in the Adolfos' car. As they got closer to the house, along the final turns up the hill, the headlights pierced the darkness, cork oaks with white limbs, years of deadfall, ghosts. An impression only heightened there inside the car in the resonant quiet, hostile, you might say, to those voices, to their laughter, their footsteps, that came to disturb the silence of memories, the flitting images that animated it like shadows of a movement, apparitions, or better yet, disappearances. Like the landscape. The low fogs of morning, clinging to the hollows, coating and insulating the hills like a balsam, the same as years before when he went out hunting after it cleared. And the same smells of autumn, shifting, nuanced, pervasive seeping emanations from the damp yellow fall, from the sickly carpet of leaves, soft under foot. While the others slept he took a walk around the property, the old plantings, the flatlands alongside the fields sown with young black poplars, slender graynesses stripped of their leaves. Heading back he saw the caretaker's kids around Polit's house, a welter of children watching him from different places. Only the recessed doorway and the window frames were whitewashed, and these touch-ups, which seemed to hollow out the deteriorated facade, and the flowerpots, gave the house the look of a skull with makeup. At the far end of the threshing ground there was now a rose tree that dropped its flowers here and there upon the empty pigsties, their gates hanging open, deep pink flowers so often growing through the fences surrounding the small gardens that town switchmen and stationmasters often plant next to railroad tracks. He returned along the winding paths through the yard, abandoned now to the weeds, invaded by creeping reptilian ivy, crouching brambles, dry creaking claws.

If the weather was inclement, the house was uncomfortable, a circumstance that perhaps influenced the general tension and bad mood. The night before, when they arrived, after having stared up at the cold sky from the porch, the moon now like wintertime, with its violet medusa halo, and those stars like ancient ice, then finding themselves in the toasty warm front room sitting before the fire, they all felt an unusual joy rising inside, an almost physical euphoria, quickly heightened by alcohol.

They explored the house, and Nuria Rivas proposed getting naked atop the altar in the chapel and celebrating a black mass, provided they warmed the place up with enough candles. They ended up playing strip poker by the firelight, and whether because they were starting to come down from the booze, whether for how the game played out, whether for the women's jealousy when facing one another—their feints, trying to gain the upper hand, settling scores—what's certain is that the tone of the party grew increasingly tense and gloomy by the moment. And if, on the one hand, the estrangement that had for some time begun to reappear between Adolfo and Federico became official that night, according to a dialectic that was rather unclear for anyone who'd not watched it develop up close, on the other, the mutual antipathy between the two Nurias—Señorita Rivas and Señorita Oller—for the first time erupted into open hostility. Later, in the icy bedroom, Nuria Rivas insisted on making love beneath that mountain of blankets, perfectly aware, no doubt, that Nuria Oller, in the next room, alone in her chilly bed, could hear her intense cries of pleasure loud and clear.

In fact, Nuria Oller, with her poorly disguised behavior, was the first to make Nuria Rivas suspicious: the silent libidinous relationship that she tended to establish with Raúl in front of others, as if the others were not capable of noticing it, or perhaps calculating, correctly, that they would notice it this way. Her emphatic messages that evinced, in the context of the gathering, a tacit understanding between them both, like one of those code words or gestures adopted by the participants in a conspiracy, too clumsy to not be decoded in time by the security agents. Raúl, why don't you put on some record by Brel? she said. Meaning: not just any record, the record. The specific record that they had heard together on such and such an occasion. Their record. A record she now wanted to hear continuously, the way one hears a marriage processional or a victory march. In only one detail, possibly, was Nuria Rivas off-track: to wonder how something that could happen was, in fact, happening. The date. The taxi. The brothel. The smooth skill with which Nuria Oller's fingers slipped into his fly, the arching feline movement with which she, both of them half-dressed, slid toward the foot of the bed, as if in haste to contemplate her work, her half-open mouth already watering like a communicant about to receive the sacrament. Her obvious knowledge of masculine eroticism, although, one could suppose, not so much from natural intuition as from experience, almost hurrying rather than going at a steady pace, almost with a desire to show off, with too much movement and accelerated rhythm that might even become annoying, although as things progressed she proved to be unquestionably effective and there was no room for such considerations, or any others, while they were hot at it, the thread of conversation lost amid their writhing, reversing position, bodies intertwining, almost suffocating between each others' legs and asses. Afterward she fell asleep. One night shortly before dawn. Their agitated awakening indicated the degree to which their erotic action came to be a continuation of that feverish state, between sleeping and dreaming, amid desires like realities, penetrating penises, brandished naked balanus, hood flush and spread wide, glans ramming forward like suckling piglets, and the fascinating scrotum, like some strange edible sea creature, cousin to both kelp and urchin, its viscous vegetable mobility pregnant with ejaculations, as if perpetually retracting, breathing, as if peristaltically displacing itself, and the erect haughty tropism of the penis that she knows so well how to arouse and put to thoroughly good use, she, hardening haughty penises, rearing back, taking stiff drinks from their stiffened lengths, manipulating, obtaining spectacular erections, nice warm hard-ons, tense, bodies hotly wedged and dovetailed together, Raúl's lance all to herself. Nuria Oller saying I don't know what's up with me but I really love you, and Raúl saying me, too, and Nuria Oller saying maybe I'm just one more girl, but you have to promise me that if you ever get tired of me you'll tell me right away, and Raúl saying you're not just one more and I see no reason why I've got to get tired of you, and Nuria Oller saying I'm so happy with you, and Raúl saying me, too, and Nuria Oller, everything is so strange and complicated but I think I love you, and Raúl, me, too. And how do you know you love me? (Oller). Tautology (Raúl). I'm happy with you.

You make me feel peaceful. But you'll soon get over it (Oller). I don't know why (Raúl). You're the first one to say that no love can last (Oller). It's just a saying (Raúl). Saying, telling, kissing, sucking, licking, embracing.

They watched their naked bodies reflected in the mirror, atop the twisted wrinkled sheets. And I thought I could never love anyone. And I think that everybody has always loved me too much. Starting with my husband. And it's not that I don't like that they love me, of course. But I wish they weren't so stuck on me, that they didn't act as stupid as sheep. And look, Peter has a nice mustache and we get along really well in every way. But it's something different. I'm not sure you understand what I'm trying to say. I wish they were like you. Everything is so different with you. For me, everybody loves me too much. My father, my brothers and sisters, I've always been the family favorite, their little pet. And then on the other hand, every woman hates me sooner or later. And usually sooner rather than later, almost just by seeing me. I don't know why but right from the start they seem to assume that I'm only looking to steal their men. And I can promise you sometimes I feel like proving them right. They start things with me, one woman almost attacked me in public, scratching me and everything. And the truth is I haven't had so many affairs as all that. In any case, it's the guys who want to fuck me. Before you notice a thing they're suddenly trying to cop a feel, groping you. You can't imagine: they drop off their wife and five minutes later they're trying to rape you right there in the car. And when I was a girl it was always flashers: on the street, in the cinema, in doorways. Really disgusting. I figure I'll end up a whore, fucking them all to see if they get sick of me. Sometimes I'm really just about to have a nervous breakdown. I can't stand them touching me that way. They almost make me feel frigid. And you know I'm hardly like that. She was talking to him from the bathroom, while Raúl lay on the bed smoking, still naked, exchanging confidences perhaps not entirely appropriate to share, given their heightened state of excitement, while possessed by that characteristic post-coital mood, when, inert and empty like the castaway who, reaching dry land, doesn't even feel capable of confirming whether or not that beach is more than just a desert island, as if struck down by fatigue, without strength to move, or to locate his clothing, confronted by the most radical questions and reproaches, what are you doing here, why do you always have to end up saying the foolish things you've said. An annoyance that would quickly increase his impatience with the incalculable and detailed routine that Nuria Oller called getting ready, showering, doing her hair, makeup, a process perhaps similar in its mechanics to that herbicidal obsession of some elderly people, who systematically dedicate their leisure time to the task of weeding their yard, purging it of weeds, raking it smooth, an obsession only interpretable in terms of being a symbolic and compensatory act.

You think I don't see she's after you? said Nuria Rivas. It's enough to see how she sits down; with her legs as wide as possible. We know each other very well. In England all she did was try to fuck every one of her friends' boyfriends. And I can promise you that Peter is an alright guy, for a while. But maybe it's better for him; that way he'll get so sick of her cheating on him so much he'll finally shake her off for good. Like me this afternoon: I hung up on her. I've already got enough going on with the Plutos to have to deal with her on top of it. She was irritable, in a bad mood; she said fuck going to see the Plutos, the Plutos were depressing, that she didn't see why they were obliged to automatically go out with them just because. And at the café, while they were waiting, she argued violently with Federico. Because if Adolfo is the Count, then you must be the Countess (Nuria). Right. And I don't like the count. A conjugal problem (the Countess). Well I don't understand why. I don't find him so bad (Nuria). But I do. The ideal thing is the hermaphrodite in the Louvre. And the Count might have enough cock but he seems to be lacking tits. The opposite of your case (the Countess). Ambiguities turn out painful for me; what you should do is define yourself once and for all, accept the reality of what you are (Nuria). The thing is reality is always ambiguous. For example, I only started to be aware of being a transvestite when I found out that my mother, when I was a little boy, dressed me up as a little girl.

They'd not started out talking about Adolfo but about M.
M. Stands for *memo*: neither cretin nor idiot nor imbecile nor
dummy nor stupid: *memo*, a fucking vegetable, said Federico.
But M. M. wasn't really the problem. Like a transvestite of a
certain age who over the years has gone about acquiring the
knowledge about things in life appropriate to an old maid, the
slightly pessimistic prudence of one who has already seen many
things and withdraws; thus, the exact personality of M. M., his
shrewd wit, his nostalgic memories, inevitably had to end up
getting on everyone's nerves. The problem was Adolfo: Nuria's
suspicion, or perhaps her desire—a pretext for venting her anxiety and pent-up belligerence—that Federico's attacks on M. M.
were, in fact, directed at Adolfo, indirect shots against the one
who had made M. M.'s presence at their meetings possible. And
Federico's intention—previous or provoked throughout by the
same attitude from Nuria—that it be understood that way, his
unequivocal desire to make Nuria upset. Speculations, relative to
his appetite for mundane life, signified, for example, in Adolfo's
case, by his continued dealings with M. M.—not so serious, after
all, however suspicious a person of supposed creative intelligence
and moral liberty dealing with a rich *memo* and with the people
from his world might be—if not by his disguised collaboration
on a vague film project, a project which, in its turn, very possibly disguised nothing more than his increasingly undisguised
literary sterility, his still-unfinished novel, his fear of finishing
it, that its publication would put an end to a myth based on the
small support generated by a few heavily promoted short stories.
Arguments beyond the reach of the Plutos, the sort of people
who were also unaware that the internal motivations for the
argument lacked any sense at all. Especially people like Marihole,
whom they had already seen in her element, overcome by moth-
erhood, plugging up her baby with bottles and suppositories, a
peepeecaca yowler of a baby, a redolent fartburper of rebellious
screams and projectile vomiting.

But also for Pluto, an expansive and witty Pluto, yes, although
more of a role imposed on him than his habitual comportment.
A role—it would be no surprise—reserved exclusively for them,

in order that everything between them all continue the same as always. And even so, like that shy fellow in love who insinuates himself only a little in hopes of the first sign of reciprocity, on certain occasions, when things were going well, allowed a glimpse of reality: how the world of business is so truly fucked, getting up at seven o'clock, slaving away for real, climbing the ladder without allowing himself a single misstep, rising at the expense of others so they don't rise at yours. Putting out feelers, to see if they caught his drift, if the others had followed his own transformation and all that was needed was for someone to be the first one to break the ice. A transformation that had possibly begun shortly before his wedding, startled by the bounced check and the volley of bills, a matter resolved by his future father-in-law in his own way and, no doubt, according to his conditions. The rest, his jokes, his stories, his way of exasperating Marihole, was rather more like telling some army camp anecdote, a kind of toll he paid when they all got together. My father-in-law is a beautiful person, he said. A man with a big heart, and a big cock. He married into such a fortune that he just pisses money and thankfully, even we can live off it. But you must tread carefully with him. If you don't do what he likes, he zips up his fly. Marihole's protests, Pluto's retort, etcetera. And nevertheless, something went wrong. Raúl tried to laugh like he meant it. But Federico had started chatting up a rent boy at the bar. And Nuria: it's weird that it doesn't bother you to talk just as if you were still in the army. Federico, very tipsy, came over with the rent boy and made the introductions, Raúl, Nuria, the Plutos, my friend Whosie-whatsit. And you, what's your name? asked the rent boy. And Federico: the Countess. They're about to close up here. Why don't we go to Castelldefels? They don't close up there (the rent boy). I don't even have money for gasoline; but we could go turn some tricks on Las Ramblas to scrape up some money. You on one side of the street, me on the other (the Countess). Alright (the rentboy). Just what the Plutos needed: that those two went off and disappeared by themselves. And they didn't take long to slip away themselves, as if they feared to be seen mixed up in something seedy. Or, more possibly, as if Pluto feared that Marihole's behavior might not rise to the occasion. A sort of reaction that a person like Leo would have never had, although it would later cost him hours of explaining things to Teresa. And it's true that just like when love comes to an end, it ends definitively, and then what's repeated is the whole scheme of amorous behavior, the same passions, the same tests, only with a different person. By contrast, all friendships created in the first flush of youth, regardless of distances and even fallings out, tend to be maintained throughout life at a level of understanding unreachable for any friendship established later on, with Pluto, for example, with Fortuny, perhaps because, in fact, one loses the capacity for making new friends and thus leaves young adulthood behind.

It was as if Leo had been rehabilitated, as if he had recovered not only his self-confidence but also his lucidity and even his sense of humor. He could crack jokes and, beyond any kind of reservation, talk frankly, almost like in earlier times. A sort of relationship which only months earlier would have seemed impossible to be reestablished someday. To tell him, for example, that his rehabilitation was a shameless case of nepotism, influenced by Floreal—a Floreal whose spectacular political career in exile, during his forced sojourn in France, so different from Fortuny's disappointing experience—was not at all safe from his ironic conjectures. Obregón's arrest kickstarted Fortuny's career, and then he had literally managed to escape the clutches of the police and reach Paris, given that without such antecedents, in another situation, he might possibly have never had occasion to deal with the leadership, to show his thoroughly discreet character, and become so perfectly well integrated with them, to secretly return to Barcelona, now become one of the key pieces in the machine, just as casually as the poet who, toying with a rhyme, hits upon a profound idea. Floreal—Federico concluded—is no small-town fellow but a man from the tough slums; some such remark like one of those local football hooligans who, from the grandstands, orchestrate scandalous mayhem, serving to whip up the home team and demoralize the visiting one, one of those goons who for his generally grotesque appearance, be it for his rather outlandish attire, or for his simian antics, seems to exercise over the spectators the magnetism of a tribal witch doctor. His loyalty is, precisely, beyond reproach. In fact, in both his case as in Fortuny's, his leaders have shown a most penetrating psychological awareness.

And Leo? As far as Leo goes, he's like that lifelong bachelor who if he's never married it's perhaps only because he can't share a bathroom with a woman, more a question of shyness than the selfishness commonly attributed to him; so, it would be equally mistaken to classify his current position with respect to the party as simple opportunism even if he himself would define it in similar terms. Because, like the person in possession of his horoscope—which he considers not only flatteringly accurate but also beneficially stimulating—he contributes what he can, from then on, so that the heavenly designs might be fulfilled and he finds in everything proofs of how much everything that happens is neither more nor less than what was foretold. Thus, in a similar way, not only Leo or Floreal himself but all militants in general tend to make every effort so that the image they offer their hierarchical superiors of the country's reality coincides as much as possible with the theoretical suppositions of the political line established by them.

The actual extent of his responsibilities—about which Leo showed himself quite reserved, although it proved no risk to link them to the neighborhood commissions, and who knows if also to the Barcelona committee—was indicated, as usual, by the details. By the fact that it was he who informed him, confidentially—and rather cheerfully—that Fortuny had fallen into disgrace, before, surely, Fortuny himself was informed—certainly coming as no surprise to him—that, now that he was back in Barcelona, it would be convenient that he abstain from all political activity until further orders. They say—and who but Escala could have said?—they've realized that his intelligence is no greater than his resolution, said Leo. A crisis whose gestation had occurred in Paris, a result of the leadership's suspicions being confirmed when they dealt with him more closely, or what he guessed about them, or both things at once, or what he began to tell or comment, or what they found out he was saying and commenting. And if personal matters, when spread, are capable of destroying a marriage, can't they certainly dissolve a political relationship? Not unlike that young newly married middle-class woman's astonished intuition of some different reality beyond her household, which usually coincides with her first explosive exposure to foul language and low-class gutter exclamations unleashed in her husband by the news of some business setback, is the similar, customary, almost incredulous reaction to the first clashing ideas voiced by the neophyte militant within the inner circles of his political organization. Doubtless, it costs him a lot of effort to get used to that dimension inherent to every kind of teamwork, objectively setting aside personal conflicts, hidden rivalries, and preeminences less related to protocol than to an effective control of power, to organizational management. It's difficult to accept that, similar to the amusing discretion with which the little local literary world circulates those anonymous letters written in the form of burlesque rhymes loaded with specific allusions to this or that writer, the work of any old gazetteer of regressive ideals and frustrated aspirations, of some slug grown rich in the solitary exercise of sleaze and defamation, wholesome brazen relief from the daily labor of newspaper reporting, universal announcement of how many universal values exist and, especially, have existed, a case of mental hygiene or, perhaps, a case of mental weakness, whose political equivalent can sometimes shorten the internal life of an organization. It's also difficult to learn to support without reservation a position according to the official political line when those muffled tensions surface, reaching his corresponding level in the organizational structure, and are resolved in a purifying disciplinary sanction, depriving the element or elements whose attitude was in error—provided they are sanctioned—of the proper number of responsibilities, leading to their expulsion if necessary, if the gravity of the case warrants it, charges that can stretch back very far, imputations that suddenly encompass his entire history or histories of militancy and which suddenly become the motive for a verbal report—if not an official declaration—about the faction's deviation, repeatedly and unanimously approved from one meeting to the next, from cell to cell, from each sector directly implicated by their former, now culpable, comrade's fall from grace, a sector where, logically, his erroneous position might have been able to spread and branch out, accusations exposed with the same nervous agitation and bitter fury with which an old man in a convalescent home shouts into the ear of his moribund roommate: Failure! You've been nothing but a failure! With that kind of rancor that comes from having to stifle too long what one was bursting to express. It's difficult—why deny it—to do all that, but no less necessary than in a marriage, dealing with all the trivial vulgarities involved in living together, without which the essential goal and proper functioning of the institution would be little less than impossible.

However, there are cases in which, according to one's experience of party life and the opportunities they've had to exercise their political tact, everything learned can be forgotten, as if from the effects of some trauma or, what's worse, turn out to be useless. A very common subjective reaction, especially when the disgraced comrade is oneself. And then they stop seeing things from the inside, which is how they must be seen, as is generally admitted, and start seeing them from outside. This makes it necessary to assess with opportune deliberation every unilateral version of the events, the judgments each person uses to defend or attack, frequently dictated by passion, a product of the subjective, observed reaction. Thus, Fortuny's stupor, not unlike the wife or husband who, after an intense extramarital erotic life, suddenly learns—inconceivable!—that their partner is fucking someone else. I assure you all that the intellectual level of a good part of the leadership couldn't be lower. The only thing that worries them now is the Chinese problem. And although it almost seems incredible, many of those leadership committee members don't know a single word of Marxism. And Federico: I assure you that this is rather an advantage. Although it must do them little good in a situation like the current one, without any objective conditions that propitiate the formation of a revolutionary vanguard capable of propitiating the objective conditions.

What a tragedy for someone like Z! To be born with a vocation to be a revolutionary hero in a time without revolutionary
heroism must be almost as bitter as not knowing how to be
heroic in a revolutionary situation. And Fortuny: but try and
imagine Floreal just all of a sudden asking you: have you seen
the sonsofbitches these Chinese are? And you ask him why. And
he says: fuck, they're just a bunch of mean dirty bastards, and
then he gets hysterical, and says that the Chinese are imperialists and racists and fascists, that you can't expect anything good
from them, that they're like the blacks, that when they manage
to produce someone good, like Lumumba, they're the first ones
to kill him. In those very words. For the love of God, do you all
think that this language is worthy of a Marxist? And look, even
by temperament I'm not really very suspicious of pro-Chinese
attitudes, personally I believe first and foremost in the struggle
of union labor. But if you just ask what's going on because you
want to stay up to date on things, that's all it takes for them to
consider you actively pro-Chinese, especially if they find out
you've got anything to do with Guillén, who's been expelled for
being pro-Chinese, but despite his radicalism he's one of the few
people there with whom you can actually talk. Poor Guillén, he's
so fucked. Comment from Federico: well, I don't know what
he's complaining about. Expelled from the party and unable
to enter Spain: the ideal situation. And Fortuny: and the stuff
about Cayetano. It also occurred to me to ask about him and
they told me he was crazy, that the tension of the struggle had
ended up disturbing his mind. And then Guillén told me what'd
happened. Alright, do you all remember Cayetano? That textile
factory manager who also had to escape when they nailed
Obregón. This was a guy who belonged to the Communist
Youth Union during the Republic, who fought in the Civil
War, who joined the Maquis in France, who returned with the
guerrillas, who was captured and tortured and condemned to
death, who had his sentence commuted at the eleventh hour and
then marched out to demonstrate along with the others who'd
been pardoned, and when Marsal went down they arrested him
again and when they got Obregón he had to go into exile. Well,

because it seems that in Paris they went after him with the same stories about the Chinese, and he said no, that they didn't make him think that the Chinese were either imperialists or fascists, and he told them all flatly that it's one thing to be a communist and another to be a Russian, and that he wasn't a Russian but a communist. And it seems they had to almost push him out of there. And he asked me: how much do you wanna bet that if the Chinese said what the Russians say and the Russians said what the Chinese say, the Russians would be the ones who would continue to be right? He was ready to climb the walls. That must be why they're saying he went crazy. Thirty years of militancy and now he's crazy. Crazy. He looked at them almost in disbelief, as if instead of seeing them he were contemplating a Gothic diptych, whose unusual story was, for example, San Cayetano martyred by his fellow martyrs followed by San Cayetano rushing into hell. New comment from Federico: sovietism, the senile sickness of communism. And Fortuny: and the worst, Z. The same thing that the Floreales repeated later on, only with more formal rigor. You can already imagine it for yourselves.

And, really, it took as little to imagine Z in action as to imagine Fortuny seeing himself as one of those movie heroes, bounced from a party—generally for having tried to flirt with a girl far above his social condition—walking off alone into the night, mortified not so much by the humiliation of having been tossed out onto the street, by the ugly scene, by the door slamming loudly behind him, as much as for imagining what must be happening inside the mansion, not only the father shrugging his shoulders, but all the servants smoothing their ruffled livery, the conversations resuming, the party continuing. The fulmination of thrashing about incoherently. The triumph of dialectical reason. And Z saying, those far left-wing mouthpieces, those extremists of yesterday and today, Maoists, Trotskyites, anarchists, sick paranoid minds, little splinter groups, disconnected from the masses, deeply entrenched in their own impotence, have no other option than blind, sterile violence, forgetting that during the Civil War it was not exactly them, but us, with the generous and fraternal Soviet assistance, who fought against Francoism and its Italian and German allies, a fight from which we might have emerged victorious instead of having been victims, besides, of an international conspiracy, of the betrayal by our supposed Western friends, of the puppets and marionettes of imperialism. So let me ask you now, aren't these revolutionaries who want to revolutionize the revolution also true counterrevolutionaries, objective allies, puppets, and marionettes of imperialism? Purported Spanish Marxists, as ignorant of Marxism as of their own country's history while they overlook the fact that it's only possible to correctly interpret the Spanish Civil War by inserting it into the general course of the Spanish people's struggle for liberty, whichever battle you're talking about, whether the Ebro or the Jarama or Bailén or the battles of Bruch, and so many other heroic struggles of our people, the people who invented guerrilla warfare—the revolutionary struggle par excellence—against the Napoleonic invader. And keeping in mind Franco's use of Moorish mercenaries, it would then make sense to extend the line of continuity back to the time of the Reconquest, with the eight centuries of continuous resistance that the Spanish people sustained against Arab expansionism, Roncesvalles and Las Navas de Tolosa, Mallorca and Seville, Valencia and Granada, milestones of our history which Spain's eternal enemies—those devious anti-Spanish pawns—prefer to overlook. In other words, our historic achievement can and should be situated along the line of other great national achievements, of those singular enterprises whose symbols are El Cid, Isabella the Catholic, Don Quixote, Cortés, Pizarro and so many other heroes whose exploits have been celebrated by our people for hundreds and hundreds of years and which, whether through historical chronicles or through oral tradition, have passed down from generation to generation, and also, from generation to generation, the people have kept alive our glorious Crusade for Liberation with new contributions of their own blood, the most recent in no way inferior to those of olden times, great feats like the siege of the Alcázar in Toledo, or the Battle of the Ebro, feats which, thanks to their literally miraculous characteristics, could have well been propitiated by the direct intervention of Saint James the apostle—Santiago. Because it's not a vain notion to believe that the History of Spain begins where Sacred History ends. A Spain already chosen by Christ when he called Santiago to become a fisher of men, assigned to the future Spaniards the mission of saving Christianity from Islam as well as from the Reformation, from any kind of reform and revolution, from any kind of subversion, the chosen people, a nation chosen since the beginning, since even before it existed as such, entity or entelechy genetically informed by a universal spirit and role, predestined to discover new worlds and Christianize them, destined to extend its blood and its values to heights and extremes that no other empire reached nor ever would reach, a history that has got to conclude with the triumph of our truth throughout the world through the final confrontation between Spain, on one side, and freemasonry and international Judaism, on the other. Sword of Rome and Bastion of the West, Defender of the Faith, whatever that might be, provided it express, in an orthodox fashion, dogmatic affirmations not very distinct, on another hand, from any other people given over to megalomaniac or simply narcissistic deliriums, like in the case of Catalunya, without going further, the fact of being Catalan, classified as a gift from God by the poet, inspired perhaps like a Tiresias, there being no evidence, with the divine gift of prophecy.

I agree, said Leo. Soviet society is currently about as revolutionary as its foreign policy. And, as far as we're concerned, the party does not follow a true revolutionary line and even if it did follow it, within current national and international circumstances, we would have only the most minimal possibility of bringing the revolution to pass. In that case: propose me an alternative. Are we going to be the first to declare that there is none? Are we going to renounce all activity and voluntarily dissolve ourselves like merchants liquidating a business? And another thing: what do you want me to do? I'm not like Fortuny. I am, or at least I think I am, a person with the party flowing in my veins. Apart from politics, and concretely from the party's politics, there's nothing that interests me. What could

I do outside the party? *Quand on n'a pas ce qu'on aime on doit aimer ce qu'on a.* Think whatever you deem best, but also think about what lies behind an attitude like Fortuny's. His belated guess that the party wasn't going to offer him the political career he was expecting. A career that his relaxed social democratic temperament must have imagined would be complemented by his legal practice and, above all, by the famous Chair of Labour Law. Also, when they nailed Obregón, he barely dodged the proverbial bullet, and this must have made him reconsider. It would be an enormous coincidence, it would go against every probability, if I were equally lucky the next time. And, finally, think what you like, but keep in mind that, in every case, I continue running risks that for him no longer exist.

They'd agreed to meet in the early evening. But Raúl had stayed longer than he anticipated at Uncle Gregorio's house and he arrived late. And, once they started talking, they decided to eat dinner in some place and keep chatting. Leo called Teresa and told her laconically that he wouldn't be home for dinner, as if to demonstrate that, unlike Pluto, he didn't need to offer his wife explanations. Raúl called his house, and Nuria and, curiously, it was Nuria who started being a pain: who was he with, and why couldn't she join them and, finally, he hung up saying he was going to Adolfo's house. Better that way. They felt comfortable and talkative, in a mood to discuss personal matters, possessed of that impunity that alcohol brings and permits you to talk about party problems right at a table in some bar. In the restaurant they went to take a piss, and Leo, as if he felt a little flushed, splashed his face in the sink and dried it with his handkerchief, looking at himself afterwards in the mirror with that expression one only puts on in front of the mirror, more how one wishes they looked than how they really look.

What objection? How to reduce to a single word something which transcends words like sincerity or cynicism, lucidity or nonsense? The fear of the quotidian, of one's own daily life, of that dimension that one intuits they are missing, which they pretend to find in others, outside of oneself, to fulfill or replace that suspected absence by entering the seminary or becoming the member of some sporting club or getting married or join-ing a political party. Something like that. The important thing is escaping from this quotidian life that is only comparable, due to the tedium it can end up producing, to the reading of one of those poems that speak of astonishment and wonder, of doubt between the perhaps and the maybe, slender distinctions between silly trifles or simply of the minor personal experience, so small that it demands consideration of the author's dry mind, the value of his oh-so-doltishly handled language, the multifac-eted emptiness of his verse, his vegetative metropolitan idiocy; thus, like just such a poem, the habits, the tics, the rhyming detritus of daily life. That's why the priest with his apostolic labor first saves himself. The soccer fan sheltered by the colors of his team. The militant engrafted with the hysterical mysteries of his ideology and its postulations. The husband and wife ensconced in matrimony, consoled, comforted, fortified, accommodated, sitting back with their feet up, safe from all the tricks and traps the world has to offer. All of them so similar to that soldier who, dispatched to a frontier fort—where he'll be stationed until retirement—is prepared to take maximum possible advantage of the situation, absolute ruler of his little kingdom, local despotic deity, with only one single idea in his head, just like Satan upon taking possession of his shadowy dominions inspects the troops who pay him honor: converting the isolation into power and confinement into strength; fortifying himself. A tendency to withdraw that only grows with the years, under the usury of time. Nothing more depressing, for example, than that married couple who stay the course, each one supporting the other half until death do them part, defeat after defeat, failure after fail-ure, beyond impotences and frigidities, beneath downfalls and surrenders, two cadavers in one single sarcophagus.

Who is it? he heard Gregorius bellowing. I'm giving him a bath, you see, said Leonor. What's going on, what's the matter, shouted Gregorius. He found him in the bathtub, without his glasses, naked, his withered peter peeking out from the bubbles. Bring him a chair, he said. And Leonor: come on, slide down a little more. Don't you see you're showing him everything?

She left them alone a little while, but as she came and went around the apartment she kept predicting the topics of conversation. Now he'll tell you about Mallorca. Now he'll talk about America. Now he'll talk about Vallfosca. She returned with a ratty bathrobe and some slippers. Good, now close your mouth, you're going to get soap in it. She knelt down next to the tub and, with a rough sponge, began scrubbing the old man from his head to his toes. If he had his way, he'd never bathe in his whole life, she was saying. And the more you scold him, the more he ignores you. He pretends not to hear and starts whistling like that cuckoo that pops out of the clock every hour, as if it really was a bird. I can't deal with him, I simply cannot. And one of these days he's going to cause a scandal with his mania for cuddling little children. The people who know him from the park still put up with him. But, someone who doesn't know him, seeing him looking the way he does, they might think anything. Doesn't change his clothes, doesn't wash, doesn't shave; he'd be happy to go around looking like a homeless beggar. Just the other day I had to finally throw away all his old clothes and shoes, they were the only things he wanted to wear.

From beneath Leonor's energetic arms, Gregorius stuck up his soapy head and, at the edge of the tub, gave Raúl a sly smile, before sinking back down, while Leonor ranted on, with the anger of that country doctor who, when examining the patient's virile member, discovers that the supposed venereal disease is nothing more than simple local irritation resulting from a lack of hygiene, relentless anger increased by the way that filthy bumpkin tolerates the doctor's shower of invective, his phlegmatic scorn, his lack of haste. In fact that very invective, Leonor's complaints, which forcefully dominated the visit, more than his chatting with Gregorius, were the reason why he arrived late at his meeting with Leo. The last one. And, as if he'd had a premonition, it was precisely that night when Leo told him about how he was worried about the confidence that Floreal seemed to have placed in Modesto Pírez, putting him in a position where, in case he were nabbed, he could implicate many people. As if he could guess what was going to happen on February 12, the holy day of Santa Eulalia of Sarriá, virgin and martyr, victim of the cruel repression decreed by the Proconsul Daciano against the Christians for their subversive activities, flogged, breasts torn off, arms and legs twisted from their sockets, her body quartered and burned in pieces before the crowd gathered in order to not miss the spectacle of torture that took place on what is now the street called la Bajada de Santa Eulalia, although perhaps the martyred maiden was not from Sarriá and none of that happened in Barcelona, but in Mérida, then called Emerita Augusta. It was all so many years ago ...

You, what are you doing here? a detective asked him. It was nine o'clock and he seemed to have just come in, active and lively, charged up with that morning energy which office managers of a dynamic temperament use to start their working day. He elbowed him, as if in complicity. You must have dragged some poor girl out into an empty lot, right?

He soon returned and, without a word, gestured for Raúl to follow him. He led him to a nearby office, more or less the same as the previous one. Stay here, he said. From different directions came the sound of conversations mixed with the clicking of typewriters. Then, some more distinct voices stood out above all the other racket. As much for their special resonance as because they kept coming closer, the chatter seemed to come from a hallway. The tone was like some friendly conversation, with jokes, laughter, one voice almost like a woman's. They were discussing the convenience of applying a fresh coat of paint. That's right, the canary sings so sweetly.

A finger pointing at him from the doorway. I'll be damned: El Pipa!

Three or four more men followed him in. Yes, it's him. You're darned right it is. Communist: you can tell right away. El Pipa! El Pipa! We've finally got him! It was me who arrested him; me. I've had to follow you around as if you were Marilyn Monroe,

you little faggot. That woman's laugh. Tell us something about
Alsina. Alsina? A box on the ear, almost the brain; the one
with the crazy laugh. And you don't know Matías, either? Or
Salvador? More blows to the ear, to his ears, from both sides,
from behind. And Leonardo Tarrés? Yes? Well, that's something.
And Floreal Conesa? And Modesto Pírez? Not Pírez? Another
blow. Wait, don't ask, let him talk, let's see if we like what he's
got to say. Nonsense; we'll clear this all up right now, you'll see.
Or maybe you know Tarrés and Conesa, but you don't know
Matías or Alsina? A hard punch right in the stomach and, as
he doubled over, stamping on his feet. They held him up so he
wouldn't fall over. What's the matter?

A bald guy with glasses was staring at him. The others made
room for him. This son of a bitch wants to play the tough guy.
Don't be stupid, kid. Here, everybody sings. If your bosses are the
top guys, you don't want to take the fall for them. Don't you see
your friend from the Canaries has sung for us, just like a canary
himself? Don't worry, I'll sing just like in the opera. That's just
how he said it. And without having to lay a finger on him, I swear.

Cackles of laughter. You don't know Pírez, eh? You never gave
him any of those pamphlets you shitty little rich college boys
write? They shoved him around from one to the other, all asking
him questions at the same time. What can you tell us about Floreal
Conesa, alias Matías? What can you tell us about your friend
Tarrés, alias Alsina? That's right, man, Alsina; you all used to call
him Serra. You think we don't know everything? You think they
haven't sung for us? You think you're not going to sing? You didn't
know the local committee's mimeograph machine was in Pírez's
flat? And that's where they ran off the pamphlets you wrote?

A knee to the groin he was able to dodge slightly, tipping
him off balance. Someone stepped in through the pushing and
shoving arms waving a photo. Look, I've got the proof right here!
Your picture! It was Raúl's photo ID card.

What do you mean what proof? A hard fist to the stomach.
Then another. He saw a pistol appear. Now they struggled with
the man with pistol, and subdued him. I'll kill him! I'm telling
you I'll kill him! Get him out of my sight or I'll kill him!

The bald man with glasses. Alright, leave him alone for later. And you, watch it, no sudden moves. Stand up, on your own two feet, no leaning on anything. Someone stay with him.

He glanced at his watch: it read ten minutes past ten, but the minute hand wasn't working. The stem or something was broken. So, you're El Pipa, eh? said the man guarding him, seated on the other side of a desk. The famous El Pipa. He spoke as if to say something, to kill time.

They moved him to another office, adjacent to the room where the bald man with glasses was, possibly his office. The man took a few steps out, just to keep an eye on the hallway. Raúl saw three detectives arrive: in a hurry, with the brusque movements of a bad mood. The birds have flown, he heard them say. What birds? Tarrés and his chick. When we couldn't reestablish contact, we decided to go in. Just what we were afraid of: they've been gone since last night. He heard a door slam. Very muffled, curses and insults, shouts sounding like a furious scolding.

Everything quieted down. Lunchtime, possibly. Still soaked with sweat, his clothes stuck to his body. Perhaps that explained why he didn't especially need to piss. But he wanted something to drink. And, especially, a cigarette.

Come over here, comrade, a gray-haired man said to him. Another move to another room. A little bit tired, right? Well if I see you move an inch, it's gonna get a whole lot worse. In Russia you're all tough, but you'll see here we know how to be tough, too. He brought a transistor radio: he sat down next to the door and turned it on. Soccer. The announcer's excited voice, the shouts, surprises, the reversals, the cheering crowd.

It was already dark by the time the detective who'd taken his statement when he'd arrived reappeared; the windows in the corridor caught reflections from the streetlights outside. You see, Raúl? If you'd been honest from the start, you would have spared yourself all that. He told the man with the radio to leave them alone. He had them bring Raúl a glass of water, and offered him a cigarette. Look, here you've got to tell the truth. You're a lawyer and you should know that, when facing the examining magistrate, the report we make about the arrestee's character has almost as much importance as your statement itself. But the thing is, apart from this, the person who doesn't adopt a reasonable attitude can have a very bad time of it. You'll see, all kinds of men work here. One maybe because it suits his temper, because he's got a passion for it, another because the Reds shot his father, or who knows, because he's got the urge, for devotion to the trade or whatever, he just gets involved and it never ends. He shoots. And then it's hard to stop him. He goes crazy and from then on the other one is just his darling, his delicate prey. Listen to what I'm telling you, believe me. There's every kind of big ape here. I don't know, they almost seem to enjoy it.

No? Raúl stood only halfway up to set the glass on the table. The heavy fist sunk him back down on the chair. They looked at each other almost in bewilderment. The glass must have rolled off the table and now he heard it shatter on the floor. Alright, you all, get in here! shouted the other man. They all piled in at once. He still wants to play the tough guy, said the other man. Arturo, you're Arturo. Well, let's get slaphappy with Arturo. They stood him up. They formed a circle around him. Right, time to torture Arturo. No, wait, Arturo's another guy, but it doesn't matter. Both of them are Reds. Laughter. Hands grabbing and shaking him hard. You've really been busting our balls. Now we're gonna bust yours. More laughter. Hands pushing and shoving him. Why don't we play seven, fourteen, twenty-one? I was starting to feel like I needed to loosen up a bit. Do you like to dance?

The questions started again, and the punches. In his stomach and his liver, especially. That's right, Armando. Let him have it.

Armando's always the first to get lively.

What'll your bosses say when they find out we nailed you? What'll Nikita say?

All yours, Armando!

They incited each other to hit him, while Raúl, for his part, tried to keep his composure, responding calmly, though haltingly, without showing signs of hatred, fear, or anger, as if interrogator and interrogated were, equally, agents of some higher power driving them against one another, protagonists of a situation that, for being out of their respective control, demands a measured response; where one sees crime, the other sees error, both points of view to the same degree fatally antagonistic. All that in the belief that if he managed it, if he could manage to modulate his reactions according to that tenor, looking at them and speaking to them with all the serenity he was capable of mustering, he'd won the match. A hypothesis of greater moral than scientific value, it's true, of inverse probability to the importance the interrogator places on getting answers, but not for that reason—even when the theory crumbles in practice—lacking in all reason. The idea that, pretending to accept the situation imposed by them, made them accept, in reality, the relationship created by him. With the certainty that even the most basic resources available to the police, floodlights in the face, etcetera, are not intended so much—perhaps without even the interrogators knowing it, only from experience but without knowing the reason why—to dazzle the suspect, making him wince and grimace, as to protect themselves from his gaze, in the same way that dark glasses, for those who wear them, more than offering a constant appearance of impassivity, serve to permit them to perform any kind of violence without having to try to make the expression accompany the act or even to acquire the proper conviction. To create an atmosphere no longer unusual but surreal. And, insofar as being surreal, capable of breaking any course of action, of turning the person being interrogated into a barely human object, of transforming him into a terrorized being, into a despicable cornered critter, abject, weeping, suppliant, crazed; or, according to his nature, enrage him, drive him to insolence, make him lose his cool, shouting insults and offenses that authority has no choice but to repel or punish; or even, manage to unleash his hatred and pique his pride, get him to declare himself a communist, threatening them with the people's justice that will come for them sooner or later, and then they, now properly hating him, give that Red his just desserts, settling the score now that he's in their hands, almost as if in self-defense, give him a proper beating, kick him, twist him, dislocate his joints, give him electric shocks, pushing the button just like on the telex machine. Meaning:

promoting within themselves a state of exasperation uniquely comparable to what a mother can feel who is especially frazzled by her baby who won't allow her any peace and when it finally does, when it finally calms down, it's she who shakes and smacks it so that it starts crying again and gives her a fair motive to keep on loathing it. Because in the same way that a pedagogical system rich in punishments and discipline reveals on the part of the educator, whether they be a family member or teacher, not only repressed sadomasochistic and, eventually, homosexual tendencies—and when involving relatives, incestuous ones— but, above all, a phenomenon of transference onto the child of their own impotences and frustrations, which tend to be more overwhelming given the intensity of the punishment applied; thus, when a policeman beats a suspect, he does so, normally, blinded by the terrors of his own conscience.

What to do then when the police beat someone until they're swollen black and blue? Not like one of those soccer or rugby players who, after falling like they've been shot and making a show of writhing around on the field, finally stand up and, after limping painfully for a few steps, take off running like greyhounds.

Because the praxis affirms the theory, because the others found themselves getting tired, and it's certain that their blows were not as virulent as the ones they'd landed in the morning, neither the hardness nor the duration of the session were like the first time. They watched him, also out of breath. This guy's not like the opera singer. This one's cold. They're the worst. What he needs is electric shocks. Don't you see he sweats cold? We've got to make it hot for him. Laughter. Yes, a little electricity will make him feel good. That's right: it's cold in Russia; a little electricity will do the trick.

The one who had taken his statement upon arrival stepped away from the others and passed the red-hot tip of his cigarette before Raúl's eyes. We're gonna crush you; you've been asking for it. He went back to the others. Take him down to the cells and tonight we'll bring him back up. This was just a dress rehearsal.

The jail cells, in the lowest basement. An iron door with a peephole or a vent. A bare lightbulb set into the wall near the ceiling. A cement bench with a wicker mat. He couldn't sleep or he wasn't sleepy. And, nevertheless, when they brought him upstairs, it was like he was dreaming. It was cold; his legs were trembling with the cold. The corridors, the offices. So much light all of a sudden was blinding. An open door here or there: Floreal. Floreal? He was sitting on a wooden armchair, barefoot, his head lolling on his breast. They pulled his head up by the hair so Raúl could see his face. His features looked Chinese. And his hands swollen, like a boxer's. And at least on one wrist, the only one visible, an encircling welt or wound between yellow and black. Do you know him? Leo's cousin? We already knew that, handsome. He thought he saw Floreal give him a wink, although it was difficult to be sure.

They took him back downstairs. The air thick and heavy: whiffs of private odors, a stench like a urinal. He didn't sleep then again. In the guardroom they'd taken away his belt, necktie, shoelaces, wristwatch, ballpoint pen, and matches. To smoke he had to ask the guards for a light. Like when he had to piss: he shouted his cell number, 18, and the guard opened the door and followed behind without taking his eyes off him. Through the peephole he saw a body slide by, dragged along by two guards, toward the cells at the far end. He called the guard to ask for a light. He was a guy of a certain age, rather taciturn. Floreal Conesa? No, son, this one's a tram driver. Another session like this one and they'll send him to heaven. Floreal Conesa? There's nobody here by that name. I'd remember a name like Floreal.

They served him a hot liquid, dark, in a grimy, dented bowl; he drank it. Later they handed him a package in the guardroom. The guard that brought him up there, a Galician, had not made it clear why he was being summoned upstairs, as if enjoying making him think that it was going to be another interrogation. Walk ahead, he had told him, like someone fulfilling a painful obligation. They opened the package in front of him and carefully examined its contents. Cigarettes. Chocolate. Cookies. Condensed milk. They made him sign a receipt.

He didn't think he had fallen asleep, but it was obvious he'd been awakened by the racket the guards made serving the meal. Afterward he began tracing and retracing, in a diagonal line, the space between the door and the cement bench. Four paces, or rather, footsteps, then turning around, touching the corner of the door with his elbows on each turn. Once in a while he ate some chocolate. The order to go upstairs coincided with the dinner ration service.

From the beginning it became evident that something had changed in the attitude of the police, the climate, their manners, not unlike the change that comes over the erotic relationships of the libertine when he employs that sudden, skillful disinterest in the pleasure he's already enjoyed. And not simply—or in spite of it—because the detective invited him to sit down before his desk, not because he offered him a cigarette. It was rather—it was in the air—as if the police were bored with the whole matter, as if they wished to be done with it once and for all the way one dispatches something grown tiresome and annoying. Look, kid, he said. We've got some undeniable facts here: you're acquainted with a member of the central committee and a deputy of the political bureau of the communist party. You also know a member of the Barcelona committee, up to his neck in matters involving the neighborhood committees. You say you don't know Folías, but we found a book of Marx in his apartment with your name in it, in your handwriting.

He tossed the book onto the table. *La Sagrada Familia. The Holy Family.* Had you forgotten that one? It often happens when people lend books. But it's yours. You wrote your name in it like in so many others you have in your house. Only this wasn't in your house, it was in Modesto Pírez's house. Besides, we followed you two. We've seen the two of you together. On the patio at the university, specifically. I'm sure you remember. And we know that you two met in Paris: through Guillén, another communist, as you know perfectly well; and although he's exiled right now, you were still classmates together. So, you must understand that all those things can't remain unanswered. That you've got to give us a coherent explanation about all that.

He listened to Raúl with a certain impatience, as if he knew beforehand what he was going to say, although what he was thinking in that moment was: alright, now this is something different. Alright. Before, they accused you of other things, of more things. And in the same flat belonging to Folías we've not found anything in your handwriting or anything from your typewriter. And before they were accusing you of writing the publications for the neighborhood committees. So what? Whether they accuse you of one thing or another is the least of it. What you've got to do is give a coherent explanation about some concrete, irrefutable facts. As a lawyer, you must know that what counts, apart from proof to the contrary, is what you say or declare. Or rather, let's see: you admit to knowing Modesto Pírez, isn't that right? Very good. But that relationship between a university professor and a person like Folías, what was that based on, what was his objective? Find a job in Barcelona for the friend of a friend. Okay. But that common friend turns out to be a communist. You can't expect me to believe that you two didn't discuss politics. And that's it, you discussed politics. And you never talked about, or he never suggested to you sometime that you get actively involved? Only theoretical problems. But Marxist ones, of course.

The bald fellow with glasses listened to them without talking, sitting on the corner of a different desk. He slapped his thigh. Alright, enough for today. Tomorrow you can start again from the beginning, make sure it all gets typed up and that he signs it. And make sure he talks about Conesa and Tarrés. He turned to Raúl. Don't you want a glass of milk? It'll do you good.

From that moment until the next day when they transferred him to the prison in the kangaroo—a blind metal cage without windows or ventilation—he spent almost as much time in the offices as in his jail cell. In the jail he slept, although neither deeply nor steadily. Perhaps that was why time passed more slowly in the offices. And although his statement was brief, there were many interruptions, and always some policeman coming by who felt like having a chat, as if from curiosity, or perhaps because he had nothing better to do, and, one might even dare say, to improve the impression that they might have made on him. Especially after he signed his statement.

When asked if he is affiliated with or belongs to the communist party, he answers no. Asked if he knows Floreal Conesa under the assumed name of Matías or some other nickname, he answers no. Asked how he came to know the aforementioned Floreal Conesa, he says from frequenting the home of his friend and former classmate Leonardo Tarrés, first cousin of Floreal Conesa. When asked if such meetings were of a political nature, he answers no, although sometimes they might have discussed politics.

An old man stuck his head in the doorway. What, has the kid started talking? he said. Also, the bald man with the glasses came over and reread the sheets. Alright, alright, but just make sure he doesn't come off sounding only like a sympathizer and nothing more. This has to include information about his complicity or, at least, of concealment. The last thing we need is for the judge to think we're a pack of idiots.

If all that is true, if you're not trying to fool us again, you don't know the trouble you've saved yourself from, said another policeman, pointing his pen at Raúl. You don't know the communists very well. And if you believed in God, because you don't look like a believer, you should give him thanks that we arrested you in time. Look, just to give you one example, the case we had a few days ago. A tram driver. A good man, at heart. But he got into trouble, let himself be fooled. And it seems now, as he realized what he'd done, he got so desperate he started ramming his head against the wall. He looked like bleeding agonizing Christ. Lucky that the guard downstairs overheard him and stopped him before he killed himself.

One of the cops who'd arrested him came in, the one who seemed to have a singer's voice. Well, you won't complain about how we treated you, right? You can see we're not a bunch of savages here. Man, I won't lie and say sometimes we don't get a little carried away, like with this Conesa; he could try anybody's patience. But, more than anything, it's just our reputation. And don't think it bothers us. That way people get frightened and talk without us having to touch a hair on their heads.

And the cop with the pen: that's right, yeah, here everybody talks. At first, they always say they don't know a thing or the really cocky ones who brag that they'll never talk. But that's just a bunch of hot air. In the end they talk.

And if sometimes we're a little hard it's because we've got no other choice. Police are the same everywhere. How do you think they act in France, or in England, or the United States?

And the cop with the pen: What about Russia? How do you think they'd treat me if they caught me there someday on an assignment?

Another cop chimed in, very young, almost like a recruit. Raúl identified him as the one who'd given him a karate chop. What about the Chinese?

Even worse. Russians aren't bad, they're good-hearted men, like us Spaniards. But the Chinese hate whites. Chinese are cruel. Chinese tortures are famous the world over.

But what do they do?

The cop who had taken Raúl's final statement patted the other man on the shoulder. You don't want to know. If I told you even a few things you wouldn't be able to sleep.

He wasn't like the others, the younger policemen of the present generation who didn't look like police exactly but more like rookies and amateur athletes, like players on the neighborhood soccer club. No, he wasn't one of them. He was one of the veterans, from older times, as Raúl remembered them or as one tends to imagine them, even without having been arrested years before; the salt and pepper mustache, the bitter face, the thin receding hairline, nicotine breath, and the unhealthy complexion of that fifty-something man who accelerates his physical and moral decline playing dice at the coffee shop bar, who has no problem with gambling or alcohol or tobacco, let alone women, but simply by spending time at the coffee shop bar.

Again the bald cop with glasses. Alright, let's get to work. What're you all doing here? He's signed it already, right? Well, let's do something else. And you, when you get out, tell your people it's not such a big deal. And that it doesn't do you any good for someone to make such a fuss over you. Of course that's the last thing they care to hear. What they want are excuses for kicking up a fuss. Intellectuals, professors, lawyers, priests, even priests from Opus Dei. La Acción Católica, the priests, there always has to be someone sticking their nose into it. Just wait till they lift the ban on celibacy for priests and you'll see how quick we sort things out. Like these four fucking monarchists. We maintain order so they can enjoy life with all its benefits, and they still protest. They want us to do what we do, but they don't want to know how it's done. They forget about the Civil War, that they'd end up being the first victims, all over again. Way before us, I can promise you that. And you? What d'you think you'd be doing in Russia? We, on the other hand, are needed everywhere. We've got colleagues who were cops during the Republic, and they still are cops, and if the Regime were to change, they'd go right on being cops. What do you expect? Don't kid yourself.

Within the darkness of the cage inside the police van, at the start of the trip that would only end when they reached the inside of the prison, where all the pilgrims find themselves surrounded by deep moats and high walls in no way surpassed by those of the city of Dis, the atmosphere of mistrust and mutual scrutiny was pervasive, all of them with something in common in both attitude and aspect. Next to Raúl, one fellow enveloped in a miasma of putrid gases he seemed unable to contain, especially with the van bumping and rattling, effluvia no less deadly for being silent as it spread persistently, as if adhering to the folds of his clothes, filthy and terrified, with the perfect mug of a petty thief, though it would not be very correct, nor very elegant, to dismiss out of hand the possibility of him being a political prisoner. Then, among those seated at the back, two or three of them started muttering about the brutal treatment they'd received, how the cops had gotten enraged with them, how they'd all had to appear before the examining magistrate. Someone leaned toward Raúl. And you, why're you here? Well, I still don't know why, said Raúl. Facing him, silent, as if stupefied, as if it took a great effort to understand what was being said, he thought he recognized the tram driver. Does the examining magistrate beat you? he heard him ask at last, just as they were arriving.

Name?

Raúl Ferrer Gaminde Moret.

Son of?

Jorge and Eulalia.

Any other name or nickname? Distinguishing marks or characteristics?

The same questions, more or less, as when they registered him at the police headquarters. The photograph, fingerprints. And, in a certain way, even the same sort of person. Specifically, the one who took his fingerprints; except that here—not so lucky—the man wore the brown uniform of a prisoner serving his sentence. If I had my way, with the Reds, I'd string 'em all up by the balls, he said, as he inked Raúl's fingers somewhat violently. He spoke while twirling the classic little gray mustache of the combat veteran, that product of the Civil War who, from his position as victor, considered in the spirit of the letter, in the absolute sense, has plunged headlong, or without the proper wits and skill, along the paths of corruption and bribery, at every available opportunity—black market, importation licenses, real estate speculation—until ending up, with increasing frequency, cooling his heels in prison, where his old friends, relations, and merits can no longer help him secure anything more than a certain situation of privilege, sufficient, notwithstanding, so that, just as when free, he always found himself among the hardline party faithful when it was time to participate in commemorative rallies, demonstrations of support, or official receptions; nor in captivity did he waste the opportunity to show his combative spirit—like that poor student in a religious academy who, enormously mistaken, believes he can make up for his habitual bad grades through his pious conduct—by keeping his distance from those who, imprisoned just the same, cannot brag about their past—the majority of the prisoners—and, with greater motivation, with respect to those doing time for political reasons, in order to be identified as much as possible with the established powers both inside and outside the prison, to be able to justify his own disgrace, attributing to the enemy all the evils that, like the mother country, beset him.

The frisking, however, also conducted by several prisoners under the supervision of an official, was much more rigorous. They let him keep his pen and his belt, his matches and shoelaces, but they made him strip naked and searched the seams of his clothing, with a scrupulousness similar to when he was arrested—which, although perhaps according to regulations, might well be interpreted as excessive zeal—and they examined his rectum and testicles. They opened up a few cigarettes and his can of condensed milk, and they gave him back his pillow, torn open with half the stuffing missing. His chocolate and tobacco had vanished, small thefts practiced by some low-level prisoners who for not failing to perform various internal prison functions cease to be what, with an obvious sentiment of pre-determination, is usually called fresh meat, instead they are that small-time crook who steals in prison and who, by continuing to do so once released is soon back inside, perhaps the same day of their release, neither more nor less—you might say—than if the police were waiting for him or if he had gone to his meeting, recalcitrant as that sodomite who, now on his knees before the executioner, upon noticing the thick bulging underneath those purple leotards, as tight as possible to allow one to clearly see the main veins of his member, asks with humility, as a final favor, permission to administer a blowjob. The men in charge of the prison peculium charged him two-hundred-fifty pesetas of the money he had on him for services. For the rest they gave him a receipt. They also confiscated all the papers and cards in his wallet that bore hand-written words and numbers. And a snapshot of Nuria on the beach, in a bathing suit, from when they went to Rosas. A ceremonial rupture with respect to the outside world similar to, in its preparatory significance, the state of mind students are made to experience as they initiate a period of spiritual exercises when they enter the residence where the retreat will take place. One of those retreats such as were developed in Manresa and which usually end with a visit to the cave of St. Ignatius of Loyola.

An impression redoubled in Raúl's case, now walking from his cell along a series of bare, seemingly deserted, corridors and galleries but full of echoes, thanks to a detail as ridiculous as his allowance of chocolate, cookies, and condensed milk, what a schoolboy carries with him when he goes on a spiritual retreat—apart from alcohol, tobacco, and banned books. A cell, on the other hand, not very different in essence—solitude and reflection—from the ones in a retreat house. Including the crude drawings and writings on the walls, despite how different their content—P. P. was here 120 days for smoking hash; I was here for smoking weed—they both responded to the same sense of expiation and purification as the professions of faith and intentions to reform that could be read on the inside of the box of the plain deal table, in the cell at Manresa. Before returning to the world, I want to write, in my own blood: I promise to never sin again.

First that lugubrious place, underground, which, despite everything, was better than the jail cells at police headquarters. Six paces instead of four. It was ruled over by an individual whose somber medieval presence only lacked a hood. His manner, however, was comforting, and he spoke almost as if excusing himself. These cells are for punishment. But you're not here to be punished but to be kept incommunicado. It seems that there was no space upstairs. And they've told me that they're already preparing a whole floor of the sixth wing for you all. You'll be better off up there. The cells there are not so damp.

A cell that would be number 243, on the third floor of the sixth wing. And one in which he would grow accustomed to the liturgy of life in the penitentiary, to its rhythms, its echoes, forever awaiting the examining magistrate. And after making his declaration, what's called the period, meaning another five or six days of isolation, maybe not even that long, in Pedro Botero's opinion, bearing in mind the ones they'd already taken away. And then, freedom within the prison. An examining magistrate who each day was going to come tomorrow.

Invaluable, the assistance offered him by Pedro Botero, the chief of the third floor, and, in his condition as both prisoner and jailer, a true incarnation of the system's ambiguity, a system in which what matters, much more than making sure the established rules are followed, is—like in all societies, on the other hand—making sure people believe they are being followed. A poor devil? An abject and subaltern demon? A Belial? Possibly, but not for that reason were his powers any less efficient and far reaching.

In fact, one of those servile beings who know how to charge for their services. One of those people who keep you informed, who protect you against thieves—here you don't trust anybody, or what they say about anybody—even as they're cleaning out your wallet. Hardened people, and at the same time sincerely human. And, something in them that always remains a failing, with a certain weakness for those people whose ignorance of the system, almost bordering on stupidity, is accompanied, as in Raúl's case, by an intuition and sense of opportunity—their proper largesse with tips, for example—so it doesn't take long for them to be seen worthy of everyone else's respect and esteem. A good disposition, formerly ephemeral and superficial, dominated by that unquestionable realism of the old sinner converted into the owner of some typical restaurant along the coast, who, questioned by the police for transporting the bodies of two accident victims in his car, recognizes them as the amorous pair who ate that day in his establishment and, witnessing those fresh corpses, cannot help thinking: what a waste of lobster.

Another admirable trait: discretion. Ask no questions and, obviously, unlike the majority of the regular prisoners, show no desire to be questioned either. Given that, like the solitary boy who interposes an adult behavior between his persona and that of his terrified companions, like the declining woman who finds the exact justification in the sicknesses she invents, like the old man who proclaims himself a victim of adversity, like the adult clinging to a childhood that protects him from his responsibilities, so, in jail, with the same helplessness, everyone tends to tell their story, everyone is sure of having done their part, except, precisely, the crime for which they're serving time or for which they must be judged. A childish reaction, at any rate, to the degree to which it ignores the fact that what the adult punishes is not some specific act by the child, but the child itself. But also, as in certain bars frequented by gay people, it's not strange to see them give themselves over to patently childish group songs and games, when the atmosphere is good and they find themselves feeling relaxed, that old *voulez voux planter de choux* sung out in a happy chorus, verses that without a doubt take them back to

the key age of their personal conflict—the simple fact of having
witnessed similar scenes, assuming their having frequented such
bars, could now well turn out to be an index of such conflict—
thus the prisoner's mere condition, so similar to those of the
student and the soldier, usually provokes a marked regression
toward typically infantile attitudes and habits. A phenomenon
doubtless exacerbated by the very structure of the penal system,
thanks to its essential formalism, similar to school or the military,
where the basic element of all classification resides in such facts
as age or height or alphabetical order of family names, and so, in
prison, although each prisoner is there as a result of something
they've done, for the specific crime committed or presumed to
have been committed, in practice, the prisoners are classified and
distributed or grouped according to previous categories, independent of all consideration unrelated to the penal system itself,
purely according to the prisoners' objective membership in any
of the categories by which, in a deductive manner, the system is
structured. Hence their being segregated into different sections:
whites, homosexuals, political prisoners, sodomites, jailbreakers,
etcetera. A division that responds to a conception not merely
idealistic but also artificial, because just as sovereignty does not
exclude lechery, belonging to a specific prison classification does
not preclude the existence of sufficient motives for belonging to
any of the others.

Raúl knocked on the door.

Number?

243.

There on the threshold, quick as a cork from a cava bottle,
appeared Pedro Botero, with his tidbits of news, his tips, his
guidance, his services. He kept him up to date not only on the
action in his section, but also about life in general throughout the
prison. About those choruses of Pardon Me Lord, or God, My
God, for example, he could hear sung somewhere far away. It's
the men in the fifth ward, he said. Spiritual exercises. They always
sing those at the end. Here, in the sixth, the session begins on
Monday. It's not required, but many attend in order to be on good
terms with the Mercedarian father. The thing is, after the warden,

the priest is the person with the most influence here. Much more influence, naturally, than the chief of services and the doctor. We call him Mother Mercedes or, because he's from Madrid, La Merche. He's not a bad person. The little girls all love him.

Sometimes his advice was spontaneous. When Raúl asked the commissary chief to beef up or change the monotonous rotating menu, lentils, beans, garbanzos, lentils. Steak or a couple fried eggs, he said, like some maître d' who takes the liberty of recommending the house speciality; that's the simplest. He brought him wine, his own ration, according to him, since the solitaries were excluded from having a share. And there was no doubt that under a less severe regimen, once his solitary confinement was lifted, it was he, Pedro Botero, who presented the clearest path toward getting hold of stronger, better quality alcohol, and even marijuana. He brought him copies of *Redención*, a kind of Sunday supplement, the only publication authorized for prisoners, as well as one of those detective novels smuggled inside that get passed from cell to cell until, in order to keep things looking normal during an inspection, they are confiscated, along with things like can openers, a hand-drawn deck of cards, and an alcohol stove fashioned out of a Nescafé can. He also provided him with an ink cartridge and toilet paper, because writing paper, unlike the fountain pen, was forbidden to prisoners in solitary confinement. A kind of assistance which, along with his self-imposed ritual discipline and the arhythmic rhythms of the system itself, had contributed, without any doubt, to his getting quickly accustomed to his cell. Sometimes it took the announcement of a headcount or the echo of some unusual movement in the passageway to remind him that he was in a cell in the Cárcel Modelo, and not in his bedroom, working, let alone in his room in Vallfosca, where, as a boy, he closed the door to think.

The prisoner in 242 liked to sing tangos. Especially "Confesión." Unlike the man in 244, withdrawn and silent, who sometimes communicated with Raúl through the wall. Naturally, it was also Pedro Botero who informed him of his name: almost like you: Farré, Ferrer, Farrés or something like that. Politician; they say he's a big fish. And Botero was almost sure that, having gotten Raúl interested, if Raúl had enough trust, not only in Pedro Botero, but also the guy in 242, he offered to transmit messages. But from every point of view it seemed preferable to continue with those necessarily brief conversations, however difficult and uncomfortable, that 242 had first initiated. Like a telephone. Tapping was the call signal. To talk, you had to cup your hands around the exact spots where the tapping had been. To listen, flatten your ear right up against the same spot on the wall. You like tangos? Yes. That's good; I even dance them. And you? You don't sing? Only inside. It's better to sing aloud. And dance. Things going badly for you? I don't think so. And you? Man, for a few years, I suppose so.

Not until the previous Sunday did he get the chance to find out what he looked like, when they brought them out onto the gallery, each one in front of his cell and with a guard behind him, to attend the Mass being celebrated in prison's Central Tower. He was about middle-aged, although his hair was already white, and he seemed quick-witted and cheerful. He glanced at the altar with a look of admiring astonishment, nodding his head in approval. Raúl did not remember having seen him before. Of course Felipe, when he came to visit, at first didn't seem to recognize Raúl either. And he himself, after nightfall, climbing up to the upper bunk to look at himself reflected in the window, also had a hard time recognizing himself. Long hair, bags under his eyes, swollen and puffy: Monte Cristo.

The visit took place after Mass, shortly before mealtime. I swear, it's just like when we visited Leo, except on the other side of the bars. How are you? Are they treating you alright? You look like you just crawled out of the catacombs. He spoke excitedly. He'd had to move heaven and earth and then some to obtain permission to be able to visit him before he appeared in front of the examining magistrate. But everybody had done everything possible. Papa is gathering signatures. And Montserrat says she's ready to disown any of her friends who try to ignore the situation. But the most effective move has been made by your girlfriend's family's lawyer, this García Fornells, who seems to have a lot of influence. Seems that Jacinto Bonet, however, has refused to talk about it. But things are looking really good. Your arrest has unleashed a real flood of protests, students, faculty, lawyers, all demanding your release. And the most important thing is that even in the factories the workers know that there's an intellectual, a university professor, imprisoned alongside their comrades. Your case has become both a denunciation and an example to follow. A denouncement of social injustice and an example of solidarity. Not words. An example.

He watched Raúl with that dazzlingly calm professional authority, not very different, in the end, from any other young clergyman's affect, more traditional in his proselytizing, when he asks his parishioners: why must you always hurry? Why is everyone in such a hurry? I never am. Why must one be? A question meant to signify: this is the inner peace of those of us who have learned to choose eternal life. However, the sermon concluded, for any attentive observer, his lightly tense smile as he withdraws, the slightly forced lightness of his steps, the volatility of his manners and gestures, seem rather to contradict the firmness of his implied principles, gravely compromising the value of a confidence more superficial than profound, allowing one to glimpse the mere mouth of what might well be an abyss of questions and uncertainties.

And with the same ineffable humor: I have to let you know that I've also got more problems with the reactionary sector of Opus Dei, from the old fogies. And concealing his laughter with his hand: when you get out, you might find they've put me out on the street, too. With that sense of humor, with that euphoric exaltation with which some people respond to an accumulation of obstacles. Another delay? Magnificent! One more problem we'll overcome. In a theological way, too. No, God's not dead, he might say, for example. He's simply drunk, sleeping it off like old Noah.

Before saying goodbye they exchanged wristwatches. The band on Felipe's watch smelled of priest.

In the afternoon, a providential storm broke up that atmosphere that felt like a small-town casino or a bullfighting club that had taken over the patios and galleries, prisoners strolling in their dress uniforms, some even wearing a hat and smoking a cigar, tipsy with the more-or-less free beer from the commissary and the paso dobles playing over and over through the loudspeakers, depressing verses from *In a Persian Market* as the only variation to that background music that set the festive mood with which the prisoners talked in small circles and played Spoof and exchanged bets on the handball games, all magically coming to a silent halt when the radio broadcast was interrupted to announce the results of the professional league soccer matches. If the storm didn't stop the revelry, it at least served to clear the patios; and seated on the upper bunk, face against the window, one could almost ignore the buzzing from the gallery. Thunder and lightning in the darkened skies, even before the rain came slashing down from the turbulent clouds, and the sensation that in a few moments, whole years went flashing by, in which time ran backward and the images floated one atop the other, as if he were not in his cell, but in Vallfosca, and different music was vibrating the glass where he rested his forehead, contemplating the landscape all blurry beneath one of those late-August or early-September thunderstorms, instead of those twisting skies above the prison's rectilinear architecture, the clouds convoluted like a mass of straining muscles in titanic combat, herculean onslaughts, centaurs with matted, tangled manes galloping away amid flashes and detonations, leaving behind them broken tensions, lightened spaces, renewed clarities, until on the western horizon there opened a crater of white sunlight, celestial glories revealing, as the rain lessened, a panorama of growing magnitude, cumulus castles, temples rising, cathedrals on the march with their violent towers, sharp naves, and labyrinthine crypts like ruined cities, violaceous shapes fading and dissolving where the Sierra Collcerola is no more than a shadowy black silhouette against the now extinguished western sky. Barcelona's violet hue, a tonality more in its light than in the city itself or in the colors of its stones and structures, like a vapor shifting from mauve to purple that emanates from its streets, from its buildings, a product of who knows what, possibly the proximity of the sea, the sombre reverberation of the encircling mountains, the trapped, stagnant humidity and the industrial atmosphere, polluted airs filtering the transparency of the elusive twilight sky—it's hard to say—of a day coming to an end.

And that liturgical purple? A Lenten color, proper to the time, but especially the circumstances. A penitent color, of tormented flesh, of cardinals, bruises, burns, and bumps, resulting from the right combination of fire red and iron blue, characteristic attributes of condemnation and damnation. The purple Mass, the Novitiate Mass, a Mass compared to which the vulgar Masses, the other Masses are only a dramatization that disguises a spectacle of much greater importance. Because, what other conclusion could an analytical spirit reach about that celebration of holy sacrifice held on the highest floor of the prison's Central Tower, above the guards' command post itself, a circular glassed-in office whose basement is the place where capital punishment is usually delivered, by garrote, to those prisoners sentenced to death? What could be the significance of its being celebrated precisely there, ostensibly for maximum visibility, except for the grandiose purpose, worthy of a delirious creativity, of giving the ritual more exemplary and authentic character, of exalting the commemorative symbolism, renewing, upon the intangible presence of so many who had really been executed there, the death of the Redeemer between the two thieves on the heights of Golgotha? Yes, right there, in the geometric center, not only the center of that series of exterior walls and moats, but also the very center of that radial layout, the confluence of the various prison wings that form the prison's internal structure. And similarly, in ceremonial terms, the axis or nerve center of daily life in the prison, in the same way that communion is the essence and synthesis of the holy sacrifice of the Mass, and the Mass, the essence and synthesis of the entire liturgical year. Concentric wings, and in each one of them, no doubt, the inmates similarly distributed. So, in the sixth ward, along the ground floor, the old and infirm in the first rows, closest to the altar and with the right to a pew because of their age and condition. Behind, already standing, the rest of the repeat offenders. And conveniently separated, the little girls, the queer prisoners, dressed up and made up in accordance with the importance of the event,

their weekly opportunity of showing off in front of the other
prisoners. And above, along the third-floor railing, those in solitary confinement, motionless before the doors of their respective
cells, each with a guard at his back.

And while the celebrant read the gospel to himself, the loudspeakers broadcast, beloved brothers, the words of La Madre
Mercedes, only a few words, most cherished and beloved sons, to
remind you that the prisons of men are not the true prisons, just
as the death of the body is neither the true death. Only the death
of the soul is death and only eternal damnation is prison. And
man's judgments, his sentences, are not what must matter to us.
For what do human judgments count for in the face of God's?
Faced with that Final Judgment which must inexorably precede
the definitive establishment of the City of God, when the final
trumpets sound, announcing the end of the world, of a world
sunk down into the slavery of sin, and the tombs are opened and
the flesh is revived and legions of angels elevate the blessed ones
into the presence of the Most High and hordes of demons drive
the reprobates headlong into the eternal fire? What will you hide
from his terrible gaze, how will you escape from his fearsome
voice when He summons you to his presence and, all simultaneously and at the same time each one individually, asking you:
what have you done with my ships? Where is my fleet? How
will you then stand a question which is in itself a condemnation?
Because you have sinned and for that you are here. Because you
have ignored Saint Paul in not obeying the law. Because you have
ignored Saint John when he told you to love the world. Because
you have failed to keep all the commandments and have trampled upon all the rules. Because you have sinned against Heaven
and against Me. You, faggots and heretics, obstinate lawbreak-
ers and fugitives from justice, communists, suicides, adulterers,
fortune-tellers, terrorists, traitors. Like Fra Garí you gave in to
the Tempter, to the Fallen Angel, and like him you have been
condemned. Like Fra Garí or Garín, the holy hermit who defiled
Montserrat, that expiatory temple that nature itself has raised up
in the heart of Catalonia, by committing rape and murder there
on the holy mountain: the holy blasphemer become wandering

beggar of those rocky peaks, those rigid royal effigies. Damned like the whore Riquilda, that little slut, that Lolita. And like her father, Jofre or Wilfredo, first Count of Catalonia, blinded, like King Lear, for his incestuous love. And like Santa Eulalia, guilty of the original lie. And like Saint George, who invented a dragon. And Saint James the Apostle, the imposter. And like Tirant lo Blanch, a coward's projection. And like Don Quixote, the creation of a sick and twisted mind. And like Cide Hamete el Campeador. And here we are, all of us, in the vaginal depths of Persephone, in the penetrating realms of Hades, where wisdom and mental retardation, weakness and strength, are all confused in the dark ambiguity of the elemental. All of them, Prometheus the pyromaniac, Sisyphus the incompetent, Vulcan the cuckold, Saturn the castrato, and together with them the thuggish Hercules and the wrathful Achilles, and Orpheus and Ajax and Odysseus and Laertes and Anchises and Aeneas and Virgil and Dante and Milton and La Merche. And I, from the center of every circle, I address my thoughts to you all, and especially to my closest companions, those who have sinned with their intelligence as well as with their sex, the enemies of God, of the Fatherland, of their governors and benefactors, to you I speak and particularly to you Raúl Ferrer Gaminde i Moret. To you and to all, princes, potentates, warriors, splendor of the heaven in which you dwelled and which you have now lost. Is it possible that such stupor can overpower your spirit? You, who in another time destroyed those giants masquerading as windmills? Is this now possible? The spirit carries its own dwelling within itself and can by itself make a heaven of hell and a hell of heaven. How many times has it not pleased the Almighty himself to reign among thick black clouds without obscuring his glory, to surround his throne with the majesty of the darkness from which burst forth the resounding thunderbolts of concentrated fury, to the point when the heavens then resemble hell? What do we fear, then? There is no longer any depth that can contain within its abysms our immortal life. Here, at least, we are free. Let us live, therefore, in this vast retreat for ourselves, free, without having to account for our actions to anyone, preferring a hard liberty to the light yoke of a pompous bootlicker. Because what is the world except a prison of darkness? What is the world but sterile land, rocky ground, a green field crawling with serpents? In which you will see, as Fray Luis de Granada said, how much this world has in common with hell. And what other name is there for paradise—if indeed it once existed—which reduced us to our current state? Wake up then, pick yourselves up, or remain forever fallen. We will build here our own paradise.

No longer the writhing multitude, the intermingling floods of passersby, colored masks and trumpets, party hats and onanistic zambombas all in their promiscuous dance, going and coming, plunging in and pulling out and spinning around, between the streamers and the confetti, between the sparkling glowing streets, wandering over the squashed grapes like blissful souls, fed up with contemplation, they might have resolved to exchange it—led on by the Almighty himself in the form of a statue of Frederic Soler, better known as Serafí Pitarra, suddenly come to life, his involuted pedestal in la Plaza del Teatro turned into an entertainer's podium—for more substantial emotions and pleasures, no longer all that, but rather, more concretely, the same horrendous scarecrow of La Venta, the same overblown waxed and painted faggot, stamping his heels and singing and clapping his hands, swaying his loose, sagging hips, almost an old man, surely, more frightening than obscene with his depressing residual synthesis of the romantic balladeer and mystic poet, his hoarse, braying rhymes, *España, mi vida, cariño, mi ser, amores, primores, morir, mi existir, olvido, perdido, entrañas, volver*— which might be rendered thus—Españya, my life, my darlingah, my beingah, my loves, my marvelous treasures, my existence, my oblivion, my abandon, my bowelsah, my return. And the lesbians' demonic laughter and the guitarist's big drunken-buddha eyes. The same one and the same ones, the Adolfos and Nuria Rivas and Nuria Oller and Pluto and Federico and even Fortuny and even that pain in the ass M. M. Everyone, maybe from the inertia of the routine, how each year they all made a date over the phone, maybe for just the opposite reason, as if they all somehow knew that, given their fraying relationships, that New Year's was going to be the definitive one, the last New Year's they would ever celebrate together.

Pluto showed up alone. Marihole had stayed home with their little boy. I think I'm gonna keep her pregnant the rest of her life. Pregnancy already takes up nine months and between bedrest and all the other stuff, it's a year. She's delighted and so am I. The great advantage with Marihole is that she's really stupid. Today, for example, I told her that I had a business dinner, and she thought it was perfectly natural. Look, it's well known that in Spain there are three forms of payment: pay, don't pay, and pay with an IOU. And Marihole is like an IOU.

Fortuny, already several drinks ahead of everyone, laughed stupidly. It shows you're what they call a man of letters. And Pluto: see? A guy like you would've been just right for Marihole, like that, sensible, just a little bit too careful. I've got to find some way for Marihole to cheat on me with you as soon as possible. That way she'll leave me in peace night and day. What this guy is proposing me to do is another one of his crackpot schemes! (Fortuny) You didn't understand me, pal (Pluto). Just an endorsement pure and simple. And with a promissory note if you like.

Federico was also pretty lit. Nuria Rivas called him Federica, a certain libidinous touch in her provocation, but he paid her no mind. As was normal when he drank, his conversation kept coming back to politics. He cornered Raúl. Why don't you just leave the party? It's absurd to let things just fizzle out by themselves. These situations have always gotta be clearly resolved, like when you get divorced. I want Leo to arrange me a meeting with Escala to request the official release. And tell him the proletariat is a kind of Frankenstein monster, a patchwork creature cobbled together from the trash of every social class.

Outrage Escala, give him a nervous breakdown, biliary colic, a coronary. The fact of the matter being, with the enraged amazement of the faithful wife who after years of marriage accidentally discovers, thanks to her girlfriends' gossip, that the frequency with which her husband performs the coital act with her is barely worthy of a eunuch and, after an initial phase in which she manages to hide her shame, so, too, the seminarian who on the eve of ordination decides to hang up his cassock, but only upon finding himself out in the wide world does he recognize the lie he has been living, and then gives himself over to all kinds of excess, so the defrauded wife, once she's been replaced, falls easily into nymphomania, and so Federico, unlinked from all political activity, seems to enjoy adopting, although only on a verbal level, the most provocative attitudes of all the orders. What's painful, he said, is thinking that humanity has had to wait so many thousands of years for its true History to begin. Oh, the poor people whose lot it was to live in a feudal, or theocratic, or capitalist society. What a tragedy, for example, to have been born a Hittite!

In fact, just like always when something occurred that seemed to lend the night a touch of the unusual, they were all rather on the same wavelength. No doubt things started to get heated with that guy from the other bar. A guy who went back and forth through the bar, sometimes stopping right in front of them. He gave them a look somewhere between friendly and defiant, with an oscillating smile. When he made sure he'd gotten their attention, his opened his shirt, now with a scorpion's triumphant gaze, showing them his chest splattered with scars seemingly from shrapnel, bare patches of red flesh amid the fine gray hair. He lit a match and, with a conjuror's flamboyant pauses began to scorch his chest hair with the small flame, meticulously scouring any areas missed at first, lighting one match from another, his belly trembling with silent laughter. Neither the bartender nor anyone else seemed to notice him. They all invited him to have a drink. When I was in the war, you all were just babies, he said. The Iron Ring of Bilbao. The Ebro. They asked him which side he'd fought on. Which side! He laughed and laughed. He pulled out a dark, worn wallet, giving them a peek inside, like someone flashing a deck of cards, the papers stuffed inside, money, identification. He ran out to the street and right in front of the bar door, threw his wallet straight into the mouth of the sewer. And then he did the same with everything he had in his pockets, loose change, a key ring, cigarettes, handkerchief, matches. He laughed, and seeing that he'd acquired a certain audience, he strolled slowly back inside, looking at them the whole while.

They invited him to have another drink. He also asked them for a Celta, delightedly filling his lungs with the smoke. They couldn't convince him to stick around with them. He turned crafty, pretending to be too clever to let them connive him. But by then they were all pretty well drunk.

¡*Vivan las revoluciones!* Federico shouted. He'd showed up with an Argentine couple, the woman was his first cousin or close relative, or at least that's what Federico said. The husband, or whatever he was, was dressed up as an Englishman; a big talker, stocky as a ram with a ram's bludgeon forehead. The cousin wasn't too bad-looking, but a real bore once she opened her mouth, too fond of trying to deliver momentous remarks. She apologized for bringing along another friend they'd run into. Not at all, it's much more fun with two women; just so long as she's a sprinkle of a dyke (Federico). The friend appeared a little more spirited or at least more in the mood for a good time, making sure to let her dress straps keep slipping off her shoulder, and then readjusting them as conspicuously as possible, expansively blowing kisses to the Buddha with the guitar.

Pluto had his eyes on her. A little prissy but definitely good for a gallop (Pluto). The cousin, however, looks exactly like a suppository. Difficult to remove once inserted.

And there was another girl, some sort of little whore, who'd also come with Federico. A model, as she explained. The cousin seemed tense with her companion, or maybe irritated with Federico, and was making eyes at Adolfo. And Adolfo, whether from morbid curiosity, or to dodge Nuria Rivas's insinuations, followed her lead.

At the Jamboree, Raúl sat apart with Aurora. How long since we talked? (Raúl). I don't know, a long time (Aurora). She leaned back on Raúl's shoulder, closing her eyes. I think it's a shame it all went to hell; I wouldn't dare tell you if I wasn't a little drunk (Aurora). Well, let's finish getting drunk (Raúl). Oh, Raúl, I do so many stupid things. But I can't take any more. I'm sick of him, of his head trips, how he likes to surround himself with a bunch of idiots, and the idiotic life we've got. Some days I think that if he's not really such an idiot then he can only shine when he's got bigger idiots around him. And if we're living this life it's not for weakness of character but because he feels incapable of doing any really creative work, and he just uses this life we're leading as an excuse. But I can't stand it. And then I do stupid things. Like how I slept with Federico just to piss him off (Aurora). Don't worry, you're not the only one. You tell me what I'm doing sleeping with Nuria Oller (Raúl). They kissed in the hallway outside the bathrooms. Then they slipped inside one together. Aurora unzipped his fly and knelt down in front of him. Come on, come on, she said next, pulling down her clothes, offering him her naked croup, propping her elbows on the toilet seat cover, the two of them spurred on faster by the door handle rattling when someone tried to come in.

Had La Rivas seen them or noticed something? In every case, it was really Aurora with whom she'd been drinking that night and not La Oller. Perhaps only because La Oller, who could not attribute Raúl's sudden coldness with her to more than an exciting cynicism, to a desire to guard the privacy of their shared secret—their tryst that afternoon in Pedralbes—was trying, with complicit dissimulation, to first make eyes at M. M. And it must also have been obvious for La Rivas that Adolfo was ignoring her, simply from being in a bad mood.

That evil bitch, with her enigmatic airs, she really gets on my nerves (La Rivas). And your nerves. You think they don't bother anybody? (Raúl). Defend her, defend her. You two would be so good together. You with Aurora and me with Adolfo (La Rivas). And you slept with him once, right? No skin off my nose. (Raúl). Well, look who's talking, the man with the golden prick. Let me tell you, it's no big deal for me either to pick up any guy at all. If I didn't have my period, I was gonna go with one (La Rivas). Do it anyway. You can always do something (Raúl). La Rivas turned away. Touché. Raúl's defenses, his capacity to be bluntly unpleasant, of replying acerbically to her hysterias and her stories, as roundly as that policeman who, the interrogation barely begun, cuts right to the chase with a few sharp blows upside the head.

Not unlike the Argentine gal with the shoulder straps. Except that the alcohol provoked a more violent response in La Rivas.

She stepped out to dance with someone, pulling him close, as tightly as possible, her tits almost falling out of her dress. And later, the scene, her compulsive need to end up starting a fight. Some greasy groper, or some wayward hand on her ass, or something like that. Go grope your mother! she screamed or she would scream. They moved aside as she barged between the tables. What do they think? They think women are like mules? She sat down unsteadily. Nerves, anxiety, a drowned, sinking, pissing wreck.

Pushy in her outbursts no less than in her chatter, capable in both cases of being exacerbating to the limit, like everything that gets repeated and repeated. When, voluble and passionate, she started chattering, or better, arguing with a taxi driver, with the waiter, with whomever, to explain her position to them about any problem, themes which she had generally seen them develop with proselytic purposes in other times, when they first met, the injustice of charity, better working conditions outside Spain, the need for political liberty, etcetera, a depressing regression directly proportional to the frequency of the chosen subject, like that hit record from years ago, years that hold nothing for us but painful memories.

On one hand, her tendency for sexual adventure was evident. Maybe to escape from Raúl, maybe for just the opposite reason, to prevent Raúl escaping from her. Preferably some happy little fling, necessarily brief as the circumstances required. Over and done with and each one back to their commitments, with the vivid memory left by all short-lived love affairs, cut short before the mutual misunderstanding of the coupling dissipates, not so much being on the same wavelength as simply a chance for each one to strip naked before the other's eyes, projecting themself onto the other like standing before a mirror, contemplating themself in the other, wrapping themself around them. Before finally discovering that the other person was someone different, a stranger with whom they had nothing in common.

On the other hand, her unfulfilled temptations. Her loss of velocity, some days barely idling along. As if now mistrustful of the vitality that formerly sustained her, of the power of her impulses; as if she had become afraid of life. The sensation of flying along the highway, about to smash flat into a wall at any moment. As if the repressive attitudes with which she'd been raised and educated suddenly became valid, no matter how much they'd been effectively exploded by her own family reality: inexorable punishment, the classic example of the family madwoman, of her fateful example, that remotely familiar aunt or cousin they talk about, one of the first to smoke in public and to go out alone with men, beautiful and uninhibited then, and now aged and impoverished and, above all, alone, one of those people who at first can be a lot of fun and entertaining when recounting their adventures, but whom everybody eventually shakes off because nobody's attracted to ruination and unhappy endings.

A slow process of inhibition, whose occasional rupture some night, fueled by alcohol, only grew worse later, upon waking up with a hangover, facing another day. A process which her relationship with Raúl, increasingly difficult, failed to explain sufficiently. Not united like a shaft of light through two windows into the same room, or like the water in a streaming current in the sea, or like the rain falling upon a river or a fountain, not even like two candles joined so closely that although being two, the flame seems one. Like water and oil.

In some way, simply the result of normal daily problems or of a specific conflictive situation, it were as if Nuria Rivas felt canceled out by something less specific, as if something were impelling and shaping her own behavior, perhaps her mother's personality. As if her childhood memories about the relationship between Doña Dulce and Amadeo, whose character she had taken a long time to understand, far from having served her as an example to follow, as a norm of conduct, they had, over time, dulled her daring and self-confidence; when they summered in Lloret de Mar and in the afternoons Doña Dulce had brought her along with her to Amadeo's house and left her playing in the garden with the chauffeur's daughter. An obvious co-dependency, even physically. Not because Doña Dulce was well preserved; because they could almost be mistaken for sisters. The difference lay, above all, in their attitude, in their bearing. Wise and mature, grave and mature fullness, impeccable presence and splendid

features, like one of those mares with brushwood and bullwhips
in her eyes.

Not yet Nuria. Amadeo's own mother, perfectly in keeping
with her own legendary amorous past. A widow, too, authoritarian, lucid, stingy, dressed with adamantine sobriety, still personally overseeing the management of her business affairs, with the
poise and class of one who moves as if the world were nothing
more than one vast Ritz Hotel. Her powdered face, taut from
cosmetic surgery. Her hair gathered under a silk turban, her eyes
behind dark glasses. The interior of her black car finished in
wood paneling and quilted leather, and she, giving the chauffeur
orders, barely looking outside through the half-drawn curtains,
imperturbable and solitary like a general or like death. What
were Nuria Rivas or Nuria Oller going to learn from a woman
like her or a woman like Doña Dulce, daughters of a time made
difficult for being anodyne and amorphous, a time of transition,
like that street thief who has neither the professional precision of
the old-time gangster, nor the natural ease of the addict who sallies forth to score his daily ration of injectables? Was a behavior
similar to Nuria's conceivable in them, in the widows, in their
good times? Might it have once been? Even if only for reasons
of social standing?

The strange loneliness of marriage, the feeling that any ordinary expression of one's spouse can suddenly create, despite the
havoc of cohabitation. The discomfort of a glance, even a loving
one, the disbelief with which one wonders who is she, who is
he, and, especially, what the fuck are they doing together. An
episodic transubstantiation of the familiar fully as unforeseen
as inevitable, the same as when the screen flashes the full moon
behind some clouds and the tormented wolf man is powerless
to stop the deadly transformation once triggered. In the same
way, in one of those parentheses of unreality peculiar to married
life, Nuria Oller spread her legs for Raúl in Pedralbes, on the last
afternoon of the year.

Perhaps Raúl was starting to get tired. Perhaps he was starting
to search for defects in her: the discordant rise and fall of her
laughter, a tone of voice perfect for roosters, her too-hungry eyes,

expressive of that perpetual state of agitation that characterized her, eager with desire, as if always walking on hot coals. And her habit of laughing with her hand covering her lips, a holdover, no doubt, from when they fixed her mouth when she was younger and she wore a bridge.

But none of all that would have been enough. The decisive turn was Nuria Oller's transformation into Nuria Hyde. When after weeks, months, years, of speaking nicely about Peter, attractive, enchanting, a good companion, one of those people whom you know you can always count on, everything suddenly changed. Peter was filthy. Peter was clumsy. He didn't know how to make love. He snored. And she had her own plans, everything figured out down to the last detail. And she divulged them, not with the simple perverse calculation of the Lolita who, out hitchhiking along the road, gets picked up by three taciturn forty-somethings, and then, once inside the car, asks suggestively, You're not all going to rape me, are you? No, not with that kind of calculation, but with something really despicable in the malign victory of her smile: divorce and, as she had managed it well, the surety of obtaining, according to English laws, a nice alimony. She held all the trump cards. She contemplated her nakedness in the mirrors, radiant like a vengeful goddess, without noticing that it really seemed, at least in Raúl's mind, like that afternoon was truly their last. Not unlike the boy who hears the ladies of the house discussing the news of the sudden death of some gloomy neighbor, commenting how the man said that he'd like another piece of gâteau, and as they were serving it to him he began to slide right off his chair, so that for the boy, for many years, the word gâteau inevitably carried the horrendous connotations of a curse whose spell he would do everything possible to not say aloud, and so for Raúl, Nuria Oller had certain accents, certain attitudes, no less traumatically dark, of which he really only became aware that afternoon.

Perhaps he had never really thought deeply about Barcelona's middle-class women. Not the current young crop, free and attractive, who'd learned to overcome so much conventionalism by themselves. Not the girls of today, or at least not them especially, but rather their mothers, their grandmothers, those women whom the young ladies today often judge rather severely for simply failing to understand their youthful behavior. What do they know about the difficulties of former times? Keeping up appearances, following protocol, appearing modest, the obstacles involved in simply finding a place to carry out an adulterous encounter. And in another area, the family, their excellent organizational qualities, their administrative gifts, their perfect control of the wardrobe and the pantry, their keys. And their awareness of the value of money, in no way inferior to that of the working woman, because if the latter will manage to get the best deal possible for what she needs to fill her shopping basket, our keen wife of a wealthy businessman will prove herself just as resourceful, relatively speaking, in playing her part, to get the discounts at shops where she is valued for being a good customer, of finding real bargains in the antique shops by paying cash, of obtaining the maximum rent on both the summer house and the furnished apartments for which she providently holds the deed in her name during the months when she doesn't use them.

Of course in a world in perpetual motion—and today's world more than ever—there are always some families who flourish while others decline. And it's in the heart of these families, the ones whose economic descent eventually shows in their social relations, where that aptitude and that competitive edge, contrary to what one might suppose, begin to be blunted. Now it's no longer the wife but the whole family that, from a lack of adequate material support, begins to lose footing, and along with the rhythm of activity, the notion of prices, finds itself trapped in a vicious circle that only turns into an ever more dizzying downward spiral. That's when that family finds the tables turning, becoming victim to antique dealers, speculators, unpaid bills, mortgages. Just like the crazed husband who arrives home denouncing today's youth—Nothing but faggots!—with the idea of psychologically preparing his wife, of better emphasizing the fortune that awaits her depending on how willingly she submits to his clumsy carnal embrace, so, too, families in decline: their progressive withdrawal and isolation is usually accompanied by some disrespectful theorizing about how impossible the world is becoming, a judgment which, more generally, is also usually the favorite theme of all people when they grow old. Thus that gentleman who, well on in years, retired from business some time ago, goes each morning to the bank to exchange, more than anything else, a few words with the assistant manager or, if the assistant manager is very busy, with the financial manager, or with the cashier, or with the porter, about his obsession, that neither his stocks nor his income are now what they once were, about being known and respected, about reaffirming his respectability, or mentioning his friendships and personal relations, of proclaiming yet again his conservative ideas, in both political and economic matters, how bad everything is, how lucky we are to have Franco, etcetera, and in passing—banks have big ears—of disregarding the fact that his son is in jail, it's what happens with students, everyone knows, it was the same when I was young.

Cabals, arrangements. In the same way that an old joke ends up turning into a real anecdote and, over time, to enhance the effect, is repeated by everyone, like something that happened to a friend or even, as incredible as it might seem, to themself, in the sincere belief that it really happened that way and that only a lapse in memory makes it difficult for one to specify the circumstances, so, too, function family histories, in their development from the past to the present. The blood ties, inheriting a personality but not a fortune. The tendency to consecrate some secret family code in the face of any less genetic explanation. An explanation that might, for example, exclude any consideration of blood relationship from the reason why Aunt Paquita's death could affect Raúl much more than anyone could have foreseen. Instead, let's imagine that the reason might be the fact that for Raúl, along with Paquita died a whole nexus of relations between the conscious past and the remembered one from their summer stays in Vallfosca, and that other more forgotten but no-less-intensely-shimmering time at Montseny during the Civil War.

In fact, that old upper-middle-class Barcelona society, now in decline, and the new large middle class share only one thing: their common uprooting, save in economic matters, from the places and lands where they were born. In one case, for devotion to a tradition that permits them to keep believing that they are still what they once were. In another, for the coincidence of their interests with those of the central power, in whose shadow they have thrived, in the heart of that monopolistic oligarchy to which they belong. And as much in the one case as in the other, although in a remote and unformulated way, their common feeling of lost identity, one of those national destinies aborted like one aborts an orgasm because of coitus interruptus.

The destiny of a people who, with its expeditions to the Orient, with its warlike Almogavars, unemployed reconquerors, technically on the dole, must prefigure the conquest of a new world for the West, in which it would not be permitted to participate. A people who, with its mariners, navigational charts, and, even, money, was going to establish the bases of that discovery, of that enterprise from which it would remain excluded. A people who, from its union with Castile, forged by its leaders, was only going to manage to be marginalized from any true center of power. Or what amounts to the same: by taking the side of the Archduke Carlos in his fight against the Prince of Viana, by embracing the cause that cannot triumph before then choosing the contrary, they end up losing just the same. And thus, at least, conserving the letter of the myth, of the unfinished enterprise. Just as the sociological pretension which holds that social context both explains and shapes a man in equal measure only begs the question, because, quite the contrary, it's man's relationship with different social contexts amid which he has developed since childhood, and his behavior in each circumstance, which must lead us to the understanding of what the subject was already essentially, including before his first memories, an understanding which in turn leads us to clarify what man is generally when removed from all specific contexts, as the component of a civilization itself, and this clarification returns us to any point in Catalonia's history. For example, its revealing identification with the prince of Viana—a poor devil, the classic born loser—will infallibly conjure up the various components of each disaster, one after another, and we now find—in this point as in any other—how many elements configure and embody the luck of the cause itself, of Catalonia's final destiny.

Well, if not, then what explains, for example, the fact of having adopted Saint George as its patron saint? Or having taken as an emblem the knight's victorious battle against the dragon? How to interpret that, if not as the projection of some internal problem, as the symbolic expression of a desire, of Catalonia's anxiety to resolve through a chimerical combat, the real combat with itself that it keeps avoiding? A struggle, of much more uncertain outcome, which postulates the triumph of order and formal rigor, the dominion of reason and the sovereignty of wisdom, over the sordid ruins of a shadowy collective unconscious. A similar impulse, in the end, to what leads a people to construct cathedrals or expiatory and votive temples.

Dragons, princesses, images very much on the level of the middle class and *le petite bourgeoisie*, the most solid nucleus of that conflictive personality called Catalonia. Because, like that young typist emotionally formed between radio serials and soap operas, so, in Catalonia, the drippy, professional-mourner mentality of its middle classes. And what other material can we point to if we discard an immigrant proletariat and an upper middle class that has renounced its historical role as the leading class, from the point of view of Catalan nationality?

The myth, the literary topic, the proparoxytonic rhetoric. Barcelona, a city proclaimed to be mirror, lantern, star, and destination of all knight-errantry, epithets accepted without even a trace of irony, insofar as they're applied to an exultant city, in the full solstice of its fiestas, which a few lines later will receive such an illustrious guest by slipping a stalk of furze under the tail of his mount and laugh behind his back after hanging a sanbenito upon him, or mocking paper dolls called *llufas* inscribed with ridicule, dirty slander, and buffoonery that could only go over the head of some idiot reader or some babbling councilman who, reader of hearsay, resorts once more to the cliché, in the course of any plenary meeting, reception, tribute, or municipal blowout party. An archive of swindles and whoring, a city that enjoys, like an open-air street party on the eve of a saint's day, the spectacle that might be offered by the unseated horseman, the fallen rider, the shipwrecked castaway on its beaches, destruction or end, form or purpose of being amused, of killing time like one kills a bandit, how he's quartered and decapitated on a scaffold. A city that injures and spits on the fallen, spits, flattens him, butchers and kills him, a killing, a bloody scalping, and the public celebrates it with 21-gun salutes and fireworks and bonfires, school of courtesans, sepulcher of strangers, and exile of messengers, the capital of a people who perhaps confronted the armies of history's greatest generals, Hannibal and Caesar, Almanzor and Napoleon, perhaps all of them, and lost. History repeated throughout time like the story of a damsel in distress repeatedly raped by successive saviors, each time between passionate promises of eternal love.

This city that can so well contemplate itself in its vastness from the heights of Mount Carmel, black weeds in the foreground, against the scintillating embers of everything far down below, and the immense sea beyond the city, and the gray vessels of the Sixth Fleet anchored in the port, and the factory smokestacks, and the flags and pennants fluttering in the sun, and the soldiers marching in file with enormous palm fronds on their shoulders, commemorating the joyful advent of the Epiphany, the reestablishment of calm, the end of the burnings, of the churches in flames, as if the heavens might have granted the bishops' prayers, heeded their Petendam Pluviam, and a saving rain would have wiped out the city from the Llobregat to the Besós, from Montjuich to Tibidabo, turning it into a plain of faint reflections, earthy water, germinative loam, a swamp surely not very different in appearance from the original, when Montjuich was a rough cape jutting into the sea, a colossal Alcides from whose side Barcelona must be born, and like Moses, emerged from the waters, born and reborn like Ilium or Troy or Hissarlik.

On the slopes of Mount Carmel we find the Gaudian Park Güell, and at the bottom of its foothills, a short distance away, in fact, although already well into the Ensanche proper, the visitor will be able to appreciate the no-less Gaudian spires of the Sagrada Familia, reaching up, one might say, like jagged crags of a sacred mountain. A work that if it were ever terminated someday would probably have very little in common, like all slow-built cathedrals, with the original design, the same thing that usually happens with a city's urban plan, always surmounted in its development by newer realities neither foreseen nor foreseeable. One of these pre-unfinished enterprises—at least according to the image its founders had made of it—to the degree to which the burden of its realization usually falls to, or is left in charge of, future generations. Sacralization of the means, the mediatization of the objective. Dominant temples, standing out in general—perhaps for their location, perhaps for their height alone—from the collective cityscape, as if so that from their summits, in the rather most exceptional case when it is not a traveler who is inspired to climb to the top of the high towers, the citizen will obtain an unprecedented panorama of their city, to which, according to their taste, they might add the dose of future they prefer.

A red city, for example, as if burning in the fires of the West. Paralyzed by a general strike of greater significance than the one in '51. A general strike that, by means of a qualitative leap forward, will lead to a true revolutionary situation. A brief notice, a small sidebar in *Le Monde*, that will suddenly dominate newspaper headlines the world over.

Revolutionary November in Barcelona. Barcelona, 9 Nov. The general strike has triumphed. Following industries, public transportation, and banks, businesses, too, have closed their doors. Demonstrations are growing throughout the whole city. More than 50,000 workers and students marched in demonstration along Vía Layetana singing "The Internationale." Army troops have been confined to barracks and public buildings appear to be protected by barbed wire and heavy police forces. After midafternoon, the city has remained in darkness due to the flow of electrical power suddenly being cut off. Unconfirmed rumors affirm that curfew has been imposed. At press time isolated gunfire can be heard in the streets. The situation is very grave.

Barcelona, 10 Nov. The revolutionary strike initiated yesterday in Barcelona seems to have displayed especial strength in the city's industrial sector. Eyewitnesses there affirm that various police stations and barracks have been attacked. There are rumors of hundreds of victims ranging from dead to wounded. In a poignant radio address broadcast early this morning, the Civil Governor of the province has called for an immediate cease-fire, at the same time explicitly offering his resignation, if that will help to calm the mood in the city.

14h. The Cabinet, meeting in Madrid in special session, after denying reports about the civil governor of Barcelona's resignation, announced the declaration of martial law in the four Catalan provinces. Reliable sources affirm that, in Barcelona, the people have taken control of the central headquarters of Telefonica, the Postal and Telegraph Office, and various local radio stations.

19h. The masses have taken barracks and official centers by storm. Among others mentioned are the City Hall and the Regional Council. Still holding out are the Civil Government, the Military Headquarters, and Police Headquarters. On the contrary, it's been affirmed that, in the barracks, soldiers are siding with the people. Radio stations are broadcasting nonstop revolutionary proclamations and exhortations.

21h. According to the latest bulletins, the Government has now proceeded to dispatch forces by air to Catalonia.

Revolution in Spain. Madrid, 11 Nov. The revolutionary strike begun two days ago in Barcelona has now spread to various parts of the nation, Asturias, Guipúzcoa, Bilbao, Valencia, Seville, and the capital itself. The actions of the masses seem to have acquired especial violence in Asturias and the Basque Country.

Official sources affirm that the Government is poised to declare a state of war in the entire national territory.

Although news reports reaching Barcelona are quite unclear, it seems that hospitals are taxed beyond their limits and the streets are littered with bodies. The situation of the last centers of resistance is classified as desperate.

21h. Madrid, urgent. Unconfirmed rumors insist that units of the Sixth Fleet are sailing at top speed toward Barcelona.

And then? A holocaust, possibly. But also the beginning of war, not just a civil war but a full-blown insurrection, the long march entailed by the development of the European Revolution. The trip to Madrid that November, the frustrated attempts to establish between the two local organizations more direct and agile contact than the habitual party mechanisms, with the goal of coordinating to the maximum the projected mass actions. The premonition of disaster that assaulted him as the plane descended over Barajas airport, between two lights, that surprising urban proliferation rising in the eroded dryness of the dusk, in the center of an empty desert horizon of mackerel terrain, conferring a character of true wonder upon the sudden flowering of such immense illumination, neon lights and skyscrapers sheltering the same old Madrid as always, hardships and dire straits, moral and economic retardation, the same propensities for barhopping as the chosen form for human relationships and as the verbal solution for all kinds of repression, black humor and basic business, simultaneously farrago and quintessence, at once crucible of Spain, of plain and simple purisms, bald-faced snubs and good-natured generosity, a smiling showplace of affected sesquipedalian raciness.

The meeting with the comrades in charge of making contact. Minds lovingly carrying the weight of eighteen ninety-eight impoverished by other ideological residue remotely translated, a mentality prone to intellectual constipation in its exhausting search for topical authenticity, more populists than scientific socialists, more provincial than puritan, more beatific than dogmatic, although also dogmatic, and puritans and scientific socialists, with the shrewdness of the meseta in its ideas and the fecundity of the wasteland. Living incarnation, in spite of his university condition, of that positive hero of social realism, of that militant example, of that worker normally called Juan or José or Pedro, simple names like the people themselves, an honest and self-sacrificing man in the factory, among his fellow workers, as well as in the neighborhood, within the vicinity, always willing to lend help to whomever needs it, whether with his strength or his counsel, to show by his example what is the correct line. The positive sort, some fellow capable of sacrificing a whole Sunday of well-deserved rest and family life, scouring half the city so as to deliver to its intended destination a package accidentally found on the street, a route that serves as inspiration for the novel that offers a true panorama of the various environments our hero feels obliged to experience, maintaining at all times an unimpeachable conduct. The sort of man who can soothe people's spirits, rightfully rebellious, like the neighbors of a property condemned by City Hall, thus preventing the municipal employees from suffering indignity or some ill because, in the end, those agents are not the ones truly responsible, but simply salaried employees like them. A fellow, in short, whose humanity leads him to mediate between striking workers and police, in order to avoid unnecessary violence, and who ends up accidentally run over by the ambulance he himself had called to take care of a little boy struck by a stray bullet. And then his companion Antonio, the individualist, the worker of anarchic temperament, almost dissolute, has an epiphany and joins the party.

And like someone who one day reflects that his devotion to a landscape, to a people, to a smell, to a wine, has got nothing to do with the word motherland, however much others would like to make him believe the opposite; in fact, they are greatly mistaken, and more real than patriotism is his being a loyal fan of this or that sports team, the result, at least, of a voluntary choice; thus Raúl's indifference, if not his impatient displeasure with the series of questions brought up at those meetings, not for any conceptual reason but for the way they were raised.

Suddenly, absolute disenchantment, that disenchantment which is confused with physical fatigue, a consequence of all activity developed around a misunderstanding. Realizing that just as he had overestimated the party's capacity to mobilize the masses in Madrid, his comrades in Madrid took for granted that in Barcelona, unlike events in Madrid, it was simply enough for the party to give the signal for the masses to take to the streets. How could he even try to make them understand that, like an old man waking up from his siesta, his return to reality in full feverish drowsiness, his awareness of the impossibility of going farther with that flaccid semi-erection, destined to disappear not only from the least physical exertion inherent to the sexual act but also from the simple fact of abandoning the warmth of his recliner, so, too, in practice, the revolutionary impulses of the Barcelonan masses seemed to vanish into thin air? Because, who doubts that in the same way that desires are based in reality, realities are based on desires? More than being about ideas, aren't ideologies about the exclusion of ideas? More than reasons, aren't ideological principles acts of will, if not of faith?

The final struggle, the transitional phase, and then, the pre-established harmonies of the new society, principles induced or deduced from the course of History, revealed on one occasion and since then hammered soundly into place on a daily basis. But if apart from that confidence in the future, it turns out that one's son has married a good girl who also works and also has socialist notions, and between the two of them they gather what's needed, and if it happens that the family's property out in a small country town, thanks to tourism, is now worth money, and the world generally seems to be on the right track, and one can finally retire with peace of mind, what more can you expect from life? This leads to a decline in one's clarity of mind, as lately evidenced by Leo's father, because just as a long stay in bed tends to aggravate an older person's condition, a bout of excessive happiness can end up affecting their normal thought patterns.

Like that old customer who drives a specific make of car, who has remained faithful to the company from the start, purchasing each new model, as far as his finances will allow, turning casual choice into habit, a habit based on principle, the principle into a proud personality trait, and that trait becomes a reason for solidarity with other drivers of the same brand; and now, after so many years, upon receiving some honorary reward for his loyalty, one of those distinctions established for publicity purposes, a medallion, for example, or a scale miniature of the first model ever produced, cast in some precious metal, the emotion overwhelms him as it's presented to him, the culmination of a dialectical process, in as much as it objectifies the dual relationship between existing reality and the sublimation of that reality, between magnification of the object possessed and jealous custody of the object magnified, a ceremony for the which, like on a Christmas holiday celebrated by the family, the tears that blur his vision seem to facilitate the dizzy series of images, the lights, the candles, the songs, the gifts, wife, children, little grandchildren, all those present and missing, the dead, the winters, the evenings, old age, a whole life of devotion and fidelity now almost concluded, while the effusions of which he is the object only serve to deepen his sweet sadness and his thoughts about the goodness of everything; thus had Raúl found Leo's father to be the very picture of such a man.

Wait, he said. And without further explanation spread out a street map of Moscow on his old cutting table, stepping back immediately, studying Raúl's reaction with a smile. The son-in-law of an old friend just brought it, a young Spanish-Soviet engineer who'd gone to spend Christmas with his Soviet family there. The old friend had played a very significant role during the Civil War. Now he had a very comfortable position and was retired from politics, but that didn't mean he was not among the ideological forefront as usual. Twelve years ago he put in a brand-new dining room. It's still untouched. You can be sure he's finally going to use it one of these days. And he arched his eyebrows in complicity.

He showed him the map. This is the Neva River. Red Square and the Kremlin. The Mausoleum. The Opera. Seems that up there the bakeries are real bread factories. The University, a kind of skyscraper. Gorky Park. A lot of people there really enjoy ice-skating. Children smile and eat shortbread.

And so, suddenly, the world. The New Society: its historical necessity like destiny, like the fruit of the divine will revealed (Moses, Christ, Mohammed), like, in its origin, any of History's other grand constructs, Rome, Byzantium, Islam, the Holy Roman Empire, Imperial Spain. And this, against any human effort to impede it, against any apparently insurmountable obstacle. The revolutionary character of the revolution will always triumph over the harsh and brutal repression of the brutal dictatorship. And the New Society will be installed. A happy age and happy centuries which our children will call golden and not because gold, so esteemed in our steel age, will be easily obtainable in that happy venture, but because those who will live in those times will not know the words "yours" and "mine."

The Milestone. And its consequence, or perhaps its cause: the New Man.

A vision that Leo's father, who struggled to express himself, had to represent in an eminently physical form, like some memorial project, from one of those allegorical group sculptures, like now, just in the moment of consecration, facing a panorama of kneeling inmates, heightened in their solemnity by the motionless concentric silence of the prison galleries, something, too, of allegorical monument in that precise instant of the ceremony celebrated upon the platform in the prison's Central Tower, which the elevated host in turn converted into its center.

A monument of monolithic composition, graduated in depth and height. A huge, vigorous work, a creation of power and fury, of love and piety, a titanic undertaking, of leaders emerged from the masses, here a young man with an angry face like a stone, there the arrogant torsion of an old man showing the lapidary law of the people, both standing out against a background in relief, a mass of muscles in ferocious battle, all of that dominated by the figure of the dialectical sybil that announces the imminence of a society void of class or contradiction, a synthesis of contraries, apotheosis or final judgment, which from on high, in the accurate unwavering scales of justice, appeared resolved, in an attitude of a pensive peace, by the image of the New Man, equally distant from extremists and wild youth, symbolized by the lewd adolescent naked feminine body, and of the crepuscular and decadent residues of the past, represented by an old man decrepit right down to the tip of his withered pecker; a New Man who with his serene calm, now rising above all conflict, seemed to preside as if from a throne, as a finishing touch, to the monumental group of sculptures.

Meaning: the culminating moment or qualitative leap, the moment of transubstantiation, when God descends and becomes the Sacred Form. The definitive consecration of the consolidation of the installation, once and for all, definitively consecrated following the decisive final battle, consolidation of the installation of the definitive conquest, once and for all, finally established, as a decisive culminating conquest, as a final consecration of the definitively installed culmination, as an installation of the consecration once and for all, a royal presence that commemorates the mystery of the incarnation, of the God who became man, and who was garroted.

The consecration. Indispensable requisite of communion, the very essence of the holy sacrifice of the Mass, a communion prepared from the evening before by the general confession that had brought to a close the cycle of spiritual exercises carried out over the preceding days. Confession or penance, a sacrament whose importance La Merche had emphasized so much in his talks, so appropriate to the expiatory weeks of Lent, the time between Epiphany and the Passion. He spoke, one might say, not through the prison's loudspeakers, but rather though a microphone, exclusively for the inmates of the sixth wing doubtless gathered on the ground floor, from an improvised pulpit, in the abstract glow of the gallery, its symmetrical architecture almost like a Masonic temple. At four o'clock sharp, during silent time, he began testing the microphone. Hello, hello, this is La Merche speaking to you all. From his cell, even though Raúl had his ear glued to the peephole, it was hard to hear. He was talking about man's principal business, his salvation.

Today I'm going to invite you all, my dearly beloved sons, that you come with me and ascend Mount Carmel, that you follow me without falling nor toppling from the summit. So, carefully, hand in hand. Let the youngest be a support to the oldest.

Let us consider. What is offered to your eyes from here in the nocturnal splendors which extend from here to our feet? A city. A city built around what was once Mons Taber, the ancient acropolis, a prominent spot to which the travelers of old, like the Apostle Saint James, had to come in their moments of anxiety to contemplate the city. Yes: that mountain no longer visible. Mons Taber. Neither Horeb nor Nebo nor Tabor. Simply Taber. But isn't that enough, now that it's converted into a cathedral? And before it, in the distance, as if pointing to the sea, Montjuich, the mountain of Jupiter, or the Jews, Mount Sinai of the law, an eye for an eye, a tooth for a tooth, a death for a death, God's mountain in every case. And behind us, at our back? That prominence of the Sierra Collcerola nowadays called Tibidabo. Tibidabo or the Devil's Mountain. That mountain to which the Tempter transported Christ and told him: all that you see shall be yours. This is, my dearly beloved sons, a mountain from whose peak one can see not only the whole city and its sins, but also catch sight of, farther away, and higher, Montserrat. From there, a ring of crags clustered together like the towers of a temple, Gothic spires, pipes of an organ played by angels, like figures frozen in movement, starting to sway back and forth, now to the left, now to the right, like in a dance, in a beautiful ring which forms and dissolves. A mountain carved by the angels themselves, pure geological eroticism, with its nests of phantoms and its golden cascades of broom and its clusters of vampires, reliefs and erections like elephants' trunks and scrotum and buttocks, in colossal copulation, a place where the deflowered virgins blossom anew like wild roses, a mountain born of the waters or by parthenogenesis, the same way a virgin is born of her rape, or a pre-Crusoe, a pre-Andrenio or any castaway reborn from the waters, who makes a sanctuary of their catastrophe.

What better watchtower for the soul, then, children of my womb? What better vantage point for Jaime the Conqueror when from there he planned to seize Mallorca, perfectly visible to his penetrating vision, more than to his sight? What better throne from which to contemplate his dominions, no longer the nearby Tibidabo, beneath whose sheltering bulwark extends Barcelona, but also, equally, Montsant, Montsech, and Montseny, with the white Pyrenees beyond, below the stimulus of that landscape of esoteric peaks and phallic protuberances? What better abode or cell, after all, than this spot which so well fosters contemplation, meditation, inspiration? A place of retreat for conquerors and prophets and saints and founders and discoverers and navigators, a sanctuary that preserves their swords, their victories, their flags, their discoveries, Lepanto and Mallorca, the Society of Jesus and America, Montserrat, primacy of a New World, as a symbolic prefiguration of the City of God.

For that reason I call on you now, my beloved children, for
you all to realize your journey to Damascus, to ride with me
like this masculine saint who after a libertine adolescence in
which he gave himself over to gambling and petty theft and
to concupiscent thoughts and acts, including unnatural ones,
rubbing elbows with bad company, stealing to go play soccer
or billiards or go to gymnasiums or attend dances or visit bath-
houses or whorehouses, later committing armed robbery with
malice aforethought under cover of darkness, in a gang, attacking
man or woman, becoming perverted and perverter, without any
kind of faith, a sacrilegious diabolical blasphemer. And then,
behind bars for his great waywardness and many vices, in the
solitude of his cell, precisely in that isolated room, far from the
noise of the world and its sins, isolated like a hermit, there, as
a result of a divine call, there, after an internal struggle with
himself, right there, overcame all his wickedness, and renounced
the world, the devil, and the flesh, drunkenness and dishonesty,
and recognizing his previous miseries, took up the banner of
Christ, surrendering himself to him like a wife to her husband,
crying out, fallen from his steed, Forgive me, oh my God, have
mercy and forgiveness, crying out, yes, crying out, Augustín,
Pablo, Saulo, Saúl, or Raúl, or whatever the hell your name is.
The world! The true prison, as the philosopher said! And what
are its shadows if not the blindness in which the wicked dwell?
What chains are these that imprison them if not the strength
of the devotion with which their hearts cling to the things they
so inordinately love? And what hunger is this they suffer, if not
the insatiable appetite they have for infinite things they cannot
reach? And they, these captives, are the ones who have built the
prison where you find yourself, which, as a negation of denial,
is an affirmation, a place of salvation and freedom. The cell!
An abode of greatness which the benign Jupiter, who calms the
heavens with his lightning, surrounded by a thousand virtues,
has created for you. For you are only in prison because the Lord
wants your indignity to bring you understanding, so that you
might know the weakness from which you suffer. And having
come to know the truth, you might lead as many fellow inmates

as you wish to also loathe that weakness, so that they might not be lost and instead reach paradise. It is not so much from your crimes as for the compassion of God that you are here. So that in this way, those of you traveling the wrong path will be able to redeem and save yourselves. And now repeat after me: oh, Lord, do you never tire of granting me mercy? Then together we will sing *Perdón, oh Dios mío.*

Outside, to judge by the sunlight pouring in through the window, forming a slanted square on the flagstones, the morning must have been splendid. One of those mornings with a strong wind, a wind that sweeps clean the stagnant city atmosphere and dissipates the noises of traffic, permitting the sun to shine brilliantly through the clean air. It gives one the desire to unbutton their overcoat and feel the already warming sun. A day that makes them forget the harsh winter weather that must naturally return, a prefiguration of the springtime that already evokes the summer. And while he remained there, motionless before the open cell door, witnessing the ceremony unfolding, everything in the street must have been movement and light. That sunny wind mussing up people's soft hair and light skirts, sudden mischievous gusts that draw from people's faces expressions like supplication or supreme pleasure, warm rushing breezes that suddenly accelerate the cycle of the seasons, the rotation of the roots, the swelling of the shoots and buds, luxurious abundance reactivated and ready to burst forth.

Like that morning when he drank a Campari in the sun with Aurora, on the terrace of a bar in the Ensanche facing the late morning sun, not far from the university. You won't leave Nuria, Aurora had told him. And Raúl: it's just that there's nothing to break. We've had some time together, without ever talking about the future. And that time is over. And Aurora: this is what makes things more difficult for you; having refused to talk about the future. And Raúl: I don't see why. Right now she's in England and I'm here, with you. And Aurora: and this summer? And Raúl: well, I don't know. I suppose we'll see each other. We're still friends. And after summer vacation, she'll go back to England. And Aurora: do what you like. I don't know if you're alright with me, but I am with you and, on the other hand, you don't seem to me to be alright with Nuria. I mean that, with her you should be how you really are.

She was wrong: he wasn't alright with Aurora either—what she was implicitly insinuating—and he didn't have the least intention that their relationship outlive the summer. However, throughout that summer, when he began to perceive the Adolfo-Aurora convergence, far from feeling the relief he'd believed he would experience upon seeing himself liberated from a connection he was beginning to grow weary of and which, in every case, he was planning to sever, the reality of the facts made him feel more like the victim of treachery. A treachery that, without a doubt, at least for his part, made him hasten the breakup, as much to push the events forward as to avoid his observation of this growing convergence from becoming something little less than obsessive.

The road that leads to these notes written upon the smooth face of rough sheets of toilet paper. A long and winding route, sometimes as if blocked, as if cut off; sometimes getting lost as one gets lost on the mountain paths leading nowhere. And, nevertheless, the first tangible result of that imprecise intuition he had early one morning, while he was standing guard next to the magazine, east of the camp. An intuition or perhaps a recovery of forgotten intuitions, precisely of that which, when he was a little boy, in his school essays, he tried not so much to reveal as to conceal, writing not what he would have liked to write but rather what he supposed he was expected to write. In the same way that perhaps that turn of standing guard by the magazine was not the decisive one. Nor that dawn. There were other hours of guard duty before and after that, and other dawns.

His first worthwhile experiments, or at least satisfactory ones, different from how much he might have written up until then. And he poured himself into them, possessed by that demented sensation of reality experienced by an explosives expert who believes he's invented a bomb that cannot be disarmed, which will always be capable of exploding at any moment, and he consumes his nights assembling it with great care. Because like the little boy with a windup toy that gets jammed, who opts to completely destroy it, so the childish sadisms or an early passion for hunting or a later vocation as a terrorist usually end up sublimated into any specific activity, always given that in such an activity the individual finds an adequate channel to give satisfactory expression to his destructive feelings that lie at the source of everything; meanwhile, on the other hand, when the individual in question does not find the ideal channel to give vent to the sentiments engendered within him, the accumulated destructiveness then turns against him and his more immediate world, giving way to the creation, both in his personal relationships as well as those with his neighbors and coworkers, of his small personal hells.

It was indisputable, however, that the army camp had acted as a catalyst in awakening those vague notions, until then dormant or undisturbed, latent in some previous phase of his mutations. That their appearance, the last stage of his metamorphosis, had been propitiated by the prevailing atmosphere there. As a reaction to a type of life that could be characterized, in general, by mental haze and moral brutalization. A world rotating around two poles—hard work and sloth—which for being simultaneously antagonistic and complementary, tended to neutralize one another in praxis, to be synthesized in a wise formula of compromise, lauded by tradition, according to which the important thing is that everyone without exception strictly complies with their duty to cover up appearances, like a present time applied by extension to the most minimal details of the system, to the most obviously impossible demands of conciliation. A world whose most prototypical fruit was perhaps the neighbor in the infirmary who just happened to be next to him, when upon emerging from a feverish delirium—produced by the flu or some other viral condition, they never informed him of the diagnosis, if indeed the doctor in charge ever established it—he found himself occupying the second-to-last bed in the row, between Fortuny and that stingy bastard who pretended to be sicker than he was so he could stay there as long as possible, in such a sordid atmosphere, reading comic books, and having lost his light gloss of scion of the middle class and future doctor or lawyer or engineer, he offered instead the aspect of an enormous and stupefied child, a halfwit somewhere between jocose and incontinent, stinking of stale piss and putrid discharges, his hands sticky, bright red cheeks like a clown, while between cyclopean yammerings he masturbated with all his might.

It was after his stay in the infirmary. Standing guard outside the magazine. Or, more precisely, that Sunday when, back from a weekend leave, it was his turn to stand the fourth watch, in the middle of the night. It was surely then. When they woke him up it was still completely dark, but the sunrise was not long in coming, the quiet clarity lightly green until the clouds began to catch light.

Upon returning from one more of so many leaves, in the end all blending into one single weekend pass. The arrival in Reus, accompanied by Nuria, after a day at the beach: *ingemisco tamquam reus*. Their last walks together, now uncomfortable, under the porticoes of the Plaza Prim, saying hello to their acquaintances who kept on showing up in those corners, awaiting the hour. The last drink shared on the patio of some bar, as a way of saying goodbye completely to civilian life. The load out, between goodbyes to girlfriends and relatives, in a dark bus driven by some fierce-looking guy, something like a degraded Virgil, turned into Charon's assistant oarsman, in his total capacity of guiding nobody anywhere except the far shore of Acheron.

And the nocturnal sea of fog in which they disappeared little by little, making their way back up the castled crenellated mountain, along a road through that harsh, uninviting landscape, where those without a weekend pass wandered about, making the most of their last gasps of Sunday indulgence, to the strains of the "Beer Barrel Polka" that would soon be silenced by the first rounds of the night watch. And disembarking in the darkness, passing before a sentinel with a glittering bayonet, the moment of jumping down from the truck, carrying his duffel bags, and, nostalgic and sad, dispersing in silence toward their respective companies, tripping over the taut guy-ropes, pushing aside the cords and canvas flaps stiffened by the fallen rain, undressing by candlelight amid the curses and complaints from fellow soldiers awakened, as well as their own, provoked by the absence of sufficient space to open up their cots, folding his heavy army jacket carefully to avoid staining it with mud, melancholically contemplating one more date crossed out on the calendar drawn on the canvas, meaning, one less date, one day less of being here, finally stepping out to piss, now in pajamas, covered with his cloak, finding his way with a flashlight, the earth sticky, the damp tree trunks shining, until reaching the latrine and, flicking off the light, looking about drowsily, as the wet papers hissed beneath his stream of piss, staring at the opaque overcast sky, searching vainly to see the stars.

Leo had been arrested, and now he and Federico could expect the same at any time. A waiting almost like ecstasy or madness. The clear ambiguity of a flame. The isolated flame of a candle that barely reveals the vague movement of its outer edges. Casting just as much shadow as light, primarily revealing the person who carries it. That black night black as a crow's wing, what, what, that enfolds and circles overhead, standing out softly against the deep blue sky, a wing that threatens and circles overhead and disappears as if scattering as it descends and blending into the black green hillsides in its descending circles, as if becoming crag and pine and low mountain in motion, only that what, what, omen or invocation or prophecy, what, what, uncertain circles, interrogations, what. What? Destruction? Creation? Immolation? Immolation and creation and destruction.

He had seen him several times in the small knots of students on the patio of the School of Humanities, entering or exiting a lecture hall, in the bar. And he had caught his attention not only for his mordant comments but also for his easy, uninhibited attitude and presence.

He came up alongside him outside the lecture hall doors and, in the tumult of students entering, commented that they were all treated like cattle or something expressed in similar terms, in the same type of acid humor the other used. And Leo said:

obviously. The last thing they're interested in is people learning how to think. Raúl sat next to him, and throughout the whole class, he analyzed the two extremes of that proposition that had made such an impact on him: the generic but concrete interest that someone, that nameless they, that third person plural, had in themselves, and the fact that their interest consisted, precisely, in preventing them from thinking for themselves.

We really look like a bunch of sheep, he said as they were leaving. And Leo: what do you expect? That's what a middle-class education is designed for. Workers have at least this one advantage: they haven't been educated and they know instinctively what interests them.

They had a beer in the bar. You would need a well-trained minority, said Raúl. And Leo: if that minority isn't the vanguard for the majority, it won't do much good. And Raúl: right. A new coup. It wasn't a question of standing apart from the majority as he had, without much interest in the problem, supposed until then—perhaps for simply shifting from literary terrain to the political—but, just the opposite, of leading them.

Federico had spoken little but astutely: he mocked his family, the stupidity of pretty girls from nice families, talked about the worker's awareness of reality, much more developed than any middle-class person, and the same with their sexual vigor. He'd become friends with Leo before Raúl had, but for Raúl it was evident that he and Leo enjoyed a certain rapport that simply did not exist between Federico and Leo.

They talked for hours and hours. Long afternoons in rambling conversation, sharing their ideas, finding out how much they agreed on. The obvious impossibility of being a true intellectual these days without being a Marxist. Dialectical materialism as key to the necessary identification or synthesis of form and matter. To make freedom and commitment compatible; even better, to discover the freedom within commitment, etcetera. The revelation that he was not alone in his dissatisfaction with the world. That his dissatisfaction responded to an objective reality and that objective reality had its ideological interpretation. That that ideology was not limited to interpreting the world; that its true end was to transform it.

They headed down Las Ramblas. The contact with reality, the feeling Raúl experienced of having touched it, derived from finding, in any old bar in the Barrio Chino, some guy whose expressions—lively and ironical or bitter and destructive—and tacit allusions, and even his laugh and his movements, revealed him unequivocally, as does a slogan or a password, as the owner of a political conscience, the exegetical key for those underworld factions organized around robbery, prostitution, alcohol, and dope, things that were so distant from the family life of the Ferrer Gaminde family as to be thought practically mythical, guilty ignorance which the middle class uses to proscribe and make exotic the inevitable result of its own existence, the face on the flip side of the coin, misery and degradation always susceptible to be transformed into precious revolutionary material in a given moment—the riffraff, the splendid and explosive riffraff, following a collective realization, in whose crystallization the voices of guys like this one, converted into leaders by the very masses from which they had emerged, were destined to serve as clarions, clarions as well as fuses. Theoretical appreciations doubtless irrefutable although frequently, at the hour of realizing them, owing to young people's natural lack of experience or to a certain hasty and arbitrary judgment, also part and parcel of youth as they tend to confuse what a thing is with what one would like it to be, easily based on some mistake; take, for example, for the sake of class conscience, the remembrances of a mythomaniac or any disgraced individual who's a bit drunk and now doesn't remember very well that time when, incidentally, he had been seen to be implicated in some way in the Republican cause; that man who fought in Teruel or in the Ebro or in Belchite, and met, to name a few, Tito, Lister, the Campesino, Clement Attlee, he's not very sure, who congratulated him. Or what's nothing more than some whore's palaver, trying to sweet-talk those three young fellows who look like students so they might buy her a drink, a maneuver whose ingenuity and calculated foresight is only betrayed by her sly flirting, the sign of someone who still doesn't know how things work. And even if that were true, said Federico, she'd be within her rights.

On the other hand, Adolfo did not make a positive impression on Leo, much less on Federico whose reservation toward Adolfo was more personal than, in Leo's case, about ideological motivations. Raúl had started getting to know him early in the semester and since then they'd gotten together occasionally and Adolfo chatted about Baudelaire, and Sartre, and the American novel. But Leo's arguments—Who in our society is free without money? And if you don't write for the people, isn't that just being complicit with the goals of the reactionary forces?—seemed to interest him insofar as they served to put a dent in his sarcasm, biting, almost disdainful, as if Leo was especially irritated by Adolfo's apparently critical and hedonistic position. Because, contrary to that petit bourgeois rudeness, particularly rooted in Catalonia, those tacky jokes and gags told for courtesy's sake, to make the other person feel comfortable, at ease, to foster a climate of cordiality and understanding, Adolfo's polite but reserved attitude seemed rather to point to a climate of separation and even antipathy, his secret formula, perhaps, for the aura of respect and prestige that seemed to automatically surround both his person as well as his opinions and even his literary projects, while the facts failed to demonstrate the contrary. A posture that lightly touched punctilious courtesy, a conciliatory character which certain people display the day after getting so drunk that they remember almost nothing of the night before. But which, from Leo's point of view, might well be interpreted in classist terms.

Nuria Rivas's case was different. She got along well with people and was accepted without reticence. What happened is that, for reasons difficult to pinpoint and in spite of her frame of mind that saw all her own political, religious, economic, social, and sexual theories as valid, or perhaps precisely for that very reason, she was not taken very seriously. At least not on her own, not apart from Raúl.

And Raúl? How could he have not discovered before, against all class conditioning, such a total conception of the world? How could he have managed without knowing it? An image of everything so real that the deeper he delved into it the greater was the feeling that he was only discovering traces, revealing to himself what he had always known deep down inside, in short, to be reading reality itself transcribed into words. An obvious consequence: ask to join the party, a party which, however clear its historical role, its actual practical functions remained unknown, an organization of mysterious and exciting character both for its members' double personalities as well as the subterranean ubiquity of its presence.

A decision that, apart from representing the logical consequence of his feelings of disgust and hostility regarding the state of the world, liberated him from all objective responsibility in relation to the true victims of the present society, workers and farmers, from the moment in which he began to form part of its political vanguard, the communist party. And, at the same time, it freed him from all the moral principles of the world in which he'd been raised that he could not attack nor, in fact, had ever attacked except on the outside. And from all the hateful schemes for resolving life's personal situations that the middle class offers its children—college education, marriage, career, blind goals if not complicit and aberrant in the face of a task like the one he'd set himself, facing the enterprise in whose development he was going to take part: the violent transformation of the world.

That feeling of coming into contact with a hidden power like the one that can be experienced in a session of spiritualism, when the medium begins to speak. There was no need for Leo to tell him he was that man. He walked ahead of them, uphill, along a deserted path in Park Güell, slowly, reading the newspaper; no doubt he'd already been there a while, surveying the terrain. And as they caught up to him he said, Hello, Daniel, without waiting, as Raúl expected—doubtless conditioned by middle-class formalities—for Leo to make any introductions. And for anyone who might have seen them from a distance, Escala seemed to be saying simply, Hey, fellas, what are you two doing here?

And the first results of his activities, the first protests at the university, the first police charges into the crowd that they watched rubbing their eyes, so to speak, more than their hands, almost incredulous that everything they were seeing was the fruit of their work to foment agitation which they had developed according to a correct interpretation of the party's political line.

The accolade: represent the Communist Party in a meeting with the representative from the Socialist Party of Barcelona. The meeting was proposed by the socialists, in order to establish a modus operandi, as his contact said, with an eye toward a boycott of public transit that was being prepared and, eventually, a general strike.

The contact took place in a chocolate café. The socialist was there, having hot chocolate topped with fresh whipped cream and ensaimadas for breakfast. A middle-aged fellow, on the mature side. He seemed surprised at Raúl's youth and appearance until—it showed in his eyes—he matched him with the right stereotype: the typical little communist rich boy. This discovery must have contributed to him regaining his self-confidence.

To the point, he said: the waiter can be trusted. But he started to ramble. He talked about the Civil War, about the French resistance, about alcohol and women, all that joined to fervent expressions about worker solidarity. He knew the communists well, he said. But he wasn't willing to be some Kerenski; that's why, during the war, he never let go of his pistol, not even when he went to sleep.

Maybe back then he didn't have such a paunch. And one thing that was certain: he wasn't carrying a pistol these days. And that stuff about the shock troops, his young socialist commandoes he spoke of mobilizing, was pure fantasy. And the character that he pretended to give to the interview, like that of gangsters dividing up the city's sectors between themselves, lacked all verisimilitude, despite the chocolate café's certain ambience—no doubt selected in order to give the impression that everything had been calculated with the goal of not arousing suspicions—despite that clientele of voracious old ladies and flabby, delighted, milk-fattened, whispering little girls. On the wall, a photo mural of a Pyrenean panorama formed of whipped cream and marmalade, the living stamp of a Catalonia as sweet-toothed and chaste as the very customers in the chocolate café, like the idyllic and socially-democratic Europe that dreaming windbag was blathering on about.

Because, like Spain, Europe also feared the true revolution.

And in fact, for them, the norms of clandestine life, the precautions they took in Barcelona with respect to their meetings, continued to be the rule in Paris. Paris, that city that came to be for him so familiar that, each time he found himself walking through the Gare d'Austerlitz, he had the impression of returning home after a trip, an impression that leads one to consider as parenthetical everything that happened since his departure. And nevertheless, dissipating the initial mistake required his time. Because, as on the Costa Brava, for example, the natives, the people from the towns, also took years even to figure out that the first tourists to come to their beaches were not necessarily any potentates, unlike what they might have assumed from a first glance, but rather, frequently, storekeepers, and even laborers, thus Raúl, in his first trips north, tended to see in all of France the complicity of a leftist militant. A mistake similar to the one he made with Obregón after several meetings, when he realized that the peaceful alternative, renunciation of an armed struggle, according to the party's political line, was not responding so much to a stratagem as to a real imposition of the circumstances.

Paris, friends male and female. And the freedom of speaking out loud on the terraces of the bars along the Boulevard Saint-Germain. And of buying the books he desired in Le Globe. Almost an obligation, like attending a certain number of sessions at the cinemathèque, after the Pantheon, completely at ease between that public of young people who looked unambiguously leftist, with a touch of the guerrilla and at the same time of the intellectual, too, from his presence and even the way he treated his female friends. To see a film by Eisenstein was like attending a religious ceremony. Eisenstein and Soviet cinema in general. Thus, that film they watched in a cinema near the Boulevard Montmartre, a film set during the war and while he's fighting at the front she's cheating on him back home, and when she learns that he's died, she goes to the station and hands out his flowers to all the returning soldiers, like a socialist Ophelia only saved from madness by joining the masses. And as the lights came up afterward he had to blink to clear his vision and he had to clear his throat and think about something else and make a show of lighting a cigarette and making as if the smoke was getting in his eyes, and walk out of the cinema saying the film wasn't too bad, without further commentary, without insisting unnecessarily, the identity of the situations was already eloquent enough, the struggle and its rupture, the problem of soldiers' wives being unfaithful, the sacrifice, the inexorability of everything.

Sessions of lovemaking carried out in sordid hotels, with crooked parquet floors, upon swaybacked beds, with stained coverlets and washed-out curtains, shoving aside the bolster pillow that kept rolling onto them, sweating and naked, in the early morning, just back from Place de la Contrescarpe or from some very interesting invasion of Montparnasse, he and she, after leaving the others absorbed in abstract discussions. The excitement of the foreplay: exploring each other, pressing, delicately testing each other out, undressing with delicate feline nicety, perfect white tits, the dark thatch of her sex, the bare cheeks of her ass. Even with Nuria it was better in Paris than in Barcelona, perhaps because of its quality of being a passing encounter, because Raúl knew that afterward they would each go their own way. The same reason, surely, that it was good for them in Rosas, when he did his second-lieutenant training in Figueres and, taking advantage of any long weekend, she came down from England and he sorted out his guard duties and waited for her at the station and they went to Rosas. It was in the springtime and, when sunny, it was already nice to swim.

Not like at first, of course, like the first times, when everything seemed to come together and harmonize so that even his relations with Nuria went marching right along perfectly and the general exaltation that possessed them was reflected equally in the erotic terrain. That night, for example, when they'd drunk quite a lot and Adolfo was insisting that they go out to see *Yerma*, and Nuria gave Raúl a blowjob during the first act, under the shelter of his overcoat folded over her head.

Like that person who after a whole night of lovemaking and, especially if it's been well done, and far from being sated with it, quite the contrary, rather stimulated, sleeplessly contemplates the city from atop a mountain and the very splendor of the morning seems only to heighten his cravings for more activity, his impatience to accelerate the triumph of the revolution, to finally abandon for good his paltry legal studies and give himself over entirely to the work of contributing to the formation—beyond simple theories, and now in the area of praxis—of a true popular army of liberation, and when the moment comes, have a good laugh at the terror-stricken stupor of the middle class, lawyers, financiers, property agents, notaries, registrars, businessmen, speculators, people who in their closed-minded routines had believed themselves busy with important things and who, suddenly, saw the earth crack, gaping wide beneath their feet, the crust of a world they had taken to be real and which was suddenly revealed to be a mere game of hypocritical appearances; thus did Raúl, facing a similar panorama of synchronous harmonizations and answers, feel at that time. Thus: like a wandering horseman or a sailor or a founder or a prophet, with that characteristic willpower of transcending oneself, of transforming oneself by transforming, only comparable to the demented lucidity with which a scientist proposes to himself to destroy the world, telling his conscience that the madness lies not within himself but within the world around him.

And just as Don Juan never feels remorse or guilt for seducing women, nor does he care about what luck might befall his victims because, like the terrorist or the thief, he's not unaware of his inevitable final damnation, so Raúl felt equally predestined to play out the role that had been imposed upon him to its final consequences. Predestined, almost like a chosen one, like that being born from the waters or from the slime or from the fruit of a tree or from the copulation of archangels or gods or, like the inverse of what happens in Ovid, from the metamorphosis of a cactus or a hawthorn tree into a boy. And then, after an obscure childhood, now grown into a man, one fine day he conceives—or it's revealed to him—a certain idea of the world, of life, of himself, a future that he designs and fills with images like one who contemplates a western sky or the heavens at dawn, the cumulus clouds shaped like castled, crenellated cities, with temples and great walls and skyscrapers reflected in the celestial seas.

What importance could all the rest hold? Everything was easier from this perspective of surrender and letting go. Including financial problems. Living a hand-to-mouth existence, without falling into a calculating, middle-class mindset. Enough to get by on, and that's all. How? By doing any old thing at all, working at whatever was available, doing enough, to keep going. The translations he wrote with Leo, for example; badly paid, of course. So what? It was no use complaining about this, this wasn't, precisely, the kind of exploitation he was worried about. Nor did they rack their brains to find just the right shade of meaning if it took them long to do it. The money was enough to help them get around and that was what mattered. And translating didn't have that childish or frivolous character common to the only solutions Raúl had found so far, the result of systematically scouring the want ads in *La Vanguardia*, how to earn money easily in his free time, etcetera, growing mushrooms, lead soldiers, taxidermy, car insurance. Or buying at a real bargain price some of the various get-rich-quick formulas sold by that crazy old man in El Clot to whomever wanted to buy them, living in a sad kitchen that smelled like gasoline and rancid bacon, while some kind of a witch gutted and sliced blue fish—barat or jureles, surely.

There were minor problems. How he felt uncomfortable with Nuria, for example. Not alone with her, but when in the presence of their friends she showed her undisguisable middle class touches, her ideological incoherence. An annoying lack of tact similar to that of the boy who, intuiting his parents' suspicion that he's running with a bad crowd, dares at last, in order to deny it as much as possible, to bring a friend home and with anxious embarrassment, incapable of reacting, becomes a witness to how his friend, with a surprising lack of awareness for situations, perhaps a result of his juvenile boasting, only confirms all the family's worst fears, for the which, quiet and watchful, their expressions and even their mere disposition are nothing but conclusive proofs of how their young offspring is addicted to wicked practices.

Problems perhaps subjective, perhaps imaginary. But just as in the geophysical world, the straight line and the flat surface are only an illusion of the senses, an excessively close and immediate appreciation of what in reality is curved and spherical. In the same way, it would be equally superficial to explain Raúl's amorous behavior, his short-lived enthusiasms, his sudden tendency at distancing if not abandoning entirely—excluding on principle all hypotheses that such behavior might seem to rule out by itself an exaggerated misogynistic aversion, for example, or a predominant homosexual component—in light of the kind of women with whom he'd had relationships, without then wondering why precisely he'd had relations with such women; or arguing that the important thing for Raúl was to safeguard his freedom, without then wondering what kind of liberty it was that made him dismiss out of hand any possibility of voluntarily continuing the relationship; or blame it on his belief, so often expressed, that there is no love which does not end, and the ends are rarely happy, without finally wondering how it could turn out otherwise when he was the first to set about hastening that end.

In fact, the idea of marriage had always disgusted him. Even more: the verb itself, *casarse*—to get married; literally, to build a house together—filled him with a sensation like shame. The same as when as a boy, without yet knowing the precise amount of sexual attraction implied by certain words, he was irritated by Felipe's jokes, about whether or not he had a girlfriend, *la niña rubita*—the little blonde girl—a girl whom he passed every morning on the way to school. And the adults talked about engagements and weddings. It seems he's proposed to her, he heard Aunt Paquita say.

No longer the uncertain and embarrassing question: do you want to marry me? Simply: I love you. Words that he could never bring himself to pronounce.

In every case, just like in a station, seated next to a little window, the soft arrival of a train on the adjacent track can produce the impression that we are the ones starting to pull out of the station, thus, in these moments it was already difficult to see clearly if Raúl's amorous relationships were dominated by a certain fatality or if it was he, with his behavior, who determined the fatal character of those relationships.

Because just as the young man from a family fallen on hard times is always a potential revolutionary, not only for the desire to see his particular domestic experience of progressive reduction and progressive straits repeated, in all the families belonging to his social class, meaning, from rancor and resentment, but also from the necessity of finding an explanation or justification of objective value and general application for the cyclical phenomenon of the splendor and decadence of human things, so Raúl seemed predisposed toward a certain type of woman or, at least, to a certain type of relationship with women. But in the same way that years must pass in order for the seducer of a middle-aged married woman to come to understand that the key to adultery does not reside within himself, in his virile attributes and in his skill at fornicating, nor in a supposed inferiority of the husband who gives rise to a coherent rationale of his own triumph, but in her and only in her, in the one presumedly seduced, in the dank well of conjugal life, in her desire to redress, in her anxieties of seeing reflected in another the unsatisfied love for herself, so that nearly the least thing is the erotic entrapment of that other, given that for her the outcome of the affair, especially if it's a short one, must be necessarily happy; so it was inevitable that Raúl should have lived so long without thinking of any question relating to the nature of love.

Neither conjectures nor interrogations: concrete plans, directed toward resolving the problem in the least traumatic way possible. According to what was possible, to the degree in which, in a young man, intuitions at once clear and imprecise are confusedly intermixed with feelings and ideas. To be with Nuria one more time and then let her fly away; let things calm down bit by bit and they could simply remain good friends. Thence the annoyance that she, as if she sensed it coming, asked him so often if he loved her. Especially when the situation began to stretch out, without any end in sight, and Raúl discovered that in front of others she called him my boyfriend and that, as a girlfriend, she hung on his arm on days when he had a leave from the camp, no sooner did she get off the bus in La Plaza de Prim in Reus, evidently proud—although she wouldn't admit it, full of that atavistic pride women usually feel when in the company of a man in uniform—of having a boyfriend of her own. Your girlfriend and mine came on the same train, Ferracollons told him.

And then, the abortion. The complication that resulted from all that, the necessity of continuing with her still once more. And the relief, the prospects for a definitive solution later supposed by her idea of leaving to study in England, who knows if with the hope—mistaken—that a temporary separation would favorably influence the course of her relationship with Raúl.

The normal thing, in principle, was that everything would turn out like in those language-learning methods, one of those courses where, through the lessons, one develops a simple theme, which serves to introduce the student to both the knowledge of the language as well as the customs and way of life of the country in question. He or she arrives. It's their first visit, but some family friends of their parents are already waiting in the station and will host them during their stay in the country. So, what better way of getting to know the country than through its people?

Sometimes, the person visiting arrives accompanied by their parents and, if it happens to be a young woman, the local couple generally has a son, also young; and vice-versa. The couple is usually grumpy, stingy, easily fatigued. The women, more active and irritating, show a profound sexual frustration. And, in any case, the final lessons usually coincide with the young couple getting engaged. Except that, in reality, things don't have to turn out like they do in the language course lessons. The girl's father, for example, can turn out to be a fearful sodomite who buggers his young foreign guest. Or the driver of the car who picks up our young friend as she walks along the road, a highway killer. And the loving couple who invite her to spend a weekend in the country, a couple of sadists who submit her, in the impunity of the cellar, to every kind of torture, outrage, and cruelty from the one hundred nights. So that perhaps the lesser evil and the fastest way of learning the language is for Nuria, of her own free will, to go to bed with anyone, and wind up forgetting, with time and distance, everything before that. Because, what better way of getting to know the people from a different country than by copulating with them?

What else could happen when something similar had already occurred, when the time and distance that separated them then were much less? With Adolfo, while Raúl was in the army camp. We were really drunk, Pipo. We'd gone out around there and I don't even know how it happened. What I can assure you is that it was a complete disaster.

She told him that story years later, during one of their trysts in Paris. The final day, in the bar at the Gare d'Austerlitz. One of those trips he made in a second-class couchette, carrying a suitcase with a false bottom. And, once over the border, in the morning, he thought that, coming from a woman with whom he had nothing in common, it was not very important. From the window, like always, the sharp young women from Montseny announced that the station at Llinás was coming up, his station, so close to Vallfosca, the pines and the vineyards, the familiar landscapes, ancient lands, of eroded contours. Some peaks that, in fact, separated his childhood from his earliest infancy.

Aunt Margarita. His mother's younger sister. She died shortly after the war. A faceless figure, in a bathrobe, eating breakfast on the verandah at Vallfosca, surely during one of those days she must have spent with them in summertime. A face he could reconstruct with the help of the few surviving photographs of her. And the room she stayed in, that room he'd entered suddenly, without knocking, surprising her as she was dressing, her breasts naked, and she told him to come in and shut the door. A room where there had once been a sink which, for some reason, was later removed. But the shoddily patched opening to the drain remained visible, a small mouth with a tiny hole plugged up with cement.

He checked out all the whorehouses, repeatedly, the same way that the lone terrorist studies the chosen target ahead of time, searching for the best spot to plant the bomb. In the end he found himself in a bed, gripped and grasping, in the act, attentive to what he was doing, like in a circle of children where any mistake in the game meant you were disqualified. Or like obeying the instructions of a gym teacher who, after warning us that he is older and stronger than us, might however, while we were performing the rhythms and movements of the exercise to the letter, add that we've got nothing to worry about. Or like that person who dreams repeatedly of being a galley slave only to be awakened by the crack of the whip next to his ear.

Only one single inhibition: dancing. Because of its inherently competitive element? Because of his repugnance for forming part of a spectacle in which, for the mere fact of knowing himself observed by those not dancing, he was going to find himself suffering by comparison to those who know how to dance and who enjoy it? A rejection, at any rate, of an operative terrain— erotically marginal—as an appropriated terrain, insofar as being synthetic and symbolic, to settle questions that were not at all symbolic or synthetic. In short, to turn the fact of not knowing how to dance into something positive, similar to that runner who leads the race but overcome by his fear of seeing himself passed up on the homestretch pretends to stumble and fall. It would be, by contrast, rash to trace that inhibition, at least wholly, back to the time when he liked Celia, for example; to the fact of seeing her dance, knowing that, given their difference in age, she could not seriously believe that a boy would dare to ask her to dance.

They were below the plane trees in the plaza, sitting along the benches, chatting, and their bicycles were resting against a wall, next to the fountain. The plaza regulars, the old men, as if displaced, had all gathered together on only two or three of the benches, and even in front of the church, sitting on the steps. They were suddenly interrupted by a little pack of excited dogs, tails quivering, ears stiff and flattened, snouts wrinkled, eyes glittering and teeth shining, running in a circle, growling and whining, all grouping up, yelping wildly, and in the middle of their circle, a bitch called Bullseye, being mounted and humped at a weird angle by an ugly mutt with big ears, both dogs looking cowed in that tense climate of barely contained violence. What a picture, said one of the old men. And one of the girls asked the typical question about why didn't they separate them. And they all pretended they hadn't heard her, obstinately talking away. An old woman stuck her head out of a doorway and faces—crafty, sullen, and lascivious—began to appear in the windows and a bucketful of water came pouring down, which, more than dispersing the pack, scattered it toward the church, leaving one poor long-haired dog a tangled mess. The old men laughed, and the people in the doorways, and from window to window. And one of the boys said: but isn't she your dog? No, said Felipe. And someone said, these dogs. And then Celia seemed to decide to stop trying to hold back her laughter, her self-absorbed expression melting all at once, a contagious laugh, which spread with the help of someone's saucy comment about how those two dogs should go get a room somewhere. And at last, the fearsome observation: look how much Lalo is blushing.

They organized an outing to the cold spring called Font Freda, a hike of a little over two hours. They packed a knapsack and took turns carrying it. They and their cousins headed out from Vallfosca and the others from the town and they met up halfway there. They talked about the cinema, the films that were already being announced for the next season. Someone commented with a severe good sense inappropriate for his age, an echo no doubt of some judgment heard at home, that they were already starting to get sick of these psychological movies where it always turns out, in the end, that what is going on is that, unconsciously, the boy is in love with his mother and although he despises his father deep down he really loves him and who knows what other stories. The conversation had that carefree tone one hears from repressed people talking about sex, as if it was something amusing and unimportant, surreal, endured, something no one could take more seriously than a joke; as if in their sweaty vigils the presence of sex were for them nothing more than some grasping octopus from which there is no escape. Had Celia noticed that Raúl hadn't taken his eyes off her for a single moment? Her laugh, her ironic look, her movements not quite so provocative as already lascivious.

An unusual case, to be sure, given the girls in those years. Because in the way that a certain anxiety in the eyes reveals a nymphomaniac even before discovering, in bed, her prolapsed flesh, her bruised vulva, her distended, misused, labia, so, in a similar way, even in her unmistakable external appearance—the good girl of those times, unlike now—she was ostensibly distinct from any other young woman of her age but of a different social level or condition.

The pretty little rich girl of those times, her modesty, her chronic display of an essentially moral upbringing, a natural product of that Barcelona middle class of the postwar era, installed in her own city as if on summer vacation, as a way of prolonging, or better yet, making last forever, the truncated summer of '36. Those youthful times of the postwar era, the posh snobs of the forties, maintained, thanks to the historical circumstances themselves, in absolute isolation from the surrounding world, the past close and remote, and the future possible, and what's worse: the present time of the adult world. An optimal situation for selfishness: once the established moral foundations were firmly inculcated, the last and most necessary principle might be assimilated by themselves without any unnecessary explanations: maintain one's own immorality in completely enclosed compartments, like any other business venture, like some additional aspect of professional life, something that occurs outside the home, away from family, social life, and summer vacations, those months of peaceful leisure in which the people of his class debut the fresh new white clothes in their wardrobe, white as innocence itself, a pleasing contrast to the dark tonalities of the poor, blacks, grays, peasant blues who hid crouched down in their vineyards like redskins, with the exclusive goal, perhaps, of spotting one distracted passerby reaching out to taste their grapes, and then falling on them in a rage, howling atrocious blasphemies, wrinkled, toothless, furtive, deformed, rapacious, looking especially rancorous when their wagons were overtaken by young summer vacationers on bicycles. And those more familiar with the life of the summer colony were no less hostile than the workers from the city, those ragged beings one glimpsed while crossing the fields of Barcelona or, in the residential neighborhoods, around the buildings under construction, their faces inconceivably brutish and ugly, almost as if alienated or mentally deficient, with their habit of eating like savages around some embers, of singing, of getting grossly drunk, of sleeping obscene siestas lying right on the sidewalk, and then, gregariously, with their lunch boxes, with their old, faded, foul-smelling clothes, clumsy, talkative, gesticulating, simian, returning to their fields, where everything is ugliness and degraded cohabitation.

The rabble that killed, set fire, looted. Why so much sacrilege? They were riding to church in the horse-drawn cart and Polit was driving, the reins soft in his hands. And Polit, as if feeling obliged to justify watching some church burn, said that, in one of these, as he approached to see what was happening, he came upon a crucifix thrown to the ground, and as it pained him to see it that way, thrown away like a piece of junk, he preferred to push it into the bonfire. Raúl stationed himself carefully, standing against a column from which he could observe Celia with equal amounts of discretion and privilege.

When did he start to lose interest in horseback riding, sword fighting, lancing shrubs and brambles, creeping and crawling along with his compressed air rifle? When did the rocks cease to be high crags above defiles perfect for ambushes, and the woods jungles teeming with tigers, forests with hidden natives in the underbrush? When did he begin to appreciate not only Celia's attractiveness, but also that of the landscape, that complex knot of hills, and the vineyards, the distances with poplars, the clean tidy architecture of the planted stands of pine trees?

One morning when the weather was bad, at Easter. And he was on the verandah playing records, a little tired of having to crank the gramophone, and he was going to listen to the *Jupiter Symphony* when he felt, first, as if he had already experienced it, the sensation of watching the cloudy roiling sky from a window, and then, that sensation of feeling himself a part of what he was watching, of the quiet skies in motion and the mountain turned gray and, at the same time, of something distant and clear, with a resonance that, like that word we feel on the tip of our tongue but which doesn't come out, becomes difficult to locate. And Papa asked what are you thinking about, Lalo, and he said, I think I'm going to go for a walk before lunch, and he walked among the oak trees with peaceful euphoria, without feeling like playing ambushes or anything, eluding the thought that school would start again in nine days.

Or perhaps before, the first time when, arriving in Vallfosca, he became conscious of the house's peculiar smell, the front hallway, the verandah, the sitting room, his bedroom, rooms in which, just by entering, unchanged since then and now when he would drop by there with his friends, he was assaulted by such an accumulation of simultaneous sensations. That smell old houses have, impossible to get rid of even when renovating and repainting them from top to bottom, only managing in the end to add one more layer to that well of lives upon lives, formed by the passing of the generations, the deterioration and the misfortune.

The house, surrounding the garden like in a cloister. A garden of peaceful thickets, softly, subtly shadowed at dusk. Then, the nocturnal emptiness, the owls, the frogs croaking, the sound of the water falling into the cisterns, much more clearly than during the day. Uncle Gregorio said that there would be a shower of shooting stars that night, and after dinner they all went out to the gazebo. And the stars rained down and they were pointing them out to each other with great excitement, each one of those shooting stars falling in silence. Look at this constellation, Raúl, said Uncle Gregorio. It's the Dragon. The hardest one.

In September the nights were already too chilly and the sky was not so clear. And from the garden one sensed the soft steps of the foxes and the snuffling of the wild boars and the cunning badgers and nearby, like a ghost, the shriek of the tawny owl.

He liked to go for walks on hot mornings, without clouds, with sunflowers in the sky. He followed the muddy paths along the creek, oozing, flowing with freshness, between the thin bamboo stalks enclosing the creek bed on both sides, along the sandy wheel tracks, continuously eroding, that centered the darkened trail of soft prints and the warm horse droppings. And with his ears alert, his air rifle ready, he penetrated the forest, opening a path between the ferns, through the gloomy mottled shade. Or maybe along the streams, poplars straight and crisp in the green clarity, reflected in the quiet, leaf-strewn water. And at midday, he went out to the parched stubble field, the sky now like zinc, colorless, hot, like a seamlessly welded iron plate above our bodies. And then, the drowsiness and heat of the afternoons, when, after lunch, the house went silent and, during the siesta, it was just right for a languid session of masturbation.

The beginning of vacations: three full months awaiting. June, with its soft greens and the warm trill of the blackbirds, trembling in the thickets, spinning through the brambles. And the storms. You could feel rain in the tense quietude of the air and the tenseness of the birds between the bristling leaves; and that horizon of moving clouds that sounded, perhaps, like a distant sea or a seashell pressed against your ear.

In general they were short rainstorms, devious fizzing cloudbursts, soon dispersed by the warm wind, by gashes of jubilant blue, by the rainbow arcing over the fruit trees full to bursting and clean in the early evening, with the last cries of the swallows and the first calls of the night birds.

Before school let out he already felt the excitement over the preparations for the trip—better yet, the expedition—to Vallfosca. Steamer trunks, provisions, clothes, suitcases, his own suitcase, his books, his weapons, everything indispensable, everything, basically, that he was going to use during the next three months. And finally, closing tight the Persian blinds and shutters and turning off the gas and water mains, by the front door and the gate, everything now loaded into the taxi, getting in and saying goodbye, not without a touch of sadness, to the trees, to the houses, the ice cream vendor who didn't even see them go by, to everything that would remain the same during his absence, reflections made while they crossed through the city riding along its most central streets, the drive to the station, where he would take the Orient Express, starting out on a long route through Central Europe, the Balkans, Asia Minor, Turkey; days and nights and more days on the train, Persia, Afghanistan and, finally, India, where there awaited him a cavalry detachment, native lancers that, among rough landscapes, were my body guards and escorted me to my unit, of which I had to take command.

One of the first things he did was to go over to Mallolet's house and let them know he'd returned. A large old country house with warm white puppies smelling of pee, with round swollen bellies, suckling away, and raucous ducks which, in a wedge formation, cut a path of clear water through the green scum atop the pond, and haylofts with wasps' nests under the roof tiles, and a horse with patient eyes in the paddock. And that dense smell of freshly-watered garden, tomatoes, peppers, eggplants, watermelons, melons, zucchini.

A note about Polit. Why did he have that premonitory intuition when they told him: Polit got stung by a scorpion just above the heart when he was picking up a hay bale? And another question: why did they call Polit "El Polit" when his name was really Josep?

Easter meant that there remained only one trimester of school. And in Vallfosca it was barely noticeable that it was Easter, apart from the Sacred Heart from the chapel that Aunt Paquita shrouded in purple, as one shrouds or covers the body of a garroted man. Raúl came back from religious services and at home said that when it came to visiting monuments he preferred to do it alone, by bicycle, through the towns of the region. There were many people from the summer colony and although the holy days came earlier, that in itself was already a harbinger of summer. April's tendernesses, marvelous exploding yellows, resurgent waters, tones, cascades of softness opening to the sun. The pathways alongside the stream appeared fluted with long reflections. He contemplated from above the poplars' serpentine undulation, the bushy tangle of flowering boughs like a pink mist. When the blackbirds stopped singing he could hear the grass breathe.

It wasn't simply that the geography and history lent him, like the cinema, creative material for his games. In his fascination with geography and history he had to seek deeper motivations until they surrendered themselves to him like absolute and unappealable realities, places that existed although he would never come to know them, totally independent from the course of his life, events unmodifiable for having already occurred, facts perhaps incredible but true and equally autonomous and unappealable, susceptible, with their mythical and miraculous elements, with their arbitrariness and incoherencies, with their essential irrevocable tragedy, of unleashing, in the spirit of the student with imaginative or neurotic predispositions, the most radical questions.

Perhaps it was the counterpart to his religious coldness. That irreligiousness appropriate to a child whose father possessed none of the typical fatherly attributes, a man defeated, his illness real or imaginary, more needful of help than capable of lending it. Surely, at times, in the school chapel, touched by a certain exultant note on the harmonium or by the oblique colorations of the stained-glass windows, he fell prey to trembling and terror, and for an instant ineffable heavens opened beneath his feet, around his irredeemably perverse reality, destined for damnation. The devil's reality, so far superior to that of the gods.

Short-lived spasms but sufficient ones, alright. Like upon returning home, when in the gloom of the hallway he practiced the exciting game of making himself panic by pulling strange faces in front of the mirror, rather more terrifying than a coconut, for example, with thick bristling hairs all around the eyes.

But something persisted, there was some constant in those crazy fits. The grief with which they marked him, as if exposing him to public compassion, for example, when his grandmother died. The shame, the rage, and the rancor toward all those watching him, their faces somewhere between intimidated and withdrawn, at school and on the street, with his everyday clothes frighteningly dyed black, humiliatingly calling attention to him, no less conspicuous than the macabre stench of the dye. Or the first day of school, when he left home accompanied by his grandmother, his valise strapped to his shoulders like a backpack, and his fountain pens rattling inside, and the folds of his school smock sticking out.

Coming out of the cinema, on Thursdays or Sundays, he was grateful for the cover of darkness, shocked as he was by the immoral baseness that every adolescent usually discovers in themself with much greater clarity at the movies than in church, as they contrast the chaste physical contact and elevated sentiments the protagonists show in their amorous encounters with the dark indecency of their own thoughts and desires.

If it was some detective thriller, afterwards he pretended to be a gangster or spy, hiding in the doorways to make sure he wasn't being followed. And Manolo signaled to him from across the street, furtively. Or together they would shadow any suspicious-looking character, perhaps a double agent.

Calle Mayor de Sarriá, the big street that served as his Ramblas in those days, ground zero for all the children in the surrounding residential neighborhoods: Bonanova, Tres Torres, Pedralbes. Axis of that nucleus of narrow russet lanes, complicated cross streets, more like a country town than an urban neighborhood, and on the outskirts quiet convents and ricocheting sparrows, garden walls overgrown with languid vines, ivy and wisteria and Virginia creeper, thick with pines, plane trees, Peruvian pepper trees, and palms, nineteenth-century touches in their townhouses and flowering almonds in their gardens.

The center of the neighborhood almost as much like a country town as always, thanks, no doubt, to the very narrowness of its streets, still redolent of bakeries, grocery stores, and dark doorways. The dairy store or the candy shop, where he bought popsicles, now closed, with lace curtains covering the plate glass windows, the door still painted the same blue, but without the sign above the lintel. Would that bell still tinkle if he walked in? And the fabric shop where his grandmother, while selecting buttons, bought him a little tin windup car that would rattle off a short distance, laboriously, like a rickety jalopy. And the cinema, the films now advertised on printed posters, not on a chalkboard; during the intermission they gathered at the bar to drink whiskey or rum depending on whether the movie was a gangster or cowboy picture, or one about pirates. And the magazine shop where he bought comic books and anise cigarettes. The shop lady, the previous owner's daughter, was sitting under the dusty lightbulb without a shade, exactly in the same spot and in the same wicker chair her mother used to occupy. Now she, too, had white hair and as she informed him that they no longer made anise cigarettes, she looked at him over the top of her glasses, just as her mother used to do, without recognizing him. That was then. Nowadays people go to the tobacco shop and buy real cigarettes.

He went back walking along the newly laid-out streets, a grid of large blocks spreading over the fields and gardens that once marked Sarriá as a separate town, back when he used to say he was going downtown, saying I'm going to Barcelona. New constructions whose implacable geometry rose up like a fortress wall above the patchwork of old roofs, tall mercury streetlights recently switched on instead of the old gas lamps converted to electricity, heavy traffic and lively sidewalks, bars with terraces and endless glittering shop windows.

Grandmother and Manolo and Emilio and Mallolet. But he got used to playing alone. Better. He preferred it. That way there was no interference and everything turned out the way it was supposed to turn out. Playing with others was like going to see a movie that everyone had already been talking about at school and which, upon seeing it, proves disappointing; the things we heard about happen but not the way we'd imagined them. And in the way that a spy or a secret agent moves in closer, he infiltrated the world of adults. That's why, when Papa took him visiting and there were also children in the house, he tended to hang around the adults until he was inevitably shooed away. Raúl, would you please go and play with the other kids?

It was as if then he already intuited the whole process, the moment when a boy, patiently shaped by a positive upbringing, appreciates for the first time the substantial sense of some key words when he thinks about getting married and having children, and begins to see himself within a historical perspective, and he begins to be seduced by the idea of someday telling his own kids how he got to climb aboard the steam locomotive or how with only a hundred pesetas they did so many different things, and furthermore the idea that someday when his kids have kids of their own they tell them all about him, and that they would even enjoy selecting their own personal future anecdotes and character traits—he was such a character!—by which he might be characterized, and so, instead of feeling blinded by his

vision of the sordid circles of this limited but infinite world, as if
complying until the end with that first appropriation of the adult
world, now coming full circle, everyone now bald and hairless,
heads, bellies, and buttocks, to end up talking about Peter Pan,
about when he was a boy, about his mischief, about the nostalgia
he felt for his memories of that time.

Nothing more hateful, nothing more loathsome, than the
figure of Peter Pan, the self-pitying sublimations he implies, his
transmutation of childhood oppressions into refuge and paradise,
his refusal to enter the world as soon as possible, becoming the
keys that, like a talisman, will permit us to confront the dragon.

Grandfather: an old mossy log; random musical creaks,
crackles, and squeaks sounding inside his body. Raúl and Felipe
spied on him from the hallway. Look, said Felipe: he's a Quaker.

The end of lunch infallibly produced a loose string of torturous intestinal gurgling and rumbling poorly masked by a dry
cough, while he moved the chair he'd been sitting in, pushing
it back under the table, feints or ploys not always effective or
executed at the right moment, although, to judge by the unruf-
fled reaction of those present, everything contributed to make
him believe that he'd carried it off.

Felipe and their cousins and the whole bunch of them
mocked his grandfather the same way they would later mock
his grandmother, just the way children make fun of old people,
about their sudden emptiness, their iguana-like faces and skin,
mocking them if not treating them tyrannically, once having
glimpsed their vulnerability and expendability.

Classification and denomination of their farts according to
their sound quality, duration, and stench: cannon, blowgun,
cornet, canary, longboat, and depth charge. Felipe proposed
more names: skunk, theodolite, noogie, and pun. The theodolite was like a kind of camera Uncle Pedro and his coworkers
were always standing next to in photos from some dam project
or another. And pun was a word Aunt Paquita was always
using. Like noogie. Do you like puns? she asked them. What
are you all laughing about, if I might know. You sound like
retards. What if I start giving out some noogies. And they all

ran away laughing. And the fava bean, said Felipe, you can also call that one the executioner.

Grandfather's death came just after the liberation, they had hardly returned to Barcelona; perhaps even before the war was over. Grandmother came to live with them; she probably died years later than Aunt Margarita. But it was like it had happened before, because she'd been a long time in the convalescent home. And Uncle Raimón showed up at the house to take care of that sad, gloomy bedroom and the belongings grandma had left behind: a somewhat ratty fur collar, an overcoat dyed black, some print dresses, her muff and mittens, her purses mildewed from disuse, a box with papers and photographs, her dentures.

It was a holiday and he and Felipe went to visit her, accompanied by Nieves. They took her an afternoon snack, some pastries. Look what a pretty garden, said Nieves. A nun, young and smiling, opened the garden gate for them. Look, how nice, Doña Gloria, you've got some visitors. They went in with her—the nun taking her by the arm—along the gravel paths, between laurel trees, acanthuses, and pines. Such lovely grandsons, you must be very proud, Doña Gloria. They sat and ate the pastries on a stone bench, and they said what Nieves told them to say. She didn't pay them much attention, as if she saw them every day and their stories didn't interest her, or as if she were busy, with other things on her mind, and they'd interrupted her. Isn't this chocolate delicious? the nun said. They went back, slowly, by the opposite path, making a circle. Well now, say goodbye to them Doña Gloria. And Nieves: come on and give your granny a kiss. And Grandma said goodbye, goodbye, looking at them for a fleeting instant. Once the gate was closed she immediately turned away, and the nun had to run after to catch her. They watched the two of them move off, Grandma with her wrinkled stockings and her felt slippers, speaking docilely about some matter that seemed to worry her, moving ahead, in the darkening late afternoon garden, of dark greens and golds. To get there you had to take a train.

Meaning: I am that sun in the leaves, I am that metal sky, I am those wheel ruts in the sand; and I am the noise of rushing water in the night and I am the snowy peaks of Montseny. And the peculiar shine of the earth when the sun strikes the garden paths, an almost blinding light, surely owing to the mica flakes in that old soil of decomposed granite. And, especially, the verandah, the attics, the wine cellar. I.

Fixed images. Impossible to think about Papa or Gregorius or Eloísa looking any different than the way they do now. And the figures from his childhood, Ramona then, Padritus, even Felipe himself, were only that, figures. Faceless figures, like the people that have disappeared or died long ago, Grandma, Grandpa, Nieves, Pilate, Quilda, Uncle Pedro. Except for Polit, maybe. Because Polit had always been the same. Or was this identity also illusory?

Because in the same way that a confidence that serves not so much to expose a motive as to disguise it, so do certain memories, and the mechanisms of memory. His initial preference for specific things about Vallfosca, the shadowy woods, the flatlands with poplars, and, almost like an obsession, the points from which you could glimpse the distant and craggy summits of Montseny. Meaning: the aspects of the landscape bearing the greatest similarity to the panoramas of Montseny itself which were the luminous setting for his first memories, liable to function as a bridge or nexus, as an intermediary scene between one epoch and another. And to the degree in which these, those nearest, affirm and establish, those others, their antecedents, tend to lose importance until they disappear, to be concealed anew by a second representation, whose attraction for us might well end up seeming to us unmotivated, arbitrary, and capricious, a question of taste.

A storybook landscape: a dark forest, with ferns and mossy green stones and cavernous tree trunks and rough boughs covered with lichen, and ragged drapes of moss, craggy dry logs, and further up, hollow layers of leaves, shadowy frondosities. And the violets between the grass and the bitter fragrance of the wild strawberries. Everything perfect for stories of enchanted princesses as well as bandits. And then, returning years later, that forest turns out to be, simply, a forest. In fact, the deeply shaded clefts of Montseny, upon whose sunny expanses lay Vallfosca.

Thus the pull that the most recondite and humid aspects of Vallfosca exercised upon him, the ones most similar to those on the other side of that massif that, as between the north and the south, stood between one period of his childhood and another. And in the same way that from Vallfosca he searched for the silhouette of Montseny, its uncertain summits frequently thrust up into the fog, from here, beyond these peaks, at the very foot of Matagalls, from Viladrau, far away, the snowy peaks of the Pyrenees could be glimpsed, almost like clouds in the afternoon sun.

Montseny. A Catalan compound: *Mont. Seny.* Mountain of common sense and reason. A mountainous massif separating not only two landscapes, but also two epochs, two worlds. And the distance between the two points, which then seemed so far from one another that the trip to either place from Barcelona meant taking a different railway line, could now be accomplished by car along mountain highways in less than two hours. Going to spend a weekend in Vallfosca, for example, passing through Viladrau.

Of course, just as when we return to the scenes of our first childhood we invariably discover for ourselves that everything is lesser, smaller, more reduced than what we remember, the adult similarly tends to minimize, to subtract importance from, and consider trivial and negligible the problems that tormented him most during his childhood. But in this latter fact he is completely mistaken, because, just as, in relation to the child he was, the objects that surrounded him were enormous and continue to be so in his memory, those problems were really no less enormous, nor the importance his impressions of those times held for him and continue to hold.

He had returned. And he saw everything accordingly, as if on a reduced scale, the sizes, the distances. But the crossroads at the highway which he could see from the house was still, in any case, quite far. How was it possible then that he could have perceived with such precision the movements of the troops at that crossroads, with the detail with which one can appreciate the people one encounters less than a stone's throw away?

The tricks and traps of memory, its empty spaces, its disguises, its appropriations. Like with Nieves. La Pilate touched Padritus, and Nieves touched Felipe and him. She laughed a lot, when she put him to bed, to see him get hard in the dim light that hung down from the fixture inside the shade. The same as that other time when Quilda was also there and some other woman from the town, all of them leaning over his bed, laughing like conspirators as they put a bit of oil on his bottom, just as if they were there to pluck a chicken, with that kind of delight that arises, when various friends are together, from the sight of the village idiot masturbating in the church plaza, and his huge, mammoth ejaculations.

For the rest, how to be sure he wasn't superimposing images? The memory of what Padritus told them: that Pilate had sucked him off. Something that Raúl then talked about at school, making it sound as if it was something that had happened to him.

And Pilate and her army boyfriends, men with a railroad look about them. And what they saw when they looked out the windows. Were they things they'd seen personally or that the others talked about seeing or having seen? The victory and its commemorations. The parade that they witnessed from the balcony of Uncle Pedro's study, all the cousins gathered together watching the steady march of the cavalry, captained, one might say, by Santiago himself, Santiago or Jaime or Jacobo or Yago or James or Santiago or Sanseacabó, meaning eternal and everlasting, patron saint of Spain, with his hosts of Moors and his legionnaires, and then the tanks and the artillery pieces and the gray companies of the military police and the Guardia Civil, armies of land, sea, and air, flags and military bands, marches sounding while on they come, on they come, the sappers to the front, those troops who appeared to have keys bristling from their shoulders, between arms raised on high and children in arms, songs and cheering, a steel orgy of sharpened blades, theirs was the victory and the full dress glory of red and golden yellow, the photo of Franco, the young Caudillo saluting the tight formations passing before his platform, on the front page of *La Vanguardia*, a full-page photo, against a sky flowering with impeccable squadrons, the picture of that happy early shining spring repeated year after year.

Because there is only one type of comprehensible war: civil war. The war that permits the individual to project the scars of his sick personality onto society. The war where one can concretize and put into practice the abstractions of their adopted ideology, for whatever the motivations might be, without having to step outside their small quotidian world, and apply them to their most immediate vicinity. That's why civil wars might be the only ones capable of exciting the people's passions, and why other wars, foreign ones, might only be felt to the degree that they suppose the prolongation or consolidation of some of the elements at play in previous civil wars: the expansion of a religious belief, an ideology, a way of life, of any common trait of the citizenry which they desire to impose on neighboring peoples. Or the inverse: the defense enacted by a people united by traits that give them cohesion the same as blood ties or a common language, their fight to remain independent from any expansions that endanger them, by safeguarding these principles which, following a phase of savage internal strife, ended up not being imposed upon the people but accepted by a citizenry persuaded of their rightness. Also because when those circumstances do not occur, it's necessary to summon the image of chains and imprisonment, as in the ancient armies of slaves, and cultivate antimilitarism anew, and pacifism, and the reason for desertion, the general lack of understanding for a cause whose motives, for being too technical and alien to the individual, are incapable of striking a spark among the people.

Not so in the case of civil war. When a phenomenon of double liberation takes place, understood not as the annihilating victory of one of the battling bands, as the end of horror, blood, and vengeance, but, quite to the contrary, as its unleashing. Better than horror: terror. Not the kind that the worker sent to the firing squad can experience, before falling, shot for nothing more than what the thick calluses on his hands testify about his condition; not for a man for whom the evil of war is nothing especially new when compared to his previous life, hunger and exhaustion and rags and unemployment, and his daughter's prostituting herself to help feed the family, and the strike or boycott or sabotage as a collective solution, with their inevitable consequences, police precincts and soldiers' barracks, mounted police charging on horseback, machine guns, gunfire, shots to the gut, and the employers' thugs awaiting him. Not that kind of terror, not at all. But the terror that makes a prisoner of a good and honest man, of the middle-class citizen, of the aristocrat, of honorable, well-educated people with money, with principles, terror, on the verge of hallucination, of those kinds of people facing the coup de grâce, no longer delivered for being a hard boss or a shrewd landowner, but now simply for attending Mass or taking a summer vacation, not to mention for simple cordiality and bonhomie. Apparent arbitrariness become the norm. Crime become spectacle, buildings on fire and dead bodies on the pavement become urban planning and landscape. Summary executions as a daily habit, madness as logic as one crumbles into the black suns of the gutter.

And that is when such a double liberation occurs: an active liberation for the executioner, a passive one for the victim. The liberation that for one and another represents everything related to the aberrant character of our relationships with our neighbor and the stickiness of things and the mummifying effects of our institutions.

A frustrated liberation, a goal never reached. And like the castaway, the one who lacks strength to reach the coast and his spent energies leave him at the mercy of the drifting tide, so too a society emerged from a civil war, like from an intense emotional explosion, whose only remaining strength seems to be inertia, whose only weight seems to be prostration, without the capacity to react, with the meekness of one who ends up half imbecile but has saved their skin, and the punitive violence of the weak victor against the still weaker loser. An extenuation even of desires, similar to the experience of one who has made love too many times in a single night, so that, upon dressing, the last thing they want is to start fucking again.

An idiotic life. More meek and placid than really peaceful. High school, college, army, girlfriend, diploma, marriage, profession, children, and then back to square one. Like a nightmare, when one dreams they're back in high school and that the teacher, although he's wearing a soutane, is the captain from his army camp.

So that, in these conditions of repressed aggression, one might well show an early love for hunting. For shooting one animal after another. Including even before the proper age. Something as clandestine as Raúl's fascination with fire, when he created marvelous lamps by burning alcohol in jars or tried turning his desk drawers into ovens.

Insufficient trials. Anguished and uncertain, Raúl's conscience was the exact inverse of that inner peace felt by the rural landowner in November, when all the crops are harvested and stored away and the new cycle of sowing begins, and who knows that the only way a year of bad weather could affect him would be increased compensation thanks to higher prices for his crop, so lacking in bad produce. The same as in adolescence, without knowing very well why, one thinks that in life everything ends in failure and that nothing is worth the trouble, and so feels proud even of his own lucidity, satisfied with his perspicacity. Until everything begins to fail and nothing really is worth the trouble. The reality of the game.

This sensation of attending a ritual performance, for example. One of those shows somewhere between carnivalesque and liturgical, with its profusion of images like fireworks, in which Moors and Christians face off each year in various festivals along the Levantine coast, mock battles in the course of which the whole town usually participates, without anybody, on the other hand, knowing with absolute certainty the heroic deeds being commemorated. A parody that doesn't even know itself to be a parody, objectified, sacralized, converted into a ceremony. A kind of consubstantial performance by some actors who stubbornly insist on repeating it again and again, even without an audience, within the ruins of an amphitheater. Or in these long straight galleries where since 19 July 1936, so many lists have been recited, so many names, so many ranks of prisoners dispatched to the firing squad, rebels, fascists, anarchists, Trotskyites, communists, years and years of life awaiting execution; fascists dead before having to helplessly witness how the dissolution against which they had fought undermined the foundations of victory in their very homes, how that dissolution was incarnated in their own children, how it was illusory to use weapons to recover time now past; anarchists dead in time to not have to get to know the workers of a consumerist society; Trotskyites dead in time to not have to see the revolution grinding to a halt in nation after nation, due to the national interest of each people more than class interests; communists dead in time to not have to fight, to save the revolution, against the proletariat itself, against the very vanguard of that proletariat, against the very direction of that vanguard, against themselves. But as if the amphitheater were not in ruins, as if the public's applause still echoed there, the actors continued their performance, some as if they were still able or still wanted to foment revolution, others as if they were preventing it from coming, as if the dissolution of values they claimed to contain were there, enclosed in that jail, and not installed in their own homes. And only the fatigue of the years that pass would prevent them from sending prisoners to the firing squad like in days gone by, in the same way that habitual duelists, once they've complied with all the requirements of the regulations, end up firing their pistols into the air.

As in a sacramental act interpreted according to the Stanislavsky method, with the verism that is derived from identification, a sacramental act in which the actors persist to the point of staying in character even after the play is finished, beginning with the Author himself and, once offstage, continue adjusting their behavior to their respective characters, the paranoid King, the schizophrenic Peasant. And especially the Author, a demented fool who believes he continues to be the garroted prisoner, with his heavy beard and his tunic or smock, now become his shroud, still sitting against the post, a cross between his stiff hands, oblique as an erect, ejaculating member.

Number?

Just as Dante, in the exposition of his journey through the darkest zones of his conscience—under the guidance of the genial pederast, whose personality is sublimated, as they wend their way upward, until being transformed into the unreachable purity of a dead little girl—does nothing but project his own repressions and venereal or sadistic perversion, and articulate them in a system, to immortalize his rancors and frustrations with his characteristic delectation, with the same vengeful spirit that permits him to judge and condemn not only the world in general, but, above all, his most immediate society, in the same way that whoever tolerates seclusion and solitude can draw from them the greatest conceivable liberty and clairvoyance.

And just as the heaven-hell relationship is one of coincident inversion, like the image of a hand against a mirror, the one a continuation of the other, but inverted, thus the relationship between God and Demon can only be understood as one of an essentially dialectical nature, insofar as, the one representing the harmonic order and the other transgression, when after various failed revolts the uprising triumphs, and with it the chaos that, as it settles down and takes hold, always makes way for a new and definitive order, the roles are exchanged: the Demon, the victorious rebel, occupies the place of God and, even as he installs a new definitive harmonic order, engenders his opposite, a new principle of dissolution, a new Demon, that ancient all-powerful overthrown one, an indomitable force conquered which, from its present Tartaric summits, will attempt again and again, disaster after disaster, the reconquest of the Olympian heights, the reestablishment of the lost Golden Age, once again the Demon against God, Saturn against Jupiter, the promised goodnesses of the new order converted with time into tyrannical arbitrariness and into a horror of the good, while the subversions of that order—transgression, evil, terror—acquire the value of liberating acts, and the Tempter's deceits become great deeds, and his agents' nature becomes archangelic, as the one who has descended to the deepest depths well knows, not like some curious traveler, like Ulysses and Aeneas and Dante, but rather like Prometheus who descended into the inferno in search of his Eurydice, who had proposed to give men freedom by eating of the forbidden fruit.

Because the diversity of the names of the Creator, the ambiguity of his origins, his confusing parental ties, Jupiter, Jehovah, Ormuz,

Elohim, Saturn, Ahriman, He. Meaning, he who has no name, the unnameable. He that is the one true self and its opposite.

This Great Narcissus with a taste for games who, as if to make a show of his power, upon giving himself over to one of those acts of onanism of the sort from which a world sprouts, seems to take pleasure in mutilating man, amputating a certain number of his components, so that, according to a demoniac calculation of probabilities, it might be just as mathematically impossible for him to find his perfect soulmate in love as to find freedom in cosmic equilibrium. His lapidary laws that made Moses ascend the heights of Mount Sinai and cry to the cloudy sky: speak, Dog!

Because in the same way that it becomes difficult to discern if it's more terrifying to consider, for example, the conditioning implied by events so remote in time and space, such as the founding of Rome, the formation of Barcino in the heart of the future Roman Empire, its conversion to Christianity following the arrival of Saint James, its reconquest by Wilfred the Hairy, the reception for which the city charged Columbus upon his return from his voyage of discovery, the departure toward that America of one Ferrer who there made a fortune and married a Gaminde, one branch of the family's return to the Iberian peninsula, settling the grandfather in Barcelona, the wedding of his son Jorge with Eulalia Moret, the birth of Raúl, the Civil War, school, the military, the party, Leo and Federico, the Sagrada Familia, Nuria and Aurora, the cathedral, Modesto Pírez, the Model Prison, I here in this instant, or on the contrary, the idea that such a chain does not exist, that the alternative of a contingent fact cannot be anything else but another contingent fact, the absolute dominion of the arbitrary.

And no less radical and traumatic than clarifying the dilemma is deciding to break one fine day, for example, with the daily grind, with its ties and servitude, with family members whom we don't even want to see, acquaintances whose behavior we can no longer stand, women whom we don't love but whom we haven't left yet, the past, in short, that we have been carrying along on our backs, a spiderweb that entangles and gets dusty and moldy, relationships which, however, generally persist and endure for life, not so much for fear of the fact itself of breaking them off as of the solitude and helplessness that come in their wake, fear of the freedom, in the same way that what frightens us is not so much suddenly conceiving of progress as a constellation, a drawing obtained by tracing an imaginary line that links stars picked out on a whim, figures, in the end, projected by ourselves. What really frightens us are the consequences that come from this idea about the conception of the world.

Because, just as with the lover, her infidelity confirmed, the problem is knowing if her tears correspond to her shame at having been found out or her rage for the mess that such a discovery means for her continued plans, so, in a similar way, it becomes problematic to know, in the diverse phases of life, if it's not more appropriate to consider what we call maturity as the end of childhood, or inversely, generalizing, if what we believe to be the start of a new epoch isn't really the end, the death throes of the preceding period.

The great difference that stands between guilt and punishment. The case of the unlucky one, for example, who when young had a brilliant idea, and while articulating it and developing it the years went passing by until he grew old, more than ever and forever down in the trenches with his handful of ridiculous ideas, a sociologist or a psychiatrist or a linguist or whatever, ever more enclosed within his personal prison, with the disastrous support of his wife and four unconditionally faithful friends. And it's then when life manifests itself with full clarity like a mountain of piety and penitence, of redemption, that we must climb up step by step. What else, if not, do those stepped pyramids, the Buddhist temples, stand for? And the cupolas on the mosques, the towers of the cathedrals, the same predilection that the gods have always shown for the mountains? A world like a mountain whose summit we must reach, given that, like on the heights of Purgatory, one still finds there the earthly paradise, from which we are only separated by the crystalline flow of the River Lethe, the river of oblivion, whose poisonous waters one must needs drink. So that, when one has served out his sentence, he dies. And heaven will be the non-existence of hell and hell the non-existence of heaven.

On the other hand, just as for our cuckolded lover, the discovery of the betrayal can be the cause, especially if his personality is prone to this, of a true neurotic crisis, with repercussions even in one's own sexual equilibrium, so for Raúl, the insecurity derived from ceasing to contemplate the world vis-à-vis a specific ideology in which every question has its response, in which everything gets explained, had momentarily affected, no doubt, not only his psychic and sexual stability but, what's worse, also his creative capacity, plunging him into uncertainty, indecision, and impotence, as if—just as the lover's infidelity can provide a splendid resolution for ending some relationships already well past their prime, one of those occasions that rarely reoccur, emancipating himself from that ideology, liberating himself from a perspective accepted not without effort—it were not capable, analogously, of widening his field of vision before reducing it.

And this all the more true given that, if on one side he couldn't say that he fully trusted the validity of those points of view he defended, no less anesthetic now than they had been during his now-past ideological crisis, nor could he trust, on the other hand, with respect to the sharpness of his mental faculties, the effects of his devotion to his practice of the accepted ideology. Because just as a good middle-class citizen compensates for his erotic dissatisfaction by collecting one thing or another or endlessly remodeling his house, or that old rural landowner who overcomes all his personal frustrations—what he might have been had he acted in time, what he might have experienced, what he might have seen, whom he might have loved, if he'd not stayed in that goddamned tiny out-of-the-way place—thinking about his properties and, especially, those not his own, those he still needs in order to finish that noose he's wrapping around the town's neck, so with Raúl, in the long run, the routine of some political activities in whose worth he didn't believe, the exercise of a militancy for militancy's sake had supplanted the development of his creative impulses, suffocating them, inhibiting them, in exchange for the protection of a moral justification that supported him in the meantime. An alternative that had not arisen at first, when it seemed that everything was unified: action and creative strength and liberty and compromise and love. Meaning: before he ended up feeling like that knight-errant who, after fulfilling all requirements, passing all required tests, and following the strictest rituals that the rules and regulations demand of one who wishes to join the order, and now knighted, goes riding and riding without ever encountering any giant or dragon, nor being able to participate in any tournament nor trade boasts with a foe nor rescue kingdoms nor princesses nor, much less, find the lost Holy Grail.

In the same way that for a person whose father played almost no role in his early childhood, due to his being weak and sick and depressed and worn-out, the last person capable of inspiring admiration and fear in a boy, in the same way that that person will always be, most likely, possessed of enormously fragile religious sentiments, so Raúl, in his childhood when he felt more moved by his fear of the Demon than by his love of God, due to the much greater tangibility of the maleficent powers in the world and, above all, of his feeling of condemnation, convinced as he was of his total incapacity to fulfill the necessary precepts to earn his way into heaven, given the dark feelings of destruction and vengeance he sensed inside himself, he began trying to conjure up as much as possible that irremediable sentence, or at least distance himself from it as much as possible, by means of ritual bets—reaching the corner of Paseo de la Bonanova before the streetcar arrived, finishing counting seven times to seventy at the precise moment of stepping through the school gates, etcetera—and, in a more general way, with his daily behavior, among whose traits his tendency to create strict obligations and responsibilities in relation to certain people, to specific tasks, and the reparative self-sacrifice in certain situations was not the least outstanding, insofar as it compensated for the regrets he failed to feel.

However: how was it possible not to relate that profound irreligiousness in a specific phase of a person's life with his previous age, not so much a lack of revolutionary conviction, as insincerity about socialism? Given that like in Dante, the Christian mysticism he shows off turns out to be obviously insincere and, in the *Divine Comedy*, scholasticism is a superimposed ideology,

so too, in Raúl, the Marxist interpretation of the world as a key
to reality had, from the beginning, been based—although voluntarily—less on rational evidence than a desire for liberation
and even for terror, far removed from any constructive purpose.

Or his patriotic indifference, which although formulated late,
was, nevertheless, already present during his years at school, mani-
festing itself with a sentiment like annoyance when, immersed in
the universal history, it collided with Spain, with the encomiastic
image which the texts ascribed to its singular role. Annoyance
if not repugnance. No greater, on the other hand, no more
intense than what a Frenchman might experience, or a Russian
or an American, with a certain critical sense with respect to their
own country. Something similar to what eventually leads one
to feel respect for his own city when he lives in it, by reason of
its very immediacy, the environs containing all the burdens that
weigh upon one's life. And if, being far away, one can remember
Barcelona almost even with a longing, being there in the city itself,
one is frequently assaulted with the desire to live in any part of
it as long as it be north of the Besós and south of the Llobregat.

Breaking with habits. No longer pretending to accept what
one really doesn't accept. Fighting petrification with stimuli,
liberating creative impulses. Because sometimes there is something unexpected inside of oneself, that has its own precise time,
like a birth, like death, like a time bomb, and then erupting like
volcanic lava or orgasmic sperm. And that is the only way we
become truly aware of the development of a woodland that's
familiar to us, or of a garden, a street, a forest, by staring at a
photo taken years earlier and making comparisons, confirming
specifically the things that have obviously changed, by seizing
upon their previous dimensions, and so Raúl, only after examining the development of such impulses from the beginning,
could establish the degree to which they had ended up imposing
themselves on his imaginative activity, his creative willpower.

The fact is that, unlike what adults seem to think when they
turn to the child telling him : that will teach you, an announcement that is usually the prelude to the application of a severe
corporal punishment, the things we forget are no less important

than the things we remember. This forest that lies before us at the start of our life, and of any other life we might find in the future, will only be a faint shadowy echo.

The paths of memory. Something similar to visiting one of those cathedrals built atop an older one, constructed in its turn from the remains of pagan temples, stones belonging to that other city excavated beneath the present-day city, subterranean ruins that one can visit contemplating what were streets and houses and necropolises and protective walls, pieced together almost always from the remains of earlier cities.

A tour, however, that one usually finds not only in the base of one's self-knowledge, but also in the full realization of all creative impulse. In these notes. Because just as Hercules founded Barcelona after being shipwrecked, and Aeneas founded Rome after the destruction of Troy, so Raúl confronted not so much his past as his future as he wrote his notes on those pieces of toilet paper, with the application and the vigor of a Robinson in recovering the notion of time or of a Monte Cristo in drilling slowly through the rock. And what he wrote there was not like what he wrote before, when instead of imposing himself on the words, the words imposed themselves on him as objective material, according to, doubtless, the repressive role of the language upon personality, to the degree to which any relationship between names and the things they designate is simultaneously an expression and a reflection of a specific external reality. And through those linguistic relationships, the prevailing relationships in the external world take shape in the child's mind. And in this way, while a specific system of relationships between names and things is established in earliest childhood, from that point on, any other kind of system of relationships is excluded.

Such a possibility, however, exists; we can intuit it during a certain number of years, sniff it, ever closer, pinpoint it. Only that its realization, meaning its birth, is not simple, nor must it necessarily be auspicious. And it almost seems necessary that some shipwreck or destruction or punishment occur as a catalyst for this phenomenon.

A surprising result. For the first time, as he stared at the words in his notes, he had the feeling of creating something and not—like that actor who one fine night discovers the tedium of repeating his role for the umpteenth time and wonders what he's doing there on stage if he was never truly interested in the theater in the first place and if, in reality, he might devote himself to something else less monotonous and repetitive—the impression of playing a game for the sake of playing it, not because it really interests him. The feeling, in other words, of creating a new reality instead of telling a story more or less in the way you would tell any other, the triumph of a strike that is, at the same time, the triumph of a growing awareness, or the moral emptiness of those who lead a dissolute life at the margin of all compromise with society and other things that are written, descriptions, dialogues, tales, internal monologues, counterarguments and clarifications such as "what's up, said Juan," or "he lit a cigarette," or "she burst out laughing," etcetera, just as boring to read as to write, including when it's all for the sake of some productive way to earn a living.

Is there any difference between a flamenco dancer who, interviewed on TV, speaks with complete self-assurance about her art, and the author rescued from obscurity by his writing and the grace of some literary prize; a national master or some small-town municipal secretary, myopic and frog-faced when he talks about the personal character of his writing or his social ideas, but later, when he gives a reading of one of his pieces, the amazed spectator discovers that beneath the ferocious appearance of that Bête who keeps the princess prisoner there beats a heart filled with love and that, behind that frog face, lives a man who loves and apostrophizes, who speaks of balconies bloody with geraniums or how the people's sovereignty fills him with vigorous inspiration? No, it's nothing remotely like that. On the contrary, one has the sensation of configuring, with nothing more than words, a reality far more intense than the reality which all that literature pretends to witness or replicate.

Even more: it was as if the words, once written, turned out to be more precise than his previous purpose and even clarified for him what, beforehand, he'd only had a vague notion of what he was going to write. A book that could be, not a reference to reality, but, like reality, an object of possible references, an autonomous world about which, theoretically, a reader with creative impulses might write, in their turn, a novel or a poem, free of themes and of forms, a creation of creations.

One might say that just as a fertilized human egg already contains the germ of everything the person is going to be, and whose development will culminate with their birth, there are, equally, moments in a man's life which, for their metaphorical strength, come to be a summary or compendium of all his conscious and unconscious perceptions, the concentration, one within another, of all implicit experience, instant and duration, a time vastly superior, in its elasticity and amplitude, to chronological time. And to secure that instant, that duration, requires a centrifugal development, successively dilating circles, spreading out like waves that grow ever larger around the spot where the stone plunged into the still water or the way that one metaphor nested within another makes a tale. The golden moment, the sensation that by means of the written word he was not only creating something autonomous, brought to life by his own hand, but that in the course of this process of objectivization through writing, he would at the same time manage to understand the world through himself and know himself through the world.

Beyond, then, the words, beyond his simple principle. Something that does not lie in them but within ourselves, although, in their turn, they are what gives us reality. The supreme union. The communicants processing to the prison's Central Tower. First the queers—the little girls—like mannequins that come walking along the catwalk. Next, only some pious being, shrunken, guilty. And some invalids and hypochondriacs, or some old man shuffling his feet quickly along, as if afraid to be left behind, of not arriving in time. And some crook desirous of ingratiating himself, of getting in good with La Merche. And the queers, with their hands together and their eyes lowered, kneel before the executioner's hood, purple as a bruise, and then the executioner raises the host. And La Merche starts muttering, let the little girls enter into me, do this in memory of me, only say the word. And the little girls, Lord, take this cup from my lips. Eating the true flesh and drinking the true blood of a Garroted man.

No one is alone, each one said to himself, under his breath. Between ourselves we keep each other company.

Just as in the course of a long journey by train, the kind of passengers who board and disembark change as slowly as the landscape outside, so that the trajectory of the trip ends up being the only point of contact between the points of departure and arrival, thus, with the passing of the years, almost everything ends up by being linked with death and very few things with life.

Nevertheless, just as birds continue gleaning without being frightened at the start of a solar eclipse, their quick chirping and peeping betraying no worry about the day's sudden unusual brevity, so goes the passing of time during youth, the innocent conviction that throughout life one more year is only one year more. But the same way that the misty glaze of our respiration begins to disappear the instant we move our face away from the glass, so just like our breath, our life dwindles and fades, as long as what we are watching remains there, on the other side of the window, outside, just as the things we tried to dominate in our lives will remain there, including those we believed to have dominated.

Allegorical drama: life is but a dream. Except, perhaps, for the one dreaming, who will then be the only one to make it out alive. *Ite missa est.*

Then the final prayers and benedictions, the final gospel, the final miserere nobis. And then the national anthem, and to its rhythm, the recession of the prisoners, gallery after gallery, past the platform in the Central Tower—now converted into something like the presidential grandstand in Red Square, where the various prison authorities sit in a hierarchical arrangement around the warden—the political prisoners coming last, without matching the rhythm, although by then, in order to avoid any unnecessary conflict, the warden had already turned away, ignoring them, alerted to their arrival by the preceding group, the little queens, who, on the contrary, attired and made up in the most exaggerated fashion possible for that great moment, approached, strutting provocatively, their formation no less tight and martial than the chorus girls in a musical revue.

Next, while the prisoners from solitary were locked away, each one in his own cell, for the others, the free time on the patios, the movie, the little queens following behind everything, apart, according to the sexual structure of the penitentiary organization, so much less arbitrary the deeper we go into the psychic darkness of its artifices. And the paella with olives and a sardine instead of the normal daily rations. And the afternoon, the Sunday binge, the betting, the loudspeakers, the scores from the official league soccer matches, *In a Persian Market*. Later, another week, another Sunday, the declaration before the examining magistrate who, despite the news from Pedro Botero, would finally arrive, only a few days behind schedule, due to the traffic jams and bottlenecks on the way. And the daily routine of Raúl's life as a political prisoner until the court-martial, after which, absolved or sentenced to a symbolic sentence, which in fact he had already served, he would be immediately released.

Motionless before the door, he turned his gaze back into the empty cell, the sun on the flagstones reticulated by the oblique projection of the bars. He was sleepy. Wouldn't he let himself be conquered by an invincible drowsiness when he found himself back inside? Or perhaps overcoming the invincible drowsiness, feeling a little bit drugged, he would take his pen and set himself to writing on the smooth side of one of his squares of toilet paper? Rambling notes, written according to some still very vague plan. Nothing in common, however, with his unconfessed poems of adolescence. Nor with the heroic prose of his time in the military. Nor with his previous frustrated attempts and, for some unexplained motive, always thematically unhappy, suicides, ill-fated love affairs, processes of deterioration. One question: When did he begin to write? Another question: Why?

Or, without any desire to write, wouldn't he, in that state
of wakeful vigilance, allow his mind to wander, to think about
when he might be released, his return home? The chaotic overgrown garden, his original design of flower beds and acacias
now completely wrecked, a mess of morning glories and geraniums and mallows and nameless flowers and volunteer dwarf
fruit trees and strange creepers with pumpkin-shaped fruit and
reptilian ivy and the honeysuckle invading everything, introducing its willful shoots between the iron bars, along the slats of
the Persian blinds, disquieting, entwining. Very healthy, Papa
would say. It's like living right out in the wild. And taking advantage of the few open spaces in that degenerative overflowing,
he'd planted thyme and oregano and southern wormwood and
rosemary and rue, aromatic plants, a vegetable proliferation whose overgrown cluster scumbled even the outlines of
the house. And each of the damp shadowy spaces inside the
house, no less present than the intangible odors, occupied its
own corresponding place in his memory. The light stink of gas
in the entrance hall, next to the gas meters, especially noticeable, the same as that moldy smell, enclosed, upon entering the
first floor, making your way through it, the vestibule, the small
sitting room, the dining room, and, upstairs, almost to the top
floor, when they returned from Vallfosca, at the end of summer.
And the closet in his room, which smelled like a rifle, and the
sideboard in the hallway like medicines, and the pantry like
dried, peeled chestnuts. And his grandparents' room, and Felipe's
room, the dampest ones, smelled like emptiness. And the attic,
filled with the dusty piles of disassembled furniture from the
conjugal bedroom Papa once shared with Mama, smelled like old
clothes and stale silk. And Papa's own bedroom that smelled like
medicinal herbs and a drugstore exactly the same as in Vallfosca;
and his desk, an accumulation of failed projects and unrealized inventions, of useless patents, of the swindles of which he'd
been a victim. And the large cracked floor tiles and buckling
molding along the walls with soft chipped coats of plaster, and
the pipes flecked with solder and the burned-out lightbulbs of
so many lamps, not replaced, and the carefully conserved ruin

of the kitchen pots and utensils. Overall, it's good enough for
two people, said Eloísa. Her old patched bathrobes, her ratty
aprons, her broken eyeglass frame fixed with a Band-Aid, her
slippers with the seams cut open on both sides so as to not
squeeze her bunions. And Papa equally disastrous: covered with
stains, clothing coming apart at the seams, as if stuck inside the
same old clothes, and his oldest pair of shoes. It was as if during
Raúl's absence they'd let themselves go, and by virtue of his very
absence, made the extent of their abandon all the more clear to
him. Why buy myself anything, son? At my age that's just throwing money away. And the small problems, the complaints, would
come. His father's mania for ventilating every part of the house,
of throwing doors and windows wide open. I don't know how
we haven't caught pneumonia yet, Eloísa would say. But he'll end
up killing us all. Eloísa's eyeglasses; now it didn't seem to bother
her to wear them all day, and not only for sewing.

Or would he take up his pen, as if hallucinating, only to set
it down again, sleeping from the geometrical splendor of those
bright slanted squares that the sun projected on the flagstones,
finally overcome by sleep, by a dream, one of those little catnaps
that, suddenly interrupted, do nothing more than leave us with
our spirit shrinking and our head heavy for the whole day, like
waking from a nightmare which, for the moment, we perhaps
do not even remember having dreamed, dreams that are not
dreams, that in the memory end up even imposing themselves
on reality, however disagreeable this might be, fixed with greater
precision in the memory?

A state similar to the one which, after waking, must have
possessed him years later, one morning, Vallfosca, Papa's room,
the early morning sun gleaming on the tiles, Papa, evidently
dead—why evidently?—coming in with this wide-brimmed hat,
his overcoat folded over his shoulder, without paying him attention, as if worried or lost in thought, and Raúl sitting up in bed
as if he had just woken up, shouting or as if he were shouting,
but what're you doing here, how did you come back, and Papa
without looking at him, looking through the things piled up on
his desk, as if browsing in a shop, well look, everybody's got their

own things, distracted and distant, looking for something, you
might say, and Raúl, wracked with palpitations, stay here, stay
here again, as if the fact that Papa had died so few days before
might allow for a solution, that it was only a question of goodwill
or determination, only four days before the boy would turn one
year old and only a few days after Raúl's own birthday, an event
that everyone thought about but which only Eloísa dared mention, the same morning of the burial, coming back, when she
saw the little boy crawling around in the garden and she picked
him up in her arms, and just as the boy was not astonished
by the adult but rather the adult by the boy, so, then she said,
poor little thing, what does he know about death and age, four
days before, a relationship between dates that had the virtue of
diverting her attention, of making her forget for the moment the
time transpired between the first manifestations of the process of
illness and the last ones, with their details, the prescriptions, the
injections, oxygen, and above all, the sentences, the words, his
words, his worries about Eloísa's sorrow when she still spent part
of her time sitting in the armchair, poor Eloísa, with her rheumatism and this problem with her leg that must be sciatica, she
would need to have a doctor check it, then, when they were still
receiving their periodic visits from Uncle Gregorio and Leonor,
and he and Uncle Gregorio talked unfailingly about the friends
of their youth and Uncle Gregorio asked him every time about
Arcadio Catarineu, you remember, I haven't seen him for a while,
and Eloísa and Leonor tried to get them to change the subject,
because Papa didn't know either that Arcadio Catarineu had
died only recently, Eloísa had spirited away the obituary page
from the newspaper, and Papa said you're looking skinny, son,
you should try to make yourself eat, and he asked him when he
would finish his doctoral thesis, and asked him about work and
told him he was a very lucky guy to have Nuria, that she was
a girl with a very good heart, and he looked at the little boy's
toys in the center of the carpet until one day he himself was
the first to say that it was better they didn't bring him to visit
anymore for the moment, that a sick man's house was no place
for a little boy, and when he got worse and Felipe showed up

again and said that they were reassigning him to Barcelona, he
said that he was very happy, pretending he believed it, and from
that moment when he could no longer get out of bed he said
he didn't want any more visits from the doctor, that they should
take care of him, who I would have liked to see is Gregorio, but
a sick man always shocks people, and with his state of health,
I don't think it would do him good, while, very possibly, Uncle
Gregorio didn't even find out about this change in his habits, at
most, someday, proposing suddenly to pay Jorge a visit, and then
forgetting about it right away, and Eloísa said poor man as they
left the doctor's office after each visit, seeing that Papa accepted
without any kind of objection all those explanations relative to
the fastidious complications that were presented, as if he were
more relaxed seeing that they saw him at ease. Only at the end,
when he began to need oxygen, taking advantage of a moment
in which he found himself alone with Nuria, he told her, help
me to take off my rings now. Later it's worse.

It was as if since he got out of prison the rhythm of time had
accelerated, events, and not only for him—his wedding, the job
that Amadeo procured for him, his son—but as if the phenomenon were obeying some general law, Amadeo's own wedding
with Doña Dulce, and Monsina's slightly more hasty wedding,
prompted—like his own wedding with Nuria—by a pregnancy,
although the motives for keeping the baby were not the same
in either case—in Monsina's case the demand and agreement of
the respective families—and the birth of Monsina's baby boy
shortly before Nuria's, followed by Monsina's immediate separation, no less hasty than her wedding, like a premonition, also,
of Raúl's inevitable separation from Nuria, not because they
quarreled as before, or for any tension or violence in their
relationship, but rather the result of a mutual indifference,
correct and even respectful, although if only the result of fatigue,
but strong enough to make them understand the lack of sense
in continuing to live together that way, in a furnished flat in
the upper streets of the city which never felt like anything more
than a way station, once they resolved the best possible way
of dealing with the problem of their little boy. A conviction

which, curiously, seemed to crystallize in both of them from the moment they found themselves married.

How to explain the process? Was it as if to Raúl, like to so many men, the helplessness of freedom had made him turn back momentarily to the fold? No, nothing so simple and concrete, nothing capable of being reduced to a single clause. Rather more as if the simple return to family locations had charged him anew with the problems of daily life, questions that he had to resolve and which, without him hardly noticing, had ended up enveloping him once more, one after another, like a chain reaction, Papa and Eloísa, his duties to them, the need to work, Amadeo's favorable disposition in that regard, his debt to Nuria, etcetera. As if only after three years he might have been able to react, recuperate, emerge from his stupor, to say, definitely, enough is enough. And get back to writing his book. And, for the moment, take a few days off to go to Rosas. And quit smoking a pipe.

His notes from prison, those notes written on squares of toilet paper, which upon his release, with the sudden rush of events and the vertigo of time, came to seem to him like those notes one takes upon waking up in the middle of the night, because the ideas seem to be extraordinarily important, but which in the morning, if they seem to make any sense at all, never usually mean what they did before. It was as if, in order to recover their meaning, it were necessary that from the many personal elements which had served as a basis for the literary material collected there, that from the many points of reference to reality he might have used, he didn't really need to keep absolutely anything, everything reduced to just that: words: as if all that he'd destroyed in his notes also had to be destroyed in reality so that his notes might acquire autonomy, become their own entity. And only then, that chaotic recording of reflections, argumentation nuclei, descriptions, evocations, dialogues, etcetera, might recover its cohesion and meaning and, above all, as if suddenly, the central idea would be revealed to him: a book like one of those paintings, *Las Meninas*, for example, where the key to the composition is found, in fact, outside the frame.

The idea of spending a few days in Rosas obeyed the necessity that the writer occasionally feels in reviewing some scene from his work. But, at the same time, the notes he'd selected to take with him, that he had to use in writing the first chapter of his book, a book still lacking a title and without any proper names for the characters, given the chosen location and the current state of his relationship with Nuria, took on an almost prefigurative character, now that he was returning precisely to Rosas and precisely with Nuria. A man fresh out of prison. His psychic state is unstable and his relationship with his lover, in a critical condition. In a final attempt to salvage the unsalvageable, they decide to spend a few days in Rosas, as in previous times, returning to the starting point. That's how he opened the book.

The visit they paid to Eloísa the day before their departure, seemed, doubtless, like an attempt to cast a spell. Not in the evening but in the morning, without taking the little boy along, as if to avoid—uselessly—what had happened the last time, on their dismal trip to Ibiza—nothing but rain the whole time—when the afternoon before they left, they went by the house so Papa could see the boy, but only after they returned from the island, upon learning that he was sick, they also found out that just before the trip, although he'd told them nothing, he'd gone to the doctor, and only then did Raúl start to make connections, realizing that the symptoms that had been showing up, the first perhaps only a few months earlier, not yet married to Nuria, the night when, arriving home, he'd found Papa vomiting into a urinal, doubled up and frail upon the bed like an eaglet in its nest. It's the antibiotics, son, they've upset my stomach. And I've had to take so many because of these damned boils. Then, as now, they'd left the little boy with his grandmother, with Doña Dulce. Now Felipe was living at home so as not to leave Eloísa alone, although she almost never stopped doing things. And Eloísa fell asleep listening to her transistor radio. They'd bought her a television set, but she said it made her eyes tired, made her dizzy, that she preferred the radio. She was most interested in the news and one day, she told them, she'd even called the radio station to see if they'd yet found poor Antoñito, the little boy who'd disappeared. It was almost unbelievable that she didn't associate, didn't relate, one thing with another: her rheumatism, her sciatica, her liver, her circulation. She listened to the diagnoses they invented without paying attention to their meaning, almost pleased, perhaps, almost proud, of the attention the doctors focused on her, of the instruments they used to examine her, of the vocabulary they used, mysterious, almost, like a prayer in Latin. The operation won't do any good, the specialist had told them. The cancer has spread everywhere. She's probably got three months at the most. But at her age you never know. She might live a few more years. He and Felipe agreed for the moment to say nothing to her son José, known as Pepe.

The other time, the trip to Ibiza had been in January, seeking—as it turns out—a bit of good weather; not like now, already springtime, after Easter. They walked without any hurry along the quiet street, and there was a boy hunting lizards with an air rifle in front of a sunny wall. Do you remember? Nuria said. And Raúl, I don't know why, but I knew that's exactly what you were going to say. It's as if we've already lived this moment. Outside the cave, of course.

Papa was organizing photos, writing on the back who was who. He showed them a family portrait taken in the living room of the chalet on Calle Mallorca: the parents, the wet-nurses and the children all arranged like in an advertisement, Jorge in the foreground sitting on a cardboard rocking horse. This is Paquita and this, Gregorio and this one, poor Raulito and, here, poor Cecilia; behind them, leaded stained-glass windows, crowded with palm fronds, the foot of a staircase. I'm writing their names, he said, because it's the only way in a few years to know who they were.

He took the child and, assisted by Raúl, held him up in front of the mirror, while the astonished little boy contemplated the double image of his two servants, at once in front and on each side, signaling to and pointing from, the cynically grotesque character of the third person who appeared there, only in front of him, perhaps the solution to the mystery.

He came out to the garden to say goodbye to them. He said that, at the least, he would come to see the child each day.

Don't worry, they'll bring him over to you in the mornings. Good, he said, so then I'll come over in the afternoons. He said goodbye to them from the gate, warts clustered around his eyes, under his white eyebrows, his eyes themselves brimming with nightfall, each pupil piercing the horizon toward infinity, with lichens and ruins, far away.

Hammer blows. From some building under construction.

THE BAY. Like two fish that swim in opposite directions. A way of being more than a sign of the zodiac. Explication of the ambivalence of our getaway. With her: more separated than ever. To Rosas: a town that is gradually no longer what it once was.

We went to the same hotel as always. Now enlarged, ruined by tacky renovations. The owner embraced us both and although she didn't say anything, by the way she did it and her liquid eyes and trembling chin it was clear she knew about my prison stint. I cut the conversation short. That's not what I came here looking for.

Her husband didn't say anything either, but as if to offset his secondary role in everything, he made sure to fulfill his obligation of speaking out against the Regime. Uncomfortable on the other hand. The fisherman's problem, a lifelong anarchist, who ends up finding himself the owner of a prosperous hotel on the coast.

THE TRANSPARENCY OF THE TRAMONTANA. To go swimming, we preferred to not follow the coast along the bay, to the right of the town, the low continuous shoreline, dunes, weeds, sand ribbed by the wind rimmed at length by the line of clinging scudded sea foam, short choppy waves obscured by the remains of rotting vegetable residue, drifting seaweed.

We took the path toward the lighthouse, to the left. As we rounded the promontory, the town was lost to sight, and the bay seemed no more like a lake as we moved toward the open sea. From there, the coast turned rough, eroded rocks, broken breakers, pure geological demolition, with sharp cliffs and basaltic coves.

The sea also changed color. Without the softness of tones seen on the bay. Much more accentuated and dense, and deep.

We swam in one of those coves. She lay on the sand bathing in the sun and I explored the rocks on both sides right at the water's edge, sunny flora flecked with foam, with something like sex, like lager beer. The water was good for swimming a few strokes and then getting out, but too cold for calmly swimming underwater.

Quiet, quiet cove. Mineral. Hardly another soul. Only one other couple: tourists, almost always. Better. Hope they speak Dutch, Norwegian.

Sheltered from the Tramontana the breaking waves are neutralized. And looking seaward it almost seems that the water is flowing away from the land, as in an estuary. A breeze, a *Briseus*, light at first, gusting from the brilliant shore, grows stronger as it moves away, unfolding and fanning out, free, accelerated, metallic glazes moving like a bird's flight, like the shadow of its flight, far away, every moment farther, toward the white madness of the horizons, one after another, like snow flurries and manes and whirling saline mists.

The clarity of the atmosphere with the Tramontana. From the hotel room, the Pyrenees are perfectly visible beyond the bay, almost nearby, snowy peaks, splendid as icicles.

À QUOI RECHERCHER LE TEMPS RETROUVE? A coastal town in the off-season, agreeably empty.

In the afternoon we went for walks, climbing up the rough paths. Between slate walls and stunted thickets, flanked by the open slopes of the lower mountain, beyond the gullies with brambles and cursed twisted fig trees.

The springtime came sooner than other years. Green and green the mountain. And the coral outcropping of the poppies in the fields. And the thistles along the edges, mauve asteroids, celestial bodies. And the solar splendor of the broom.

Our walks. We would depart the town walking between whitewashed walls, the wisteria along the patios growing sparser. And further on, the white, narrow, curbed roads. A landscape

of vineyards and olive trees and serpentine walls of slate. And
the green slopes of the lower mountain. In the distance, upon
a promontory, dominating the entrance to the bay, the ruins
of Trinidad castle, little more than an eroded crag, perfectly
integrated into the orthographic stone of that promontory, the
whole thing crumbling apart. One more alluring spot for the
new urbanized surfaces.

The inner town remained almost intact. We meandered,
snooping along the white windswept streets, smelling of tar and
then just as strongly, salted fish; and the same cats grooming
themselves in the doorways. And the swallows. Their golden
descent upon the church plaza, winging sharply, plummeting
straight down, cheeping pitilessly. Their flashing disappearance
into the vespertine limpidity, as if sucked into a vortex and shot
out by a centrifugal force, after spinning and spinning like gusts
of wind around the church.

We walked along the breakwater, roaming the seafront of
the town from point to point, like tourists in search of local
color. The setting sun an immense pupil upon the bay. Fluid
gleams, crucibles, multihued agates, from purple to turquoise,
crepuscular tonalities, a sunset of tattered skies like a furnace or
an eruption, eyelids squinting as tightly as possible. The same
chromatic expansion that must accompany the sun wherever
else, in the same instant, it was dawning, even as it sank down
here. A dawn that is a sunset.

We walked as far as the dock, ambling along the wharf,
almost lifeless this time of year. Some man fishing with a pole,
some tourist taking advantage of the fading light to snap their
photo of that flaming horizon on the white synthesis of the transit, blue waters burning yellow, red skies burning blue, pinkish
greens, orange-hued violets and lilacs and indigos and mauves,
an iridescent sunflower of oily spots in the calm opaline bay, still
warmed by the fading colors, now translucent rainbows, now
colorless translucence, now gray, now heavy, now lead.

We visited the ruins of the citadel or, on the opposite end of
town, Trinidad castle. We went into town, we followed the paths
that lead to the mountain. We walked along the breakwater.

To the dock. The church plaza. The swallows.

Now dark, we returned. It was as if with each walk we sought a new proof of the failure of our relationship.

I couldn't fall asleep until daybreak. She slept peacefully, and this always makes the one who can't sleep more anxious. I finally went out to the terrace wrapped in a blanket. Perhaps I needed to see the dawn. Hoping that another parenthesis would open, and banish my insomnia. Inverting the terms of the metaphor.

A plain of glittering phosphorescences, with flakes of light, bit by bit transformed into cloudy hazy blues. Still water, and the wake of a boat like a vanishing point, opening up the quiet sparkles of spreading rings, circles more and more colored in those first lights of dawn like mercury, more and more amber, the decreasing vibration of the motor marking the silence. And in the emptiness the coppery mountain slopes began to take shape, polished, glowing in the first rays of dawn.

Only then did I sleep. Until midday.

THE SUPREMACY OF THE LANDSCAPE. Now dark, we returned. Smoothness of steel in the distance and a descent of nocturnal forms, saline hills, quartz trees, stark branches, the moon spinning fantasies.

Blue night sky. And the taut crackling firmament, crystalline pinpricks.

Or the moon. The moon flowering above the stony shoots, glowing pink like a jellyfish. And, in the town, a proliferation of windows in the massing shapes, illuminated windowpanes, interlocking shadows and whitenesses.

The description must predominate at the start. To give the sensation of serenity, of something peaceful and relaxing. What he wants to find. In contrast to the newspapers he doesn't buy, the radios he flees from, the television, a motive for walking out of a bar when they turn it on.

Avoid local color: fishing boats arriving, the fish auction, etcetera.

However, now in the course of the first chapter, the descriptions must shed their objective almost enunciative character.

They will become subjective, surreal, in a certain way. Like the landscapes one images when contemplating the clouds from an airplane. Contradictory repetitions.

In the following chapters, the same as with the dialogues, they will slowly disappear.

THE CAPE. Going to Cabo Creus by boat, from Rosas, is a problem. Not a technical one; simply finding a person who's willing to take us. But the hotel owner found us a fisherman, an old man willing to take us if the weather that day was good.

It's not that I don't feel like it, just the opposite, she said. But it's three or four hours if the sea is calm. And that many more to come back. And I: but you can only get to the cape by boat. And she: what I don't understand is what you hope to see from there. And I: the other side. And she: we've already seen that: France, the Gulf of Lyon. Let's rent a car and we'll see it all in one morning. And I: but not like we'll see it from the cape.

PENTECOST. In the morning we made love, with the sun shining on the bed. It was bad.

A splendid day, almost like summer. Cerulean atmosphere, igneous in the zenith, burning bramble, and the moving incandescence of the distances.

Ideal for the town to seem like summer holidays, too, invaded by cars, travelers, mostly day trippers from Barcelona, and also French from the Midi-Pyrenees. It took us a while to find a free table on the bar's terrace.

It was time for their aperitif in the sun. Catalan petite bourgeoisie, avid and porcine, showing off the family style, obscenely prosperous, with the respectability of appearances of those who want to make their social ascension absolutely clear, their right to be accepted by those who are already wealthy, and along with them close ranks against those who still aren't, the respectability of those who meet all the requirements, wife, children, stroller, little parcel of land, all manifestations, just like a certain excess weight, of the country's general economic development, but above all, of their own personal triumph, external signs for those who are willing to pay, if necessary, even more taxes!

But not only Sunday drivers. Sunday is usually also the best day to formalize certain kinds of business negotiations. Speculators, promoters, salesmen, contractors. Talking about real estate properties the way others talk about slaughtering a pig: you get him with the hook, you tie him up really nice and tight, you cut him to pieces, and then, sausage for everyone.

At the next table, French couples, young married couples surely. *Mon petit trésor*, said one of the group as if suddenly effusive, drawing close, smooching, like suction cups, applying his lips to her rough cut scallop of a mouth, to her defiant contempt, a contrasting attitude of the two elements of copulation, derived, no doubt, from what was for her an unsatisfactory ending of the habitual amorous exercise, unyielding, in consequence, to the heat of such transports, incapable of sharing any allusive gesture to such non-reciprocal pleasures, only worthwhile for him, for him hidden in that stubborn little body and only for him, his particular practices, his intimate manipulations, *ces petites cochonneries*. Anal erotic.

And the charnegos all dressed up in their Sunday best. And the pairs of hikers, lively and garrulous under their backpacks. It seemed that more than the commemoration of the descent of the Holy Spirit in the form of a tongue of flame, it might have been ultimately the meaning that the holy day held for the Jews, commemorating Moses's going up the mountain. And once atop, each one disappearing to shit behind a shrub.

Bird-beaked old people, frightened away by all that activity. Too many years old now to not lose out, to follow the rhythm of the changes experienced by the town in recent times. What they have seen, what they have heard, what the television says, what's being built, the millions the land is worth, the millions of tourists who show up, their children's habits, their grandchildren's, the external appearance they've acquired, they almost seem like tourists too, confirmations that they've been reaching until losing all capacity for surprise, for discerning the possible from the impossible, accepting as such the impossible without other

disruption than a greater propensity for paranoia and megaloma-
nia. But the euphoria past, if in fact it happens, the eyes increasingly wide open and demented in their nests of tiny wrinkles, so
much transformation ends up shrinking them, by making them
feel, each summer that passes, that the world is ever stranger, that
they are ever stranger. And it's then when they become bird-like;
the facial skin almost transparent; the scarecrow body twisted
and limping, doubled over at the kidneys; their hands made to
grasp hoes and pull nets, almost already molded to their shape;
their voices made to speak in shouts, in the field, out at sea, at
home, shouting at his old lady, at the kids, at the dogs, a voice
which, from shouting so, is reduced to little more than a hoarse
crackling, stridencies that go twisting around the few slobber-
ing teeth they show us when they smile, unsure whether they've
greeted us or not. So, in full season, they only venture out to the
fish auction, doing everything possible, as if they intuited their
role, to seem typical. Old people are birds already.

That afternoon I went out walking alone. Watching the
clouds that were forming: bright perfect stratocumulus alternating with clear patches of sky, forming orographical vastnesses,
shaping islands and oceans, peninsulas, mountains or valleys like
craters, crests, more crests, islands, peninsulas, shorelines, plains,
rivers, isthmuses, capes, bays, and below, cloudy skies and, above
all, between the cracks, a yawning terrain, like the ocean floor
when one goes diving down.

NOCTURNAL BROUHAHA. They only saw the end of it.
Others told them about the rest. They'd had quite a lot to drink
and took a while to catch on. It was cold to be sitting at the
tables outside.

El Roc was drunk. The town bohemian: half-fisherman,
half-alcoholic, with sufficient artistic gifts to paint oil paintings, copied from postcards, which he sold to tourists. He'd
drunk his fill in some other bar around there and that night
he started to kick up a scandalous row. Then the policeman on
night watch showed up. The barman said nothing was wrong,

that he'd sort things out with El Roc. But the cop had already made up his mind because El Roc, when he drank, started trouble with every mother's son and the gods they worshipped, and wished long life to communism. At other times he'd had problems with the Guardia Civil, but they'd always preferred to let him off, and take no notice of him. What happens in small towns: everybody knows each other. One night in the jail and that's it.

And El Roc, they said, seeing that the cop was raising his billy club, wrenched it out of his hand and threw it out into the street, and the cop's peaked cap fell off. Strong fellow, El Roc, stout. And then the cop fired two shots into the ceiling and told him to get out of there, to go stand and face the front of the building, with his back to him. He smacked him in one of his knees with his club, from the side, and when he saw him double over, gave it to him in the other one. El Roc grabbed hold of the iron bars outside a window, his legs limp as dishrags. And then the cop smacked one hand, and then the other, and dislodged him. And once he had him laid out on the street, he kept working him over, kicking him.

They arrived at that very moment, just in time to see the final blows to El Roc stretched out on the ground, and a couple of Guardia Civil arrived, and as they dragged him away he was spitting out his loose teeth. The people looked on in silence. A silence that became hostile when they heard them say: that's right, let him cool his heels in the cell. A good taming is what he needs. A fat Andalusian smoking with a cigarette holder.

We returned to our bar, to our table. I realized that she was leaning against me, crying, her face buried in my shoulder. I can't stand to watch them beat a man like that. That monster, just because he's got a pistol and a uniform, beating a man like that. I can't stand it. I can't stand it. I can't stand it. She went running to the bathroom.

Develop the scene stripping away all kinds of atmospheric elements. Principal features of the prose that must be included in this first chapter: density, tension, intensity. A syntactic stretch. A semantic entwining.

METAPHOR. How to contemplate the landscape from the lighthouse, the rocks beaten by the breaking waves barely visible above the sea foam, dripping with anemones and mollusks and black urchins, overflown by the seagulls, savagely beaten, rearing up in white. And beyond the crumbled promontory, beyond the ruins blending back into the stony slopes, the bay dissolved and calm below the saline sky, and the bright jellyfish floating and drifting, carried by the clear western breeze. And the town, between the ruins of the castle and the fortress. And the port, the boats anchored in the shelter of the dock, the piers, the wooden gangways perpendicular to the wharf, and the rigging and the radar antennas and the woven texture of all the gear bordering the footbridges, curtains of nets and of brown corks and the rough rope along the gangways, and the smell from the gangways like piss and tar and fresh paint, and the muted splashing under the gangways, against the ships' hulls, against the stones of the jetty. And the town, the whitewashed walls and the vertebrae of the lizard-hued roofs; and farther on, the long dirty beach, dry seaweed, sinuously accumulated, and driftwood and branches like bones and organic flotsam and indestructible plastics and footprints leading nowhere, footprints erased by the swirling sand, undermined by the deliquescence.

The rocks discolored in the midday sun, below the waxen zenith, the coast like saltpeter or gunpowder. And a front of clouds advancing menacingly, like flocks or dust clouds or the white eyebrows that sharpen the sight of a madman scrutinizing, scrutinizing like a lighthouse in the night, again and again, again and again like a lighthouse lamp turning, an obsessive gaze that encompasses 360 degrees, not so much to be seen from the sea intermittently as to scrutinize, to watch over it as it watches the wild windswept coasts, coasts that turn the way a sardana turns or the way the whole bullring revolves around a slain bull, stones tumultuously set, protean masses which, to a penetrating eye, quickly show themselves to contain, perfectly identifiable, petrified battles, cavalry charges, city walls besieged, ships foundering, everything immobilized by the centuries of an eternal instant, like Pompeii or Machu Picchu, everything turned to stone as in a grotto the dripping water turns to stone, phantasmal forests of stalactites, chaotic rocks like a madman's brain, aeolian demolition and eroded ruin below those wrathful skies and the violent crashing waves, a bay roused to fury by the storm, devastated directly by the east wind, that tense line which on clear days like today, the weather calm, cloudless, and bright, rising in the far distance, clearly, sharply visible, the ruins of Empúries, Iberian, Greek, and Roman stones, towns swept clean by the wind-driven sand, buried by the beckoning sea, that wind and that sea which brought here the battles and the shipwrecks like those ships that smash and founder, horsemen and horsemen galloping, besiegers of walls upon walls, these waters and this air that are barely an image of the impulse which brought them here, of the gales, of the seas they carried inside, the ultimate key to the landscape. And the diaphanous sapphire of the cierzo wind blowing cold and hard from the north and the arid zenith high above the protean relief of the coast, rocky excrescences, stony disintegrations. And the dirty ashen sky and the black sparkling water, hidden rocks, reefs, boulders hurtling down and smashing to pieces upon the defenseless plain, upon the short, storm-chopped waves, implacable foam and roaring air. And the gray hangover, that current that detaches a person from terra firma, pulling him out into the gray sea, into his brain.

FIGURES ON THE BEACH. I don't like sunbathing lying still on the beach. I don't even like the sand. I prefer the rocks.

She was talking to me while lying on her stomach facedown, her bikini straps loose. She said that they hadn't been able to locate the house from the years when they used to summer there, after the war. She only remembered that it was a fisherman's house, on one of those streets parallel to the sea inside the town. Then we started going to Lloret. Papa had more money and he thought it was more elegant. But I've always had better memories of Rosas.

It's as if with everything there had to be something that came between us, I said. Why? she said. Well, because I had spent a summer just around the other side of the cape, in Port de la Selva. Before the war. I don't remember anything, of course. But there's a photo of me there. I must have been just a little more than a year old.

A pebble beach, with boats. And I'm on a boat, and she's holding me. You can barely notice but, given the season, she must have been quite pregnant. It might be the last photo of her. She's looking at the camera, smiling more with her eyes than her lips.

Luis Goytisolo was born in Barcelona in 1935. The author of more than a dozen novels, as well as several collections of stories, fables, and essays, he is best known for his tetralogy of novels *Antagonía*, of which *Recounting* is the first book. Goytisolo has been awarded the Premio Nacional de Narrativa, the Premio Nacional de las Letras Españolas, and is a member of the Real Academia Española.

Brendan Riley is a teacher, translator, writer, and editor. His translations of Álvaro Enrigue's *Hypothermia* and Juan Filloy's *Caterva* are both published by Dalkey Archive Press.

MICHAL AJVAZ, *The Golden Age.*
The Other City.

PIERRE ALBERT-BIROT, *Grabinoulor.*

YUZ ALESHKOVSKY, *Kangaroo.*

FELIPE ALFAU, *Chromos.*
Locos.

JOE AMATO, *Samuel Taylor's Last Night.*

IVAN ÂNGELO, *The Celebration.*
The Tower of Glass.

ANTÓNIO LOBO ANTUNES, *Knowledge of Hell.*
The Splendor of Portugal.

ALAIN ARIAS-MISSON, *Theatre of Incest.*

JOHN ASHBERY & JAMES SCHUYLER,
A Nest of Ninnies.

ROBERT ASHLEY, *Perfect Lives.*

GABRIELA AVIGUR-ROTEM, *Heatwave and Crazy Birds.*

DJUNA BARNES, *Ladies Almanack.*
Ryder.

JOHN BARTH, *Letters.*
Sabbatical.

DONALD BARTHELME, *The King.*
Paradise.

SVETISLAV BASARA, *Chinese Letter.*

MIQUEL BAUÇÀ, *The Siege in the Room.*

RENÉ BELLETTO, *Dying.*

MAREK BIENCZYK, *Transparency.*

ANDREI BITOV, *Pushkin House.*

ANDREJ BLATNIK, *You Do Understand.*
Law of Desire.

LOUIS PAUL BOON, *Chapel Road.*
My Little War.
Summer in Termuren.

ROGER BOYLAN, *Killoyle.*

IGNÁCIO DE LOYOLA BRANDÃO,
Anonymous Celebrity.
Zero.

BONNIE BREMSER, *Troia: Mexican Memoirs.*

CHRISTINE BROOKE-ROSE,
Amalgamemnon.

BRIGID BROPHY, *In Transit.*
The Prancing Novelist.

GERALD L. BRUNS,
Modern Poetry and the Idea of Language.

GABRIELLE BURTON, *Heartbreak Hotel.*

MICHEL BUTOR, *Degrees.*
Mobile.

G. CABRERA INFANTE, *Infante's Inferno.*
Three Trapped Tigers.

JULIETA CAMPOS, *The Fear of Losing Eurydice.*

ANNE CARSON, *Eros the Bittersweet.*

ORLY CASTEL-BLOOM, *Dolly City.*

LOUIS-FERDINAND CÉLINE, *North.*
Conversations with Professor Y.
London Bridge.

MARIE CHAIX, *The Laurels of Lake Constance.*

HUGO CHARTERIS, *The Tide Is Right.*

ERIC CHEVILLARD, *Demolishing Nisard.*
The Author and Me.

MARC CHOLODENKO, *Mordechai Schamz.*

JOSHUA COHEN, *Witz.*

EMILY HOLMES COLEMAN, *The Shutter of Snow.*

ERIC CHEVILLARD, *The Author and Me.*

ROBERT COOVER, *A Night at the Movies.*

STANLEY CRAWFORD, *Log of the S.S.*
The Mrs Unguentine.
Some Instructions to My Wife.

RENÉ CREVEL, *Putting My Foot in It.*

RALPH CUSACK, *Cadenza.*

NICHOLAS DELBANCO, *Sherbrookes.*
The Count of Concord.

NIGEL DENNIS, *Cards of Identity.*

PETER DIMOCK, *A Short Rhetoric for Leaving the Family.*

ARIEL DORFMAN, *Konfidenz.*

COLEMAN DOWELL, *Island People.*
Too Much Flesh and Jabez.

ARKADII DRAGOMOSHCHENKO,
Dust.

RIKKI DUCORNET, *Phosphor in Dreamland.*
The Complete Butcher's Tales.

FOR A FULL LIST OF PUBLICATIONS, VISIT: www.dalkeyarchive.com

RIKKI DUCORNET (cont.), *The Jade Cabinet.*
The Fountains of Neptune.
WILLIAM EASTLAKE, *The Bamboo Bed.*
Castle Keep.
Lyric of the Circle Heart.
JEAN ECHENOZ, *Chopin's Move.*
STANLEY ELKIN, *A Bad Man.*
Criers and Kibitzers, Kibitzers and Criers.
The Dick Gibson Show.
The Franchiser.
The Living End.
Mrs. Ted Bliss.
FRANÇOIS EMMANUEL, *Invitation to a Voyage.*
PAUL EMOND, *The Dance of a Sham.*
SALVADOR ESPRIU, *Ariadne in the Grotesque Labyrinth.*
LESLIE A. FIEDLER, *Love and Death in the American Novel.*
JUAN FILLOY, *Op Oloop.*
ANDY FITCH, *Pop Poetics.*
GUSTAVE FLAUBERT, *Bouvard and Pécuchet.*
KASS FLEISHER, *Talking out of School.*
JON FOSSE, *Aliss at the Fire.*
Melancholy.
FORD MADOX FORD, *The March of Literature.*
MAX FRISCH, *I'm Not Stiller.*
Man in the Holocene.
CARLOS FUENTES, *Christopher Unborn.*
Distant Relations.
Terra Nostra.
Where the Air Is Clear.
TAKEHIKO FUKUNAGA, *Flowers of Grass.*
WILLIAM GADDIS, JR., *The Recognitions.*
JANICE GALLOWAY, *Foreign Parts.*
The Trick Is to Keep Breathing.
WILLIAM H. GASS, *Life Sentences.*
The Tunnel.
The World Within the Word.
Willie Masters' Lonesome Wife.
GÉRARD GAVARRY, *Hoppla! 1 2 3.*

ETIENNE GILSON, *The Arts of the Beautiful.*
Forms and Substances in the Arts.
C. S. GISCOMBE, *Giscome Road.*
Here.
DOUGLAS GLOVER, *Bad News of the Heart.*
WITOLD GOMBROWICZ, *A Kind of Testament.*
PAULO EMÍLIO SALES GOMES, *P's Three Women.*
GEORGI GOSPODINOV, *Natural Novel.*
JUAN GOYTISOLO, *Count Julian.*
Juan the Landless.
Makbara.
Marks of Identity.
HENRY GREEN, *Blindness.*
Concluding.
Doting.
Nothing.
JACK GREEN, *Fire the Bastards!*
JIŘÍ GRUŠA, *The Questionnaire.*
MELA HARTWIG, *Am I a Redundant Human Being?*
JOHN HAWKES, *The Passion Artist.*
Whistlejacket.
ELIZABETH HEIGHWAY, ED., *Contemporary Georgian Fiction.*
AIDAN HIGGINS, *Balcony of Europe.*
Blind Man's Bluff.
Bornholm Night-Ferry.
Langrishe, Go Down.
Scenes from a Receding Past.
KEIZO HINO, *Isle of Dreams.*
KAZUSHI HOSAKA, *Plainsong.*
ALDOUS HUXLEY, *Antic Hay.*
Point Counter Point.
Those Barren Leaves.
Time Must Have a Stop.
NAOYUKI II, *The Shadow of a Blue Cat.*
DRAGO JANČAR, *The Tree with No Name.*
MIKHEIL JAVAKHISHVILI, *Kvachi.*
GERT JONKE, *The Distant Sound.*
Homage to Czerny.
The System of Vienna.

JACQUES JOUET, *Mountain R.*
Savage.
Upstaged.
MIEKO KANAI, *The Word Book.*
YORAM KANIUK, *Life on Sandpaper.*
ZURAB KARUMIDZE, *Dagny.*
JOHN KELLY, *From Out of the City.*
HUGH KENNER, *Flaubert, Joyce and Beckett: The Stoic Comedians.*
Joyce's Voices.
DANILO KIŠ, *The Attic.*
The Lute and the Scars.
Psalm 44.
A Tomb for Boris Davidovich.
ANITA KONKKA, *A Fool's Paradise.*
GEORGE KONRÁD, *The City Builder.*
TADEUSZ KONWICKI, *A Minor Apocalypse.*
The Polish Complex.
ANNA KORDZAIA-SAMADASHVILI, *Me, Margarita.*
MENIS KOUMANDAREAS, *Koula.*
ELAINE KRAF, *The Princess of 72nd Street.*
JIM KRUSOE, *Iceland.*
AYSE KULIN, *Farewell: A Mansion in Occupied Istanbul.*
EMILIO LASCANO TEGUI, *On Elegance While Sleeping.*
ERIC LAURRENT, *Do Not Touch.*
VIOLETTE LEDUC, *La Bâtarde.*
EDOUARD LEVÉ, *Autoportrait.*
Newspaper.
Suicide.
Works.
MARIO LEVI, *Istanbul Was a Fairy Tale.*
DEBORAH LEVY, *Billy and Girl.*
JOSÉ LEZAMA LIMA, *Paradiso.*
ROSA LIKSOM, *Dark Paradise.*
OSMAN LINS, *Avalovara.*
The Queen of the Prisons of Greece.
FLORIAN LIPUŠ, *The Errors of Young Tjaž.*
GORDON LISH, *Peru.*
ALF MACLOCHLAINN, *Out of Focus.*
Past Habitual.

The Corpus in the Library.
RON LOEWINSOHN, *Magnetic Field(s).*
YURI LOTMAN, *Non-Memoirs.*
D. KEITH MANO, *Take Five.*
MINA LOY, *Stories and Essays of Mina Loy.*
MICHELINE AHARONIAN MARCOM, *A Brief History of Yes.*
The Mirror in the Well.
BEN MARCUS, *The Age of Wire and String.*
WALLACE MARKFIELD, *Teitlebaum's Window.*
DAVID MARKSON, *Reader's Block.*
Wittgenstein's Mistress.
CAROLE MASO, *AVA.*
HISAKI MATSUURA, *Triangle.*
LADISLAV MATEJKA & KRYSTYNA POMORSKA, EDS., *Readings in Russian Poetics: Formalist & Structuralist Views.*
HARRY MATHEWS, *Cigarettes.*
The Conversions.
The Human Country.
The Journalist.
My Life in CIA.
Singular Pleasures.
The Sinking of the Odradek.
Stadium.
Tlooth.
HISAKI MATSUURA, *Triangle.*
DONAL MCLAUGHLIN, *beheading the virgin mary, and other stories.*
JOSEPH MCELROY, *Night Soul and Other Stories.*
ABDELWAHAB MEDDEB, *Talismano.*
GERHARD MEIER, *Isle of the Dead.*
HERMAN MELVILLE, *The Confidence-Man.*
AMANDA MICHALOPOULOU, *I'd Like.*
STEVEN MILLHAUSER, *The Barnum Museum.*
In the Penny Arcade.
RALPH J. MILLS, JR., *Essays on Poetry.*
MOMUS, *The Book of Jokes.*
CHRISTINE MONTALBETTI, *The Origin of Man.*
Western.

NICHOLAS MOSLEY, *Accident.*
Assassins.
Catastrophe Practice.
A Garden of Trees.
Hopeful Monsters.
Imago Bird.
Inventing God.
Look at the Dark.
Metamorphosis.
Natalie Natalia.
Serpent.
WARREN MOTTE, *Fables of the Novel:
French Fiction since 1990.*
*Fiction Now: The French Novel in the
21st Century.*
Mirror Gazing.
Oulipo: A Primer of Potential Literature.
GERALD MURNANE, *Barley Patch.*
Inland.
YVES NAVARRE, *Our Share of Time.*
Sweet Tooth.
DOROTHY NELSON, *In Night's City.*
Tar and Feathers.
ESHKOL NEVO, *Homesick.*
WILFRIDO D. NOLLEDO, *But for
the Lovers.*
BORIS A. NOVAK, *The Master of
Insomnia.*
FLANN O'BRIEN, *At Swim-Two-Birds.*
The Best of Myles.
The Dalkey Archive.
The Hard Life.
The Poor Mouth.
The Third Policeman.
CLAUDE OLLIER, *The Mise-en-Scène.*
Wert and the Life Without End.
PATRIK OUŘEDNÍK, *Europeana.*
The Opportune Moment, 1855.
BORIS PAHOR, *Necropolis.*
FERNANDO DEL PASO, *News from
the Empire.*
Palinuro of Mexico.
ROBERT PINGET, *The Inquisitory.*
Mahu or The Material.
Trio.
MANUEL PUIG, *Betrayed by Rita
Hayworth.*

The Buenos Aires Affair.
Heartbreak Tango.
RAYMOND QUENEAU, *The Last Days.*
Odile.
Pierrot Mon Ami.
Saint Glinglin.
ANN QUIN, *Berg.*
Passages.
Three.
Tripticks.
ISHMAEL REED, *The Free-Lance
Pallbearers.*
The Last Days of Louisiana Red.
Ishmael Reed: The Plays.
Juice!
The Terrible Threes.
The Terrible Twos.
Yellow Back Radio Broke-Down.
JASIA REICHARDT, *15 Journeys Warsaw
to London.*
JOÃO UBALDO RIBEIRO, *House of the
Fortunate Buddhas.*
JEAN RICARDOU, *Place Names.*
RAINER MARIA RILKE,
The Notebooks of Malte Laurids Brigge.
JULIÁN RÍOS, *The House of Ulysses.*
Larva: A Midsummer Night's Babel.
Poundemonium.
ALAIN ROBBE-GRILLET, *Project for a
Revolution in New York.*
A Sentimental Novel.
AUGUSTO ROA BASTOS, *I the Supreme.*
DANIËL ROBBERECHTS, *Arriving in
Avignon.*
JEAN ROLIN, *The Explosion of the
Radiator Hose.*
OLIVIER ROLIN, *Hotel Crystal.*
ALIX CLEO ROUBAUD, *Alix's Journal.*
JACQUES ROUBAUD, *The Form of
a City Changes Faster, Alas, Than the
Human Heart.*
The Great Fire of London.
Hortense in Exile.
Hortense Is Abducted.
*Mathematics: The Plurality of Worlds of
Lewis.*
Some Thing Black.

RAYMOND ROUSSEL, *Impressions of Africa.*

VEDRANA RUDAN, *Night.*

PABLO M. RUIZ, *Four Cold Chapters on the Possibility of Literature.*

GERMAN SADULAEV, *The Maya Pill.*

TOMAŽ ŠALAMUN, *Soy Realidad.*

LYDIE SALVAYRE, *The Company of Ghosts.*
The Lecture.
The Power of Flies.

LUIS RAFAEL SÁNCHEZ, *Macho Camacho's Beat.*

SEVERO SARDUY, *Cobra & Maitreya.*

NATHALIE SARRAUTE, *Do You Hear Them?*
Martereau.
The Planetarium.

STIG SÆTERBAKKEN, *Siamese.*
Self-Control.
Through the Night.

ARNO SCHMIDT, *Collected Novellas.*
Collected Stories.
Nobodaddy's Children.
Two Novels.

ASAF SCHURR, *Motti.*

GAIL SCOTT, *My Paris.*

DAMION SEARLS, *What We Were Doing and Where We Were Going.*

JUNE AKERS SEESE,
Is This What Other Women Feel Too?

BERNARD SHARE, *Inish.*
Transit.

VIKTOR SHKLOVSKY, *Bowstring.*
Literature and Cinematography.
Theory of Prose.
Third Factory.
Zoo, or Letters Not about Love.

PIERRE SINIAC, *The Collaborators.*

KJERSTI A. SKOMSVOLD,
The Faster I Walk, the Smaller I Am.

JOSEF ŠKVORECKÝ, *The Engineer of Human Souls.*

GILBERT SORRENTINO, *Aberration of Starlight.*
Blue Pastoral.
Crystal Vision.

Imaginative Qualities of Actual Things.
Mulligan Stew. Red the Fiend.
Steelwork.
Under the Shadow.

MARKO SOSIČ, *Ballerina, Ballerina.*

ANDRZEJ STASIUK, *Dukla.*
Fado.

GERTRUDE STEIN, *The Making of Americans.*
A Novel of Thank You.

LARS SVENDSEN, *A Philosophy of Evil.*

PIOTR SZEWC, *Annihilation.*

GONÇALO M. TAVARES, *A Man: Klaus Klump.*
Jerusalem.
Learning to Pray in the Age of Technique.

LUCIAN DAN TEODOROVICI,
Our Circus Presents...

NIKANOR TERATOLOGEN, *Assisted Living.*

STEFAN THEMERSON, *Hobson's Island.*
The Mystery of the Sardine.
Tom Harris.

TAEKO TOMIOKA, *Building Waves.*

JOHN TOOMEY, *Sleepwalker.*

DUMITRU TSEPENEAG, *Hotel Europa.*
The Necessary Marriage.
Pigeon Post.
Vain Art of the Fugue.

ESTHER TUSQUETS, *Stranded.*

DUBRAVKA UGRESIC, *Lend Me Your Character.*
Thank You for Not Reading.

TOR ULVEN, *Replacement.*

MATI UNT, *Brecht at Night.*
Diary of a Blood Donor.
Things in the Night.

ÁLVARO URIBE & OLIVIA SEARS, EDS.,
Best of Contemporary Mexican Fiction.

ELOY URROZ, *Friction.*
The Obstacles.

LUISA VALENZUELA, *Dark Desires and the Others.*
He Who Searches.

PAUL VERHAEGHEN, *Omega Minor.*

BORIS VIAN, *Heartsnatcher.*

FOR A FULL LIST OF PUBLICATIONS, VISIT: www.dalkeyarchive.com